Dorinda Balchin

Heronfield

This edition published 2014 by Dorinda Balchin

ISBN 978-0-9574218-2-0

Cover Design © Lorna Gray www.saltwaydesign.com
(Cover design runner-up in Authors Database
Book Cover Competition 2013)

Visit www.dorindabalchin.com
to find out more about the author and her works

Praise for Heronfield

The course of six years is spanned here, from the beaches at Dunkirk to the liberation of the Concentration Camps in Germany...The characters are so incredibly realistic that it is extremely difficult to put Heronfield down. It wouldn't be possible to write a story about the bravery of the soldiers or the Resistance without making sure that the reader is aware of just why they were so brave and this is put across tactfully, but still gives the reader an idea of the horrors faced by these people.

Heronfield is not a book you should let slip by. It is an amazing read.

Rachel Malone

Historical Novel Society Indie Reviewer

MAY - JUNE 1940

1

Tony felt as though he were fighting against a sea tide as he tried to make his way east. The narrow hedge-lined road was crammed with a heaving mass of humanity, all heading west, pushing and jostling the young man, slowing his progress to a crawl. He saw old men and women, young mothers with children at their skirts and babes in their arms, all moving at a maddeningly slow pace in the crush, weariness apparent in every movement and dull fear in their tired eyes. Everyone carried bundles of their most treasured possessions - a few photographs, money, clothes, food. Many pushed handcarts ahead of them, all their worldly possessions in a muddled heap and their homes left far behind. A lucky few rode on farm carts, drawn by horses which should have been at work out in the fields. But although it was less tiring for those who rode than those who made their way on foot, they could go no faster, the road was so thronged with people that it was impossible for the carts to pass them. The few motor vehicles were reduced to a crawl, until they reached a place where the weary refugees could step aside for a moment to let them pass. Yet with all that pressing mass of humanity there was no noise, save for the shuffle of feet and the rumble of wheels and, infrequently, a baby's hungry cry.

Tony and his companions, a lieutenant and three privates from the beleaguered British Expeditionary Force, had joined the road from a narrow country lane some half a mile back.

"We'll never rejoin our company at this rate." Private Watson, a veteran of the Great War, re-adjusted the Lee Enfield rifle on his shoulder. "We never had this trouble on the Somme."

Private Phillips smiled grimly. "'Arf of France weren't tryin' to go t'other way at the same time, was they, mate?" He was a short man in his early twenties, who had joined up when Hitler invaded Poland. He had never been far from home before, let alone in the middle of a war, but he was taking it all very calmly. "What we needs to do is find an easier route."

"That's true, but a route to where?"

Lieutenant Briggs shrugged at Watson's remark. "I don't rightly know, private. The last I heard was that we're falling back towards a place called Dunkirk. No doubt we'll be launching a counterattack from there."

Tony brushed a stray lock of wavy brown hair from his forehead. He stood up on tiptoe and tried to see over the heads of the people in front of him. As far as he could see, the road was like a column of ants at a summer picnic. He turned to Briggs, who was trying to force his way past a hay cart laden with household goods.

"I'm afraid I don't know this area of France too well, so I can't lead you overland. I know Dunkirk is somewhere on the coast, but I don't know its exact location. Still," he stepped aside to let an old woman pass, her only possession a small bag of bread and cheese, "it would be better to get off the road or we'll never get anywhere. Why don't we just go into the fields next to the road and walk along beside it?"

Briggs nodded. "My thoughts exactly. Who'd have thought it would come to this so soon? It's only eleven days since the Germans launched their attack, and we seem to be completely outmanoeuvred." He led the way over a ditch, then through a narrow gap in the hedge which bordered the road. His companions followed close behind.

They found themselves in a field of newly sprouted wheat, bright green in the warm spring sunshine. A gentle breeze passed in waves across the fields, as though in obscene parody of the fleeing mass thronging the road on the other side of the hedge.

"What the hell happened to the bloody Maginot Line? That's what I'd like to know. I thought it was supposed to be strong enough to hold back the enemy for months, if not years."

Briggs turned to the man who had spoken. "As far as I can tell, Smith, they just went round the ends."

"Bloody 'ell!" Phillips spat into the hedgerow. "That means the whole German army is runnin' around 'ere in France. No wonder we're retreatin'."

"Enough of that talk, Phillips. This is a strategic withdrawal, not a retreat. Now, let's get moving."

Briggs led the way, with Kemshall at his side. Their pace was swifter now that they had left the road, the hedges and walls that they had to cross from one field to the next barely slowing their brisk pace. They had been moving along in this manner for almost half an hour, when the muffled drone of airplane engines could be heard, approaching from the east.

"Ours or theirs?"

Briggs shrugged at Tony's question. "Have to wait and see."

As the sound of the planes drew nearer, the people on the road halted their shambling progress to turn and gaze heavenward, eager to identify the approaching machines. Three black dots in the sky, flying in a V formation, approached swiftly. They were still too far off for the men on the ground to see their markings, but Briggs had seen that ominous shape before, when he and his companions had become separated from the rest of their company.

"Stukas!" He turned towards the men behind him as he shouted. "Into the hedge!"

As one man, the three soldiers leapt for the relative safety of the newly leafed hedgerow while Tony, untrained in military matters, hesitated. Briggs pushed him as he passed. "Come on! Run!"

As they hit the ground and rolled beneath the hedge, Tony saw the planes bank and plunge into a steep dive. The sirens fitted to their undercarriages produced a terrifying scream. It was echoed by hundreds of human voices, as the refugees on the road panicked. Those at the edge dived for the comparative safety of the ditches. Most milled about in total confusion, unsure of what to do or where to go. The screaming of the planes rose to a terrifying pitch as the Stukas swept along the road, machine guns blazing. Cries of pain mingled with the sounds of fear. As Tony watched in horror from his hiding place, he saw a boy, no more than five years old, who had become separated from his parents. His cries of "Mamma! Mamma!" rang out shrilly. Tony would have rushed to his aid but for the spouts of dust which reached out ahead of him, the impact of bullets which raced along the road and intercepted the frightened child before the Englishman could do more than climb to his knees. Screams of pain filled the air as the small body was spun around by the impact of the bullets, then crumpled and fell to the ground.

The Stukas were climbing high now after their first pass, and began to execute a tight turn. Tony felt a restraining hand on his shoulder.

"You can't do anything to help those people! The planes are coming back! For God's sake, get down!"

Tony looked up. The planes had completed their turn and were beginning to dive again. Bullets whistled in all directions, and many of those who had failed to find shelter in the ditches and hedgerows now fell, screaming. The initial panic was over, the only sounds were the high-pitched screaming of the planes as they swooped in, the thud of bullets and the cries of the wounded. As the planes passed overhead Tony saw a carthorse rear up in the traces. Blood poured from its neck and back as it keeled over and lay screaming in the dirt, kicking ineffectively. The cart it had been pulling turned over, crushing the family who had been sheltering beneath it. Tony felt sick.

He closed his eyes as the planes climbed once more, and found he was praying.

"Please God, let it be over. Don't let them come back."

But his prayers remained unanswered. The planes turned and swooped once more. This time the chatter of machine guns was replaced by the whistle of bombs. One fell close by. Tony felt the earth shake a moment before the heat of the shock wave hit him. Shrapnel flew everywhere, and he crouched low to avoid it. Another stick of bombs fell ...crump...crump...crump.... Tony buried his face in last year's leaf mould and covered his head protectively with his arms. His terrified mind retraced the events which had led to his being there, in the midst of so much death and destruction, seeking safety in the memory of people and places that he loved.

2

The family gathered around the radio in the drawing room, intent on the voice which issued crackling and hissing from the speaker. It was a Sunday morning, and the first time the family had all been together since the eldest son, David, had joined the Royal Air Force. Sir Michael Kemshall stood with his back to the warm September sunshine, which flooded through the window. His hands were clenched tightly behind his broad back, and sweat stood out on his brow and the balding patch on his head. His thoughts were many miles, many years, away, on the bloody battlefields of Flanders where he had fought as a young man. He silently prayed that his sons would be spared the need to fight for their country as he had done. Louise Kemshall, Sir Michael's pretty French wife, seemed to have aged little in the twenty-three years of their marriage. She sat with her slim hands folded in her lap; fair hair framed her strained features as she listened to the radio and prayed for her two sons. David Kemshall stood beside the fireplace. At twenty two, he was a tall slim man with dark hair reminiscent of his father at that age. His RAF uniform lent an air of threat to the uneasy family gathering. He gazed across the room at his brother, Tony, who was two years younger. He was leaning forward with barely concealed eagerness to hear the words from London.

It was two days since the German army had invaded Poland. Now, on Sunday September 3rd 1939, the whole nation waited to hear what the Prime Minister, Mr. Neville Chamberlain, was about to say.

"I am speaking to you from the Cabinet Room at Ten Downing Street..." The voice that issued from the crackling speaker and spoke directly to thousands of homes sounded tired but not defeated. "This morning the British Ambassador in Berlin handed the German Government a final note, stating that, unless the British Government heard from them by eleven o'clock that they were prepared at once to withdraw their troops from Poland, a state of war would exist between us."

Louise's hands clenched tightly together as she held her breath. Her eyes darted to her two sons, then swiftly away again so that she need not meet their gaze.

"I have to tell you that no such undertaking has been received, and that consequently this country is at war with Germany."

Tony watched his mother close her eyes, as though in pain. He knew she was thinking of her two sons, who would have to fight. His heart went out to her. She had lived through one war and lost people she loved, so her fear was understandable. Yet he felt this war would be different. Underlying his sorrow for his mother was an upwelling of excitement and anticipation at the thought of going to war. The family listened on in silence.

"You can imagine what a bitter blow it was to me that all my long struggle to win peace has failed..."

David unconsciously straightened to attention as the words of the Prime Minister amplified the expectant silence in the room. His mind was on his squadron. He needed to rejoin them as soon as possible, leave or no leave; this is what they had been preparing for for so long, and he was ready. Sir Michael looked across at his firstborn son, already in uniform and willing to fight for his country. A mixture of a fathers pride and anxiety was apparent in his gaze. The voice on the radio continued.

"We have done all that any country could do to establish peace. The situation in which no word given by Germany's ruler could be trusted, and no people or country feel themselves safe, has become intolerable..."

Sir Michael stared at the dust motes dancing in the sunlight with unseeing eyes. He felt strangely detached. His sons would be going away to fight as he had done in his youth. Yet his home was still so peaceful, everything apparently unchanged, belying the fact that his country was now at war and nothing would ever be the same again. He closed his eyes, slowly coming to terms with the changed world.

"We have resolved to finish it. It is the evil things which we shall be fighting against - brute force, bad faith, injustice, oppression, and persecution... and against them I am certain that the right will prevail."

The Prime Minister finished speaking. The three men stood to attention as the National Anthem began to play whilst Louise sat numbly in her chair, barely hearing the music as her troubled mind envisaged the bloodied and broken bodies of her sons, lying lost on some Godforsaken battlefield. As the Anthem came to an end, Sir Michael walked slowly across the room, switched off the radio and turned to face his family. There was silence as the full import of the words which they had heard registered for each of them. Then Sir Michael spoke.

"Well, this is it then. After all the talk of appeasement, we are at war again." His gaze took in his two sons, his hopes for the future. His voice choked with emotion at the possibility of losing them. "May God go with you both, and bring you safe home at the end of this."

But nothing happened. David was recalled to his squadron where he flew endless training flights. A Law of Conscription was passed, enabling the Government to call up all men aged eighteen to forty-one when the need arose. The grounds of the house were defaced with the construction of the obligatory air-raid shelter, and the family carried their gas masks at all times. Sir Michael would never forget his experiences of mustard gas in the trenches. He prayed fervently that nothing so horrific would be unleashed upon the citizens of England in their homeland. Still no attack came, and the Government sent no aid to Poland. By the end of September it was all over. Poland was now a part of the Third Reich. England was at war, but no one seemed to know what to do about it.

The winter passed. The Kemshalls listened intently to the news of the British Expeditionary Force being sent to France. Yet no battles took place, none of the expected air raids materialised. They began to join with the rest of Britain in talking of the Phoney War. There was a cautious optimism in the air; surely it would all soon blow over and no Englishman would be called upon to fight. Tony, like many young men of his age, was filled with frustration. He desperately wanted to fight, wanted to take part in heroic deeds, like those he had heard and read about in his childhood. But the opportunity never came. He continued at university with the other undergraduates, eager for something, anything, to happen to relieve the boredom of lives which had promised so much excitement in September and delivered nothing. As spring progressed, lives began to return to normal. Tony reconciled himself to the inevitable fate of completing his university studies before joining his father in the family engineering business.

Then it happened.

In April, Germany invaded Norway and Denmark. There was little that Britain could do to oppose them. On 10th May 1940, Hitler turned his attention to the west, and threw his war machine into Holland and Belgium. The thoughts of Britain turned to the government, the resignation of Chamberlain and the appointment of Churchill as his successor. But not so the Kemshall family at their country home just north of Marlborough. Here all thoughts turned to France, to Louise's mother, Madame Chanterelle de Thierry, and her home in Saint Nazaire. Old and alone now, unable to face the decisions which war might thrust upon her without the support of her family, she needed someone beside her. As David's squadron was on standby, Tony volunteered to travel to France to be with his grandmother until the situation was resolved.

The young man set out the following day, his uneventful journey slowed by troop movements once he reached mainland France. Madame de Thierry was glad to see him, although she thought the concern behind his visit was totally unnecessary, and said so in her usual brusque manner, which belied the warm heart and nature Tony loved. Then the news began to come in from the Front. The Germans were sweeping through France at an amazing speed. There seemed little that the French and British forces could do to oppose them. Tony's concern grew with each passing day. Finally, against all her protests, he managed to get his grandmother onto a ship bound for England. Only the promise that he would bring her home again as soon as it was safe finally persuade her to leave the country house, which had been home since her marriage fifty years before. She had been a young woman in that house, loved her husband, mourned him and their son, grown old there. She had not deserted even in the darkest hours of the war with Germany, the war which had brought so much pain and loss to her family, yet also much happiness in the form of Michael Kemshall. Tony decided not to travel with his grandmother but headed east towards the fighting, to see what was happening and if there was anything he could do. Somewhere out there were the adventures he had dreamed of, which might be waiting for him just around the next bend. He met up with Briggs and his companions three days later, and headed east with them, in search of the remainder of their company, and adventure.

Maybe it would have been better for him if he had returned to England by sea with his grandmother.

3

The planes dived once more. Their engines screamed like lost souls from hell, and Tony tried to bury himself deeper in the leaf mould. The ground shook and heaved. The chatter of machine guns accompanied the roar of exploding bombs. At the end of the run, the three planes climbed high into the sky. Turning gracefully like three enormous birds of prey, they disappeared into the east. The air was still and quiet for an endless moment of time. Tony tentatively raised his head to look through the branches at the road beyond. For a moment he thought that his ears might have been injured in the raid, for no sound accompanied his vision of people pulling themselves slowly, incredulously, from the ditches and hedges and staring open-mouthed at the devastation. Then the sounds began. Anxious voices calling the names of lost friends and relatives; the moans and cries of the wounded; cries of anguished disbelief from those who found loved ones amongst the dead.

Tony forced his way through the hedge and onto the road. His feet, guided by instinct rather than thought, led him unerringly to the little boy's broken body. As he reached the pathetic remains, the child's mother found him, and fell to her knees in shocked silence. A young man, perhaps the boy's father, laid a comforting hand on her shoulder, as they stared in dry-eyed horror at the child. Sensing that he could be of no use to them, Tony turned away. He looked around at the horrific scenes. There were a number of smoking craters where the bombs had fallen, ripping the road apart. The torn earth was surrounded by bodies, or parts of bodies; broken cases from which personal belongings were strewn; dead animals. Between the craters lay many people, injured or killed either by shrapnel from the exploding bombs or the deadly accurate machine-gun fire that accompanied them. Everywhere was red with the blood of the dead and dying.

It was a scene of utter carnage. Tony felt sick. Fighting down the nausea, he forced his leaden feet to move, and approached the nearest body to see if he could be of any assistance. It was a woman, her ancient lined face which had seen so much life was streaked with blood and dirt, now peaceful and still in death. He moved on. A man twisted and broken by the force of the explosion which had lifted him and thrown him against a tree; a horse, still in the traces, its hooves pointing in the ugliness of death towards the sky. Then, to his left, Tony heard a baby cry. Spinning round on his heel he heard the cry again, muffled as though something covered it, a strange eerie sound amidst so much death and destruction. For a moment he could not see where the sound came from, was unsure whether he had heard aright, then he saw the edge of a shawl protruding from beneath a woman's body. Carefully he rolled her over, to find a tiny infant clasped tightly to her breast. Loosening the arms of the woman who had died shielding her daughter, he gently lifted the child and looked around, uncertain what to do next. A girl of fifteen, maybe sixteen years of age, gently touched his arm.

"Parlez-vous francais, Monsieur?"

Tony nodded, and the girl continued to speak in French.

"The dead woman is my brother's wife, he is at the Front with the army. I will care for my niece."

Tony frowned, his eyes moving constantly between the baby and her dead mother.

"Monsieur? The child?" The girl held out her arms, and what she was saying finally registered on Tony's traumatized mind. He gently handed the child to the girl, who turned and walked away without another word.

"God go with you," Tony whispered to the retreating back.

The young Englishman did not know how long he spent on the road tearing cloth for bandages, binding wounds, comforting the dying, before he felt a gentle hand on his shoulder and looked up into Briggs' concerned features.

"Come on Kemshall. We must be going now."

"But what of these people?" Tony's tired gaze swept the scene of carnage. "There are many more who need help."

Briggs nodded. "I know. But we must leave them to their own people. I've got to get back to my company." His voice was filled with compassion. "Stay if you wish."

Tony looked around him, his face filled with pain and anguish at the death and destruction which had rained down upon them from the skies, then he shook his head. "No, you're right. There's not much I can do here. I'll come with you, and if I can get hold of a gun I'll pay the Germans back for this." He stood up and took a final long, hard look at the carnage around him. His voice was filled with anger and bitterness when he spoke. "I want to remember every detail of what those animals have done. Waging war on innocent refugees who can't fight back. I'll remember this and do all that I can to avenge these people."

His face held an unfamiliar harshness and maturity as he turned and followed Briggs back through the hedge to where the remainder of their small party were waiting. They too had been doing what they could for the injured, each emergency medical kit was empty, and their grim faces told Tony that they all felt the same as he did. Briggs turned and led the small group of Englishmen silently on their way.

They travelled in saturnine silence for two long hours before Briggs called a halt. A fire was hastily lit and water boiled to brew tea. As they sat, sipping the steaming liquid which revived their tired minds and bodies, the young lieutenant spoke to Tony.

"Do you plan to join up when you get back, Kemshall?"

Tony nodded. "Yes. And the name's Tony. After what we have been through together today, formality seems so unimportant." His face was grim. "But yes, I intend to fight the Germans. The war seemed so clinical to me back in England, almost like a story from the books I read as a child, but to have seen what we have seen today fills me with anger and hatred. If we came across the Germans now I would fight them with you, Briggs, never mind the formality of joining up."

"I'm James, Jim." Tony smiled and nodded in acknowledgement but said nothing as Briggs continued. "I was impressed by the way you handled yourself today. Never having been in action before, you must have found it frightening, yet you handled it like a veteran."

Tony nodded. "I'm not ashamed to admit that I was scared, but my anger was greater." He finished his mug of tea and rose to his feet. "Shall we get moving, Jim? The sooner we join up with your company, the sooner I can begin fighting."

They had not been on the move for long when they noticed a change in the movements of the refugees on the road. The exodus to the west slowed then stopped. People stood around in small groups talking and gesticulating wildly; many looked westwards along the road then back towards the east from whence they had come, all looked confused and unsure of the direction which they should take.

Jim Briggs looked westwards, but could see nothing that might possibly be responsible for the confusion of the refugees.

"Something must be happening." He turned towards the low stone wall which formed the border between the field they were crossing and the road. "You men wait here, and I'll see what I can find out."

"Do you want me to come with you? You might need someone who can speak French."

"That's all right Tony, I'll manage," Jim replied in perfect French, and Tony smiled as he watched the young officer vault the wall. Jim spoke for a time with an old man who gesticulated wildly first to the east and then to the west then, with a shrug which seemed to say 'so what do we do now?' he fell silent. Jim spent long moments gazing westwards, a frown of concentration furrowing his brow, then he turned to look over his shoulder to the east and distant Dunkirk. After a few moments he nodded, as though concluding an argument with himself and coming to a decision. Vaulting the wall once more, he made his way back to the small group of men waiting for him, and began to speak as soon as he reached them.

"There's a rumour that the Germans have reached a place called Noyelles."

"An' where the bloody 'ell is that?"

Jim smiled grimly. "That, Phillips, is on the coast to the west of us."

"But I thought the enemy were coming down the coast from the east?" Tony frowned; he did not like the way things were turning out.

Jim nodded in answer to his comment. "That's right, but apparently they've swung round to the south of us and then pushed up to the coast at Noyelles."

They were silent for a moment, each thinking the same as his companions, but not one of them daring to speak. At last Watson broke the silence.

"That means that the whole British Expeditionary Force is surrounded."

Jim nodded. "That's assuming that the rumour is correct. I don't think we should rejoin the company with nothing but unsubstantiated rumours to report, so I intend that we go back westwards and find out what is really happening. Tony," he turned to the only civilian in their group as he spoke, "I suggest that you continue towards Dunkirk, and we'll meet up with you there."

Tony shook his head. "No. I'm coming with you." He turned to look at the bewildered refugees as he spoke. "At least we have somewhere to aim for, but what about them? They left their homes to escape from the Germans only to find the enemy waiting for them down the road. Where do they go now?"

Where indeed? Few people were now moving on the road. Some stood in silent bewilderment, many sat on their packs and cases, heads bowed in despair. Women wept as they thought of the long miles they had covered, all for nothing; children lay in the road too tired to do anything but sleep.

Private Smith shook his head sadly. "The only thing we can do to help them is to push the Jerries back out of France." He turned to Jim. "Shall we get moving then, sir?"

Jim nodded silently and led them back along the way they had come.

They had been on the move for less than an hour the when they heard an ominous rumbling sound.

"What's that?" Phillips looked puzzled. "Sounds a bit like a train, but I don't think it is though."

Watson nodded. "I've heard that sound before. Tanks. Either they're ours or that rumour's true."

Jim led them away from the road and into a small wood some fifty yards further on. As they crouched in the undergrowth the rumble became louder. The squeal of metal grating on the surface of the road accompanied the sound then, above the brow of the hill, the muzzle of a gun appeared. The long slender gun barrel was closely followed by the main body of the tank, and the few refugees left on the road fled before it. A moment of sick fear filled Tony, would the tanks attack helpless civilians as the planes had done? But no, the tanks continued along the road as though the refugees did not exist, the turret hatches were thrown back and the commanders rode with their heads and shoulders in the fresh air, to escape the suffocating atmosphere of the Panzer's interior. The commanders paid little attention to their surroundings, and Tony realised that they must believe themselves to be invincible to be moving so swiftly through enemy territory, without fear of reprisals from either the French or the British. He counted twenty tanks as they breasted the hill and made their swift way eastwards. As the last one passed them, Jim turned tight-lipped towards his new comrade.

"The bloody nerve of them." He was angry, partly at the attitude of the Germans but also at his own helplessness. "By God, I wish we could do something."

Tony nodded. "You're right. We have to do something, not only to show them that we might not be as easily dismissed as they think, but also because now that they've passed us we are behind enemy lines. We've got to get past them to rejoin our own army."

Phillips was obviously afraid at the thought of being cut off, and Watson laid a comforting hand on his shoulder.

"Don't worry, lad. Those tanks are sticking to the road. We can bypass them through the fields."

Jim nodded. "We'll get in front of them and then try to lay some kind of ambush. I know there are only four of us..."

"Five," interrupted Tony. "I intend to fight as well."

Jim perused him thoughtfully for a moment, then nodded. "...only five of us, but if we find the right place and plan the action correctly, we should be able to make an impact." He watched the tanks advancing swiftly along the road. "If we want to pass them we'd better get moving, or we'll never catch up with them."

Tony felt a cold knot of fear in his stomach. It was one thing to say in the heat of the moment that he was willing to fight, but quite another to lie here concealed beneath a hedge, grenade in hand, awaiting his first participation in an action in which he might actually be killed. The small company had passed the tanks soon after midday, while the crews were stopped to eat. Phillips had wanted to attack them there while the crews were out in the open, but there had been no cover for the Englishmen and it would have been suicidal, so Jim led them on.

Some two miles further along, the narrow road, now flanked by tall trees, took a sharp bend to the left, concealing the way ahead. Jim ordered two of the trees to be felled by grenades about thirty yards from the bend and the road was soon blocked by their leafy bulk. When the tanks came round the bend, they would have to stop either to move the trees or to find a way around them. That was when the Englishmen would attack. Each soldier lay concealed, a grenade in his hand and a rifle by his side. Tony still had no gun, but Jim gave him two grenades. 'Just treat them like cricket balls' he said, 'aim for the tracks as though they're wickets. That way I should hope that we could cripple at least a couple of them.' Tony now nervously licked his dry lips and waited, hoping fervently that he would not let his new friend down. He did not have long to wait.

The heavy squeal of metal on tarmac soon reached them and, moments later, the first of the enemy tanks rounded the bend. Seeing the obstruction the vehicle halted, those following drawing up close behind. Three tanks were fully round the corner and the officers reviewed the scene. The leading commander leant down into the turret to consult his driver at the very moment that Jim leapt to his feet and threw the first grenade. It took the tank square on the front axle, and the resulting explosion rocked the vehicle dangerously but did not overturn it.

Tony found himself leaping to his feet and throwing his grenade with the others. He could feel his heart thumping rapidly as adrenalin flooded his system, washing away the fear and replacing it with a strange exhilaration. He was doing something positive at last! He watched as the first of his grenades hit the second tank a little too high to do much damage, but his second throw was much more accurate and he saw the projectile fall on the tank tracks, shattering a couple of the links. The air above him was suddenly filled with smoke and shrapnel from the other grenades, and he dived for cover, the exhilaration of being part of the action now beginning to give way to a creeping fear as he found himself unarmed and unable to do more to inflict damage on the enemy. The British soldiers, hands free now that their grenades had been thrown, took up their rifles and began to fire at the commanders of the Panzers, who were retreating into the turrets which turned inexorably towards their attackers. The machine guns positioned on the front of the hulls began to chatter, bullets smashing violently through the hedge which concealed the five men.

Rifles cracked to his right and left, and Tony fervently wished that he had one too and could do more than just lie there impotently watching as the skirmish unfolded. His mouth was dry, his hands shaking and his breath coming in ragged pants as he watched Jim beside him, firing rapidly and with great accuracy at the machine gun slits. His face was a mask of concentration, yet he still had time to speak.

"All three have been damaged to some extent, and we can't do anything more now that they have the lids on those things. It's time we were going." He rose to his knees as he spoke. "Come on lads, let's get out of here." His voice was loud enough for all of the party to hear. "Stay parallel to the hedge, and for God's sake keep your heads down!"

Watson led off, closely followed by Smith, then Tony and Jim with Phillips bringing up the rear. The machine guns still raked the hedges, shattering branches in the process, and Tony felt a large splinter embed itself in his cheek. With his head hunched low between his shoulders and blood trickling from his cheek he followed the man in front as quickly as he could. None of them saw the 75mm gun of the first tank being brought to bear, the first they knew of it was the report of the gun firing, then the ground in front of them rising up in a cloud of earth and debris. In front of him Tony saw Smith stumble and fall to his knees, and beyond him the sickening sight of Watson, a large bloody hole in the centre of his chest and sightless eyes staring at the sky. He stopped in his tracks, head spinning and bile rising in his throat. This was a man he knew, a man who had been vibrant and alive seconds before, now lifeless and still in a spreading pool of blood. Tony felt himself beginning to shake as his body reacted to the excitement, fear and horror of the previous few minutes, minutes in which he had experienced more than in many a year of his previous existence. He felt his knees beginning to weaken and crumble. He wanted to sit down and weep.

"For God's sake keep moving, or we're all done for!" Jim's voice reached Tony as though from a great distance, yet it brought the civilian back to reality and he took a deep breath, ready to move on. "Pick up Watson's gun. I'll deal with Smith!"

Turning his horrified eyes away from the corpse of the man who had survived the Somme only to die beneath a French hedge twenty years later, Tony picked up the Lee Enfield and moved on. He glanced over his shoulder to see Jim and Phillips, each with one of Smith's arms around their shoulders, half carrying, half dragging the man whose left leg trailed uselessly behind him. Tony turned again and fixed his gaze on the wall ahead, which separated this field from the next. If they could get over that, they would be able to use its cover to reach a small wood further away from the road.

The tank gun spoke again and another section of the hedge exploded, but this time no one was hurt. Tony reached the wall and paused for a moment to regain his breath then, as he flung himself frantically upwards, bullets thudded into the stone, showering him with chips but leaving him unharmed. He landed safely on the other side and looked up to see Smith being pushed over the wall by his companions, amidst much cursing and swearing. Grabbing the young soldier by the voluminous material of his greatcoat, Tony dragged him down into the comparative safety of the wall, and the last two surviving members of their party quickly followed. Phillips was bleeding from a wound in the arm, but seemed not to notice it as he helped Jim lift Smith to his feet and, head down, made for the safety of the woods.

The gun roared again and a section of the wall behind them was demolished, but the Germans could not see them and were obviously loathe to waste ammunition on the gamble of perhaps getting another lucky shot. So, after two minutes of running with the fear of an explosion that never came, the four men entered under the eaves of the wood.

Once under the protective cover of the trees, the small party stopped to regain their breath and tend their wounded. Smith's leg had been shattered above the knee and was bleeding profusely. The small party had used all of their emergency field dressings after the Stuka attack, and so the wound was dressed with a strip of cloth torn from Tony's shirt; a rough splint was improvised from the branch of a tree and a crutch fashioned from a forked branch. Then they turned their attention to the flesh wound on Phillips' right arm, which was soon bound up. When the splinter was pulled from Tony's cheek, it began to bleed again but soon stopped as he pressed his handkerchief against it. Jim was the only one who had escaped unscathed, and he watched as Tony uneasily turned Watson's Lee Enfield over in his hands.

"Do you know how to use that?"

Tony nodded. "We often went shooting at home, and I'm sure I can handle this. It's just that..." He paused for a moment and looked back towards the road. "Well, this isn't how I'd planned to get a gun. I'd rather be unarmed and still have Watson here with us."

Jim nodded. "It's never easy to lose a fellow soldier." He too gazed back at the road. "At least it must have been over instantly, and he would have felt no pain."

As they looked back at the road they saw movement, as the crews of the three damaged tanks set to work on repairs. The three commanders spoke together in a huddled group before moving back round the bend and out of sight of the British soldiers. Moments later the sound of tanks revving up reached them, and there was a crash as one of the behemoths forced its way through the confining hedge and trees into the field. It moved slowly across the pastureland, by-passing the stricken tanks, before regaining the road through the gap in the hedge caused by the shell which had killed Watson. The remaining tanks followed the first through the field, and Jim smiled grimly.

"We obviously did a fair amount of damage if they're not waiting until the repairs are finished." His voice was grim. "That's three less tanks to bother our boys while we're re-grouping. Now," he stood as he spoke and helped ease Smith, grimacing in pain, to his feet, "let's get moving and try to meet up with the rest of our lot at Dunkirk."

They spent the night huddled around a fire to ward off the chill May night air, greatcoats pulled tightly around their shoulders, weapons and gas masks close at hand. Tony woke in the small hours to the damp and chill of the night. He stretched stiffly before placing more wood on the embers of the dying fire, then lay on his back to gaze up at the star-studded sky above. There was not a cloud in sight and the stars sparkled like diamonds. Tony though wistfully of the many nights he had camped out with David before the war, with nothing to disturb his nights save the hoot of an owl or the rustling of some small creature hunting in the undergrowth. Now all that his imagination would allow him to see was the torn and bloodied body of Watson. There was the sound of movement and he reached hurriedly for the Lee Enfield rifle beside him as an increasingly familiar fear gripped him. When he recognised the slim frame of Jim Briggs, he let go of the rifle and relaxed.

"Couldn't sleep?"

Tony shook his head. "No. I was thinking about Watson."

Jim sat beside him and gazed sightlessly into the flames, his mind reliving the last few hours.

"I know it was your first action Tony, and you did well. You should be proud of yourself."

Tony shrugged. "At times like this you do what you have to." He looked across at Jim and frowned. "What I don't understand though, is how you could just leave Watson there."

Jim turned towards Tony and, for the first time, the younger man saw the pain which the more experienced soldier had been hiding from him.

"It's as you say. We do what we have to do. If we'd stopped to bring him away more of us could have been injured or killed; and he wouldn't have wanted that. He'll be found and buried, whether by the French or the Germans we'll never know. But they will take care of the body, just as we will if we find a German dead beside the road and time permits it."

"I guess you're right, but it doesn't ease the pain." Tony sighed as he looked across at the sleeping soldiers. "War isn't what I'd expected it to be. I was so excited last September, so eager to fight. Now, after the last few days, I look back and can't recognise the boy who thought like that."

Jim nodded. "War makes us grow up. Fast." He laid a comforting hand on the young man's shoulder. "Now try to get some sleep, we've a long way to go tomorrow."

The young lieutenant lay down and wrapped his greatcoat tightly around himself to keep out the cold as Tony nodded. "I'll sleep soon."

He sat for a while longer gazing up at the stars. Although he had not even officially joined the army, here he was, an accepted member of a combat group, desperately searching for a way back to the retreating BEF and safety. The war was not turning out how he had expected it would. There was none of the glory he had read about in his boyhood, none of the excitement, only pain and death and the cold of the night. He hoped that the war would not last long. At last he lay beside the fire and drifted into a fitful, troubled sleep.

4

It took them five days to reach Dunkirk, moving slowly because of the wounded Smith and Phillips, and because of the need to stay hidden from the enemy who were now close on their heels. For some reason the German tanks seemed to have slowed their advance and did not pass the small group of men, but there was always a chance of being spotted by the Stuka patrols and their days were filled with apprehension and fear. On the third day they reached their own lines and watched as Smith was whisked off ahead of them by field ambulance; Phillips, although his wound was slight, could have gone too, but decided to stay and walk the rest of the way with Tony and Jim.

The road was thronged with people. Children pulled boxes on wheels, the boxes laden to overflowing with their few possessions; old folks mixed with women and children; and now and then a group of French soldiers would be seen, as weary and dejected as the rest. They now knew that General Lord Gort had ordered a full retreat towards Dunkirk as the victorious German army gradually moved closer on all sides save that of the open Channel coast. Whenever they stopped to rest and talk with other retreating soldiers, they were assured that there would be ships at Dunkirk to take them back to England. But there were so many soldiers! How would they find enough ships? And what about the civilians?

Tony felt as though he had been retreating with the soldiers for most of his life. He was no longer concerned by the looting he saw; at least things were taken without violence. He himself had acquired the odd loaf of bread and piece of cheese from deserted houses where the food would only have rotted if left. Yet, no matter how much a soldier he felt, he could not get used to the constant strafing by Stukas. They attacked in the same manner as before, shallow shrieking dives which sprayed the road with bullets, tight climbing turns and then back again from the opposite direction. Now people ceased to help those they did not know, saving themselves for friends and family; few had the energy, or means, to be of assistance to the wounded, the lost, the insane. Burning vehicles littered the road and the smells of burned flesh, rubber and metal were everywhere, clogging the throat and making breathing difficult. The men spoke little, for their throats were raw and they were bone tired. The only thing keeping them going was the blind hope of Dunkirk and a boat home.

They saw the pall of smoke above Dunkirk long before they reached the port. The air above them was frequently filled with aircraft, mostly German, which seemed to be bombing and strafing something on the edge of the land. Somehow the civilians were being weeded out by the military police, who directed the soldiers onwards, but the roads were still crowded and progress was slow. At last they reached the outskirts of the town, and made their way towards the sea on a tidal wave of helpless humanity. Then they were there, on the promenade, and stopped in stunned surprise. The sight that greeted their eyes was so unexpected that they could barely take it in. The long beach was a seething mass of waiting soldiers, wounded and weaponless, though the new arrivals could not see what they were waiting for.

"My God!" Phillips spoke in an awed whisper. "The whole bloody army is 'ere! 'Ow the 'ell are we supposed to get away?"

Jim shook his head. "God knows! Though something must be planned or we wouldn't be waiting here like this. Come on," he led the way down onto the beach as he spoke, "let's see if we can find someone who can tell us what's going on."

They found a young lieutenant, directing new comers to move along to make room for others who followed close behind. His uniform was filthy, his face drawn and haggard, but he seemed to know what was going on so they stopped to talk to him.

"It's called Operation Dynamo," he explained. "The navy has been ordered to pick us up off the beaches and take us back home. From what I've heard and seen they weren't ready for anything like this, and only had about forty destroyers available."

"Forty! But it will take weeks for them to get us off!" Jim was appalled at the prospect and the young lieutenant shook his head.

"That's just it though. They started picking us up three days ago and I've seen all kinds of ships - destroyers, personnel carriers, fishing trawlers, even paddle wheelers and Thames barges. It seems they put out a call for all available shipping and even the local yacht clubs have turned out." He shook his head again, as though still unable to accept the enormity of it all. "Many of the boats out there are manned by civilians, and many of them have made upwards of half a dozen trips already. Look, another lot's coming in now." He pointed down the beach and the newcomers peered through the clouds of smoke in an attempt to see what was happening.

Then they saw them. Boats of all shapes and sizes moving into the beach under cover of the smoke. Soldiers rose wearily to their feet and formed orderly queues out into the water where they were helped aboard. Those too far away to have a chance of boarding this time just shuffled a little closer to the sea, then sat down to continue their wait. It was all so quiet, so orderly, like waiting to embark on a summer pleasure cruise.

"You say it's been like this for three days?" Tony was incredulous.

The lieutenant nodded, then seemed to notice for the first time that Tony was not in uniform.

"Are you a civilian?"

"Yes."

The young officer looked uncomfortable. "I'm afraid we're only allowed to take troops off from here. You can't go with us."

Tony felt a cold knot of fear in his stomach and his hands began to shake. Not go? Would they really just leave him behind to be picked up by the Germans? He knew that would mean imprisonment until the end of the war and he felt sick. Why had he not gone with his grandmother from Saint Nazaire? He must have paled at the thought of what might lay ahead of him, for he felt a comforting hand on his shoulder as Jim spoke.

"Don't worry Tony, you're coming with us." He turned to his brother officer and explained. "This man has been with us through Stuka attacks and helped us to ambush a convoy of Panzers. He took part in the action and his grenade helped disable one of the tanks. He also helped to carry a wounded soldier out of enemy held territory to where he could get medical aid. I say he should get the same chance as the rest of us."

The young lieutenant nodded. "He's one of us all right if he's done all that, uniform or not." He turned to Tony and smiled. "See if you can get hold of a greatcoat or something to make you look more like a soldier, then you and your mates can move on down the beach. Just be patient and take your turn when it comes. Though heaven knows when that will be."

With that he turned away and began wearily to direct the next group of newcomers.

"Come on." Jim led his tired companions further along the beach as he spoke. "This way looks as good as any."

Above the muffled sounds coming from the beach, the unmistakable sound of diving Stukas filled the air as they started to move. All around them men dived for cover beneath the promenade wall. Further down the beach, where there was no cover, men crouched in shallow fox holes scraped out of the sand. Some just sat and waited, praying that this time the gouts of sand thrown up by machine gun bullets would not reach them. Bombs fell, throwing huge fountains of sand into the air, and the ground shook.

The attack only lasted a few minutes, although it seemed like hours to the vulnerable men on the beach, then the planes moved swiftly away to re-arm in preparation for their next attack. The men sat up, shaking off a loose covering of sand, and Phillips looked round at the calm acceptance of the men on the beach. Some soldiers were already carrying the dead up towards the promenade. They no longer needed a place on the ships. Others were treating their wounded companions in the open.

"Some of these men have been here for days. God knows how they can stand it," Phillips said to no one in particular as two men carried a dead comrade past them. Jim stood up.

"Can we have his coat please? I'm afraid he won't be needing it any longer."

The two privates looked hesitant.

"Is that an order, sir?"

Jim shook his head. "No, but our companion here will need something warm tonight if it gets cold."

The two men thought for a moment, then nodded and stripped the coat from the body.

14

"Here you are, sir."

Jim took the coat with a word of thanks and held it out to Tony. The young man looked at the dead soldier with half of his head blown away, then back at the coat. The collar was still wet with his warm, sticky blood and Tony shook his head, praying that he would not disgrace himself by being sick.

"I can't wear a dead man's coat."

"It's the only way you're going to get one, and you won't get off the beach without it."

Jim still held out the offending article and finally, reluctantly, Tony reached out and took it.

5

David sat in the cockpit of his Spitfire, the roar of the Merlin engine filling his ears, as he followed closely on the tail of his flight commander. At last the coast of France came into sight. This was it, the moment of truth. Yet David felt no fear as he approached his first taste of battle, just an intense exhilaration at the thought of the contest ahead of him. As the planes approached the black pall of smoke which hung like a shroud over the beaches of Dunkirk, he looked down at what he could see of the shattered remnants of the British Forces. They all seemed so remote, spread out down there before him like ants at a summer picnic, as though the retreat was part of another world. He did not stop to think about the fact that this was a fight to the death.

"Look out! 109's!"

The voice through the intercom startled him and David looked wildly about. Then he saw it. A Messerschmitt Bf 109E, grey and evil-looking with the black crosses along its sides. With the sound of his blood pounding in his ears, David turned towards the enemy plane, hoping to approach it unseen. He wondered if the opposing pilot was also facing combat for the first time. The German must have seen him approaching from behind for the plane began to turn a tight circle to the right, and David followed it. His whole being seemed to be concentrated on the plane as it tried to evade him, and David could see the pilot crouched in his cockpit, as though to urge extra speed from his machine. Then the 109 was in his gun sight. With hands slick with sweat, holding his breath in utter concentration, David pressed the trigger which set his eight machine guns roaring, and he watched the flash of his bullets as they ripped into the wing and tail-plane of the 109. Suddenly David felt bullets thudding into his Spitfire and his stomach churned with fear.

"For God's sake, look out behind you!" a voice yelled through the intercom as David swerved away to the left.

Out of the corner of his eye David saw another Spitfire in a steep dive on an intercept course with the German plane that he had been attacking. His comrade fired and hit the 109 with a burst of gunfire which tore off the left wing and caused the Messerschmitt to plummet towards the earth in a spiraling dive. David did not have time to see if the pilot bailed out, as he turned to fire on the plane which was pursuing him. Two rapid bursts of machine gun fire and he saw smoke pouring from the German aircraft. His fear was suddenly replaced with a wild exhilaration. He felt he could do anything. He had shot down his first enemy aircraft, and now the whole world lay before him. Then he looked at his instrument panel and noticed his fuel gauge. He spoke into the radio.

"Blue 2 to Blue Leader. Blue 2 to Blue Leader. Am returning to base. Low on fuel. Over."

"Roger, Blue 2. See you in the bar. Over."

David turned and headed back towards England. The flight was uneventful after the hectic dogfight above the beaches. He flew straight and true, man and machine at one with the sky, his mind filled with images of the recent battle. When he landed at Hornchurch with only a few gallons to spare, his heart was still thumping with the excitement of combat, head aching from the smell of cordite, mouth dry. Now it was all over, reaction to the combat began to set in and he felt a deep weariness. As he made his way towards the Dispersal Hut to report to the intelligence officer, his knees were weak with the relief of being back on the ground again.

Over the next fifteen minutes the remainder of the planes landed, and it did not take the intelligence officer long to add up how many German planes had been confirmed or probably destroyed by the two flights of No. 74 Squadron. No sooner had he finished than the pilots were ordered to return to their aircraft, which had already had their bullet holes swiftly but expertly patched. The squadron took off again, their planes completing the journey across the Channel in a tight formation which was swiftly broken when they ran into the enemy above the beaches. David felt a knot of fear in his stomach as he saw the mass of Heinkel bombers approaching like a gaggle of grey geese. Flying a little above these were a close escort of countless Me 110's while, high above these, was formation upon formation of Me 109's, betraying their presence by their smoke trails at such a high altitude. How was their squadron, only twelve planes, to combat such a huge number of the enemy? Then the RT crackled.

"B Flight, take on the top cover. A Flight, stick with me and we'll show these bombers what we can do."

David pulled back hard on the stick and climbed rapidly, the force of his climb pushing him back into his seat like a heavy fist. Suddenly he found himself in the centre of a milling mass of Me 110's. Locking in on the nearest enemy plane, the Spitfires machine guns began to live up to their name. The first burst missed, and David turned swiftly to stay on the tail of his prey. Tracer bullets from the rear gunner crept closer and closer to David, and he crouched down as though to make a smaller target as he depressed the triggers again. This time he scored a direct hit, and the enemy plane fell like a stone, both engines blazing.

Licking his dry lips and wiping the sweat from his brow, David turned back into the dogfight. The sky was filled with tracer and flying bullets. He had lost count of the number of ominous thuds that he had heard ripping into the fuselage of his plane, and he offered a silent prayer that the damage was not too great, that he would make it home. Another enemy plane, this one with a shark's jaw painted on its nose, passed in front of him. Pushing his fears aside, David tacked onto its tail and fired from about forty yards' range. He could not miss, and felt a surge of exhilaration as he emptied the last of his ammunition into the plane. As the enemy began to fall from the sky, David pulled out of the aerial combat and headed for home.

6

Sarah Porter stood with the other VADs and nurses on the steps of Heronfield House waiting for the casualties they had been warned to expect. This would be her first experience of dealing with wounded people, and she chewed nervously on her lower lip.

Sarah turned towards the VAD beside her.

"Something's happening at last. When I joined up the day after Chamberlain declared war, I didn't think it would be nine months before I saw my first patient!"

Jane Scott grinned. "Yes, but the training has been fun, hasn't it?"

Sarah nodded and smiled. "Yes. And I'm so glad we've both been posted here."

"Yes, but it's been bloody hard work this last week. Typical of administrators I'd think. We're supposed to be at war for nine months, and we do nothing. Not till the Germans are chasing our boys right across France do they send us here to set up the convalescent homes, and only give us a week to do it. Bad planning if you ask me."

"Stop moaning, Jane! At least we're going to see some patients at last!" She looked behind her at the old mansion house. "I don't suppose many of the wounded would expect to be treated somewhere like this."

"I bet it's only for the officers. Ordinary soldiers will probably go somewhere a little less plush."

"You are a cynic. Still," Sarah perused the edifice which was Heronfield House, "you have to admire the Kemshall family for giving all this up to be used as a hospital for the duration, and moving into that little lodge at the end of the drive."

"Little lodge! It's much bigger than my home!" Jane laughed. "How the other half live, hey. I never thought I'd find myself in a place like this in a million years!"

"Then let's make the most of it while we're here."

Sarah looked around at the people assembled on the steps. The nurses and doctors were ready to greet their patients, and a number of men had been called in from the nearby village to act as stretcher-bearers. She frowned to see so many people gathered there together.

"You know, I expected the wounded to come in ones and twos, but it looks like they're expecting far more than that today. Do you think the rumours that our men in France have been defeated are true? I've heard the whole army is being evacuated under fire, but surely that can't be right?"

"Of course not. It's only been a few weeks, there's no way the Germans could have defeated us yet."

"Then what's this all about?"

Jane shrugged. "I don't know, but I think we're soon going to find out. Look, here they come."

Sarah checked that her auburn hair was neatly arranged, and smoothed her starched white apron as she craned her neck to see down the sweeping driveway that led to the house. Sure enough two, no three, buses had just passed the Lodge and were making their way towards them. Sister Freeman, as senior nursing officer present, made her way down the steps to greet the new arrivals. As the first bus halted at the bottom of the steps, Sarah licked her dry lips and put on a welcoming smile. As Heronfield House was to be used as a convalescent home, the wounded would already have been treated at field dressing stations before being brought back to England; thankfully she would only have to change dressings and help to re-build the strength of the men as they were made ready to return home. It would have been a far different prospect if she had to deal with wounded straight from the battlefield. But she was wrong.

The first casualties to be helped from the bus were a group of officers. They were dirty, disheveled, some wore only part of a uniform and everywhere - on arms, legs, bare torsos - were bloody bandages.

"Good God!" Sarah was stunned. "What has happened to the usual casualty routine? These men should have had their wounds cleaned and properly dressed at a field dressing post somewhere along the line, but they look as though they've come straight from the battlefield. What the hell is going on out in France?"

As she made her way down to help the walking wounded while the stretcher cases were carried inside, Sarah noticed the dirt and the smell, a miasma of sweat, blood, putrescence. She felt physically sick. Never had she expected to see anything like this! What were the conditions like further down the line, if these men had come all the way to a convalescent home in the heart of England in this state?

Putting an arm around the waist of a young man who struggled to mount the steps with a swollen leg smothered in bloody bandages, she quickly assessed his condition. He was unshaven, his face haggard from pain, lack of food and sleep. Blinking away the tears which pricked her eyes, she smiled a welcome.

"Come on now. You're home at last. Everything will be all right. You're in England now." She talked to him as though he were a child, not really knowing or caring what she said. The words were as much of a comfort to herself as to him.

Heronfield was not prepared for such an influx of men in need of emergency treatment; the small operating room was soon in constant use, while those less seriously injured had to be tended in the wards. The crisp white sheets on the beds were soon filthy as uniforms were removed and bodies, unwashed for many days, carefully sponged down. The men were dead tired, some did not even wake when their uniforms were removed and they were washed. They soon awoke with cries of pain though, as the field dressings which had stuck to their wounds were soaked and then peeled away.

Sarah helped her casualty onto a bed and he lay down thankfully. His leg was swollen to an unbelievable size, and Sarah saw that it would be impossible to remove the trousers. A sister hurrying past with a tray of syringes noted her hesitation.

"Cut them off down the seam. They may have to be used again."

Sarah took a pair of scissors and began to cut the uniform away to expose the leg, bloody and mangled. The wound had obviously been dressed on the battlefield days before, and then not looked at again. The sickly-sweet smell of putrescence rose from it and she fought to control her churning stomach. As the dressing stuck to the wound, she began to soak it in warm water. The soldier winced in pain. His face was ashen and his eyes tightly closed when Sarah looked at him.

"How long has it been like this?"

"Six, maybe seven days. It's hard to remember."

Sarah was aghast. "You couldn't get treatment in all that time?"

The soldier shook his head. "Treatment wasn't the most important thing on my mind, I was just glad to get away with my life. You can't imagine what it's like out there." He closed his eyes as though to try to drive the scene from his mind, but the images were obviously still there, for he continued to speak. "The whole bloody army is stuck on the beaches at a place called Dunkirk, and it looks as though every ship in England has sailed to help us. I was brought off by a Thames barge."

Sarah felt rather than saw someone at her shoulder, and turned to look. It was Sir Michael Kemshall, owner of Heronfield House. She had seen him before but only at a distance, and had not realised that he had come to the main house to greet the casualties.

"Can I help you, sir?"

"I would like to talk to the soldier, if I may."

Sarah was not sure what to do. She shrugged her shoulders.

"Well, I suppose it will be all right as long as he wants to. But don't tire him."

The soldier opened his eyes, and looked at the balding man in front of him.

"Are you the doctor?"

Sir Michael shook his head.

"No. I'm just trying to find out if anyone has seen my son. His name is Tony. Tony

Kemshall. He's a civilian, and he's somewhere out in France at the moment. Have you seen him?"

The soldier shook his head.

"Can't say I have sir, but there's hundreds of thousands of men on those beaches. Most can't even find their own company again, so there's no chance of me remembering a stranger. They all seemed to be strangers to me."

Sir Michael muttered his thanks and moved on in an attempt to find someone, anyone, who might know the whereabouts of his son. A doctor took his place and lifted a corner of the now loosened dressing. He turned to the nurse who accompanied him.

"I think you should get this one prepared for surgery. You," he turned to Sarah as he spoke, "there are more being brought in all the time. Can you get another one cleaned up for me, please?"

Sarah nodded and moved across to the next bed, where two men carrying a stretcher had just deposited a soldier. His eyes were covered with a blood-soaked bandage, his uniform torn and bloody. Feeling desperately sorry for him, Sarah laid a hand on his shoulder, and he started at the unexpected touch.

"Hello." Sarah's voice was cheerful, though her eyes filled with tears as she began to help him out of his uniform. "Let's see what we can do for you."

7

David sat in the mess with a half-empty pint of beer, his second so far, in his hand.

"It was far more exhilarating than I'd anticipated." He smiled grimly. "Once we actually came into contact with the enemy I didn't feel afraid at all."

"I know what you mean." Martin Ritchie signed a chit for the drinks. "The planes seem so impersonal, as though you're not really shooting at people. It's only when they bail out that their humanity sinks home."

The door burst open and the rest of their flight came in.

"Good news." Ted Browne walked up to the bar. "Philip and Ken are both all right. They were shot down, but they're reported to be with the army on the beaches."

"Not bad, considering how many of them we shot down." David turned so that he could see the station band, who had grouped together around the piano in the dining room, and were beginning to play. "Still, they did some damage to us. You should have seen my kite!"

Martin laughed. "It's the best impression of a sieve I've ever seen! But you're not the only one. We'll be lucky to get a dozen planes in the air tomorrow."

David finished his drink and called for another round. It was funny how the combat seemed to have stirred up a terrific thirst in them all. Perhaps it was a way of coping with the excess adrenalin, for the drinking went on late into the night as they swapped tales of confirmed kills and near misses. All the time the band played lively dance tunes, as though attempting to make the men forget that they must be up again early the next morning, to fly once more against the enemy.

The next day dawned to find a depleted squadron out on the airfield. Of their sixteen aircraft only eight were serviceable enough to fly.

"Even less than we thought!" Martin grinned nervously. "What good will eight of us be able to do?"

"Don't worry." David grinned at his friend as they made their way towards their planes. "We'll do all right, just like yesterday."

The engines roared into life, and the flight took off for the uneventful trip across the Channel. It was only as they crossed the French coast that they ran into about fifty German bombers with their fighter cover and, regardless of the odds, attacked from below. All was a whirling confusion of planes and tracer bullets. There was no chance of avoiding the enemy, all they could do was to hope for the best as they picked a target and stuck to it until it went down.

"That's two to me!" David's voice was ecstatic as the adrenalin flooded his system. "One has gone down, I saw it flaming as it went; the other's limping away with both engines smoking. I don't think we'll see him again today!" He looked down at his fuel gauge. "I'm getting low. Heading for home." As he turned his plane in a sweeping curve back towards the Channel and home, the RT crackled.

"I've been hit!"

It was Martin's voice, and David frantically scanned the sky to see where he was. At last he saw him. The plane was in a shallow dive as it headed north towards England. David dived in pursuit, imagining the fight that Martin must be putting up to bring her under control, and praying desperately that the damage wasn't too bad.

"Hang on there, Martin. Your engine is smoking, but it will get you home in one piece."

"No chance of me making it in one piece, David." Martin's voice was strained." I've already lost the bottom half of my leg."

For a moment David closed his eyes, in an effort to bring his whirling emotions under control. At last, head spinning, bile rising in his throat, he was able to speak.

"Come on Martin, pull her up." He tried to force a little joviality into his voice. "You drank so much last night that you can't be losing any blood yet, just alcohol!"

A strangled sound, almost a laugh, came over the RT.

"We must have drunk enough to float all those boats down there."

David looked down, and realised that they had now dived perilously close to the heaving grey waves.

"Come on, Martin. You can do it." His voice was encouraging and at last he saw the plane responding, coming out of the dive into level flight some thirty feet above the waves.

"Escort me home, David?"

"Of course. It's your round first though. Don't ever give me a scare like that again."

They flew slowly towards England, talking briefly at times, but the silences between their comments became longer and longer, and David could feel Martin slipping away.

"How are you feeling, Martin?"

There was no reply.

"Martin?"

At last a whisper.

"I'm tired, David. The floor's swimming with blood."

David felt a lump in his throat.

"You can make it, Martin. I know you can."

"Thanks mate." Talking was obviously an effort. The words were coming slower now, and slurred. "Do me a favour. Phone Mum and tell her it was all over very quickly. I don't want her to think I died in pain."

David felt tears in his eyes, and dashed them away with the back of his hand.

"I'll tell her."

"Good luck, David. Kill one of those bastards for me."

David could say nothing as he watched Martin's Spitfire waver in the air, as though the pilot were losing control.

"I'm tired. I'll be glad to sleep."

The plane banked to the left and fell into the cold embrace of the sea, while David continued grimly home alone.

It seemed strange to David to be flying without Martin. They had not seen much action, but they had been together for some time and immediately hit it off. It is rare to find such a friend, and David found his mind wandering as he flew towards France, thinking of the good times they had spent together, wishing he had been able to help Martin by intercepting his attacker, praying that he would not die in the same way. Martin had not been the only one who had failed to return from the previous day's sortie, but at least the two other pilots had been seen parachuting down, and it was hoped that they were still alive. Now just one flight of six planes could be mustered due to the missing pilots and the number of bullet-ridden planes, but one flight seemed to be enough.

As they approached the coast of France, David tried to focus his attention on what lay ahead. This could be his opportunity to avenge Martin, or if he was too distracted, his last flight. As the six planes scanned the skies for enemy aircraft, they were amazed to find themselves virtually alone after the crowded skies of the previous day. Only three enemy aircraft were sighted during the patrol. Two were shot down and, as the other limped away home over France, David found himself wondering, for the first time, what the German pilot might be going through. He was in the same situation that Martin had been in, crippled and hoping to make it home. Yet David did not find himself sympathising with the pilot, only hoping that his plane would not make it, that he would die as Martin had, that it would go some way towards avenging his friend's death.

With fuel running low and magazines still half full of ammunition, B Flight turned for home and landed at Hornchurch without further incident.

They were just downing their first pint in the officers' mess when Flight Lieutenant Reynolds walked in. His shock of blond, almost white, hair was responsible for his nickname of Polar Bear, or sometimes just Bear. When David first met the Canadian, he had thought him a little too old for a fighter pilot, already thirty, yet he had soon come to respect the man's superb flying skills and excellent marksmanship. With an aggressive flair for leadership that was going to be very useful in the months ahead, Reynolds was proving a popular squadron leader with his men.

Although a born leader, his manner was quiet. As he approached the bar, he carried himself with an air of confident authority, and the strong face broke into a broad grin.

"Well lads, look at this!" He held out a flimsy piece of paper as he spoke. "It's from Dowding, the C in C Fighter Command, to all you brave lads of No. 74 Squadron. Apparently we're considered to have put in a magnificent performance, and are ordered to retire to RAF Leconfield to rest, and try to find a few Spitfires that are not full of holes!"

"When do we leave?" Ted Browne's face was wreathed in smiles. The last few days had been exhausting, and he felt desperately in need of a rest.

"First thing in the morning."

There was a whoop of joy and a rush to the bar.

"Although the Expeditionary Force has been defeated, this is not the end of the war." Browne took a long draught from his glass. "Hitler is sure to try to invade England next, and we'll be ready to push his Luftwaffe back where it belongs. He won't have the upper hand for long."

"Right, lad. And Leconfield will give us a chance to prepare for what's ahead." Bear looked grim. "Let's not kid ourselves, we've got a difficult few months in front of us."

David stared glumly into his half-finished pint.

"It's a shame Martin won't be coming. His mum lives up in Yorkshire, you know."

Reynolds laid a comforting hand on his shoulder.

"We all know how close you were, David. We miss him too. God alone knows how many of us will go down before this is all over, but we have to try to put it all behind us. What we must do now is concentrate on defeating Hitler. The grieving will come later."

David emptied his glass, and caught the barman's eye to ask for another.

"I suppose so. But right now I'm just wondering what I'm going to tell his mum."

8

It was their third night on the beach. Behind them, the buildings of Dunkirk were still burning fiercely, but far from being a problem this actually helped the evacuation. By day, the huge roiling clouds of black smoke hid the beaches from the ever-threatening Stukas, and at night the fires lit up the quays, or what was left of them, making it a little less dangerous for the lucky ones who were embarking. Tony looked around at the now familiar scene. The beach seemed to him like a field of fireflies as each soldier sat quietly smoking, waiting for the slow process of reaching the ships to be over at last. He huddled deeper into the dead man's greatcoat, glad now that he had it, for the wind coming in from the sea was cold, and the lack of food made him feel its keenness even more.

"I'll be glad to get back home, where it's warm and my clothes aren't full of sand."

Jim gave a weary, understanding smile.

"I know what you mean." He looked up the beach, back towards the burning buildings, almost unable to comprehend the huge numbers of men behind them. "Still, we've come a long way down the beach, and we'll get off long before those poor blighters behind us."

Tony turned towards the sea. It was difficult to see the water for the number of small boats bobbing upon it, and the men wading out waist-deep to reach them. Some of the smaller boats were ferrying soldiers out to those whose draught was too deep to allow them to come close into shore, and then coming back for more, time after time after time. Tony was still surprised by the orderliness of the evacuation. For two days now they had moved with agonizing slowness towards their only hope of escape from either death or imprisonment, yet there had been no fighting, no attempt to get there ahead of those who had been waiting longer. It made him feel proud to be British.

"With a bit of luck we should be able to get away tomorrow."

Jim nodded.

"As long as the Germans don't get here first."

With that depressing thought in mind, Tony lay down on the beach, shuffling to find a comfortable position before finally falling asleep to dream of Heronfield, before the war.

9

Sarah woke slowly to the whispering of her name.

"Sarah! Sarah! Come on. Get up. We have to be on duty in half an hour."

Sarah opened her eyes. "Oh, it's you, Jane." She stretched tiredly and sat up. "Can you get me a cup of tea while I'm dressing?"

"It's on its way." Jane smiled, turned and left the room which the two girls shared. Yesterday had been their first full day of caring for the wounded, and they had not left the wards until well after midnight. It was now half past six in the morning and Sarah had to be on her ward by seven o'clock. She washed quickly, and was in her uniform adjusting her cap when Jane returned with the promised cup of tea.

"Thanks. That should wake me up!" She sipped the scalding liquid, then yawned "I'm exhausted after yesterday; I never thought we'd have to work that hard." She shook her head sadly. "I thought we'd be dealing with one or two new patients each day, but there seemed to be no end to the number of poor men they brought in. It's sad, but after a few hours I was so tired that their condition didn't seem to worry me anymore. The sight of dirt and blood and gangrenous flesh all came to feel part of normal life." She shuddered. "I hope I'm not going to become immune to suffering. I don't want to lose all feeling for others, but I was glad that I couldn't feel anything. They made me so sad, so much pain and suffering. I wanted to heal them all and comfort them all, but there was so little I could do."

Her friend, already in full uniform, rubbed her tired eyes.

"I know what you mean. Those men had been waiting for so long for help, and what we could do for them just seemed like a drop in the ocean." Her face was serious. "By the looks of things we must have been defeated in France, which means that the Germans will be trying to invade us next. I'm scared."

Sarah nodded. "So am I. If those poor men who were brought here yesterday are anything to go by, we can't have much of an army left." They left their room and made their way down to their wards while they were talking. "Seeing them made me glad that Joe was found unfit." She stopped and turned to face her friend. "I suppose that sounds terribly unpatriotic of me."

"No." Jane's voice was understanding. "It's only natural to want someone you love to be safe, and it's not as though Joe isn't doing his bit. He's still working in the aircraft factory isn't he?"

Sarah nodded. "As soon as I get some more leave, I'll be going home to see him."

They walked the few remaining paces to the head of the stairs, where Jane went up and Sarah continued along to her ward. She pushed the door open as the clock in the hall downstairs began to strike seven. As Sarah entered and looked around she let out a deep breath she had not realised she had been holding. All the mess, smell and confusion of the day before was gone, to be replaced by an orderly, if small, ward in what had once been the nursery of Heronfield House. During their first few hectic days converting the old country house into a hospital, she had helped to clear this room, making sure that everything that was not needed for convalescing soldiers, including many toys that had not been played with for years, was boxed and stored in the stables for the duration of the war. She wondered what Sir Michael Kemshall's children would think of their old nursery if they saw it now. Would they even recognise it?

To the left of the door, Sister Freeman was arranging a sheaf of notes on a small desk. She looked up as Sarah entered.

"Ah, Miss Porter. Will you get the patients' teas for them, please; then we'll freshen them up for breakfast."

"Yes, Sister." Sarah left the room and went down to the kitchen where the tea trolley was ready and waiting.

The hospital which had been established at Heronfield relied heavily on the work of the VADs. Sarah had anticipated that it would be a calm, quiet environment with the convalescing soldiers, but the unexpected influx of untreated evacuees from Dunkirk had left a controlled business-like atmosphere about the place that was unexpected, though strangely invigorating. The one doctor assigned to the hospital, Dr. Henry Millard, was able to perform some operations, although his main task was to see that wounds healed cleanly when the men were sent for convalescence after a period in a more specialised hospital. The unexpected arrivals of the previous day had left him rushed off his feet, and two local doctors had been called in to help treat the wounded. The Senior Nursing Officer, Sister Freeman, was wondering how she would manage with just five nurses to aid her in the medical work of changing dressings, administering medication and re-habilitating amputees. She was thankful for the VADs who would carry out the remainder of the work, washing the patients, issuing bed-pans, bringing up food and drink, cleaning the wards and any other work which she deemed necessary. So it was that Sarah passed a busy morning, first bringing tea for the patients then washing them and preparing them for Dr. Millard's rounds. While he assessed the patients, with the aid of Sister Freeman and a nurse, Sarah thankfully took a quick break for breakfast before providing breakfast for her charges and washing the floor. It was after eleven o'clock before she was able to put her duties aside and spend some time talking quietly with the patients.

The first soldier she had helped into the ward the previous day was in the bed nearest the door and so she spoke to him first.

"Hello. How are you today?"

The young man turned haunted eyes towards her, his hands clutching convulsively at the sheets as a nod of his head directed her gaze to the cage which held the bedclothes high above his wounds.

"How do you think I'm feeling? How's a man like me supposed to go about getting a job with only one leg?" His words were bitter and angry.

Sarah did not know what to say, so said nothing, just laid a comforting hand on his shoulder. The soldier turned his face away, ignoring the hand that tried to soothe him.

"I don't need your sympathy, miss," he said at last. "Just leave me alone for now."

Sarah nodded. "All right, but I'll be back to see you later." She moved on to the next bed. The occupant had fresh clean bandages over his eyes, and she recognised him as one of the patients she had prepared for Dr. Millard the previous day.

"Hello. Can I sit and talk with you?"

The head turned towards her. "Yes, please. It's rather lonely not being able to see. Can you tell me where I am?"

Sarah smiled. "Of course. You're at Heronfield House. It's the home of Sir Michael Kemshall, but he's allowing us to use it as a hospital. This ward was once his children's nursery, and there are now twelve beds in it, all occupied."

The soldier was silent for a moment. "What's your name?" he finally asked.

"Sarah. What's yours?"

"Bob." He sighed. "Your voice sounds a bit like my girl's. Her name is Brenda, and she's waiting for me at home." He reached up to touch the bandages, which swathed the top half of his head. "They say I've lost the sight completely in one eye, and may only be able to see light and shade with the other. I wonder if Brenda will still want to wait for me when she knows?"

Sarah's eyes pricked with unshed tears as she took his hand in hers. "I'm sure she'll

24

still want you. I've got a man of my own, his name's Joe. I know that if this happened to him I wouldn't love him any less. I would just want to care for him to show him how much I love him."

"I don't want Brenda's pity."

"She won't pity you Bob, but you'll have to be careful not to confuse her love and concern for you with pity. It's probably self-pity you'll be feeling, and only seeing others' feelings as a reflection of that. It's you, the person inside, that Brenda loves, not just your body."

He squeezed her hand tightly. "You're a good girl. Your Joe is a really lucky man." He took a deep breath, as though to prepare himself for some ordeal, then he spoke again, his voice shaky. "Could you write a letter for me, please? To Brenda? She must be worried, and I think she really ought to hear about this from me."

Sarah nodded, then realising that he could not see her gesture, she spoke, her voice choking with emotion.

"Of course I'll write for you. Just hang on while I get some paper and a pen."

As she made her way to the desk by the door, she glanced out of the window into the gardens and stopped when she saw a figure standing motionless, gazing south towards the Channel and distant France. There was a world of loneliness in his stance, as though part of him was missing, and his heart and mind were reaching out in an attempt to draw that part back to himself, and make him whole once more. It was Sir Michael Kemshall, and she recalled from the previous day that his son was still in France. Her heart went out to the man as she sent up a swift, silent prayer that his son would soon be safely home.

10

The relentless intensive bombing by German planes had destroyed most of the quays at the port of Dunkirk, leaving only 'the mole', one of the two breakwaters which surrounded the harbour, for the larger ships to tie up against. From what Tony could see, the mole was about two thirds of a mile long, its main bulk constructed of rock, whilst most of the upper surface was boarded over with timber. A protective railing had been placed on both sides to prevent people falling into the icy water. It was not wide. Men could not walk along it more than three abreast, but it was their only way out to the larger ships which could not come close inshore. From a distance its surface was a dark seething mass of men.

As the hours passed slowly by, Tony saw that the water rose fifteen feet at high tide, so that the men merely had to cross makeshift bridges from the mole to board their escape vessels. At low tide they jumped down onto the heaving decks below, careless of danger to life and limb, only wanting to be away from the beaches at last. The line of men, three abreast, stretched back along the full length of the mole and then across the beach like the sinuous curves of a snake. They were gaunt, unshaven, expressionless with exhaustion. Many supported comrades who no longer had the strength to stand alone. When the Stukas came in there was nowhere to hide. Men just lay down on the boards and watched bullets splatter across the harbour towards them, praying that this time they would escape. The Stukas bombed the waiting ships whenever they could dive below the heavy pall of smoke which hung permanently above the harbour, and the water was full of burning wrecks, which made the task of evacuating the beaches even more treacherous.

Although thousands of men made their way out along the mole, Tony could see that the vast majority of the stranded army had no such aid to reaching the ships, and would have to leave the beach directly into the water. Tony, Jim and Phillips were amongst that group, and he envied those who were close to the mole and able to board without entering the cold waters of the Channel, which would draw all heat swiftly and surely from their bodies. Too long in the water could be almost as fatal as waiting on the beach for the next German attack. Evening was drawing in, and soon their fourth night on the beaches would begin. Thankfully they knew that it would be their last. Now only three or four men stood between them and the water's edge; one of the boats out there, one of the ones which they could now see, would take them away from this living hell and back to the rolling green hills of England. As the light faded on the evening of June 2nd, the Stukas came in for one final attack. Tony pointed out towards the mole as the planes screamed in a shallow dive. Many soldiers were lying down to avoid the bullets, while those nearer to the ships continued to leap aboard.

"That trawler's low in the water." Tony watched as the boat pulled away into the narrow channel of water leading out to the open sea. "It looks as though she might go over." As he spoke bombs began to fall and, although none of them hit the trawler, the huge shock waves caught her broadside, lifting her and slowly but inexorably pushing the overloaded ship onto her side. The screams and cries of the soldiers, who now found themselves struggling for their lives in the cold water, were drowned by the roar of Stukas and the evil chattering of machine guns. Many of the men trying to escape the sinking trawler were dragged from the water onto an already dangerously overloaded yacht, which rolled heavily in the swell for a moment before taking a direct hit from a bomb. The mast was hurled high into the air, along with flailing bodies and burning sails. When the smoke cleared, wreckage was still falling - a spar, planks of wood, a tattered strip of burning sail fluttering in the wind.

"The poor devils." Phillips crossed himself as he spoke.

Tony was thankful that night was falling fast, forcing the Stukas to withdraw, although the beach itself was not left in darkness. The burning port behind them and the dozens of ships afire ahead of them cast an eerie glow on the scene. A small pleasure cruiser appeared out of the smoke, bobbing on the waves in indecent parody of its peacetime duties. A cheerful sounding voice called out from the wheelhouse.

"Come on, you lot. Let's get you back home to a nice cup of tea."

The men in front of Tony began to ease their way forward, and were soon being helped aboard. Tony counted sixty-four men going aboard a boat that could only have been built to carry a quarter of that number, and marveled at the bravery of the civilians who had made this trip so many times before, yet still came back to aid the beleaguered army. When the small boat began to pull away Tony realized that there was no one else in front of him. The next boat to come to this part of the beach would be his ticket home.

He found himself standing in water up to his waist, the waves reflecting the flames of the burning ships in rainbow hues. Tony realised that the whole of the water's edge was coated with a thin film of oil from the wrecks. It clung to their clothes, and the stench of it invaded their nostrils as they stood as still as they possibly could, for the oil made it slippery underfoot. Tony had never felt so weak and tired before in his life. The constant shaking of his legs was due only in part to the low temperature of the water, and at times black dots danced before his eyes. He had slung Wilson's rifle onto his back, for he knew that he could not hold onto it much longer, and his hands hung limply at his sides. Jim noticed how weak his new friend was, and understood exactly how he felt. They had had nothing to eat for three days, and since their water had run out the previous evening they had existed on what they could gather from condensation. They had an unspoken agreement that none of them would go back up the beach, for that would mean losing their hard earned place and starting the endless waiting all over again.

They had been standing in the cold water, which seemed to drain the last reserves of their energy from their exhausted bodies, for almost an hour when Phillips pointed a shaking hand out to sea.

"Look at that. It's our ride home."

Making directly towards them, through the oil slick which covered the sea, was a small private yacht. For a moment it looked as though it might run them down before running aground, then it tacked beautifully and halted inches from the waiting soldiers.

"Come on lads."

A man in his thirties and a boy of about fourteen, perhaps his son, leant over the side and began to drag the exhausted men aboard. Tony watched as one soldier after another was hauled from the water, and prayed that he would not be left behind. At last, after what seemed like an eternity, he felt strong hands lifting him and laying him on the deck. The small, two-berth, cabin was already crammed with thirteen men so that Tony, Jim and Phillips were moved to the back of the boat. Another five men were helped onto the deck, a total of twenty-one evacuees in all, when the boat's owner took hold of the tiller and ordered his son to ready the sails.

"Don't worry lads, we'll be back," he said comfortingly to those left standing in the water. Some of them did not want to wait for the next vessel and, thinking that there might be room for just one more, began to swim out after the yacht. As they got out of their depth, the heavy uniforms began to drag them down. A dazed Tony saw three of them disappear beneath the surface of the water, before helping hands pulled their companions back to the comparative safety of the shallows.

Nothing was said as the yacht picked her delicate way through the harbour, past the burning wrecks that blocked most of the safe passages. The owner of the yacht sat at the stern, steering them carefully around obstacles, while passing quiet instructions to the boy at the sails. As they moved further from the shore Jim was able to see, for the first time, the full horror that was the beaches of Dunkirk and wondered again at the bravery of the men who came back time after time to do what little they could to help. He gazed off to port for a moment, a puzzled frown furrowing his brow, then his eyes opened wide in horrified understanding of what he saw.

"Look at that!" His voice was a hushed whisper and the others followed his pointing finger to see what could have affected him so.

At first they saw only what they thought was a causeway, some eight feet wide, extending far out into the sea. Then understanding dawned. It was not a causeway but a column of men, six abreast, standing as if on parade. Those at the front were standing up to their necks in water, calmly waiting for the Thames barge which slowly approached them. The yacht swung wide to avoid a burning pleasure cruiser, and the column of men was lost from sight. Moments later they rounded the end of the shattered harbour wall and were in the open sea.

"We're heading for Portsmouth." It was the first time their rescuer had spoken to them since they left the beaches. As Tony turned towards him he noticed the deep shadows under his eyes, and the weary stoop of his shoulders.

"How many times have you been to the beaches?"

"This is our nineteenth trip. Twenty-one soldiers at a time means that when we get you lot home we'll have brought back nearly four hundred men." He rubbed his eyes tiredly. "I'll try to get back one more time tonight, but it's not easy. The navy has only cleared three narrow channels of mines, and with all the buoys and lightships blacked out it's easy to wander from these. So if you gentlemen would like to keep an eye open for any strange objects floating near us, I would be most grateful."

For a time Tony watched the heaving grey waves for any sign of mines, but his tiredness, coupled with the relief of being away from the beaches at last, must have overwhelmed him, for he woke to find Jim shaking him gently by the shoulder.

"Tony. We're home." His voice was full of relief at an ordeal safely overcome, and Tony sat up to look around him. They were sailing into Portsmouth harbour, but not the harbour he knew from peacetime, for there were no lights shining, and the yacht had to maneuver carefully between other vessels before coming to rest beside the quay. The soldiers rose gratefully to their feet.

"Here you are then, lads. Home at last."

Tony turned to their rescuer and smiled a weary smile.

"I don't know how to find the words I want to say. 'Thank you' seems so inadequate after what you've done for us."

"No need for thanks, lad. I'm just doing my bit for king and country, same as you are. Now, if you'd like to go ashore, I think I'll get turned around and head back to France."

The soldiers climbed wearily onto the quay to be greeted by smiling women, civilian volunteers again, who handed out mugs of steaming tea and doorstep sandwiches.

"Move over to the warehouse, loves, and when you've rested a bit you can register, so that the army knows what to do with you. There are some postcards there as well, so you can write to let your families know you're safe."

They smiled their grateful thanks and moved off. Phillips noticed a friend nearby whom he had thought to be dead, and the small group said an emotional farewell as he went to rejoin his comrade.

"Just the two of us now." Jim sipped the scalding tea. "I'm glad about the postcards. My family must be worried sick about me. They'll be glad to hear I'm all right."

"I shan't bother with a postcard." Tony sat down on a packing crate. "Don't forget I'm still a civilian. I'm catching the first train home, and I'll be there long before any postcard can arrive."

Jim nodded. "I don't blame you. Do you still intend to join up?"

Tony nodded, images of dead civilians mingling with the beaches of Dunkirk in his mind. There was nothing else he could do.

"Well, I can't say too much at the moment, but just before all this blew up in France I was given a posting to a new unit, to take effect at the beginning of July. They said they needed men like me who can speak French and know parts of France quite well. You made a good showing of yourself out there Tony and I think they might be interested in you. I'll speak to my superiors and see what they say. I can't promise anything, but if you can postpone joining up for a month or so I'll be in touch. All right?"

Tony nodded. "Just as long as it's not some desk job translating French papers. I want to get some action against the Germans, after what I've seen out there."

"I know what you mean," Jim agreed. "I'll let you know as soon as I can."

11

The Tony Kemshall who walked towards the steps of Heronfield House that evening was very different from the smart young man who had set out on his journey to France. He was still wearing the bloodstained greatcoat that Jim had acquired for him on the beaches of Dunkirk. His trousers were stained with seawater and oil, and his shoes were splitting at the seams. He had landed at Portsmouth, and caught the first train for London at six a.m., changed at Guilford and again at Reading before taking the branch line to Marlborough. It was now almost six in the evening and the journey, together with his exhausting activities of the previous two weeks, left Tony so weak that he could barely stand. He was lucky to find a delivery van going his way and it dropped him off at the end of the drive. As his feet crunched on the gravel of the sweeping driveway, and he approached the house which had been home to him for all his twenty years, he felt a lump in his throat and tears in his eyes. There had been times over the last few days when he had thought that he would never see his home or his family again, never walk the driveway to the safe haven which awaited him. He smiled as he pushed the door open. It would be good to see his family again, and then to get some rest.

A frown began to furrow his brow, and he stopped. Something was wrong. It was the same hallway, with the same familiar furniture and pictures, but there was a subtle smell, like a hospital, in the air and he could hear the murmuring of many voices upstairs. A door closed down the hallway and, to his surprise, a nursing auxiliary approached, although Tony was too tired and bemused to notice the auburn hair, lively green eyes and clear skin. The woman, however, noticed his dark hair and complexion and the tired brown eyes. Her professional gaze also took in the tattered and bloodstained clothes, and the smell that had accompanied all of the soldiers who had come to Heronfield directly from the beaches.

"Hello." She greeted him with a warm smile. "I'm sorry there was no one here to meet you, but we weren't expecting any more wounded. Are you just back from Dunkirk, like all the rest?"

He nodded, trying to work out what this nurse was doing in his home. "I arrived in Portsmouth this morning, but I'm not wounded. Just tired."

Sarah frowned. "Not wounded? Then what are you doing here?"

Tony managed a weak smile. "I could ask you the same question. This is my home. Where's my family? What's happening here?"

Sarah's eyes opened wide. "Are you Sir Michael's son, Tony? He was in my ward, trying to find out if anyone had seen you at Dunkirk. He's been very worried about you. He'll be so glad you're safe."

"I'd like to see him, if you'll only tell me where he is."

"Oh, I'm sorry." Sarah noticed the young man swaying on his feet, and pulled up a chair. "You must be exhausted. Sit down while I explain." She waited while Tony thankfully lowered himself into the chair, then continued. "Your father has given up Heronfield House for the duration, to be used as a hospital and convalescent home."

"Yes, I vaguely remember him talking about it before I left." He smiled wearily. "I'm so tired and I was so eager to see them all again that I'd forgotten. Where are my family? Have they gone up to London?"

Sarah smiled. "No, they've not gone that far. They're at the lodge. I'll get someone to take you down there. I'm sure you..."

Realising that he was safe at last, Tony could stay awake no longer and slumped from his chair. As Sarah rushed to the side of the unconscious young man, she called for aid. Two more VADs came hurrying to help her carry him into the drawing room, where he was laid on a sofa. One of the girls went to summon the doctor, while the other ran down to the lodge to inform Sir Michael that his son had arrived safe home at last.

Sarah had already removed the greatcoat and was loosening Tony's filthy clothing, when the doctor arrived to conduct a swift but expert examination. He was just putting his stethoscope away as Sir Michael burst into the room.

"Tony? Is he all right?"

Dr. Millard nodded. "He's fine, just exhausted. I think it will be best if we let him sleep, then he can come down to the lodge with you when he wakes. A few days' rest and food and we'll soon have him back to his old self."

Sir Michael nodded his thanks as the doctor and Sarah left. Kneeling beside the couch he took his youngest son's hand in his own.

"Tony. Thank God you're alive." His voice was little more than a whisper. "I'm so proud of you. So very proud."

Sir Michael was glad he was alone with his son so no-one could see the tears of relief coursing down his cheeks.

It was lunchtime just three days after Tony had returned from Dunkirk. Sarah and Jane were taking a well-deserved break from work, sitting in the warm summer sun in the gardens of Heronfield House. Jane had been reading the newspaper, and sighed deeply as she put it down.

"Even Mr. Churchill admits we've suffered a great defeat. He says we must prepare for an invasion any time."

Sarah nodded sadly. "I wish I could go home and see Mum. She must be worried sick. And I'd like to see Joe again, just in case..."

Jane took her hand reassuringly. "I'm sure we'll be all right. Hitler won't get us without a fight." She picked up the paper again. "We can all do our bit. Listen." She began to read from the paper. "All signposts and place names are to be removed or painted out, so that they will not help enemy paratroopers to find their way. Defences along the coast-line have been extended, and many beaches are now off limits. It's now an offence to leave a car unlocked, or a bicycle not immobilised, or anything else which might help a German paratrooper."

Sarah laughed bitterly. "Much good that's going to do us without an army!"

Jane shrugged. "It's not over yet. We ought to be less pessimistic."

Sarah sighed. "I suppose you're right. Hitler hasn't won yet. But it all seems so hopeless after Dunkirk. How on earth are we going to defeat the German army, when most of our soldiers are in hospital, or a prisoner of war camp?"

There was the sound of footsteps on the gravel path, and the two young women turned to see Tony Kemshall approaching. He smiled warmly at them.

"Excuse my interrupting, but aren't you the nurse who met me when I came home?" Sarah nodded and he continued. "Can I speak to you for a moment please?"

Jane rose from the bench where they had been sitting.

"Well, I must get back to work. See you later, Sarah." With a quick wave of her hand she turned and ran across the lawn.

Tony looked more like his old self after three days of rest and home cooking. He was clean, freshly shaven and well dressed, and no longer so tired that his skin was pale and black rings circled his eyes. Unlike his first meeting with Sarah, he was now able to take note of her looks and the warm smile. He felt an instant liking for the young VAD.

"May I sit down?"

Sarah nodded. "Of course." She turned towards him with a puzzled frown. "I hope you don't mind me asking, but how did you get involved with the troops at Dunkirk, if you're a civilian?"

Tony found himself responding to her quizzical look with a smile.

"Of course I don't mind. I went out there to help my grandmother to get to England, and foolishly stayed behind. I suppose I thought it would be just like the books I used to read as a boy, but I couldn't have been more wrong." He frowned. "War is not all heroics, with the goodies always defeating the baddies. Still, I managed to get away in the end, and I wanted to thank you for being so helpful."

Sarah was a little embarrassed. "It's all part of the job, sir."

"Gosh, 'sir' makes me sound so old!" His face held such a look of mock horror that Sarah had to laugh. "Please call me Tony," he continued, "and may I call you Sarah? That is what your friend called you, isn't it?"

Sarah was not quite sure what to say. It was strange, but she already liked Tony. He was friendly and seemed in many ways to be just like her friends at home. Yet he wasn't. He was a member of the aristocracy, a class of people who would never dream of speaking to her under normal circumstances, and she felt uncomfortable to be talking so freely with him. Finally she shrugged her shoulders. What did it matter? They would probably never meet again and, after all, there was a war on.

"Of course you can call me Sarah."

She smiled across at him, and Tony's heart raced. That smile was something special, and he decided there and then that he wanted to get to know her better. Searching for some sort of common ground, he began to enquire about her family.

"Are any of your family in the Forces?"

Sarah shook her head. "No. There's only me and my mum. My dad died two weeks before the end of the last war, shortly before I was born."

"Oh, I'm sorry."

"That's all right. I never knew him, and I never really missed having a father as a child. I suppose it was a case of not missing what you've never had."

"What about your boyfriend? A pretty girl like you must have one. Is he in the army?" As he asked the question, Tony hoped that she would say no, there was no boyfriend, she was unattached and free to be courted. His brief hopes were soon dashed.

"My boyfriend is called Joe. The day after war was declared I joined the VADs and he tried to join the army, but they found him unfit. He has a weak heart. They say it's a result of the rheumatic fever he had as a child. He's taken a job in an aircraft factory, so he can feel he's doing his bit, 'though he'd prefer it if he could join up and fight." Sarah smiled. "I'll be going home to Coventry in a couple of weeks. It seems ages since I've seen him."

Tony noticed the extra brightness in her eyes and the softening of her smile as she spoke of Joe, and for some reason it saddened him. Here he was talking to a total stranger, yet she was making him feel things he had never felt before. He longed to get to know her better; and found that he was jealous of a man whom he had never met, and probably never would meet. Maybe he was still tired from his ordeal in France, still emotionally fragile after what he had seen and experienced, or maybe he had just found someone who could hold a special place in his life. Whatever it was, Tony was confused at his churning emotions, and felt that he needed some time alone to think.

"Well, thanks again." He rose as he excused himself. "I must go now. I promised to help my father with some paperwork. Good-bye, Sarah." He smiled at his new acquaintance. "Perhaps we can meet again sometime?"

Sarah smiled politely in return. "Yes, I think I'd like that. Good-bye, Tony."

As Sarah watched the young man walk back across the lawns, her smile deepened. Somehow she knew they would be friends.

Sarah arrived in Coventry on the nine o'clock train. It was dark and the blackout caused some difficulties for her, but she knew that she would soon get used to it. There were very few vehicles on the road. The inability to use headlights and the shortage of fuel kept most people at home, or if they had to go out they went on foot. Sarah walked along the edge of the pavement where every other kerbstone had been painted white, and used these as a guide through the streets to her home. It seemed strange walking up to the door of a house where no light peeped out from behind the curtains. As a child she had always thought of the lights as a loving welcome home but now the house seemed dark and eerie. Sarah knocked at the door and, after a few moments, heard the sound of footsteps coming down the hall. They stopped on the other side of the door.

"Who is it?"

Sarah smiled at the sound of the familiar voice. No matter that the house was dark, this was home.

"It's me, Mum."

"Sarah! Hold on a minute!"

There was the sound of a heavy curtain being drawn back and a bolt pulled, then the door opened.

"Come in love, I wasn't expecting you until tomorrow!"

Sarah went in and her mother closed the door behind her, shutting out the night. She drew the blackout curtain again and switched on the light.

"Hello, Mum."

Sarah smiled at her mother. Alice Porter was plump, and exuded a feeling of love and warmth to all around her. Since the death of her husband in late 1918, only six months after their wedding and four months before the birth of Sarah, she had provided for herself and her child by any number of jobs, usually cleaning. Although she had had to work long hours to make ends meet, Sarah had wanted for nothing and knew the kind of loving home which many people would envy. Sarah reached out and hugged her mother.

"I managed to get a train as soon as I got off duty, and didn't want to waste any more of my leave than I needed on travelling. Besides, I couldn't wait to see you."

Alice laughed. "You mean you couldn't wait to see Joe! He'd have been at the station to meet you if he'd known you were coming today. At least tomorrow is Sunday, so he'll be able to spend the whole day with you. It's his only day off, you know."

Sarah nodded as she put down her small case and took off her coat.

"You don't seem to have brought much with you love, how long are you staying?"

"I have to go back on Friday."

Alice led the way down the narrow hall into the familiar kitchen, and put the kettle on as she listened to her daughter talk. As they sat at the old wooden table and drank their tea, Sarah told her mother all about her work at Heronfield House, of the wounded and dispirited soldiers she had seen after Dunkirk and her fears for the future. Alice took her daughter's hand and gave it a gentle squeeze.

"Don't worry, love. The Germans didn't get to England last time and I'm sure we can keep them out now. The worst they can do is drop a few bombs and we're well prepared for that." She indicated the gas mask which Sarah had placed on the kitchen table when she sat down. "Apart from those infernal contraptions which we have to carry at all times, we now have an air raid shelter."

"How did you manage to get one?" Sarah asked. "I thought they were being given to people with large families first?"

Alice nodded. "True, but I agreed that if I had an Anderson shelter in the garden I would share it with the neighbours, so old Mr. and Mrs. Cook from number 27, and Mary Norman and her two children from number 31 will be using it too. We've decided to work as a team and do our bit for the war. Both of their gardens, and what's left of ours after that huge corrugated iron monstrosity was put in, have been dug over and planted with vegetables. It's been hard work, but worth it. We'll be able to provide ourselves with at least half of the vegetables we'll need, so we'll be able to use our ration coupons for other things."

"I'm impressed, Mum." Sarah took her empty cup to the sink and washed it. "You know," she said as she turned off the tap, "it seems strange to stand here at the sink and only see the blackout curtain. I'm so used to looking at the garden."

"You won't recognise it now, love. There's a lump in what used to be the lawn, where the Anderson shelter is, and the rest is all vegetables." She sighed. "I had to dig up my roses."

Sarah laid a comforting hand on her mother's shoulder.

"Surely not everything has changed?"

Alice laughed.

"No, not everything! Joe is still the same! He often calls to see how I am, which is really kind of him. You've got a good man there, Sarah."

Sarah nodded, barely able to suppress her excitement at the thought of seeing Joe again.

"Yes, I know."

Sunday morning dawned bright and clear, and Sarah was up early to be ready when Joe came round. It was just before ten o'clock when he called to ask Alice if she knew which train Sarah would be on, only to be greeted at the door by the one he had missed so much.

"Sarah!"

Sarah laughed, a gay abandoned laugh, and threw herself into the arms of the young man at the door. She kissed him happily and ran her fingers through his silky fair hair.

"Oh Joe! It's so good to see you again!"

"Really? I'd never have guessed!" He laughed, but made no effort to extricate himself from her arms.

"Come on." Sarah pulled away and took him by the hand. "Let's go for a walk. I've got heaps to tell you."

So they walked and talked in the warm summer sunshine, Sarah relating all that had happened in the twelve weeks since she had last seen Joe, and he describing his work at the aircraft factory.

"I don't mind the work," he concluded. "I just wish I could take a more active part in things."

Sarah squeezed his hand.

"I know how you must feel, but your job's as important as any soldiers. Without the armaments from the factories there'd be no chance of us winning this war. And now the army has had to get out of France, I'd think that the planes you're helping to build will be our main defense against invasion." She smiled lovingly at Joe. "You're doing as much for the country as any man in uniform."

Their steps had brought them to the beautiful cathedral in the centre of Coventry. The sun shone brightly on the yellow stone spires and the sound of voices raised in praise to God drifted out to them on the breeze.

"Isn't it beautiful." Sarah's voice was almost a whisper as she stood quietly absorbing the atmosphere. "I've always loved this place."

Joe nodded.

"So have I. I'd hate of think of the Germans invading, walking down our streets and worshipping in our cathedral. That's why I've done something about it."

Sarah turned towards him in surprise.

"What have you done, Joe?"

"Joined up."

Sarah frowned.

"But they found you unfit. Didn't they give you another medical?"

Joe shook his head.

"I didn't need one." He led her to a grassy bank dotted with daisies and buttercups. "Sit down and I'll tell you."

Sarah sat, curious to know what Joe had been up to. He sat too, facing her so that he blocked out her view of the cathedral.

"Did you hear Mr. Eden, the new War Secretary, on the radio a few weeks ago?"

"You mean when he warned about the danger of German paratroopers?"

Joe nodded.

"Well, he also talked about something called the Local Defence Volunteers. He wanted men who are not in the forces to join the Volunteers to prepare to push back an invasion, or spot enemy planes, or any number of jobs like that. It's part-time, so those who do join up don't have to give up their jobs; we don't get paid to be in the Volunteers either." He smiled. "The best part of it is that I don't need a medical. Any lads like me with a slight heart murmur or something else that keeps them out of the regular forces can join up, and feel as though we're doing our bit."

"And so you volunteered?"

Joe nodded. "Yes. I've got a uniform but no gun as yet, there aren't enough arms to go round. My duty is aircraft spotting three nights a week." He paused and looked at Sarah. "You don't mind, do you?"

Sarah smiled. "Of course not, Joe. I'm glad you can feel involved in the war effort. If only all men were so patriotic." She put her arms around him and hugged him tight. "I'm so proud of you."

"And I'm proud of you, Sarah." He kissed her gently and held her close, murmuring softly against her hair. "I hope this war will be over soon. I miss you so much when you're away."

They kissed again, and the peace and beauty of their surroundings faded into insignificance as Sarah clung tightly to the man she loved.

Sarah's leave passed quickly. Time spent with Joe seemed short, for his work at the factory and with the LDV could not be put aside for her, but it did give her more time to spend with her mother. Alice always seemed to exude confidence. For her there was no doubt as to the eventual outcome of this war. No matter that the British Army had suffered a grave defeat, they, and the civilians who had rescued them, had shown themselves to be courageous and resourceful, and Alice lived with the conviction that Hitler's Germany would eventually be defeated. Sarah was never to forget the afternoon they sat together listening to the radio and hearing an inspired Churchill speaking to a people rocked by defeat but not bowed down. The two women, like everyone who heard those words, listened in silence to the man who was to lead their country into battle. His praise for the men who had fought with the British Expeditionary Forces was uplifting, and his thanks to the civilian sailors left people in no doubt that all men and women in the country could play their part in the conflict which lay ahead.

"We shall fight on the beaches, we shall fight in the fields and in the streets, we shall fight in the hills; we shall never surrender."

Sarah reached across the table and took her mother's hand in her own.

"Is this what it was like in the last war? Did you prepare to stop an invasion too?"

Alice shook her head.

"No love, it never came to that. Our men, and theirs, were bogged down in northern France." Her eyes had a distant look, remembering the man she had loved and who never returned from the fields of death and destruction. "This war is different", she continued. "It's so unpredictable. But with a man like that leading us, how can we fail to win? His words are an inspiration to us all."

Sarah nodded. Yes, Churchill could thrill and uplift with his words. She thanked God that He seemed to have placed the right man in a position of power just when he was needed most.

13

The sun flooded the drawing room with its yellow morning light, as the family sat in quiet preoccupation after breakfast, each deep in their own thoughts and barely conscious of those around them. Chantrelle de Thierry gazed into the distance as though her eyes could see nothing but the destruction of her beloved homeland; Louise was reading the papers and trying to glean any information that she could about what was happening on the continent, while Tony gazed out of the window of the lodge towards the imposing façade of Heronfield House. It seemed strange to be so close to his home yet not living there, especially when he thought of Sarah being there and treating it like home. He wondered when he would see her again, and if she was looking forward to their next meeting as much as he was. Probably not. After all, she still had this 'Joe' who seemed to be so important in her life. He sighed. Life seemed so frustrating at the moment. He wanted to get to know Sarah better, but that seemed impossible: and he wanted to get back to France and fight; the need to do something seemed to burn in his heart like the flames he had seen surrounding the beaches of Dunkirk.

Tony could hardly believe that he had been home for three weeks already. He was feeling physically rested after his experiences in France, but found that his emotions were still in turmoil and he could not relax. At any moment of the day or night his mind would fill with images of the refugees, the tanks, the Stukas, the beaches. As he reflected on his experiences, he knew that he could not sit at home while the rest of the country prepared for war. He was restless and eager to fight, keen to join up at the earliest possible moment. Yet he had promised Jim that he would wait to hear from him before he joined up, and now that promise weighed heavily on him. What was taking so long? He remembered their last conversation together as they said goodbye in Portsmouth. He replayed the words again and again in his mind. Jim had definitely said that he would call, and that there would be a job he could do. What was taking so long? He wanted to join up now, to pay the Germans back for the dead boy on the road, the wounded and dead soldiers he had seen, the beaches of Dunkirk. He frowned deeply in frustration. What was taking Jim so long?

Sir Michael put down the letter he was reading and turned towards his son.

"That was a letter from David. It seems that my two sons both had their first taste of action at Dunkirk."

"David was at Dunkirk?" Tony turned towards his father in surprise. Just the name conjured up the feelings of tiredness, hunger, fear, hopelessness and dread which had been his all-encompassing experience of Dunkirk. He heard the sound of the Stukas again, the chattering of their machine guns and the thud of their bombs as they fell among the crowds of humanity thronging the beaches. Somehow he had not been aware, amidst all the chaos, of any British planes involved in the evacuation. He shivered as he remembered the horror he had experienced on the beaches, and hoped he would never have to face anything like that again. "You know, Dad, we saw very few of our aircraft there. The sky seemed to be full of Stukas. They kept bombing and strafing us, but we saw hardly any fights between British and German planes. It was as though they had complete control of the skies, and our boys were nowhere in sight."

Sir Michael nodded. "I can understand how you might have got that impression. From what David says in his letter they flew high and engaged the fighters above the clouds, sometimes above the beaches and sometimes inland, trying to stop the enemy planes reaching the evacuation point. He says that they couldn't see anything of what was going on on the beaches under the clouds of smoke."

"How is David?"

"He's fine. He survived Dunkirk with no injuries, just like you." Sir Michael gazed thoughtfully at his younger son. "He asks in his letter if you've joined up yet and, frankly, I've been wondering about that myself. You know more about what's going on in France than most people. I thought you'd have joined up by now, instead of waiting to be called up."

Tony frowned across at his father. "I hope you're not implying that I'm trying to avoid joining up, Dad. I want to get out there and fight after what I saw. You're no more eager for me to join up than I am myself! I was going to join up as soon as I got back, but something stopped me. The fact is, a young lieutenant I met in France thinks that a new unit he's been posted to might be able to use me. I'm not sure what it's all about, but I promised not to join up for a month or so, to give him time to make enquiries." The young man turned to look out of the window again. "You didn't see those Germans killing civilians like I did. Nor the chaos on the beaches. Now Paris has fallen, and more than half of France is under German control. I mean to get out there, free Grandmother's home and drive the Nazis back to the holes they came from. If I haven't heard from Jim Briggs in a couple of weeks I shall be joining up anyway, and if his unit wants me they'll just have to arrange a transfer."

Sir Michael walked across to his son and laid a hand on his shoulder.

"I'm sorry son, I didn't mean to suggest that you're a coward. I just thought that a young man like you would have joined up sooner. Now you've told me about this lieutenant I quite understand. Let's review the situation in a couple of weeks, shall we?"

Tony turned and smiled at his father.

"Yes. And thanks for being so understanding."

The two weeks were almost up when Tony finally heard from Jim Briggs.

JULY 1940

14

The phone call was brief and to the point.

"Tony? It's Jim here."

Tony relaxed at the sound of the voice. Although he had not been aware of feeling such tension, its easing was almost visible to the naked eye.

"Jim! At last! I was beginning to think you weren't going to call. How are you?"

"I'm fine, Tony. It didn't take them long to get me back in harness, and we're working hard to get ready for the next confrontation with Jerry." There was a brief pause. "Have you joined up yet?"

Tony smiled grimly.

"No, and I have to admit it's been difficult not to. Apart from wanting to join up myself, I've been under quite a lot of pressure from my father. He seems to think I've been putting it off because I'm afraid to fight after what happened in France, but my feelings are exactly the opposite; I can't wait to get out there and do something to put things right. I have to join up soon, or I'll go mad. Do you have any news for me about joining your unit? If not, I'll go and join up tomorrow. I want to be ready to fight when the invasion finally comes, not stuck in some barracks doing basic training."

Tony's eagerness was transmitted down the telephone line so that Jim smiled on the other end. "As it happens, I do have some news. A Mr. Jones wants to see you the day after tomorrow at 10.30, in Room 34 at the Northumberland Hotel in London. Do you know it?"

"Yes, we often use it. But why a hotel?"

"We don't want people to know who you are seeing and why, so a hotel is the best place."

Tony smiled. "It sounds intriguing."

"It is." There was a pause. "Tony, you must realise that no-one, including your family, is to know about this at this stage. Do you understand?"

A frown furrowed Tony's brow.

"Yes, I understand. But why? What is it that you people get up to, Jim?"

"I can't tell you that. Mr. Jones will explain if he thinks you are suitable; if not then you'll never know. I can't say precisely how long the process will take, but if I were you I'd make arrangements to be in London for about a week. Any questions?"

Tony laughed. "Hundreds, but I'm sure you won't answer them! Will I see you when I'm in town?"

"Sorry Tony, not this time. I have to go away on a training course, but I'm sure we'll meet again soon."

"All right Jim, I'll be there. And thanks for calling."

"Good luck, Tony. I hope it all works out."

The phone went dead and Tony put the receiver down, the light of anticipation in his eyes.

The family were seated around the table as the one remaining servant entered with a small roast chicken. The rest of the help had joined up, and the family were doing their best to take on some domestic chores themselves. As Sir Michael said, 'we can all do our bit, even if it's just the washing up!'

He sipped his wine and sighed. "We'd better be careful with this. Who knows when we'll be able to re-stock the cellar again?"

Tony grinned. "I'll pick you up some wine while I'm in London if you like."

"I was thinking more of when we shall next get wine from France." His father looked across at him, a quizzical expression on his face. "When are you planning to go up to town?"

"Tomorrow." Tony reached across for the potatoes.

"What for? Are you enlisting at last?"

"Er…well…not exactly." Tony was at a loss as to what to say. Jim had asked him to say nothing about his meeting and what it entailed, although he knew little enough himself, and he knew just how much his father wanted to see him join up and 'do his bit'. "I'm just going to meet up with a few university friends before we all join up and go our separate ways," he said, hoping his father would not detect the lie in his voice.

"What? You mean you're going to London to meet up with your friends and have some fun?"

Tony recognised the confrontational tone in his father's voice but could do little to ease the tension. He had told the lie and now he must live with it. He nodded reluctantly.

"Yes, I suppose so." His voice was subdued as he looked down at his plate. "Once we join up we could be sent all over the place. We may never see each other again; some of us may not come back from this war. I think we have a right to have one final outing together." He hated lying, but he had to tell his father something.

"And will you enlist while you're there? You should have plenty of time for that too, you know."

Louise looked across at her husband, recognising the rising anger in his tone, and tried to mollify him.

"Come on now, Michael, you know that Tony will join up eventually. Give him this one last piece of freedom."

"One last bit of freedom? When I was younger than he is now I was fighting so that he could have this freedom, and many of my friends died so that he could go up to London for a bit of fun. Now all over the country other people are preparing to fight, and to die, for this country. All I want to know is when he thinks he'll have the courage to do his bit. Is that too much to ask?"

Tony looked his father in the eye.

"No, it's not too much to ask. I will join up and I will fight in this war, but I have to do this first. You lost friends, surely you understand the need to say goodbye?"

"Of course I do, but I also understand the need to stand up and be counted."

"Are you calling me a coward, Dad?"

Sir Michael was silent. The red flush in his cheeks began to subside, and he sighed. At last he spoke.

"No, of course not Tony. I suppose part of it is that I want to join up and do my bit myself. But I'm too old, and I can't understand why you won't go in my place."

"I will, Dad. Just give me time. You do trust me, don't you?" Tony desperately wanted to tell his father about Jim's call and the meeting that he would be attending in London but it was impossible. He had promised. He felt a gnawing anxiety that this impending interview might somehow sour his relationship with his father, but he didn't know how or what to do about it.

Sir Michael frowned.

"I've never had any reason not to trust you son. But I can't say I like this. I shan't be happy until I see you in uniform."

"Are you so eager to send him into danger?"

Sir Michael looked across at his wife.

"No, of course not my dear. But it's a matter of duty." He looked across at his youngest son. "I thought you would understand that Tony."

Tony lowered his eyes to his plate once more.

"Yes Dad. I won't let you down."

The rest of the meal was conducted in a frosty atmosphere. Unable to say anything about his secret meeting, Tony had remained silent, replaying his father's angry words over and over again in his mind. His heart was heavy. Sir Michael's words had cut him deeply, and for the first time in his life Tony had felt that he was a disappointment to those he loved the most. Somehow, he did not know how, he would show his father that he knew the meaning of duty, and was as prepared to lay down his life for his country as the next man.

How he longed for the meeting, and the secrecy, to be over.

Tony walked down the drive with his small suitcase in his hand his. His eagerness at finally making some headway towards enlisting was tempered with sadness as he thought of the words which had been spoken over dinner the night before. He wanted to make his father feel proud. He knew that once he joined up he would do so, but for now his father was feeling angry and frustrated, and there was nothing that Tony could do about it.

As he looked back over his shoulder he saw Sir Michael watching him silently through the drawing room window as he began his journey, though it was obvious from the sullen expression on his father's face that his opinion of his younger son had not changed overnight. As far as he knew, this Jim Briggs whom Tony had spoken about had never been in touch, and Sir Michael was beginning to think that his youngest son was using the expected telephone call as an excuse to keep out of the fighting. As he looked at his father Tony longed for the chance to explain where he was really going. Still, come what may, he would be a member of the armed forces by the end of the week, either with the people he was to see the following day or in some other capacity, and the domestic friction would be over at last. With a sigh he turned his back on his home and set off for London.

Tony checked into the Northumberland Hotel, just behind the War Office, early that evening, and after eating a dinner somewhat below the usual standard for the hotel, no doubt due to the rationing, he went for a brief and depressing walk through the blacked out streets of London. Returning to the hotel, he retired early to bed, but he could not sleep with his mind a whirling jumble of thoughts about what the morrow might bring.

As the hands of his watch reached 10.30 the following morning, Tony raised his hand and knocked at the door to Room 34. It looked the same as all of the other doors in the hotel, so he was not prepared for what greeted his eyes when the door was opened. The room was completely bare, its only furnishings two folding chairs, a naked bulb and a blackout curtain. One of the chairs was occupied by a middle-aged man, wearing civilian clothing but with the unmistakable air of the military about him.

"Anthony Kemshall?"

Tony nodded. "Yes, sir."

"Come in then, and close the door." The man indicated the other seat. "Please sit down, Mr. Kemshall."

Tony sat down, eager to find out what it was all about.

"You met a Lieutenant Briggs in Northern France during the evacuation. Is that not so?"

Tony nodded. "Yes, sir."

"He spoke very highly of you. It seems you handled yourself very well."

"Thank you."

"Parlez vous francais?"

Tony was startled to hear the man he had come to see speaking such fluent French, with a distinctly Parisian accent.

"Oui, Monsieur."

"Then we shall continue our conversation in French, if you don't mind?"

Tony shook his head, and from then on the conversation was carried out in French.

"How is it that you speak French so well?"

"My mother is French. She met and married my father during the last war. We spent a good part of each summer at Grandmamma's estate just outside Saint Nazaire. I learnt to speak French there."

"And your accent is that of the area?"

"Yes, sir. I believe I could pass for a native."

"Do you know the area well?"

Tony thought of the lazy summer days he and David had spent exploring his grandmother's estate, and the nearby port in the company of her estate manager. Places which were now occupied by the Germans. Places he thought of as his second home. "Yes. I know the area well."

"And what do you do when not holidaying in France?"

"I'm at university. When I graduate, I intend to go into my father's engineering business."

The officer nodded slowly. "An admirable ambition. But what about Dunkirk?"

Tony was not surprised by the sudden change of direction. After all, this was the purpose of his visit.

"What would you like to know?"

"How did you manage to get involved with the army?"

"I went to Saint Nazaire to bring Grandmamma to safety in England, but once I had got her on board a ship I decided to stay and see some action." He smiled grimly. "It wasn't what I was expecting. Nothing like my preconceived ideas of war. Seeing the Germans murder innocent civilians, women and children. There was really no option but to get involved and help Lieutenant Briggs."

"You could have turned and walked away."

Tony shook his head. "The thought never entered my head."

"Lieutenant Briggs said that you took part in an attack on some tanks. How did that happen?"

Tony's mind flew back to France and he closed his eyes for a second as he relived the scene, then he looked at his companion as he began to speak, trying to explain what had happened and how he had felt. His feelings threatened to overwhelm him as he recalled his experiences in France – the strafing and bombing, the violence and death, fear, hunger, exhaustion. The officer watched the emotions play across the young man's face as he recounted his experiences, but said nothing to interrupt the flow of recollections as Tony recounted the attack on the tanks.

"So how did you feel after your first action?"

Tony struggled to find words to express the mixed emotions he had felt. "Elated. Scared. Exhausted. It's hard to say really."

"It didn't put you off joining up?"

Tony's face was grim. "On the contrary. I was more determined than ever. After what happened to Watson, to the civilians, to the men on the beaches." He closed his eyes as though to escape the sight, but the images still haunted his mind.

"And after the tank attack?"

Tony opened his eyes and looked at the officer. He took a deep breath.

"That was it really. From there we began to make our way towards Dunkirk."

"What have you been doing since?"

"I wanted to join up, but I was waiting for a call from Jim, to see what he could come up with."

"Your first taste of action didn't put you off the army?"

Tony was incensed.

"No! Of course not!" His face was grim. "It may seem strange as I haven't joined up yet, but that would have felt like disloyalty to Jim and the others." His eyes took on a faraway gleam as he thought of his time in northern France. "The attack on the tanks was frightening, but the beaches of Dunkirk were the worst part. The waiting. The attacking planes. The cold and hunger. But it only made me more determined to do my bit as they say." He gazed thoughtfully at the officer. "If you'd seen what I saw, especially the strafing of civilian refugees, you would understand. I'm determined to do everything in my power to help defeat the Nazis."

He sat looking at his companion for a moment, wondering what his role was in the scheme of things. "May I ask a question?" he ventured at last. At the other's nod of approval, he continued. "What's this all about? Jim, I mean Lieutenant Briggs, said it was something to do with the military. You've checked out my French, so I assume that must be important. I just want to say that I have no intention of spending the war sitting behind a desk translating. After what I've been through, I want to see some action. Can you guarantee that?"

His companion smiled.

"I can't tell you what the job involves at present, as I need to check out one or two things about your background first."

Tony frowned, but said nothing as the other man continued.

"That's all for now Mr. Kemshall. If you could be here again at 10.30 three days from now I would be most obliged." He stood up as he spoke and held out his hand. "Goodbye Mr. Kemshall, and please say nothing of this conversation to anyone."

Tony shook the proffered hand and left, more deeply puzzled than he had been when he arrived in Room 34.

Tony spent the next three days in a kind of limbo. There was no need for him to be in London other than for the unusual interview. He had no work to do and no people to see, so he spent his time walking and absorbing the strange sights of a city at war. Barrage balloons floated overhead like the huge bloated carcasses of dead whales, the muzzles of anti-aircraft guns pointed menacingly at the cloudless blue of the July sky, signs directed the way to air-raid shelters, and there were men in uniform everywhere. After his first evening in the city he decided not to venture out of the hotel at night again. His memories of London after dark consisted of bright lights and laughter, not the dark brooding of a city under blackout and awaiting the next move from an enemy poised to strike. He supposed he would get used to it all if he had to live and work in London, but he preferred the peace of Heronfield; even with the influx of nurses and wounded soldiers, its isolation from the big cities encouraged the aura of peace and tranquility in which he had grown up.

Tony was glad when the three days of endless waiting were finally over, and he found himself seated once again opposite the mysterious 'Mr. Jones' who had now forsaken his civilian clothes for the uniform of a major. Room 34 was as bare as it had been before.

"Mr. Kemshall, I'm sure you're wondering what this is all about."

Tony nodded at the uniformed officer. "Yes, sir."

"Well, since our last meeting I have had your background carefully checked by members of the Intelligence Service and am pleased to say that you came out of it all without a blemish."

"Did you expect anything else, sir?"

The officer noted the disapproval in Tony's voice and smiled thinly.

"I know that you find it disturbing that we've checked up on you like this, but don't forget that we're at war. We can't be too careful about choosing the people we recruit."

Tony nodded.

"Yes sir. I understand."

"Good. Now let's get down to business. As you are well aware, we no longer have any armed forces in France, and if we are to defeat Hitler it is in France that we must work. The only way we'll be able to do this for the foreseeable future is to send men, undercover, to France to try to organise some sort of resistance. It goes without saying that it will be a dangerous undertaking, and we are liable to lose many of our agents, but that is the nature of war."

Tony's thoughts were racing, leading him to a conclusion that he thought was surely impossible. The officer smiled.

"I see that you have grasped what this is all about. We'd like you to work for us in Occupied France. You speak French like a native, and have detailed knowledge of Saint Nazaire and the surrounding area. You are also known to a number of locals, which will give you a head start in any work you have to do." He held up a hand to silence Tony who seemed about to speak. "I don't want you to make up your mind too easily," he continued. "It is a difficult decision to make. It's a life and death decision for both of us. I have to decide whether I can risk your life, and you have to decide whether you are willing to risk it too."

"I understand, sir."

"I'm not sure that you do, Kemshall. This operation is Top Secret. No one, and that includes family and friends, is to know about our approach to you. You must make the decision alone, bearing in mind that there's no more than a fifty-fifty chance that you will come out of this alive."

"Can't you do an intelligence check on my family? They would come out clear, and it would be so much easier for me if I were able to discuss this with them." Tony frowned slightly. "My father won't understand if I'm not seen to be in active service. It could prove…difficult."

"I know. But it's something that all agents must face. I don't doubt that your family would prove to be perfectly safe if we were to check them out, but that's not the point. Secrecy is vital for your safety, and the safety of hundreds of other operatives. If your family know about you, they could let something slip when talking to friends, with catastrophic results. I'm afraid that the decision has to be yours alone. And if you choose to join us, you may not speak to your family about your work until after the war, if at all."

Tony nodded, reluctantly accepting the logic of the argument, as the officer rose to his feet and offered him his hand once again.

"I'll see you again in two days' time, Mr. Kemshall. And I'll want your decision then."

Tony stared out of the window, without seeing the beautiful gardens of Heronfield spreading out before him. He had spent two days thinking endlessly of the proposition that had been put to him, barely able to believe that his country placed so much trust in him. He knew the dangers involved, he was aware of the fact that if he joined he probably would not live to see the end of the war, yet he found that there was no decision to be made. He knew that he would go, and had been proud to say so to the mysterious 'Mr. Jones' at their final meeting. Once his decision had been accepted by the authorities, he had been given the rank of lieutenant in the Ministry of Economic Warfare, to counter any suggestions that he was not 'doing his bit' for England. Yet he knew that this would not please Sir Michael, who would want to see him out there, fighting for his country. The decision to become an agent in France had been easy in comparison with the confrontation which Tony would now have to face with his father. As if on cue, the door opened and Sir Michael entered.

"Well, Tony. Back from gallivanting about London, I see." His voice was gruff, uncompromising, and Tony steeled himself as he turned to face his father.

"Yes, and I've joined up. Jim's people did want me after all."

His father beamed as he stepped forward to shake his son by the hand.

"At last! I can't tell you how glad I am to hear it, my boy! Which regiment are you with?"

Tony licked his dry lips and took a deep breath. This was it.

"Actually, Dad, I'm not with any specific regiment. I have been made a lieutenant with the Ministry of Economic Warfare."

Sir Michael released his son's hand, a frown beginning to furrow his brow. He slowly shook his head.

"Never heard of it. What's your job?"

"Well, they knew about my background, and thought I could be best used as a liaison officer between the military and the armament factories."

There was stony silence for a moment as Sir Michael took this in. His voice was tight with emotion when he spoke at last.

"You mean you won't be fighting?"

Tony nodded.

"I'll be doing much the same job Grandfather did in the last war. After all, it was his turning the bicycle factories over to the production of aircraft that made his fortune, and won him his knighthood."

"But your grandfather was old! I was your age and I fought in the trenches. It's your generation who should fight, and leave the running of the factories to people like me who've already fought one war." Tony watched the conflicting play of emotions on his father's face as he spoke. "You know how worried I was when you were missing in France. I thought I'd lost you, and I was so glad to get you back alive. I don't really want to go through that again, but I must, that's what war is all about. It's my duty to be willing to give up my son for my country, and it's your duty to be willing to fight, no matter how difficult we may both find it."

Sir Michael struggled to put across his mixed emotions, hoping that in some way he could influence his youngest son. Tony thought he understood his father, a man from a different generation where every action was based on honour and loyalty, a man who had lost family and friends fighting in the war to end wars. A war that had left him in no doubt that, if the younger generation did not fight to preserve their freedom, then the losses of his youth would have been in vain. Tony could feel the depth of his father's emotions, it was not hard to sense how important it was for him to see his son fighting to defend his homeland, but the decision had already been made and could not be undone.

"I know, Dad." Tony's voice was conciliatory. "I want to fight, but I must accept that the military know what's best, and if this is what they want me to do, then I shall do it."

Sir Michael was barely able to control his frustrated anger.

"The military know best? You should have been in the trenches, boy, then you'd have seen that the military often knows nothing! Certainly nothing of honour and loyalty; just glory and protecting their own positions." He glared at his son. "You could have said no, couldn't you? You could get a transfer now, if you wanted to? But you won't, will you?" Tony silently shook his head. "Then the only conclusion I can come to is that you somehow engineered this, because you're afraid to fight. After all my generation went through, all the horror of war in the trenches to buy your freedom." He turned and strode angrily to the door before glaring over his shoulder at Tony. "I must face the fact that my youngest son is a coward."

With that he turned and left the room.

Tony was breathing heavily, fists clenched, his body rigid. It had been far worse than he had anticipated. To be called a coward by his own father, and not be able to defend himself. He had never imagined that, nor the pain it would bring, and it cut him to the core. Yet, for all that, he knew where his loyalties lay. He kept his silence for the sake of his country, though it broke his heart to do so.

15

David stared glumly at his half-finished pint of beer. 74 Squadron had arrived at RAF Leconfield in Yorkshire the previous afternoon, for a rest period after their action over Dunkirk. True to his promise to his dying friend, David had been to see Martin Richies' mother and had just returned. He had hated lying to her, but felt that he owed it to Martin to say that his death had been quick and painless; what was worse, he could see from the look in her eyes that she did not quite believe him, but was grateful for the attempt to ease her loss. Martin's home was very different from David's, a small trader's house filled with inexpensive ornaments and pictures, yet steeped in a feeling of family love and unity. On the sideboard had been a photograph, draped in black ribbon, of Martin in his RAF uniform. Beside that was another photograph of a young man, so like Martin that David knew it had to be his younger brother. The young man was standing proudly beside a Tiger Moth, one hand placed possessively on the wing. Mrs. Richies had noticed David looking at the photograph and forced a wan smile. David could still hear the echo of her words in his head.

"That's Andy, Martin's brother. He's joined the RAF too, you know. He only has two more weeks of training then he'll be joining his squadron." She had stood and walked slowly over to the sideboard where she had picked up the photograph. Her fingers lovingly traced the outline of his face as she spoke quietly. "He was so proud of Martin, his death hit him badly. He's applied to join your squadron in some mad hope of being able to avenge his brother." Her eyes filled with tears as she picked up Martin's photograph too. "My boys were all I had, and now I only have one." She turned to David. "You were Martin's friend. If Andy does join your squadron, will you look after him for me? I couldn't bear to lose him as well."

David shivered and drank the rest of his beer. He had promised to do his best to look after Andy, but he knew that there would be very little that he could do to protect the boy. He hoped that Andy would not be assigned to 74 Squadron, that way he would not have to feel responsible. With a strange sense of foreboding, David ordered another drink.

The week at Leconfield passed quickly; days spent at leisure at the airfield, nights in the local pubs or in the arms of the local girls at the dances held on the base. There was a feeling of excitement in the air. Now that Hitler had control of the Continent, he would be making his move against England, and the boys of the RAF knew that they would be in the front line when it came to defence. No one said anything, but they had all lost friends over Dunkirk, and knew that when the Luftwaffe came many more of the RAF would be lost. Would it be them? Their friends? How long had they left to live? 'Forget the questions and live life to the full' seemed to be the general conclusion. When the squadron returned to RAF Rochford on June 6th to await new aircraft and pilots, the men were ready for action.

Life on the front line continued in much the same vein as it had in Yorkshire; there was little combat, which gave the pilots time to get to know the local girls, and a chance to experience all that life had to offer. New aircraft and new pilots continued to arrive over a period of days, so the squadron was soon almost back to full strength. They were only waiting now for one more pilot to join Blue Section, and when the notice of the posting came through, David Kemshall felt a dull weight settle in the pit of his stomach. His prayers had not been answered. Andrew Richies was to join 74 Squadron.

David lay back in his deck chair, eyes closed against the harsh glare of the sun. A shadow passed across his face, and he opened his eyes to see the silhouette of a man standing beside him. Sitting up, he turned to face the young man who smiled down at him.

"Are you David Kemshall?"

David nodded. "You don't need to tell me who you are, I recognise you from your photograph. Welcome to Tiger Squadron, Andy." He stood and shook the young man by the hand as he spoke. "You've just finished basic training, haven't you? Have you seen any action yet?"

Andy shook his head.

"No. But I can't wait to get up there, and pay those bastards back for what they did to Martin."

David nodded and pointed over to the hangar.

"Come on, Andy, I'll show you around and explain how we do things here." He pointed to a row of aircraft, which stood gleaming in the intense sunlight. "They're our new Spitfires. They haven't seen action yet, so they're as new to all this as you." He smiled encouragingly at the young man, barely eighteen years old, trying to put him at his ease. "Each fighter squadron has sixteen aircraft and twenty six pilots, so we can maintain a standard combat formation of twelve fighters in the air. We're part of Number 11 Group, and our assigned area is the air space over London and the southeast. The Squadron is divided into two flights. The inventive boys at H.Q. have called them 'A' Flight and 'B' Flight." David smiled as he continued. "When we're operating at full strength, each flight is split into two groups of three aircraft which we identify by colour. A Flight is split into Red and Yellow Sections, while B Flight is split into Blue and Green. I'm in A Flight Red Section and you are in B Flight Blue Section."

"What was Martin in?"

David still found it difficult to talk about Martin in the past tense, and took a deep breath before replying.

"Red. With me."

"I don't suppose I can be in Red as well?"

David shook his head.

"Sorry, Andy. I don't have any say in the matter. Anyway, perhaps it's best that you don't follow too closely in Martin's footsteps."

David felt that Andy was tempting fate in wanting to emulate his dead brother so closely, and was glad that they would be in different sections.

"Let's get back to flight details," he said, wanting to turn the conversation away from Martin and the memories of their last flight, which still haunted him. "Pilots have to identify themselves over RT, Radio Telephone, by stating their position in the formation. For instance, your leader will be Blue 1; Blue 2 will be on his right and Blue 3 on his left. We never mention the squadron number when we're up in the air. That way the enemy are less likely to identify who we are. We are known as Dysoe."

They had reached the aircraft and were looking around at the peaceful scene. One or two mechanics worked on the planes, but nothing else moved in the hot summer sun. The pilots could be seen lounging in the shade of the buildings on the edge of the airfield. Even the squadron's pet dog was lying in the shade, its only sign of life the slight movement of its tail.

"There doesn't seem to be much going on at the moment."

"We've had the odd encounter, but the main battle hasn't started yet. When it does, you'll need to be familiar with the various states of preparedness. If you are 'Released' it means you're not required for operations. 'Available', which is what we are at at the moment, means be ready to take off in twenty minutes. 'Readiness' is take off in five and 'Stand By' is take off in two, which means you must be strapped in your plane ready for the order to scramble. We need thirteen minutes to scramble and climb to twenty thousand feet, so every second counts."

"I've heard this new radar can see planes from miles away. How can it tell the enemy from us?"

"We carry a small transmitter called IFF which means Identification, Friend or Foe. It shows up on the radar screen so that the boys at Ops. know who we are. Whatever you do, don't forget to switch on your IFF when you go up, or you'll be in for some stick. We also have a device called 'Pip Squeak' on board. It switches on a high-frequency radio signal for fourteen seconds every minute. The transmission is picked up by three ground direction finding stations, and they fix our positions by triangulation, so there's no chance of you getting lost up there."

David looked at his watch. "Almost lunch time. I'll take you over to the mess to meet the rest of the boys, then give you the rest of the low-down this afternoon."

It was a pleasant lunch. Reynolds welcomed Andy to the squadron, and introduced him to the other members who were relaxing at the bar. Dysoe Squadron had seen little action since returning from Leconfield. Although they were expecting the main battle to begin soon, they still had time to relax and fly training flights, one of which would be going up that afternoon with Andy as Blue 3.

After lunch David took the new recruit back out onto the airfield and led him across to his Spitfire.

"Each fighter has its own ground-crew, an air-frame rigger and an engine fitter who check over the plane after each action. There are also armourers, wireless, electrical and instrument mechanics allotted to each flight. So unless a plane is really badly shot up, we should be able to get it back up into the air again, if the ground-crew work through the night."

Andy had donned flying overalls and Mae West life jacket in the crew room. He carried his helmet, gloves and parachute with him, and David showed him how to stow his gear in the Spitfire and arrange his straps for a quick getaway. After being introduced to the ground crew, Andy climbed up the wing root and into the cockpit. By the time he was strapped in, the rest of B Flight were taxiing out; he turned to David.

"Aren't A Flight going up?"

David shook his head. "No. It's only a training flight. We stay here in case there's a scramble." He noticed the young man's nervousness and smiled encouragingly. "I know it's your first time in a Spit, but just stick with your section leader and, if you should come into contact with the enemy, don't forget the 'Hun in the sun'."

David turned and ran, as tongues of flame and clouds of smoke burst from the exhausts of the Spitfire. Andy spotted his section leader and taxied across to take up position. B Flight lined up in battle formation across the width of the airfield then opened up their engines. With an ear-splitting roar, the planes rolled forwards together and then were airborne. David watched the planes circle the airfield, then turn south and climb swiftly into the clear blue sky.

<h2 style="text-align:center">16</h2>

Sir Michael, Louise and her mother were in the drawing room when David arrived on leave. Sir Michael merely smiled warmly at his eldest son but his wife could not contain her feelings, and rushed over to embrace him.

"It's so good to see you, mon cher. But why are they giving you leave now? I thought that Hitler was planning to invade? Should you not be ready to fight?"

David smiled. "We are ready, Mamma, and they can call me back at any time." He walked over to the window where he looked out over the peaceful gardens of his home, He wondered what was happening in the occupied lands, less than an hour's flight away. "We don't know much about what's happening out in France at the moment, but we do know that the Luftwaffe are building up their numbers just beyond the coast. I don't think Hitler will begin the full invasion until his air force has done as much damage as they can to our ports, airports and radar stations in the south."

"Will the invading forces come soon?"

"Our squadron leader doesn't think so. He thinks Hitler will try to wipe out all our air resistance before sending his invasion forces across the Channel."

"So shouldn't you be with your squadron?"

David turned to his father. "He thinks Hitler's almost, but not quite, ready. That's why Fighter Command have given us front-line pilots forty-eight hour passes. It might be the last chance we get for some time."

"I wish you could stay for longer."

David turned back to his mother and smiled. "So do I. It's so good to be back home again after the action we saw over Dunkirk. You won't believe how much I've missed you all."

"We are so glad you came safe through all that." She tilted her head back to look up at her son and smiled. "I am so proud of you David."

"Yes. So am I, son." Sir Michael indicated a chair as he spoke. "Sit down and tell us all about it."

David went across to Chantrelle de Thierry, and bent to kiss her cheek.

"Hello, Grandmamma. I'm glad to see you safe."

The old lady hugged her grandson tearfully.

"Welcome home, David."

The young man made his way across to the chair, sat down and smiled at his assembled family. "There's not much to tell, really. I'm sure I told you everything in my letter. The RAF saw a lot of action over the beaches and kept the big bombers away, but the soldiers down below couldn't see us because of all the smoke. We've taken some stick for that from the army over the past few weeks."

Sir Michael nodded.

"Yes, Tony said he saw little of the RAF from the beaches."

"Tony?" David was stunned. "He was at Dunkirk? But I thought he came home with Grandmamma?"

Chantrelle de Thierry shook her head and smiled wistfully. "Your younger brother packed me off on a boat, then went to see what was happening further east. It is a long story and you must ask him all about it yourself."

"Where's Tony? Has he joined up yet?" the elder brother asked eagerly. "I can see that I've got a lot to catch up on."

Sir Michael frowned, and David wondered what was wrong.

"You certainly have got a lot to catch up on," his father said at last, his voice bitter and harsh. "Tony is in the army; in a strange capacity." He could see that David wanted to ask a question, and held up a restraining hand as he shook his head. "No, don't ask me. It will be better coming from your brother. He's out in the gardens somewhere at the moment. Why don't you go and look for him?"

David rose with a puzzled frown.

"All right, Dad. I'll go and find him, and swap notes about Dunkirk."

David found his younger brother sitting with his back against a pine tree, gazing up towards the imposing presence of Heronfield House.

"Hello, Tony. It's a bit of a come down living at the lodge, isn't it!"

Tony leapt to his feet, laughing delightedly as he hugged his brother.

"David! It's good to see you!" He looked back towards the house in which they had both grown up. "Actually, I was thinking how strange it is not to be able to use our own home, and how much more difficult it must be for Grandmamma to know that her home is in enemy hands."

David nodded as they both sat down on the cool grass. "Yes, it must be hard, but she seems to be taking it well."

"I think she just hides her feelings. I'm sure the incident at Mers-el-Kebir has upset her deeply. I know we had to fire on the French Fleet to stop it falling into German hands and all that, but it still meant British fighting French, and I'm sure she finds that hard to accept. A betrayal, really."

David nodded gravely. "I see what you mean. Still, she's lucky to be out of it and safe here with us. It was good of you to go out there to fetch her. I'd have gone, but I couldn't get leave. We were too busy trying to defend the beaches."

"What was it like to fly into battle?"

David looked across at his younger brother, wondering how he could explain the mixed emotions which had engulfed him as he flew, and as he watched his best friend die.

"It's hard to explain." His eyes took on a faraway look as he thought of his encounters with the enemy. "At first it was so exhilarating, there was so much happening that it was hard to be afraid. Then I lost a friend."

"How?" Tony's voice was soft, sympathetic.

48

"Shot down." David was silent for a moment, then shook his head as though to clear his thoughts. "But I don't want to talk about that. After…after we lost Martin I lost all the feelings of excitement, I just wanted revenge. It seemed strange to be flying without him. We'd not seen much action but we'd been together for quite a time, since training." He smiled sadly. "It's rare to find such a friend. Flying back to France the day after his death I couldn't help thinking of the good times we'd spent together, wishing I could have done more to help him." He turned an anguished face towards his brother. "Perhaps if I'd been able to intercept his attacker, he might not have died. But I have to admit that's not all I felt when I flew that day. I was scared, scared that I might die the same way as Martin. It was so hard to focus on what lay ahead, all I could think of was Martin, that this could be my opportunity to avenge him. But I knew that if I only thought of Martin and revenge and didn't concentrate this could be my last flight. I shot down an enemy that day. I didn't find myself sympathising with him though, only hoping that his plane wouldn't make it, that he would die like Martin, that it would go some way to avenging my friend's death." He turned towards Tony. "I suppose that sounds cold and heartless."

The younger man shook his head. "No. It sounds perfectly human. How else were you supposed to feel?"

David smiled. "Thanks, Tony. I knew you'd understand. It's as though you experienced it yourself." Realising what he had said, he turned excitedly to his brother. "That reminds me! What were you doing at Dunkirk? I didn't think there were any civilians on the beaches?"

So, for the second time in a week, Tony found himself giving an account of his experiences from the time he had placed their grandmother on board ship for England, through the horror of the Stuka attack and his revenge attack on the Panzers, and through the desperate days heading towards the beaches and the hope of a ship home. He found himself struggling for words to explain the horror of the beaches to his brother, even though he could still see, and hear, and smell it all if he closed his eyes and let his thoughts drift back. David listened intently to his younger brother's harrowing account of the beaches, the endless bombing, the waiting, the deaths.

"How long were you on the beaches?"

"Four nights."

"Four nights! My God, Tony, it must have been hell!"

Tony nodded.

"You can't imagine how it felt when we realized that it would be our last night on the beaches." He looked across at his brother and David was shocked to see the pain and horror in his eyes. "You might find it hard to understand, but I was so desperate to see green fields and rolling hills again after the dirt and smoke and blood of the beaches." Tony shuddered as he recalled his experiences. "As the light faded the Stukas came in for one final attack." His gaze was distant as he relived the scenes. "God, it was awful, David. They sank a couple of ships. I could hear the screams and cries of the soldiers struggling for their lives in the cold water, but then they were drowned by the roar of Stukas and their machine guns. I'll never forget that sound. Evil incarnate." He shuddered and David was shocked by the pure hatred he heard in his brothers voice, shocked but able to understand after what had happened to Martin. He said nothing as Tony continued his nightmare tale, his voice little more than a whisper now. "I saw them strafing the wounded in the sea; another boat was hit and there were bodies, and bits of bodies, everywhere." He was silent for a moment, remembering.

"The poor devils."

Tony nodded. "I was so thankful that it was getting dark. Then our lift home arrived.

It seemed so odd, David, a little yacht which should have been giving kids a trip from the end of the pier floating in that living hell. It was almost surreal." He laughed, but without any humour and David was saddened at the change in his younger brother. Not wishing to disturb the train of thoughts he remained silent as Tony continued.

"It was incredible, the bravery of those men. They were all civilians you know; they'd made the trip so many times before yet still came back to help us, to help me. I felt so small, as though I wasn't worthy of the risk they were taking. I guess we all felt like that." He shivered as he remembered the cold which had seemed to eat into his very bones. "I was standing in water up to my waist, and I had never felt so weak and tired before. I've never prayed so hard in my life."

"You poor sod."

"Yes, but at least I got away on that boat. I just couldn't believe that those men, and boys, would make the trip to England and back time after time to help us. They were so brave, David, they all deserve bloody medals."

"So that was it then?"

"Yes, thank God. I was so lucky to get off." There were tears in his eyes as he looked across at his brother. "I never want to experience anything like that again. It was a living hell and I'm so glad I'm out of it."

David reached out a comforting arm and the brothers embraced silently for a while, each thinking their own thoughts and struggling to bring their emotions under control. At last Tony pulled away, wiped his eyes and smiled at his brother.

"So there you have it. Seems like we've both seen our fair share of action already."

"Well, it seems to me that you had your first taste of action before I did!" David smiled proudly at his brother through the residue of his tears. "It sounds as though you did well Tony, I'm proud of you. I suppose Dad is proud of you too, but he seemed a little strange when I spoke to him just now. He said you'd joined up, but he wouldn't tell me about it. What's that all about?"

Tony took a deep breath and closed his eyes. Talking about Dunkirk had been cathartic, he felt exhausted and just wanted to rest, but he couldn't ignore David's question. After his father's reaction to his cover story, he knew that David would not be pleased. He dreaded telling him, but it had to be done. He opened his eyes and looked at his brother.

"You're in the RAF, David. You understand about taking orders and accepting that those above us know best, otherwise you would never have joined up."

David nodded, but said nothing.

"Well," Tony continued shakily, "I was approached by a certain ministry who feel that the best contribution I can make is to work for them. After listening to them, I was convinced. I'm now a lieutenant in the Ministry of Economic Warfare."

David frowned. "Never heard of it. What's your job?"

"Liaising between the Ministry and the armaments factories." Tony took a deep breath and squared his shoulders as he awaited the expected outburst from his brother. There was silence for a moment as David thought hard about what his brother had said. When he spoke his voice was disbelieving.

"Do you mean that you'll be doing an office job? You won't see action at all?"

Tony nodded, well aware of his brother's thinking, and feeling his own tension mounting. "Yes, but the job's vital. We can't win the war without the right weapons."

"I know that!" David's voice betrayed his anger. "But that's the sort of job for men too old to fight, men like Dad. After what you've just told me, I'd have thought that you of all people would want to see action against Jerry."

"Believe me, David, I do; but I have to accept that my superiors know best."

David frowned. "If I didn't know you better, Tony I'd say that what you've seen and experienced in France has got to you. I think you're afraid to go back out there and face Jerry again."

Tony's gaze was steady as he looked his brother in the eye. "You must believe me when I say that I'm not afraid, at least no more than the next man, no more than you. I want to see those bloody Nazis wiped off the face of the earth, and I'll do everything I can to help accomplish that. I'd be happy to go out there and fight today, but this job is vital. I'm just doing the job that I'm most suited for, like you are. We're not all cut out to be fighter pilots, David. My work is just as important as yours."

David shook his head in puzzlement, and rose to his feet. "I really don't understand you, Tony. I thought you'd want to fight. No wonder Dad seems so disappointed."

"He called me a coward." Tony's voice was filled with anger and pain as he spoke.

David thought of Martin's smiling face, his eagerness to face the enemy, his quiet dignity as his lifeblood ebbed away in the plane which was to be his coffin. He thought of Martin's younger brother, eager to serve in the same squadron, eager to fly and to fight to avenge his brother's death. Then he looked back at his own brother, so keen to take a desk job, so keen to stay away from the danger which he and his comrades faced daily. There were none of Martin's, or Andy's, qualities there.

"Maybe he's right."

Without another word David turned and walked away.

Tony gazed longingly at the retreating back of his brother and then turned to look up at Heronfield House, though his eyes saw little of what was before them. The people he loved most in the entire world believed him to be a coward, when he knew his actions would prove the very opposite of that. Yet no matter how much he wanted to, he could not explain to them. How he hoped that the war would soon be over and he could tell them the truth, but there seemed little chance of that. If only there were someone he could talk to who would understand, someone who would accept him for who he was, and see that there is more than one way of fulfilling your duty. Then he saw a familiar figure walking in the gardens and his heart felt lighter. He remembered his earlier talk with Sarah and thought that perhaps talking to her now would help. He rose quickly to his feet and crossed the gardens to intercept her path.

"Hello, Sarah. I hope I'm not disturbing you."

Sarah smiled in greeting. "No, not at all. It's good to see you again, Tony."

"It's good to see you too." Tony smiled. He realised that he was glad to see Sarah again. Her infectious smile had made him feel better almost immediately, and he knew she would understand.

"I've just been talking to my brother," he said as he led her down towards the river where the herons fished in summer, and from which the house had derived its name.

"Was that handsome young man in the Air Force uniform your brother?" asked Sarah.

Tony smiled and nodded. David usually had that effect on women.

"Yes. I'm afraid I've upset him, and my parents, and I'm feeling rather bad about it."

Sarah frowned but said nothing. After a moment's silence Tony spoke again.

"You said your boyfriend works in an aircraft factory?"

"Yes. Joe wanted to join up, but he was unfit. At least he feels he's doing his bit for the country in his own way. Why do you ask?"

"You think that his work is as important as the armed forces then?"

"Of course I do!" There was unconcealed anger in her voice. "Where would your brother's squadron be without Joe? I hope you're not implying that he's not doing his bit?"

Tony reached out and took her hand. "No, Sarah! On the contrary! You see, the Ministry of Economic Warfare has made me a lieutenant, and I have to liaise with the armament factories. I think it's a vital job." He turned his face away to look towards the river, but did not let go of Sarah's hand. "The problem is that my family think I'm trying to avoid fighting. They think I'm a coward."

Sarah could feel his sadness and, sensing his need for reassurance, she squeezed his hand.

"You're not a coward, Tony. I suppose they were just expecting you to fight like your brother. I'm sure they'll get used to the idea when they see the value of your work."

Tony turned questioning eyes towards her. "You don't think I'm a coward then?"

"No. I'd have thought you'd want to fight, but I don't know anything about your job. I'm sure it's important to the war effort. I'm sure you wouldn't do anything against your conscience. I suppose if you ever feel you're not doing enough, you could always get a transfer to an active unit."

Tony let out a strangled laugh. An active unit! He would see all the action he wanted in his present job, yet he could not explain that to the people he cared about. He noticed Sarah's puzzled expression and stopped laughing.

"I'm sorry, I shouldn't have laughed, but you have no idea of the irony of that. Yes, I could get a transfer if I wanted to, but I'll do my best to make this job work first." He smiled. "Thanks for making me feel better. Shall we walk a little further?"

"I'm sorry Tony, but I have to get back on duty."

"Maybe some other time?"

Sarah nodded and looked down, suddenly aware that Tony was still holding her hand and that she was enjoying the sensation. Withdrawing her hand gently from his she turned away so that Tony would not see the blush on her cheeks. How could she enjoy holding Tony's hand when she was in love with Joe?

"I'll see you again soon," she called, as she hurried away in the direction of Heronfield House.

Tony said nothing. He, too, was conscious of the pleasure he had gained from holding her hand. He realised with a jolt that what he felt for Sarah was a deeper friendship than should be possible on such a short acquaintance. As he watched her hurry away, he hoped that it would not be too long before he saw her again.

17

David returned to his squadron, now back at RAF Manston, feeling in some way betrayed by his brother. That feeling was only emphasised when he was greeted by Andy who, though younger than Tony, knew where his duty lay and was proud to fight for his country. Over the next few days, David began to realise that his earlier antipathy towards the young man had been as a result of Martin's death. They had been good friends, and the death had hit him hard. He did not want to get that close to a fellow pilot again, in case that friendship was destroyed in aerial combat too. Yet Andy was Martin's brother, and Martin would have been proud of him. David found himself beginning to treat Andy in the way he would have liked to treat Tony, not only as a brother in arms but truly as a brother to be proud of. As their relationship grew closer, David made a private vow to do all he could to protect Andy, and he buried his feelings of sadness at Tony's actions deep within himself.

One week into July, and the pace of life at Manston began to quicken. At 10.46, the Operations Room at Sector Station picked up an approaching airborne attack on RDF. Four minutes later the speed and direction of the raid had been plotted, and was appearing on the Operations Room's plotting tables. Fighter Command had been informed and were making decisions as to which squadron to send up. It appeared to be a small raid, so control was passed to the Section Controllers, and at 10.53 Blue Section of 74 Squadron was ordered to scramble.

The pilots of Blue Section reached their planes at a run as the Tannoy blared out the scramble alarm. Within moments the three planes were airborne, the directions from Section Control ringing stridently in their ears. Andy was nervous, his palms sweaty and his mouth dry as his Spitfire climbed steeply towards his first taste of action against the enemy. 'Remember the Hun in the sun'. The memory of David's words echoed hollowly in his head and he gazed wildly around for some sign of the enemy, but saw nothing.

Flight Lieutenant Pellow led his section up into a layer of low cloud, and as they broke through on the other side his loud "Tally Ho!" signaled to Control that he had seen the enemy some two thousand feet above his Spitfires, and was now taking over control. He led his section in a fast climb towards the lone He 111 bomber and opened fire from below the plane.

"Blue Leader to Blue Three. Blue Leader to Blue Three. Hold back and keep your eyes peeled for any more of the enemy."

"Roger, Blue Leader." Andy began to weave back and forth, scrutinising the sky for any signs of the enemy.

"Blue Leader to Blue Two. Follow me."

"Roger."

Andy watched as the two Spitfires began a series of attacks astern of the bomber. The rear gunner returned fire and tracer filled the air. By the time the two Spitfires had used their limited ammunition, the rear gunner of the bomber had been silenced and the port engine was afire. The plane began a banking turn to take it back towards the Channel.

"Blue Leader to Blue Three. She's all yours."

"Roger."

Andy's hands clutched tightly at the controls as he swung in behind the stricken aircraft. His finger was poised above the button that would send a stream of deadly bullets into the enemy, and he took a deep breath. This was it. His first action, and he hoped he would not let his section down. Depressing the button, he watched the bullets rip into the Heinkel. It shuddered under the impact then rolled over into a dive. The last time he saw the plane it was disappearing into the clouds below, undercarriage down. With a whoop of joy he turned his plane, and followed Blue Leader back to base.

David was waiting at the Dispersal Point to meet him when he returned, a beaming smile on his face.

"Well done, Andy. I hear you got a kill."

Andy smiled proudly at the compliment. "Yes, I suppose so. It was my bullets that finished him off, but he'd already been disabled by the rest of the section."

David slapped him on the back. "Good work anyway. Martin would have been proud of you."

Andy made his way to debriefing with a happy smile on his face. That was all the praise he needed.

"Red Section Scramble! Red Section Scramble!"

David was on his feet and running, his mind in a whirl. The second scramble of the day. Maybe this was it, the beginning of the real battle. He was soon airborne and climbing swiftly.

"Hello Dysoe Leader. Hello Dysoe Leader. Angels over Dover."

"Dysoe Leader. Message received. Over."

The three Spitfires headed for the coast, still climbing, and before long they were over Dover. Sergeant Brennan spotted four Bf 109's on his starboard beam.

"Tally Ho! Red Section into line astern!"

The three Spitfires broke their normal Vic formation and came in one behind the other. David climbed beneath one of the enemy and opened fire, causing the 109 to do a half-roll and dive steeply to ground level. Determined to get his man, David dived too. The blood pounded in his head and spots began to appear before his eyes as the g-force increased, but he was not about to give in. The pressure proved too much however and he blacked out for a moment. When he came to, the ground was approaching at a terrifying speed and he pulled back sharply on the stick, watching as the nose of the Spitfire slowly, but surely, rose above the horizon.

"I've got it, Red Two," came a voice over the RT, and David saw his quarry being pursued by Brennan. Another enemy fighter was flying at low level, and David went back down to attack it. The German fighter began contour chasing along the valleys behind Dover and Folkestone, with David desperately trying to follow each rapid twist and turn. Time and time again David thought he was about to get it into his sights, but the enemy veered away at the last moment. Sweat beaded his brow with the intensity of his concentration, but all the time he was drawing gradually closer to his quarry. Twice he had it in his sights, but only long enough to fire a short burst; the third time he was lucky, and his bullets found their mark. The 109 began to trail vapour as it banked steeply away and made a belly landing in a field where haymaking was in full swing. As David climbed back into the sky he saw farm workers rushing across, pitchforks held grimly before them, to take charge of the downed airman. Then his attention was focused once more on the battle which raged all about him.

Amidst the confusion of racing aircraft, he saw that the enemy which Brennan had been chasing was enveloped in thick oily smoke, which trailed behind it as it plummeted to the ground. The sky was fast clearing of enemy aircraft as the squadron manoeuvred rapidly into superior attack positions. The Section Leader's voice rang out over the RT.

"That's two down, boys, and the rest are heading for home. Well done!"

With a whoop of joy Red Section re-grouped and returned to Manston.

It was a beautiful morning two days later. The sky was a pale summer blue, flecked here and there with a wisp of white cloud. A Flight were patrolling the skies above base and David was engrossed in the peaceful scene down below him, so much like his flying days before the outbreak of the war. It was so relaxing, and he wanted the peaceful interlude to last forever.

"Dysoe Leader. Dysoe Leader. Convoy under attack two miles east of Deal. Engage."

The voice on the RT brought David's thoughts back to the present as he heard Freeman acknowledge that they were on their way. Turning eastwards, the six Spitfires headed swiftly towards the conflict. Flying at twelve thousand feet they spied the enemy below them, a single bomber escorted by some thirty 109's, and, flying line astern, Red Section dived towards the enemy.

There were planes everywhere. Over to his right David saw Freeman dive down to within fifty yards of one of the fighters before firing a short burst into it. The plane dropped like a stone, pilot obviously dead at the controls, but David did not have time to watch it fall. A swarm of the enemy flew at Freeman to avenge their fallen comrade, and the air was alive with bullets and flying tracer.

"Get out of there, Red Leader!" David found himself yelling as Red Two swooped in and began to fire at one of the attacking planes.

"I've been hit! I'm losing control!" Freeman's voice was tense over the RT. "Keep them occupied, boys, I have to get out of here."

Freeman turned away and coaxed his ailing aircraft homewards as David entered the fray in an attempt to draw some of the fire from Brennan, who was flying Red Two. His sights were trained on a fighter whose pilot became aware of him at the last moment, and began a steep left hand turn as David opened fire. David watched as the line of bullets flashed through the air, ripping into the enemy wing, but before he could move in for the kill he had to climb swiftly away to avoid the German's wingman. He fired on a second fighter which was diving towards Brennan's rear.

"Look out! He's on your tail! I'm coming in!"

The enemy made a half roll and dived away, evading David's guns but relieving some of the pressure on Brennan.

"Thanks, David. I owe you a pint for that. I'm losing control here; the plane looks like a sieve. See you back at the bar."

With that Brennan dived away, leaving David as the sole member of Red Section engaged. Over to his left he could see Yellow Section having a busy time of it, but then he had to turn his attention back to the battle in hand.

An enemy fighter dived past him, probably hoping to latch onto Brennan, and David plunged vertically after him, guns blazing. A deep satisfaction filled him as he saw smoke pouring from the engine. As he watched it fall, he felt the impact of bullets in his tail. Out of ammunition and flying alone, he turned and raced for home.

"Red Three heading for home. How are Red One and Red Two? Over."

Relief washed over him as Control's reply came over the RT.

"Both made forced landings, but are down all right. Over."

David landed without further incident, closely followed by Yellow Section who returned with all their planes intact and two kills to their credit. The exhausted pilots made their way to debriefing, before taking what rest they could at the Dispersal Point. This seemed to be the long awaited battle, and no-one doubted that they would see more action before the day was out.

In the middle of the afternoon, while David was still waiting for Freeman and Brennan to be brought back in a ground transport, Yellow and Blue Sections were sent up, to reinforce the air cover of a convoy steaming past Dover. David watched as Andy leapt onto the running board of the truck which sped him across to his aircraft on the other side of the field. He prayed that he would come back alive.

The bar of the Black Swan was noisy. Locals sitting quietly at the corner tables watched the crowd of young RAF officers clustered around the bar, loudly celebrating the day's victories. The landlord smiled as he refilled the empty glasses on the bar, while a pilot began to pound out dance tunes on the piano in the corner.

David led Andy to one side, a friendly arm around his shoulders.

"How did it go then, Andy?"

The young man smiled happily. "It was fantastic! There must have been a hundred planes up there. Bombers at four thousand feet with fighters stacked above them to about twelve thousand. Pellow hit a fighter and a bomber before running out of ammo. I don't know how he managed to get back to the coast. A swarm of fighters tacked on to him, but he made it somehow. Etheridge managed to hit two fighters before he broke off. He managed to get back without a scratch to his plane, though I don't know how he did it. I tagged on to a Vic of three bombers and managed to disable one, though I got no kills.

"It was incredible!" he continued breathlessly. "The air was full of planes, enemy everywhere, but I didn't have time to feel afraid, I was just so excited. I would have stayed up all day if I'd got unlimited ammo. Anyway, I eventually broke off and came back to base with Yellow Section, apart from Yellow One who only just managed a wheels-up landing at Lympne. They got a few good hits as well, but no confirmed kills."

"Yes, Yellow Section has been busy today." David emptied his glass and ordered another round. "I can see that this sort of fighting is going to go on for some time. I only hope we don't lose too many planes in the process."

Andy smiled. "We came off best today, and I'm sure we will again. We'll beat the Hun yet!"

David raised his glass to toast this comment, as the door to the pub opened and two young women walked in. David winked at Andy.

"That's enough about flying. I think it's about time we relaxed."

Andy looked towards the door, then smiled.

"OK, let's get some action!"

With confident strides, the two young officers made their way over to the door and introduced themselves. It was not long before the four young people were sitting happily with their drinks, all thoughts of the coming conflict far from their minds.

Two nights later, Manston was quiet and dark with all the pilots taking a well-earned rest when David was awoken by an ear-shattering crash. There were two more crashes as he sat up in the room that he shared with Andy and Etheridge.

"Damned ack-ack," he said as he lay down again and tried to get back to sleep. The gun battery kept firing for most of the night. At times he could hear the desynchronised motors of the enemy aircraft passing overhead, but more often than not the heavy pounding of anti-aircraft guns drowned it out. Every now and then the whistle of descending bombs could be heard, followed by the crash as they hit the ground. He felt he would never be able to get to sleep, yet sleep he did eventually.

At dawn he rose with the other pilots of 74 Squadron and, after a swift breakfast, collected his parachute and made his way to the Dispersal Point. It was all peaceful after the night's bombardment, and he felt an intense relief. Suddenly, as he remembered the barrage of the night before, he thought of Tony on the beaches of Dunkirk. He had been under fire, not only for a few hours but constantly, night and day, for four days, with nowhere to shelter and no way to defend himself. As he tried to imagine himself in his brother's position, David was surprised that the younger man had managed to keep his sanity, and wondered if the constant bombardment was the reason why Tony was now behaving in such a cowardly manner. For a moment he felt he had a clearer understanding of his brother's motivation, yet he still felt that he could not forgive him for accepting an office job. He sighed deeply. It was a strange dichotomy, to love his brother and want to keep him safe, yet resent him for not putting himself into danger. Maybe they would have time to discuss it together during his next leave; right now he had to keep his mind focused on the job in hand, ready to take to the skies at a moment's notice.

David looked up at the overcast sky and saw what he took to be an Oxford Trainer circle the field. He watched as it began to dive towards the Dispersal Point, and only realised as the machine guns began to blaze that this was no training exercise. A stream of bullets ploughed into the ground behind him as he dived behind a wall of sandbags. A stick of bombs fell, tumbling in slow motion from the belly of the aircraft. Thump...thump...thump. The bombs hit and the air was filled with dust, smoke and debris. The plane began a steep climb into the clouds, the rear gunner firing a parting burst as it went.

David rose to his feet, coughing to clear his lungs of the choking dust, and made a dash for his Spitfire, closely followed by the other members of Red and Blue Sections. The engines roared into life and the planes taxied swiftly across the airfield, but by the time they were airborne the enemy aircraft had disappeared. They returned dispirited to an airfield marred by three bomb craters but where, thankfully, no planes or pilots had been hit.

After lunch, Red Section were scrambled to investigate a raid plotted some fifteen miles north east of Margate. They took off eagerly, keen to avenge the morning's attack on the airfield, and were ready for action when they arrived on the scene, to find a ship under attack, anti-aircraft guns blazing.

"Tally Ho!" Reynolds voice rang over the RT. "Let's get him, boys!"

Reynolds led the attack, silencing the mid-upper gunner of the Heinkel on his first pass. Red Two and Three then joined the attack, their bullets thudding into the fuselage of the enemy plane in tremendous numbers, until the Hun at last fell away, spiralling slowly down towards the distant grey mass of the sea. Two parachutes mushroomed in its wake as the huge plane hit the water, sending a fountain of spray into the air. As David circled over the scene, he saw a boat launched from the ship and head out to where the parachutes were falling.

"Well done, lads!" Reynolds' voice was triumphant. "Another kill for Red Section. Let's go home."

As they flew back to base, David found himself praying that if he were ever brought down over the sea, there would be a ship within easy reach, just as there had been for the two German airmen. Somehow he did not relish the idea of dying slowly in the cold embrace of the waters off the coast of his homeland.

David leant against the stone wall, gazing across the fields full of ripening grain, which moved gently in the breeze. He sighed deeply.

"What's wrong?"

David turned to Andy. The two men had grown closer during the days of conflict, and David felt even more that Andy was a surrogate younger brother.

"I was just thinking of home," David replied. "The hedges, the fields full of corn, the woods; it's all so much like where I grew up. I just hope home will still be there when this damned war is over."

Andy nodded. "I know what you mean. It seems impossible to imagine that peace will ever come again after days of fighting."

David turned to look back across the open countryside. "It would all be over quicker if everyone did their bit." His voice was bitter and Andy frowned. For a moment David remained silent, wondering if he could confide in his new friend. Then, with a shrug, he turned once more towards Andy. It would be better to get his worries off his chest, rather than taking them into battle with him.

"It's my brother," he said softly. "I'm not sure he's doing his bit for the war."

Andy raised a quizzical eyebrow. "Wasn't he at Dunkirk? And isn't he a Lieutenant now?"

David nodded. "Yes. He acquitted himself well at Dunkirk and I thought he would be eager to get back into action, but now he's taken some desk job with the Ministry of Economic Warfare."

"What does he do exactly?"

David shrugged. "I'm not really sure. Some sort of liaison between the armaments factories and the forces."

"Is he qualified for that?"

David nodded.

"Then what's the problem? He's in uniform and he's doing the job his superiors think he's fit to do, the best he can contribute to the war effort."

David turned an astonished countenance to the young man beside him.

"I thought that you, of all people, would understand!" He was shocked at Andy's easy acceptance of Tony's job. "After losing your brother to the Germans, I thought you would be against anyone who was avoiding action."

Andy shrugged. "I want to avenge Martin's death, but I can't expect complete strangers to feel the same as I do. We all have different skills. You and I can fly planes, while your brother can make sure that there will always be planes there for us to fly. I wouldn't say that one job is more important than the other."

"But your brother wasn't a coward."

Andy was struck by the bitterness in his friend's voice and laid a comforting hand on his shoulder. "Are you so certain that your brother is?"

David frowned but said nothing. Andy's words gave him plenty to think about. Tony had certainly not proved himself a coward in France. On the contrary, it appeared that he had fought well, so maybe he did see his present job at the Ministry as being important rather than as an excuse to avoid fighting. Deep down he loved his brother, and really wanted to give him the benefit of the doubt; after all, they had always been so close. Yet his anger and shame at Tony's actions remained, and he had no idea how he was ever going to come to terms with his feelings.

It was now the third week in July, and the battle for air supremacy was still localised. The main targets of the Luftwaffe were the Channel convoys and any military installations on the south coast. Sorties were being made inland in attempts to disable the airports and radar stations in southeast England, ready for the all-out offensive which the Germans planned to launch in early August. Beyond the south eastern sector, few civilians saw the air battles which raged throughout July. As David flew high above the white capped waves, he hoped people appreciated what the Air Force was doing for them.

"Red Three to Dysoe Leader. Hun below."

David had spied three bombers flying low over the sea in an attempt to evade the RAF patrols. Freeman, leading A Flight, acknowledged David's transmission.

"Well spotted, Red Three. Let's get them, boys."

The six Spitfires banked and dived steeply down towards the slate-grey waters. Someone on the bombers must have noticed the fighters, for the three planes executed a tight turn and headed back towards France, bomb bays full.

The airwaves were full of the crackle of radio transmissions.

"Look at the cowards go!"

"Come on lads, they can't outrun us!"

"The one on the right is mine!"

David smiled grimly as the six fighters drew slowly but inexorably closer to the fleeing bombers. As the range closed, he slipped off the safety on his guns and began to train his sights on the planes.

"They're heading for the clouds, boys." Freeman had noticed the low cloud off Gravelines and seen the bombers alter course towards it. "Stay on their tails!"

The Spitfires were still some two thousand yards from the bombers when the German rear gunners opened fire. As he flew towards the hail of bullets, David's thumb moved to the firing control. Freeman must have sensed that A Flight were preparing to fire, for his voice came over the RT again.

"Hold your fire lads. Wait till we can't miss."

As the six planes drew closer to their quarry, David found himself crouching down in the cockpit to try to minimise his target. He was sweating now. The air was full of bullets, and he felt the thuds as one or two hit his plane, but he flew on, praying they would reach the bombers before they entered the cloud which was drawing swiftly closer. At last the order came.

"Let them have it, boys!"

Six sets of guns fired simultaneously. The smell of cordite filled the cockpit, and David's eyes began to sting as he watched the hail of bullets tear into the enemy planes. One of the bombers fell in a steep nose-dive, too low for the crew to bail out. The starboard engine of the second burst into flames as the plane disappeared into the cloud, followed by the third, apparently undamaged, bomber.

By this time 'A' Flight had been in the air for a long time.

"Red Three to Dysoe Leader. I'm getting low on fuel."

"We all are," came the reply. "This cloud stretches for miles, and we'll be damned lucky if we spot those bombers coming out the other side. All right boys, let's head for home."

18

Sarah had arranged her leave to coincide with the nights when Joe was not spotting for the Home Guard, as the Local Defence Volunteers were now called. It felt good to be back in the familiar surroundings of Coventry once more, and she was smiling as she walked into the kitchen to find her mother scrubbing potatoes at the sink.

"I see you're doing that as well!" she laughed. "This war will put the manufacturers of potato peelers out of business!"

Her mother smiled. "That's true, but they say on the radio that this way is more nutritious, and there's less waste. With the rationing we need the best value for money we can get."

"I know." Sarah sat at the familiar kitchen table. "It's the same down at Heronfield. Even the wounded soldiers are eating exactly the same as everyone else. There is no favouritism at all."

"That's as it should be. They didn't live too well, when your father was at the Front in the last war, you know."

Sarah nodded. "Let's just hope this war will be shorter than the last. I don't think this country could stand to lose another generation of young men."

"And to think we called it the war to end all wars." Alice shook her head sadly. "God knows why men have to keep fighting like this."

"Joe's taking me dancing tonight," Sarah said gaily, in an attempt to get the conversation back onto less morbid lines. "There's a dance on in the canteen at the aircraft factory."

Alice laughed. "You'd think he'd have enough of planes what with making them all day and looking for them all night." She turned from her work and smiled fondly at her daughter. "You've got a good man there, Sarah. He's always popping in to see if I'm all right. You just make sure you don't let him get away."

Sarah's eyes were shining as she smiled back at Alice.

"I don't intend to, Mum."

The canteen at the aircraft factory was festooned with bunting, a band had set up at one end while light refreshments were laid out on the serving counter at the other. When Sarah and Joe arrived, a number of couples had already taken to the floor and were dancing with gusto. Smiling at Sarah, Joe took her by the hand and led her out onto the floor. The band was playing a fast popular dance tune, and Sarah was laughing breathlessly when it finally ended.

"Oh, Joe! I must sit down!"

Joe laughed. "I thought you'd be fitter than this, now you're running around on your feet all day!"

"Nursing does make you fit Joe, but tired as well. Besides," she squeezed his hand as she smiled up into the laughing blue eyes, "I want a chance to talk to you and find out what you've been up to these last few weeks."

"All right." Joe led her to a table, before fetching drinks for both of them. He sat close beside her and put an arm around her shoulders. Sarah leant happily against the warm bulk of his body. "Now tell me everything."

Joe shrugged. "I suppose I've told you just about everything in my letters. Between work and the Home Guard I don't get much time to myself, and what little I do get I usually spend resting. The last couple of weeks have been extra busy. We've had to increase the output of fighter planes, and the repair facilities have been working flat out. There must have been a lot of action going on over the coast, more than the BBC let on."

Sarah nodded. "David Kemshall, the eldest son of the house where I'm working, is stationed down there. His brother Tony seems quite worried about him."

"I bet." Joe chuckled. "On first name terms with the nobility now, I see. Soon I won't be good enough for you."

"Don't be daft," she said gently. "You know that you're the only man for me."

Sarah's head was still resting on his shoulder so Joe did not see her blush and Sarah was thankful, she was not sure how Joe would react to her friendship with Tony.

Joe kissed her soft curls.

"I'm glad to hear it. So, what's this Tony Kemshall up to then?"

"Well, that's rather strange." Sarah was not quite sure how much she should say. "He's working as a Liaison Officer for the Ministry of Economic Warfare. It's a sort of desk job really. He won't be called on to go into action, and his family seem to be taking it rather badly."

"I'm not surprised. I'd jump at the chance to be able to fight for my country. Desk jobs and factory work are all right for old folks and people like me who can't get into the army, but any fit young man should be out there doing his bit. Unless he's a coward, that is."

"Oh, I don't think so. He was at Dunkirk and did quite well there by all accounts. He said he just thinks that if this is what the bosses want, then they must know best."

"That's a good excuse." Joe looked quizzically down at Sarah. "You're rather quick to jump to his defence, aren't you?"

Sarah shrugged. "I don't think so. I suppose it's so quiet out in the country that the only thing you can do with your spare time is to poke your nose into other people's business! But that's enough about other people. I don't get enough time with you as it is, so let's not waste it. Aren't you going to dance with me again?"

"I thought you'd never ask!"

The band was playing a waltz, and Joe smiled lovingly at Sarah as he took her hand. As Joe enfolded her in his arms all thoughts of Heronfield House and the problems of the Kemshall family were banished from Sarah's mind. Here in Joe's arms was where she wanted to be more than anything in the world, and as the music played on she wished the night would never end.

A nurse's leave in wartime was all too short. As Sarah rose on the morning after the dance, her happiness at being able to spend time with Joe was tempered with sadness at the thought of returning to Heronfield that afternoon. It was not that she did not enjoy her job, she did, in fact Sarah was beginning to think that once the war was over she might train as a proper nurse. It would be far more rewarding than an auxiliary helper. She would put the idea to Joe, once she had more time to think about it.

Joe called round early, as eager to make the most of the little time remaining to them as Sarah herself. It was a bright, sunny morning, the kind of day that filled one with a joy of life, and they enjoyed the morning walking and talking in a Coventry comparatively untouched by the war. True, there were patriotic posters everywhere warning that 'walls have ears' and encouraging people to 'dig for victory'. Anti-aircraft guns pointed their muzzles to the sky, and there were signs pointing the way to public air raid shelters, but around all this life went on as normal.

Sarah sighed sadly.

"What's wrong love?"

"I was just thinking how different things must be in the towns and cities of Northern Europe, the ones which have already been overrun by the Germans. Swastikas in the streets, German uniforms. It must be so strange to have those things in your home town."

"Don't worry." Joe's words were comforting. "That won't happen here. The RAF will stop the Germans from landing, but if they do, by some miracle, set foot on British soil, they will never get past the beaches. Our homes here in Coventry will be quite safe."

Sarah looked about her at the familiar streets and houses. "I hope you're right Joe. I never want them to touch us here."

Joe leant down and silenced her fears with a tender kiss.

They lunched at a small café and Sarah wished that the hours would pass more slowly so that they could spend more time together, but the hands of the clock moved inexorably round. Soon it was two o'clock. Sarah smiled at Joe, her eyes filled with sadness.

"I have to go now or I'll miss my train."

Joe nodded as he rose to his feet and led the way out of the cafe. Sarah had already said goodbye to Alice, and had her overnight bag with her so that she did not need to go back home. They made their slow way to a station full of noise and bustle, as people met friends or said fond farewells. A train pulled into the platform, enveloping the couple in a cloud of steam as the brakes screamed and the engine settled with a whoosh beside them. Joe carried Sarah's bag to a vacant carriage and placed it inside before helping her up and closing the door behind her.

Opening the window, Sarah leant out to say goodbye as Joe reached up and kissed her tenderly.

"Take care of yourself, Sarah." His voice was little more than a whisper.

She reached out a hand to gently caress his cheek. "I'll miss you, Joe." Her voice caught in her throat. Who knew in these uncertain days how long it would be before they were able to see each other again? A whistle blew and the train began to move slowly away.

"I love you, Sarah!"

With tears in her eyes Sarah withdrew her hand as the train drew them further apart.

"I love you too, Joe, with all my heart."

Suddenly he was gone, engulfed in a cloud of steam which billowed from the train. Sarah pulled her head into the carriage and slowly sat down. It almost broke her heart to leave Joe on the station platform, yet she was only going away to the comparative safety of a convalescent home. In that moment, Sarah had her first inkling of how it must be for soldiers and their families as the war called more and more men from their homes. She understood fully, for the first time, just what her mother must have felt when she said goodbye to Sarah's father on that very same platform. He had gone to his death without even knowing that his wife was expecting a child, and Alice had been left alone. Sarah felt the weight of maturity settling upon her shoulders. She had thought that she had grown up when she left home to join the VAD, but now she was beginning to realise that life was not as simple as she had thought, that love and pain often go hand in hand, and there is nothing that mere mortals can do about it. As the train headed southward, Sarah prayed that the war would stay far away from Coventry and that Joe would be safe.

19

The long hot month of July was drawing to a close at last. It was early afternoon when the scramble alarm sounded, and the pilots of 74 Squadron, who had been enjoying a few moments' relaxation in the warm summer sun, leapt to their feet and raced for their planes. In a matter of minutes they were airborne and heading for Dover.

"Tally Ho! Huns at three o'clock!"

David looked over to his right, to see a flight of bombers escorted by at least thirty fighters headed towards the coast.

"Looks like three to one against us." Reynolds voice rang through the RT. "Shouldn't be a problem, hey boys? Follow me!"

He led Red Section down onto the tails of eight 109's which had failed to spot the incoming Spitfires. Opening fire on one, he disabled its controls then switched his attention to attack another fighter, which had crossed right in front of his nose. As he fired into it, the plane began to go down in a steep spiral, trailing smoke behind it.

"Good hit, Red Leader," David called as he fired on an enemy to the left of Reynolds. The German broke away from the fight and headed towards the French coast, engine smoking. Turning to attack two more of the fighters, David called "That's one for me, lads!"

As David threw his plane expertly from side to side in swift pursuit of the enemy, he saw his bullets tearing into both his targets and gave a whoop of elation. Three damaged planes in one sortie! This was the life! Suddenly his euphoria evaporated as his plane was attacked from behind. Bullets thudded into the fuselage of his Spitfire as he broke away, desperately trying to climb to avoid his pursuer. Then the heady smell of glycol fumes entered the cockpit. The Merlin engine began to run roughly, coughing and spluttering. With a sinking feeling deep inside, David realised that this was no minor damage to the plane. The moment he had been dreading had arrived at last.

"Red Three to Red Leader. Red Three to Red Leader. Engine about to seize! I've got no control, so I'm baling out!"

"Red Leader to Red Three. Good luck, David. I'll have a pint waiting for you on the bar."

"I'll need it." David's voice was tense as he reached up to pull back the cockpit hood. With one last look at the useless controls, he threw himself from the plane. Suddenly he was falling through a world which tumbled all around him, so that he could hardly tell sea from sky. Then he was pulled up sharply by the opening of his chute. As he hung suspended in limbo between the heavens and the earth, he watched his plane fall towards the sea. Then he lifted his eyes to the dogfight raging high above him. It was an unwritten law with both the RAF and the Luftwaffe that pilots who had bailed out should not be fired on, so David felt safe from direct attack, but he prayed fervently that no stray bullet from the battle above would find him in this vulnerable position.

Above him and to his right David saw Freeman lead Yellow Section against a second flight of fifty fighters. One of the enemy was brought down before the three Spitfires turned and headed for home, one trailing smoke, their ammunition gone. Away to his left, Blue Section were in the thick of things and under heavy fire. The air was filled with the roar of their engines and the chatter of their machine guns as they brought down a fighter, before they too were heading for home to re-fuel and re-arm.

David looked down at the murky water towards which he was falling, then looked up again to see a Spitfire of Green Section in a head-on pass with the enemy. They missed colliding by a matter of feet and the Spitfire turned to attack again, but David could not watch the outcome. He had to concentrate on the water racing up to meet him.

'Feet together and keep stiff,' he thought, remembering the training exercises he had been through. Then he was down. The cold waters of the English Channel engulfed him, forcing the breath from his lungs as he fought to release the harness of his parachute. At last it gave. With lungs bursting, he kicked away from the billowing mass of wet silk, before striking upwards towards the surface. Finally his head broke through, and he gulped in mouthfuls of precious life-giving air. Gasping for breath, yet now in control of himself once more, he inflated his Mae West and began to float on his back, looking up to where the dogfight had taken place. The Spitfires had all gone now. He assumed that they must have used up all of their ammunition, and the German fighters were headed back towards France. Only a few smoke trails in the sky showed that a life and death struggle had raged so recently overhead.

As David floated, he wondered how long it would be before an Air Sea Rescue craft could reach him. Reynolds would have reported his position, and he was still within sight of the white cliffs which flanked Dover. Maybe an hour, he thought, as he shivered with the cold. He began to swim slowly towards the shore, the movement bringing a little warmth to his chilled limbs as he fought against the retreating tide. In fact it was only a little over thirty-five minutes later that he heard the approaching craft. Waving his arms vigorously, David was relieved when the boat turned and headed towards him. As it drew alongside, eager hands reached down to grab him and help drag him aboard.

"Thanks, lads. Boy, am I glad to see you!"

The boat turned and headed swiftly towards the shore, and a blanket was placed around David's shoulders.

"Are you hurt?"

David shook his head. "No. Just cold."

David huddled down in the boat, trying to avoid the chill breeze and to get warm again as they sped back towards the shore. None too soon he found himself sitting in a staff car in borrowed clothes with his wet uniform in a bag at his feet, heading back to RAF Manston. The tension of the dogfight coupled with the cold of the English Channel even in the height of summer, the relief of being picked up safely and finally being warm, all conspired to lull David into a deep sleep. He was unaware of the journey back. It was almost dark when a hand shook his shoulder and brought him back to wakefulness.

"Come on, David, you're home now."

He opened his eyes to see Andy Richies bending over him.

"Andy? What are you doing here?"

"I live here, remember!" Andy laughed. "You're back at Manston."

As the young man helped him out of the car, David came fully awake. The shadowy bulk of the buildings was familiar, and David felt he had come home. With a cheery smile and a wave, he thanked the driver, who turned and headed back towards Dover while Andy led the way to their sleeping quarters.

"Boy, am I glad to be back." David smiled at the young man. "I don't mind admitting, it was rather scary out there."

"You're one of the lucky ones. Brennan has been wounded; he'll be all right though. But I'm afraid Youngs is dead."

David stopped for a moment, and Andy waited quietly while his companion assimilated the news. It was hard, but the war must go on. Trying to bury his relief at being safe, yet sadness at the fate of his colleague, David turned to his young friend.

"What are you doing here, anyway? I thought you'd be down at the pub with the other lads."

"I wanted to wait for you. Now that I don't have Martin, I feel almost as though you're my elder brother. I hope you don't mind." Andy's voice was soft, nervous; David could sense his fear of rejection.

"Of course I don't mind, Andy. To be honest, I've already come to think of you as part of my family. Now let's get my wet stuff put away, and I'll buy you a pint."

As the two men made their way companionably towards an evening of drinking and dancing, David placed a friendly arm around Andy's shoulders, secure in the confidence that their new found relationship would see them through whatever trials might lay ahead.

The pilots of 74 Squadron, like so many other pilots, spent the day at their Dispersal Points from one hour before dawn until it was too dark to fly. Some slept, particularly if they had already been in action once that day. Others sat and talked quietly while waiting for the now almost inevitable call to combat. The last day in July was a day like all the rest. It was hot, and a brilliant sun rode high in a cloudless sky. It all seemed so quiet, so restful, but the peace was shattered by the call of the Tannoy.

"Scramble! Scramble! Raid over Dover!"

The pilots of A Flight ran to their planes, and were already airborne by the time the pilots of B Flight, whose planes were parked on the far side of the field, had their engines running. As Reynolds led his Section out over the coast, he sighted a formation of enemy aircraft out at sea.

"Tally Ho! Let's get them, lads!"

Red and Yellow Sections followed their leader out to sea, pouring on every ounce of power they could get, yet never seeming to get any closer to the enemy. At last Reynolds' voice came over the RT.

"Looks like we've had it, boys. Let's head for home."

The six dispirited pilots turned their planes in close formation, and headed back to Manston.

"It's damned frustrating," David said vehemently to Reynolds as they made their way to de-briefing. "If only we could follow them further over France, we could have wiped them out."

"Never mind, lad." Reynolds smiled. "We'll get them next time. Anyway, B Flight might have had better luck than us."

"I hope so."

David followed Reynolds into the de-briefing hut, and was surprised to find Squadron Leader Grey waiting for them. The two pilots stood to attention and saluted.

"Relax, lads." Squadron Leader Grey was smiling. "Before you make your reports, I want to give you a little good news. Reynolds, you got your DFC over Dunkirk, didn't you?"

"Yes, sir."

"Well, now you have a Bar to add to it. Congratulations." He shook hands with Reynolds, then turned towards David.

"As for you, David, you're a credit to this Squadron too. Fighter Command obviously agrees with me, as they've awarded you the DFC."

David was stunned. The DFC! He had never expected that. His face broke into a broad grin as he took the Squadron Leader's proffered hand.

"Thank you, sir."

"It's no more than you deserve. Well, I must get back to work. Put your reports in and I'll see you in the Mess this evening to celebrate." With that, Grey turned and left the hut.

"Well done, sir! The Bar! You deserve that. We couldn't hope to have a better leader."

"Thanks, David. The DFC, hey? You're a damned good pilot, and deserve the recognition. I'm proud of you, lad."

"Thank you, sir."

They were still in the midst of this back slapping and mutual congratulation when Green Section came in to report.

"How did it go, lads?" Reynolds turned towards the newcomers. "I hope you did better than us, we didn't even manage to fire a shot!"

Sergeant Bartlett nodded. "We did all right. The enemy hit Blue Section, so we climbed above them and attacked. We got a couple of probables and a few damaged."

"Great." David felt the day couldn't get much better. "What about Blue Section? How did they do?"

Bartlett shrugged. "I don't know. We lost contact with them once we joined with the Hun. Sounds like they're coming back now."

The sound of a plane engine, obviously struggling to keep going, was heard, and the pilots rushed out to see who it was.

"That's Bickell's plane," came a voice from behind David as he watched Blue Leader bring his plane in for a landing.

"His wheels are up!"

The plane was weaving from side to side as though Bickell was having trouble with the controls. Just before touchdown, the nose of the plane was pulled up and the labouring engine took the aircraft in a tight turn around the airfield.

"He's going to try again. That last pass was too fast."

As the Spitfire approached the runway again, its engines cut out and the plane banked steeply to the right. Bickell was obviously fighting furiously with the controls. The Spitfire levelled off just as its belly touched the ground. The plane skidded uncontrollably and hit the shell of a truck, one of a number placed on the airfield to discourage glider landings by the enemy. As the right wing was torn from the plane causing it to veer towards the hangers, David found himself running across the field with the other pilots. The plane had barely stopped moving, only feet from the hangars, when they caught up to it. Bickell was already throwing back the cockpit hood and climbing shakily down.

"Are you all right?" Reynolds helped him down from the plane.

Bickell nodded. "Just a few bumps and bruises."

Glad to see that Bickell was all right, David searched the sky for the final two Spitfires but saw no sign of them as his companions continued to congratulate Bickell on his narrow escape.

"Where's the rest of your Section?" David asked as Bickell sat down, obviously more shaken than he cared to admit.

He shook his head. "We were at eighteen thousand feet, still climbing for altitude when they hit us from above. About fifteen 109s, I'd say. Andy and Steve were both hit in the first pass, then Green Section came in and took some of the heat off us. I was fired on from behind and hit badly; I was lucky to get back in one piece. As I pulled away, I saw Steve hit again and go into a dive. I couldn't get him on the RT. I think he must have been dead already. I saw no chute when he went down."

There was silence for a few moments. It was David who finally voiced the unasked question.

"And Andy? What happened to him?"

Bickell was well aware of the friendship between David and Andy, and could not bring himself to look at his questioner. David knew then to expect the worst.

"When I was disengaging, Andy went spiralling down quite close to me." Bickell was obviously shaken, and took a moment to compose himself. "He'd been hit. He said on the RT that his right arm was useless. His plane was on fire, and I saw him struggling to open the cockpit. He never made it. I'm sorry."

David was speechless. No! Not Andy! he wanted to cry, but the words would not come. He turned and walked slowly back to the Dispersal Point, wondering at the perfidy of fate. Here was a young man with everything to live for. He had given up his life in service to his country and in memory of his brother while David's own brother, Tony, was skulking at home like a coward. In that moment of irrational grief and anger David knew he would never be able to forgive his brother for taking a desk job, while others lay down their lives to preserve all that was good and honourable in the world.

And what was he going to say to Mrs. Richies?

AUGUST 1940

20

Sarah and Jane walked side by side along the shady lane, the summer sun dappling the path beneath their feet. The air was clear and warm, birds sang in the trees and butterflies filled the air. It seemed strange to Sarah that they were a country at war, when everything around her was so peaceful.

"You know, Jane, I'd never been out into the countryside until I was posted here." She sighed. "It will be hard to live in the city again after all this."

"You don't have to live in the city." Jane smiled at her friend. "You could always stay here when the war's over."

Sarah shrugged. "I suppose so. But what about Joe? I couldn't live here without him."

"Perhaps he'll move out here too. Who can tell what will happen after the war?"

"Will you please stop mentioning the war!" Sarah snapped as she turned to face her friend. "I've come here to try to forget about it before I have to go back on duty. I know we only have a few men convalescing here now, but things are sure to get worse before they get better. Hitler's bound to try to invade this summer, he'd be mad to give us the whole winter to prepare ourselves. From what Joe told me, the initial air battles have already begun. We'll soon be fighting the Germans on English soil." Sarah shuddered, her voice coming softly now. "I'm afraid, Jane. Afraid that the Germans will come; afraid that Joe might be hurt; afraid that I might not be able to cope with the job when things get tough."

Jane put a comforting hand around her friend's shoulder.

"You don't need to be afraid, Sarah, you showed after Dunkirk that you can cope with this job. As for everything else, try to put it at the back of your mind. Take each day as it comes. Don't worry about things that might never happen. If the Germans land, and I for one don't believe that they'll be able to, then we won't go under like the French did. Eventually we'll defeat the Nazis, even if we have to fight to the last man."

"That," said Sarah, a frown creasing her brow, "is what I'm very much afraid of."

The two young women crossed the stile back into the Heronfield estate. Jane pointed out a young man in lieutenant's uniform, not an uncommon sight in a convalescent home.

"Isn't that Tony Kemshall?"

Sarah took a closer look and nodded. "Yes, he said he'd joined up. It looks as if he's being posted somewhere now he's in uniform."

"Will you miss him?" asked Jane, smiling mischievously. "I'm sure he'll miss you. He seems to have taken quite a fancy to you!"

"Stop it, Jane!" Sarah found herself laughing at her friend's ridiculous statement. "He's too rich, and his family is far too important for him to be interested in me. Besides, I'm in love with Joe. I like Tony's company, but I could never think of him as anything more than a friend."

"Well, as you enjoy his company so much, I think I'll leave you two alone together. He's heading this way." Jane turned to leave as she spoke.

"Don't be silly, Jane. I'm sure you'd enjoy his company too. Why not stay here with me?"

"Are you frightened your feelings might run away with you if you're left alone together?" Jane laughed.

"If you're going to say ridiculous things like that, it's probably better if you do go!" said Sarah, trying unsuccessfully to hide her laughter.

Jane said no more. With a quick wave, she ran through the trees towards Heronfield House. Moments later Tony strolled up to Sarah, his eyes on the form of the retreating nurse.

"Was that your friend?"

Sarah nodded in reply, still struggling to control her giggles.

Tony smiled an open, boyish smile that Sarah found rather endearing. "Did I say something funny?"

Sarah shook her head. "No. Not you. It was Jane. She has a peculiar sense of humour at times."

"I hope I didn't scare her off, although I'm glad she's gone." He smiled at Sarah's wary frown. "I have to leave this afternoon, and I wanted to see you to say goodbye."

"Surely you could have said goodbye to me in the company of my friend?"

Tony nodded. "Yes, but it wouldn't have been as easy. You see I have a bit of a confession to make. I've become rather fond of you since I got back from Dunkirk, and I enjoy spending a few moments alone with you. I hope you don't mind." Tony waited breathlessly for her response, hoping that she would give some sign that she cared for him. He was beginning training in a few days, and the atmosphere at home left him needing someone to be close to, someone who could understand him and help him through the bad times ahead. After what seemed like an endless silence, Sarah spoke.

"I'm flattered to think that you're fond of me" she said carefully, beginning to think that maybe Jane had been right about Tony's feelings after all, "and I enjoy your friendship too. Though I'm not sure what Joe would say if he knew we kept spending time alone together."

"Is it really that important to you, what Joe thinks?" Tony did not want to hear the answer yet knew that the question had to be asked.

Sarah nodded and smiled, and seeing the happiness in her eyes Tony did not need to hear her reply.

"Yes, it's very important to me what he thinks. I'd never do anything to hurt him."

Tony's heart felt heavy with the realisation that this beautiful young woman, whom he had known for such a short time, belonged to someone else. He forced a smile to hide his feelings.

"Our friendship can't hurt him though, can it, Sarah?" he questioned. "All I ask is that you allow me to talk with you from time to time. You understand me so well, better than my own family."

Sarah noticed the hurt in his voice. "Don't worry," she said gently. "They'll come round in the end. Until they do, you can come and talk to me whenever you like."

"Well," Tony was smiling again, "I won't be back to Heronfield for some time. I begin work tomorrow. That's what I really came to tell you."

Sarah nodded. "I guessed as much when I saw you in uniform. It suits you by the way." Sarah realised that this was perfectly true. She observed his slim figure in dress uniform, and sadly wished that Joe could wear something similar. Not realising the turn of her thoughts, Tony leant forward and kissed her gently on the cheek.

"Thank you, Sarah. It's nice to be appreciated. Now I really do have to be off, or I'll miss my train."

Sarah was still blushing after the kiss, and found it difficult to raise her eyes from the leafy floor. At last she had her feelings under control, and was smiling again when she looked up.

"Goodbye, Tony. I hope the job turns out to be all you want it to be."

Tony nodded. "I'm sure it will." He was suddenly serious, his thoughts turning to what might lay ahead for him in France. Then with a laugh and a quick wave he turned and ran back towards the lodge. "'Bye, Sarah. See you again soon."

Sarah waved back, feeling unsure of herself, as she always seemed to after talking with Tony. He seemed so open and outgoing, yet she felt that there were depths to his character that few, if any, knew about. With a shrug she turned again to the path through the trees, and made her way back to Heronfield House and her waiting patients.

21

The barbed wire caught on the shoulder of Tony's tunic as he struggled to crawl beneath its lowest strand, and he heard the material tear. With a muffled curse, he continued to drag himself towards the end of the tunnel. His hands and knees slipped in the slimy mud which clung to his clothes, weighing him down and making his task all the more difficult. His breathing was laboured when he finally pulled himself free of the wire and struggled to his feet. Yet, without pausing to regain his breath, he ran on towards the river which flowed swift and deep between its banks after the previous night's rain. As he broke from the cover of the trees into the bright sunshine he heard someone crashing through the trees behind him, and redoubled his efforts. The riverbank was only a few yards away now, and after stumbling breathlessly across the intervening space he plunged down the steep, slippery slope into the cold water, which stretched ahead of him for some twelve yards. He found himself struggling to keep his head above water. The weight of his clothing was already dragging him down. He would normally have swum the narrow stretch swiftly and without difficulty, but in his exhausted state every stroke was a painful struggle, every breath an agony. His breath was coming in short, harsh gasps when he reached the other side and, despite the need for speed, he rested on his hands and knees for a moment, head down, oblivious to the water which coursed from his body in shinning rivulets. Finally, with a massive effort of will, he dragged himself to his feet and began to pull himself laboriously up the riverbank.

A meadow stretched before him, and on the far side of it he could see an army truck parked in the shade of the spreading branches of a large oak tree. Forcing himself into one final effort to overcome his exhaustion Tony broke into a run once more and headed for the truck, his aching muscles screaming to be allowed to rest as he forced one tired foot in front of the other. At last he was there. The shadow of the tree stretched invitingly as Tony threw himself down beside the truck, thoroughly exhausted.

"Not bad, Kemshall." Sergeant Hopwood jumped down from the truck. "First back. But the others aren't too far behind."

Tony rolled over and looked back across the meadow to see a rag-tag group making their way towards the truck, each as filthy and exhausted as himself. Within five minutes the whole group were back, sprawled beside the vehicle in the shade of the tree, their laboured breathing gradually easing, their bodies aching. Sergeant Hopwood climbed up onto the tailgate and looked down at his new charges.

"Right, you lot, that was just a taste of things to come. By the looks of you all you're totally unfit and ill prepared for what lies ahead of you. But mark my words," he glared down at them as he spoke, "by the end of these three weeks you'll be running the course in half the time it took you today, or I'll want to know the reason why!"

The new recruits looked at each other in disbelief as Hopwood's voice barked again.

"Now up you get, you lazy lot. Into the back of the truck. When we get back to Base you'll have ten minutes to change into dry clothes before meeting me in the lecture hall for basic map reading. Understood?"

"Yes, sir" came the tired chorus.

"I didn't hear you!" The Sergeant's yell brought them all to their feet.

"Yes, sir!" they shouted as they scrambled tiredly into the back of the truck.

As the truck pulled into the drive, Tony caught a glimpse of the old country house that was to be home for the next three weeks. It was older than Heronfield but built along the same lines, and it was owned by a similar family. Like Sir Michael, the owner of this house had given up his home for the duration of the war. But unlike the Kemshalls, this family had to vacate the property altogether. It was one thing to allow a family to stay within the grounds if the house was being used as a convalescent home, but quite another if its purpose was to train spies. Tony had been told this would be just the first part of his training, concentrating on his physical fitness. After this morning's performance he was beginning to realise that it would not be as easy as he imagined.

The truck crunched to a halt on the gravel drive, and Hopwood jumped down.

"Ten minutes!" he reminded them, "and anyone who's late will go for a six mile run before dinner."

No-one was really sure if he meant what he said, but neither were they willing to put his words to the test. Hair still dripping and bodies damp inside their dry clothing, they were all assembled in the lecture hall as the ten minutes drew to a close. It was not really a hall, merely the family music room. Pianos and music stands had been removed, and replaced by desks and chairs. A bust of Beethoven still stood on a pedestal at one end of the room, and Sergeant Hopwood stood beside it. He glanced at his watch.

"Well, gentlemen, you made it. Now sit down and pay attention."

The group of twenty young men found seats at the desks, each with its allotted map and compass, notepad and pencil.

"You'll keep the pad and pencil for the full length of your stay with us," Hopwood explained. "The map and compass are there because you're going to be 'dropped' this afternoon within six miles of this Base. You'll have to find your way back by dinner time. Now, I'm assuming that you are all total beginners at this, so today you'll be allowed the luxury of being dropped on a road. Next time it will be in the middle of a field, or a wood. Now, pay attention."

As Hopwood began to explain the intricacies of the compass and how to use it in conjunction with the map, twenty heads bowed over notepads, twenty pencils scratched and a quiet of extreme concentration settled upon the room.

The twenty new recruits to the SOE, the Special Operations Executive, met together in the bar after dinner. The map reading had gone well for a first attempt, and they all managed to make the six miles back to base in time for dinner. But on top of the morning's assault course the walk had left them feeling totally exhausted; and this was just the first day.

Tony sat on a comfortable sofa, a small scotch on the table in front of him, and smiled at the young man opposite.

"How did you find the map reading?" he asked.

Len Haines shrugged.

"All right, I guess. I was a bit confused at first, but I think I'll get it all sorted out by the end of the course." He emptied his glass and signalled the bar steward for another double whisky. "This is like being in the boy scouts," he laughed. "If only my mates could see me now!"

Tony frowned. "You wouldn't tell them what you're doing would you?"

Len laughed. "Of course not! But wouldn't it be great to see their faces! Len Haines, super spy! What an adventure we're going to have!"

The steward brought Len his drink and hovered close by, wiping down tables. Len picked up the glass and emptied it in one swallow.

"You ought to take it easy with that whisky," Tony advised. "I bet we'll need to be wide awake tomorrow."

The young man shrugged. "I'll be all right in the morning. I can hold my liquor better than the average man. And why pass up the chance of free booze? You never know when you'll get another opportunity."

Tony's brow furrowed into a frown, but he said nothing. His companion's attitude puzzled him. The way he was behaving it was likely that he would be unfit for anything the following morning. Len Haines ordered another drink, and Tony wondered what special abilities he must have to have been chosen to join the SOE.

The next morning found the recruits out on the range, practicing with pistols. Their number was down to nineteen. Len Haines had been found 'unsuitable' and dismissed. Tony felt sure it must have been because of his excessive drinking and bragging the night before, and found himself wondering if the steward who had hovered close by was actually more than he appeared. Putting this from his mind, Tony concentrated on the task in hand. He had never used a pistol before, and had to concentrate hard on the target before squeezing off the two shots necessary to ensure a kill. By lunchtime he was mentally exhausted; by the end of the afternoon's cross-country run he was physically exhausted too.

So the days passed, half of each day on assault courses and cross country runs, each seemingly longer and more punishing than the one before; the rest of the day with map reading, or pistols, or machine guns. By the end of the first week the recruits had pushed their bodies to the limit and beyond. Tony felt that, no matter how hard he tried, he would never be able to make it to the end of the course. He would have to leave in disgrace. Yet, by half way through the second week his muscles ceased to ache at the end of each run. He found himself hitting the target at the range more and more frequently, and map reading was no longer a total mystery. He was feeling fitter than he had ever done before, and as each day passed he grew more confident that he would finally pass this part of the course, despite his earlier misgivings.

It was the night before the final test and the remaining nineteen recruits were relaxing in the Mess.

"It's the big one tomorrow. Twenty miles back to base, from wherever they decide to drop us." Tony smiled. "Last one back buys the drinks!"

A chorus of assent greeted this; after all, there was no harm in a little healthy competition. One of the men at the bar spoke up.

"Did you see that air battle while we were out on cross country this afternoon?"

There were some nods, but the majority said no.

"There must have been at least a dozen aircraft, flying too high for me to see what they were. There were a lot of smoke trails and the sound of an engine now and then, but nothing more. It was quite eerie really, to know that men were fighting for their lives up there, and we were almost totally oblivious to them down here. I don't know what the outcome was. I saw one plane go down in flames, but I can't say if it was theirs or ours." He shook his head reflectively. "Those pilots must be pretty special people."

Tony nodded. "They are. My brother's a Spitfire pilot. From what I gather he seems to be fighting every day now. They're just holding the Nazis back until we're ready for them."

"You must be pretty proud of your brother."

Tony nodded.

"I certainly am."

'I just wish I could make him feel proud of me,' he thought sadly. Still, once the war was won he would be able to explain everything to David, and they could resume their previous close relationship. He hoped that day would not be too far away.

Tony climbed down from the back of the truck, wearing full fatigues and carrying a haversack on his back. It did not feel too heavy, but he knew that before the twenty miles were over he would be wishing he did not have it with him. Sergeant Hopwood smiled grimly down at him.

"This is roughly where you are, Kemshall," he said, pointing to a broad area on the map. "See you back at Base."

With a roar, the army truck sped off down one of the two lanes which crossed here in the woods. Tony had a choice of four routes. The trees grew closely together, and he knew that it would be foolish to try to force his way through them. Compass in hand, he studied the map, carefully finding the position of the Base and orientating himself towards it. The track which led in roughly the right direction, according to both the map and his own inbuilt sense of direction, lay to his left. Placing the compass in his pocket and carefully buttoning the flap, Tony began to run at a slow, steady trot down the track.

It was a hot, sunny day and Tony was glad to be in the shade of the trees, although he knew from the map that these would soon end and he would have to cover the majority of the twenty miles in the full glare of the sun. As if to prove him right, the trees came to an abrupt end and Tony was faced with a field glowing yellow with ripened heads of corn, bending low to the ground. It looked like it would be a good harvest. Unclipping his water bottle from his belt, Tony took a swallow of the warm, tasteless water before setting off around the edge of the field.

It was almost midday and the sun beat down mercilessly. The haversack was already a crushing weight on his shoulders, and sweat soaked his heavy uniform, but Tony kept up a steady pace, forcing one weary foot ahead of the other across the uneven ground. At last, he reached the smooth surface of a road. A quick glance at the map was all he needed to determine which way to go, then he was off again. As time passed, his pace slowed. Tony was tired and his muscles ached, yet he felt that he was making good time. He forced himself on through sleepy villages, across slow moving streams, past fields where hay-makers stopped their work to watch the fool run by in heavy clothing on such a hot day.

At last the familiar and welcome sight of the gates to base greeted his eyes, and Tony smiled wearily. Straightening his back, he increased his speed a little and ran up the driveway to halt on the gravel forecourt in front of Sergeant Hopwood.

"Well done, lad." The Sergeant smiled his first truly friendly smile of the course. "There are a few back before you, but not many, so it won't be you who has to buy the drinks."

Slipping the haversack from his shoulders, Tony leant forward and placed his hands on his knees. As he drew in huge gulps of air, his laboured breathing began to ease and the pain in his chest to dissipate.

"You'll have to wait to see the CO to get your official report," Hopwood continued, "but unofficially I can tell you that you have passed this course with flying colours. Now, go and get changed."

With a smart salute and a grateful smile, Tony headed back to his quarters for a bath and a rest.

22

Operating from the forward Base at Manston, 74 Squadron's pilots had barely reached their Dispatch Points when the scramble alarm sounded at 07.49 hours on 11th August. Reynolds was the first to reach his plane, and they were swiftly airborne with his Squadron's twelve Spitfires leading the way out towards Dover. Not long into the flight they surprised a formation of German fighters.

"Tally Ho! There they are, boys! Let's get them!"

The German planes dived to avoid the Spitfires, and soon the sky was a whirling maelstrom of individual dogfights. David saw Reynolds heading south towards France on the tail of a 109, then broke away from his Section to help another Spitfire with a fighter on its tail. Taking the enemy by surprise, he poured bullets into the plane until the pilot veered away to avoid further damage. With a whoop of joy David was after it, adrenalin pumping. He felt no fear as he fired into the plane again. Suddenly bullets ripped into him from behind. This time it was his turn to climb steeply away to avoid the man on his tail.

The sky was filled with vapour trails, smoking planes, the scream of engines, planes climbing, diving, turning; it was almost impossible to keep track of what was happening, although David got the distinct impression that the Spitfires had the upper hand. Diving into the melée once again, he fired his guns repeatedly until his ammunition was exhausted, then headed for home.

The pilots, all except Etheridge who had bailed out into the sea just off the coast from Dover, were still in debriefing when the Tannoy blared again at 10.15 hours. A reserve pilot and plane flew where Etheridge should have been as the Squadron headed out over the Channel, where they intercepted another flight of Meschersmitt fighters.

"Look out, Tim!" David yelled, as he saw a plane dive towards Green Three, but there was no reply, just a crackle and hiss over the RT.

"Can anyone hear me?"

The RT hissed again.

"Damn!"

Reception must have been bad for all of the Squadron, for David noticed that there were very few co-ordinated attacks on the enemy, but that did not deter the Spitfires. The air was full of de Wilde burning bright pathways towards the enemy. David knew he had scored hits on two planes, but both had limped back towards France and, as his ammunition ran out, he knew he would be able to claim no kills at all on this sortie. With one last look at the planes still engaged in combat, he turned and headed for home.

David's legs were shaking with tiredness as he climbed down from his bullet-ridden plane at Manston. He made his slow way across the airfield to debriefing. His shoulders were stiff, his head ached, and he rubbed gently at his eyes, which were tired and heavy from the fumes. What he wanted more than anything was a chance to sleep. He made his report concisely before heading for his Dispatch Point and the chance to rest. The ground crew had the kettle boiling, waiting for the Squadron to return, and David thankfully poured steaming tea into his tin mug before sitting down in the corner, feet up on the chair opposite. With a sigh he raised the mug to his lips, just as the scramble alarm sounded again. It was 11.45. With a groan of dismay, David put his mug down on the arm of the chair and ran out to his plane.

"Is she ready to go?" He climbed up onto the wing root.

The ground crew nodded. "Your tank's full and you have a full load of ammo, though we've had no time to make any repairs."

"Never mind, that'll give you something to do this afternoon!"

David slammed the cockpit hood closed and pressed the ignition. The Merlin engine roared into life, and he was airborne again. Making a slow turn, he headed east with ten other Spitfires to give air cover to Convoy 'Booty', which was steaming twelve miles east of Clacton.

"Right, lads." Reynolds voice came over the RT as they sighted the convoy. "Contrary to rules, I want to fly in fours instead of our usual Vic of threes. Red and Blue Sections into fours. Numbers One and Three, and numbers Two and Four, fight as pairs."

"About forty Hun at four thousand feet, Red Leader."

"Thanks, Freeman. Right. Let's get them, lads."

David felt tired as he dived down on the low-flying enemy. The day had been a round of constant tension, no moments to rest, let alone relax, and he felt drained. Yet as battle was joined and the adrenalin flowed it was as if he were reborn. Everything became clear, the action appeared to happen in slow motion. He found himself totally attuned to his surroundings, aware of all that was happening around him. Feeling at one with his plane, David felt completely in control and this time he made two kills, watching them fall into the heaving grey seas below. To his amazement, he found himself sympathising with the enemy pilots after his own experience of ditching.

As the battle raged, David's feeling of euphoria began to fade, and his tiredness became more apparent. His body ached, and it was getting more and more difficult to control the plane. His hands shook with fatigue, but at last the enemy broke away and the convoy was safe. The Spitfires turned as one, and headed for home.

"Some way to celebrate your twenty-sixth birthday, hey, Yates?"

Silence greeted Freeman's remark.

"Yates?"

"He won't be celebrating." Reynolds voice was grim. "I'm afraid he's bought it. So has Jones."

The pilots returned to Manston in silence. No one thought of the fight they had just won or the number of enemy they had brought down. All their thoughts were with their two companions who would never fly with them again, of friendships forged in combat now shot down in flames.

The nine Spitfires landed at Manston at 12.45.

"You fought magnificently up there," Reynolds complimented the pilots on their way to debriefing. "I know we've always fought in the traditional Vic formation, but that requires a great deal of skill and absolute concentration. I thought that as we were all so tired, flying line astern might be safer."

David nodded. "Forming pairs seemed much easier, and gave us all greater cover. I, for one, appreciated that."

There were murmurs of agreement from his colleagues and Reynolds nodded. "I'm convinced we'd have lost even more planes if we had been flying the old Vic formation."

His words brought to mind their fallen comrades, and the pilots continued on their way in silence.

After debriefing, David made his way back to his Dispatch Point, praying that the action was over for the day. A dark scum had settled on the surface of his mug of cold tea, and he poured it away before refilling the mug and taking a thankful drink.

There is a limit to what the human mind and body can take in a short space of time. David was fast asleep within moments of sitting down, his exhausted body recouping what little it could in the time available. Shortly before 14.00 hours the scramble alarm sounded again.

For a few moments the sound did not register in David's tired brain. Then, with a groan, he opened his eyes, rose to his feet and ran for his plane, fighting back his lethargy. As he gunned the engine into life and took off to join the other seven planes which were to be sent out, David felt as though his hands had not left the controls all day. His muscles ached, and there was a throbbing behind his tired eyes as Reynolds led the aircraft towards Margate.

"We'll be flying in two Sections, lads, Blue and Red. Four apiece." Reynolds stopped talking as he sighted planes in the distance and tried to distinguish them.

"Dysoe Leader to Control. Dysoe Leader to Control. Have sighted about ten bombers with twenty Bf 109's. We're going in." David had heard, and was ready when the order came. "Right, lads. Blue One, take your boys down and deal with the bombers. We'll take the fighters."

As the planes closed with the enemy, Blue Section failed to peel away and stayed alongside Red.

"Hartley, can you hear me? Take your men down to the bombers." There was no response, and Reynolds swore expressively as the bombers disappeared into cloud cover.

Reynolds was firing wildly at a plane. It burst into flames and fell spinning towards the ground as he turned to attack four fighters above him. Over on his left he saw David firing into a plane. David felt once again the exhilaration of battle, but knew it would not last for long. Desperate to return to base and rest, he fired once more at the plane as they dived through the clouds. Suddenly the Germans' engine stopped and fragments broke away. It fell to the earth like a stone.

David was exhausted and had forgotten his own rule about the 'Hun in the sun'. As he pulled up from the dive, a cannon shell exploded behind the armour-plated seatback, punching him forward with the impact. A bullet whistled as it cut through his helmet, grazing the top of his head before smashing his gun sight. Other bullets punctured the oil and glycol tanks, and David watched through a red mask as a 109 flashed by.

Trying to wipe the blood from his eyes, he fought desperately to turn the damaged plane away from the enemy. Fumes were filling the cockpit causing him to cough. His blood filled eyes began to sting, and he fought frantically against an overwhelming dizziness. The plane had had it, and he was too low to jump. Praying that the enemy would leave him alone for long enough, David headed for a field where it looked as if he might get away with a forced landing. Stick-like figures ran from the centre of the field to take cover in the hedgerows as the plane screamed towards them. At one hundred feet the engine blew up.

David felt himself being thrown through the air, the wind of his passage roaring through his ears, and he knew this was the end. Unable to see through the curtain of blood which covered his eyes, David was unaware of the haystack until he hit it. Instead of hard unyielding earth, he fell through the softness of the hay and lay still.

Minutes that seemed like hours passed before hands reached down to pull him clear.

"Are you all right, mate?"

David nodded, still a little groggy. Someone prodded his head.

"It's all right. Just a flesh wound. There's a lot of blood, but it looks worse than it is."

A jug of water was proffered, and David drank gratefully.

"The police will be here soon, they'll get you back to your base."

David nodded his thanks, and slipped into oblivion.

Whoever had looked at his head was right. The wound was not serious, and David came to as it as being bandaged by the local police. With grateful thanks, the pilot allowed himself to be led to a patrol car. It ferried him back to Manston where he sank gratefully into his bed and slept the night through.

Within a period of little more than seven hours on 11th August, No. 74 Squadron had fought four engagements with the Luftwaffe. They had destroyed thirty-eight enemy aircraft, as well as damaging many more. The battle for air supremacy over Britain was now raging. Civilians were becoming more aware of just how much depended on these brave men, who went up time after time to do battle with the an enemy determined to add their country to its long list of conquests.

David was pronounced fit for action again immediately. There were few enough pilots without giving sick leave to those with only minor injuries. At the airfield, no-one now grieved openly for the dead. Deaths were inevitable during such concentrated fighting. None of the airmen doubted that the RAF would be victorious in the end, but would they personally be there to enjoy the victory celebrations? David found himself secretly watching the others, wondering who would be next, searching their faces for signs of fear. He thought they were looking at him in the same way too, but no-one spoke about their fears. They were all afraid that, if they did, it would give such nightmares a living, breathing reality, and leave them unable to do their job. As he sat in the Dispatch Room two days after his crash landing, watching the early morning mist rising from the damp grass, David wondered if he would ever see his home and family again. Fear gripped him tightly, yet it allowed him to be totally honest about his feelings for the first time in weeks. He recognised his own fear, his desperation to see his family again, his longing for a return to the peace he had known in his youth. All these things helped him to see that although he would never be able to forgive Tony for his cowardice, he still loved the younger brother who had always been such an important part of his life. He was determined to give Tony the support to face up to his own fears, and to try to get him to do something a little more worthwhile in this war. At peace with himself, David leant back in his chair and relaxed.

"Scramble! Scramble!"

The Tannoy howled and twelve pilots ran for their machines. Moments later, the squadron rose into the air, like giant birds of prey lusting for their next meal.

"Dysoe Leader to all Sections." Reynolds' voice came over the RT. "There are about seventy bombers over the estuary without fighter cover. Let's go get them!"

The Squadron headed out for Whitstable. The early morning sun was low in the sky and obscured their vision. At last the enemy were sighted.

"Tally Ho! It's everyone for himself today!"

The Spitfires broke formation and dived at the bombers who returned fire, though not as effectively as they would have been able to if they had fighter cover. As David entered the fray, he was conscious of individual combats all around him. Reynolds was carrying out a beam attack on three bombers, Taylor had disabled the port engine of the first plane he attacked, Freeman hurtled through the cloud to attack a plane from behind and send it crashing into the sea.

David fired into one of the bombers from slightly above and astern, riddling it with bullets. Two of the crew bailed out, and he watched the pale mushrooms of their parachutes as they followed the plunging death-dive of their burning plane at a more leisurely pace. David found it almost relaxing. It was easy to attack the bombers with all the speed and manoeuvrability of the Spitfire, without having to constantly look over his shoulder for an attacking fighter. Although the bombers could, and did, fire back, the damage to 74 Squadron was slight and they returned to Base able to claim five bombers destroyed and seven damaged.

In the bar that evening Reynolds set up the drinks. "Well, lads, a good days work. And I've got some good news for you too." He smiled at the ring of expectant faces around him. "We're being withdrawn to RAF Wittering in Northamptonshire for a rest period."

Cheers and whoops of delight greeted this remark while uniform caps were hurled into the air. Reynolds laughed. "That's not all. Everyone gets one week's leave before we have to begin training the replacement pilots in the way we like to do things. Now, pick up your drinks and let's celebrate!"

The pilots needed no second bidding. Glasses were raised in hearty toasts and more drinks were downed than would normally be acceptable in the Mess. But who cared? No-one needed to stay sober, for tomorrow they would be out of it, able to sleep well at night and relax during the day, without the scramble alarm lifting them from their seats at a moment's notice. Knowing that he would finally be able to relax, David began to realise just how much pressure he had been under for the last few weeks. Many of his colleagues had shown signs of cracking, and he wondered if he had appeared the same to them. A spot of leave was just what they all needed.

23

David drove home the following morning in the small red sports car that had been his coming-of -age present from his parents. As he turned into the sweeping driveway that led to Heronfield House, the young man found his eyes pricking with tears, and roughly dashed them away with the back of his hand. It would not do for the homecoming hero to be seen crying like a baby. David parked outside the lodge, still feeling uncomfortable at being denied access to the big house, yet proud of the sacrifice his father was making. Not bothering to open the low-slung door, he climbed out of the car just as his parents appeared on the top step of the flight leading up to the door of the lodge. The three people looked at each other, too full of their emotions to do or say anything, then Louise Kemshall rushed down the steps to embrace her son. Tears glistened in her eyes as she looked up at him.

"I am so proud of you, David." She hugged him again, as though afraid that he would be called away before they had a chance to spend some time together. Sir Michael followed his wife more sedately down the steps and laid a comforting hand on her shoulder.

"Well done, lad." Sir Michael waved a hand at the blue and purple-striped ribbon sewn beneath the wings on David's uniform. "The day I heard you'd got the DFC was the proudest day of my life." Throwing all decorum to the wind, he reached out and embraced his son. "It's good to have you home again."

"Let us have our lunch in the garden!"

David noticed that his mother's gaiety was forced, and raised a questioning eyebrow at his father. Sir Michael shook his head as if to say 'not now'. Louise seemed not to notice this exchange as she started back into the house.

"You two go round to the side. I have laid a table in the shade. It is a cold lunch, so I will join you soon."

She disappeared in the direction of the kitchen.

"Come on, lad." Sir Michael led his son round to the side of the house. "You'll have to bear with your mother, David. Although she hasn't said anything, I know she's been really worried about you. The newspapers are full of how you boys are fighting the Battle of Britain alone, and we can't switch on the radio without hearing more news. Each morning your mother waits for the post, hoping for a letter from you. And every time the doorbell rings during the day she jumps like a scalded cat. I'm sure she expects to get a telegram, because when it turns out to be a friend or neighbor, not the postman, the relief on her face is enormous."

"I'm sorry, Dad. The last thing I want to do is make Mamma suffer like that, but it's all part of the job. I don't think I'll tell her much about it though, if that's all right with you."

His father nodded. "Yes. I think the least said about it the better. This week will go too quickly as it is. Just try to forget and enjoy yourself."

"That's easier said than done, Dad."

David sat down, his back to a tall pine tree, and Sir Michael noticed the tiredness and strain etched on his eldest son's face.

"It's that bad, is it?"

David nodded. "The losses are so high. Planes are repaired and replaced quickly enough, but it's harder to replace pilots. They take a year to train, and even by cutting the courses at Operational Training Units from four weeks to two, we can't fill all the places. So many of the new pilots sent to us are unready for combat, and we don't have time to train them. You know, some of the new lads never return from their first sortie. I don't even remember the names of some of them, they weren't with us long enough for me to get to know them." He closed his eyes as though to shut out the world. "Some of them are so young, Dad, not much more than boys." His voice was soft, and he felt himself near to crying again as he thought of Andy. Fighting to get his emotions under control, he opened his eyes and listened to the homely sounds coming from the kitchen.

"You look tired, lad." Sir Michael remembered his service in the trenches, and knew just how hard it was to constantly face the enemy without any hope of respite. Unaware of his father's thoughts David nodded.

"Yes, I'm tired. You can't know what it's like, Dad. We can fly up to half a dozen times a day. We often fly when we're totally exhausted or wounded. We try to snatch a few moments' sleep between emergencies, but it's hopeless. While it's daylight we have to be ready to fly, and the days are awfully long at this time of year. Sixteen hours on duty seems to be the norm at the moment." He closed his eyes and ran his hands through his hair. "I know we'll win, Dad, we shoot down far more of them than they do of us, but we get so tired. I sometimes think it will never end."

Unsure of what to say to comfort his son, Sir Michael sat in silence. When he looked back, he saw that David had fallen into the sleep of the exhausted.

Cups rattled on a tray as Louise made her way around the side of the house.

"Here I am at last. Sorry I took so long but..." She stopped speaking as Sir Michael held a finger to his lips and took the tray from her, placing it gently on the table. He inclined his head towards their sleeping son.

"Let him rest."

He took his wife in his arms and this time the tears came freely.

"I am so frightened for him, Michael. I wish he did not have to go back."

"I know. I'm as frightened for him as you are, Louise, but we both know that he must go back." He looked down at the sleeping form. "I'm proud that David is willing to give so much for his country."

Holding his wife close he gently wiped away the tears, and prayed this would not be the last time that they would see their son.

Nothing more was said of the pressures under which David was working. His parents tried their best to make him forget, to divert him with trips to his old haunts, or just spending time quietly with him. Outwardly, David seemed to be recovering. He was no longer so tired, and was able to spend less time catching up on the sleep he had missed at Manston. But the worry lines still etched his face. His eyes held a haunted look, as though even away from his squadron, David was still fighting the battle.

Five days into David's leave, Tony arrived home from his physical training course. Despite his anger at his brother's choice of duty, David was immensely glad to see him. Maybe he could share his experiences with his younger brother, just as he had done when they were boys. Maybe it would help him to exorcise some of the ghosts that haunted him, and maybe it would bring the two brothers closer together again. He certainly hoped so.

The atmosphere at home was tense, as though Sir Michael was comparing his two sons and one of them was found wanting. It was impossible to talk.

"Shall we go out for a drink tonight?" Dinner was over and David smiled across at his brother. Tony nodded.

"Come on, then." David led the way from the room. "It'll be good to see the old places and old faces again."

"If there are still any here. I would think most of them have joined up by now."

"Well, we won't know if we don't go and look!"

The two young men climbed into the red sports car and David headed off towards the local pub in the village. On the way he stopped, got out of the car and leant on a gate, gazing out over the beautiful countryside. After a moment's hesitation, Tony climbed out of the car to join him. There was silence for a time, not the companionable silence of their childhood but one filled with expectancy, waiting for words to be said that could never be taken back. At last David broke the silence, his words soft, questioning.

"Were you afraid at Dunkirk?" He continued to gaze across the fields as though he had not a care in the world, but Tony could see how tense he was.

"Yes. I was afraid. The beaches were so open, and there was nowhere to take shelter. But I didn't show my fear, if that's what you're thinking." Tony's voice was filled with hurt and anger and David turned to face him.

"No, that wasn't what I was thinking; but it sounds as though Dad must have said something like that."

Tony nodded. "You must have noticed the atmosphere at home. He still hasn't forgiven me for accepting my present job."

"I can understand that."

Tony tensed at David's words, waiting for the attack, but it never came. Instead... "I can also understand how fear might have played a part in you deciding to take the job. You see, Tony, over the last few weeks I've known what it is to feel fear." David took out a cigarette and lit it, hands shaking. "I've lost a lot of friends in this. I told you about my friend who died. I tried to talk him home over the radio but he was wounded, and all the time he was talking his blood was pumping out of him. His cockpit must have been awash with it. Eventually he passed out and crashed into the sea." Tears appeared in David's eyes, but he ignored them, desperate to unburden himself to Tony. "That friend's brother then joined my squadron. He was shot down in flames. I was told that he was conscious but couldn't get out. I don't know if it was the flames or the crash that killed him. He was younger than you, Tony."

David buried his head in his hands, forgotten cigarette falling to the ground where Tony swiftly stamped it out.

"I dream about those deaths. Then I dream that it's me in those planes." He looked up, and Tony was shocked by the pain and loss in his eyes. "We've lost so many men. There are hardly any of the original squadron left, and most of the new boys are so inexperienced that they don't last for long. I don't think I'll ever be able to forgive you for not making a stand and fighting for your country. But in a purely selfish way, I'm glad you didn't."

Tony frowned, puzzled by his brother's contradictory words. "What do you mean?"

"There won't be many of us left by the time this is all over. I want to live, but being realistic I know my chances aren't that good. If I die, that means that you're all Mamma and Dad will have left. If doing an office job will keep you safe for them, then I'm glad. Though saying that makes me feel like a traitor to all the other young men who have died."

Tony did not know what to say. He wanted to comfort David in the loss of his friends, tell him that he wasn't going to die and that there was no need to be afraid, tell him that far from being ashamed of Tony, he should be proud of the job he had taken on. Yet the words would not come. There are no words to say such things. Tony reached out and put an arm around his brother's shoulders.

"You'll be all right, David," he said softly, "and I want you to know that I'm not a coward. This job isn't totally lacking in danger. Although I may not be at the front shooting at the enemy, I'll have to travel abroad to some war zones, to liaise with the army and find out what they need." Tony found the words of comfort flowing from some inner source, and prayed that he would be forgiven for what he saw as necessary lies. "There will be danger involved for me, though perhaps not as much as being in the front line. I still believe this is what I'm best suited for in this war."

David seemed to relax a little, leaning against his brother, and Tony wondered at this strange trading of places. In the past it had always been David who was the strong one, David who comforted little Tony. Now the roles were reversed.

"You should have told us more about your job. Maybe Dad would have been more understanding then."

Tony laughed bitterly. "I don't think Dad will be satisfied unless I'm driving a tank through Berlin in an attempt to capture Hitler myself!"

David laughed and straightened up. "Maybe you're right, but I'll have a word with him, see if I can get him to ease up on you a bit." He smiled at Tony. "I still don't totally approve, but I love you, and I'm glad you're out of the worst danger." He breathed deeply. "Thanks for listening tonight, little brother, it's been a big help. We get so tired at base that fear takes hold of us all too easily. But after this spot of leave I'm sure we'll be fit and ready to go again. The battle will be over before you know it, and we'll laugh at the times we were afraid!"

Tony reached out to touch his brother's shoulder again. "I'll always be here if you need to talk David. I love you, and I'm immensely proud of you. I'll do my best not to let you or Dad down. By the time this is all over, maybe you'll all appreciate my contribution too."

David nodded. "I'm sure we will. Everything is so black and white in wartime, brave or coward, loyal or traitor. It won't be until this damned war is finished that we'll be able to see the shades of grey." He grinned, more like the David that Tony knew from before the war. "Now come on, let's get down to the pub!"

The two brothers climbed into the sports car and the engine roared into life, but before pulling away David turned to his brother once more.

"I'm glad we had this talk. You don't know how much it means to me that we're friends again."

As the car pulled out into the road and headed for the village, the two young men were smiling happily.

It was David's last morning at home before rejoining his squadron at Wittering, and the family were together in the drawing room. Sir Michael had noticed the change in the relationship between his two sons, and felt that if David, whose life was in constant danger as he fought for his country, could come to terms with Tony's apparent cowardice, then he, too, should make an effort. The atmosphere had eased slightly, much to the relief of Louise and her mother, and the family could meet once more without fear of arguments.

The two young men were playing chess at a table placed in front of the window, so that they could look out at the pleasant sunlit gardens. Madame de Thierry and her daughter were both engaged in writing letters, while Sir Michael sat in his favourite armchair reading the morning newspaper.

"Mr. Churchill has been giving another one of his speeches," he said to no-one in particular. "That man does have a way with words. He seems to be able to bring out the best in us, and to say what each of us feels."

"What did he have to say this time?"

Sir Michael turned towards his son. "He's been praising the work that you and the other brave boys in the RAF are doing."

There was silence for a moment, and Tony feared that Sir Michael might make some comment about his younger son's reluctance to fight. But the moment passed and nothing was said.

"Read it to us, mon cher."

Sir Michael smiled at his wife. "Of course, dear. I'm sure you'll like it." He cleared his throat and rustled the paper as though he were about to make a speech to Parliament, not read one that was already a day old. His two sons smiled indulgently at each other as Sir Michael began to read.

"'The gratitude of every home in our island, in our Empire, and indeed throughout the world, except in the abodes of the guilty, goes out to the British airmen who, undaunted by odds, unwearied in their constant challenge and mortal danger, are turning the tide of the world war by their prowess and their devotion. Never in the field of human conflict was so much owed by so many to so few.'"

"Never was so much owed by so many to so few? He must have seen our mess bills! "David winked at his brother, and they both laughed.

"Do not make a joke of it, cher." Louise was smiling indulgently at her son. "This shows just how much the people of England appreciated what you are doing. I am so proud of you."

"Me too. What you're doing will go down in history as one of the greatest battles ever. And if you fly your plane like you play chess, Hitler doesn't stand a chance!" Tony indicated the board where his white king was almost surrounded by black pieces.

"That's always assuming Hitler is as bad at planning his battles as you are at playing chess! Come on, let's go for a walk before I have to leave."

As the two young men left the room, they failed to notice the frown which furrowed their father's brow. As the door closed he turned to his wife in exasperation.

"I don't know how David can be so friendly with Tony, while he's taking the easy way out in this ghastly war."

Louise gave a typically French shrug. "Perhaps he knows more about Tony's job than we do, and can appreciate its value. Or perhaps he merely loves his brother. Whatever the reason, I am glad to see them friends again. They should not part as enemies in wartime. Life and love are too precious to waste, mon cher."

Sir Michael nodded. "Perhaps you're right; but I don't mind admitting that I find it hard to keep my relationship with Tony friendly."

With a sigh, Louise turned back to her letter-writing.

24

Four days after David rejoined his squadron, Tony was reading the morning paper in the gardens. The headlines filled almost the entire front page, and what they said filled him with a deep anger. 'German bombs fall on London'. In his mind's eye he saw once again the refugees bombed and strafed in France, the horror of the bombing on the beaches at Dunkirk. He transferred the vision of fear and pain to the civilians in London, his own capital city. If it could happen there, it could happen anywhere. Would the Germans dare to bomb other civilian centres?

A shadow fell over the paper, breaking into Tony's black thoughts. He looked up.

"Sarah!" He leapt to his feet at the sight of the girl beside him. "It's good to see you again. I was going to come looking for you later on. I have to be back at work soon and I wanted to see you again before I left."

Sarah's smile was forced, holding none of its usual sparkle and Tony frowned. "Is there anything wrong?"

Sarah indicated the newspaper lying at his feet. "Why did they do it Tony? Why bomb London? Do you think it was deliberate?"

"I've been thinking about it, and I don't think it was. Maybe the pilots got lost, and with the blackout they wouldn't have known they were dropping their bombs on a city." He took Sarah by the arm and began to walk with her across the lawns. "Maybe this will be just an isolated raid."

"Do you think we will retaliate?"

Tony shrugged. "If we're wise we won't, at least not until they do it again, and we know that it wasn't an accident. But I don't think we'll take the sensible course; there'll be calls, from all sides, for us to bomb Berlin. If we do retaliate then the Germans will bomb our cities again. It'll be a vicious circle, with no way out."

Sarah felt a shiver of fear run up her spine as she tried to imagine how the civilians must have suffered.

"Do you think they'll bomb other cities, apart from London?"

"I guess so. Especially the ones involved in the war industry." Tony felt Sarah's arm stiffen beneath his hand and turned towards her. "I'm sorry, Sarah. Your family are in Coventry, aren't they?"

Sarah nodded. "There's just my mum, she's all the family I have. Then there's Joe." Deep down, Sarah had been glad that Joe had failed his medical, feeling that he would be safe at home. Now, with the prospect of the Luftwaffe bombing civilian centres, she realised just how insecure her loved ones really were. Tony took her gently in his arms and held her close.

"Don't worry, Sarah, I'm sure they'll be all right. The Germans might not bomb other cities, but if they do there are plenty of air raid shelters. People will be safe."

Tony found it hard to concentrate on his words. Holding Sarah in his arms and feeling her soft hair brush his cheek, he was in heaven, and hoped the feeling would never end; but at last it did. As he knew she would, Sarah pulled away.

"Thanks, Tony. I feel a little better now." She turned towards the river, making a conscious effort to change the subject and to forget how good it felt to be held in Tony's arms.

"I see your brother's been home on leave, too."

Tony smiled and nodded. "Yes, and I'm glad to say we parted as friends. David seems to have come to terms with the importance of my job, which is more than I can say for my father. He still seems to think I'm taking the easy way out."

"Do you feel that you are doing the right thing? I mean, civilians are in danger now as well as the military. Don't you think you should be out there doing your best to put an end to this, as soon as possible?"

"But that's what I am doing! I thought you at least understood that!" Tony was exasperated. He had thought Sarah understood him, but now he was not so sure. Even she seemed to be criticising him now.

Sarah smiled at him, the old warm smile that had first attracted Tony to her, and he felt his anger melting away.

"I'm sorry, Tony. I suppose I'm just worried about the people I love."

Tony knew she meant Joe, and he felt jealous. Never before had he cared so much about a woman, and the woman he cared for belonged to someone else. He fought to keep his emotions under control and not to let his feelings for her show in his face.

"Of course your job is important. After all, where would the army be without weapons? When do you have to go back?"

"In three days."

"Maybe I can see you again before you go?"

Tony smiled happily. "I certainly hope so!"

The two young people met every day during Sarah's short lunch break, talking of the war and their hopes for a peaceful future. Tony had no more opportunities to hold Sarah and he regretted that. But at least he had her friendship to treasure as he set off north to Scotland and the training grounds at Arisaig.

As Tony had foreseen, the RAF bombed Berlin in retaliation for the raid on London. The evil circle was completed when the Germans came back and deliberately bombed more cities. There were many civilian targets, but at the end of August it was Liverpool which suffered the most, with heavy night raids between the 28th and 31st.

Then, at five o'clock in the afternoon on Saturday September 7th, the deliberate mass attacks on London began.

25

September 7th began like any other Saturday morning. Children played in the streets, mothers did their shopping and chatted to neighbours over the garden fence. Then the Home Guard Stations received the signal they had been dreading - 'Cromwell'. They all knew that this was the code name for 'invasion imminent'. Every man in the Home Guard stood to arms, though often those arms consisted of little more than pitchforks, axes, antique weapons and anything else they could get hold of. In diverse parts of the country, from the borders down to the south coast, the coastline of Wales to the Wash, church bells were rung, in the mistaken belief that German parachutists had already landed. Remarkably enough, there was little panic. Mothers ushered their children down to the air raid shelters for a while; but as time passed and no attack came, they soon returned to life in the open, filled with hope that it was all a mistake. Then, at five o'clock, the bombs began to fall in London's East End.

26

David stretched languorously. "In a strange way it's good to be back, but the changes are going to take some getting used to."

Watson nodded. "Six new pilots." He sighed. "It wouldn't be so bad if it didn't mean six others won't be coming back." He looked across at the new recruits, laughing together on the far side of the airfield. "I wonder how many of those will still be with us in a week or two?"

David shook his head. "Who knows. It looks like this is going to go on forever. You know how we got withdrawn from the front line after six weeks? Well, rumour has it that's not going to happen anymore. We're going to need every plane and pilot constantly, if we are to win. I was talking to Bear, and apparently we're all now classed as Category A or Category B squadrons. B's will be on standby to replace the frontline Category A squadrons, whenever their losses become too great. And we all know what that means."

The two pilots sat in silence for a moment as they thought of the continued action and pressure that faced the Category A pilots. Each unit would have to fight on indefinitely, without the prospect of relief, their only chance to rest coming with twenty-four hours leave each week. They would be too tired to do more than sleep for that one day.

"Thank God we're B. At least that gives us some time to put these new lads through their paces, and give them a better chance of surviving their first combat."

Watson nodded but said nothing.

"It's not just the new boys but the changes in command as well. We could do without that in the middle of a conflict. Freeman deserves his promotion. He'll do well as commander of Red Section, but I'm going to miss Sykes. He's a good pilot and they need men like him in the Operational Training Unit, but I'd rather he was back here with us. It was comforting to have him fly on your wing, knowing he was there to support you. Many's the time he's got me out of trouble up there."

"You're right. But I try not to think of the changes too much. Once we get sent back to the front line, the changes will come thick and fast. Being realistic we're bound to lose more planes and men, though hopefully our losses will be less with those new Mk. II Spitfires we flew down here yesterday." He looked around at the bustling airfield at Duxford. "From here we'll be able to support the squadrons defending the south-eastern corner of England. It'll be good to get back into the air again."

David smiled. "You know, you're right. There was a time when I thought I could never face combat again, but now I'm raring to go. I guess the rest did me good."

"It was what we all needed."

"You know, I never thought I'd complain about it being too quiet! When we were in the front line, we'd have flown at least two sorties by midday, yet here we are in the middle of the afternoon and the Mk. II's still haven't seen action. I just want to get up there and fly!"

As David looked out at the new aircraft he felt much better now that his leave was over. Perhaps his fear had been compounded by exhaustion, for now that he was rested he knew that he would be able to face the enemy again in the same cool manner as he had approached his first action over Dunkirk.

"Scramble! Scramble! All Sections rendezvous with No. 19 and No. 11 Squadrons!"

As the Tannoy blared, David and Watson raced for their planes and were soon airborne, joining the three four-aircraft sections in line astern which linked up with the rearmost squadron in the flight.

"Dysoe Leader. Enemy over London Docks. Your boys take out the bombers, while we deal with the fighters."

"Roger." Reynolds' voice echoed over the RT. "You heard that, boys. The bombers are ours."

As the planes approached the docks, David saw about thirty bombers at twenty thousand feet. He was cold. The skies at high level were always bitterly cold, and he was glad of his fur-lined flying jacket, but the cold was the least of his problems. As usual at this height, the inside of the perspex canopy had misted up and frozen over, leaving David semi-blinded. Frantically scrubbing the ice away, he peered out and saw the bombers below him. But as fast as he cleared the ice it reformed, and he could not wait to reach lower levels and warmer temperatures.

"Dysoe. This is Dysoe Leader." Reynold's voice again came over the RT as the planes dived towards the enemy bombers. "Position yourselves for a head-on attack."

The Spitfires raced towards their targets, screens clearing steadily in the warmer air.

"Bogies at one o'clock!"

Freeman's voice broke through the silence, and David turned to see the enemy fighters bearing down on them.

"Dysoe. Turn in and attack from the beam." Reynolds was already carrying out the manoeuver as he spoke. "Good luck, lads."

Attacking from the beam, David saw his bullets hit two aircraft before he continued down in a fast spiral to evade the fighters. As the g forces caught hold of him, he pulled back on the stick and climbed rapidly to rejoin the fight, where he attacked a lone bomber head-on from out of the sun. The German pilot failed to see him until it was too late, and as David's Spitfire raced past he saw the bomber's port engine catch fire. As he watched, he felt the impact of bullets ripping into the fuselage of his own plane, and dived away to avoid the fighter on his tail.

The sky was filled with aircraft. Like participants in some strange aerial dance, the Spitfires and Hurricanes moved in and out of the enemy bombers and fighters. Climbing, diving, weaving back and forth in an intricate ballet of the sky, lit by streams of de Wilde incendiary bullets which created delicate patterns of living death in the air. Yet for David and the other participants in the engagement, the tapestry of the battle was too broad. They saw only their own individual movement, and the occasional corner of a life and death struggle close by.

David fought on until his ammunition ran out, then dived away and headed back towards Duxford, one kill, two probables and one damaged to his credit. As his Spitfire touched down, he threw back the cockpit hood and climbed out to be greeted by the ground crew.

"You look a bit of a mess, sir."

David turned to look at his plane and smiled grimly. Two lines of bullet holes stretched the length of the fuselage, but by some miracle there had been no hits on vital equipment.

"I guess I've been lucky again." David removed his flying helmet and goggles and sauntered over to report to debriefing. It was good to be back in the air again.

It was the beginning of the second week in September. As 74 Squadron did not form a regular part of the Duxford Wing, life was not as hectic as it had been at Manston. David and his fellow pilots lounged in chairs or stretched out on beds, waiting for the order to scramble. From time to time the Operations Room phone rang, as the Sector Controller checked on aircraft and pilot readiness. Each time it rang the pilots would look across, waiting for the order to scramble. When the phone was replaced in its cradle with no message issuing from the Tannoy, they would relax once more.

David was just dozing off when the phone rang again. This time the operator called his orders before replacing the receiver.

"Blue Section Scramble. Lone enemy fighter over the Norfolk coast!"

As the members of Blue Section leapt to their feet and raced for their aircraft, the remaining nine pilots relaxed again.

David smiled across at Lewis from Yellow Section. "Looks like things are going to be fairly easy for us here, if we only have to face the Hun one at a time."

Lewis nodded. "Yes. But let's not forget that these planes must have got past the front line squadrons to reach us. It must be hell for the boys in Category A."

David stood up and stretched. "You know, I think I'd rather be with them at the moment. The sooner we smash the Luftwaffe, the happier I'll be."

Blue Section returned in time for lunch after bringing down the enemy plane, and in the early afternoon it was the turn of Yellow Section to scramble. David watched the three planes speeding off in the direction of Great Yarmouth to intercept another lone fighter. He turned to Lewis.

"God, but I hope we'll be going up soon. You know it's funny, but when I went home on leave I wouldn't have minded if I'd had never flown against the enemy again. Now here I am feeling jealous of those boys who get to go up instead of me!"

The rest had left him clearheaded and ready to do his bit once more. He waited eagerly for the 'Scramble' alarm; but when it came it was Green Section who headed off in the direction of Suffolk. With a sigh, David turned back to the other two pilots of Red Section, and joined them in a deck chair in the shade cast by the Operations Hut. It was cooler there, offering some relief for the men who, still wore their heavy fur lined flying jackets which would be so essential to them when flying at height. Freeman took a pack of cards from his breast pocket.

"Anyone for a game?"

David nodded. "It'll help pass the time." He pulled his deckchair closer to Freeman.

"I hear that Green Section ran out of fuel and had to land at Wattisham."

Freeman nodded as he shuffled the cards. "That's right. We seem to be spending all day chasing individual raiders all over the place. What I wouldn't give to be in a big fight again, it's far more exhilarating. I..."

"Red Section Scramble! Bomber in the vicinity of Lowestoft!"

The three pilots were in their planes and taxiing away before the Tannoy had ceased to blare. David felt the familiar rush of adrenalin as the wheels lifted, and he took his plane to its position in the formation. The new Spitfire Mk. IIs performed well, bringing them over Lowestoft in record time.

"Tally Ho!" Freeman's voice signalled that he had sighted the Hun. "He. III at eleven thousand feet. He's just above that thick cloud-layer, lads so let's get him before he has a chance to duck in there."

Freeman opened the attack from astern, closely followed by David. The bomber returned fire from the fringes of the cloud, where it was only intermittently visible. The two Spitfires fired again and again as the plane came into view.

"I keep hitting the damned thing, but it just doesn't seem to be doing any good!" David was frustrated. "If only we could get it out of the cloud!"

"It's all academic to me." Freeman broke contact with the raider. "I'm out of ammo."

David fired a half-second burst into the tail of the plane. "Me too. Let's head for home."

"Red One to Red Three. It's all yours Ted, we're heading back to Duxford."

"Roger."

The two Spitfires headed back to base while Ted followed the He. III out to sea. He chased it in and out of the cloud until, twenty-five miles further on, he lost contact and returned to Duxford, leaving the damaged bomber to limp home.

Life continued in this vein for 74 Squadron for the remainder of the month. Time and again the sections were sent up to intercept lone enemy planes, rarely flying as a full squadron. Their only losses were when two of their number were posted as instructors to Operational Training Units, and one to take command of a squadron. So, while the battle for the airways of Britain was at its height, David remained comparatively safe at Duxford.

27

Tony gazed out of the window at the russet-coloured bracken that stretched all the way to the pine forest on the horizon. He had been at Arisaig, on the western coast of Inverness-shire, for four weeks now, learning the tools of his new trade. Days were spent on small arms training with every imaginable weapon - German, Italian, British and American - ranging from pistols through rifles, machine guns and sub-machine guns. After his initial confusion, Tony was now able to strip, reassemble, load, fire and maintain any weapon the staff gave him; and after hours of working blindfold, he could strip and load them all in total darkness with little loss of speed. Knowing the names of weapons and how to maintain them was not, however, enough. The trainees practiced firing on a small range and also at snap targets, after a long and arduous obstacle course that left them breathless and shaking. Unnecessary aiming was discouraged. All potential agents were taught to fire with knees bent and two hands on the pistol, which was aimed by instinct from the waist. The action of pulling the trigger twice in succession was almost second nature to Tony now; there was no chance of him risking his life on one shot which might miss.

Tony found the silent killing the most difficult, yet most rewarding, part of the course. At first the thought of using his bare hands to kill a man sickened him, but as he became more skilled he found his self-confidence increasing, along with his feeling of power and security.

Any task which might face Tony in France, from blowing up a train to storming a house, or laying a simple ambush, had been practiced constantly, along with intensive map-reading and cross-country work. Tony now felt ready for anything, and was anxious to prove himself. He looked down at the piece of paper on his desk.

'You will come ashore from a submarine and destroy the local train tomorrow. It will be carrying senior SS officers.'

The times of the trains were laid out in front of him, as were the maps of the locality. Tony knew that attempts would be made to stop him, and he had only twenty-four hours until the train was due. With a frown of concentration he picked up a pencil and began to make his plans.

Tony paddled the tiny one-man canoe silently towards the shore. He had disembarked from a small fishing boat, the training course's substitute for a submarine, now he made his stealthy way towards the rocky cove he had chosen as his landing site. Although there were no lights to be seen, Tony knew that between him and the railway track were a number of army personnel posing as Germans; their brief was to guard against attack on an important train due to pass through their area. Although it was only a test, Tony's heart was racing. 'This is what it will be like in France,' he thought, 'only there I'll be facing real Germans, and real bullets.'

The bottom of the canoe grated against the shingle as Tony climbed out, dragging the boat ashore and stowing it behind a boulder. Dried seaweed, left high up the tideline after the winter storms, festooned the rocks, and Tony used it to camouflage his canoe. Then he shouldered his heavy pack and began the slow ascent of the low cliff.

It would not have been a difficult climb in the light of day, but on such a moonless night it was difficult to find hand and footholds amongst the rocks. He slipped a number of times, and wondered if his time in the SOE would end here and now with a broken leg if not something worse. At last, Tony dragged himself over the edge of the cliff and lay concealed behind a bush, as he carefully surveyed the area. He was just about to move on when he heard footsteps. Peering into the blackness on his right, he saw two men walking slowly along the cliff path, rifles slung on their backs. A cliff patrol! He waited silently, hardly daring to breathe, but the two men passed by without seeing him. As soon as they were out of sight, Tony ran for the cover of the pine trees.

The railway he was looking for was some three miles away on the other side of the woods. It took him the rest of the night to get there, for although the woods were not patrolled, it would have been all too easy for him to get lost amongst the dark, crowded trees. The rosy light of an early Scottish dawn found him crouched on the edge of the wood, surveying the railway half a mile away over the bracken-covered ground. It was three hours before the train was due, and he wondered if the track had been checked. Almost in answer to his unspoken question, four men made their way along the line, looking carefully at the tracks to see if they had been tampered with. Tony watched them until they were out of sight then, conscious of how conspicuous he would be if he stood up, he crawled slowly through the bracken until he was close to the rails. Taking off his pack, he removed the small packet of plastic explosive. He moulded it around the tracks before inserting a detonator and retreating towards the trees, playing out the line behind him as he went. It was then a matter of waiting.

He waited as patiently as he could beneath the trees. The time the train was due came and went, but there was no train. Tony found it difficult to control his nerves. He wanted to jump up to see if he could see the train coming, or maybe abandon the task, as it seemed that the train might not come at all. Then there it was, the obsolete rolling stock which was often used in SOE training. The throttle was jammed open to allow the train to move down the track at a reasonable pace without the need for a driver. Behind it came another engine and carriage, carrying soldiers. They would be the guards on the SS train for the purpose of the exercise. Tony knew that if he managed to destroy the train, they would be after him.

As the train approached the position of the explosives, Tony nervously licked his lips and tightened his grip on the detonator handle, then the moment came. With a quick downward thrust, he detonated the explosives. The whole front end of the engine was lifted from the rails and fell to one side, dragging its single carriage off the rails with it. With the sound of the explosion still ringing in his ears, the scream of tearing metal shrill in the still air, Tony quickly re-packed his haversack before looking once more at the train. It had come to rest with the carriage at an obscene angle, lying against the boiler of the engine. Tony smiled, but as he put his pack on his back and watched the second engine screech to a halt, his smile faded. Between twenty and thirty soldiers leapt from the carriage and fanned out, heading for the trees which were the only place a saboteur could be concealed. Tony grimaced. His task would not be over until he had reached his designated safe house, without leading the 'enemy' there. He turned and ran swiftly into the trees.

To right and left of him, Tony heard the crackling of undergrowth as his pursuers searched for him. Shunning the pathway ahead where he would be all too easily seen, Tony ran on through the trees, hoping that his noise would be mistaken by the following men for one of their own. The would-be spy slowly turned his path southwards, making for the edge of the forest. Finally, across the wide space of bracken ahead, he could see a small village. Somewhere over there was his safe house.

Turning back towards the trees, Tony listened carefully. The sounds of pursuit were still well north of him, and seemed to be moving away. He waited a moment to make certain, then ran out from the cover of the trees. The half-mile to the village was the longest he had ever covered. He pushed himself on and on, not daring to slow in case the pursuit turned his way and he was seen. By the time he reached the shelter of the first houses, his breath was coming in painful gasps and his head was reeling, but he had made it. He carefully scrutinised the tree line for long minutes which seemed like hours until, with no pursuit in sight, he felt that it was safe to move on. Trying to compose himself and blend into the surroundings, Tony sauntered down the main street until he came to a small house, number 25. He walked up the pathway, knocked on the door and anxiously awaited a reply.

"Who's there?"

"The nine fifteen is running late," Tony replied.

"Then catch the nine thirty to Deauville."

Relief flooded through him as he heard the hoped for reply.

The door opened and Tony slipped inside. The man who had been waiting for him peered intently out of the window for a moment, then turned with a broad smile towards the breathless Tony. The young man smiled in return as the chief training officer took him by the hand.

"No sign of pursuit. Well done, Kemshall. You pass with flying colours."

28

September had been a quiet time for David. A few sorties were flown, but as back up for the front line they did not fly even a small percentage of the hours that Category A pilots put in. Then things began to hot up once again, as September turned to October and the air battle for Britain continued to rage.

"Still on standby. It's getting frustrating." David turned to Freeman. "Would you mind if I took up a training mission? Stanford has only been with us a few days. He could do with a bit of combat practice."

Freeman grinned, recognising in David the same frustrated energy he felt himself.

"Be my guest."

The men were soon suited up and on their way. David thrilled at the feel of the plane as its engine throbbed, ready for take-off. The power of the Merlin engine communicated itself to him through the fuselage, and David felt some of the excitement of his earlier flying days, when his only reason for taking to the air was to revel in the feeling of power that controlling a plane gave, and to enjoy the views of the land below him.

"Right, lads. Let's go."

David's plane shot into the air with Stanford on his right wing and Williams on his left. David pulled back on the stick and the Spitfire rose at a terrific rate.

"Come on. Up to twenty thousand, then we'll try some battle tactics. Stanford, you watch me and Williams first, get the feel of things, then you and Williams can have a go."

The three planes broke through a layer of cloud into the clear skies beyond, and David banked away to the left.

"Right, Williams. You're a Hun on my tail, and I'm going to break away from you. Let's get going."

The two planes roared off, Williams clinging tightly to the tail of the plane in front of him. David banked right and left, then put the plane into a steep dive before pulling up the nose and heading for the open spaces above. The g forces were terrific, causing his head to spin, but he held on as the plane went over onto its back, performing a perfect loop which placed him right on the tail of Williams' plane.

"Bang. Bang. I've got you!" David's laughter echoed over the RT. "Right, Stanford, your turn now. Show us what you can do."

David watched as the two planes sped off. Stanford tried to turn to the right to avoid his pursuer, but with no success.

"You must make your turns tighter if you want to shake him off."

Stanford executed a sharp turn to the left, drawing away from Williams a little, but the more experienced pilot soon made up the lost ground.

"Well done, that was much better."

As David spoke Stanford began to pull his plane up into a steep climb, trying to force it over into a loop. David shouted a warning.

"Don't try to loop! You don't have enough speed!" But his warning came too late. As the plane reached the apex of its loop, the engine failed and it fell away.

"Williams! Look out! He's coming down on top of you!"

David watched in horror as the two Spitfires drew closer and closer together. He could hear no sound above the roar of his engine, but as he saw the two planes come together, he imagined the sound of tearing metal. Stanford's plane crashed directly into the cockpit of the other Spitfire, and pieces of plane began to fall away.

"Jump! Do you hear me? Bail out!"

David listened, but no sound came to him over the RT. He watched in speechless horror as the two planes fell rapidly towards the earth and disappeared into the layer of cloud. There were no parachutes.

The long summer was fading into autumn. 74 Squadron was back on the front line, and David stood at his Dispersal Point, once again experiencing the long hours, the tension, the fear and the exhaustion that went hand in hand with front line flying. Despite all that he was glad to be back in a position where he could feel part of the battle once more. He wondered how much longer the battle would continue. He shivered. He did not relish flying against the enemy in the middle of winter. As he viewed the battered airfield, complete with bomb craters and damaged aircraft, he felt a great pride in the way the RAF had stood up to the superior numbers of the Luftwaffe. He knew he would remember these months of hardship and comradeship for the rest of his life.

"Scramble! Scramble! Enemy bombers approaching London!"

As the Tannoy blared, David broke into a run towards his waiting aircraft and was soon airborne. He followed Squadron Leader Reynolds into a position where the early afternoon sun was behind them, screening them from the enemy.

"There's ack-ack fire out over the estuary. Let's take a look."

Reynolds banked his plane to the right, and the other eleven planes followed closely behind. They were over Maidstone when the Squadron Leader sighted about sixty German fighters, all unaware of the presence of the Spitfires. Two Bf 109's flew across the front of the squadron. Reynolds surprised them, diving at them from out of the sun. He fired at the nearest plane, which pushed its nose straight down to avoid him. Reynolds followed him down, his engine cutting in the negative g's, then catching again. He fired at the enemy and saw it fall, smoking, as he pulled up from the dive. The air around him was full of bullets as the remaining planes in his squadron joined the conflict.

"Red Section, stick with me. We'll take on these four."

"Red Two to Red Leader. Roger." David took up his position as he spoke. He saw Red Three fly in close to Reynolds' other wing. The three Spitfires opened up on the enemy.

"Look out, Red Leader! Four Huns on your tails! I'm coming in to help!"

Jameson broke away from Yellow Section to fall in behind the attacking Messerschmitts, guns blazing.

"Let them have it, boys, then let's get out of here." Reynolds opened fire and the two other members of Red Section followed suit. David saw his bullets rip into one of the enemy, and prepared to fire another burst. His thumb pressed again on the button, but nothing happened.

"Red Two to Red Leader. My guns have jammed. As soon as we've shaken off these boys on our tails, I'm heading for home."

As David pulled his plane into a steep climb to avoid the enemy on his tail, he cursed angrily. The usual battle high was upon him, and to be unable to fire on the enemy galled him immensely. As he climbed higher, he saw Jameson bring down one of the raiders who had been on their tails.

"Well done, Yellow Two. I'll buy you a pint when we get back to base!"

Jameson laughed. "I'll hold you to that, David!"

David watched the battle raging around him and turned back towards Biggin Hill. He would make up for it next time he was sure, just as long as his guns did not jam again.

The thud of bullets ripping into his fuselage broke David's reverie, and he glanced in his mirror to see two fighters on his tail. Calling on all his experience and expertise, he rolled to the left to avoid them, but they stayed with him, firing all the time. Smoke began to pour from his engine, and a knot of fear settled in David's stomach.

"This is Red Two. Red Two. I've been hit and I've got no guns. Anyone free to help me?"

His words were flippant, but his anxiety was transmitted over the RT.

"This is Red Three. Hang on, David. I'm coming to get you."

Another burst of fire hit the Spitfire. David felt a pain like a fist punching him in the back. A warm wetness began to seep through his flying jacket as a wave of agony shot through him. His scream echoed over the RT. With a terrific effort of will, David forced himself to stay conscious.

"David? Are you all right? David?"

His head was spinning. He felt his control of the plane slipping. Flames were now pouring from the engine. He knew that he did not have long.

"I've taken a hit in the back. The plane is going down. I'm baling out."

"Good luck, David." Reynolds' voice echoed in David's headphones.

"Thanks, sir." David unbuckled his harness as the plane began to fall forwards into a dive. He threw back the cockpit hood and tried to pull himself clear.

"I can't move my legs! I can't get out!" His mouth was dry and his hands shook. His vision was becoming blurred as the blood loss took hold.

"Come on, David! You can do it!"

David shook his head to clear it. "No. Not this time. When you write to my parents, tell them I love them."

The Spitfire was in a steep dive now. As the pain in his back expanded to fill his whole being David heard the scream of his plane rising in pitch. He watched the ground race closer, spiralling in a dizzying pattern that added to his disorientation. Soon, too soon, the green and brown of the land took on recognisable shapes - fields, roads, a stream. A clump of trees raced towards him, and David closed his eyes.

"I'm glad we parted as friends, Tony," he whispered.

He felt the first impact as the Spitfire ploughed into the trees and began to cartwheel. But long before the plane came to rest he knew no more, and would know nothing ever again.

29

Tony stood between his mother and grandmother, starring numbly at the wooden casket containing the final remains of his brother. He had returned home on leave before the next stage of his training, to be greeted with the devastating news of David's death; the funeral was planned for two days later and now here they stood, David's close family and a few friends from his youth, to pay their respects and say their final goodbyes.

Louise Kemshall stood dry-eyed at the graveside. For some time now she had been expecting to hear the dreadful news that her eldest son had not survived the battle for air supremacy over England, but the telegram had still numbed her and put her in a state of shock from which she had yet to recover. Tony placed a comforting hand on her arm and looked past her at his father, stony faced and silent as he stared at the heap of dark earth which would soon cover his son forever. He had said no more than a few words to Tony over the last two days, and seemed to have shrunken, withdrawn within himself with the thought that all his hopes and dreams for the future were now shattered. Tony turned his attention back to the minister at the head of the grave.

"He was a brave man," he was saying. "Without men like David the evil of Hitler and his Nazi regime would engulf the whole world. But with one man like David Kemshall willing to fight the tyrant, then the light of the Lord will not be overcome by the darkness of Germany's dictator." He opened the Prayer Book in his hand and began to read from Psalm 27.

"The Lord is my light and my salvation; whom shall I fear? The Lord is the strength of my life; of whom shall I be afraid? When the wicked, even my enemies and my foes, came upon me to eat up my flesh, they stumbled and fell. Though a host should encamp against me, my heart shall not fear: though war should rise against me, in this will I be confident. One thing have I desired of the Lord, that will I seek after; that I may dwell in the House of the Lord all the days of my life, to behold the beauty of the Lord, and to inquire in his Temple. For in the time of trouble he shall hide me in His pavilion: in the secret of his Tabernacle shall he hide me; he shall set me up upon a rock. And now shall my head be lifted up above my enemies round about me; therefore will I offer in His Tabernacle sacrifices of joy; I will sing, yea I will sing praise unto the Lord. Hear, O Lord, when I cry with my voice: have mercy also upon me and answer me..."

Sir Michael bent down to take a handful of earth and throw it down on the coffin. Louise did the same. As Tony knelt in the damp earth to say a final farewell to his brother, he felt the hot wetness of his mother's tears fall onto the back of his hand and knew that she had broken through the barriers of shock at last.

When the family returned from the graveside, Chantrelle de Thierry gently led her daughter up to her room. The final release of her emotions left Louise feeling drained both physically and emotionally, and her mother had wisely decreed that she should rest. Sir Michael was left in the drawing room with his only surviving son. After pouring and handing him a whisky, he shook his head grimly.

"I suppose it had to happen eventually. We've lost so many good young men in these air battles. It was too much to hope that David would survive."

Tony sipped his whisky. "He was a hero, Dad. I shall always remember him with pride."

Sir Michael nodded. "I suppose that's some consolation, but it doesn't heal the pain." He looked at Tony in silence for a few moments, then took a deep breath. "Last time you and David were home you seemed to get on well; just like when you were boys."

Tony nodded and smiled sadly.

"David and I discussed your job," Sir Michael continued. "He seemed to think it was important, and asked me to give you the benefit of the doubt. I've tried to do that, mainly for the sake of your mother."

Tony took a deep breath. 'Not now!' he thought. 'We've just buried David, and now he's going to have a go at me!' But then he saw the steely look in his father's eye. 'Here it comes' he thought. He took another swallow of whisky.

"I suppose things will change now that David's dead."

Tony boldly faced his father. "Why?"

Engulfed by grief, Sir Michael struggled to keep from shouting at the only child he had left.

"Why? Your only brother is dead! Killed by the Germans! You've just said that he was a hero. Surely you want to avenge him? I know that I do, and if I were young enough I'd be out there fighting now!" He gestured wildly towards the window. "Don't you feel like that too? Don't you feel a burning pain, an emptiness where David should be? He'll never fill that emptiness again, Tony; don't you want to fill it, with anger and hate and killing? Don't you want to avenge his death?"

"Yes, I want to avenge him. I loved David dearly. I'm truly proud of what he did, but I see my present job as the best way I can make a contribution, the best way I can pay Hitler back for what he's done to us. David understood."

"Did he really, or was he just humouring you? You think the best you can do to avenge your brother's death is to hold down a desk job that a man of my age could do? What's the matter with you, Tony? Are you really such a coward? You make me ashamed to be your father!" Hurt, pity, pain but most of all grief shone from Sir Michael's eyes as he spat out the words. But Tony was too wrapped up in his own pain to see, too buried in his own heartache to reach out a hand and bring the two of them close together again.

"I've had enough of this Dad!" Tony could contain his anger and frustration no longer. He slammed his glass down on the table and turned to face his tormentor. "You're constantly criticising me! Even today, when we should be honouring David and all that he has done, you still take the time to tell me what I'm doing is wrong! I happen to believe that my job is worthwhile, and David felt the same. You've been in the army, Dad. Surely you don't think that those in authority would have given me this job, if they didn't think it was the best contribution I could make to the war effort?"

"I don't know what to think anymore!" Sir Michael was shouting now. "I was so proud of you when you came back from Dunkirk. I felt that both of my sons were heroes. Now you're content to sit behind a desk and let your brother's death go unavenged! I don't know how you managed to persuade them to give you this job. All I can say is that I am ashamed of you. If I had my way I would never see you again!"

All the bitterness at the loss of David was in Sir Michael's voice as he turned away and looked out of the window, the view clouded by his tears of anger and grief. Tony stood in silence and stared at his father's unrelenting back. The urge to tell his father the truth was almost unbearable. When he joined the S.O.E. he had expected difficulties at home, but never anything like this. He closed his eyes tightly and clenched his fists, fighting to control his feelings. At last he spoke, his voice little more than a whisper.

"Do you want me to leave, Dad? Are you throwing me out of the only home I've ever known?"

For a moment Sir Michael said nothing, then his shoulders slumped slightly as he sighed deeply and shook his head. Not able to turn back to face his son he continued to gaze out at the gardens.

"I would rather not see you again, but David asked me to be kind to you. For his sake, and for your mother who has just buried one son and could not face losing her last remaining child, I can't throw you out. You can continue to live here, but don't expect to resume your old relationship with me. As far as I'm concerned you're a disgrace to this family. I'll speak to you no more than is absolutely necessary. Now leave me."

Tony stood in silence for a moment before turning to leave the room. His heart, already pained at the death of his brother, was now nearing breaking point at his father's rejection. As he slipped quietly from the room, he did not see the tears in his father's eyes. If he had, things might have turned out differently.

The slamming of the lodge door behind him did nothing to assuage the hurt and anger Tony felt. He stormed down the steps and headed towards the river, his pent up emotions adding speed to his steps. Here he was, not yet fully through training, almost wishing he had never heard of the SOE, never joined its secret ranks. True, he knew that the work was vital and he also knew he would not resign. But how he wished he could tell his father what it was all about. He knew that Sir Michael would be proud of him, for it takes a special kind of courage to live amongst the enemy, in constant danger of discovery, knowing that if you are caught you will be shot as a spy. Yet his father believed him to be a coward. Tony kicked at an old tree stump in frustration, and groaned as the pain jarred his foot. Turning around he gazed up at the warm, welcoming facade of Heronfield House. For a time his thoughts turned away from the war, and in his mind he re-lived his childhood. Suddenly it struck him; the one thing that angered him more than anything else about this situation was that he would never be able to tell David about his work with the SOE. His brother had died thinking Tony was trying to avoid active service. Slowly his anger was replaced by sadness and a keen sense of loss. No-one had ever been closer to him than David. No-one had ever known him quite so well. Now he was alone.

Tony turned back to the river and sat down, the peaceful flowing of the waters helping to soothe him. He had no idea how long he had been sitting there, when a shadow fell across the grass in front of him and he looked up.

Tony rose to his feet, the ghost of a welcoming smile lighting his face. "Sarah. It's good to see you."

Sarah smiled.

"I'm glad to see you too, Tony, though I wish it could have been under happier circumstances." She stopped smiling and laid a comforting hand on his arm. "I was so sorry to hear about your brother's death. From what I've heard, he was a very brave man."

Tony nodded, trying desperately to control the tears.

"I shall miss him terribly, Sarah. Life just won't be the same without him."

Though Sarah said nothing, Tony could feel the warmth of her sympathy and all his pent up emotions broke through at last. As his tears flowed, Sarah reached up a hand to wipe them softly from his cheek. Tony felt his heart melt. After all of the confrontation at home here was someone with whom he could share his grief. Slowly he lowered his head, until it rested against Sarah's shoulder. For a moment she did not know how to respond then, almost of their own volition, Sarah's arms moved. She cradled him to her, then began to stroke his hair as she whispered words of comfort. After a time, Tony's tears ceased to flow and he became aware of himself being held in the comforting embrace of Sarah's arms. He wished that he could remain there forever, safe from his father's anger and rejection, safe from the emptiness of life without David, safe with someone who understood and cared. As if aware of Tony's thoughts, Sarah ceased to stroke his hair and gently stepped back. She gazed out over the river, giving him time to compose himself.

It was Tony who eventually broke the strained silence between them.

"Thank you, Sarah. You'll make a good nurse. You know just what to do and say to help your patients!"

"I hope you will never be a patient of mine." Sarah turned to Tony. "I hope you will never be injured in this ghastly war."

Tony smiled, thinking of the courses he still had to attend before he could go out to France.

"Thank you for your concern, but I should be quite safe for the time being."

"Haven't you decided to transfer to an active unit?" Sarah asked. She was shocked by

Tony's grim response.

"No. I have not. I'll continue to do the job that my superiors think I'm best qualified to do. And if you or my father, think you can make me change my mind, then you can just think again!"

"Just a minute!" Sarah protested. "I thought you would want to fight to avenge your brother, but I wouldn't dream of trying to influence your decision. That's not my place."

"Do you think I'm a coward?"

Sarah was silent for a moment, her gaze reflective, then she slowly shook her head. "I hardly know you, Tony, but you don't strike me as the cowardly sort. But I don't understand your reluctance to fight."

Tony sighed sadly. "I had hoped that you, of all people, might understand; or at least just accept me as I am." He reached out a hand to touch her cheek. "Please don't judge me until this war is over, Sarah. I may surprise you yet."

Sarah frowned, troubled by the strange inconsistencies in Tony's character, and stepped back so that his hand no longer touched her cheek. After a hesitant moment, Tony let his hand fall limply to his side.

"It's not my place to judge you, Tony. After all, I hardly know you. Now, if you'll excuse me, I must return to work."

Without waiting for a reply Sarah turned and walked away. As he watched her retreating figure, Tony realised that no matter how short their acquaintance, nor what she thought of him, he was in love with Sarah Porter. As he contemplated the lie he must live until the end of the war, he knew that he would not be able to compete with her boyfriend in Coventry. He realised that the price he would have to pay for working with the SOE was going to be far higher than he had ever anticipated.

NOVEMBER - DECEMBER 1940

30

Tony was glad to be posted closer to home for the third part of his training, which took place in the New Forest. It felt good to be in familiar countryside and within reach of home, and of Sarah, even though he could not visit. The officers in charge were living at Beaulieu Manor while the agents in training, of whom Tony was just one of many, stayed in a group of country houses in the vicinity. They had all been vacated for the duration in the same manner as Heronfield, and he felt strangely at home. On his first morning there, Tony found himself in the company of nineteen other trainees in a small drawing room, which had been converted into a lecture hall. To his immense surprise, the man who stood up to speak to them was Lieutenant Jim Briggs.

Jim gave no sign of recognising Tony as he embarked upon a talk which he had obviously given before.

"You have all been through the first two stages of training," he began, "and can now be considered fit enough and capable enough with weapons to be of use to us overseas. Now we come to the most important part of your training. If you fail to learn all we have to teach you here, then you will not survive behind enemy lines." He surveyed the grim faces ranged in front of him.

"You all know France well enough for one reason or another, that's why you've joined us; but before now you have always been an Englishman in France. You must now learn how to be a Frenchman, for it is the little things that will give you away to the enemy. The life of an agent won't be filled with endless excitement. There will be long periods of inactivity; but you must never forget that you're playing a role, never forget your cover story or how to behave like a Frenchman. For instance, don't forget that the French drive on the right. You must look left then right before crossing the road, not right then left as you do at home. We lost agents to that simple mistake during the last war."

"Apart from how to live as Frenchman, we shall also teach you the tools of your craft, from how to pass on a message to how to stand up against interrogation. You will need to know how to handle the French police. The Milice work closely with the Germans and will prove hostile; never, ever approach them, although you might find that some of the ordinary Gendarmes will be quite helpful. If you approach a police control point, be brisk, polite, perhaps a little dull, but never offer extra information. That will only make them suspicious."

Tony was finding it all difficult to absorb at one go, and felt his confusion must show in his features. Many of the trainees must have displayed the same feelings, for Jim smiled.

"Of course, we will cover this all again in much more detail over the next few days. For now though, it's important to start living as a Frenchman. To help you in this, all conversations here will be in French, not just at lectures but twenty four hours a day. You will eat French food, adopt French customs and habits, wear French clothes. You will each be given a cover identity. Study it for the rest of today. From tomorrow you are that man; you must react exactly as he would, be able to answer any questions about his life history without hesitation."

He looked around the room, meeting the gaze of each one of the trainees. "Remember, this is not a game. Once you get to France, even the slightest slip-up could cost you your life. Consider that you are no longer in England. From now on we all live, breathe, eat and sleep as Frenchmen."

Without another word Jim stepped down from the podium and left the room, while other training officers handed out the files containing the cover identities of the agents. Tony retired to his room to study his new identity, the man he would be for the rest of this war. As he spent hours reading and memorising the details of the fictitious man into whom he must transform himself, the dangers that lay ahead of him in France became acutely clear to him. He realised that his chances of coming out of this alive were slim indeed.

"I knew they'd accept you" Jim smiled across the breakfast table at Tony. "You're ideal material for this work."

Tony nodded. "I like to think so." He was glad to be able to renew their friendship, forged during those never to be forgotten days in northern France. "What have you been doing since I last saw you? So much has happened to me that it seems more like five years than five months."

Jim shrugged. "I haven't done much, I've spent most of my time running courses here." He smiled grimly. "That's not as easy as it sounds. None of us knows what it's really going to be like out there. We just have to do our best to think of all the possible pitfalls, and then try to train against them." He took a sip of tea and smiled at Tony. "I suppose you've been busy with your training most of the time. Has it been hard?"

"Yes, but not nearly as hard as life at home."

Jim frowned. "Problems?"

Tony laughed sardonically. "You could say that. Dad seems to think that working for the Ministry of Economic Warfare is a safe desk job that I've taken to keep me out of the firing line. Basically, he thinks I'm a coward."

Jim shook his head sadly.

"It must be really difficult for you to keep your real job a secret."

Tony nodded but said nothing.

"Of course, it's different for me," Jim continued. "I'm a regular. I was in the forces before this ghastly war broke out, so my family just accept that I'm a soldier and can't tell them everything I do. Surely your brother, David isn't it? Surely he understands?"

Tony closed his eyes and bowed his head for a moment at the thought of his brother. Then, taking a deep breath, he spoke.

"To begin with, he thought like my father; but then he came to understand a little more. I'm sure he came to the conclusion that I'm not a coward, and he tried to get Dad to lighten up a little."

"Did he?"

Tony shook his head.

"Still, with David on your side it should relieve the pressure a little."

"David's dead."

Jim was silent for a moment, then placed a comforting hand on his friend's arm.

"I'm sorry."

"His Spitfire was shot down and he couldn't bail out. We buried him last week." In his mind's eye Tony could still see the clods of dank, dark earth falling upon the coffin, the thud they had made as they hit the wood still echoed in his mind. He buried his face in his hands. "I'm doing this for him, Jim. I still remember the air attack we saw on the civilian refugees, and the mess on the beaches of Dunkirk; but when I go into France it will be to avenge David."

"I understand your feelings, Tony, but don't let the need for revenge get too big a hold on you. It could cloud your judgment. It could cost you your life."

Tony looked up, straight into Jim's eyes. The eyes of a friend conveying concern, compassion, support, the love of a comrade. He took a deep breath and nodded.

"Don't worry. I won't let you, or David, down."

Jim smiled.

"Now come on, it wouldn't do for us to be late for the lecture. After all, I'm giving it!"

With a laugh the two friends left the table and made their way to the lecture room. Jim took up his position at the front, while Tony took one of the two remaining empty seats. He expected Jim to wait for the late arrival, but he began to speak immediately.

"Good morning, gentlemen. Before we begin, I feel I must explain the empty seat in your midst. This morning I had the unfortunate duty to inform one of your comrades that he had failed his training."

There was a buzz of interested chatter and Jim held up his hand for silence. "It was difficult for me to do. This particular young man had excelled in everything he had been asked to do so far, he failed only on the fact that he could never live in France as a Frenchman. You are wondering how I know this and I shall tell you. Your rooms are bugged, and because of this we learnt that this trainee talks in his sleep. In English." Jim looked long and hard at the remaining trainees. "That may seem excessively harsh to you, but something like that could cost you your life in France, and maybe the lives of others too. That's why you will be under such close scrutiny over the next few weeks. It's our best chance of ensuring your survival in the months, maybe years, that it will take to win this war. Now, down to business.

"Many of the skills you will need in France will take a lot of learning. They will need to be constantly practised until they are second nature to you. How do you drop a pre-arranged password into a casual conversation? How do you hand over a written note unobtrusively? How do you spot, and lose, a tail? How do you deal with Germans at checkpoints? The list of things you need to know is endless. Today you will learn how to turn up for a meeting." He smiled at them. "That sounds pretty straight forward, doesn't it? But it isn't as easy as all that. You must always, and I stress - always - be punctual. If you arrive early, you could be arrested while hanging around waiting. If you're late, your contact could be arrested while waiting for you. Don't arrange to meet at times like midday, or on the hour. Why not 12.17, an odd time when no one would be expecting a meet to take place? Arrive a few minutes early, walk past the rendezvous to check it out, make sure it's safe then go into a shop or something before walking back to arrive exactly on time."

Jim talked for a long time about how to conduct a meeting. By the time the trainees went outside to put his advice into practice, their heads were spinning.

Tony had been at the training centre for almost a week, living the life of a young Frenchman, when he was awoken in the dark hours before midnight. He barely had time to notice the silhouettes of three people crammed into his small room, before sticky tape was slapped over his mouth to muffle his cries, and a black hood was pulled roughly over his head. Tony struggled to fight off his attackers, but they were obviously professionals and his brain was clouded with sleep. Within moments his hands were tied securely behind his back and he was bundled roughly from the room. With a man at each elbow, he was steered along corridors and down stairs. In his confused state the walk seemed to take ages but, less than five minutes from when he had first awoken,

Tony felt hands roughly forcing him down into a seat. The hood was ripped from his head along with the tape that had covered his mouth. He winced in pain.

A bright light shone directly into Tony's eyes, drowning out the interior of the room in which he found himself. He had no idea where he was, or how many people were present. Screwing up his eyes, he turned his head to avoid the glare. As his eyes began to adjust he saw three men in the room, all in the uniform of the SS. Tony was stunned. What was going on? Had enemy paratroopers taken over the training centre? A voice boomed at him from the dark shadowy man behind the light.

"Name?" The interrogator spoke French with a thick German accent.

Tony gave his cover name. "Albert Fouqet."

"Address?"

"22 Rue Blanc. St. Nazaire."

"Liar! You are a spy."

Tony shook his head. "No."

The voice screamed at him again. "You are an English spy! What is your name?!"

"Albert Fouqet."

The shadowy figure waved an arm, and his two companions dragged Tony to his feet. Standing him against the wall, they threw buckets of ice-cold water over him. Tony drew an involuntary deep breath as the cold hit him like a physical blow. His pyjamas were drenched and, as the water poured from him, he felt the material clinging clammily to his kin. Tony shook the water from his eyes.

"Stand to attention, spy!"

Tony stood to attention.

"English spy, what is your name?"

"Albert Fouqet."

"How many were with you when you attacked the checkpoint?"

Tony shook his head. "I don't know what you're talking about."

"Liar! You killed two German soldiers, so you must die. Where do you live?"

"22 Rue Blanc. St. Nazaire."

"Who was with you?"

"I didn't do it."

The questions went on, hour after hour. Tony was frozen; his wet clothes clung to him; his arms ached where they were still tied behind his back; his head ached from the bright light which was still directed into his eyes; his legs were stiff from standing to attention with his back against the wall; and still the interrogation went on. For one brief moment Tony was tempted to tell the truth, to say yes he was English. But then he remembered the dead civilians on the French country roads and the beaches of Dunkirk, remembered David. His head lifted slightly.

"I am Albert Fouqet. I live at 22 Rue Blanc, St. Nazaire. I am not English. I am not a spy. I don't know what you're talking about."

Six hours after being so forcefully removed from his bed the hood was once again placed over Tony's head and he was dragged from the room. The same three men led him, exhausted and stumbling, upstairs and along corridors. Tony had the vague feeling that he was heading back in the direction of his room, but he could not be sure. At last he heard a door open and was ushered inside. His hands were untied and he rubbed his numbed wrists with relief. He heard the door close quietly behind him and stood in silence for a moment, wondering what would happen next.

"You can take the hood off now."

Tony took the hood off to find himself facing a smiling Jim sitting on his bed. He was stunned.

"What's going on, Jim?"

Jim stood up and held out a towel. "Get out of those wet clothes while we talk."

Tony began to peel off his sodden pyjamas. "I suppose this was all part of my training." It was more of a statement than a question and Jim nodded.

"You performed very well. Not once did you deviate from your story."

Tony began to towel dry his hair. "But was it really necessary?"

Jim nodded grimly. "Yes. We had to be sure that you could stand up to it. But don't feel too pleased with yourself. We were very gentle compared with what the SS will really be like if you're captured in France. The interrogation will go on for days, not hours, and they won't stop at buckets of cold water. The SS are renowned for physically torturing their captives."

"Do all trainees have to go through this?"

"Yes. Some fail. They can't keep their French going or stick to their cover story under pressure. So far everyone on this course has done well."

"I hadn't heard of this exercise. I thought I must be the first."

Jim shook his head. "No. Those who have already undergone interrogation are sworn to secrecy. How can we test you fully if you know what to expect?"

Tony nodded. "I see what you mean. So I must remain silent about tonight's little adventure?"

Jim smiled. "Yes. Now go to bed and get what sleep you can. You have to be up again in a little over an hour. It's going to be a busy day."

Jim gave Tony a playful slap on the back, then turned and left the room.

31

On their evenings off, Jane and Sarah often went into Marlborough to the cinema. It was a change of scenery from the hospital, giving them the opportunity to forget for a while the smell of carbolic soap and the sight of wounded soldiers and airmen. After one such evening, the two young women walked slowly down the dark road to the bus stop. The last bus to pass Heronfield House would not be along for another half-an-hour, so they had plenty of time to spare. Jane frowned as she pulled her coat more closely around her against the cold night air.

"I enjoyed the film tonight, but the newsreel was too disturbing for me."

Sarah nodded. "I know what you mean. I've never been to London, but I hate to see all that damage. It must be awful for the people who live there and have to spend most of their nights in the shelters."

"Yes. We're lucky to be out in the country."

Jane turned to her friend. "How's Joe?" she inquired, wanting something to take her mind from the images of indiscriminate bombing on the civilian centres of England. Something to bring a little normality back into her world.

Sarah shrugged. "He seems all right according to his letters, but I'll be glad to get home to see him. So far there've been no raids over Coventry, but I do worry about him and Mum."

"At least he's doing his bit. You should be proud of him."

"I am. And I'm glad he's relatively safe where he is."

Jane nodded. "I suppose I'm lucky that I don't have anyone really close. At least I don't have anyone to worry about."

"Surely you don't mean that?"

Jane smiled. "No, not really. In fact I rather fancy that Tony Kemshall!"

Sarah laughed. "You're not serious?"

Jane giggled infectiously. "Of course I am! He's good looking and rich, what more could I want in a man? But seriously though, I don't think I'd stand a chance with him. He's only interested in you."

"Don't be silly!" Sarah laughed. "I hardly know the man; and besides, I'm in love with Joe!"

"That doesn't prevent Tony showing an interest in you though, does it?"

Sarah blushed. "I suppose not. He's a nice enough man but I'm not interested in him in that sort of way. And he knows it."

"I know, I'm only teasing." Jane laughed. "We're a very small community up at the hospital. We need something to gossip about!"

"So what are you going to talk about when I'm on leave?"

"Don't worry, we'll think of something!"

Jane laughed and led the way towards the bus stop.

32

Coventry without lights no longer seemed as strange to Sarah as it had done at the outbreak of the war. She smiled happily as she made her way swiftly through the blackout to her home, thinking of her mother, and of Joe. The house looked dark and forlorn when she arrived, but she knew that there would be a warm welcome awaiting her. She pushed open the unlocked door and entered the dark hall. Closing the door and pulling the blackout curtain across to cover the cracks, she switched on the light and placed the small bag holding her necessities for the next three days on the floor.

"Mum! I'm home!"

She made her way along the hall, an enticing aroma drawing her towards the kitchen. The kitchen door opened, and Alice reached out her arms to embrace her daughter. The two women hugged each other for a moment then pulled apart.

"It's good to see you, love."

"You too, Mum." Sarah sniffed. "Something smells good."

Alice smiled. "I've been saving up my meat rations. We've got pork chops for dinner."

"Mum, you shouldn't! You need your meat rations for yourself!"

"Please indulge me, Sarah. You're home so rarely that I like to do something special. Besides, the vegetables cost nothing. Remember we dug up the garden? Well, all the crops have been harvested now. I've a store of carrots and parsnips, there are onions hanging in the air raid shelter and potatoes stored under the stairs. They won't last for the whole winter, but at least I'm doing my bit towards growing food for the country."

Sarah took off her coat and hung it up. "I suppose it's hard to cope with the rationing. It's not too bad for us at the hospital, we just hand over our coupons and the kitchen staff are responsible for providing our meals; but it must be difficult for you."

Alice shrugged. "I cope, just like everyone else."

The two women sat down at the kitchen table and Alice poured them each a cup of tea. "How is work gong?"

"The rush after Dunkirk has passed now. We don't have any of the soldiers who were on the beaches; the beds are now full of airmen who've been shot down in the last few months. Things are rather slow, I'm glad to say. But once ground fighting picks up again we're sure to be busy."

Alice nodded. "We owe a lot to those young fliers. They've held the enemy planes back long enough to stop an invasion, but they're just too few to hold back the night bombers."

"I know." Sarah frowned. "Jane and I saw the newsreel a couple of days ago. It must be horrible to live in London at the moment."

"Yes, we've been lucky so far. We've had a few planes over, but no big raids. I wonder how long we'll escape them?"

"Don't be a pessimist, Mum." Sarah finished her tea and began to set the table for dinner. "They might not bother us here."

Alice shrugged.

"Maybe. But Joe seems to think that we're bound to get a raid sooner or later, with all the war industry."

"Is he coming round tonight?"

Alice glanced across at her daughter and smiled. She had tried to sound unconcerned but Alice knew how much she longed to see Joe again.

"I'm afraid not love. He's on duty tonight and working at the factory tomorrow. But he'll be free tomorrow night. He'll come round to see you then." Alice laughed. "Don't look so glum! It's not the end of the world!"

Sarah laughed too, "Sorry Mum, it's just that I was really looking forward to seeing him again."

"Well, waiting one more day won't do you any harm. Now come and get your dinner."

Alice was right. Waiting another day did Sarah no harm at all, in fact it merely increased her anticipation of the coming meeting. Joe duly arrived the following evening, muffled against the cold November air. He took a radiant Sarah in his arms.

"It's good to see you again, my love."

Sarah smiled happily, needing no words to express how she felt at seeing Joe once again.

"How's life in the country?"

Sarah shrugged as she took his coat and hung it up. "All right, I suppose. We get quite a few pilots in at the moment, but it's nothing like as bad as after Dunkirk. At least our present patients are over the worst. They're only coming to us to convalesce." Sarah shivered. "Getting them straight off the boats from Dunkirk was awful. I hope I never have to go through anything like that again."

Joe took her hand gently. They settled on the sofa in front of the roaring fire.

"I think it's going to be a long war, love. We have a lot to do before we can go back into France, but I doubt whether anything like that will happen again – we're too prepared now."

"I hope so."

Sarah gazed into the fire, watching the dancing flames as they ate the logs, listening to the crackle and feeling warm in the gentle yellow glow. She sighed.

"Why does it have to be like this Joe? Why do men have to fight?"

"That's a question women have never stopped asking."

Alice's voice came from the doorway and the two young people turned to see her struggling into her overcoat.

"I'm just popping next door for a cup of tea."

Sarah smiled gratefully, sensing that her mother remembered the precious stolen moments she had shared with Sarah's father during the last war. "Thanks, Mum. We'll see you later."

Alice left the room, then they heard the front door slam behind her.

"You've got a very thoughtful mother, Sarah. Not many women in her position would leave their daughter alone in the house with a young man!"

Sarah laughed. "You're right! But she realises how little time we have together, and how precious that time is to us." She snuggled close. "Will I be able to see you tomorrow?"

Joe shrugged. "I doubt it. I'm at work all day and on duty all night."

Sarah pouted

"Some leave this is going to be! Don't you have any free time at all?"

"Well, I have an hour or two after work before I begin spotting, but I have to eat then."

"Why not come and join us for dinner?"

"Won't your mother mind?"

"What do you think?"

Joe laughed. "I suppose it will be all right. Don't let me forget to give her my ration coupons though. I can't expect her to feed me on hers."

Sarah snuggled closer.

"Have there been many raids here?"

Joe shook his head. "No. The odd plane has been over, but I wouldn't be surprised if they were lost. There have been no mass raids so far. But I don't suppose we can escape them forever."

"It all seems so heartless, bombing innocent civilians like they are in London. Do you really think they'll do that here?"

"I'm sure of it. Remember, it's not only innocent civilians in Coventry. We have aircraft factories and other war industries. The Germans would be mad not to bomb us."

"Don't say that!" Sarah was appalled at the thought and pulled away to look him in the eye. "You're talking of them bombing our homes and families! How can you be so matter of fact about it?"

"Because it's bound to happen. I don't want it to happen and I'm frightened of how I'll react when it does, but I know it will. I just try to hide my feelings and face facts."

Sarah leant her head against his shoulder and snuggled close again. "I'm sorry, Joe. Let's not talk about the war any more tonight. We have so little time together. We really ought to make the most of it."

Joe smiled down at her upturned face and gently brushed back a stray lock of hair that had fallen across her eyes.

"You're right as usual," he whispered softly as he leant forward to kiss her.

His lips were soft and warm against hers, and Sarah reached up to run her fingers through his silky blond hair. It felt so good to be in his arms again. She did not resist as Joe's kiss became stronger, more insistent. As his tongue found its way into her mouth and began to gently caress her own, a low moan escaped from Sarah's lips. Encouraged by her response, Joe's hand moved up from her waist until it was cupping her left breast through the thin cotton of her blouse. Sarah tensed at the touch, excited yet not sure how to respond. Her breath caught in her throat.

Pulling gently away, Joe gazed down into the face of the woman he loved. A small frown puckered her brow, and there was a questioning look in her eyes. He smiled gently.

104

"Just relax, Sarah. It will be all right. I promise."

He leant down and began to kiss her again. His lips were slow but sure, and Sarah found herself beginning to respond again. Joe's hand began to move more firmly against her breast and his thumb to stroke the hardened nipple. Sarah felt her head spinning. His touch excited her in a way that she had never experienced before. She wanted it to continue, yet was afraid of the consequences. With an effort of will she pulled away and sat up. Joe's hand slipped from her breast and fell to the sofa between them.

"What's the matter?"

"I...I'm not sure." Sarah's cheeks felt hot, and she knew she must appear flushed. She found it difficult to lift her eyes to Joe's.

"Didn't you like it?"

Sarah said nothing. How could she tell him of how his touch had made her heart pound and want for more? What would he think of her if she told him that she wished his touch would never end?

"You know I'd never do anything to hurt you, don't you?"

Sarah nodded. "It's just that...I'm not sure what to do. I don't think I'm ready for this."

"Look at me, Sarah."

She lifted her eyes slowly, afraid that she might she rejection in his but found there only love.

"It doesn't matter if you're not ready Sarah. We can wait. We have our whole lives to wait."

Sarah's features relaxed into an answering smile. Joe leant forward and kissed her softly, gently. They had all the time in the world.

For a while the crackling of the logs on the fire was the only sound to be heard.

The evening of November 14th was cold and clear. The bright moonlight lit the streets and Joe hardly noticed the blackout as he made his way to the Porters' home. It was a lovely evening, and he wished he did not have to go on duty. At least he would be able to spend some time with Sarah.

Sarah answered his knock and led him along to the kitchen, where Alice was busy at the stove.

"Hello, Joe. Just make yourself comfortable. Dinner won't be long."

"Thanks, Mrs. Porter."

Joe took off his scarf and gloves and hung his coat up before sitting at the table where Sarah poured him a cup of tea. He blew the steam gently, cradling the cup in his hands, then took a sip.

"Thanks, Sarah, I needed that. It's cold out there. The grass is already beginning to whiten with frost."

"And you've got to be out there on duty all night long. Poor Joe."

Joe smiled warmly. "It's not that bad. We work in teams so we each get a break now and then to rest and warm up. Besides, you know I like to feel that I'm doing my bit."

"No one could do more than you." Sarah's intense gaze held his. Slowly, their hands crept across the table to clasp each other.

"Come on, you two!" Alice bustled over to the table. "That's enough of that. Now you let go of his hand, Sarah, he needs both of them to eat his dinner."

Sarah laughed, blushing, and took the plates from her mother.

"That smells good, Mrs. Porter."

"It's only shepherd's pie I'm afraid, and more vegetable than shepherd at that. But

I'm sure it will taste all right."

It certainly did taste good. In what seemed like no time at all the meal was eaten and the plates cleared away.

"I'll wash these for you, Mrs. Porter."

"You'll do no such thing!" Sarah laid a firm hand on Joe's arm as she spoke. "I'll do these after you've gone. Do you want anything else?"

Joe shook his head. "No thanks." He looked up at the clock on the kitchen wall and frowned. "I'm afraid I'll have to be off in a moment. It's six thirty already, and I have to be on duty by seven."

Sarah sighed. "I really love it out in the countryside. Heronfield is a really nice place to live and work, but I do wish it was nearer to Coventry. I might get to see more of you."

Joe nodded as he slipped his coat on. "I know what you mean. But this war won't go on forever. Then we'll have all the time in the world."

Sarah smiled wistfully as she wrapped his scarf around his neck and handed him his gloves

"The sooner it's over the better, as far as I'm concerned. Do you think you'll be busy tonight?"

Joe shrugged. "Who can say?"

"Well, if you find yourself at a loose end you can always think of me."

"I always do." Joe smiled. "I always do."

The love shone clearly in his eyes and was reflected in Sarah's own. With a smile, Sarah handed him his gas mask and led him towards the front door.

"Come on, or you'll be late."

"Goodnight, Mrs. Porter, and thank you for the dinner," Joe called over his shoulder as he was ushered along the hall. Sarah closed the kitchen door and turned out the light, before drawing back the heavy blackout curtain. She reached up and kissed Joe tenderly on the lips.

"Goodnight my darling. Take care of yourself."

Joe smiled and returned the kiss, a little more forcefully.

"Goodnight. I'll get over to see you tomorrow. Somehow."

Sarah opened the front door and watched the young man make his way out into the cold November night. He turned at the corner to wave, his breath like a plume of smoke in the moonlit air, then he was gone. Sarah closed the door and pulled the blackout curtain back across it before rejoining her mother in the kitchen, rubbing her hands.

"Is it cold out there, love?"

Sarah nodded. "The blackout curtain is of some use after all. It certainly cuts down the draughts!"

Alice laughed. "Every cloud has a silver lining!"

The two women chatted happily as they washed up after their meal. The clatter of plates and saucepans transported them back to the less worrying times they had enjoyed together before the war. The chores done, they retired to the sitting room and settled down for the evening. Alice picked up her knitting and the sound of clicking needles vied with the music coming from the radio. Sarah snuggled down in an armchair to read the paper. She had barely got past the first page when the sirens sounded.

Alice looked at the clock on the mantelpiece as she stood up and placed a guard in front of the fire.

"Ten past seven. Well, at least it should all be over by bedtime." She glanced at Sarah, who had jumped nervously to her feet. "I forgot, this is your first air raid warning, isn't it?"

Sarah nodded.

"Don't worry love, we often get them. They usually only last an hour or so, and there are rarely any bombs dropped. Going to the shelter is no more than a formality really." She inclined her head towards the newspaper. "Bring that with you if you like, it'll give you something to do. I'm going to take my knitting."

They put on their coats and picked up their gas masks before making for the back door, switching off the lights as they went. As they made their way down the path in the cold night air, Alice smiled.

"At least we can see where we're going in this moonlight. I wouldn't like to tell you how many times I've come off the path and landed in the vegetable patch!"

Sarah laughed. They made their way towards the pile of earth covering the Anderson shelter in the centre of the garden. The dark mass of its bulk was silhouetted grotesquely against the star-filled sky, like a beached whale. As they made their way down the steps, the drone of aircraft could be heard above them. Sarah looked up.

"Ours or theirs?"

Alice shrugged.

"I don't know. Come on."

Barely had they entered the shelter when they were joined by Mary Norman from next door, with her children, Tommy aged six and Lucy who was little more than a babe in arms. She smiled in greeting.

"Hello, Sarah. It's good to see you again. Though I wish it was under more pleasant circumstances."

Mary settled her children on the top bunk which ran along the side wall of the shelter as Mr. and Mrs. Cook from the house on the other side of Alice's carefully made their way down the steps. Alice closed the door and lit the kerosene lamp, which threw their features into sharp relief. Mary handed blankets from the lower bunk to the old couple.

"It's cold tonight. Wrap yourselves in these."

Mrs. Cook, looking every day of her seventy-three years, smiled gratefully.

"Thank you, Mary."

They were soon settled. Alice, Sarah and Mary sat on the lower bunk while Mr. and Mrs. Cook made themselves comfortable in a pair of old, but serviceable, armchairs. Sarah smiled across the small intervening space at the Cooks. They had lived next door all her life and, to her eyes, had always been old. It was comforting to have two such familiar figures in the shelter with her. Mr. Cook smiled.

"Don't worry my dear. The All Clear will sound before you know it."

As though to prove his words a lie, they heard the first bombs begin to fall.

.

33

Joe met up with Bob Dean at seven o'clock. They made their way to the roof of the factory which was their spotting position for the night. Bob rubbed his hands together briskly.

"It's going to be a cold one tonight."

Joe nodded as he picked up the binoculars and slowly scanned the sky for enemy planes. "It's just the sort of night when I'd prefer to be snuggled up close with a pretty girl to keep me warm!"

"And we all know which pretty girl that would be!" Bob laughed.

Joe smiled ruefully. "It wouldn't be so bad if I could see her more often, but she's hardly ever here."

Bob's reply was lost in the wailing of the siren at the other end of the roof. The two men covered their ears with their hands until the deafening sound ceased. Even then their ears still rang, and they felt the echo of the siren roll round inside their heads. Joe shook his head to clear it, then pointed out over the city.

"My God, Bob! Look at that!"

Away to their left the sky was full of planes, like clouds of midges in the air above a still pond on a hot summer's day. But these midges grew and grew until the shape of the enemy bombers could be see distinctly in the clear, moonlit sky.

"How many do you think there are?" Bob had to raise his voice as the awesome roar of the plane's engines reached their still smarting ears.

Joe shrugged. "I don't know. At least seventy or eighty, I would think."

In fact there were a hundred, closely followed by three waves of equal number. The two members of the Home Guard watched the leading planes drop flares attached to parachutes, to light the targets for those who followed. Then the bombs began to fall.

Joe saw the ack ack open up, sending what looked like little puffs of cotton wool into the air, and the shells seemed to have no more effect than cotton wool on the armada of aircraft above them. The roar and thump of falling bombs was still distant, but as the planes drew closer Joe felt the vulnerability of their position.

"I don't think we'll be much use up here spotting tonight," he called over his shoulder to Bob, as he ran towards the roof door that led to the stairs. "Let's get down to ground level and see if we can be any help there."

"Don't worry! I'm right behind you!"

Within moments they were running out into the street and away from the tank factory, which must surely be a target for the enemy aircraft. There was a high-pitched screaming sound as a bomb hurtled down close by. The two young men dived into the relative safety of a doorway just as the bomb struck. It destroyed the end house of a terrace and left the adjoining one only half standing. As they left the doorway and ran through the clouds of dust, Bob saw the first flickering flames of fire spread along the fallen roof timbers.

"Quick! Let's put that out before it spreads!"

It was easier said than done. The two men ran to the area of devastation that had once been a kitchen, and began carrying water from a ruptured pipe in two bowls they found lying nearby. It was hard, hot work, running backwards and forwards across the heaps of broken bricks, tables, chairs and pictures. At last they had the flames under control and, finally, they were out. All the time, Joe had been aware of the roar and thunder of the planes, the echoing explosion of bombs, the thump thump thump of the ack ack and the wailing of sirens. Now he stopped for a moment to look around him and stood rigid with horror. The factory where they had been on watch was situated high on a hill, and the whole of Coventry was spread before him like a map. The air was alight with searchlight beams, and full of aircraft raining down bombs in an endless stream. On all sides he could see the yellow glow of fires started by incendiary bombs. He saw that the raid was not confined to Coventry's factories alone. Fires were burning in all areas of the city.

"There's no point trying to make it back to HQ through this lot," he muttered. "Let's just get down there and see what we can do."

As the two men made their way down the street a woman ran round the corner ahead of them, screaming as she came.

"My baby! My baby!"

Joe ran to her. "What's wrong?"

"My baby was asleep so I didn't go to the shelter. My house is gone! Where's my baby?"

She turned and ran back around the corner. Joe followed close behind. A whole row of houses had been flattened by a stick of bombs, leaving little recognisable behind. The woman ran to the rubble and began to dig with her bare hands.

"She's here somewhere! I know she is!"

Joe pulled her gently away.

"Wait in the street, love. Bob and I will see what we can do."

Over to his right a ruptured pipe spurted flaming gas into the air. Somewhere behind a weakened wall toppled, and fell with a crashing of bricks as the two men carefully began to remove the rubble. It was not long before their bodies were soaked with sweat, their hands bruised and bleeding. After almost half an hour they found the family's pet dog, a mongrel whose skull had been crushed by falling masonry. Joe looked at Bob, but said nothing. They both knew that the chances of a child remaining alive in this were remote. They dug on, slowly clearing an area of the more moveable debris. Then Joe stopped, his head to one side as though listening to something.

"What is it?"

Joe held up his hand, and Bob fell silent. Then Joe began to dig frantically, a little to the right of where they had been before.

"I'm sure I heard a baby cry," he whispered as he removed part of a roof timber. Sure enough there was the edge of a white lace shawl, covered in red brick-dust. They were close to the child. Joe began to move more carefully now. A door had fallen against a partially demolished wall, leaving a small triangular space at its base. Joe reached carefully inside. To his immense relief his hand made contact with a warm, moving bundle. Gently he eased the child from its sanctuary and handed it up to Bob.

"She must be the luckiest baby alive. There isn't even a scratch on her. That door saved her life."

Bob made his way carefully across the rubble. He handed the baby to her sobbing mother.

"There you are, love. Now you get yourself and your little girl to a shelter. Fast."

She smiled up at him through her tears.

"Thank you."

Bob turned and called to Joe. "Come on. Let's see what else we can do to help."

The hours passed quickly. Sometimes the two men helped to dig in the rubble for survivors, though they lifted out more than one for whom the raid had spelt death. At other times they helped fight the fires which raged throughout the city, a task made increasingly difficult now that the water supply was totally unreliable. Clouds of choking black smoke hung in the air obliterating the stars, and also the waves of the enemy, but the drone of their engines could still be heard, along with the explosions of their bombs. Joe lost all sense of direction and had no idea where he was. The scale of destruction was so awesome that he was lost in the city which had been home to him all his life. Midnight came and went with no slackening of the raid. Dirty and exhausted, Joe thrust his face into a bucket of water for a moment, then shook it to send drops of water flying in all directions. Feeling only a little revived by the icy water, he surveyed the carnage surrounding him, and prayed that Sarah and her mother were safe.

34

There was a shocked silence in the Anderson shelter as the first bombs fell. Then Alice spoke.

"Well, it looks like this is going to be the real one we've all been waiting for."

"How far away are the bombs, Mummy?"

Mary smiled reassuringly at Tommy.

"Don't worry, love. We're quite safe here."

"Can Daddy hear the bombs?"

Mary shook her head.

"I shouldn't think so, he's in the army now. Remember?"

Tommy nodded.

"He's a long way from home, so a few bombs here won't worry him."

There was the sound of more explosions, seeming to be closer, and Sarah felt a tingling in her feet, as though the very earth was trying to tell her of its pain.

"How long will this go on for?"

Alice looked at Mrs. Cook and shrugged. There was no answer.

For a time they listened to the droning aircraft and the crash of bombs, at a loss for words. Then they heard the screaming sound of a bomb tearing through the air close by. It landed not far away with a terrific explosion. This time Sarah did feel the earth shudder. Moments later, debris rained down on the shelter, the thumps and bangs waking little Lucy who began to cry fearfully. Mary lifted her down from the top bunk and held her close.

"There, there, darling. There's nothing to be afraid of."

The strange noises, and obviously nervous adults, filled the child with fear, and she continued to cry, despite her mother's best attempts to quieten her. For a time the child's sobbing was the only accompaniment to the awful cacophony from outside. Then a small, frightened whisper came from the top bunk.

"I'm scared, Mummy."

Mary's hands were full with little Lucy. She looked pleadingly at Sarah, who nodded reassuringly. She got up from the lower bunk and climbed up next to the little boy, having to lie down so she did not hit her head on the curved roof.

"It's all right, Tommy. We're quite safe here."

The six year old looked at her with frightened eyes.

"Really?"

"Really. Would you like me to tell you a story?"

The small boy nodded and snuggled close to Sarah as she began to tell him the tale of Goldilocks and the Three Bears.

35

The whole city seemed to be ablaze. Streets were blocked by rubble, hampering the fire engines and ambulances in their work. Even if the vehicles were able to get through, there were far too few to make the slightest impact on the devastation. Joe and Bob attached themselves to a fire-fighting team and their whole world shrank to the size of the small road where they were working. It was a world of heat and flames, roiling black smoke, screams and cries, the shouts of men trying to bring order to the chaos. All the time the planes droned overhead. The barrels of the anti-aircraft guns followed them through the sky until, locked in the cross beams of the searchlights, they fired at the monsters which were spewing so much death and destruction on what had so recently been a calm, ordered world.

Joe was exhausted after a day of working in the aircraft factory and half a night lost in the confusion of the air raid. Working under the orders of the senior fireman on the scene, he moved from one task to another like an automaton. The carnage no longer broke through the barrier his mind had erected to carry him through the night. The sight of a doll, its head crushed by a falling brick, touched him with a tinge of sadness, but as he helped yet another injured person from the ruins of her home and bandaged her wounds, the pain and blood moved him not at all. Joe wondered at this total detachment. He could only see it as a mental escape valve to enable him to preserve his diminishing energy.

The dark night was moving slowly and inexorably towards dawn when the 'Raiders Past' signal finally sounded at nineteen minutes past six, almost twelve hours since the first bomb dropped on the unsuspecting city. For a moment the rescue workers paused and raised their weary eyes in relief. The sky was now empty of planes, but they did not halt for long. The raid might be over, but the task of clearing the devastation would take days, probably weeks, of continued backbreaking effort.

Joe and Bob were directed into a house with part of the roof and wall missing. Their instructions were to search for survivors. Initially there seemed to be little damage. Dust hung in the air like a midsummer haze, but it did little to impede their view. The front room was undisturbed. The embers of a fire glowed in the hearth, a mug of cold tea stood on the table. As the two men moved out into the hall they heard a sound, perhaps a groan, coming from the direction of the partially demolished staircase.

"Is there anybody there?

Joe listened to the silence for a moment, then the groan came again. Within seconds Bob and Joe were at the staircase, carefully removing the shattered remnants of the banisters. They had soon uncovered part of a torso, a man, and Joe began clearing towards the head. The injured man was old and frail. A blow to the head had rendered him unconscious, but Joe did not think he was seriously hurt. A sudden intake of breath from where Bob was uncovering the man's legs caused Joe to turn and look.

"What is it? Are his legs badly hurt?"

Bob shook his head. "No. They're just trapped under the thing that made such a bloody great hole in his roof, and demolished this staircase."

Joe felt his throat go dry and his hands clammy. He licked his lips.

"You don't mean...?"

"Yes." Bob nodded. "A damned great German bomb. I doubt it was brought all the way over here just to make a hole in a roof, so I guess that it's liable to explode at any moment."

"Then we've got to get this old fellow out."

Bob sucked in his lower lip thoughtfully, then nodded.

"I think we can do it. The bomb's resting on a pile of timbers and tiles and is trapping the leg against the wall. If I prop it up with a few more timbers, we should be able to ease him out."

Joe nodded. "The poor old fellow must have been sheltering under the stairs."

"That bomb certainly seems to have had his name on it." Bob gently eased the timbers aside, his forehead beaded with sweat, his brow furrowed with concentration. Joe watched, unable to offer more help than to hold the man's shoulders and keep him still. The seconds ticked by, each one seeming an hour, each minute a day. At last Bob looked up.

"I think we can get him out now."

Joe released his breath. He had not realised he was holding it. Gradually he dragged the old man clear. One of his legs was lying at an awkward angle, obviously broken, and Joe was relieved that the unconscious man could feel no pain.

"Come on then, Bob. Let's get out of here."

"That could be a bit of a problem."

Joe looked across at his companion, who spoke fearfully through gritted teeth.

"The timbers have slipped. The bomb is only supported by me now. I'm afraid that if I move it will go off." He licked his dry lips. "Get the old fellow out of here. Then send someone in to prop up this bomb."

Joe hoisted the man over his shoulder. "I'll be back before you can say Jack Robinson."

"You don't have to come back, Joe."

"I do. You're my mate. Now just hang on a minute."

Joe began to make his way along the hall. His burden was light, for the old man was frail, and it only took him a few seconds to reach the front door. The blast took him there, throwing him and the old man through the door with the force of the explosion, leaving them lying there on the pavement like two discarded rag dolls.

36

Tony lay on his stomach, his back brushing the lowest branches of the hedge. It was a cold, cloudless night; the stars shone brightly and he knew there would be a frost before morning. His face and hands were blackened with streaks of river mud, so that his pale skin would not give him away. Ahead of him was a stretch of open ground leading to a barbed wire fence. At each end of the fence, which stretched for about half a mile, was a tower with a sentry. At frequent intervals, a foot soldier walked slowly along the inside of the fence, rifle slung across his shoulder. As Tony watched, the shadowy figure of the guard passed in front of him. He looked at his watch. Twenty-eight minutes. The same as last time. He licked his dry lips and reviewed the events which had brought him to this damp hedge bottom.

Jim had called Tony and Adam Banks into a small room two days before to explain their final passing-out test.

"You have three days to break into the army camp five miles down the road, where you will find and steal a machine gun. The idea is that you're in France, trying to get the weapon for your local resistance group." He smiled as he took in the two impassive faces across the desk. "We obviously don't want to make it too easy for you, so the local police and the army camp have been given your description. Imagine that they are the local Gestapo and do your best not to get noticed. The soldiers will be armed with live ammunition; after all we are at war. The camp CO has been warned that you'll be trying to break in sometime in the next three weeks. He's issued instructions that all intruders are to be taken alive if possible. So take care. If you're spotted, give yourselves up immediately, or you risk being shot."

The two men opposite frowned and Jim nodded.

"I'm glad to see that you are taking this seriously. It's as close to the real thing as we can get without actually sending you to France. All that remains for me to do is to wish you good luck in your mission."

Tony glanced across at Adam, who lay beneath the adjacent bush. They had thought

112

and planned hard and, after observing the camp for two days, had decided that the best way in would be under the wire at night. The sound of the sentry's footsteps diminished. Tony signalled to Adam, who ran forwards, crouched low to the ground, then threw himself flat against the earth, his hand tightly clutching a pair of wire cutters, painted black so that they would not reflect any light. He began to cut the lowest wires in the fence; each snap seemed like rifle fire to his ears, but the sentries in the watchtowers did not appear to hear. Within moments there was a gap large enough for a man to slither through on his stomach. He beckoned to Tony. From his concealed position, Tony glanced at both watchtowers. The sentries were not looking his way, so he ran at a crouch across the open space, and wormed his way through the gap in the fence which Adam held open for him. Once through, Tony turned and held the wires for his companion. Within moments they were both inside the fence and running towards the shadowy buildings ahead of them.

They had entered the camp in the south-west corner, and knew that the ammunition store, the third building on their left, was their best chance of getting a machine gun and getting out again unseen. Tony looked at his watch. Seven minutes had elapsed from the time the guard had appeared. That left them eighteen minutes to get out again before the sentry checked the fence and found the hole. Adam was now working on the padlock of the ammunition store. Two minutes later they were inside. It was a dark, windowless shed so Tony was able to switch on a pencil torch and swing it around amongst the cases of munitions. Adam touched him on the shoulder and pointed to their left.

"Machine gun."

His voice was a whisper. Tony turned to look as Adam picked up the gun.

"Let's go."

Tony shook his head. "Hang on. What use is a gun without ammunition?" He lifted a box of ammunition for the gun. It was heavy but he did not think it would slow him down on the way out. He looked at his watch. Fifteen minutes.

"Let's go, then." he said as he moved towards the door. On the way he passed a box of grenades and, on impulse, forced it open and put three grenades into each coat pocket. Then they were outside again, pressed against the side of the building. Their dark clothes and blackened skin made them all but invisible. Everything was quiet, the only sound and movement coming from the northeast, where the Mess was situated. The two men looked at each other and nodded, then raced towards the fence. It was not so easy to get through, encumbered as they were with their booty. But they managed it and were soon back under the welcome cover of the trees, a hundred yards from the fence.

Tony looked at his watch once again. Twenty-one minutes. They had five minutes or so before the sentry discovered their entry point. The two men ran for half a mile to the bushes where they had hidden their motorbike and sidecar, borrowed from a local garage. Adam loaded their booty into the sidecar and climbed in with it as Tony gunned the engine into life and roared off down the road. Behind them the wailing of a siren rent the air as the break-in at the camp was discovered. But they were well away now. As the two men roared off down the little country lane towards the training centre they were both laughing.

Jim was in the middle of some paperwork when Tony and Adam knocked at his door.

"Come in." He closed the folder and screwed the top on his pen as he spoke. The door opened to admit the two very dishevelled, but smiling, young men. He took in their blackened faces and the bulky objects wrapped in sacking and smiled.

"I take it that you two have accomplished your mission?"

Adam nodded. "Yes, sir."

"Did you get the gun?"

Tony grinned boyishly as Adam unwrapped the gun and laid it on the table.

"We thought the gun would be useless on its own, so we brought a few extras." Tony unwrapped the sacking around the case of ammunition and placed it on Jim's desk. Then he took the grenades from his pockets, and placed them on top.

Jim laughed. "It seems that your mission was a success. You should both make good agents. Now go and get yourselves cleaned up, I'll see you down in the mess later."

"What about the gun?"

"Leave it with me, Tony. I shall have to return it to the army camp. The CO is no doubt reviewing his security at this very moment."

The two young men, their blackened faces clean, and dressed once more in dry clothes, were drinking a warming whisky in the mess some forty minutes later. Adam sipped his drink and gazed at his companion.

"You seem rather friendly with Lieutenant Briggs."

Tony nodded. "When you have been through what we've been through together, you're bound to build up a relationship."

Adam raised a quizzical eyebrow but said nothing. Tony took a sip of whisky while deciding what to say, then placed his glass with great care upon the bar.

"We were at Dunkirk together."

"Dunkirk!" Adams eyes widened in amazement. "I didn't think you were a regular!"

Tony shook his head. "I'm not. I was a civilian at the time."

"How come you were there, then?"

"It's a long story."

"What was it like?"

Tony felt a shiver run down the length of his spine and took another sip of his drink before speaking again. "It was awful. I never want to go through an experience like that again. That's the main reason I'm here. The sooner this war is over the better pleased I'll be."

Adam inclined his head towards the door. Jim was just entering. "I guess you two won't be seeing much of each other once you finish here. I'll leave you alone."

"You don't need to."

Adam smiled. "I know, but some of the others have just come in. I think I'll go over there and brag about our successful evening's work!"

Tony laughed as Jim arrived to take Adam's place. The Mess Officer placed his usual whisky on the bar and moved away.

"It sounds as though you're not the only ones to have been busy tonight."

"Has someone else done their final test?"

Jim shook his head. "No. Apparently the worst air raid of the war so far is going on at this very moment."

"Where?"

"Coventry. I suppose they're trying to hit the war industry. There's little news at the moment. It seems that there are hundreds of planes involved. It's already been going on for hours." He shook his head sadly. "It's going to be a mess up there tomorrow."

Tony frowned. Sarah's family were in Coventry. He hoped they were all right.

Jim noticed his expression.

"What's wrong?"

"One of the nursing auxiliaries at Heronfield comes from Coventry."

"Is she at home on leave?"

Tony shrugged.

"I doubt it. I just hope her family get through it all right, that's all."

"Do you know where all the nurses come from?"

Tony turned towards Jim who smiled at his puzzled expression.

"What I mean is, if you know where she comes from, she must be pretty special."

Tony smiled. "Yes, she is. She's really beautiful, and has a lovely personality with it."

Jim smiled broadly. "This sounds serious!"

Tony shook his head. "No. I wish it was, but she's already got someone." Tony frowned. "He's in Coventry too. I guess she must be pretty worried about him."

"He's that special to her, is he?"

Tony nodded. "I wish I'd met her first. I don't stand a chance with her while he's around."

Jim shrugged. "Just hang on in there, Tony. There's a war on. Anything could happen. Just make sure you're there if she ever needs you."

"That won't be easy if I'm out in France."

"What about her fella? Has he joined up yet?"

Tony shook his head sadly. "He's unfit. I could be away for months at a time, while he'll always be at home and available." He smiled grimly. "Sounds hopeless doesn't it?"

Jim shrugged. "It'll work out. Don't worry."

Tony forced a smile. "It's easy enough for you to say that."

He emptied his glass and, believing Sarah to be safe at Heronfield, put all thoughts of her aside.

37

The All Clear sounded at last. In one long night, four hundred enemy planes had dropped flares on parachutes to light the way for the first wave of planes which had dropped incendiary bombs with explosive charges; after that the flares were no longer needed for the fires raged incessantly. Guided by the destruction below them the enemy planes passed over again and again, dropping land mines and high explosives. In all thirty thousand incendiaries and five hundred tons of bombs and land mines had been dropped, nearly fifty thousand houses had been damaged and twenty thousand rendered totally uninhabitable. Three quarters of the city's industry had been put out of action; telephone, water, electricity and gas supplies were all totally disrupted. The tram system was unusable and one hundred and fifty six out of one hundred and eighty one buses were out of action. During the attempts to bring the chaos under control twenty six firemen were killed and over two hundred injured; almost one thousand civilians were seriously injured, five hundred and fifty four killed.

After what seemed an endless night. Sarah looked at the watch Joe had given to her the previous Christmas. 6.16. As she gazed at the watch her thoughts were centred on Joe. Where had he been through the long, dark night? Was he safe? For a moment her anxiety for him held her frozen. All night long she had prayed for the air raid to end, and now that it had she was afraid to leave the shelter to face the unknown. None of the others moved. Eventually it was Tommy who broke the tense silence.

"Can't we go now, Mummy? I'm hungry."

His mother smiled indulgently

"Of course. Come on, my dears."

She picked up little Lucy, still sleepy and clinging tightly to her mother. Tommy climbed down from the top bunk and took her free hand. Alice rose stiffly to her feet as Sarah opened the door of the Anderson shelter. The early morning air was cold, and she shivered. It should have been dark, it was still over an hour before dawn, but an eldritch orange glow streaked the night sky lighting it so brightly that Sarah could see her surroundings clearly. Her home still stood, though the force of an explosion had blown some of the windows in. On one side Mary Norman's house was intact, but on the other, where the Cooks lived, some of the walls were cracked and all the windows were shattered. The house next to the Cooks' had no roof left, and the walls leaned at dangerous angles. One of the bombs that had landed close by, probably the one that had shaken the very foundations of their shelter, had scored a direct hit further down the street. It had demolished three houses and badly damaged four more. In others curtains billowed out from shattered windows. For a moment the small group of people stood in silence; then Sarah spoke.

"If it's like this here, what will it be like in the city centre?"

Alice shivered. "Worse no doubt. Let's get our place cleaned up first, before we go to look."

Sarah shook her head. "No. You should stay here. The fewer people wandering about the better. But I must go. I have a feeling my training is going to be needed."

Alice looked long and hard at her daughter. She feared for her safety, yet knew she was right. Finally she nodded.

"Just be careful." Without waiting for a reply she turned to the old couple, who were staring speechlessly at their damaged home. "Come on, Mr. and Mrs. Cook, there's plenty of room for you in my house."

Sarah watched the small group split up, Mary Norman taking her two children home while the elderly couple gratefully followed her mother up the garden path and through the kitchen door. Sarah turned and made her way towards the centre of the city.

There was death and destruction everywhere. Houses lay in ruins. Shops and factories burned furiously and there were not enough people to put out the raging fires. People wandered injured and shocked through the streets, and Sarah felt she had awoken in hell. She was stunned and walked aimlessly through the destruction, not knowing where to go or what to do. Then she saw two ambulance men carrying a stretcher towards a bombed house and ran towards them.

"Wait!" she called. The two men stopped and turned towards her.

"If you're looking for someone, I'm afraid we can't help you. We're very busy."

The young men looked exhausted. Sarah guessed they had been working all night.

"No, you don't understand. I'm an auxiliary nurse at home on leave. What can I do to help?"

The young man smiled gratefully. "Thanks, love. We could do with all the help we can get. Injured people are being taken to the local schools. Do you know where the nearest one is?"

Sarah nodded.

"Good. Go there. I'm sure they could use your help."

Sarah watched the two ambulance men making their way towards the bombed house, and wondered if Joe was as tired and dispirited as them. That was if he was still alive of course. As Sarah made her way towards the school buildings her fears for Joe increased, and she was tempted to try to find him. But where should she look? Where could she start? His job of spotting would have been over as the first wave of planes came in. What had he done for the rest of the night? Sarah looked around her at the destruction, which stretched away in all directions. She realised that to search for him would be a waste of time and energy. If he had survived Joe would go to her house. She hoped and prayed that would be the case.

As Sarah rounded the next corner, she saw the local school. Part of the classroom block was destroyed, but the hall was still standing. She was in a state of mild shock as she made her way across the piles of rubble and through the open door where she stopped, stunned by the sight which greeted her eyes. Those not too seriously injured were seated on children's chairs, waiting patiently. A doctor and four nurses laboured incessantly amongst the more seriously injured, who were stretched out on tables that had recently held nothing more gruesome than school dinners. After a moment's hesitation, Sarah made her way over to the doctor. He was completing the amputation of the leg of a teenage girl. It was a mercy she was unconscious for Sarah could see no anaesthetics and precious few other medical supplies. The doctor spoke without looking up.

"Wait with the others please."

Sarah did not want to spoil his concentration but knew that she must speak. "I'm a nursing auxiliary. What can I do to help?"

This time the doctor did look up. His face was haggard but determined, and there was a look of intense gratification in his eyes.

"Thank God. Do you think you could deal with some of the less seriously wounded, while we do the operating?"

"Of course."

Sarah picked up a nearby first aid kit and made her way towards the injured. Most had superficial cuts which she could deal with, and she set to work. The number needing her attention seemed endless, and she worked long and hard, the needs of those around her driving all fears for Joe from her mind.

Sarah worked unceasingly throughout the day and on into the night. Long before the injured ceased to make their way to the makeshift hospital, they had run out of everything - dressings, sutures, disinfectant, bandages, painkillers, antiseptics. The list was as endless as their needs. Able-bodied people who had brought their relatives for treatment were sent home to search for any first aid supplies they could find. Clean sheets were brought in and torn up for bandages, then sterilised in an old tin bath of boiling water placed over a fire made from roof timbers. Water was collected from broken pipes, which dripped incessantly. There was no electricity, so light was provided by a few candles scavenged from nearby houses, but their light was barely sufficient. The windows were broken allowing the chill November wind to sweep in, and the hands of the doctor and nurses were numb from the cold. Some of those who were uninjured came to offer their aid. The blankets they brought were gratefully received, some being used to cover the windows, while the rest were distributed to the patients. There seemed little chance of evacuating any of the wounded to a proper hospital. So far there had been no communication with anyone in authority, and the destruction was so great that it seemed unlikely that there would be any improvement in communications for some time. An able-bodied young man in his twenties was sent to the Town Hall, in the hope that someone there could tell them what was happening and send them some aid. But as the day wore on they were still awaiting his return.

With facilities so limited, all those not seriously injured had been sent home, including those with broken limbs, but that still left almost fifty seriously wounded people laid on the school tables: a baby with a fractured skull and severe internal injuries, the teenage amputee, a mother who had given birth in the debris of her home and almost died from loss of blood, a man with a broken back, an old woman suffering severe shock and pneumonia. The list was endless. By late evening, more than twenty-four hours after the bombing had begun, there had been six deaths, two of them during emergency operations. The bodies were removed to a small classroom to await identification and burial.

The night drew on. Sarah had been working in the school for sixteen hours when she looked up to find that no one else was waiting for treatment. She straightened up slowly, her back aching from so many hours bending, her fingers numb with the cold, her head aching with a pounding, throbbing pain that had been going on for hours. As she rubbed her tired eyes, she looked around her at the people whose lives had been so dramatically changed in the space of just one day, but she could find no tears for them. She did not know why. Perhaps she was too exhausted, maybe she was in shock. She did know, however, that her family had been remarkably lucky, and for this she was extremely grateful. Mixed with this gratitude was a gnawing fear about what had happened to Joe. There had been so much death and destruction. Everyone who came into the school had their stories of bombed houses and shelters, raging fires, rescuers injured by booby trapped bombs and land mines. Her fears for Joe's safety increased.

As she rubbed her freezing hands together, Sarah was approached by the doctor she had spoken to when she first arrived. He looked exhausted, his face haggard and grey, his clothes covered with his patients' blood.

"I'm sorry, but I don't even know your name." His voice was weak and shook with exhaustion. Sarah guessed he was little more than thirty, but the day's experiences had aged him immeasurably. She wondered if she looked as bad as he did; perhaps that was why she could find no tears for the suffering around her.

"My name's Sarah Porter. I'm based at Heronfield House near Marlborough. I was home on leave last night."

The doctor took a deep breath. "I'm Charles Bailey. I'm just an ordinary G.P., but somebody had to do this." He looked around him. "God knows how long it's going to take to make some sort of order out of this mess. If we don't get some of these people to a proper hospital soon, they're going to die."

"Have you heard anything from the messenger you sent to the Town Hall?"

Bailey shook his head. "I doubt if he'll be back before morning. I told him not to come back until he had some firm news."

"I'll stay on as long as you need me."

Bailey smiled weakly for the first time. "Thanks, I don't know what I would have done without your help, or that of the other nurses who came here. They all live locally. I suppose you do too?"

Sarah nodded.

"Is your house damaged?"

She shook her head. "No. We were lucky."

"Then I suggest you go home and get some sleep. I've sent two of the nurses home too, the other two will stay and help me tonight. Perhaps you can come back in the morning to relieve them?"

Sarah smiled weakly. "Thanks. I don't mind admitting I'm exhausted." She looked around at the patients. Some were unconscious, many more sleeping, others lay groaning in unrelieved pain. "I'll see if I can get hold of some food when I come back."

Bailey's eyes lit up. "That would be fantastic. These people must eat if they're going to survive." He smiled warmly at her. "Now get off home. I'll see you again in the morning. Goodnight."

"Goodnight, Doctor Bailey."

Sarah wrapped her coat tightly around her against the cold night air, and made her way over the mounds of rubble in the school playground. When she reached the road, she walked down the middle where there was less rubble to impede her progress, though still enough to prevent motor vehicles from knocking her down in the blackout, though the blackout was in no way complete. Fires still burned where houses, shops and factories had once stood. Rescue teams still worked amongst the rubble, although with diminishing hope. Work parties were beginning to clear some of the rubble from the roads. Sarah could not believe that these were the streets where she had played as a child, where she had shopped with her mother and walked with Joe. Coventry was unrecognisable. She had an empty feeling deep inside when she thought of how long it would take to get things back to normal. As she turned into her own road she saw for the first time just how bad the damage from the bomb had been. Six houses were totally demolished, while the Cooks' next door to her mother's was in very poor condition. The damage to her own home was superficial, and she was glad that her mother still had somewhere to live.

As she walked tiredly through the front door Alice came out of the kitchen.

"Sarah! Where've you been? I've been so worried about you!"

Sarah hung up her coat and made her weary way to the kitchen. She slumped down at the table.

"I've been at the local school, they're using it as a makeshift hospital." She looked across at her mother, who was filling the kettle. "It was awful, Mum. There are so many people injured and nothing much we can do to help."

Alice took her hand and helped her up from the table. "I'll have to boil the kettle over the parlour fire, there's no gas. Come on, love."

The two women made their way to the front room, where they sat in front of the fire as the kettle began to heat.

"Have you heard anything from Joe?"

Alice shook her head.

"Sorry love, I've heard nothing. But don't worry, I'm sure he's out there helping to sort things out. We've been busy here today, first clearing out the glass and boarding up the windows, then helping to clear the road. Mr. and Mrs. Cook are upstairs asleep at the moment." She smiled encouragingly. "Your Joe is a good man. He'll know you're worried, but he'll put his duty to help others first. He'll be back, when things begin to get sorted out. Wait and see."

Sarah nodded. "I'm sure you're right, Mum. I suppose I'm just tired." She tried to bury her fears deep inside as she began to tell Alice of all she had experienced during the day. The death and destruction, the pain and suffering, the feeling of helplessness. The tears began to flow at last, partly for Joe but mostly for Coventry, her home; for its people, for what they had been and what they had become.

38

When Joe regained consciousness he was lying on a stretcher, gazing up at the cloudless sky. He tried to sit up, and groaned. His head hurt badly. He was covered with cuts and bruises, but apart from that he was in one piece. As he turned his head, his gaze fell on the house where he and Bob had been working. There was nothing left of it but a pile of rubble. Joe staggered to his feet and felt a hand on his arm.

"Don't go back in there."

Joe turned to the fireman beside him. "Bob?"

The fireman shook his head. "No chance I'm afraid. The old man is dead too. His body over your shoulders protected you, but he took most of the blast." He looked at the ruin. "He was a brave man, your friend."

Joe was numbed. Bob's death seemed so senseless, just one more casualty in a city filled with death. They had not even managed to save the old man. He sat down on a heap of bricks and cradled his head in his hands.

"Are you all right?"

Joe nodded slowly. "I'm fine. Just give me a few moments to let my head clear. Then I'll be back to help you."

"Thanks. We need all the help we can get."

As he watched the fireman walk away to rejoin his colleagues fighting a fire a little further down the road, Joe checked his injuries. Every bone in his body ached, he was exhausted, his head throbbed and his vision blurred when he moved quickly. Despite all this, he knew that he would not take a rest. The last thing he wanted to do was think about what had happened that night. Never in his wildest imaginings had he thought that the Germans would pour out so much devastation on innocent civilians. He found a deep hatred for the enemy, and knew he must do his utmost to minimise the effects of their brutality. He was unfit to fight, but needed no fitness test to help in the aftermath of the worst bombing raid the world had ever seen. Rising unsteadily to his feet, the young man made his way through the clouds of smoke and dust to rejoin the others in their work.

39

Sarah made her way back across the school playground She had risen early, her fears for Joe preventing her sleeping. After a breakfast of bread and jam, with tea brewed once again over the fire in the parlour, Alice helped her fill a bag with the vegetables stored for the winter under the stairs. The bag hung heavy in Sarah's hand, just as her heart hung heavy in her breast. In the cold light of day the destruction of her beloved city stood out stark and clear. In the distance she could still see a few columns of smoke curling into the air, but it seemed that most of the fires were out now. But it was obvious that the chaos caused by the bombing was going to take much longer to sort out. Most roads were still blocked by heaps of rubble. Occasionally she heard the crash of falling bricks as a weakened wall finally gave up its unequal struggle with gravity, falling in a cloud of mortar and dust, to add to the confusion on the ground.

As Sarah made her way into the old school hall, she was met by the bleary-eyed Dr. Bailey.

"I'm glad to see you. The two nurses who have been on all night really need a rest. One of the other nurses has already arrived, so they can go now."

"What about you?"

"Me?"

"Yes, you, Dr. Bailey. When are you going to go and get some rest?"

He shook his head. "I've got to stay here with the patients. Besides" he spoke wistfully, "my house is no longer there. I'll grab a few moments sleep when I can."

"Good. How did it go last night?" Sarah's eyes strayed over the blanket-wrapped forms on the tables.

"We lost another three." The doctor looked exhausted. He was still wearing his blood stained clothes from the previous day, and was dirty and dishevelled, with black shadows circling his eyes. Sarah could see he would not be able to stand up under such pressure for much longer. He needed food and rest just as much as his patients. Bailey caught the sympathetic look in her eyes, and smiled weakly. "What have you got in your bag?"

Sarah returned his smile warmly. "Home grown vegetables. Some potatoes and carrots, a few parsnips and a turnip or two. Now, it's quiet here for the moment, so you get a little sleep while I make some broth. I see the fire is still burning. I'm sure I'll be able to find plates and saucepans somewhere. Some hot broth will do the patients, and you, the world of good."

Charles Bailey laughed. "Are you sure you're only a nursing auxiliary and not a matron?!"

"Oh, I'm sorry. My mum always says I'm too bossy." Sarah joined in the laughter. "Now get some rest."

"Thank you, Miss Porter." He ran a hand over the rough stubble on his chin. "If one of my patients needs me, you will wake me, won't you?"

Sarah nodded. "Of course." Turning towards the school kitchen she hurried off. Bailey found a spare blanket and settled down in a corner to sleep.

The morning passed swiftly. While Sarah prepared the broth, the two nurses made sure that the injured were comfortable, and then helped her to feed them. After clearing up the dirty dishes Sarah collected more roof timbers for the fire. Then she woke Bailey with a bowl of broth.

"Here, eat this."

He rubbed his reddened eyes. He was obviously still tired but the edge of exhaustion had left him and he looked able to face the trials ahead once more.

"What time is it?" He spooned broth into his mouth, and smiled appreciatively. "This is good."

"It's just after one."

He looked surprised. "I must have slept longer than I thought. Are the patients all right?"

Sarah nodded. "So far there seems to be little infection in their wounds, but we could certainly use some pain killers."

Bailey nodded. "I wonder if any of the hospitals are undamaged? There's the danger of pneumonia if they stay here much longer."

Sarah shrugged

"It's still chaos out there. Haven't you heard from your messenger to the Town Hall yet?"

Bailey shook his head and stretched. "I'm sure we'll hear something soon. Now, I think I'll go and take a look at my patients."

It was late in the afternoon when the messenger finally returned. To their immense relief, he had brought some medical supplies with him.

"It's a real mess out there. There was no organisation at the Hall 'till the army arrived this morning. They sent these medical supplies. They said the first priority will be to clear the roads to this school, and other make-shift hospitals so the wounded can be got out of the city. Then they can have proper treatment." He shook his head sadly. "The hospitals here are all unusable."

Sarah was shocked by his words. Things were obviously much worse than she had feared." How are we going to manage?"

The young man smiled reassuringly. "So far six hundred soldiers have been drafted in, to help with demolition, clearing streets and keeping order. There are more to come, and they're talking about releasing building workers from the army to help."

"What about food?" Bailey glanced around the room as he spoke. "We've got to feed these people somehow."

"Army field kitchens have been set up in some areas, and the WVS are moving in today to provide what food and help they can. Somehow they'll manage to let us know where the kitchens are. Any shops that have still got undamaged food are to sell as normal, but not to demand to see ration books. At least half of them must be missing. There's been a special issue of tinned corned beef from the Ministry of Food. As I was there on behalf of the wounded, we got one of the first consignments."

He opened a sack at his feet to produce his treasure and Bailey relaxed visibly.

"With this, and the medical supplies you brought, we should be able to hold out, as long as we can keep the patients warm."

40

It was three days before the army finally managed to evacuate the school building, three long cold days and even colder nights, in which they lost three more of the wounded. As Sarah watched the last ambulance pull away she sighed gratefully. With proper care and attention, all those who had left the school alive should survive.

"What will you do now?"

Sarah turned to Bailey. "I suppose I'll go back to Heronfield. I've already extended my leave for far too long without permission. I hope I don't get into trouble."

Bailey smiled. "I'm sure you won't, when they find out what you've been doing for the last four days." He perused her thoughtfully for a moment. "Do you intend to continue with nursing after the war? You seem supremely adapted to the job."

Sarah nodded. "I hope to study once this is all over. When I'm looking after ill people I really feel useful. You do understand, don't you?"

Bailey nodded. "Indeed I do. Thank you for all your hard work over the last few days. It's been invaluable." He held out his hand. "Take care of yourself, Miss Porter."

Sarah took his hand, smiling warmly. "Thank you Dr. Bailey. Goodbye."

"Goodbye, my dear."

Sarah began to make her way home. The streets were cleared now and a few army vehicles moved back and forth, though the shells of houses looking down upon her deflated Sarah's spirits. She realised that she would be glad to get back to the clean fresh air of the countryside. Heronfield seemed to beckon her from the destruction, back to a place where she could forget for a while the pain and suffering she had seen over the last few days. The country estate seemed to call her weary body, and she knew it was her duty to return, but her heart was still full of fears for Joe's safety. It was now five days since the bombing, and Sarah had no news of him. She was beginning to fear the worst. She wanted desperately to remain until she knew for certain what had happened to him. Suddenly Sarah turned away from her home and made her way towards the city centre and the Cathedral. She could not face leaving without seeing its beautiful soaring towers once more. Her step lightened. She remembered how she had walked to the cathedral in the summer, with Joe by her side. It was a place of happy memories, and she knew that seeing it again would fortify her for the days ahead. She was not prepared for the sight that met her eyes as she turned the final corner.

The beautiful walls lay in heaps upon the ground. The delicate strained glass of the windows lay shattered amongst the rubble. At one end part of the wall still stood forlornly. It was a disaster, and Sarah's heart sank. It was as though all her hopes for the future lay here in the midst of the shattered symbol of her city. She was unable to halt the tears. Then Sarah's eyes were drawn to where the altar, which had served so many worshippers over the centuries, now stood open to the elements. Someone had taken two charred and blackened timbers from the ruins of God's house, and placed them in the shape of a cross, a symbol of love and forgiveness. Opposite the cross, the tower stood alone, like a finger pointing through the clouds to the abodes above. Sarah saw that there was hope for the future. The cross and the tower of the ruined cathedral lightened her heart, and with a firm resolve to look to the future with hope, she dried her tears. Coventry would rise again from the ashes. One day, the cathedral would rise again too.

With lightened step Sarah turned for home.

It was getting dark when Sarah opened the door and pulled back the blackout curtain. "Mum! I'm home!"

A smiling Alice came out of the kitchen with a cup of tea in her hand. "I've just made this dear. Drink it, it will do you good."

Sarah hung up her coat and reached for the cup. "They moved the wounded out today, so I'm going back to Heronfield tomorrow." She sipped the tea. "I've already overstayed my leave, and they'll be worried about me." Her laugh was harsh, with a tense edge which caused Alice to frown in concern. "That's if I'm not on report for overstaying my leave!"

Alice reached out an arm and hugged her daughter. She led her down the hallway to the kitchen where she could rest.

Sarah focussed her concern for those she loved on her mother, trying to put her fears for Joe to the back of her mind.

"You'll be all right, won't you, Mum?"

"Of course I will. I've been all right so far, haven't I?"

Sarah nodded. "Yes, you've done well."

Sarah heard the front door opening and closing, but did not look round. It was probably only Mr. and Mrs. Cook returning after trying to salvage more clothes from their home next door. Sarah's heart was heavy, and she sank wearily into the inviting chair.

"I'm really worried about Joe, Mum. I should have heard from him by now."

Alice knew what her daughter was going through. She had suffered in the same way during the last war, and she knew there was little she could do or say to help.

"He'll be all right, love. I'm sure of it."

Sarah sighed deeply. "I hope you're right. If ..." she paused, "...when you see him, will you tell him that I stayed as long as I could? And that I love him and miss him very much?"

"Why don't you tell me yourself?"

Sarah leapt to her feet and turned towards the kitchen door where a dishevelled, bloodstained young man smiled wearily at her.

"Joe! Oh Joe! I've been so worried!"

She threw herself into his open arms and hugged him tightly as though afraid that it might all be a dream and he would disappear if she was foolish enough to let him go.

"I'm sorry, Sarah." Joe bent to kiss her tear-stained cheeks. "I wanted to come to see you, but I had to stay and help. We're almost certain that no-one is still buried alive, so I've taken time off." He hugged her tightly. "I've been worried about you too. You can't believe how difficult it's been for me not to drop everything and come rushing over here."

Sarah smiled up at him. "It doesn't matter Joe. Nothing matters at the moment. I'm just so relieved to see you safe and sound."

As Joe leant down and gently kissed Sarah on the lips, Alice left the kitchen, quietly closing the door behind her, her eyes bright with tears of happiness.

41

As Sarah turned through the gate, Heronfield House held out welcoming arms towards her. Its walls were a dusty yellow in the autumn sunlight. The trees which bordered the drive were a riot of colour, red and gold, russet and brown. The scene was breathtaking, like a picture in a fairytale book, and Sarah realised just how much she had come to love the countryside. Maybe Joe would be willing to move out into a country village, once the war was over.

As she walked up the drive, gravel crunching underfoot, Sarah's features were wreathed in a broad smile. Alice and Joe were safe and she was returning to work; she could not have been happier.

"Sarah? Sarah! Is it really you?"

Sarah turned at the sound of the voice just in time to see Jane burst from the trees and run towards her. Sarah smiled. "Yes. It's me."

Jane hugged her friend enthusiastically. "You don't know how worried we've all been! When we heard about the raid on Coventry and then heard nothing from you we feared the worst. How bad was it?"

Sarah gave an involuntary shiver. "It was awful. Like the description of hell I used to hear at Sunday school." She smiled sadly. "I'm sorry you were worried, but there was no way I could get in touch with you. There are still no telephone lines."

"What have you been doing since the raid?"

"Working. We set up a makeshift hospital in the local school. There were no windows, no heating, and no medical supplies." She closed her eyes but the images her words had conjured up did not leave her. "Can you imagine what it was like?"

Jane shuddered. "No. And I don't want to have to find out, either."

The two girls turned and walked, arm in arm, towards the big house.

"Am I in trouble for not coming back when I should have?"

Jane laughed. "No, you're not in trouble. Everyone knew that if you hadn't come back it was because you were needed there." She did not add 'or dead' but that was what she had been thinking for the last week. The best way to cope, she thought, was to act as though the whole thing had never happened.

"Are you and Joe still going strong?"

Sarah nodded. "As strong as ever."

Jane laughed and Sarah caught a hint of mischief in her voice.

"All right, what's so funny about me and Joe?"

"It's not you two. It's Tony Kemshall."

"Is he back again?"

Jane nodded, still grinning broadly.

"Not only is he back, but he's been up to the house every day to see if we've had any news of you!"

Sarah groaned and lowered her head but not before Jane saw the hint of a blush stain her cheeks.

"You still think he's soft on me, don't you?"

"Of course." Jane's voice was full of mischief. "Why else would he be so worried about you?"

'Why indeed?' thought Sarah, but said instead "We're just good friends, that's all."

They reached the steps leading up to the front entrance to the house. As they made their way up, the door opened and a figure in nurse's uniform stepped out.

"Sarah Porter! I'm so glad to see you!"

Sarah smiled. "And I'm glad to be back, Sister Freeman."

As she entered the hall, engulfed by the familiar smell of disinfectant. Sarah felt as though she had come home.

It was a cold day. The frost which had rimed the windowpane when Sarah arose still patterned the grass when she gazed out of the window at lunchtime. She had been back at Heronfield for just one day, yet was already fully engrossed in her routine. She was glad to be part of the team once more. She looked across at the patients in her ward, mainly burns cases from the RAF. They had all had lunch and were as comfortable as could be expected, so she smiled at them gaily as she made her way over to the door.

"I'm off for my lunch now. See you all in an hour."

Those who were well enough waved or called after her. Others lay still upon their beds, seeming to see and hear nothing. Sarah made her way down to lunch, a thick vegetable soup with freshly baked bread, which she ate quickly before returning to her room. Jane was stretched out on her bed as Sarah walked in, chin on hand and book on the pillow in front of her. Sarah reached down her coat, scarf and gloves.

"I think I'll go out for a walk. Are you coming?"

Jane rolled over onto her back. "Are you joking? It's freezing out there!"

Sarah laughed. "Being home again made me realise just how much I've grown to love trees and open spaces. Besides, the fresh air will do me good!"

"Rather you than me." Jane stretched lazily. "I don't know where you get your energy from. We have to be back on the wards in less than an hour."

"In that case I'll be off. See you later."

Sarah left the room and went down the back stairs to a side door that opened into a small kitchen garden. The air was crisp and clear, knifing her lungs as she breathed deeply. The cold air clearing her head of the woolly feeling that a morning on the wards so often left her with. She turned left and made her way beneath the bare branches of some apple trees in the small orchard. One or two wizened fruits still clung to the topmost branches. She stopped to watch the starlings pecking hungrily at them, their iridescent feathers shinning in the weak sunlight.

"They'll be even hungrier by the end of the winter."

Sarah recognised the voice but did not turn; instead she continued to watch the birds.

"You don't know how lucky you are to have grown up here with the opportunity to watch birds like this. In Coventry we only get sparrows and pigeons!"

"Are there many of them left?" Tony moved round to stand beside Sarah as he spoke. "I hear it's pretty bad up there."

"There's not much of Coventry left, let alone its bird life." Sarah tried to keep her voice light, but the experiences of the last week still clung heavily to her. Tony noticed her tension and spoke softly.

"I was worried about you. We all were."

Images of devastated buildings and shattered lives crowded her mind, and Sarah shook her head sadly.

"You can't imagine what it was like. So much destruction, so little we could do to help." She shivered. "No one can know what it felt like."

Tony laid a comforting hand on her arm. "I believe I can. Don't forget I was at Dunkirk."

Sarah turned to face him. "I had forgotten. I'm sorry. You know as much about bombing, and the pain and misery it brings, as I do."

"I also know that the images which haunt you will recede in time. You won't forget, but you will be able to think about it without breaking into a cold sweat."

"You do understand." Sarah found that sharing her feelings with someone who had been through something similar helped enormously. The relief was like the snapping of a taut wire. "Thank you for your concern. I hear you were asking about me while I was away." She could still feel his hand on her arm. Not knowing how to pull away without appearing rude, she was glad the cold air had put some colour into her cheeks so that Tony would not see her blushing.

"It's the same concern I'd feel for any friend in a similar situation." Tony smiled and removed his hand. "I was so relieved when I went up to the house yesterday and they said that you were back, safe and sound." He frowned. "They couldn't tell me much about what happened. What about your mother? Is she all right?"

Sarah nodded. "Yes, she's fine. Our house only had superficial damage, so she's taken in some of the neighbours."

"I'm so glad. What about Joe?"

Sarah smiled brightly, her whole face lighting up and her eyes sparkling. With a lurching feeling inside Tony thought 'this is surely the look of a woman in love.' His heart ached, because the smile was not for him.

"Yes, Joe's all right. He's helping to clear the bomb damage. It will be months before his factory is back in production again."

"I'm glad everything turned out so well for you. I can see how much Joe means to you, and how awful it would have been if he had been...injured."

"You were going to say 'killed' weren't you?" Sarah smiled sadly. "I used to be thankful that he had been found unfit for active service, but this last week has taught me that it doesn't matter who or where you are, or what you are doing, this dreadful war can bring death to you, at any place and any time."

Tony took her elbow and turned her back towards the house.

"Don't let that get you down, Sarah. We can't live our lives worrying about what might happen tomorrow. Let's just enjoy today."

"You're right." Sarah smiled. "I'm glad to have you for a friend, you always help me to get things back into perspective."

With a quick wave Sarah darted off.

"'Bye Tony. And thanks!"

"Bye."

She slipped in through the side door, closing it quickly behind her to keep out the cold November air. With a sigh Tony turned away and made his solitary way back through the orchard and on down to the river, which is where he had been heading when he had first noticed Sarah. He could see that she was glad of his friendship, and to be honest he was glad to have her friendship too, but what he really wanted was something much deeper, something which she was not prepared to give to him for from the smile which had lit her face when he had mentioned Joe he knew that she had already promised it to someone else.

126

42

The weeks passed by, and 1940, the first full year of what looked like being a long war, was drawing to a close. The wards at Heronfield House were no longer full. As those convalescing from wounds received earlier in the year went home there were fewer to take their place. But this did not result in a feeling of over optimism amongst the staff; they knew it was only the calm before the storm. Britain was an island under siege. The help that people had hoped would come from the rest of the world, notably America, had not materialised. Hitler's armies were poised on the French side of the Channel, ready to invade in the new year, while Britain was frantically training the men drafted into the army to replace the heavy losses suffered at Dunkirk. Hitler's U-Boats patrolled the waters of the Atlantic making any trading with the outside world hazardous. Supplies of imported luxury items were running low. Rationing had hit people hard, but they had endured in the hope of a swift end to the war. Now the war looked set to continue for some years, if Britain was not overrun in the near future, and the prospect of more severe rationing loomed ominously on the horizon.

Throughout the latter part of the year Tony spent much of his time away from home. His basic training was complete, but he had a number of other courses to attend in the New Year. He was left with time on his hands and no idea what to do with it. He would have liked to have remained at home, but he had to keep up the appearance of working for the Ministry of Economic Warfare. He moved around the country from city to city, town to town, always visiting places with munitions factories so that his family would really think that he was working. He spent nights in cheap hotels and days walking unfamiliar streets in the cold winter wind. He realised that this strange way of life was good for him. He was getting used to being alone, to wandering around strange places looking as though he knew where he was going and what he was doing, to living a lie. The experience would be invaluable to him when he finally reached occupied France.

Tony returned home each weekend, eager to see Sarah and to spend time with his mother. Now David was dead, she placed all her hopes for the future in him. Tony would not have returned so often if it were not for his mother. The situation with his father was growing more strained all the time. Sir Michael had not spoken to him on his last two visits, so Tony approached the Lodge with some trepidation on the morning of the second Saturday in December. He opened the front door to find his mother waiting for him in the hall. She had obviously been watching for him from the window. With a warm smile, Louise hugged her son.

"Hello, mon cher."

Tony kissed her forehead. "Hello Mamma. You're looking well. How is Grandmamma?"

Louise shook her head sadly. "She misses her home. She hates the thought of those Nazis going through her things. But she is well."

Tony nodded. "And Dad?"

Louise's eyes clouded. "Still the same. Do not expect too much from him, mon cher. He is finding it hard to cope with the loss of David."

"We all are, Mamma."

"But at least we talk about it. Your father is a typical English gentleman, and will not speak of such deep feelings. It is hard for him."

"Not as hard as he finds it to accept my work."

Louise laid a restraining hand on his arm. "Hush, mon cher. Try not to talk about it. Now, go and tidy up. Lunch is almost ready."

Tony joined his parents in the dining room some fifteen minutes later. He was determined to make an effort to get on better terms with his father over the weekend, but it was not easy. As they ate, Louise and Sir Michael talked of everyday things. Louise talked with Tony about the approaching festive season, but not once did Sir Michael direct a remark to his son. As the soup bowls were cleared away and the bowl of fruit, mainly apples from their own orchard, was placed on the table for dessert, Sir Michael said something which grabbed Tony's attention.

"Did you know that one of the auxiliaries up at the House was in Coventry during the bombing?"

"Yes, mon cher."

"I hear she worked in a makeshift hospital until things got sorted out. The doctor she worked under has written to the doctor here to say how well she did. He suggests that she should train to be a proper nurse if the opportunity arises."

Tony took a deep breath. This seemed an ideal opportunity to try to improve things with his father. "She is to be congratulated. I'm sure she deserves the praise."

Sir Michael threw a withering look at his son. "Yes, she knew where her duty lay, and she was not afraid to carry it out."

Tony clenched his fists beneath the table in an attempt to control his temper.

"It's only the medical staff, along with the Air Force and Navy, who can do their bit at the moment. Our ordinary soldiers are stuck in their camps waiting for a chance to fight. They are bored while at least I'm occupied in useful war work."

Sir Michaels face reddened. "But when the time comes they'll fight for their country, not like you."

"But what will they fight with, Father? How will they get their weapons, if people like me don't do our jobs?"

"People like you should be at the forefront of the battle!"

"I'm sure Mamma does not agree. She sees the value of my work, and she has already lost one son. Do you want her to lose the other as well?" Too late he saw the shake of Louise's head and the rising anger in his father's eyes.

"How dare you, boy! How dare you speak of your brother and yourself in the same breath! He was a hero and you...you..."

"And I am a coward."

Tony rose from the table, his anger draining from him as he realised the futility of any attempt on his part to rectify the situation with his father. With a sad, weary look he leant down and kissed his mother's forehead.

"I'm sorry, Mamma. I think I'll go up and see Grandmamma."

As the door closed softly behind her son Louise turned angrily towards her husband.

"Michael! Was that necessary? The boy has already been in action at Dunkirk. The officers feel he is best suited to his present job. As he says, at least he is doing something. Why can you not accept that his work is valuable?"

"Because in the last war men of his age, and younger, died in the mud and filth of the trenches so that he could grow up in the privileged surroundings he has enjoyed. He owes them.."

"He is paying that debt in the best way he knows how!"

"Is he?"

"Would you be happier if he were to die?" Louise looked across at her husband in silence for a moment, then threw up her hands in exasperation.

"Oh Michael, please be careful. I have already lost one son, do not drive the other away so that he is lost to me too."

Seeing the tears in his wife's eyes, feeling the same deep hurt at the loss of their son, Sir Michael rose and went round the table. Kneeling beside the woman he had met while fighting in the last war, he took her in his arms and kissed her ,hair.

"Forgive me my darling. I suppose times have changed, and I must change with them. I'll try to be kinder to Tony." He sighed deeply. "I only wish I could know for certain that he's not a coward."

Louise lifted her tear stained face to look deep into his eyes. "He is your son, Michael. He cannot be a coward."

43

Christmas approached rapidly. A tree was brought up to the big house by Sir Michael, who helped to set it up in the main hallway. Boxes of decorations were brought down from the attic. Most were used to brighten the wards, while Sir Michael took a few down to the Lodge. He did not really feel like celebrating Christmas this year, but he knew he must go through the motions for the rest of the family. Some of the nursing staff had been given two days leave, but the remainder were to stay on. Their celebrations would begin at the dance in Marlborough on Christmas Eve, and continue with dinner at the hospital with all the patients. With rationing, Christmas dinner would not be the same as in pre-war years, but the kitchen staff were working hard to make it a memorable one.

Christmas Eve dawned clear and bright, and an air of expectation pervaded the whole hospital. The rounds were completed early and the auxiliary staff had completed their work once dinner had been served to the patients and cleared away. All that remained was to serve tea to the patients later in the afternoon, then the women would be free to go into Marlborough. The afternoon was spent bathing, washing hair, beautifying, for the chance to go to a party was rare in the secluded precincts of Heronfield House.

Sarah was sitting in front of the mirror. She smiled wistfully. How she wished she could be back in Coventry for the next few days. She had never been away from home at Christmas before. She would miss the midnight service followed by a glass of sherry before bed; then the excitement of opening presents under the tree after breakfast. She was glad that Mr. and Mrs. Cook would be with her mother. She would hate Alice to be alone on Christmas Day. Sarah began to brush her hair vigorously. She knew that she would miss seeing Joe most of all.

The door opened and Jane entered, quilted housecoat tied tightly around her waist and hair wrapped in a towel.

"I can't wait to get to the dance." She waltzed excitedly across the room as she spoke. "I hope there are plenty of handsome young men there."

Sarah laughed. "None of them will dance with you if you look like that!"

Jane sat down on the bed and began to towel her hair dry. "You wait till you see me tonight! They won't be able to resist me!"

"I hope so. Then at least you'll have a happy Christmas."

Jane stopped towelling her hair and gazed thoughtfully at her roommate. "Won't you?"

Sarah shrugged and smiled. "I suppose so. It's just that I'll miss Mum, and Joe."

"There'll be so much going on here, you won't have time to be homesick."

Sarah put down her hairbrush and made her way over to the wardrobe. She took out the red dress she intended to wear, and hung it on the back of the door to let the creases fall out. There was a knock on the other side of the door, which startled Sarah and made Jane laugh.

"Who is it?"

"It's Carol. Is Sarah there?"

"Yes. Come in," Sarah replied. She opened the door to the young nurse who came in, smiling broadly.

"There's someone to see you. I think he's come down from Coventry."

Sarah's eyes widened in surprise. "Joe? Joe!" She turned and rushed over to Jane. "It's Joe!"

Jane laughed. "I'd gathered that! Now get down there before he goes back to Coventry!"

As Sarah rushed from the room, Jane smiled mischievously at Carol.

"It must be love!"

Sarah stopped at the head of the staircase and looked down into the hall. She knew it was a moment that she would remember for the rest of her life. The tree was bright with baubles twinkling merrily beneath the lights, holly hung above the mirrors and picture frames, streamers hung from the ceiling. In the midst of it all, standing straight and tall beside the green, silver and gold of the tree, was Joe. Smiling radiantly Sarah made her way down the stairs and into his arms.

"Joe! It's so good to see you! What are you doing here?"

Joe smiled down at the girl in his arms. Her happiness radiated from her like the light from a candle in a darkened room. He felt a surge of pride that she was his.

"I couldn't face the thought of Christmas without seeing you, so I came down. I can't stop long, the last train leaves at six o'clock."

"But that only gives us an hour or so!"

"Then let's not waste it. Can you get away?" Sarah nodded. "Then get your coat and let's go for a walk."

Sarah rushed upstairs for her coat, and was back in minutes. Breathlessly she took Joe by the hand and led him out of the house and down the gravel drive.

"You didn't tell me Heronfield House was so big and beautiful."

Sarah smiled. "It's another world, isn't it." They passed the lodge as she spoke. "The Kemshall family are living in the lodge for the duration. It must be quite a change for them."

The two young people were so engrossed in each other that they did not see Tony Kemshall, who stood a little way from the drive and watched them walk out through the big wrought iron gates, a frown furrowing his brow as he realized that his plans for the day had suddenly disrupted by the appearance of his rival.

Sarah and Joe walked slowly down the road going nowhere in particular, just glad to be together.

Sarah sighed happily. "This is one Christmas I'll never forget."

Joe stopped walking. They were beneath the spreading branches of a chestnut tree, bare now in the winter sunlight.

"Perhaps I can give you another reason to remember today." Joe reached a hand into his coat pocket. "I realised during the bombing that life wouldn't be worth living for me if you weren't there to share it." He took a small blue velvet box from his pocket and opened it. Sarah could see the ring nestled inside, a diamond shining brightly. "Would you do me the honour of becoming my wife?"

Sarah said nothing. Her eyes were fixed on the ring, her throat constricted by emotion.

"You don't have to answer me now. You can think about it, and give me your answer when I next see you."

"Oh, Joe." Sarah's voice caught in her throat. "I don't need to think about it. You know I love you. I can't think of anything I'd like more than to be your wife."

Joe smiled happily as he took the ring from the box and placed it on Sarah's finger.

"Oh, it fits perfectly!"

Joe grinned.

"I thought it would. I asked your mother what your ring size was when I told her I was coming down. She took a guess and seems to have got it right!"

As he took Sarah in his arms and placed his lips on hers Sarah thought that her heart would burst with happiness.

Joe left Sarah at the gates to Heronfield House. She watched him walk away towards his bus to Marlborough, where he would catch the train to Coventry. With a quick glance at her watch she realised she was late and rushed inside to serve tea to the patients. Sarah worked in a dream, her actions purely mechanical as her hands passed out plates and cups. Though she spoke cheerfully to the patients, her thoughts were not with them but many miles away. She was going to marry Joe! She had known for some time that Joe was the only man for her and she had thought he felt the same. This confirmed it. The war seemed so far away, almost insignificant as her brain raced with ideas for the wedding and plans for the future. Being Joe's fiancée gave her a different perspective on the conflict. No longer was it a war that blocked out all normality in life, but something which infringed on life for a time. It would eventually go away, to leave her and Joe to enjoy life as any young married couple should. The time seemed to fly by, and Sarah soon found herself back in her room sitting once again in front of the mirror, gazing at her reflection and contemplating the rosy future which lay ahead of her.

The door opened and Jane came in. "Has Joe gone already?" she asked in surprise.

Sarah nodded dreamily. "Mmmm. He had to get the last train back to Coventry."

"It was hardly worth him coming so far for such a short visit."

Sarah smiled happily. "Oh yes it was!"

She held out her left hand. Jane gasped.

"Sarah! Is that an engagement ring? Of course it is! Oh, how wonderful!" She hugged her friend. "I'm so happy for you. This is certainly one Christmas you won't forget in a hurry!"

Sarah laughed. "I'll never forget it! Now, come on and let's get ready. We have a party to go to!"

44

The trip into Marlborough and the early part of the dance passed in a whirl for Sarah. Her friends and colleagues at the hospital were full of congratulations and she had danced with almost every young man at the party. Sarah had never been happier.

Tony came late to the dance. He had wondered if it would not be better to stay away. He did not want to watch Sarah with Joe for the whole evening, but in the end he decided he would be even more depressed if he could not see her at all. So he took David's red sports car and drove to Marlborough. It seemed strange to be in the car without his brother, but Louise had said that she was sure David would have wanted him to have it. Reluctantly, he had accepted the gift, wishing David were there and there was no gift to give. He felt conspicuous and alone as he walked into the hall. It was a whirl of swirling colours. Couples danced energetically to the band playing the latest dance tunes. Some people stood at the refreshments table, while others admired the huge Christmas tree. He stood quietly by the door watching the festivities, and it was some time before he noticed Sarah sitting alone at a table. His eyes widened with surprise to see her unaccompanied, but he soon had his feelings under control and made his way across to join her. Sarah's thoughts were miles away, reliving the time she had spent with Joe that afternoon. She jumped when she felt a hand upon her shoulder.

"Merry Christmas, Sarah."

As she turned in her chair and looked up at him, Tony had never seen her looking so beautiful.

"Hello, Tony. Merry Christmas."

"Are you alone? I thought I saw you with a young man this afternoon. I assumed it was this Joe you've told me so much about."

Sarah smiled radiantly at him. "Yes, it was. But he's already gone back to Coventry."

Tony smiled as he envisaged the evening stretching before them. If he could only spend time with her, maybe she would see how much he cared and choose him instead of Joe.

"Would you like to dance?"

Sarah nodded, and Tony's heart was thumping as he led her onto the floor. It felt so good to hold her in his arms. They seemed to move together as one, as though they were made for each other. The fresh, clean scent of her hair intoxicated him, and he wished the night could last forever.

"Did Joe bring a Christmas present from your mother?"

Sarah shook her head. "No he only decided yesterday that he'd come down, so Mum had already posted my present. But Joe did bring me something."

"Oh?"

Sarah stopped dancing and held out her left hand excitedly.

Tony saw the ring and knew he had lost her. He felt the blood rush from his face, and his breath catch in his throat. He forced himself to smile. Hiding his dismay as best he could, he took her hand in his.

"Congratulations. I can see you couldn't be happier." He swallowed hard, then continued. "I wish you and Joe every happiness. You deserve it."

"Thank you, Tony." Sarah tipped her head to one side. "Are you all right? You seem a little unhappy."

A little unhappy! Tony almost laughed at the understatement, but there was no way he could explain his feeling to her. He shrugged his shoulders.

"I suppose it's because this is the first Christmas I'll spend without David," he half lied.

"I'm sorry, Tony. I'm so engrossed in my own happiness that I'd forgotten how you must be feeling."

"There's no need to apologise. Now, let me congratulate you properly."

As the dancers whirled about them Tony leant down. He kissed Sarah on the lips for the first and, he assumed, the last time in his life. It was a bittersweet experience, a gentle kiss, soft and lingering. A kiss to lock away in his memory and cherish forever.

JANUARY - APRIL 1941

45

The war was not waged solely in the skies above Britain. Air units had been deployed to mainland Greece during the latter half of 1940, along with ground troops to Crete and some of the Aegean Islands. On the night of 11th November, as Sarah was preparing to go on leave to a still recognisable Coventry, a Royal Naval Task Force from the aircraft carrier Illustrious sank three battleships at their moorings with a surprise attack on the Italian base at Taranto. On 9th December General Wavell launched a counter-offensive against the Italian army in North Africa which was so successful that in three days they had captured thirty-eight thousand Italians, with the loss of only six hundred and twenty-four British and Indians killed and wounded. The Army of the Nile continued to advance. Tobruk fell to them on 21st January 1941, yielding another twenty five thousand prisoners and providing an essential supply port for the army. The dawn of 1941 brought with it an optimism for the British which had been lacking during the long, dark months of 1940. If the Italians could be pushed back so swiftly in North Africa, maybe the Germans could also be held and repulsed in Europe. No one had yet heard the names of Rommel and the Afrikakorps.

46

It was at the end of a cold February that Tony Kemshall reported to S7533 Altrincham for parachute training. He knew that, for him, this would be the most difficult part of his training so far. Each time he thought of going up in a plane his mind was filled with images of David, with memories of his love of flying and of how flying had led to his death. Now he was to get into a plane and face the hazardous skies which killed his brother. Tony was not afraid of jumping from the plane. He was sure his training would enable him to cope with that. It was the thought of flying itself that made his throat go dry and his hands break out in a clammy sweat. He knew he would have to overcome this irrational fear if he was ever to qualify to become an agent in France. Tony took a deep breath on his first morning at Altrincham and joined his comrades on the airfield.

"I know you're here to learn how to jump out of a plane," Sergeant Keegan began, "but I thought we'd spend this morning looking at some of the aircraft from which you won't be jumping." He smiled at their puzzled faces, and led the group of ten men and three women across the airfield in the direction of two light aircraft.

"Our first agents into France will jump blind so to speak. That means that there will be no Reception Committee for them, because we don't have good enough contact with the Resistance. It will be their job to make this contact, so that later agents can be met as soon as they hit the ground and taken straight to a safe house. Much better than wandering about in the dark, not quite knowing where you are."

Sergeant Keegan stopped beside a small, sturdy, high wing monoplane. "This is a Lysander." He placed a hand firmly on the fuselage. "We've been experimenting with it, to see if it's possible to land agents rather than making them jump. Our tests have proved it to be very good, so once the Reception Committees are set up you could actually find yourself landing on French soil in one of these."

Tony looked the plane over doubtfully. "It seems rather small."

"That's its major asset. As you can see it has a small front cockpit for the pilot. There's no room for a navigator, so that job falls to the pilot as well. This ladder here," he placed his hand on the rung of a small ladder fixed to the fuselage, "leads up to the second cockpit. It holds two passengers side by side facing aft. At a pinch it will hold three or, in a crisis, four."

"Won't that limit its range?"

Keegan nodded at the young man who had spoken. "That's right, but if your cover has been blown and the Gestapo are hot on your tail, you'll take off immediately and leave the worrying about where you're going to land till later."

"What's its range?" asked Tony.

""With an extra tank fitted it can cover seven hundred miles. That means that if you take off from Tangmere, we could just about get you to Lyons."

"What about landing?" asked one of the women.

"The Lysander can land and take off in three or four hundred yards of flat grass or clover. As agents will be going in at night, the field will need lights. That's why the Reception Committee is so important, and why the first agents will have to jump."

Tony compared the plane to the Spitfire David had flown. It was much slower, not as sleek in its lines, but then it was made to perform a different task. He supposed the difference was something like that between a racehorse and the horse which pulled the milk cart. With the picture of a Spitfire in his mind, a sudden thought struck Tony. "What about armaments?"

"It's unarmed, but the pilot carries a pistol."

"She can't outrun a Messerschmitt?"

Keegan shook his head. No one spoke as they absorbed the fact that if they were spotted by the enemy, they were very unlikely to survive.

"Right, come on." Keegan broke their reverie. "Let's get this tour over with, then we can get down to some real training."

For two days the agents-to-be practiced jumping through a hole in the fuselage of a crashed plane until it was second nature to them. They would not be allowed to make a jump from the air until they could exit the plane without thinking - sit down, put your legs into the hole, watch for the red light to turn green, watch the dispatcher's arm sweep down as he shouts 'go', jump forward and spring to attention. Sergeant Keegan drummed the routine into them. Leap to attention immediately or you will be entangled in the cords of the parachute as it is opened, land with knees bent, and roll. Slowly but surely the trainees acquired the skills necessary to drop into enemy territory. Sergeant Keegan was finally satisfied with the results.

"After lunch tomorrow," he said with a broad grin "you'll make your first jump. Just to put you a little more at ease though, I'll take you over to Ringway in the morning."

Ringway held a large hangar in its centre and Keegan led the trainees towards it.

"When you jump," he said as he led them through the door, "you place your life in the hands of the person who packed your parachute." With a sweep of his arm, he indicated the huge interior of the hangar. There was row upon row of long tables, where women worked with intense concentration folding the yards of silk upon which men's lives would depend. Tony watched, fascinated, as the huge sheets of diaphanous white material were folded along with the lengths of cord, and packed into the small harness he would wear. It was an intricate job, and an important one, and Tony wondered at the weight of responsibility placed on the shoulders of the young packers. After watching for a time his eyes were drawn to words painted a yard high along both sides of the long walls

REMEMBER A MAN'S LIFE DEPENDS ON EVERY PARACHUTE YOU PACK

He smiled grimly. With a constant reminder like that, the women would make very few mistakes. Sergeant Keegan was right, watching a parachute being packed did instil confidence in you. Tony knew he would have no worries about jumping from a plane and depending on a parachute. His only fear was that he might not have the courage to go up in the plane in the first place.

A weak winter sun was shining as Tony made his way towards the Halifax waiting at the end of the runway. Its engines were already roaring. Tony licked his lips nervously as he approached the huge bulk of the plane. The other trainees were ahead of him, and he watched as they climbed aboard; he stood for a moment thinking about how the enemy had shot down David's Spitfire and wondering if they would attack this plane too. Sergeant Keegan leaned out of the plane.

"Come on, Kemshall. We're all waiting."

Tony took a deep breath and stepped closer. 'I'm just as likely to be killed on the ground as in the air' he mused. 'I'm just being silly.' Stiffening his spine, he climbed aboard and seated himself as the Halifax began to taxi down the runway. He had a sinking feeling in his stomach as the wheels lifted from the ground and they were airborne at last. It was a strange, though not unpleasant, sensation and Tony found himself beginning to relax. After all, if David had died in a car crash he would not be afraid to get into a car again, so there was no cause at all for his fear of flying. The plane climbed steadily then levelled off as it reached cruising altitude. Sergeant Keegan, dispatcher for the afternoon, rose to his feet.

"Right then, time to go." He smiled reassuringly at the nervous faces ranged before him. "There's nothing to worry about as long as you follow the routine we practiced when you jumped from the back of the moving truck. Just watch the light and don't worry. I promise you, you'll enjoy it."

All eyes were on the red light that burned above the door as the Halifax banked to the right and headed back towards the airfield. At a nod from Keegan, the trainees stood and attached their ripcords to the static line before shuffling over to the open door. The red light turned to green, and Keegan swept his arm down.

"Go!"

The first trainee jumped.

"Go! Go! Go!"

One more and it would be Tony's turn.

"Go!"

Tony found himself sitting in the open doorway, the wind whipping at him and trying to drag him out. Keegan swept his arm down.

"Go!"

Tony jumped, arms by his sides, legs straight. With a jerk the static line pulled his cord. He heard the 'whoosh' as his parachute pulled out above him. Then, with a sharp tug, the canopy was open and he found himself hanging in space. At last, Tony was able to look around him. It was breathtaking. Below him were the pale chutes of those who had jumped before him. Below them, way way below, were the fields and hedgerows of England, spread out like a patchwork quilt at his feet. Tony had the most glorious sensation of freedom, hanging between earth and sky with no sound but the wind in the flimsy silk above his head. Pulling on the lines, first one side and then the other, he experimented with manoeuvring in the air and found it surprisingly easy. Tony was swiftly approaching the airfield at Altrincham; with intense concentration he pulled the lines to steer himself towards his chosen landing site. As the earth drew closer his speed seemed to increase, though he knew this was only an illusion. Then he was almost down.

'Feet together' he thought as he crossed his arms on his chest and braced his lower legs together. Then he was down and rolling as Keegan had shown him, almost as though he had been doing it all his life. Seconds later he was on his feet, pulling the slowly deflating canopy towards himself. He turned a little to his left, a broad grin on his face as he watched the Senior Training Officer approaching.

"That was great!" he laughed. Perhaps being a spy would not be so bad after all.

47

Sarah returned to Coventry in March, four months after the devastating raid. As she made her way from the station towards her home the sight of the bomb sites depressed her. There was so much destruction that could not be made good until the war was ended, whenever that might be. From Alice's letters, Sarah knew a massive effort had been made to get the city's war industries running once again, but there were no resources available for rebuilding homes destroyed during the raid. As she approached her own front door, Sarah felt once again a great sense of relief that her mother still had a roof over her head. She opened the door to be greeted by the smell of cooking, and called out happily.

"Mum! I'm home!"

Alice came out of the kitchen, wiping her hands on her apron. "Hello love! It's good to see you again." She kissed her daughter on the cheek. "Now, let me have a look at the ring that Joe gave you. You won't believe how much I've been longing to see it."

Sarah held out her left hand, smiling.

"It's beautiful, dear! Now come into the kitchen and I'll make you a cup of tea."

Sarah hung up her coat and left her small bag in the hall. She hadn't brought much with her as she was due to return to Heronfield the following day. She made her way to the kitchen, where she sank happily into a chair at the table. She sniffed.

"Dinner smells nice."

"Rabbit stew. Joe will be joining us." She looked up at the clock. "In fact he should be here any time now."

"Great! I can't wait to see him!" Sarah perused her mother thoughtfully, she was looking a little pale and tired, not her usual robust self. "Are you all right, Mum? It must have been difficult for you over the last few months."

"Oh, I'm fine dear. Things aren't as bad as you might think. Those who've been injured are being treated under the new Emergency Hospital Scheme. Casualties of the raids are treated free, so that's a great weight off everyone's mind. Of course rationing is still making it difficult to get hold of some things, but I'm sure we'll cope."

There was a knock at the door and Sarah leapt to her feet, a radiant smile on her face.

"I'll get that, it's probably Joe!"

Within moments Sarah had opened the door and was in Joe's arms. They kissed for a long moment, the unspent passion of four months' separation lending a hunger to their embrace. Sarah felt as though she were being devoured by Joe's lips, and wanted the feeling to last forever. Joe's hand crept upwards until it was cupping her breast. His thumb brushed the hardened nipple and he groaned softly.

"I can't wait until we're married, darling. I want you so badly."

Sarah ran a hand through his hair as she pressed against him. "I know. I feel the same way too Joe, but it won't be long to wait now."

Joe pulled away, smiling. "I'll wait as long as you want me to, Sarah. You know you're the only one for me."

Sarah smiled, her love for Joe reflected in her eyes.

"It'll be worth waiting for. Now come on, Mum's cooking dinner."

The young couple walked hand in hand into the kitchen, where two cups of tea stood steaming on the table.

"Sit down and have a cup of tea. Dinner will be about half an hour."

Joe sat down opposite Sarah.

"How are you love?"

"I'm fine. I really enjoy my work, but I've missed you so much. How about you?"

"I'm fine too. We're making planes again at the factory, which I'm sure the RAF will be glad about. Most factories are working again now, but the new Lend-Lease system will be an enormous help to the war effort."

"Lend-Lease? I'm not sure I've heard about that." Alice stirred the stew as she spoke. "What does it mean?"

"Well, the Americans still won't join us in the war, but they've agreed to let us have some of the things we need - planes, tanks, guns and so on - on a Lend-Lease system. It means we get the goods now, but we don't have to pay for them until after the war.

"Well, at least they're doing something." Alice sniffed haughtily. "I suppose they'll 'sit on the sidelines until we have taken all of the fight out of the Germans, then come in at the last minute and try to take all of the glory. Just like they did last time."

Alice had never said anything, but Sarah was sure she blamed the Americans, in part at least, for the death of her husband. If the Americans had entered the war sooner it might have been much shorter and maybe Sarah's father would not have died. To get her mother's mind back onto a more pleasant tack, Sarah turned to Joe.

"How soon do you want to get married?"

Joe smiled. "As soon as possible."

"Good. How does June suit you?"

"Fine."

"June!" exclaimed Alice. "Can we be ready in time? I'll need to save up ration coupons for the cake and reception, as well as for the dress. And where will you live?"

"The reception should be easy." Sarah smiled. "We'll only have close family and friends, twenty people at most, just a small buffet. I'm sure people will understand, they may even contribute."

"But that's not the way it should be!"

"We're at war, Mum. I'd rather have a small wedding now, than have to wait who knows how many years till things are better."

Alice smiled indulgently at her daughter. "You're right, of course. But where will you live?"

Sarah shook her head. "I'm not sure. I don't suppose I'll be in Coventry much. Even if I was able to get back more frequently, there are no houses."

"If it's all right with you, we could live with my Mum." Joe said with a smile.

Sarah grinned happily. "I'll be happy anywhere as long as I'm with you."

"That's settled then." Alice put the onionskins into the bin for edible waste as she spoke. There were four bins in the kitchen now, the edible waste one for pig swill, bones (for glue), paper and cardboard, and one for tins and other metal (for planes and tanks). She turned to her daughter.

"Now, getting back to more mundane matters, can you set the table please, Sarah? Dinner's almost ready."

Sarah's twenty four hours in Coventry passed all too swiftly. Time spent alone with Alice was utilised in planning the wedding ceremony. The pattern for the dress was decided on, and Alice promised to find some suitable material. A guest list was made up, a menu for the buffet prepared, and a note made of how many ration coupons they would need. Time spent alone with Joe was passed walking in the unseasonable March sunshine. They wandered through the changed streets and parks of their childhood, yet even the destruction of her city could not dampen Sarah's happiness. Her life seemed to stretch before her like a welcoming, tree-lined avenue. Every step she took along the path would be in the company of the man she loved, the man who meant more to her than life itself. When the footsteps of the young couple finally brought them to the station and the train that would take Sarah south to Marlborough, they clung to each other for what seemed an eternity. Sarah finally boarded the train, knowing that the next time she saw Joe she would be walking down the aisle to take her place beside him for the rest of her life. The train began to move, slowly at first then with gathering speed, and Sarah leant from the window to watch the tall figure of her fiancé grow smaller as the platform receded. Finally he disappeared in a cloud of steam. Sarah stayed at the window for some time, before finally closing it and throwing herself into one of the empty seats. She was sad to be leaving Joe, but a smile of happiness lit her face as she thought of him. One day the war would be over, and they would never have to part again.

48

Heronfield House was busy during the month of March. While England waited for Hitler to launch his invasion across the English Channel, the Army of North Africa fought on. Some of the wounded found their way to the hospital in the country, away from the London Blitz and the bombing of other industrial sites, in the peace and quiet of the English countryside where wounds and shattered nerves could take the time to heal.

Sarah's professionalism increased, which did not go unnoticed by Sister Freeman who decided that once the war was over she would recommend Sarah for a course that would give her full nursing qualifications. Sarah was unaware of this as she tended her patients, wondering at the conditions they must have been serving in. Where their uniforms of short sleeved shirts and shorts had covered their skin they were as white as milk, but wherever it had been exposed to the burning African sun, their skin had taken on a rich golden hue. Sarah found herself dreaming of the places they must have been and the sights they must have seen.

Some of the patients in the hospital were not wounded, but suffering from unaccustomed illnesses picked up in North Africa. It was one such soldier who fired Sarah's dreams of travel as he lay weakly in his bed and talked of the historical places he had seen.

"We don't get much time to look around," he told Sarah, two weeks after her return from Coventry, "but I was lucky. I arrived in Egypt just before Christmas, before the big push started, and had three days before joining my unit. So I travelled up the Nile for a bit." His eyes held a dreamy, faraway look. "Those pyramids are really something, reaching right up into the sky. From a distance they look really smooth. But as you get closer you can see that they're really made up of steps, tapering up to the top."

"Did you walk out to them?"

The young soldier laughed. "No. Believe it or not I went on a camel. Me, an ordinary bloke who wouldn't normally get to leave England, and I've ridden a camel round the pyramids of Egypt!" He sighed happily, as though he could still feel the blazing sun burning his skin and taste the desert sand on his lips. "I saw some beautiful temples too. They look almost as though they were carved yesterday, but they're supposed to be thousands of years old." He shook his head in awe. "It makes you want to find out what made those old Egyptians tick, you know what I mean? Why did they build all of those beautiful places? I saw the Sphinx you know, a lion with a man's head. How am I supposed to know what that's all about?"

Sarah laughed. "This war has certainly broadened your horizons!"

The young solder laughed too. "It's certainly given me an interest in history! When I get out of here, I'm going to find out all I can about the Egyptians."

"Why wait till you get out? Heronfield House has a wonderful library. It's bound to have some books on Egypt."

The soldier frowned. "I doubt if they'll let me use such a posh library."

"Don't be silly!" laughed Sarah. "Sir Michael has turned over this whole house to you patients, and that includes the library. Do you want me to see what I can find for you?"

"Really?"

Sarah nodded.

"Oh, yes, please! That'll give me something interesting to do, until I'm back on my feet again."

"Right. Just wait here and I'll be back in a minute."

"I'm not going anywhere!"

Sarah made her way downstairs to the library, where she soon found a small section of books on ancient Egypt. Taking two down from the shelf, she went out into the hall. She was just about to start back up the stairs when she heard Sister Freeman calling her.

"Sarah! There's a phone call for you. You can take it in my office."

A phone call? Sarah frowned as she made her way into the office. Who could be calling her? A cold ball of icy dread settled in her stomach as she picked up the receiver.

"Hello? Sarah Porter here."

"Sarah, love. It's Mum."

"Mum! Are you all right?!"

"I'm fine, love." There was a pause. Finally, "It's Joe."

Sarah's heart seemed to stop beating. She closed her eyes and breathed deeply.

"What is it, Mum?"

"There was another raid last night. I'm afraid Joe's dead, love."

The books slipped unnoticed from Sarah's fingers, falling to the floor with a dull thud.

"Sarah? Are you still there? Sarah?"

But Sarah could not answer. Life had ended for her when it ended for Joe. What use were words now?

49

Sarah was granted compassionate leave, and took the first available train home to Coventry. As the train made its way north she looked out at the countryside and thought it strange that everything looked the same, that life went on as normal. For her, life stretched endlessly, hopelessly ahead. The crops, which were just beginning to show, would grow swiftly and ripen, the farmers busy producing food for a hungry country. Sarah comforted herself with the thought that she, too, had work to do. But what would she do when the war ended? What would she do to fill the long, empty years? She saw them stretching ahead of her, like the tracks for the train stretched ahead of them until they disappeared into the distance.

At last the train pulled into a Coventry station scarred from the bombing. Sarah alighted with her small case, and began to make her way through the familiar streets of her hometown. The trees which had survived the bombing were breaking into leaf, softening the harsh lines of the damaged buildings. The daffodils waving their heads bravely in sheltered corners reflected a lightening mood in the city as repairs were completed, work resumed and life began again. There was a feeling of optimism in the air. The people of the city had worked together and come through the terrible months after the November bombing, now they felt they could face anything that might confront them during the remainder of the war. Sarah felt none of this optimism. Her feelings were numbed, her emotions buried deep where they would not threaten to overwhelm her. She hardly saw the changes in the city. She walked numbly through the streets until she stood, finally, on her own doorstep. For a moment she waited with eyes closed, summoning all her self-control, before opening the door and stepping wearily into the hall. The door closed behind her, and she heard the scraping of a chair on the kitchen floor. Then Alice appeared in the doorway.

"Sarah?"

Sarah's bag slipped from her fingers and fell with a thump to the floor.

"Mum." It was little more than a whisper, and at last the tears came as Alice rushed forward to take her daughter in her arms.

"Sarah, love. I'm so sorry." She led her daughter into the kitchen, whispering words of comfort as she sat down beside her. She held her hand tightly as the silent tears fell. After a time Sarah was able to speak again.

"What happened, Mum?"

"He was on duty with the Home Guard. A raid came over at about ten o'clock. After he gave the warning, he went down to see what he could do to help. It was a small raid, only a dozen planes, and the area of destruction was small." Alice wiped the tears from her own cheeks. "It seems that he was helping to make a bomb-damaged house safe when he stood on a mine which had been dropped by a plane. They say he died instantly."

Sarah closed her eyes.

"He didn't suffer?"

"No."

There was silence for a moment, a silence laden with sadness. Then Sarah opened her eyes.

"Why, Mum? Why did Joe have to die?" She stood up and began to pace the kitchen. "I didn't believe it, to begin with. Not Joe. Not my Joe. Not my love." The tears coursed down her cheeks. "I thought he'd be safe when they found him unfit. After the bombing in November, when we'd all survived I thought nothing could ever touch him. Why, Mum?"

Alice shook her head. "Who can say, love?"

She put her arms around Sarah, holding her close as the tears came freely.

"What am I going to do without him? How can I live without Joe?"

Alice had no answer.

It was a cold, wet day when Sarah followed Joe's coffin to the graveside, as though the sky itself wept at his passing. Sarah was still numbed by it all, unwilling to accept that the wooden box in front of her contained all that was left of her Joe. As she watched the casket being lowered slowly into the ground she toyed with the diamond ring on her finger, as though seeking comfort. He had given it to her, his hands had touched it. She closed her eyes and could see again the spreading chestnut tree arched over their heads, as Joe had placed the ring on her finger and kissed her. Life had been so full of promise then. Now there was nothing to look forward to but loneliness and desolation.

The first spadeful of earth hit the coffin with a dull thud. She opened her eyes and looked across the ugly scar of the grave towards Joe's parents. They seemed old and bent, not like the lively people she had known, and Sarah realized she was not the only one who was going to miss Joe. His older brother was already in the army, somewhere in North Africa, and his safety was a constant worry to his parents. The fact that Joe was still in England had been a comfort to them. But now he was dead. Alongside the grief etched on their faces, Sarah could see the fear that their other son would be taken from them too.

As the earth continued to rain down on Joe's coffin, and the skies to weep their sorrow, Joe's parents turned and led the small funeral party towards the waiting cars. There they stood, looking small and alone, as they waited for Sarah and Alice. The small group remained in silence for a time, not really knowing what to say. Then Alice reached out a comforting hand; taking Joe's mother's hand in her own, she squeezed gently.

"I'm sorry about Joe. He was a really good man."

Joe's mother nodded. "Thank you." She turned towards Sarah. "I know you love Joe as much as we do and this is just as hard for you. After he...after it happened, I went up to his room, to try to be with him once more. I know it sounds foolish, but I just wanted to say goodbye."

Tears welled from Sarah's eyes as she spoke. "It's not foolish. I wish I'd been able to say goodbye to him, but I couldn't. Now he's gone, and I don't know what to do."

Fumbling in her bag for a moment, Joe's mother brought out a large, neatly wrapped bundle.

"I found these in his room. Every letter you have sent him since you went away. I thought he'd want you to have them."

Sarah's heart stood still, an ache spreading through her chest as she thought of all the words of love she had written. They were all there, in that one neat bundle. They, and the letters that Joe sent to her were all that remained to show that he had once lived, and had loved her. With a look of deep anguish, she reached out a tentative hand to touch the bundle.

"Please. Take them."

She took them and held them close to her heart, eyes closed and head bowed.

"Thank you." Her voice was little more than a whisper. She was hardly aware of her mother's hand at her elbow, guiding her towards the car they had hired. All she was aware of was the bundle of letters in her hand, and the deep abiding sense of loss, an emptiness in her life where Joe had once been.

50

Tony gazed out of the window at the spreading acres of Thame Park, some miles east of Oxford. The March sunshine highlighted the vibrant green of the newly-budded leaves on the trees which he could see stretching across the parkland.

"God, we're lucky." He turned to the young man beside him. "When you think of the places ordinary recruits go for their training, and here we are again, in another beautiful old house."

"Yes, but we have to work for the privilege!" Adam smiled grimly. "You know, I'm really dreading this. I've never been much of an academic."

"Don't worry!" Tony smiled encouragingly. "I'm sure communications training won't be all that bad."

"Well, we're about to find out." Adam inclined his head towards the door as he spoke, and Tony quickly found a seat as the training officer entered. He stood for a moment at the front of the room, perusing the expectant faces gathered before him.

"Right, lads. You've proved yourselves to be the calibre of men we need by getting this far. And now you're facing the last stretch. Not far to go now. But what you learn here will be vital, and you won't be able to go behind the lines without it. Understand?"

Twenty heads nodded in unison.

"Good. Now, let's get down to business. Communications with base are vital if you're to know what we want you to do, and if we're to know what you've been up to. The ideal circuit will consist of four - an organiser, a courier, a wireless operator and a sabotage instructor - though there will be times when four agents aren't available, so you'll have to double up on your jobs. Sometimes you might be sent out in teams of two, or even alone. The system has to be flexible, which means you all need to be able to do all of the jobs." He smiled encouragingly. "You'll find that you have a penchant for one particular field, and we will always try to use you in that capacity; but believe me, if you're a courier and your cover's been blown, you'll want to get out of there fast. You'll be eternally grateful that you listened to me, and learned how to use a wireless!

"Right. First off you will be learning Morse code. Each sender has a distinctive style. Anyone know what I mean by that?"

Twenty heads shook in the negative. "Well, you'll all send at different speeds and in different rhythms. It's a bit like talking really, you'll be the only one to communicate in that particular style."

"Is that important?"

The instructor nodded grimly at Tony's question.

"Yes. Very. We'll be able to identify you by your style, but if the Germans have been listening in to your transmissions and then capture you, they will be able to train someone to imitate you."

"Can that be done?"

"Yes, Banks. We can do it so there's no reason to believe they can't."

"So you can never be sure if it's us sending a message, or the Germans?"

"That's right. A tricky one isn't it? That's why you must always include a security code in each message, and only send to Grendon Underwood and Poundon. Never, ever send a message direct to another agent. That could cost you both your lives. Is that understood?"

"Yes, sir."

He nodded at the chorus of assent.

"Good. Now let's get down to business. Morse code. A serious of dots and dashes which make up letters of the alphabet…"

"Well, Adam. Morse code over and done with and you survived!"

His young companion laughed. "Perhaps I'm not as academically challenged as I thought!"

Tony stretched tiredly. "Yes, I found that surprisingly easy, but these ciphers, on the other hand, are giving me hell!" He sighed heavily. "I sometimes wish that damned Leo Marks had never invented the things! I've spent hours of extra time working on them!"

"You're not the only one! But at least it's all beginning to make sense now. The test this morning showed we can both do it. Twenty minutes to encode a short message of eight words and transmit it, without needing to check our notes. I didn't think I'd be able to do that a week ago!"

Tony smiled. "You're right. It feels good to know we'll be able to communicate with home." And it did feel good. Tony had a feeling of deep satisfaction at a difficult skill well mastered, and he knew this would help him to face the next task. This was the Barn Code, a written message that could be taken by courier. It would have to seem incongruous if the courier was stopped, but the receiver would be able to pick out the real message from the text. He found himself waiting eagerly for the next group of lectures to begin.

After his initial difficulties, Tony found he had a hidden talent for coding and sending. His technical ability with the small Paraset wireless also surprised him and he felt ready for whatever might lie ahead, although he did not allow himself to minimise the dangers. If he became a radio operator he was more likely to be caught. They had been told that it was possible for the Germans to track down a wireless set within twenty to thirty minutes of it beginning to send. The set would have to be constantly on the move. Under no illusions about what lay ahead, he continued to study hard, determined to be as well-equipped as possible for whatever faced him in France.

In mid-April the course was completed, and Tony was ready for action. He knew it could be months before he was needed, or he could be called upon tomorrow. He left Thame Park in a high state of nervous tension, heading for Heronfield House and four days leave before beginning his cover job. The first agent from Section F had been dropped into France three days previously. He was filled with pride, knowing that he, too, would soon be called upon to serve his country, in a job so few were capable of doing.

51

As Tony turned through the gateway of Heronfield House, he noticed that the huge iron gates were missing. Another casualty of the war, torn down to be melted in the furnace, forged into something more useful to the war effort. He smiled to himself, maybe he would find himself firing a gun made out of Heronfield's gates! As he parked his small red sports car in front of the lodge, his gaze was drawn up to the main house.

He wondered what Sarah Porter was doing. He hoped she was not in Coventry on leave, or he would not get a chance to see her while he was home. The door to the lodge opened, and Tony turned to see his mother on the steps, a smile of welcome lighting her face. He clambered out of the car, not bothering to open the door, and rushed up the steps to embrace her.

"Tony! It's good to see you!"

"Hello, Mamma." He kissed her lightly on the cheek. "How are you?"

"I am fine, mon cher."

"And Grandmamma?"

"She is still so sad to be away from home. But she is well."

"Good." Tony took a deep breath. "What about Dad?"

Louise frowned slightly. "He is well, Tony. But he is feeling useless at the moment."

"Useless? But the factories are doing useful war work aren't they?"

His mother nodded. "Yes, but he is not personally involved." She shrugged. "You must judge him for yourself."

Tony followed his mother into the drawing room, where the tea was set out. He smiled happily at the sight of cake.

"You always manage to produce such nice things, despite the war."

Louise frowned. "I am afraid it does not taste quite as good as it looks. It is the dried egg, you know."

"I'm sure it will taste lovely, Mamma."

"Yes, of course it will."

Tony turned to see Sir Michael standing in the doorway.

"Hello, Dad."

"Hello, Tony." Sir Michael's voice was gruff as he made his way across the room to his favourite armchair and sat down. "Can I have a cup of tea please, my dear?"

Louise complied happily and Tony sat down, aware that his father's attitude to him had changed in some subtle way. As the tea continued he realised that the animosity had gone. He still said very little to Tony, and Tony still felt his father disapproved of what he thought he was doing. But there was no longer the feeling he was waiting to explode if Tony said or did the wrong thing. Maybe he was coming to terms with David's death at last. Maybe Louise had managed to convince him that his son's job was worthwhile, or maybe he did not want to upset his wife any further by arguing with their one remaining child. Tony did not know what had caused it, but he was glad of the reduced tension in the atmosphere. Maybe he would enjoy this leave after all.

Once tea was over he rose with a smile. "I've missed home. It's good to be back." His gaze strayed to the window and the expanse of the estate beyond. "I think I'll take a walk by the river." He really wanted to find Sarah and speak to her. He knew she was engaged to someone else, and that knowledge was like a knife in his heart, constantly twisting and turning each time he thought of her in Joe's arms, but he knew that he could not let this leave pass without seeing her.

Tony walked for over an hour through the familiar places of his childhood, but his hope of seeing Sarah was disappointed. There were a few nurses out walking, but none with her distinctive hair, or the slim figure that made his heart race. With a discontented sigh, he turned back to the lodge, and home.

52

Sarah lay on her bed, gazing at the ceiling but not seeing it. Instead she saw Coventry cathedral as it had been before the bombing, when she had sat with Joe and listened to the voices raised in praise to God. She spent most of her off duty time alone now, remembering her times with Joe and trying to come to terms with life without him. The door opened quietly, but Sarah did not look towards it. It would only be Jane.

"Sarah, are you awake?"

"Yes."

Jane made her way to the bed and sat down beside her friend. She had watched Sarah sink deeper and deeper into despair over the weeks since Joe's death, and felt so helpless at being able to do nothing for her.

"Come on, Sarah. Joe wouldn't want to see you like this. He'd want you to get on with your life."

Sarah turned lethargically towards her friend, her eyes dark rimmed. "What's the point?"

"Oh, Sarah." Jane's voice was filled with compassion. "Did your mother think that, after your father died? There's always some point."

"She had me to live for. I have nothing."

"You might think that now, but you will learn to love again."

Sarah frowned. "I'll never love anyone the way I loved Joe."

"Of course not. He was your first love. He'll always have a special place in your heart. But life goes on."

Sarah sighed. "It doesn't seem to go on for me."

"It won't do, if you coop yourself up in here. You used to love being in the countryside; the trees, the birds, the fresh air; yet you haven't been out for a walk since...for weeks."

"You were going to say, since Joe died." Sarah sighed sadly. After a moment's thought she sat up. "I suppose you're right. I can't spend the rest of my life in this room." She walked over to the window, and looked out over the gardens, bathed in the warm April sunshine. The spring scene held a promise of new life, of hope for the future, a hope which she did not feel she could share, but which beckoned her nevertheless. She turned her sad gaze towards her friend. "I think I'll go for a walk."

Jane watched as Sarah put on her coat and quietly left the room, the old vitality and love of life gone, her movements now slow and heavy. She felt so sorry for her friend, but she felt there was nothing she could do to help her, just be there for her when she needed a shoulder to cry on.

Sarah made her way downstairs, through the back door and out into the orchard. The trees were in full leaf. Some of them had blossoms, and the heady scent filled her nostrils. She reached out to one of the apple trees, placing her hand on the warm bark and feeling its strength and solidity, its permanence. Slowly she leant forward, resting her head against the trunk and closing her eyes.

She was still standing there when Tony saw her. For three days he had been hoping to see Sarah, but without success. He had almost resigned himself to not seeing her at all before his leave was over when he walked into the orchard. For a moment he was not sure that it was Sarah. It looked like her, but she seemed to have shrunk. Her shoulders sagged, and she seemed to be drawing strength from the tree against which she leant. He walked slowly across to stand behind her.

"Sarah?"

She did not move. He was not even sure she had heard him. He reached out a tentative hand and placed it on her shoulder.

"Sarah?"

She straightened up slowly and turned towards him. He was shocked by the change in her. Her face was pale and drawn, her eyes dark from lack of sleep. A feeling of love and compassion welled up from deep within him, and he wanted to take her into his arms. Sarah looked at him almost without recognition for a moment.

"Tony?"

Her voice was little more than a whisper. He tried to smile, but the smile did not reach his troubled eyes.

"Yes, it's me. I'm on leave. I've got to go back tomorrow, so I'm glad I've had the chance to see you."

Sarah said nothing.

"What's wrong? Is it your mother?"

Sarah shook her head.

"Joe?"

Sarah closed her eyes and tears began to seep from beneath the lids.

"Is he…dead?"

An almost imperceptible nod.

"Oh, Sarah. I'm so sorry."

He gently put his arms around her and pulled her close. She was stiff, unyielding, and then she seemed to crumple. His arms tightened around her, and he began to rock her gently.

"Oh, Sarah. Sarah."

She buried her face in his shoulder and sobbed, deep racking sobs. The sound almost broke his heart. He stroked her hair gently, realising, perhaps for the first time, just how deeply she had loved Joe.

"It will be all right," he whispered. "I know it hurts, but the pain will go, and leave just the happy memories. You will be able to think of Joe and smile."

Sarah continued to sob, yet took some small comfort from his words and the strength he transmitted through his comforting arms. She relaxed a little, glad of his friendship and understanding.

"I've got go away tomorrow Sarah. I wish I could be here to help you."

Slowly she lifted her face to look at him.

"Thank you, Tony."

The tear -streaked face tugged at his heart, and he wished with all his heart that he could stay.

"Write to me whenever you need to, Sarah. I'm your friend and I want you to feel that you can always confide in me."

Sarah smiled, a sad smile which did not reach her eyes.

"Thank you."

He put his arms around her once more, and held her close. He wished he did not have to leave, for here was something he could do for Sarah. He felt her pain and loss. He knew it would take a long time for her to come to terms with Joe's death, but along with the sadness was a glimmer of hope. She was free now. While he would never have wished for Joe's death, maybe he would be able to fill a part of the gaping hole which his going had left in Sarah's life.

53

On 3rd February, Hitler had chosen Rommel to lead the new Afrikakorps. By 24th March they were ready to embark on the offensive. The year that had started with the British moving swiftly across North Africa now saw them retracing their footsteps, with Rommel in close pursuit. By 3rd April, Rommel had captured Benghazi. Tobruk, held as a fortress by the Ninth Australian Division, was surrounded in the German-Italian rear. Rommel, in the hope of shortening his supply line, tried but failed to take Tobruk, while the Royal Navy managed to re-supply the Western Desert Force from Convoy Tiger. Wavell went once more on the offensive to try to unseat Rommel, but the Germans were now well dug in. The British advance shattered like waves against a breakwater. The year's earlier victories in Africa had brought hope to an island community besieged and awaiting an enemy invasion. Now those hopes were diminished as people began to realise that the war would be a long and bloody affair. As Britain settled ever more deeply into rationing and isolation, the casualties of the desert war began to return home.

SEPTEMBER - OCTOBER 1941

54

After the reverses of Britain's earlier good fortune in North Africa, 1941 continued in a disastrous vein. May 20th saw a German parachute attack on the island of Crete. Although the defenders were forewarned, communications between the different posts were atrocious. On the first day of the attack, a massacre of German paratroops took place, but the British let their advantage slip away. While confusion reigned on land, the Royal Navy were suffering heavy losses in the attack on the seas around Crete. To the despair of people at home, avid for news of victory, the British began to retreat on May 18th. The Navy managed to take off eighteen thousand retreating soldiers, but an almost equal number were left on the island, thirteen thousand prisoners and two thousand dead.

Wavell attacked Rommel in North Africa. In a battle that began on 15th June, Britain lost ninety-one tanks to Germany's twelve before breaking off the engagement on the 18th. Churchill was in depressed but firm mood, thinking that nothing else could go wrong when, four days later, Germany invaded Russia. This meant the creation of a Second Front and, hopefully, a withdrawal of some enemy troops from Western Europe. But no-one really expected the Russians to hold out for long. Once they had fallen, their vast mineral and material wealth would flow west to bolster the German war machine. That night, Churchill spoke to the people of Britain on the radio in an attempt to raise their spirits. No one who heard him speak ever forgot those stirring words. "Can you doubt what our policy will be? We have but one aim and one, irrevocable purpose. We are resolved to destroy Hitler and every vestige of the Nazi regime...It follows, therefore, that we shall give whatever help we can to Russia and the Russian people."

To begin with, events in Russia proceeded much as Churchill had foreseen. The battles were fought with a brutality and ruthlessness so far unseen in the war. The Russian forces, despite their tenacious defence of every inch of their homeland, were forced back until, six weeks after Operation Barbarossa began, the Germans were within two hundred and twenty miles of Moscow. The German advance continued relentlessly. On 26th September six hundred and sixty-five thousand Russian prisoners were taken in one pincer movement, the largest single mass ever taken in one operation of war before or since. By the end of September, nearly three million Russians had been taken prisoner. Leningrad, the vulnerable former capital, was mobilised to construct concentric lines of defence, which included four hundred miles of anti-tank ditch, six hundred and twenty miles of earth works, three hundred and seventy miles of barbed wire entanglement and five thousand pill boxes, all built by three hundred thousand members of the Young Communist League and two hundred thousand civilian inhabitants, both men and women. The defences were completed only just in time. The German siege of Leningrad had begun.

55

After completing his training in April, Tony had begun his 'cover job'. He spent two weeks at a time away from home, returning to Heronfield every second weekend. As time passed, his nervous energy increased. Now that he was fully trained, he wanted to be in France fighting the Germans, not wasting time at home. Home itself, however, was a relatively peaceful place to be. His father was still cool towards him, although he said nothing about Tony's job. His mother was happy thinking he would remain in England, and so be in no greater danger than anyone else in this war. Tony felt more guilty about deceiving her than his father. After all, once the war was over and he was able to explain about his work, his father would be proud of him, while his mother would chastise him for putting himself in unnecessary danger. He knew how much she missed David, and he was worried how she would cope if he, too, were killed. Although Tony enjoyed being with his parents, the main attraction of home was Sarah.

Over the months, Tony managed to see Sarah every time he was home. He noticed a gradual easing of her pain. He knew she still mourned Joe deeply, but she was coming to terms with his death, and remembering their times together with a poignant happiness. In her turn, Sarah had come to rely on Tony's support. He seemed to understand the depth of her loss, maybe because the loss of his brother was still a fresh scar on his heart; and he was able to make her smile again. Slowly, imperceptibly, Tony began to forge a place for himself in her life. It was still far too early for her to think of love. She still wore Joe's ring, and often wept when she contemplated life without him. She did not even have a child of his to remember him by, for she had refused him when he wanted to make love to her. How bitterly she regretted that now. In the dark of the night her body cried out for his touch, wanting him with an ache which could never be assuaged. She cried herself to sleep, knowing she had denied Joe this one happiness with her wish to remain a virgin until she married. How wrong she had been. She would now never know that intimate touch of love; never hear him whisper her name at that ultimate moment of passion; never take his seed to herself and create a new life, a part of him to love and cherish for the rest of her days.

The real depth of Sarah's loss was kept hidden, a secret part of her which she would never share. No one would ever take the place of Joe, but as her friendship with Tony deepened, she found herself looking forward to his weekends at Heronfield when she could forget, for a while, her sadness and loss.

56

Tony faced Captain Dawson across the green leather expanse of the desktop. The officer's face was stern as he told Tony why he had been called to London.

"As you know, one of our major problems at the moment is supply, both to this country and to our forces overseas. U-boat packs are making it difficult for convoys to cross the Atlantic, and we can hardly afford the losses we are currently sustaining."

"Yes, sir."

"Since early this year, we have come to believe that the Germans have been constructing submarine pens on the Atlantic coast of France, Brest, La Rochelle, Lorient. Now we have reason to believe they may be building pens in the region of Saint Nazaire." He smiled grimly at Tony's expression. "I think you've probably already guessed what I'm going to ask of you, Kemshall. You have intimate knowledge of the Saint Nazaire area, so we want you to go there and find those pens."

"And when I have found them?"

"Destroy them." Dawson leant forward, resting his arms on the desktop. "I don't have to tell you how vital this is to our war effort. Find those submarine bases,

Kemshall, and call down an air attack on them. We have to reduce the number of U-boat packs out in the Atlantic, if we're to survive long enough to win this war."

"Yes, sir."

The Captain leant back in his chair as he perused the eager young man opposite, and hoped that he would not be sending him to his death.

"You will be flown into France in two days' time, weather reports are not good enough until then. On your way down south call in at your home for an hour or two. Give them some excuse as to why you won't be visiting for a while. Perhaps you could tell them you're going to Scotland."

Tony nodded.

"I don't have to tell you not to mention where you're really going, of course. Now, don't spend too long at home, they'll want to brief you before you go."

"Yes, sir."

Tony stood and saluted. Dawson rose to his feet and took Tony's hand across the table.

"Good luck, Kemshall. God go with you."

"Thank you, sir."

As Tony drove from London to Heronfield his mind was in turmoil. This was it. At last he would be able to go out and do the job he had trained so long and so hard for. Deep within himself was the permanent knot of hate which he felt towards the Germans. Hate for the way they had treated the French refugees, hate for Dunkirk, hate for the way they had killed David. He knew he must keep his hatred and anger under control, but he found it difficult now he was actually preparing to drop into enemy territory. 'I'll avenge you, David;' he thought, 'and I'll make Dad proud of me.'

The red sports car pulled into the drive of Heronfield House and sent gravel flying in all directions as it came to a halt. Louise Kemshall rose from her knees beside a small rose bush with a mass of yellow blooms and smiled happily at Tony. As the sound of the engine died away, she waved and called out in greeting.

"Tony! I was not expecting you!" She laid down the bunch of roses she had been picking, and made her way across to hug her son. "Are you all right, mon cher?"

"Of course, Mamma. I have to go away for a few weeks, that's all. I thought I'd drop in and say goodbye."

Louise frowned. "It will not be dangerous work?"

Tony laughed, a gay laugh which hid his true feelings of excitement, nervous tension, fear.

"Of course not. I just have to go up to Scotland to liaise with some factories there. I won't be able to get back until the job is done. They don't issue travel passes for that sort of distance, unless it's absolutely necessary."

Louise smiled. "Scotland? Then that is all right. Come on in, and I will make you a cup of tea. Your father is at the factory at the moment and will not be back until later this evening."

"Then I shall miss him. I can only stay for an hour or so, and I want to say goodbye to someone at the main house too."

"One of the nurses?"

Tony coloured slightly but said nothing and Louise nodded knowingly, a smile on her lips.

"I thought so. A mother knows these things. Do you think I have not noticed you sneaking up to the house every time you are home?"

150

"It's not what you think, Mamma. We're just good friends."

Louise laughed gaily. "Of course, mon cher. Now you go and say goodbye to your friend, while I make some tea."

Tony waited for Sarah in the orchard. He had asked Sister Freeman if she could spare the nurse for a short while and she reluctantly agreed, although he could see she would not let him make a habit of it. He was watching the back door intently, hardly able to control his eagerness to see Sarah. It opened and she emerged crisp and neat in her nursing auxiliary uniform, the beautiful auburn hair pinned up beneath the starched white cap. Tony noticed that the five months since Joe's death had changed her. She now walked with some of the old joy of living in her step, and a smile came more frequently to her lips. Tony felt a large lump in his throat, and tears pricked his eyes. This might be the last time he ever saw Sarah. Blinking the tears away, he walked rapidly towards her and took her hand in his.

"Tony! Is anything wrong? Why did you ask Sister Freeman to release me?"

Tony laughed, trying to sound as though this was just another ordinary day.

"One question at a time, please! Nothing is wrong. I asked Sister Freeman to release you so I could say goodbye."

"Goodbye?"

Sarah was conscious of his strong hand holding tightly to hers. She felt again the strange mixture of emotions which he had stirred in her of late. For a moment she feared for his safety, and the fear was evident in her eyes.

Tony smiled reassuringly. "Don't worry. I'm only going up to Scotland, but I don't know how long I'll be gone for and I wanted to see you before I left."

Sarah smiled. "Scotland is relatively safe."

"Do you care so much for my safety, Sarah?"

"Of course I do, Tony. We're friends."

Tony took a deep breath, trying to marshal his mixed emotions. If things went wrong in France, he might never see Sarah again. This could be his last chance to tell her how he felt, but he was fearful of her rejection. He watched the dappled shadow of the apple tree play across the smooth clear skin of Sarah's face, and licked his lips nervously.

"Are we just friends, Sarah? Don't I mean more to you than that?"

Sarah tried to pull away, but Tony held tightly to her hand. "You're more than just a friend to me, Sarah. I know you're still mourning Joe, and it will be a long time before you're ready to fall in love again. But I wanted you to know how I feel."

"Why now, Tony? Why tell me this now?"

Tony shrugged, trying to hide his true feelings.

"I don't know. Perhaps it's because I will be away for some time. I don't want you to find someone else while I'm gone."

Sarah laughed, almost the gay laugh of their earlier friendship before Joe's death. Tony was glad to hear it.

"I won't find 'someone else' as you put it, Tony. There's no room for any man in my life at the moment."

Tony smiled. "Good, then I don't have to worry about competition while I'm away!"

Sarah was suddenly solemn. "Don't read too much into that, Tony. I'm not ready for a relationship with anyone yet, and that includes you. It's still too soon. I don't know if I'll ever be ready for another relationship."

Tony nodded understandingly. "I know."

He stroked her cheek with his free hand, his mind churning with the things he wanted to say to her but could not. Slowly he leaned forward and kissed her on the lips. A gentle, lingering kiss to which Sarah found herself responding against her will. After a moment she stepped back, breaking the contact, yet still feeling the touch of his lips against hers. Feeling unsure of herself, she gently extracted her hand from his.

"Goodbye, Tony."

"Goodbye, Sarah. May I see you when I get back?"

Too full of conflicting emotions to say anything, Sarah merely nodded.

Tony smiled. That was confirmation enough for him. Without another word, he turned and walked away.

Sarah watched him walk down the orchard path and out of the gate. She stood there for long minutes remembering his kiss, so unlike Joe's, but awakening similar emotions in her. Could her feelings for Tony Kemshall be deeper than she had realised? With an angry toss of her head, she turned away. Of course not. She loved Joe. She would always love him, even though he was dead. No-one could ever take the special place he held in her heart.

57

Tony sat with his back pressed hard against the fuselage of the Whitley. He examined the gold watch given to him at his final briefing. A solid, accurate timepiece, its purpose was twofold. A gift such as this showed the faith which the leaders of Section F placed in their agents. And if it became necessary for the agent to raise extra funds while in enemy territory, any item of gold could be sold easily on the black market. Placing the watch in his breast pocket, Tony withdrew his false papers and ration cards, painstakingly produced for the SOE by forgers who had been, or were still, in prison for their crimes. In the dim light of the aircraft interior, he carefully studied the papers his life might depend on. Albert Fouquet. 22 Rue Blanc. Saint Nazaire. He knew all there was to know about Albert Fouquet, could recite it in his sleep. Date of birth, details of education and employment, parents' names, mother's maiden name. The list of details was almost endless, but Tony knew them as though they were the details of his own life. That was what they must be if he wished to return home again. As he put the papers in his breast pocket with the watch, and carefully buttoned it up so that nothing would get lost during his jump, his eyes were drawn to the two objects on the floor near his feet. There was a small case containing a few clothes similar to those he wore at the moment, French-made from the socks to the jacket, nothing to show that he was English. Amongst the clothing was a not insubstantial sum of money to aid him in the task ahead. The other case, slightly smaller than the first, contained his wireless set. Tony knew that if he were caught with it in his possession, his life would be forfeit. A familiar churning sensation began in the depths of his stomach. He breathed deeply, trying to control the nervous tension.

"We're crossing the coast now, sir. We should be over the drop zone in fifteen minutes."

Tony nodded at the dispatcher, too engrossed in his thoughts and feelings to reply. Was he really good enough for this job? Would he be able to do what was asked of him? As the plane droned on above the darkened countryside of Occupied France he realised that stronger than his fear of death was his fear of failure. He wondered if David had felt this, too, each time he had taken his Spitfire up against the enemy.

Time ticked by slowly. Each minute seemed an hour as they flew deeper and deeper into enemy territory. At last the dispatcher spoke again.

"Five minutes to the drop, sir. You can get ready now."

Tony tied a length of rope around each case and then fixed the other end securely to his harness. This way there was no possibility of him losing the items during the jump, the length of rope should ensure that the cases hit the ground first, minimising the chance of them injuring him. He watched the airman lift the cover from the hole in the floor of the fuselage, then stood up and fixed his ripcord to the static line, lifting the cases and holding them tightly against his chest. Carefully he shuffled over to the open hatch, just as the red light winked on.

"Two minutes to go, sir."

Tony felt the plane banking to the left to bring it in on its approach run. This was it. He glanced nervously at the dispatcher, who smiled grimly.

"I don't envy you your job, sir. It's a dangerous place down there."

Tony nodded. "Yes. But nowhere will be safe until this war is won. That's why I'm going."

The dispatcher nodded. "Good luck to you, sir."

"Thanks."

As Tony smiled his reply the red light went out and the green winked on. The dispatcher's arm fell in a swift chopping motion.

"Go!"

Tony stepped forward through the open hatch and found himself falling, only to be pulled up with a jerk as his chute opened. He looked up, and when he was satisfied that the mushroom of silk was fully opened he let go of the cases, feeling the jerk seconds later as the ropes were extended to the full. Looking down at the ground below him Tony realised that this jump was not going to be as exhilarating as jumping in the daylight, over home ground. It was dark. The blackout meant he could see nothing at all, he realised he would be almost down before he would be able to see anything. Would he have enough time to avoid any obstacles once he saw them? The unfamiliar weight of the two cases suspended from his harness dragged at him, and made the parachute sluggish to respond to his pulls on the cords. All the time he fell, there was a knot of fear in his stomach. Had the enemy heard the plane? Was a patrol out looking for him at this very moment? Would a beam of light suddenly pierce the night, to expose him to the fire of the enemy? All his fears proved groundless and, moments later, he could see an open space rushing towards him and he was down, knees bent and rolling to prevent injury.

Tony's training had been thorough. All his actions after landing came as second nature to him. He quickly dragged the chute in close and bundled it up, then dragged in the two cases still fixed to their ropes. With a quick look around him, he headed for the nearest shelter he could see, a small stand of trees on the far side of the field. Once inside their protection, he found an old rotting log and pushed the parachute and ropes inside, as far as he could reach, before filling the remainder of the hollow with dead leaves and ferns. He stepped back and looked at the log critically for a moment, then nodded in satisfaction. No one would suspect that something was hidden there. Tony picked up the two cases and made his way along the edge of the trees, until he reached a road.

He looked around for a moment, trying to get his bearings. He was to have been dropped to the north of Saint Nazaire, about a mile from his grandmother's estate, so if he headed west he should eventually reach familiar territory. He made his way through the field bordering the road, making sure that he kept it always in sight but keeping out of sight himself. If he were found on the road during curfew, he was likely to be shot. Once a motorbike roared along the road and he lay flat amongst the tall grass, but the bike passed straight by and he was on his feet and moving again swiftly. He must be under cover by first light.

At last, Tony came to a crossroads and knew where he was. His jump had been a little off course but not too much to worry about. He had less than a mile to go to reach his intended destination. He left the road and cut across the fields, until he spied a small cottage. Moving closer, he hid among the trees which bordered the small vegetable patch beside the cottage, and watched. No signs of life. No lights. But that was only to be expected at four o'clock in the morning. The cottage was the home of Jean-Paul Boues, a worker on Chantrelle de Thierry's estate, someone whom Tony knew from before the war and who, he hoped, would be willing to shelter him. There was no time to waste. If Jean-Paul could not, or would not, help him he must find somewhere else to hide during the day. Concealing the two cases in the middle of a holly bush, Tony made his way over to the front door and knocked loudly.

No reply.

He knocked again.

"Who is it?" The voice was muffled with sleep. Tony knocked once more.

"All right. I'm coming."

The door opened a crack. "What do you want at this time of night?"

Tony looked at the eye which peered around the door at him, not enough to identify the speaker by.

"Jean-Paul Boues?"

"Yes. Now who are you, and what do you want?" Jean-Paul asked gruffly. He perused the young man in peasant's clothes who stood outside his door. There was something vaguely familiar about him, but he could not be sure what. He frowned.

"Well?"

"Don't you recognise me, Jean-Paul?" Tony smiled warmly. "I used to spend the summers at the big house with Grandmamma."

Recognition flooded Jean-Paul's features. He threw the door wide, his face incredulous.

"Monsieur Tony? It is! Monsieur Tony! What are you doing here?"

"Can I come in, Jean-Paul? It will be safer for us. Then I can tell you everything."

Jean-Paul nodded enthusiastically.

"Of course, Monsieur Tony. My home is yours!"

"Thank you, Jean-Paul. But please don't call me by my real name. Call me Albert."

"Yes, Monsieur...Albert."

Jean-Paul closed the door behind them, then lit a small oil lamp and placed it on the table. He smiled warmly.

"It's good to see you. But what are you doing here, and dressed as a peasant too?"

"May I sit down, Jean-Paul? It's been a long night."

"Of course! Please forgive me! It's just that it was such a shock to find you knocking at my door!" He went over to the cupboard and rummaged inside for a moment before returning with a bottle of wine and two glasses. "Now tell me all about it."

The two men sat down, and as Jean-Paul poured the wine Tony began to talk. He told his companion how he had put his grandmother onto a boat bound for England, before heading east towards the evacuating army at Dunkirk.

"Then Madame is safe?"

"Yes, Jean-Paul. She's with my parents and will remain with them until we have driven the Germans out of France."

"What about Monsieur David? When you came to take Madame away you said that he was in the Air Force."

Tony nodded. "He flew Spitfires through most of the air battles last summer, until he was shot down. He was killed."

"I'm so sorry, Monsieur...Albert. How are your parents taking it?"

"As you might expect."

Jean-Paul was quiet for a moment, sharing the sorrow of Madame de Thierry's grandson then, "What about you? What are you doing here?"

"I'm working for a secret section of the army. Trying to fight the enemy behind their lines."

"A spy?"

"Yes, Jean-Paul. A spy. What I want to know is, are you willing to help me? If not, I'll leave now so as not to implicate you."

"Leave? My family has worked for your mother's family for generations. I hate to see the Germans living in your mother's home. I hate to see them walking the streets of my country. I have felt so useless, unable to protect my country and my family from the enemy. It will be an honour for me to work with you."

"What about your family? I don't want to endanger them."

Jean-Paul raised his eyes towards the ceiling.

"They're sleeping at the moment, but I know they will feel as I do. We are willing to take the risk. After all, we are at war."

Jean-Paul refilled their glasses, and raised his high in a toast.

"To the day when France is free once more."

Tony raised his glass. "To a free France."

The two men drank their wine, Jean-Paul deep in thought. After a moment he spoke again.

"Do you have papers?" Tony produced the forged papers which Jean-Paul perused critically. "These are very good. You can stay here. I'll tell the authorities you have been employed to work on the estate. I have friends who will be willing to help with your work, whatever it is."

"I'm looking for U-boat bases on the coast. When I have found them, I'll call in a bombing raid."

"How?"

"I have a wireless set. It must be hidden safely away."

Tony watched the swarthy Frenchman while he sat deep in thought. He was in his mid-thirties, a strong man used to working on the land. Tony knew he would be useful. Jean-Paul's face broke into a broad grin.

"I have just the place to hide your radio, Albert. Where is it?"

"I left it in the trees."

"Then let's get it now, and hide it before daylight." Jean-Paul led the way outside. "You get the radio while I get the other things we need."

Tony retraced his steps to the trees and retrieved his two suitcases. By the time he had returned to the cottage, Jean-Paul was waiting for him with a pitchfork, planks of wood and a sheet of rubber. Tony raised a quizzical eyebrow.

"What's all this for?"

"Come with me and see."

Jean-Paul led Tony to an enclosed space. Tony knew before they reached it what it was used for. The stench hung thick and heavy in the air, and he wrinkled his nose.

"A manure pile?"

"Of course. I don't think the Germans will look there. Do you?"

Tony laughed. "Not if their noses are as sensitive as mine!"

Jean-Paul climbed the low wall and used the pitchfork to clear a space which he then lined with the boards.

"The radio, please."

Tony passed the suitcase containing the radio to Jean-Paul, who wrapped it in the rubber sheeting and put it in the space he had created. Tony passed him another small package from the other suitcase.

"Bury this as well."

Asking no questions, Jean-Paul placed the package next to the wireless. More boards were placed on top to protect them, then Jean-Paul used the pitchfork to cover the hiding place with the noxious contents of the manure pile. When he climbed out of the heap, it looked untouched. Tony smiled gratefully.

"Thank you, Jean-Paul."

The Frenchman looked towards the rising sun.

"Come inside now, and let's have some breakfast. I'll then show you your duties around the estate, so that you are able to answer any questions the authorities might put to you."

They re-entered the cottage to find Marie Boues preparing breakfast. She had heard Jean-Paul talking to someone and, although curious, had refrained from going to see who it was. Now that she recognised their visitor, her eyes widened in surprise.

"Monsieur Tony!"

"My name is now Albert Fouquet, Marie. Jean-Paul says I may live and work here, if that's all right with you."

"Of course it is!" She studied him for a moment, then nodded thoughtfully. "I won't ask what it's all about, though I'm sure I can make a guess."

Before Tony could reply, the door to the kitchen opened to admit Jean-Paul's two daughters. Theresa was eleven , while Jeanne was just nine years old. They smiled in welcome.

"Hello, Monsieur."

"Hello, girls."

Jean-Paul stepped forward.

"This is Albert Fouquet. He will be living and working with us for a while."

Theresa made as though to say something, then frowned. After a moment her face cleared, and her eyes widened questioningly. Tony caught a strange look in her eyes as she opened her mouth to speak then turned quickly away, and the moment was lost.

"Did the Germans send him?" Jeanne frowned thoughtfully as she spoke.

Jean-Paul smiled at his younger daughter. "No Jeanne. They did not."

The young girl smiled brightly. "That's all right then. Welcome to our home, Monsieur Fouquet."

58

Tony worked on the estate during the day and was glad to have something to keep him occupied until he could make contact with the Resistance. His tasks took him near his grandmother's home, and he could not help stopping to look at the house that held such a special place in his heart. The great old house looked as beautiful as ever. Tony stood in silent contemplation for a time, remembering the happy times he had spent there during his childhood. The old mansion house stretched its wings wide around the edges of the gravel courtyard lined with rose bushes. But to Tony's eyes the beauty, and the memories, were marred by the huge swastika which flew above the roof, flapping in the gentle breeze, and the row of army vehicles which stood in front of the sweeping curve of the steps. As in many other places the conquering Germans had taken over the best properties for the officers to use, and they had settled in well. Tony bit his lower lip angrily as he thought of the enemy using his grandmother's precious possessions. He wanted to rush down there and throw the invaders out, but he knew that was impossible. Still, when the war was over the Germans would leave and he would be able to restore the house to his grandmother's possession once more.

"Hey, you! What are you doing!"

Tony spun hurriedly around at the sound of the heavily accented French. A young German soldier stood, rifle levelled at Tony's chest.

"Me?"

"Yes. Of course you! What are you doing here?"

"Working."

"I do not recognise you. Do you work on the estate?"

"Yes. Monsieur Boues employed me this morning."

"Papers.

Tony hurriedly produced his forged papers which the German perused carefully.

"Name?"

"Albert Fouquet."

"Address?"

"22 Rue Blanc. Saint Nazaire. But I'll be staying with Monsieur Boues while I'm working here."

"Why?"

"It saves travelling time. I can work right up to curfew."

Tony's nerves were on edge at his first close encounter with a German, but he tried to appear calm. The questions were frighteningly similar to the time when he had been interrogated during training. But this time it was for real. A mistake could cost him his life. The young soldier stared at him thoughtfully.

"If you are working for Monsieur Boues, why are you standing here looking at the house?"

"This is my first day on the estate, the first time I've seen this house. It's beautiful. I just wanted to look at it."

The soldier frowned for a moment, then nodded. "That sounds reasonable. I too found it a beautiful place on first sight. But I shall be watching you, Monsieur Albert Fouquet."

Tony nodded. "May I go now?"

"Yes." The German handed back Tony's papers and lowered his rifle. "Now get back to work and do nothing else to draw my attention to you. Understand?"

Tony nodded, turned and walked away. He knew things would be different in Occupied France, but this was worse than he imagined. Jean-Paul had told him that German officers were using the big house but he had not expected a guard to challenge him for just looking. Although the experience had shaken him, he realised it was a good thing. It had brought home to him in no uncertain terms that the Germans really were everywhere and he must be constantly on his guard if he was to survive. At least his papers had passed inspection, and he had not stumbled over his cover story. The meeting with the young German soldier instilled a feeling of cautious confidence which Tony felt sure would see him through the difficult days, and weeks, ahead.

Dinner was ready on the table when he returned to the Boues' cottage after his day's work. He had been able to survey the estate, and the changes which had taken place since the Occupation began. Tony breathed deeply the aroma of cooking, and smiled at

Marie.

"This smells good."

She smiled in return. "It's the best we can do. The Germans take all of the best food. Though we are better off than those who live in the city."

Tony was washing himself at the sink when Jean-Paul entered. He turned and picked up the towel, drying himself briskly.

"How was your day, Albert?"

"I was questioned by a German soldier, but there was no problem. When it's dark, I must make radio contact to let my superiors know I've settled in safely."

Jean-Paul nodded. "I understand. But before that, I would like you to meet some people. A Resistance organisation is being formed in France at the moment. Our aim is sabotage and anything else that will help to get rid of the Germans. So far we have done little other than get ourselves organised, but we should be able to help you. I'd like you to meet the other three members of my group and have set up a meeting for tonight."

Tony grinned broadly. "Jean-Paul! You're a marvel! I had been wondering how I could make contact with the Resistance, and here you are, already a member! I didn't know just how lucky I was, choosing you as my contact!"

Jean-Paul smiled. "Good. Now eat your dinner before it gets cold."

It was well after dark when Jean-Paul led Tony through the trees at the back of the house, to the small clearing where he had arranged to meet the other three members of his group. There was a thin sliver of moon in the sky which gave a little light to help them on their way, and illuminated the leaf-strewn floor of the glade. As they crouched in the undergrowth which concealed them from any prying eyes, the Frenchman carefully observed the open space, looking for anything out of the ordinary.

"Everything looks normal."

He whistled softly, and seconds later an answering whistle came from the other side of the clearing.

"All right. Let's go."

Jean-Paul rose to his feet and, with Tony following close behind, made his way into the empty clearing. Three shadows detached themselves from the trees and came forward. Jean-Paul smiled warmly.

"Bonsoir. This is Albert Fouquet, who has come here to help us fight the Germans. Albert, this is Claude Corver. He owns a garage, so he could be useful in providing transport."

The man, in his late thirties and losing some of his hair, smiled and held out his hand.

"Bonsoir, Albert."

Tony shook the proffered hand warmly.

"Bonsoir, Claude. I'm pleased to meet you and hope that we can work together."

A young man, much the same age as Tony, stepped forward with a welcoming smile.

"Bonsoir Albert. My name is Charles Durand. I have no specific skills like Claude, but I'll do anything to get rid of the Germans." His face clouded, anger flashing in his eyes. "You have no idea how much I hate to see the invaders in my city, walking down the streets as though they own them."

Tony smiled. "Bonsoir Charles. I can see we'll get on well. We think in the same way."

The third person stepped forward, a slim figure whom Tony took to be another young man, until the moonlight caught the features. He realised it was a woman in her late twenties.

"Bonsoir. I'm Madeleine Thibault and I'll do anything I can to help." Her face was harsh, though Tony felt it looked like the result of suppressed anger and that if she were to relax, she could be beautiful. "My husband was killed during the invasion. I intend to pay the Germans back for what they've done."

Tony nodded.

"I understand. I too have lost a loved one in this war. But we must not let our feelings get the better of us. If we allow our anger to take too big a hold, it could cost us our lives too. Are you prepared to follow my orders, even if you don't think it's the best way to fight the enemy? If not, if you think that your feelings will interfere with my work, then I can't use you."

Madeleine frowned, deep in thought, then nodded.

"I understand what you are trying to say. I'll do my best to keep my feelings under control." A slight smile touched her lips. "I know I'll find it difficult, so please tell me if you think I'm overstepping the mark. I have to work with you. Do you understand?"

Tony nodded. "Yes, and your honesty convinces me that we can work together."

"Right." Jean-Paul led the way over to a log and sat down. "Now the introductions are over, let's get down to business. The less time we spend here together, the less danger there will be."

The others sat down and Tony began to explain what he was doing there.

"You will know me as Albert Fouquet, but that's not my real name. I'm an Englishman, and I'm here to find some submarine pens on the coast, then to call in an air strike to destroy them."

"You have a radio?"

Tony nodded at Claude's question. "Yes. It's in a safe place. I'll only use it when necessary. The German detection system is bound to be good."

"What can we do to help?"

"Well, Charles, we need to check the coast carefully. Every crack in the cliffs must be investigated. There may be underwater entrances to caves or hidden passageways. Jean-Paul and I will take the coast north of the city, while you and Claude check the south."

"What about me?"

"I need you to keep us in touch, Madeleine. You're to make arrangements to be at a certain place at a certain time each day. If Claude and Charles find anything, they are to meet you there and you must bring the news to us. Jean-Paul will come to you if we find anything. The important thing is for us not to meet together again, until we have found something. The more times we meet, the greater the danger of the Germans finding out about us."

Madeleine frowned and Tony smiled.

"You're thinking that this is not the work you had in mind. But it's the best job you can do for us at the moment."

Madeleine nodded. "All right."

Tony stood up. "Now we had better split up again. I hope I'll be seeing you all again soon, with some good news. Good luck."

The others stood too. "Bon chance."

As the words of encouragement hung in the air, the five figures slid into the trees and the clearing was empty once more.

After leaving their fellow conspirators and making their way back through the trees to Jean-Paul's cottage, Tony helped his companion to uncover the radio and his other, smaller, package. They lifted it carefully from its hiding place in the manure pile.

"Will you transmit from here?"

Tony shook his head. "No. The Germans will be monitoring constantly. They would soon be able to track us down, especially if we transmit from the same place more than once. I shall go some two or three miles east of here. Next time I'll go in a completely different direction."

Jean-Paul nodded thoughtfully. "Do you want me to come with you?"

"No. There's no need for both of us to risk being caught. It's dangerous enough breaking curfew, without being found in possession of a wireless set."

Jean-Paul nodded. "I'll wait for you in the cottage, and help you to rebury the wireless when you return." He turned and walked away, his confident step masking his fears for his young friend.

Tony unwrapped the smaller package and checked it over carefully. A Bren light machine gun, which could fire off five hundred rounds per minute and was accurate up to eight hundred yards. It was clean, well-oiled and working smoothly. Fitting a full magazine into the clip, and a spare into his jacket pocket, Tony picked up the suitcase containing the radio and made his way into the trees.

The wind had risen slightly, blowing clouds across the face of the moon so there was little light to see by, but Tony did not mind. Although he had to take greater care of where he was walking, he was less likely to be seen by any German patrols. He walked for almost an hour until he came to a dense thicket of trees which he felt was far enough from the Boues' home to be safe. After carefully reconnoitring the area to make sure that there were no signs of life, he forced his way into the centre of the thicket and set to work.

Tony opened the suitcase to reveal a cadmium steel box eight-and-a-half inches by five-and-a half by four-and-a-half, and a six-volt battery. As he removed a small bakelite box from his breast pocket, a detached part of his brain wondered at his coolness. It was so much like being on a training exercise that it was easy to forget this was enemy territory. Moving swiftly and surely, he opened the small box and used the pair of tongs inside to lift out the postage-stamp sized crystal, which was cut to a precise wavelength. He plugged it into the set, checked the battery connections and, when he was sure everything was in order, took a deep breath and sat back on his heels for a moment. This was it then. He placed the headset in position, rubbed his hands together, took a final look at the pre-encoded message, took another deep breath and began. His fingers moved easily as he tapped out his name and code.

"Albert. KHURQILHOG."

He sat in total stillness for a moment, wondering at his own calmness as he waited for acknowledgment of his code, the letters of Heronfield transposed three places. Then it came, the regular beep...beep...beep... of Morse in his headset.

"Receiving."

Tony's fingers began to briskly type out the message.

"Arrived safely. In safe house. Contact made with Resistance. Over."

The reply was swift. "Received. Will continue listening. Over."

"Understood. Out."

Tony removed the crystal and replaced it in its box, before slipping it into his pocket. The headset was put back in the case and the battery disconnected. In moments the case was closed, and he was making his way back towards Jean-Paul's cottage. It had all gone like clockwork, and he should have felt good, but reaction to the evening's tension was building up. Half-way back to Jean-Paul's, Tony had to sit down. His legs and hands were shaking as though he had been exposed to extreme cold, and a slight throbbing at his right temple told him that he would soon have a headache. He leant back against a tree for a few moments, eyes closed and breathing deeply. He was scared now, far more so than on his way to make contact or during the transmission. What if his transmission had been intercepted? There could be Germans out looking for him at this very moment. He rose to his feet and continued towards Jean-Paul's at as fast a pace as was possible in the darkness. He was breathless when he finally reached the edge of the trees and stopped to look carefully around for any signs of movement. When certain that all was safe he ran over to the cottage and knocked on the door. It was opened immediately.

"Albert. Is everything all right?"

Tony grinned. "Yes Jean-Paul. It was easy. Now let's hide the stuff and then have a drink."

59

Tony and Jean-Paul began their search of the coastline soon after dawn the following morning. Tony did not like the idea of working in daylight but, by the very nature of the task ahead of them, this was the way it had to be done. The submarine pens would be well concealed, so they could easily miss them if searching in the dark. To the north of the city was a stretch of sand which shelved gently into the sea, a totally unsuitable place for U-boats, so they began their search just north of this where the cliffs fell sharply to the sea and the deep blue of the waves indicated deep water. Each man carried a pair of binoculars. Lying flat on the cliff edge, they carefully scrutinised every inch of the cliff face below them. There were so many cracks and crevices that their eyes soon became tired. After three hours they had covered little more than two miles of the cliff face, and the tide was coming in rapidly. Tony rubbed his eyes and rolled over onto his back. Seagulls wheeled overhead, calling shrilly, and Tony hoped they would not attract the attention of German patrols. He turned towards Jean-Paul.

"We may as well give up now. As the water's rising it may cover a secret entrance. We'll have to come back again when the tide turns."

Jean-Paul nodded. "Let's go."

The two men crawled along the cliff top until they reached a stand of trees, then rose to their feet. Tony led the way silently to where the trees bordered the road and listened intently.

"Trucks."

The two men crouched down. The sound of the engines drew closer and Tony felt a shiver run down his spine. It was just like waiting for the Panzers on the road to Dunkirk; but this time the idea was to remain undetected. As he crouched lower, the first truck rounded the corner and came towards them. It was a covered truck, carrying supplies of some sort, followed by another half-dozen similar vehicles. The trucks disappeared northwards, and an idea came to Tony. He smiled.

"Jean-Paul, perhaps we're going about this search in the wrong way. It's true that the U-boat pens will be well hidden, but they will need supplies and spares for repairs. They must be accessible from the cliff top."

Jean-Paul grinned and struck his forehead with the heel of his hand.

"But of course! We should be looking for the tracks of heavy vehicles leading to the cliff edges, or perhaps a cliff path!"

"That's right. It will certainly be easier than searching the whole cliff face inch by inch." Tony was thoughtful for a moment. "Can you get in touch with Madeleine, so she can tell the others what to look for?"

Jean-Paul nodded. "I can go into Saint Nazaire on estate business this afternoon. I'll see her then."

Jean-Paul made contact with Madeleine later that day, and she promised to speak to Claude and Charles later the same evening. Tony spent the reminder of the day working on the estate to establish his cover story in the eyes of the German soldiery. It was not until early the next morning that he and Jean-Paul began to search the cliff-top for tracks which might indicate a supply point for the U-boat pens. The cliff-top the north of Saint Nazaire was barren, which made the task more difficult as they could not approach the edge without being observed from the road. So far they had seen no German patrols, but if the U-boat pens did exist there would be some sort of security for them; this might well be hidden so they had to proceed cautiously. By mid-afternoon they had moved some five miles further up the coast, with no sign of a well-used track or path leading to the cliff edge. It was a very disheartened and tired pair who made their way back to the Boues' cottage that evening. Theresa and Jeanne were curious about what their father was doing.

"Why haven't you been working as usual today, Papa?"

Jean-Paul gently ruffled his younger daughter's hair. "I've been showing Albert around. He wants to get to know the area around the estate better."

"Why?"

Jean-Paul shrugged. "Why not? He's living and working here now."

"What about the Germans, Papa? Won't they expect you to do your work?"

Theresa nudged her younger sister, whispering "Perhaps they're doing something the Germans won't like. You shouldn't ask so many questions Jeanne."

Jeanne gazed at her father, wide eyed. "Are you and Albert fighting the Germans, Papa? Can I help?"

Tony laughed, trying to change the subject. "How can we fight the Germans, Jeanne? We have no weapons, and there are only two of us."

"I wish you would fight them, Albert. I hate them."

"Me too," said Theresa.

Tony looked at Theresa. Although she was only eleven, he saw something in her eyes which gave him pause for thought. Jeanne had just been chatting, like all small girls do, but Theresa's face was deadly serious. Had she guessed who he was, and what he was doing? Would the girls be a danger to his mission?

Jean-Paul noticed Tony's frown and rose to his feet.

"That's enough of this chatter, girls. Time for bed."

Jeanne rose to her feet and flung herself into her father's arms, placing a huge wet kiss on each of his cheeks.

"Goodnight, Papa."

"Goodnight, my little one." He put the child down and patted her gently on the bottom. "Now, off you go to bed."

As Jeanne's footsteps were heard thumping up the stairs Theresa turned to face her father.

"Are you working with the Resistance, Papa?"

Jean-Paul frowned. "Why do you say that?"

"Because you've changed your routine since Albert arrived." She directed her serious gaze at their guest. "I recognised him on the first day. I remember Madame's house in the summers before the war. But don't worry, Jeanne doesn't remember. I think you're working with the Resistance to try to get rid of the Germans, and I want to join the Resistance too."

"Who do you think I am?"

Theresa turned to Tony. "I know you're the grandson of Madame de Thierry. But don't worry Albert, I won't give you away. This is my country and I have the right to fight if I wish." Her eyes were pleading. "Please trust me. I won't let you down."

Tony's heart was in his mouth. What should he do now? He knew that Theresa had every intention of keeping his secret, but what if things went wrong? Would she be a liability? Would her life be in danger too? He frowned as he took in the serious expression on the child's face in front of him. At last he nodded slowly.

"I don't know why you think I'm the grandson of Madame de Thierry, but if I was, I would trust you as your father's daughter. But I have no rights over you, Theresa. If your father knows anything about the Resistance it is up to him to decide what he wants you to do."

The young girl turned eagerly towards her father.

"Please let me help, Papa."

Jean-Paul's frown deepened. "What do you know about the Resistance?"

Theresa shrugged.

"Nothing much. There are rumours at school." Her face was grim. "I hate the Germans, Papa. If you are helping the Resistance, perhaps you could find work for me. There must be many things someone my age could do. The Germans wouldn't suspect me."

Jean-Paul was thoughtful. Tony did not envy him his problem. Finally he broke the silence.

"You are old enough to understand something of this war, Theresa. You understand it is dangerous, and it will probably take us years to defeat the Germans. Any work that the Resistance does must be kept a secret. It could cost the lives of many brave Frenchmen and women."

Theresa nodded. "I understand, Papa. I don't think Jeanne understands or even knows about the Resistance. But I do, and I want to help."

Jean-Paul took his elder daughter's hand in his, and squeezed tightly.

"You're very precious to me, Theresa. I wouldn't want to put your life in danger..."

"But Papa!"

Jean-Paul held up his hand to quieten her. "I was going to say that I wouldn't want you to put your life in danger, but if I ever have contact with the Resistance, and if they can use you without endangering you then I shall consider it."

Theresa smiled. "Thank you, Papa. I understand." She turned to their guest. "Goodnight Albert. I won't let you down."

"Goodnight, Theresa."

She turned back to her father and hugged him tightly. "Goodnight, Papa."

Jean-Paul closed his eyes and held her tightly. "Goodnight, Theresa."

The young girl made her way towards the door then turned back.

"Papa. Albert. Please be careful."

Then she turned and was gone.

Jean-Paul sighed deeply and turned to Tony.

"I'm sorry about that. I had thought that Theresa was too young to recognise you. If I'd known that she remembered you, I could have found somewhere else for you to hide."

"That's all right, my friend." Tony smiled. "You have a very remarkable daughter there. So perceptive, and so brave."

"Do you wish to find somewhere else to hide? I'm sure she won't betray you, but if you wish to go I'll understand."

Tony shook his head. "No. I don't think Theresa will speak of this to anyone else. I trust her." He frowned thoughtfully. "Would you be willing to let her help us?"

Jean-Paul rose and poured each of them a glass of wine to give him time to think. Finally he turned back. "I don't want to, Albert, but she is French, as I am, and she loves her country. If she's willing to help, then it would be wrong of me to stand in her way. I would rather she helped us than try to do something stupid on her own."

Tony nodded. "I understand. You must be very proud of her."

Jean-Paul nodded. "I am."

"I'll be honest with you, my friend. I won't ask her to help in anything that I would consider to be too dangerous."

Jean-Paul smiled. "Thank you."

"Well." Tony stood and stretched as he spoke. "I'm for bed. We have a lot of work tomorrow."

It was a dull day. A light drizzle fell steadily, soaking their clothing and depressing their spirits. Tony and Jean-Paul made their way slowly through a narrow stand of trees, stopping frequently to study the cliff top with their binoculars. Jean-Paul noticed the tracks first, and pointed them out to Tony. He trained his binoculars on them and studied them carefully. The tyre marks made a well-defined track through the trees and out over the grassy cliff edge. They were deeply rutted, signifying that heavy loads had passed that way, and puddles gathered in the ruts as the rain increased.

"They seem to go right over the cliff edge."

Jean-Paul nodded. "I believe there's a narrow cliff path there, but it's not large enough for vehicles. I can't imagine how they could get supplies down there if this is the place we're looking for."

"What's down there? Caves? A beach?"

Jean-Paul frowned. "I haven't been here since I was a child. If I remember correctly, there's a cave, but the approach to it by water is very narrow. There's also a wide rock ledge at the base of the cliff path."

"Sounds promising, but we can't get any closer now. If there are U-boat pens down there then there are bound to be security patrols around. We'd better come back when it's dark."

Jean-Paul nodded and the two men made their way back through the narrow stand of trees, following the tracks to find out where they joined the main coast road. As they approached the edge of the trees, Tony placed a hand on Jean-Paul's arm and pulled him down into the undergrowth.

"What's that?" He inclined his head towards a small building.

"It's just a small hut that was used by the local gamekeeper some years ago. But it's empty now."

"No, it isn't. Look."

A thin column of smoke was rising from the chimney.

"Who could be there?"

Jean-Paul shrugged. "I don't know."

"It could be the Germans."

Jean-Paul nodded. "We watch?"

"Yes Jean-Paul. We watch."

They were there for almost half an hour, the water from the trees dripping down on them, leaving them wet and uncomfortable. But their perseverance was rewarded when the door opened and two men came out swathed in cloaks. Each man carried a rifle. The field-grey of their trousers left the two watchers in no doubt about their identity. Germans. The two soldiers turned and spoke to someone else inside the hut, then closed the door and made their way down the muddy pathway, passing within feet of the hidden men. The Germans splashed through the deep ruts towards the cliff edge. Once they were out of sight, Tony and Jean-Paul retreated into the trees.

"There was someone else in the hut."

Tony nodded. "More sentries. At a guess I'd say that there are four of them. There should be two on guard at any time. This rain has probably driven them all inside the hut, and they're only patrolling at intervals. Getting wet has probably been to our advantage after all."

"Do the sentries change your plans for tonight?"

"No, I must come back and check this out, but I'll be all the more wary now I know where the sentries are. Now let's get back to the cottage. I'd give anything to be warm and dry."

60

The rain stopped early in the evening, just as Tony and Jean-Paul were setting out to reconnoitre the cliff top. They wore dark clothes to make them as inconspicuous as possible, and carried ropes in case they were unable to use the cliff path because of the patrols. Jean-Paul, being more familiar with the lie of the land, led the way. Barely an hour after setting out they found themselves in the narrow band of trees, surveying the gamekeeper's hut. A small beam of light escaped from a crack in the curtains. Tony smiled grimly.

"They're careless. They don't seem to be expecting trouble. Look at that light. They aren't even afraid of air raids!"

Jean-Paul nodded. "These Germans are so full of themselves. And in my country too!" His voice, although merely a whisper, expressed all his pent up anger and hatred for the enemy. "Let's get to work, Albert."

Tony nodded. "Come on."

They made their way cautiously along the rutted track until they reached the edge of the trees. The tracks stretched ahead of them for some two hundred yards to the cliff edge, and Jean-Paul frowned.

"There's no cover for us out there. What if we meet a German patrol?"

"It's a risk we have to take, Jean-Paul. Can you see any movement out there?"

The Frenchman shook his head.

"Right, let's go."

Tony led the way, crouched low to the ground and running as fast as he could, Jean-Paul was right behind him. Moments later, the relieved men found themselves at the edge of the cliff, still undetected. The tracks halted some three yards from the cliff edge. The ground around them was disturbed, as though a great many goods had been unloaded there. Tony made his cautious way towards the edge of the cliff and gazed over. The cliff path went down steeply, weaving back and forth but accessible to men on foot. It varied in width from three to five feet, plenty wide enough for supplies to be man-handled down, although that would be time consuming and a little dangerous. Tony let his eyes wander further. A large flat expanse of rock at the base of the cliff led to a dark shadow. A cave? But access to this from the sea looked almost impossible. The cliff walls curved round here, creating a small bay ending in a narrow cleft where the waves crashed along the sides even though the sea beyond was smooth and calm. Tony was uncertain. Could the U-boat captains actually negotiate such a passage? It seemed impossible to his untrained eye.

He turned to Jean-Paul. "I don't know what to think. It looks impossible to me."

"What do we do?"

"Go down. It's the only way to find out for sure."

"The cliff path?"

"No. If it is a submarine base I might walk straight into the hands of the Germans. Look over there." He pointed away to their left. "That outcrop of rock seems to go most of the way down. If I use the rope and go down behind it, I'll be hidden from anyone below."

Jean-Paul nodded. "Let's go, then."

Tony led the way further along the cliff edge until they reached his chosen spot. He tied their rope to an outcropping of rock.

"I'll go down alone, Jean-Paul. You stay here and keep watch."

The Frenchman nodded as his companion slipped silently over the edge of the cliff. As Tony lowered himself carefully down the cliff face he was thankful for all the night exercises he had endured in Scotland. There was little moonlight, but he found his hands and feet working almost independently, seeking out the best route to the cliff base. Within five minutes he was down, peering round the rocky outcrop. The rock platform at the base of the cliff path seemed deserted at first glance, but as he watched he saw a flicker of movement away to his right. A guard. He turned his head towards the end of the narrow cleft. The dark shadow which he had seen from above was not the depths of a cave, but huge iron doors painted matt black, the same shade as the surrounding rock. His mind was a whirl. If there were metal doors here, it was the right place, but it would be totally invulnerable from the air. This base would have to be destroyed from the ground. He would have to get a closer look. He watched the guard closely. Surely the huge sea doors would not have to be opened to admit a single man. There must be another entrance.

Time passed slowly, but eventually the shadowy figure made his way towards the doors, and then disappeared. One moment he was there and the next he was gone. Tony crept out from behind the rock, and made his way to where he had last seen the soldier. A narrow crack in the rock led to a cleft, which disappeared into the cliff. After a moment's hesitation, Tony entered. His heart was beating rapidly, and the palms of his hands were sweating. If this led to a U-boat base, he was likely to meet an enemy any time. If he came across another guard in the cramped confines of the passageway, he would have no choice but to fight. He would be outnumbered and have little chance of getting out of there alive. Tony pressed on, moving as quickly as he could as the passageway turned to the right. He found himself gazing into a huge, well lit cavern.

The place was a hive of activity, with uniformed soldiers and workers in overalls moving purposefully about. To his left Tony saw a pile of boxes and slid behind them. From his new position he could see without being seen, and he studied the chamber. A large expanse of water was surrounded on three sides by a wide rocky ledge, much of it seemingly recently blasted from the raw rock of the cave. On this ledge, set back against the walls, were piles of boxes, stores and spare parts, and huge drums of diesel fuel. To the rear was a broad passageway which, judging from the activity around it, led to a smaller cave which was possibly used as sleeping quarters for the scores of men employed here. But what caught and held Tony's attention were the two huge black shapes lying at rest in the water. U-boats!

Tony closed his eyes for a moment, attempting to control his feelings. He had found it! He had not failed after all! He opened his eyes again, and watched the activity all around him. One of the submarines was covered with a swarm of men - mechanics and fitters in overalls worked steadily while boxes of supplies were passed along a long chain of men and down into the hull of the submarine. The other U-boat was quiet. There was no one aboard as far as he could see. A klaxon sounded, echoing loudly in the huge rock cavern. The lights went out and the great expanse of the sea doors began to open, creating an area of grey light in the darkness of the cave. Everyone in the cavern stopped what they were doing as the mooring ropes on the second U-boat were cast loose. As the doors finished opening, the engines of the sinister shape roared into life and the U-boat moved steadily out of the cavern and into the sea cleft. Tony was unable to see it manoeuvring itself out to sea, for the door closed immediately, the lights came on and the workers resumed their jobs as though nothing out of the ordinary had happened. Perhaps it had not. Perhaps this happened most nights. Tony was more convinced than ever that this base must be destroyed. He looked carefully around him. There were plenty of places where explosives could be concealed, and in such a confined space they would cause the maximum amount of damage. With a final look around, Tony slid back into the rocky defile which led outside. In no time at all he was back out in the open air, concealed behind the outcrop of rock.

The Englishman sat against the rock for a moment, trying to control his excitement. He realised it was later than he had thought. He must have been in the cavern for almost an hour. Aware that Jean-Paul was probably worried by his prolonged absence he gave two tugs on the rope, a pre-arranged signal, and began to climb.

The ascent took longer than the descent, but it was not too arduous and he was soon back on the cliff-top. Jean-Paul began to haul in the rope.

"You don't have to tell me what you found down there, Albert. I saw the U-boat leaving. What an incredible sight! If I'd not seen it with my own eyes, I wouldn't have believed that it was possible to manoeuvre a boat in such a confined space."

"Yes, I found it." Tony's voice was grim. "But there's no way an air attack can damage what they have down there."

"What do we do then?"

"I'll send to England for explosives and weapons. We will have do it ourselves."

Jean-Paul looked surprised and a little fearful. "Whatever you say, Albert."

"You're a brave man, Jean-Paul. Now let's get going, it's only about two hours till dawn."

"Wait." Jean-Paul laid a hand on Tony's arm. "Look."

Lights could be seen moving through the trees, and the sound of heavy engines reached their ears.

"Supply trucks?" Jean-Paul was bemused. "Why come in the night? It's too dark to get anything down the cliff path."

"Let's watch."

They had little choice but to remain hidden. To break cover now would mean almost certain discovery by the troops who accompanied the trucks. The area around the summit of the cliff path was a hive of fevered activity as boxes of food and supplies were unloaded, along with large drums which Tony guessed must contain diesel, or drinking water for the submarine crews. The supplies were piled up, no attempt was made to carry them down the cliff, and less than an hour after appearing, the trucks turned and retraced their tracks, leaving just one of their number behind. A guard of eight soldiers remained with the supplies so the two watchers were still unable to leave their hiding place.

"What are they doing now?"

"I would guess they're waiting for sunrise," Tony replied. "They obviously want to keep this base secret, so the supply trucks come at night. With the curfew no one will see them leaving the road loaded with supplies and returning some time later from an apparently deserted cliff top without their heavy loads. But it's too dangerous to move the loads down the cliff face in the dark, so that must be accomplished during the first daylight hours. Very clever."

The two friends continued to watch in silence until the pale light of dawn began to tinge the sky. The soldiers, who had been sitting on the supplies, chatting as though they did not expect any trouble, now rose to their feet and moved to the cliff edge. Two of them remained on guard. The remaining six set to work assembling a block and tackle arrangement which came with the supplies. Tony smiled grimly.

"So that's how they do it," he whispered as the first of the huge drums was lowered over the cliff edge. The sound of voices and laughter reached them as a number of men ascended the cliff path to join the soldiers. With shouts of greeting they picked up the smaller bundles and boxes, and disappeared over the cliff edge. The work continued for more than an hour. Groups of men carried supplies while the block and tackle creaked incessantly as heavier loads were lowered directly onto the rocky shelf below. Empty drums and boxes were raised, and loaded into the remaining truck. When all the supplies had been dealt with, the soldiers dismantled the block and tackle, loaded it onto the truck and clambered aboard. The engine roared into life and the truck disappeared into the trees.

"A very neat operation." Tony was impressed. "The only weakness is that they don't think anyone will be able to find this place. If the lax security at the keeper's hut is anything to go by, an attack by land on this base should be possible."

Jean-Paul nodded. "Yes, Albert. Now let's go home."

The two men rose stiffly from their hiding place, and made their way back into the cover of the trees as the morning sun rose higher in the sky.

Later that evening Tony began to encode his message for England. No matter how hard he tried he could not keep the message as short as he would have liked, but that was unavoidable. He was relieved to find that his mastery of the Playfair Code had not deserted him, and finally the message was ready. Jean-Paul helped to retrieve the wireless set and gun from the manure heap, and Tony set off. He was two miles from the cottage when he looked at his watch and realised that his call-in time was fast approaching. He was already in deep cover, far enough from the Boues' home that suspicion would not fall on them, so he set up the transmitter and waited. The five minutes' wait seemed to stretch to eternity, but finally the time was right and he began to tap out his message on the key.

"Albert. KHURQILHOG."

The headset crackled.

"Receiving."

"U-boat pens found. Invulnerable to air attack. Drop container. Brens. Plastic. Limpets. Reception Committee and zone will be organised. Over."

"Received. BBC next contact. Over."

"Understood. Out."

Within moments the wireless set was dismantled, and Tony on his way back to the cottage. He was thankful that the hiding place for the wireless was so close to the cottage, for now he would have to listen in every evening until his code call came through telling him to make contact. That would mean the container was ready, and they needed dropping co-ordinates. Tony was excited. This was what he had looked forward to and trained for, ever since those days on the beach at Dunkirk. Within days, weeks at the most, he would be striking a blow against the enemy, to avenge the deaths of the refugees on the road, the soldiers on the beaches, and David. As he rubbed his tired eyes he smiled grimly at the thought of David and home. If only his father could see him now!

As he approached the cottage all thoughts of home fled from Tony's mind. It was almost forty-two hours since he had last seen a bed. All Tony wanted to do now was sleep.

Jean-Paul got a message to Madeleine the next morning. She was to find Claude and Charles, and arrange for them all to meet with Tony and Jean-Paul at the same rendezvous as before, at ten o'clock that night. When Tony and Jean-Paul arrived, warmly wrapped against the cold night air, the other three were already waiting for them. Tony smiled in greeting.

"Bonsoir."

"Bonsoir" chorused the members of the Resistance group.

"Have you found anything yet?" Charles' question was eager and Tony smiled.

"Yes, Charles. We've found the U-boat base."

Smiles and congratulations greeted this statement. Tony held up his hand.

"It's not all good news. The base is well hidden. Any attack from the air would cause little or no damage. That means we must destroy it."

"Us? But we have no weapons; no ammunition."

"I know, Claude. I've been in touch with London, and they'll supply everything we need."

"How?"

"Parachute drop. That's why I've called you here. We must find a suitable drop zone and be clear of our procedures before the drop comes."

"Will they send us much equipment?"

"I've requested one container. It will be one foot in diameter and almost six feet long. It'll take the four of us men to carry the contents."

"What about me?"

Tony smiled at Madeleine. "Once we have unpacked the container we'll take its contents to a store. Jean-Paul will organise that. You'll remain at the drop zone and bury the container, Madeleine. But you must be careful. There must be no sign left."

Madeleine nodded. "Yes. I can do that."

"The main question is where should the drop take place."

Claude frowned thoughtfully. "You will be needing an open space, with cover close by?"

A nod from Tony.

"Up in the hills, where we can hide what they send with less fear of discovery?"

Another nod.

"Then, Jean-Paul," he turned to the other man, "what about the high meadow where we used to go hunting before the war?"

Jean-Paul hit his forehead with the heel of his hand. "But of course! It's ideal! Why didn't I think of that?"

"Can you show me on a map?"

Jean-Paul nodded.

"Then it's settled. We'll get word to Madeleine when we know the date and time and we will meet there. Can you find a place to cache the goods nearby?"

Jean-Paul nodded.

"Good. Madeleine, you must bring a small spade. The rest of us will need back packs, the bigger the better." He turned to Jean-Paul. "Is there material up there for starting a fire?"

"Yes."

"Good. We'll light a fire to aid the plane. Madeleine," he turned to the young woman, "you'll be responsible for hiding all traces."

She nodded. "Of course, Albert."

"Good. Then it's agreed. Do nothing to attract attention to yourselves. We'll meet at the high meadow sometime in the near future. Good luck and good night."

The group chorused their farewells. Soon the clearing was empty once more.

61

Every evening for a week, Tony took Jean-Paul's radio, which had been hidden away when all such items were confiscated by the Germans, and went into the barn to listen to the news and messages which followed. There were not many. As yet there were few agents in enemy territory, though each seemingly senseless message was full of meaning for its recipient. It was on the eighth day that a relieved Tony heard the message intended for him.

"The heron returns to its nest in spring."

Tony returned the radio to Jean-Paul, and set out with the suitcase containing his wireless. Contact was easily established and brief, home station notifying Tony that the drop would be at eleven p.m. the following day. Tony relayed details and co-ordinates of the drop zone.

Early next morning, Jean-Paul made contact with Madeleine who promised to pass on the message to Charles and Claude that afternoon. At last, all was ready.

The night was bright and clear, ideal conditions for a parachute drop. Tony found the walk to the high pasture invigorating. He and Jean-Paul arrived a little before ten p.m. in plenty of time to build a bonfire ready to light as soon as the plane's engines were heard. It was ten thirty when the others arrived, and the small group settled down to wait. As Tony watched them he could see their attempts to control their nervous excitement. He sympathised with them. He was tense himself, though he had been trained for just such a situation as this. For the others, it was a new experience which each of them would have to come to terms with in their own way. He looked up at the cloudless sky, where stars twinkled brightly. The plane would have left England by now, was probably already over France. He hoped it would get through all the air defences safely. Time passed slowly. He hated the waiting. Would the plane never come?

Madeleine heard it first. Soon they were all aware of the humming in the distance which gradually grew louder, heading in their direction but a little to the left. Tony checked his watch. 11.02. He leapt to his feet.

"Jean-Paul. Claude. Light the fire."

The fire caught quickly, and they heard the plane circling above them. Tony spotted its dark silhouette blocking out the light of some of the stars, then saw the mushroom open beneath it.

"There it is!"

He led the others in the direction of the falling container calling back over his shoulder. "Madeleine! Get that fire out!"

There was little wind and the chute came down straight, drifting a little to their right but still in the open meadow. By the time it landed, they were waiting for it. They rushed across to gather in the yards of silk that made up the parachute. The large metal cylinder, its four carrying handles giving it the appearance of a coffin, was lifted and carried into the shelter of the trees, as swiftly as its two hundred and twenty pound weight would allow. Once in the trees Tony showed the others how to open it along its hinged axis, and began to unload the contents. There was a quantity of plastic explosives, pencil fuses and limpet mines, all of which would be crucial to the destruction of the submarine pens. To Tony's delight, the packers had also included two Bren guns with plenty of ammunition. The munitions were divided into four equal piles and loaded into the backpacks. The four men were rising to their feet and adjusting their burdens, when a breathless Madeleine arrived.

"The fire is out. Ashes and unburnt wood in the trees. I've replaced the turfs."

Tony smiled. "Good. Put the parachute in the empty container, then bury it here. Cover it well with dead growth so that the disturbed earth will not be seen. We'll meet you back here in one hour."

Madeleine nodded and set to work as the four men disappeared, Jean-Paul in the lead, to conceal their supplies. Jean-Paul led them up the side of a hill to a deep gully, which led to a cave. It was not very large, but was dry and well hidden. Tony smiled broadly.

"Well done, Jean-Paul. This place couldn't be better."

The stores were concealed and the men made their way back to Madeleine, re-joining her about an hour after they left. By the time the first light of dawn broke over the hills, the five conspirators were in their beds and there was no sign at all that they had ever been up on the high meadow.

They met up at the cave again the following evening, to give Tony the opportunity to acquaint his companions with what was in the container. He had thought long and hard about how the submarine pens were to be destroyed and now he wished to convey his plans to his colleagues. Tony opened one of the packs, and took out a large lump of a putty-like substance. He began to mould it in his hands.

"This is plastic explosive."

"Explosive?" Charles eyebrows were raised in surprise. "Isn't it dangerous to handle it like that?"

Tony smiled at the young man, so like himself. "Don't worry, Charles, this is one of the safest of all types of explosives. It won't explode even if struck by a bullet, so it's perfectly safe to carry around with you. It requires a detonator embedded in the mass of the plastic to make it explode. It can be moulded like dough, so we can use it in many different ways."

"What about the detonators?"

"Well Claude, they should be here somewhere." Tony rummaged in another of the packs, then smiled. "Ahhh." He held up a handful of slim tubes. "These are pencil fuses. They are colour coded. Each colour has a different timer, ranging from ten minutes to one month. See this ridge at the end? When it is depressed it releases acid, which burns through a wire. The wire breaks, and a pin springs back and fires the detonator."

"Ingenious." Claude's mechanical mind was impressed. "What other interesting things have you got?"

"This." Tony held up a bulky object about the size of a steel helmet. "This is a limpet mine. Two pounds of plastic explosive, surrounded by half-a-dozen magnets, with a waterproof fuse. Put a few of these below the waterline, and a ship will be sunk." He smiled broadly. "Ideal for submarines!"

The others laughed. It was Madeleine who dampened the gaiety.

"We obviously have everything necessary to destroy the submarines, but how do you plan to do it, Albert?"

Tony sat down. "The fewer of us who actually go down into the base the better. Less chance of getting caught." He turned to Claude. "Will you be able to supply a car from your garage?"

The Frenchman nodded. "Yes, of course."

He turned to Madeleine. "Can you drive?"

A nod.

"Good. We'll hide the car in the trees, about half a mile north of the base. You'll wait there to drive us away." He smiled ruefully. "I don't envy you your job either, waiting is always the worst part. Charles," the young man looked up eagerly, "How good are you at climbing?"

"Quite good, Albert."

"Good. I thought we two, as the younger and fitter men, should go down and plant the explosives. Jean-Paul and Claude will wait at the top of the cliff, to haul us up and protect our backs."

"What with?"

Tony turned to Jean-Paul. "This." He held up a package. "Two Bren guns came with the drop." He showed them as he spoke. "Jean-Paul, do you think you and Claude can handle these?"

Both men nodded silently.

"Good. Before we leave tonight you can test-fire them. We won't be heard, will we Jean-Paul?"

"No, Albert. No-one lives near here."

"Good." He breathed deeply. He now had to commit himself to the plan and he was beginning to realise how difficult it was to lead. The lives of these four people were in his hands. "I don't see any point waiting. We do the job tomorrow."

There were murmurs of surprise at this.

"Any questions?"

There were none.

"Good. Madeleine and Charles, you make your way back home now, while Claude and Jean-Paul have a go with the Brens. Jean-Paul and I will pick up the stuff tomorrow and meet you all with the car, at the end of the lane leading to White Farm. Ten p.m."

The others nodded and disappeared into the trees. As they made their way down the steep hillside the sound of gunfire reached their ears.

62

The following night was cloudy and cold, but at least the rain held off. They met as planned and Madeleine drove without headlights to their rendezvous point. Once the car was safely hidden in the trees, Tony turned to his co-conspirators.

"Well, this is it. Anyone want to back out? If so, now is the time."

The others shook their heads, but Jean-Paul spoke for them all.

"No, this is for France. I won't pretend I'm not afraid because I am. I would be surprised if the others don't feel the same. But it's something we have to do, Albert, and if you can come from England to do this job, then the least we can do is help you."

Tony was touched. "Thank you, Jean-Paul." He looked up at the sky. "I think it may rain later so we'd better get going. I don't want to leave wet footprints when we enter the base."

The others reached for their packs. Tony carried plastic explosives and the fuses, as well as his Bren gun. Charles carried the limpet mines, the heavier of the four packs. Jean-Paul and Claude each had a pack containing plastic, a rope slung over their shoulders and their Bren guns. Tony handed out pencil flashlights.

"The beam of these is very narrow, but only use them in an emergency. Understood?"

The others nodded.

"Right. Let's go."

The four men made their way through the trees, Tony in the lead, and they soon found themselves crouched down, gazing at the open space bordering the edge of the cliff. Tony pointed to the rocky outcrop.

"That's where we go down. We'll be hidden from the guards, or anyone on the cliff path."

He carefully surveyed the cliff -top but could see no signs of movement.

"Let's go."

They ran, crouched low, to the large rock where Jean-Paul had anchored Tony's rope on their previous visit. Claude and Jean-Paul shrugged off their packs and secured the two ropes, while Charles and Tony picked up the spare packs and slung them, uncomfortably, from their shoulders. Tony turned to look at Charles who nodded silently.

"Right. I'll set the timers for two hours. When we're ready to come back up I'll give three tugs on the rope."

Jean-Paul nodded. "We'll be ready, Albert."

The two young men slid over the edge, and began to lower themselves down the cliff face. It was more difficult than Tony's previous descent for now he was encumbered with packs and weapons, but there were no mishaps and the two men soon found themselves crouched in the shadows at the base of the cliff. Tony peered cautiously around the outcrop. He studied the approach to the narrow passageway that led through the cliff wall and into the cavern beyond. There was a movement away to his right, a dark, man-sized shadow. He slipped behind the rock and placed his mouth close to Charles' ear.

"A guard. Wait."

Charles nodded.

Removing his packs, and laying them quietly on the rocky ledge, Tony put down his gun and drew a knife from his belt. He watched the guard for some time from behind the rock. When his back was turned, Tony crept up behind him. His left hand snaked out around the man's face and covered his mouth, silencing the gasp of surprise. The guard reached up his hands to try to loosen Tony's iron grip, and the Englishman's right hand came round, sliding the blade of the knife between two ribs and into the German's heart, just as he had been shown in training. This time, however, it was different. This was a real knife and a real man. As the life drained from the guard, he slumped heavily in

Tony's arms. He stood for a moment, shocked. He had killed a man with his own hands. He had probably been a good man. Maybe he had a wife and children, a father and mother to mourn? Tony clamped down on the thoughts whirling round his head. The man was the enemy. If Tony had not killed him, then he would have tried to kill Tony. Forget the personal details. Tony hurried back towards the outcrop of rock, dragging the body with him. As he hid the guard's body, he noticed Charles' pale face and grim expression as he looked at the bloodstained knife.

"Are you all right?" he whispered.

Tony nodded, but said nothing. For a moment he contemplated taking the German's uniform, but the bloodstained jacket would attract too much attention. They would be far less conspicuous in the blue overalls they had acquired for the night's work. Tony retrieved his packs and gun, his face grim.

"Come on, Charles."

The young Frenchman followed closely behind Tony as he slipped silently across the rocky ledge and into the narrow passageway. Again his heart was in his mouth. What if someone was coming the other way? But there was no one there, and the two saboteurs were soon hidden behind the huge piles of supplies lining the cave walls. Tony had carefully tutored Charles in what was expected of him, and they set to work swiftly and silently. Charles passed the plastic explosive to Tony who moulded it and attached it to the supply cases, while Charles took out a pencil fuse ready for when Tony needed it. The Englishman held out his hand, and Charles passed the fuse. Within seconds it was embedded in the plastic charge and the ridge depressed, releasing the acid. Tony paused to look around.

The cavern was busy, but the movement was not as frantic as on his last visit. Perhaps there was no U-boat going out tonight. Although the centre of the huge space was well lit, there were deep shadows against the walls. The two men should be able to make a complete circuit without being seen. Tony picked up his packs and led Charles to the next pile of supplies. They worked methodically, paying little attention to the activity around them, their whole being concentrating on the job in hand. As they passed the huge metal drums, Tony sniffed at them carefully. The first stack contained water. They ignored these, but the second and third piles had the distinct smell of diesel about them. Tony smiled grimly as he placed explosives in the middle of each one. When these went up, they would certainly help to maximise the destruction.

By the time they had worked themselves round to the far side of the cavern, taking great care when passing the entrance to the crew quarters, forty-five minutes had passed. Three of the packs were empty. All that remained now were the limpet mines. Tony looked at the two sinister black shapes moored to the rocky shelf. There was little activity around the U-boats. Most of the workers seemed to have retreated to the crew's quarters. The majority of the remaining Germans were uniformed soldiers. They probably did not understand what work was in progress and Tony felt that, if he acted confidently enough, they probably would not notice him moving around the cavern. He emptied a toolbox which he found abandoned in a dark corner, and placed four limpet mines carefully inside.

"What are you doing?"

"I'm going to try to get these onto the submarines. You hang on to my gun, and be prepared to use it if necessary."

Charles nodded as Tony rose to his feet. He sauntered towards the U-boat, toolbox in hand, his heart beating wildly yet showing an outward confidence which amazed the Frenchman. Tony did not know how he managed to cross the narrow space to the submarine without giving himself away, but there he was. Kneeling down, he slipped the first of the mines below the waterline and heard the dull thud as the magnets made contact with the hull. He hoped that there was no one on board. If there was, they would surely have heard. He continued working until all four mines were attached along the length of the submarine, then rose and sauntered back towards the pile of supplies. Once out of sight he slid to the ground, heart racing. He leant back, breathing deeply. Charles quickly joined him, obviously impressed.

"I've never seen such courage!" he whispered.

Tony smiled weakly. "Courage? I was terrified!"

"Let's get out of here, then."

Tony shook his head. "No. I still have to mine the other U-boat."

Charles was wide-eyed. "Haven't you done enough?"

"I have to be sure they'll both be destroyed."

Charles nodded. "OK. Come on."

They made their stealthy way back round the cavern until they reached their starting point. Tony placed four more limpet mines in the toolbox. He walked nonchalantly towards the second submarine. As far as any observer was concerned, he was just another worker going about his business. This U-boat was deeper in shadow than the first, and Tony completed his task swiftly before rejoining Charles behind the supplies. Two of the empty packs were slipped into a third, Charles carried this, while Tony took the pack with the two remaining limpet mines. The two men carefully surveyed the cavern. There was no evidence they had ever been there. As long as their luck held, the Germans would not know what had hit them when the charges exploded. They smiled victoriously at each other and shook hands.

"Come on." Tony's voice was little more than a whisper. He led the way back out of the cavern. A soft drizzle had begun to fall soon after they had entered the cavern and was still falling, leaving the rocky ledge wet and slippery. The two men made their way cautiously towards the huge sea doors through which the U-boats entered the base. Tony removed the final two mines from his pack.

"These must be fitted below the waterline. I'll have to swim."

Charles looked doubtful. "Is that wise? Look at the way the waves are moving, there's probably a strong undertow there."

"I have to risk it."

Tony slipped into the water, and Charles passed him the first of the mines. As Tony submerged, he felt the pull of water trying to drag him away. He clung desperately to the rocks with one hand, while fixing the mine with the other. He surfaced, gasping for air, his wet hair plastered to his skull, and reached out a hand for the final mine. Charles handed it over and watched as Tony disappeared beneath the waves once more. It was long, worrying moments before he re-appeared, and the grateful Frenchman dragged him from the waves.

"If you don't mind, Albert, I think I would like to go home now."

Tony smiled. "I agree, wholeheartedly."

They made their way back to the outcropping of rock, the drizzle becoming heavier by the minute. They were so emotionally drained that the sight of the German whom Tony had killed moved them not at all. Tony looked at his watch. An hour before the first explosion. They would have plenty of time to get away. He reached out and tugged the rope, signalling Jean-Paul and Claude that they were coming back up. He frowned.

"The ropes are wet, Charles. Take care."

The Frenchman nodded and began to climb his rope swiftly and surely. Tony began his ascent too, but his hands were wet and slippery from the seawater and he found it difficult to get a grip on the rope. He struggled upwards, concerned by his physical and mental exhaustion, but knowing he had to get to the top. He looked up and saw Charles, almost at the top now, reaching a hand to the cliff edge to draw himself up. Part of the cliff came away in Charles' hand. For a moment the young Frenchman teetered on the edge, before welcoming hands reached down to pull him up. Jean-Paul and Claude dragged him over the edge as a large rock broke away and came hurtling towards Tony. He hunched down, lying as close to the cliff face as he could, trying to minimise his body and avoid the falling rock, but he knew it would hit him. When it came, the impact was on his left shoulder and he felt the whole of his left arm go numb. His fingers could no longer cling to the wet rope, and his left hand fell away. Tony closed his eyes as the pain suffused his body. He looped the rope about his good arm, hoping he could hang on until help reached him. Anxious voices called softly from above.

"Albert? Are you all right?"

"No." Tony's voice was little more than a whisper, and he doubted if they heard him up above. He looked up. Charles was coming back over the edge of the cliff. If he could only hold on for a few moments longer. His right hand and arm were tiring and, as he felt the wet rope slipping, he knew he would not be able to hold on long enough.

"Charles!"

The Frenchman looked down.

"I can't hold on. Go back. You and the others must get clear!"

The rope finally slid through his fingers, and he found himself falling. He closed his eyes and braced himself for the impact, willing himself not to cry out as he fell. He must not give the others away. The fall seemed to take forever, then the impact came, and he knew no more.

Up on the cliff edge three horror-struck faces gazed down at the broken body on the rocks below.

OCTOBER - DECEMBER 1941

63

Sarah walked amongst trees now clothed in red and gold. Fallen leaves rustled underfoot as she made her way through the orchard and down towards the river. A heron rose into the air, huge wings beating, long neck pulled in and long legs trailing behind. Sarah smiled. She always wondered how such a large bird could raise itself from the water, and fly so gracefully. It seemed almost impossible that it should be able to fly at all, yet it could, and she saw it as a symbol of hope. No matter how impossible things might seem, no matter how far the Germans advanced in North Africa and Russia, no matter how many young men lost their lives fighting for freedom, there was still hope for the future. Things, however impossible they seemed, would be accomplished and freedom regained. As the heron winged its way over the low hedge into the fields beyond, Sarah breathed the chill autumn air deeply, thankful she had been posted to such a beautiful and tranquil place. She had no doubt that the slow healing of her heart after Joe's death was partly due to the peace of her surroundings. She would never forget Joe, and there would always be a secret corner of her heart devoted to his memory, but she could now face the future without him. She looked down at her finger and saw the ring he had given her. It glittered in the weak sunshine. Was it really almost a year now since he had placed it there? A slow smile played upon her lips as she toyed with it. She remembered Joe's happiness, and her own, when she agreed to be his wife.

"Penny for them."

Sarah was startled and turned quickly. She had been so lost in her thoughts that she had not heard the sound of approaching footsteps.

"Jane! You made me jump!" She laughed. "What did you say?"

"I said I'd give a penny for your thoughts."

"Oh." Sarah looked down at the ring upon her finger. "Well, if you must know, I was just saying goodbye."

"Goodbye?" Jane frowned. "I don't understand. There's no-one here."

"Yes, there is." Sarah tapped her chest. "Here in my heart. I've decided to stop dwelling on what might have been, and face the future." She took off the ring, and as she saw it laying in the palm of her hand her eyes glistened with unshed tears. "I won't wear his ring anymore. It's a constant reminder of what might have been. I'm sure Joe wouldn't want me to waste my life living in a dream."

Jane reached out to embrace her friend. "Oh, Sarah. I know how hard this must be for you, but you're doing the right thing."

Sarah pulled away and nodded. "I know. But it isn't going to be easy."

"You'd be surprised!" Jane laughed. "I've seen the way some of our patients look at you. Now that you don't wear his ring anymore, I'm sure the men will come flocking!"

Sarah laughed. "Really, Jane! I didn't mean that and you know it!" Her face resumed its serious expression. "Seriously though, I'm not ready to fall in love again. Especially with the uncertainty of war. I couldn't bear to fall in love again, only to lose that man like I lost Joe."

"Do you wish you'd never loved Joe?"

"Of course not! How could you... Oh, I see what you mean. If I loved and lost again, it would be better than not loving at all."

Jane nodded. "Something like that." She sighed. "I often think I'll never fall in love."

"Don't be ridiculous! You've had more boyfriends than I've had hot dinners!"

"But I've never been in love." Jane chuckled. "Still, I can keep looking! Which reminds me, there's a dance on in Marlborough tonight. Do you want to come with me?"

Sarah looked at Joe's ring once more. "No. I don't think so."

"Come on, Sarah. I may be looking for the man of my dreams, but that doesn't mean you have to! Just come along and enjoy yourself."

Sarah thought for a moment then nodded emphatically, closing her fist around Joe's ring in a strangely final gesture.

"All right. I will!"

It felt strange to Sarah to be walking into a room full of men and women laughing and dancing, and so obviously having a good time. She had not been to a dance since Joe's death. She had hardly left the grounds of Heronfield in all those lonely months, and though she was grateful for the peace and healing of that place, she now realised how close she had come to burying herself there, to allowing her work to become her whole life. Watching the couples dancing, she was aware of what a waste that would have been. Jane turned towards her friend, and was cheered by the smile which lit her face.

"Glad you came?"

Sarah nodded.

"Come on, let's find a seat."

They edged their way around the dance floor to a vacant table in the corner, but had barely seated themselves before two young airmen came to join them.

"Hello, Jane. Who's you're new friend?"

Jane smiled up at the two.

"Graham, Nick, I'd like you to meet Sarah Porter. We work together at Heronfield."

The two young men grinned. "Pleased to meet you," they chorused

Sarah found their grins infectious and smiled in return.

"Hello."

Nick took Jane by the hand and led her out onto the dance floor. Graham watched them go, then turned to Sarah.

"Would you like to dance?"

She nodded and followed him onto the floor. She had forgotten how good it felt to be in the arms of a man, moving to the rhythm of the music.

"Are you new at Heronfield? Only I've never seen you before. I would certainly remember you if I had."

Sarah shook her head. "No. I've been there since the hospital opened eighteen months ago."

"Eighteen months! Then where have you been hiding yourself?"

"Oh, I've been busy."

"You should never be too busy to go out and enjoy yourself. Come on."

Graham began to swing her energetically around the dance floor. He was an excellent dancer, and Sarah began to enjoy herself, but after four dances she pulled away from his arms, laughing breathlessly.

"Enough! Please, I must sit down!"

Graham laughed too, and led her towards the table where Jane and Nick were already sitting. As the breathless couple sank into their seats, Nick indicated the glasses on the table.

178

"I got some drinks for you."

They reached gratefully for the glasses and murmured their thanks. Sarah turned to Jane, her face glowing.

"No wonder you find it hard to get up in the mornings if you dance like this all night!"

Jane smiled warmly at her friend. "Enjoying yourself?"

The nod was superfluous, the shining eyes and smiling face said it all.

Sarah danced more that evening than she had done since the outbreak of war, sometimes with Nick, but mostly with Graham who seemed fascinated by her. While she was dancing with Nick, Graham took the opportunity to move closer to Jane.

"Who is she, Jane? And why has she never been here with you before?"

"I'm sure she's told you who she is. She's been here once or twice, though not for the last six or seven months."

"Why not?"

"Hasn't she told you?"

Graham shook his head, and Jane gazed thoughtfully at her friend on the dance floor before making a decision.

"It's no secret I suppose, but don't let her know I've told you. She's not looking for sympathy."

"Sympathy?" Graham was intrigued.

"Yes. Her fiancé was killed in a bombing raid earlier this year. She's only now coming to terms with it. This is her first time out."

Graham looked at Sarah and Nick enjoying themselves on the dance floor.

"Poor girl. But she seems to be over it now."

"Don't let her fool you." Jane's face was serious. "She's decided that she must get out and about again, but she's not looking for another relationship yet."

"Maybe I can make her change her mind."

The music stopped, and the dancers began to make their way back to the table.

"Don't be too hasty Graham," Jane warned with a whisper. "And don't you dare hurt her, or you'll have me to answer to."

Graham turned to her in surprise. "I've never seen you so serious Jane. You're that concerned for her?"

Jane nodded. "Just be careful."

Nick reached the table, and took Jane's hand with a welcoming smile.

"It's time for the last dance. Come on."

Jane shot a warning look at Graham as she rose and left the table, then she turned away from the other couple as her whole attention was centred on her partner.

Graham smiled at his companion. "Can you manage the last dance?"

Sarah nodded and allowed herself to be led onto the dance floor, where Graham held her closely for the last waltz.

"I've enjoyed this evening."

"Me too." Sarah nodded.

"Can I see you again?"

"Maybe."

"How about tomorrow?"

Sarah pulled away slightly so that she could see his face. He looked eager, almost too eager, and she shook her head.

"I don't think so, Graham. I've had a lovely evening but that's all there is to it. Maybe we can spend the evening together if we meet here again, but I won't make any promises. I'm sorry."

Graham smiled and pulled her close once more. "That's all right, I'm used to girls saying no. But you can't blame a man for trying can you?"

64

Jean-Paul watched Tony's body twisting silently in the air as he fell, only to be halted by the rocks below with a sickening crunch. Through the horror he also felt a deep admiration for the man who had not cried out as he fell. It would have been so easy to shout out in pain and fear, but that would have alerted the Germans and Jean-Paul realised that Tony put the safety of his colleagues and the destruction of the base before everything else, even his own life. He had heard his final words to Charles urging them to escape, but Jean-Paul knew that he could not leave Tony at the base of the cliff. Not only was he a brave man and the leader of their group, he was also the grandson of Madame de Thierry and his family had served hers faithfully for generations. There was no way he could leave the young man down there at the mercy of the Germans.

"Charles." Jean-Paul's voice was a hoarse whisper. "Come up. I'll go down to Albert."

Charles looked up from his position six feet down the cliff face.

"No Jean-Paul. I'll go down. I'll tie the second rope around him and you can pull him up."

"Won't that compound his injuries?"

Charles glanced up at Claude. "Possibly. But what else can we do? Leave him to the Germans, or to be blown up by our own explosives? I must go."

Claude nodded and watched as the younger man descended the cliff. He moved cautiously down until his feet touched the cold wet ledge, then quickly crossed to kneel beside the inert Tony. For a moment he feared the young man might be dead, but as he leant closer he saw the gentle movement of his chest. Tony's left leg was tucked underneath him at an unnatural angle, and Charles assumed that it was broken. There was also a deep gash above his left eyebrow which was bleeding freely. The young Frenchman had no time to check for other injuries as he bandaged the gash and straightened the leg, praying that he would not injure Tony further. He was glad the Englishman was unconscious. The task of raising him up the cliff face would be painful. Charles took the ends of the rope and tied them securely around Tony's body, just beneath his arms. He tugged the rope to signal that he was ready, and the two men on the cliff top began to haul on the rope. Charles supported Tony as the slack was taken up and he was raised up the first few feet of the cliff face. Another tug signalled Jean-Paul and Claude to wait, and Tony hung, swinging gently, his head on his chest and his limbs hanging loosely. Charles climbed a few feet up the cliff and tied the other rope around himself so it was too short to reach the ground, that way he could trust it to save him if he fell while trying to get Tony to the top of the cliff. When he was ready, he signalled his two friends and the slow ascent began.

Jean-Paul and Claude hauled away on the two ropes while Charles braced himself, using his body as a buffer between Tony and the rock face. His feet slipped frequently on the wet stone, but he somehow managed to keep going, trusting to Jean-Paul who took up the slack and kept him from falling. It was hard, tiring work, but eventually the two men were at the top of the cliff. Charles scrambled up onto the grass before helping his two colleagues to pull Tony up behind him.

For a moment they rested, then Jean-Paul spoke. "Is he still alive?"

Charles nodded. "Yes. But I don't know how bad his injuries are. What do we do now?"

"We get him down to a deserted fishing hut I know of, some five miles down the coast. Then we will have time to think about what to do next. How long until the first explosion?"

Charles looked at his watch.

"A little over thirty minutes. We'll have to move quickly if we're to be clear of the area by then."

The three men rose and lifted Tony between them, before moving off into the trees. The half-mile from the edge of the cliffs to where Madeleine was waiting seemed endless. It was so dark they could hardly see where to put their feet. They were careful not to jolt Tony too much, grateful that he was still unconscious for they had to move as swiftly as possible and knew that their movements were likely to be aggravating his injuries. Twenty minutes had passed before they saw the black shadow of the car amongst the trees, and thankfully placed him on the rear seat.

"What happened?" Madeleine's face was white in the darkness as she looked at the unconscious man.

"No time to explain." Jean-Paul climbed in beside her, Charles and Claude close behind him. "Drive out onto the road and head north."

Madeleine complied, and the engine roared into life. Slowly she manoeuvred the car through the trees and out onto the road where she picked up a little speed, though it was impossible to go too fast on the unlit country road without any lights. The road was empty. The curfew kept all civilians in during the night and they knew that if they met anyone at all it would be a German patrol. Their nerves were on edge as they drove into the dark of the night. There were only moments to go until all the Germans in the vicinity would be aware of their night's work. Time seemed to drag by as Madeleine made the best speed she could. They had covered only four miles when an explosion rent the night. Jean-Paul looked back over his shoulder to see a brilliant flash light the sky followed almost immediately by another explosion. He smiled grimly.

"Whatever else happens, it looks as though you and Albert planted your explosives well."

"That was all Albert's work, Jean-Paul." Charles' face was grim. "He'll be glad to know that the submarine pens are destroyed when he wakes."

Claude looked up from where he was sitting beside Tony, trying to cushion his body against the jolts of their progress.

"If he wakes. His breathing is becoming shallower. I fear he may have internal injuries. We must get help for him. Fast."

Jean-Paul nodded. "I know. Turn here."

He indicated a small track as he spoke, and Madeleine swung into it. It was rough. Even though she took it with care they were jolted from side to side in the vehicle. Jean-Paul looked back at Tony and frowned. The Englishman's face was pale and blood-stained, looking younger in unconsciousness than he had before, and Jean-Paul realised that this brave man was not quite twenty-four years old.

"Is this it?" Madeleine's voice brought him round to face the front. He nodded as he saw a small, one-roomed fishing hut loom out of the night.

"Yes. Stop and let Charles and me out here. We'll take Albert inside and do what we can to help him. You and Claude go to the village a mile further on and bring back Dr. Leclerc. I'm sure he'll help us. But be careful. The Germans will be out searching for us by now. You may have to leave the car and go on foot."

Madeleine nodded as Jean-Paul climbed down. Charles carefully lifted the heavy weight of the unconscious man, and slid him across the seat until Jean-Paul could get a hold under his arms. Slowly, the two Frenchmen carried Tony to the hut. Claude opened the door and placed sacking over the window, before lighting a small oil lamp which illuminated the interior of the hut. It was small, a bed set against one wall and a small table and chair against the other were the only furnishings. The two men laid their burden down on the bed.

"I'll go with Madeleine." Claude turned and left the hut. The door closed behind him, and Jean-Paul turned his attention to Tony.

His face was ashen. Blood was seeping through the rough bandage that Charles had tied on, and was now matting his hair. Charles took a bowl from the table and left the hut, returning a few minutes later with water he had fetched from the stream a few paces from the door. Gently he began to bathe the hair.

"Don't take the bandage off until Leclerc gets here," Jean-Paul cautioned. "The less we do the better. Unless you know more about medicine than me."

Charles shook his head. "No. I'm afraid not." He gazed worriedly at Tony. "All we can do is wait. And pray."

Madeleine drove back along the twisting lane. Away to the south, the sky was lit with the burning of their night's work. As she imagined the destruction, she smiled grimly. Approaching the junction with the main road, Madeleine cut the car's engine and listened intently. All was quiet then, just as she was about to restart the engine, a low rumbling reached her ears. Three trucks approached at speed, heading south towards the burning, each truck full of soldiers.

Claude's face was grim.

"They will soon be searching down this way. Perhaps we should leave the car."

Madeleine shook her head. "No. I'm not a doctor but Albert looks really bad to me. If we don't get the doctor to him quickly, it might be too late." She turned towards the older man. "There's no point in risking both our lives. You can get out now if you like."

Claude smiled grimly. "And leave you alone with my car? No, I think I'll come with you."

Madeleine nodded as she turned the key. The engine roared into life. Swinging north onto the coast road, she accelerated away into the dark. It only took minutes to complete the mile to the village. Madeleine left the car hidden in the shadow of a clump of trees, and went on foot to the doctor's house, closely followed by Claude. They made their way cautiously down the garden path towards the shadowy bulk of the darkened house. When they reached the ivy-covered walls, Madeleine lifted a hand and tapped gently on the window. After a few moments without an answer, she knocked again a little louder. At last footsteps were heard approaching the other side of the door.

"Who's there?"

"My name is Madeleine, Dr. Leclerc. Jean-Paul Boues sent me. We have an injured man."

The door opened a crack, and the face of a man in his latter years peered out. His gaze darted around the empty night then looked back at the two people who stood outside his door, a frown furrowing his brow.

"An injured man? Where?"

"Before we tell you that, may I ask you something?" Claude spoke in little more than a whisper. "How do you feel about the Germans?"

The doctor's face was grim.

"The Germans? I hate them, like all true Frenchmen should. Especially since they killed my only son. Why do you ask?"

182

"Well..." Madeleine began slowly but continued with a rush. "The injured man is an English spy. Tonight we helped him to blow up a submarine base six miles from here. We need to know if we can trust you. And you need to decide if you are willing to risk your life to help."

Leclerc's eyes were wide with astonishment. "An English spy? A submarine base? Of course you can trust me! I'll get my bag."

The doctor disappeared for a moment, then came back buttoning up his coat with one hand and clutching his bag with the other.

Madeleine led the way down the path, back to where the car was concealed.

"Are the roads safe?"

Claude shrugged at Leclerc's question.

"Who knows? There are bound to be soldiers all over the place, now that the explosives have gone off. But we must risk it if we are to save Albert."

Without another word the three people climbed into the car. The engine was gunned into life and they headed back towards the south, where the sky was alight with the flames of their night.

Jean-Paul listened intently, his nerves on edge as he waited to hear the sound of the returning car. At last the sound of the engine reached his ears, and he opened the door in relief. He did not know how much longer he could have stood the inactivity of waiting while his friend lay injured. His relief showed in his voice.

"Doctor! Thank goodness you've come!"

Leclerc climbed out of the car and joined the others in the hut. He faced his friend across the expanse of the room.

"What happened, Jean-Paul?"

He indicated the bed.

"A rock fell onto his shoulder while he was climbing a cliff. It caused him to fall. His left leg is broken, but we don't know what other injuries he has."

Leclerc began to examine Tony, starting at the head and working down to the broken leg.

"I'll leave the bandage for the moment," he said as he gently felt Tony's shoulder. "His left collar bone is broken and there is much bruising." He frowned as he examined the torso. "He has broken some ribs. I hope they haven't caused any internal bleeding." He continued his explorations. "The left leg is broken in two places, and there is a great deal of bruising." He looked across at Jean-Paul. "It would be better if this man were not moved. Will he be safe here?"

Jean-Paul shrugged. "As safe as anywhere else, I suppose. This hut is normally only used in the summer, so no one should come here. As for the Germans, I have no idea where they will search." He looked at his watch. "Its three a.m. now. I think it would be best if we all stay here until morning, then make our way back into Saint Nazaire with the workers. Madeleine," he turned to the woman as he spoke, "will you be able to stay here and look after Albert?"

Madeleine nodded." "Of course."

"Good. I'll come back when I can. What do you say, Leclerc?"

The doctor nodded slowly. "That will be all right. I'll have to come back, so I'll bring food and medication." He turned to look at the patient. "Now I must get back to work."

Leclerc worked slowly and steadily, straightening the broken leg and splinting it with a broken broom handle. The broken ribs were bandaged, the collar bone treated and the arm placed in a sling. Finally he removed the bandage, washed the gash on Tony's head and stitched it together. At last he looked up from his work.

"That's the best I can do for him, Jean-Paul. What he really needs is hospital treatment."

"We can't get him to a hospital."

"I know. What about getting him back to England?"

Jean-Paul shrugged. "I don't know. I'll bring his radio tonight. If he's well enough he can get in touch with his superiors and organise something."

Jean-Paul stood over his friend gazing gravely down. What were his chances of getting back to England for treatment? Jean-Paul did not know what contingency plans, if any, Tony had and he knew the days ahead would be long and difficult.

When Jean-Paul returned to his cottage, he found his wife and daughters filled with fear at his prolonged absence, and they were immensely relieved at his safe arrival.

"Oh Papa! I'm so glad to see you!" Theresa flung herself into her father's arms and hugged him tightly.

"We were so worried about you."

Jean Paul looked across at his wife and smiled tiredly.

"No need to worry about me now. I'm safe."

"Where's Albert?" Theresa pulled away as she spoke. "Why hasn't he come home with you?"

"Albert has moved on to work somewhere else." Jean-Paul's eyes found those of his wife as he spoke. Marie frowned, but said nothing. He looked down and saw the concern in the eyes of his older daughter, concern and a determination to find out what was really happening. He sighed deeply before turning to Jeanne.

"Well, my little one, have you collected the eggs this morning?"

Jeanne shook her head.

"Well, off you go, then." Jean-Paul patted her affectionately on the bottom as she ran towards the door. "I'd like an egg with my breakfast today."

When the little girl had gone and the door was closed behind her, Jean-Paul turned back to his wife and older daughter.

"I will be honest with you two, but you must say nothing of what I reveal to you to anyone, especially Jeanne. It could be very dangerous. Do you understand?"

His words were meant chiefly for Theresa. She nodded.

"Yes, Papa."

"Then this is what happened. Albert and I, with some friends from Saint Nazaire, blew up a German submarine base last night."

Marie's face went white, and her mouth gaped, but Theresa was not silent. Her face was radiant, eyes sparkling.

"Oh, Papa! I'm so proud of you!" She ran to her father and kissed him. "Is Albert hiding? Will you be safe here?"

Jean-Paul frowned. "The Germans are likely to search thoroughly for us, but they don't know who we are. They'll probably centre their search on the city. Albert is further up the coast, and as long as no-one says anything I think he will be safe."

"Will he come back then?"

Jean-Paul took her hand and sat her on his knee. "I don't think so, little one. You see, Albert was hurt, very badly. We must care for him until the Germans stop looking for us, and then try to get him to a hospital."

Marie's eyes filled with tears.

"Poor Monsieur Tony," she said softly. "Will you try to get him back to England?"

Theresa was thunderstruck. "Mamma! You called Albert Monsieur Tony, and you mentioned England as well!"

Marie raised her hand to her mouth in horror. "Oh Jean-Paul, I'm sorry. I wasn't thinking."

Jean-Paul frowned. "There's no harm done Marie, but you must be more careful. Another slip like that could cost him, and me, our lives."

Marie said nothing while Theresa frowned for a moment, deep in thought. "Papa, you have work to do on the estate and you'll be missed if you're not there. Is it the same with your friends?"

Jean-Paul nodded. "Yes."

"Then who will look after Albert?"

Jean-Paul smiled grimly at his daughter. "You have a keen mind, little one. A doctor has already seen him and will visit again. One of my friends is staying with him today, and I'll go to him tonight. I'll spend most nights with him." He looked across at Marie, who nodded.

"That's how it should be, Jean-Paul."

"Can your friend look after him every day?"

Jean-Paul shook his head. "No, she must go back to work tomorrow. We will do the best we can though to care for him."

"What about me?"

"You?"

"Yes, Papa. I could go and look after him. The Germans wouldn't miss a little girl like me, and if other people asked, you could say I've gone to stay with someone, maybe Aunt Yvette."

Jean-Paul frowned. "I don't know."

"Please, Papa."

"It sounds a good idea, Jean-Paul."

The Frenchman looked at his wife. "You wouldn't object?"

"Not for Albert. As long as we can be sure that Theresa is safe."

"That is just it. Until the excitement from last night's raid dies down and the Germans stop searching, it will not be safe."

"But Papa!"

Jean-Paul held up his hand. "Wait. I was saying that until the search is over it will not be safe. After that you can help to look after Albert."

Theresa's face was solemn.

"Thank you, Papa. I understand how dangerous it is. I will not let you down. I promise."

Jean-Paul looked at his daughter. Only eleven years old, yet she seemed so mature. He was proud of her, and hoped that he was doing the right thing in including her in his plans. His heart was gripped with a sudden fear for the safety of, and a deep love for, his brave little daughter He smiled to chase away his fears, and gently pulled her plait as he had done when she was smaller.

"Theresa, you are a good French girl. I'm proud of you and..."

The door burst open and they all turned fearfully towards it, only to see Jeanne carrying a large basket laden with eggs.

"Here you are, Papa!"

Jean-Paul laughed with relief.

"Good. I don't think I have ever felt so hungry!"

65

That night was dark as Jean-Paul made his careful way by bicycle, down the coast to the small fishing hut where he had left Madeleine and Tony. He watched from the trees for a time to make sure that all was safe. It was dark, silent, seemingly deserted. Slowly he crept forward, and put his ear to the door. There was no sound. He closed his eyes and took a deep breath. Either everything was all right and Tony and Madeleine were sleeping, or the Germans had found them and were waiting in ambush. There was only one way to find out. His grip tightened on the Bren gun in his hand, and he slowly opened the door.

The hut was lit by the pale glow of an oil lamp. Jean-Paul entered quickly, closing the door behind him so no light would escape. He swung his gun round the interior of the room, his eyes taking in the occupants.

"Please don't point that thing at me!" Leclerc's face was white. "I'm on your side. Remember?"

Jean-Paul smiled. "Sorry doctor. Just being careful. Where's Madeleine?"

"I came late this afternoon and sent her back to Saint Nazaire. I thought it would be better for her to travel before the curfew."

"You were right. Thank you for staying with Albert." He turned towards the inert form on the bed. "How is he?"

"He regained consciousness a while ago, and is sleeping now. I gave him something for the pain." He frowned. "I don't think he has any internal injuries, but I wish I could get him to a hospital."

"That's not possible, doctor." Jean-Paul was worried. "I don't know how we're going to care for him while the Germans are still searching for us. I can come at night, but we will all be missed during the day. For the next few days we should do nothing out of the ordinary. It may even have been a mistake to leave Madeleine here today. She might have been missed in the city."

Leclerc shrugged. "There's nothing we can do about that now." He looked at Tony. "I don't like to leave him alone, but I'm afraid that will be necessary. If you stay until just before dawn, I'll come back as soon after surgery as I can, midmorning at latest, and be here until early afternoon. Can you come back before nightfall?"

Jean-Paul nodded. "It's a good job it's now late in the year, and night comes early. Will he be all right for those few hours alone?"

"He should be, but who knows?" The doctor rose to his feet. "I must be going before I'm missed."

Jean-Paul shook him warmly by the hand. "Thank you, doctor. I don't know what we should have done without you."

Leclerc smiled. "No thanks are needed. I'm glad to help."

The doctor slipped silently from the hut.

Jean-Paul checked that the fire burning in the small hearth was not giving off any smoke, then turned towards the bed. The fire gave some heat but not enough. Tony's still form was lost beneath a pile of blankets, more of Leclerc's work, Jean-Paul assumed. As his gaze fell on Tony's face he noticed that the Englishman's eyes were open.

"Albert! How are you feeling?"

Tony grinned weakly. "Never felt better!" His voice was weak. It seemed an effort for him to speak. "I heard you talking with the doctor."

"I'm sorry I woke you."

"No, that's all right." Tony closed his eyes for a moment, then opened them again. They were worried, questioning.

"What happened last night?"

"We managed to get you back up the cliff and down here. The doctor is a good man and he has done all he can for you but, frankly, you should be in hospital."

"The base?"

Jean-Paul smiled. "It went up like a rocket on Bastille Day! We heard the explosion and saw the flames from three miles away. I don't know how much damage was done, and the Germans certainly aren't telling, but by the way they've been rushing around today, it must have been serious! They're questioning people and searching local farms and such like, but they have nothing to go on."

"Have they been this way yet?"

Jean-Paul shook his head. "They seem to be concentrating more on the area round the base. I get the impression they think it was perhaps a commando team coming in from the sea, as there were so many munitions involved and they've found no sign of us. I suppose they will continue searching for a few more days, though they must realise that if they didn't get us straight away, they're not likely to catch us at all."

"As long as they don't find me here." Tony's face was anguished. "I'm a liability, Jean-Paul, a danger to you all. You should have left me at the bottom of the cliff."

"And how was I supposed to explain that to your grandmother at the end of the war? No, my friend, I couldn't leave you just as, if our places had been reversed, you couldn't have left me."

Tony smiled weakly. "You're right. Thank you." He groaned. "I hurt all over, Jean-Paul. What's going to happen to me now"

"I've thought of that. I've brought your radio and hidden it in the trees. You could call England and ask them to send a plane, or a submarine if they can, for we are right down on the beach here. Can they do that?"

"It's possible, Jean-Paul, but I'll have to wait a while before using the radio."

"Why?"

"The Germans will be monitoring more closely for the next few days. I won't be able to move after using it, so we must wait until some of the panic has died down. And I don't think I have the strength at the moment to encode a message and transmit it."

"I'm sorry, Albert. I didn't think."

"That's all right. At least the radio will be close by when I need it. Can you bring a map of the area next time you come, so I can work out map references?"

Jean-Paul nodded.

Tony's eyes closed. The talking had tired him more than he had thought possible. He felt the acute pain of the injuries to his head, shoulder, ribs and leg, and behind all that the dull ache of his many cuts and bruises. He had never felt so much pain before. The insecurity of the situation filled him with dread, yet underlying those feelings was a satisfaction at a job well done, and he knew that if he did nothing else in this war, this one action would avenge David's death, and prove to his father that he was not a coward.

"All I want now is to rest," he muttered. And with that he slipped into a troubled sleep.

"The Germans have been searching for three days now. Have they found anything?" Marie's anxiety showed in her eyes.

Jean-Paul shook his head. "No. For all the passes they've checked and the restrictions they've put on the movements of people, they're no nearer finding us than on the night of the attack."

"How long will the searches go on?"

Jean-Paul shook his head. "I don't know, but they already seem to be removing some of the restrictions. The Germans probably don't think there were any locals involved. The Resistance isn't that organised. If they think the people who did it have got away, they should stop searching soon." He smiled reassuringly at his wife. "I went into the city today. One of my friends said things are returning to normal, or as normal as can be expected. They've not been near the fishing hut yet, so I am guessing that Albert's hiding place is safe."

"How is he?"

"He seems to be mending, but the doctor is still worried that he might have internal injuries. He wants him to get to a hospital."

"But that's not possible."

"No. And I can't keep asking the doctor to go out there every day. It could draw attention to him, and he has other patients to look after."

"Then it is time for Theresa to go and look after Albert."

Jean-Paul turned his solemn gaze towards his wife. "I think so. If you still agree."

Marie nodded. "Of course I shall worry about her. But it is a duty. He is Madame's grandson, and he has done so much for us."

"Then I'll take her with me tonight."

"Hello, Theresa. I'm glad you're here. I'm getting bored lying here all day with no-one to talk to."

"Don't worry, Albert. I'll talk to you or read to you. And I can help you with your food, or whatever else you need."

Tony nodded. "You're a good girl, Theresa."

"Are you feeling any better?"

Tony smiled. "Much better, thank you." Four days of enforced inactivity had allowed Tony's body to begin the slow process of repair. The minor injuries were mending well, but he still suffered greatly with the cracked and broken bones, although the painkillers given to him by Leclerc helped.

Tony turned his attention back to the girl's father. "Could you fetch my transmitter for me? I've encoded a message that I need to send home." He looked at Theresa, who smiled.

"I guessed you must have some way of contacting home. I won't say anything."

Jean-Paul slipped quickly outside and returned with the radio.

"Bring the chair across, and place the transmitter on it," Tony instructed. Theresa put the chair next to the bed, within easy reach of Tony's good hand, while her father placed the case on it. "Now open the case for me please." Jean-Paul opened the case and, following Tony's instructions, fitted the crystal into the set and placed the headphones over his ears.

"Right. Now I want you both to leave. Go way back into the woods and stay there. If the Germans manage to track me down they'll be here quickly. If they're not here in one hour we should be safe, and you can return."

Jean-Paul nodded and led his daughter from the hut. Tony watched them go and waited for five minutes to give them some time to get clear. Then he tapped out his code.

"Albert. KHURQILHOG."

He did not have long to wait before he heard the beep...beep of a reply in his headset.

"Receiving."

He tapped out his message, slower than usual due to his injuries, and he wondered if the receiving station would find it too suspicious.

"Mission accomplished. Albert injured. Need transport from coast. Hospital needed. Over."

There was a pause. Tony's heart raced. Hurry, hurry, he thought, wondering if the Germans were on to him yet. Then the reply came.

"By sub possible. BBC message to confirm. Co-ordinates? Over."

Tony sent the map references for the nearby beach.

"Received. BBC 'Three men in a boat'. Pick up 9.13. Over."

"Understood. Out."

Tony switched off the transmitter and lay back on his bed, tired by his exertions. So they would try to send a submarine. If he listened to the BBC broadcast every evening, he would receive the message 'Three men in a boat' on the day they were to pick him up. Now he had wait and see if the Germans had picked up his transmission. The minutes dragged by. The wait seemed long, much longer than an hour. Tony was tense, knowing that if the Germans had traced his message to the hut he would be unable to escape them. By the time he acknowledged that his transmission had gone undetected and that he was safe, his head throbbed and he longed to sleep.

The door opened to admit Jean-Paul and Theresa.

"Is everything all right?"

Tony nodded.

"Good." Jean-Paul turned to his daughter. "Make yourself a bed on the floor, and try to get some sleep. I'll sit with Albert tonight. You don't need to watch until morning."

"All right, Papa."

Theresa took some blankets and made herself a bed on a pile of nets in the corner. They smelt of stale fish and were not terribly comfortable, but it was better than sleeping on the floor. Jean-Paul turned to Tony.

"I'll hide the radio again, then I'll sit with you." But Tony was already sleeping the sleep of the exhausted

66

The days, and nights, passed slowly. Theresa proved to be a good nurse, washing Tony, feeding him and keeping him company through the daylight hours. Leclerc managed to visit the small fishing hut at least once a day, and he was content with his patient's progress. Much of the swelling in the abdomen had gone down, and he no longer feared that Tony was bleeding internally. The cut on his forehead was healing well and the broken bones seemed to be knitting together. But Leclerc was still worried about the leg; it had been a bad break and he wished he could X-ray it to make sure that it was set properly. Tony was slowly regaining his strength and sat up for short periods, although this tired him out and often led to a headache. He had been worried about this, but Leclerc assured him that headaches were quite normal after such a blow to the head, and the concussion he had suffered. Jean-Paul visited the fishing hut each evening, and spent the night there so Theresa was able to get some rest. On the first evening after Tony had radioed England, Jean-Paul brought his small family radio to the hut and the two men listened together to the BBC broadcasts. The news of how the war was being fought in North Africa and the situation back in England lent some interest to the long, boring days for Tony. But what really captured their attention and had them leaning over the radio in anticipation were the messages put out by the BBC after the news, at the instigation of the SOE. There were not many messages each evening, and Tony always felt a keen sense of disappointment when they were over and the music programmes resumed without a message to say that his transport was on the way. To hide his disappointment, Tony would talk for a while with Jean-Paul, of happier times in the past, and of the present situation in Saint Nazaire after their successful raid on the U-boat base.

Tony noticed a change in Jean-Paul as the days progressed. He was looking paler, and dark shadows rimmed his eyes.

"Are you all right, Jean-Paul?"

The burly Frenchman nodded. "I'm fine, just a little tired. It's six days since your accident and I've had too little sleep in that time." He smothered a yawn. "The Germans are still being heavy-handed and keeping a close eye on everyone, even though they still seem convinced that it was a commando raid. Nevertheless they are watching us closely for any break in routine, so I must continue with my normal work on the estate as well as spending my nights here."

Tony nodded. "I understand Jean-Paul, and I don't know how to thank you. I would be dead or rotting in some German prison now if it wasn't for you. I'll never forget it.

Jean-Paul shrugged. "You don't need to thank me. I'm here for the sake of our friendship, and for your grandmother." He frowned, his anger showing in his steely gaze. "I love my work on the estate. It's what I've always done, it's what my family have always done for the de Thierry family. But how I hate working there under the supervision of the Germans, providing food for them to eat in Madame's dining room, watching them drink her cellars dry and lord it in her home!" He smiled ruefully. "Sorry, I'm getting a little carried away, but being tired is the least I can do if it will help to rid Madame's estate of the Germans."

Tony smiled. "Your loyalty to the family will not be forgotten, Jean-Paul. Nor will your bravery and devotion to your country. Now get some sleep. I'll call you if I need you."

Jean-Paul smiled. "That's the best idea I've heard in a long time!"

Taking a blanket against the chill of the early November night, he lay down in front of the fire and immediately fell into the sleep of the exhausted. Tony watched the sleeping forms of father and daughter for some time, reflecting on his good fortune in having such stalwart friends. Then he, too, drifted into the oblivion of sleep.

Tony sat eagerly listening to the radio. The news was over and the SOE messages to its agents were in progress. Tony listened intently.

"The red car is lost... Daffodils bloom in June... The gate is locked... Three men in a boat..."

Though the messages continued Tony didn't hear them. He looked eagerly at Jean-Paul.

"Did you hear that?"

"Yes. 'Three men in a boat'". Jean-Paul replied in heavily accented English. "That means they'll pick you up tonight?"

Tony nodded. "From the beach outside at 9.13." He looked at his watch. "It's 6.30 now. We must make sure we're out on the beach by 9 p.m. at the latest. Do you have your torch?"

Jean-Paul nodded.

"Good. I can use it to signal the submarine."

"How will you get down to the beach?"

Tony turned to Theresa and smiled. "I'll crawl if I have to!"

"You're not fit enough even for that. I'm not sure that Papa and I can carry you between us."

Jean-Paul nodded. "My ever practical Theresa. You're right, of course. I'll fetch Doctor Leclerc. He'll help us."

Theresa smiled happily at her father's praise. She watched him wrap himself against the chill night air and set off in the direction of Leclerc's house. Theresa sat beside the bed and the young girl and the spy tried to talk, but their minds were elsewhere, and the conversation soon died. Time passed slowly, each minute felt like an hour. Tony frequently consulted his watch only to find that the hands had hardly moved at all. A little before eight o'clock, Jean-Paul returned with Leclerc. The doctor smiled warmly at his patient.

"Sorry I took so long, but when Jean-Paul told me that you were going home I thought I'd better make some notes for your English doctor." He handed Tony a small package wrapped in oilskin to keep it dry. "I hope they can read French over there."

Tony smiled in gratitude. "Thank you, Doctor Leclerc. I'll translate it for them if necessary." He shook the doctor's hand." Thank you for all that you've done for me, and the risks you've taken."

Leclerc smiled. "What else can a Frenchman do?"

Tony turned his attention back to Jean-Paul. "I've been thinking, my friend. I may come back if my leg heals properly, but if not it's likely that another agent may be sent. Would you agree to be his contact?"

"Of course, Albert. You don't need to ask."

"Good. Then I'll leave the radio, guns and remaining explosives here. Hide them well. Don't try to use the radio or you might get caught, but feel free to use the explosives if the opportunity arises. But don't take too many chances."

"Thank you. I, and the others, will continue your work if we can. It is our country we are fighting for."

"Before we go out into the cold, I have a little something to help us keep warm." With a triumphant flourish, Leclerc produced a small hip flask and passed it to Tony. He sniffed the contents curiously, then with a smile he took a deep swallow.

"There's nothing like cognac to keep you warm." He passed the flask to Jean-Paul, who savoured a long swallow.

"The Germans seem to get most of the good stuff these days. Where did this come from?"

Leclerc laughed. "I keep it for medicinal purposes!"

In such a jovial atmosphere the final hour passed swiftly. It was almost 9 p.m. when the two Frenchmen helped Tony into a sitting position, before raising him onto his one good leg. Tony's head swam. It was the first time he had stood up for a week. Although he had put no weight on his injured leg, it was already beginning to throb painfully, and the cracked ribs felt as though they were ready to tear him apart. Jean-Paul and Leclerc supported him, one on either side. They took care not to jolt his left arm, which was still in a sling to aid the healing of the collarbone. Tony leant heavily on Jean-Paul as they made their laborious way out of the hut, and down to the beach some fifty yards away. Theresa followed closely behind with a bundle of blankets and the torch. On the beach the two Frenchmen lowered Tony slowly to the ground and wrapped the blankets around him. Then they seated themselves to await the submarine. Four pairs of eyes anxiously surveyed the stretch of water opposite them, but nothing moved, save the silver moonlight reflected from the rolling waves. The night sky was clear, there were no clouds to hide the moon which was almost full. Tony wondered if the light would deter the submarine captain from coming in tonight. He hoped not. The short journey from the hut down to the beach had been an agony for him, only endurable because of the hope of returning home at the end of it. If the submarine did not come, he did not think he could make it back to the hut.

At 9.13 precisely, a light flashed out to sea.

"That's it! Help me up!"

The two Frenchmen helped Tony to his feet and supported him while he used the torch to flash a coded message to the submarine. The other light flashed again. In the bright moonlight, Tony's companions could see his smile.

"They're coming in."

He turned to Theresa, his face serious for a moment.

"This is goodbye then," he said gruffly. "I don't know how I can thank you, Theresa. I never thought I'd find such bravery and strength in one so young. Your father must be very proud of you."

There were tears in Theresa's eyes as she looked up at Tony.

"Get well quickly, Albert, and come back to us."

Tony leant down, ignoring the pain in his ribs, and kissed her lightly on the forehead.

"You can count on it Theresa."

He turned to Leclerc and shook him warmly by the hand. "Thank you once again, doctor. I don't know what I'd have done without you."

"All in a day's work, Albert." Leclerc's tone was light, but Tony knew it hid the strong emotions of a man who had lost all that he loved to the enemy, and was now fighting in the only way he knew how. Finally he turned to Jean-Paul.

"What can I say, my friend? We worked well together, didn't we?"

Jean-Paul nodded, trying to control his emotions. He reached out and kissed Tony briefly on both cheeks. "God go with you, my friend."

The small party on the beach turned their attention to the water's edge where a light canoe was beaching. One of the sailors in it remained seated, while the other leapt ashore.

"Where's our passenger then?"

It seemed strange to Tony to hear a voice speaking in English. He smiled, glad to be going home at last.

"I'm here."

The sailor looked at him. "Are you injured, sir?"

Tony nodded as the two Frenchmen helped him down the beach. It was not easy for them to get him into the boat, and by the time he was seated, his face was white and his teeth clenched against the pain. The sailor climbed in behind him. He was about to push off when Theresa ran forwards.

"Wait Albert! Don't forget this!" She thrust Leclerc's notes into his hand and he smiled.

"Ever practical, Theresa."

Then the boat was moving out into the waves to where the dark shadow of the submarine awaited them. Tony turned and waved to the three figures on the shore, who waved back before turning and disappearing into the trees.

"Are you badly hurt, sir?"

Tony grimaced. "Bad enough."

The young man shook his head in wonder. "I really admire blokes like you, you know. Going and living among the enemy and fighting him there. It must be really frightening."

Tony nodded. "Yes, I suppose it is. But you cope with the fear, when you find friends like I did."

They continued in silence. The dark bulk of the submarine became more distinct as they drew closer. The paddles dipped into the water with a gentle slapping sound, until the canoe came up against the hull of the submarine with a gentle thud. Eager hands lifted the injured spy up the conning tower, but speed was of the essence, and they were none too gentle. Tony's leg was jolted against the hull and he cried out in pain. His shoulder was wrenched as they lowered him through the hatch and by the time he reached the bottom of the ladder he had slipped into unconsciousness.

Tony opened his eyes to find himself lying on a narrow bunk in a small, enclosed space. A steady thump...thump...thump communicated itself to him through the vibrations of the wall to his left, and he realised he was in the submarine. He turned his head to the right, and saw a man in naval uniform showing the rank of captain.

"How are you feeling?"

Tony smiled weakly. "Sore."

"I'm sorry we hurt you getting you aboard, but an enemy patrol boat had been sighted and we had to dive quickly."

"You mean we're now under water?"

The Captain nodded. "Does that bother you?"

Tony thought for a moment, imagining the tons of water above him and on either side, pressing in, trying to crush them. Then he shrugged painfully.

"I suppose not. I'm just as likely to die in a plane as in a submarine."

The Captain laughed. "You'd be surprised how few people see it that way!" He looked thoughtfully at Tony. "You look as though you've been in quite an accident. What happened?"

Tony smiled. "Sorry, but I'm not allowed to talk about it. All I can say is I'm glad you were able to break off your patrol to come and pick me up."

"We wouldn't be able to break our patrol for anyone. It just so happened that we were on our way home and were in the area. We only had to divert fifty miles to pick you up."

"So you're on your way home now?"

The Captain nodded, and Tony smiled in relief.

"Good. It's not that I'm not grateful for your help, but I'll be glad to get to a hospital and rest."

"By this time tomorrow we'll be back at base." The captain turned to leave. "Now get some rest."

Tony smiled wearily. "Thanks Captain. That's just what I need."

The submarine stole into base during the long hours of darkness the following night. An ambulance was waiting, and Tony was carried aboard to be greeted by the welcoming smile of Jim Briggs.

"Jim! It's so good to see you! You know, there was a time when I thought I'd never see you or my family again."

Jim smiled, though his eyes were full of concern for his friend. "It's good to see you too, Tony. You deserve a long rest, but before that I'm afraid I must ask you for a full report; we only have your brief report that your mission was successful. We need more."

Tony nodded. "I understand."

As the ambulance made its way through the dark countryside Tony told Jim all about his time in France, the contacts he had made, the discovery of the U-boat base and how the explosives had been placed, while Jim took copious notes. When Tony came to the part where he had fallen down the cliff, his hands were sweaty and he was shaking.

"You know, Jim," his voice was soft, almost a whisper, "I thought that was the end for me. If it hadn't been for the bravery of my companions I wouldn't be here now."

"Your bravery had a lot to do with it too." Jim smiled. "Your father would be proud of you."

Tony returned the smile. "Yes. It's a shame I can't tell him about it." He frowned. "What do I tell him when I see him?"

"Your cover story is that you were caught in an air-raid in London a week ago. You look as though your injuries will fit in with that."

"That reminds me." Tony fumbled in his sling with his good hand and extracted Leclerc's notes from their place of safety. "The French doctor gave me these notes for my doctors over here. Do you want them?"

Jim shook his head. "No, I'm afraid I'll be leaving you in a short while. I won't be coming all the way to the convalescent home with you. Though I will drop in and see you if I get the chance."

"Do you know where they're taking me?"

Jim's smile was mischievous. "Can't you guess?"

Tony thought for a moment then opened his eyes wide in surprise. "You don't mean... home?"

Jim nodded. "It was my idea. I thought it might be more conducive to your recovery and the bosses agreed." His grin widened. "Of course, I didn't tell them that you would be benefiting from the ministrations of one nurse in particular!"

Tony laughed, then winced at the pain it caused in his cracked ribs.

"Thanks Jim! I owe you one!"

67

Dawn was breaking as the ambulance drew to a halt in front of the sweeping facade of Heronfield House. As Tony was carried on a stretcher up the steps and through the open doors, he felt a peculiar mixture of emotions. He was coming home, yet to a home that was strange to him. Instead of his family to greet him, there was a doctor, and the smell of disinfectant stung his nostrils. But the hall looked the same as it ever had, and the sweeping curve of the staircase led up to the room which had once been, and would be after the war, Tony's own.

Doctor Millard smiled in welcome at Tony.

"Welcome home, Lieutenant." He nodded towards the two stretcher-bearers. "Follow me please."

The doctor led the way up the stairs to the first landing where he turned right. The two stretcher-bearers followed him until he stopped in front of a door and opened it.

"In here, please."

The two men carefully deposited their burden on the bed, before folding the stretcher and withdrawing. Tony looked around in surprise. His was the only bed in the room, the remainder of the furnishings consisted of a desk and chair, dressing table and door to a closet. He turned in amazement to his companion.

"This is my own room!"

The doctor smiled. "Yes, I know. I received a visit from a Lieutenant Briggs yesterday to say you were on your way, and to get this room ready for you."

Tony was curious. "Did he say anything else?"

The doctor nodded, his face becoming serious. "Yes. I had to sign the Official Secrets Act before he could tell me everything, but he felt it necessary for your doctor to know how you came by your injuries." He frowned. "He was still rather vague about that, although he did say that you were injured in France while carrying out a secret mission. I must say, Lieutenant, that I admire your courage in going out into such a situation."

Tony, not knowing what to say in answer to the compliment decided to ignore it.

"The reason Jim, I mean Lieutenant Briggs, didn't give you too many details about my injuries, is that he didn't know himself. You see, until last night I was still in France. I was brought off by submarine, and here I am."

Millard was amazed. "They certainly put themselves out for you. So, how did you get your injuries?"

Tony frowned. "I know you've signed the Official Secrets Act, but I think it would suffice to say that I fell down a cliff."

"Interesting." Millard was thoughtful. "What is the extent of your injuries?"

"Broken leg and collar bone, fractured ribs, gash to the head and concussion along with numerous other minor cuts and bruises. Can you speak French?"

Millard nodded, puzzled. "Yes. Why?"

Tony retrieved the oilskin package from his sling and handed it to Millard. "These are my notes from the doctor who treated me in France."

The doctor shook his head in disbelief. "This is incredible! It's hard to believe I'm not dreaming!" He took the package and unwrapped it, before sitting at the desk and beginning to read. There was silence for a time as he slowly translated Leclerc's notes, then he looked up.

"You seem to have been a remarkably lucky young man, Lieutenant. You should have been in hospital long before this." He looked down at the notes. "I agree with this doctor though, a few X-rays would be in order to see that everything is knitting together properly." He looked at his watch. "We'll do that in an hour, after you've had breakfast, then I'll let your parents know that you're here." He frowned. "How are you going to explain your injuries?"

"My cover story is that I was injured in an air raid in London a week ago. That'll explain why my head is healing so well."

Millard nodded. "Yes, but it doesn't explain why you haven't been in touch with them before now."

Tony frowned. "I hadn't thought of that."

"May I make a suggestion?"

Tony nodded.

"We'll tell them that you suffered from loss of memory. When you regained your full faculties yesterday you were brought straight here."

Tony smiled. "Brilliant. I like it."

"Good." Millard rose to his feet as he spoke. "I'll see that breakfast is brought to you, then we'll get you X-rayed."

With that he turned and left the room.

Tony lay back upon the pillows, eyes closed wearily. The door opened some five minutes later to admit a nurse, who carefully divested him of his clothes and dressed him in clean pyjamas before bringing him breakfast. It seemed strange to Tony to be eating breakfast in his own room again; it was so familiar yet so different. The room had been prepared as a private ward for officers. He wondered how many other wounded men had lain in his bed, sat at his desk or gazed from his window. He smiled. Few men in hospital can feel so at home! he thought. Finishing his breakfast he put the tray to one side. His injured body craved sleep, particularly after the long and painful journey from France, but he struggled to stay awake until the X-rays had been taken. He heard the door opening and turned towards the sound. At the sight of the young nursing auxiliary, he smiled.

"Hello, Sarah."

Sarah's mouth dropped open in amazement. For a moment she felt she could neither move nor speak as she gazed at the recumbent form on the bed. Finally her voice found its freedom.

"Tony! What are you doing here?" She pushed a wheelchair into the room, then moved briskly over to the bed. "What happened to you?"

Tony was overwhelmed by his feelings of joy and relief as he looked at Sarah. He realised just how close he had come to never seeing her again, and the relief at seeing her face once more washed over him like a flood. Through blurred eyes that threatened tears, he smiled up at her.

"Oh. I'm all right. Just a few minor injuries from one of Hitler's bombs."

Sarah's hand had somehow become tightly entwined in Tony's, but she did nothing to release it. Her mind was a whirl of thoughts. She was shocked to see Tony suffering from more severe injuries than he cared to admit to, more shocked than she would have expected to be. She thought he was up in Scotland, far away from the threat of bombs; but her overriding feeling was one of joy at seeing him. She frowned. When had his friendship become so important to her? She had never felt such a conflicting jumble of emotions - fear, sorrow, pain, concern and above all joy - for anyone else before. Except for Joe. Could her friendship for Tony have developed into something far deeper without her even being aware of it? She thrust the thought aside. Time enough to dwell on that when she had her emotions under control. She gently squeezed Tony's hand.

"Dr. Millard asked me to bring a new patient along to X-ray, but he didn't tell me who it was." She smiled brightly, a smile which warmed Tony's heart. "I'm so glad to see you again, though I wish it was under different circumstances."

"Me too." Tony grimaced as he tried to sit up. Sarah, conscious once more of the duties she was there to perform, helped him. "Bring over the wheelchair, then let's get to X-ray. Dr. Millard will be wondering where we've got to!"

Sarah smiled as she fetched the chair. "I have so many things to ask you, and to say to you, but I suppose they can wait. It looks as though you'll probably be with us for some time to come."

Tony grinned. Being wounded had its compensations after all!

While Tony was being X-rayed, a message was sent down to the lodge to inform his parents that he was now a patient up at the main house so that when Sarah wheeled him back into his room, his parents were already waiting for him. Sir Michael was gazing out of the window, hands clasped tightly behind his back, while Louise sat stiffly at the desk, her face white. As the door opened she rose to her feet.

"Tony!"

Sir Michael turned at the sound of his wife's voice, his face inscrutable.

Sarah's gaze roved from one face to the other as she pushed the chair closer to the bed. She could feel the pent -up emotion in the room. Such a reunion should be held in private

"If you will excuse me, I have work to do."

Tony watched her as she left, closing the door quietly behind her, then turned to face his parents. "Hello, Mamma. Dad."

Louise crossed the room and knelt on the floor beside her son's chair.

"Are you all right, Tony? What happened?"

"Yes, son. How are you?"

Tony looked up at is father; his face was set, but the anxiety in his eyes betrayed him. Tony smiled. Perhaps his injuries could bring the two of them closer.

"I'm all right, Dad. Just a few cracked ribs, and a broken leg and collarbone. It's a bit painful at times, but I'll be all right."

Sir Michael indicated the stitched gash on Tony's forehead.

"That looks to be healing well. When did all this happen?"

Tony frowned. Would his cover story stand up?

"They tell me I was injured a week ago."

"A week? But why did you not contact us?" Louise's voice was troubled, and Tony reached out a hand to comfort her.

"I'm afraid this gash on the head is responsible for that, Mamma. I lost my memory and only really knew who I was yesterday."

"Why didn't the hospital contact us? You were wearing your dog tags, weren't you?"

Tony's mind worked fast. He had left his dog tags behind when he went to France, and Jim had not returned them to him. He hoped his father would not want to see them.

"Whatever broke my collar bone must have broken the chain because I wasn't wearing them when they got me to hospital. I'd still be there now if I hadn't got my memory back."

Sir Michael crossed the room and placed his hand on Tony's shoulder, the first physical contact he had initiated between them since Tony had said that he was joining the Ministry of Economic Warfare.

"I thought you said you would be safe up in Scotland, son?"

"Oh, that job had finished. I was just reporting back to London when this happened."

"Were you on leave, then?"

Tony felt a tightening in his father's hand. Could he resent Tony's apparent lack of active service so much that he was willing to argue about whether he was injured on or off duty? Tony vowed to do his best to build up the tenuous link his father had initiated.

"No. I was on my way to the office when the raid happened." He looked up at his father. "War work, Dad."

Louise watched her husband's face. Their son was injured. Surely all that mattered was getting him well again? Then Sir Michael smiled.

"Perhaps your job isn't as safe as I thought it was." He walked over to the chair and sat down. "Now, my son, how long are your injuries going to keep you cooped up in here?"

"I'm not sure, Dad." Tony relaxed as he held his mother's hand in his and smiled at his father. Getting well now seemed immaterial to him. It looked as though the real healing had already taken place. "I'll have to wait and see what Doctor Millard makes of the X-rays."

As if on cue, the door opened and Millard entered, smiling.

"Good morning, Sir Michael, Lady Kemshall. I've just got the results of your son's X-rays. You'll be pleased to hear that all the broken bones are mending nicely. The leg was quite bad, so it will be some time before he can return to work. I'd like to keep an eye on him here for the next week or so, then he can move down to the lodge with you." He turned to Tony and smiled. "You're a lucky young man, and have been receiving excellent medical attention. I'd like to meet the doctor who has been treating you one day."

Tony smiled. "I'm sure he would like to meet you too. Let's hope it's not too long before that's possible."

Sir Michael frowned, convinced that there was something in the exchange which he was missing but unable to put his finger on what it was. Millard turned towards him.

"Now I think the patient needs some rest."

Louise rose and kissed her son on the forehead. "I'll come in and see you later, mon cher."

"Thank you, Mamma."

Sir Michael merely nodded as he moved over towards the door. "See you later, son."

"See you later,

As the door closed behind them Tony was smiling happily. It was good to be home.

68

The speed of Tony's recovery surprised, and pleased, Millard. Maybe it was due to the reduction of tension and anxiety. He found it almost impossible to imagine how Tony must have been feeling, unable to move unaided, in hostile territory, knowing that the enemy were on the lookout for him after his work of sabotage. The fear would have been enough to hinder the healing process; now in familiar territory with no worries and with caring parents to watch over him, Tony was improving in leaps and bounds. Little did Milliard know that the improved relationship between Tony and his father, as well as the constant attention from Sarah, also contributed to the speed of his recovery. A week after his arrival at Heronfield, Millard was sufficiently satisfied to allow Tony to move down to the lodge. Sir Michael volunteered to push the chair down the driveway, and Tony was glad of his company. He still found it hard to believe that the animosity between the two of them had been brushed aside by his injuries, and was keen to continue the improved relationship. The wind blew coldly. Sir Michael tucked a blanket closer around his son's legs as he made his way down the drive to be greeted by Louise at the door to the lodge. She smiled warmly to see Sir Michael supporting Tony as he made his painful way up the steps.

"Come in. I have a hot cup of milk waiting for you in front of the fire."

"Mamma!" Tony laughed as he leant against his stick and hobbled into the sitting room. "I can remember you doing that for me when I was hurt as a child!"

He seated himself in the comfortable armchair, close to the fire, and Louise wrapped a blanket round his knees.

"Surely you don't want milk at your age, son. How about something stronger?"

Tony looked at his mother, realising her need to express her love and concern for him in the only way she knew how. He turned to his father and smiled.

"No thanks, Dad. I'll have something stronger later. Right now, milk sounds wonderful."

Sir Michael nodded, realising that Tony was doing his best to please his mother, and wondering, as he had done so many times over the past week, how he had ever allowed his feelings to drive such a wedge between them in such uncertain times. He stood with his back to the window, looking thoughtful as he gazed at mother and son.

"You know, Tony, I think I owe you an apology."

Tony looked up. "Dad, it's not necessary. I..."

"Yes it is, son." Sir Michael interrupted. "I thought you should have volunteered for active service, especially after you saw that mess at Dunkirk. Then when David died I thought you would want to avenge him. I still think your job is suited to an older man and that you should be fighting for your country, my views about that haven't changed, but I should never have allowed my views to come between us. This war is different from the last one; anyone anywhere can be killed or injured, civilians as well as the military. The danger here is not as great as the front line, but I suppose you know what you're doing. This is the last time I'll bring the subject up, son, though I do hope you will volunteer for active duty some time."

Tony smiled.

"There was no need to say all that, Dad, but thanks." He was thoughtful. "I do intend to come face to face with the enemy before this is all over, Dad, perhaps when we invade France I'll ask for a transfer. But right now I must obey orders."

Sir Michael crossed the room and laid a hand upon his son's shoulder.

"That's good enough for me, son."

Tony turned as he heard the sound of the door opening. Chantrelle de Thierry entered, smiling broadly, and Tony felt his heart stand still. He had pushed his experiences in France to the back of his mind while in hospital but now, seeing his grandmother, the memories came flooding back. He could tell her all she wanted to know, and more, about her home and friends, but he must remain silent. He found himself at a loss for words, but Chantrelle de Thierry did not notice as she crossed the room and kissed him on both cheeks.

"Tony! It is good to see you. I am sorry that I did not come up to the big house, but it is so unnerving to see strangers there, it makes me think of my home and the strangers who must be living in it."

Tony reached out and took her hand.

"That's all right, Grandmamma. I understand."

He looked around at the room full of smiling people. It was good to be home. This was where he belonged.

As Tony grew stronger he was able to walk for a while each day in the gardens, and Sarah walked with him. She had thought long and hard about her reactions when she saw Tony in the hospital bed, and had at last admitted to herself that he was special to her. Yet she was still not ready to admit it to him. Tony, however, noticed a subtle change in their relationship. She smiled more, and seemed more relaxed in his company; she spoke of Joe less frequently, as though she had now let go of him. Their daily walks assumed great importance to each of them, a time when they could talk about the war and how things were going. But as time passed, they talked less about the war and more about themselves. Slowly they came to know each other better. If the weather was inclement and they were unable to walk, it felt as though an important part of their day had been lost.

So time passed. The leaves continued to change colour and fall from the trees, rustling and crunching underfoot. In the mornings, the grass and trees were edged with white crystals of frost, and the windowpanes were patterned with its fine etchings. So November turned to December. A year of setbacks in the war was drawing to a close and people were looking forward to the New Year, hoping the combined might of England and Russia would finally bring Germany to her knees.

69

Sarah and Jane sat in the nurses' common room, relaxing over a cup of tea after a busy day on the wards. It was 8th December 1941. The dreary sounds of rain drumming against the windows hardly registered as the two young women laughed and talked. As usual, Jane was teasing Sarah about the number of men she attracted when they went out dancing.

"I shouldn't take you with me!" The smile on her face belied the harshness of her words. "You always get the best looking ones and leave the rest to me."

"That's not true!" Sarah laughed. "You know very well I don't go there looking for men!"

"You don't go looking, but you always find them." Jane's gaze was quizzical. "What have you got that I haven't? Is it something to do with that red hair of yours?"

"Now you're being silly." Sarah rose from her seat and crossed the room.

"Why not pick one of them, and leave the rest for me?"

"I haven't found the one I want yet." Sarah grinned as she switched on the radio ready for the evening news.

"Really?" Jane eyebrows rose in mock surprise. "Are you sure you haven't found one man you like more than all the rest?"

Sarah turned away, her cheeks burning. "No. Now stop it, Jane, I want to listen to the news." She sat down again and sipped her tea as the radio hissed into life. The invigorating sound of a dance band filled the room for a few moments. When the record came to an end there was a moment's silence, followed by the voice of the newsreader.

"This is the BBC news. Yesterday morning at 7.55 Eastern American time, the American Fleet at the naval base of Pearl Harbour was attacked by the Japanese."

The two women looked at each other, stunned. Turning their attention back to the radio, they picked up the voice once more.

"...first attack lasted for thirty minutes, and was followed fifteen minutes later by a wave of dive bombers and high level bombers. Details are still unclear, but it appears that the first wave of torpedo bombers were the decisive factor. Of the eight American battleships the Arizona, Oklahoma, West Virginia and California were sunk, while the Maryland, Nevada, Pennsylvania and Tennessee were severely damaged. Three destroyers were also sunk with at least four smaller vessels, and many more were badly damaged. Casualty figures have not yet been released, but are estimated at being over three-and-half-thousand. The Prime Minister has condemned the attack, which came without a declaration of war by the Japanese. Mr. Churchill stated that we would stand by our American friends in their hour of need, and has consequently declared war on the Japanese Empire."

Sarah turned her troubled gaze towards Jane.

"So we are at war with Japan. As if we didn't have enough to contend with, fighting Hitler."

Jane reached over and switched off the radio. The sound of rain echoed dismally in the common room.

The rain ceased to fall during the night, but it was still a dull morning when Sarah walked beneath the trees, water still dripping from their bare branches with a depressingly monotonous sound. Tony limped slowly beside her.

"What do you make of it?" she asked, her brow furrowed. "For a long time now we've been hoping the Americans would come into this war and help us defeat Hitler. But I didn't expect that would mean fighting Japan."

Tony shrugged. "It was bound to come to that, I suppose. Japan and Germany are so closely linked. We would have been fighting the Japanese sooner or later. What I don't like is that we've jumped to America's defence by declaring war on Japan, but they still haven't declared war on Germany." His eyes flashed. "Do they expect us to keep the Nazis from conquering the world, and fight their battles too?"

Sarah stopped walking and turned towards her companion. Her eyes were troubled, and she laid a hand on his arm as though to draw the answers from him.

"They will declare war on Germany. Won't they?"

Tony smiled gently, covering the cold fingers of her hand with his.

"They'll have to, eventually. I can't see how they can avoid it now." He frowned. "Have you heard this morning's news?"

Sarah shook her head. "What's happened now? Surely things can't get any worse?"

"I'm afraid they can. Japan launched an attack on Hong Kong yesterday. Our battles in the Far East have already begun."

Tears started in Sarah's eyes, as she thought of the fighting taking place. It was two years now since war had been declared. They had hoped to win quickly, but it had dragged on and was now escalating. It seemed that the whole world would soon be one great battlefield. She thought of the soldiers who would return to England maimed by the great battles to come. There would be thousands passing through Heronfield on their way home, and thousands more who would never return.

"When will it all end?" The tears began to fall. "How many more years of this can we endure?"

Tony put his arms around her, and gently drew her close. It was good to feel her in his arms once more. He was glad she turned to him when she needed comfort. He stroked her hair as she buried her tear-stained face in his shoulder.

"We can endure as many years as it takes, Sarah," he said softly, "and we won't be defeated. America will come out on our side. Hitler can't stand against us both. And when this is all over, it will be up to people like us to continue to be strong, and to build a peaceful world where nothing like this ever happens again."

Tony heard the cawing of a rook. He looked up to where the bird wheeled in the mackerel grey sky above him. Its cry seemed to echo Sarah's hopelessness, and his arms tightened around her as though he could protect her by the strength of his arms alone.

70

So the days passed and Christmas approached once more. When preparing to celebrate the previous Christmas, people had hoped and prayed that it would be the last of the war. But here they were again, desperately trying to instil the holiday spirit into a country ravaged by war and stark with rationing. It would certainly be a Christmas unlike any that the British had known, but they determined to make the best of it with the limited food and gifts in the shops. It was a time of improvisation. A time to make gifts instead of buying them, creative cookery, making the most of what little they had. On 11th December, Germany declared war on the United States, bringing a strong ally to Britain's side at last, although many still resented the fact that America had not come into the war earlier, and it had been left up to Hitler to drag them into the mele. The prospect of America's strength being lent to the war in Europe was uplifting, but this was countered by continuing bad news from the Far East. On the 10th, the Prince of Wales and the Repulse had been sunk off Singapore, while the battle for Hong Kong seemed a one-sided affair, in favour of Japan. So Christmas Eve dawned amidst a welter of hope and despair, of promise and dread.

Jane entered the room which she shared with Sarah to find her friend sitting deep in thought, a small velvet box in her hand. Jane threw her wet towel on the bed.

"Come on, Sarah. Hurry up or you'll be late."

Sarah turned her serious gaze towards Jane. "I don't think I'm coming."

Jane's eyes widened in surprise. "Not coming? But why not? It's Christmas Eve. It will be one of the best nights of the year."

"I can't come because it is Christmas Eve."

Jane frowned, then her eyes fell on the box in Sarah's hands and she understood.

"Oh Sarah. I'm sorry. I forgot." She knelt down beside her friend. "It was Christmas Eve last year when Joe proposed to you, wasn't it?"

Sarah nodded. "It just brings back so many memories." Her voice was filled with sadness. "I was so happy last Christmas Eve. I thought I had everything to look forward to, and now I have nothing."

"That's not true," Jane spoke comfortingly, "and you know Joe wouldn't want to hear you talking like that. You have your work. You're a born nurse and you'll have a future in nursing even after the war. You have life and health, and you have friends who love you. Just because you don't have a man to share your life at the moment is no reason to give up." She grinned. "Look at me. I haven't got a man, and I haven't given up!"

Sarah laughed. "Oh, Jane! I'm so glad I've got you for a friend! You certainly help me to keep things in perspective." She looked down at the ring nestling in its velvet box. "Christmas Eve will always be a special day for me. I shall never be able to let one pass without thinking of Joe. But I'll try to remember what we had together, not what we were never able to share." She closed the box lid and smiled at Jane. "Is the bathroom free? I want to wash my hair before the dance!"

The two young women entered the dance hall amidst a crowd of other nurses who had travelled with them on the bus to Marlborough. The room was a swirl of colour. All the women wore their best clothes, some saved from before the war, while others were made with material bought with hoarded coupons. Many of the men were in uniform, obviously home on leave, but even with the farm workers they were outnumbered by the women. It was one of the difficulties of war. With most of the men away on active service, there were few left to keep the women company. But this did not stop any of them from having a good time.

Sarah led the way to the only empty table in the room, close beside the band, and they sat down. Her eyes took in the gay streamers and the bauble bedecked tree, and as she watched the couples dancing energetically she was glad that Jane had persuaded her to come. They had only been there for a few minutes, yet Jane was already dancing with one of the young men. Sarah smiled. Although her friend often complained of having no man in her life, it wasn't through lack of choice. Sarah supposed she was still looking for the right one. As Sarah watched she became aware of someone standing at her shoulder and looked round. For a moment she did not recognise the man in uniform, then she smiled.

"Tony! I didn't expect to see you here!"

She had not seen him in uniform since he had returned to the hospital, and had forgotten how well it suited him. He stood tall and straight, his boyish grin seemingly incongruous to one in uniform. Sarah thought he had never looked so handsome. She blushed slightly and turned away, so that Tony would not see the colour in her cheeks. He smiled.

"Aren't we soldiers allowed to enjoy Christmas?"

Sarah laughed. "I didn't mean that! I just didn't think you would bother with a dance, as your leg isn't fully healed yet."

Tony shrugged. "It's getting better all the time, and I'm sure I can manage a dance or two." He smiled broadly. "Would you like to dance?"

Sarah nodded and rose to her feet. As he led her onto the dance floor, Tony thought how good her hand felt in his and as she came into his arms he felt as though he had come home. They danced well together, as though they were one, and Sarah was glad she had come.

"When do you have to go back to work?"

"I suppose my leg will be good enough early in the New Year. I'll be glad to be out and doing things. I've been bored at home over the last few weeks." He grinned. "The only thing that has kept me at home for so long is our walks together."

"Has it been that bad? I thought you were getting on better with your father?"

"Yes, but I still want to get back to work. I've a lot to do before this war is won."

"Are you thinking of applying for a transfer to active duty?"

Tony looked down at her questioningly. "Why?"

Sarah shrugged. "I just wondered if you were getting fed up of an office job."

"The work is interesting," Tony replied defensively, "and even if it wasn't, I would still do it. It's what my superiors think I am best at."

"How do you know you won't be better in an active unit?"

"Are you trying to get rid of me?"

Sarah shook her head vigorously. "Oh, no." She was surprised by the way her heart thumped at the thought of Tony in danger. "I just thought you might prefer it."

"Who knows?" Tony smiled. "I must admit I'm glad that my job keeps me in England at the moment, so I can see more of you. But I've told Dad I'll apply for a transfer when the invasion of Europe comes, and it will." Tony breathed in the scent of Sarah's hair and felt her soft and yielding in his arms. "Enough of this talk of war. Let's enjoy ourselves."

The couple danced for a while. When Tony's leg ached too much they sat and talked, before dancing again. As the evening drew to a close, Tony led Sarah outside to gaze at the brilliant winter stars in the cloudless December night. They were standing there, enjoying the quiet after the noise of the dance hall, when the clock in the church across the square struck twelve.

"It's Christmas Day," Sarah murmured. She turned to Tony. "Happy Christmas, Tony."

"Happy Christmas, Sarah."

Their eyes met and held in the darkness. Slowly Tony leant down until his lips lightly brushed hers. For a moment Sarah's thoughts were centred on the fact that this kiss was unlike Joe's, then she gave herself up to her feelings. As Tony felt her lips move beneath his, he drew her close, his heart full. It felt as though she were made to fit in his arms. He vowed silently that now they had found each other, he would never let her go.

Tony's heart filled with hope on that Christmas morning. Far away, on the other side of the world, night fell over Hong Kong, and all hope died in the hearts of the twelve thousand British soldiers who were taken into captivity.

71

Tony looked out of the window at the snow-covered lawns. He sighed deeply.

"What's wrong?" Tony shrugged as he turned towards Jim.

"Don't get me wrong. It's good to be back here at Beaulieu, but I asked Dawson to send me back to France and he said no. It's so frustrating."

"Why did he say no?"

Tony grinned sheepishly. "For all the right reasons! He said my request was denied because he didn't want to send me back to France suffering from a disadvantage. The doctors still haven't passed me as A1 yet."

"But you still want to go back?"

"Of course! You know I've been ordered to spend a few months telling the new recruits about my field experiences. I can see the value of that, but it doesn't stop me chafing at the decision!"

He sat down at the small table in the mess, which overlooked the winter gardens.

"I know this job is worthwhile, Jim," he swirled the brandy around the balloon of his glass, "but I do wish I could go out there again." His voice was quiet, introspective. "You can't imagine what it's like to be out there. The constant tension, knowing that one small slip could cost you your life, yet the satisfaction of knowing what you're doing is worth the risk. And the French people." He smiled at Jim. "There are a few traitors and a few who seem to have given up hope, but not the majority. There's a spark in them, buried deep so that the Germans can't see it, but it's there, only waiting for the right moment to burst into flame, then nothing will be able to stop them. The few members of the Resistance that I worked with know the risks they're taking, but take them nevertheless. Even the children are willing to risk their lives to oppose the Germans." He sighed. "I wish I could go straight back out there."

"Stop feeling sorry for yourself!" Tony's eyes widened at Jim's tone. "How do you think I feel? At least you've been out to France, while I've been stuck here instructing people like you."

"Sorry, Jim. I didn't think."

Jim smiled reassuringly. "That's all right; but don't forget you're not the only one eager to get out into enemy territory instead of sitting here at home. As it happens," his voice was smug and he smiled broadly as he spoke, "I'll be going out next week."

Tony grinned, genuinely pleased for his friend. "Great. Where are they sending you?"

"Dinan. I'll be setting up a network there with the aid of the local Resistance."

"Then we won't be far apart; if they ever send me back that is!"

Jim laughed. "Right, but I doubt that we'll get a chance to meet for a pint!"

The two men laughed at the thought. Two British secret agents meeting for a drink in enemy territory: how the Germans would love that!

"Getting back to more serious matters," Jim picked up his whisky and took a sip, "meet me in the weapons room at 9a.m. tomorrow. I'm to instruct you in the use of our new master weapon for secret agents."

Tony raised a quizzical eyebrow, but Jim would say no more.

Tony met Jim the following morning, eager to see what he had to show him. Jim was carrying a small bag with an object concealed within its folds.

"It's a Sten gun," he said by way of explanation. "We started getting them just before you went out to France. Have you heard of it?"

Tony nodded. "Yes, but I know little more than its name."

Jim inclined his head towards a table, the only furnishings in the otherwise bare room.

"Come over here and I'll show you."

The two young men leant over the table, and Jim removed the gun from the bag.

"As you can see," he said as he worked, "it comes in three pieces. The barrel, the body and the butt. Added to this is the magazine. Three or four are usually provided with each gun." In seconds the completed gun lay on the table between them. It was short and stubby, with the magazine sticking out at right angles to the left of the gun. "Whatever you do don't grip the magazine, or it will misfire." He pushed a spare magazine across the table to Tony, who picked it up and examined it.

"9mm?"

Jim nodded. "Yes. The same as the Schmeisser MP 30. The boffins thought that if agents were to take a weapon with them, they should have one with the same ammo as the Germans. That way there'll always be fresh supplies at hand!"

"You mean steal from the Germans?"

Jim grinned and nodded. "Got it in one."

He passed the gun to Tony. He hefted it and nodded appreciatively at its balance and lack of weight. The barrel was only seven-and-a-half inches long, making the whole weapon very short and compact.

"It can fire either single shots or bursts," Jim continued, "but with such a short barrel, single shots are liable to miss. In bursts it can fire five hundred and fifty rounds a minute, though the magazine only holds thirty two." He frowned. "One of the drawbacks is that when the magazine is almost empty the breach can jam and cause a misfire, so it's better to use only twenty-eight of the rounds." He removed the magazine, then reloaded it. "It takes a little time to reload, but keeping it loaded weakens the spring. So it's best to load it when you're ready to use it. The bolt also works on a strong spring." He demonstrated the movement with a satisfying click. "Be careful if it jams, or you could lose a fingertip trying to free it."

Tony frowned. "Won't it be better to stick with the Bren if the Sten has all these problems?"

Jim shook his head.

"Of course it has its drawbacks, but the advantages far outweigh those. It's not much good over distances of more than a few yards, but for close range work this machine is deadly. It's also suited to our type of work, because mud and water do it little harm." He smiled broadly. "I'll be taking one with me next week. Do you want to try it now?"

Tony nodded and the two men wrapped themselves against the icy cold before venturing out. Jim led the way to a sandbagged area, where he hung a straw dummy from a meat hook. The dummy was dressed in German uniform, and swung listlessly in the wind. Tony held the new gun at hip level, carefully drawing the bolt, then pulling the trigger. The rat-a-tat-tat of the magazine discharging and the satisfying thump of bullets hitting the target raised his adrenalin. After one short burst he stopped firing and looked at the dummy. There was a line of holes across its chest from which straw was gently falling. He realised that, if it had been a man, he would have been almost cut in two. Tony turned to Jim with a broad smile.

"You're right! That's just the kind of weapon we need in France. Book one out for me!"

So the weeks passed with Tony instructing new agents in the need for surprise, in swift and sudden attacks at the enemy's weak points, in knowing the line of retreat before attacking. He emphasised the need for all agents to know their area well, and to have reliable guides, all of which he knew were essential from his own experience. The students looked up to him. He was one of the few men who had already seen action behind enemy lines and they hung on to his every word, knowing that what he told them could save their lives. As Tony taught them tradecraft and how to deal with enemy controls, he found himself warming to the task. A year before, he had been sitting where they now sat, but the information he had received from the instructors lacked the bite of experience and was, in some areas, speculation. Now he could tell them what it was really like to work behind enemy lines, and was able to channel their eagerness and temper it with caution.

Early in February Jim left Beaulieu, heading for the south coast of England and a plane to France. Tony watched him go with mixed feelings. Since he met Jim during the disorganised retreat to Dunkirk, they had become close friends. Tony had never felt closer to another man, except David. As he said goodbye, he was fearful for his friend's safety, yet envied him the opportunities and experiences which awaited him across the narrow expanse of the English Channel. Despite the dangers, Tony longed to be out in France again. He was determined it would not be long before he followed Jim back into enemy territory.

72

The war in North Africa was fluctuating back and forth. Early in January, the British forces were back in Benghazi after a German retreat, but Rommel counter-attacked, pushing them back to Gazala. The fighting had been fierce with many casualties on both sides, and some of these casualties eventually found their way back to Heronfield. It seemed strange to Sarah that Britain was at war with Germany, yet most of the injured she was seeing came from North Africa or the Far East. When war had first broken out she had expected most of the fighting to take place in Europe but the Germans now seemed to have almost complete control there, and there was little, if any fighting.

It was late one February afternoon when Sarah met a typical group of patients who had just arrived at the hospital and were settling in. Two of the patients had been assigned to her ward, and she bustled about cheerfully in an attempt to make them feel more at home.

"Hello, lads. How are you feeling?" Her concerned gaze met the eyes of a young man, hardly more than a boy. He smiled wearily in response.

"Glad to be back in Blighty, miss."

Sarah returned the smile of the slim form encased in bandages. "What happened to you?"

"Our tank took a direct hit and caught fire." The young man frowned as though reliving the experience. "It was like an oven in there, and we were all fighting to get out. Not all of us made it." His eyes clouded as he thought of his comrades who had burned to death then, with a shrug and a smile that looked old on his boyish face, he spoke again. "Still, now I know how a Christmas turkey feels!"

Sarah was moved by the young man's attempt at humour, a defence against the horrors which must inhabit his mind. She straightened the bedclothes and took a quick look at his notes.

"Lieutenant George Scott." She smiled. "Well, Lieutenant, I hope your stay with us won't be too long. With a bit of luck, you'll be able to go home to your family soon."

"Are you trying to get rid of me already?"

Sarah smiled a sad smile as she gently patted his bandaged hand. "No, not at all. You're welcome to stay here as long as you like."

She turned to the other newcomer in the adjacent bed. "And who are you?"

"Lieutenant Graham Brown. I was luckier than my colleague there." He glanced across at Scott. "My tank was disabled. I was shot while trying to get from it to cover."

Sarah noticed how still and straight his legs were and looked at his notes, which hung from the end of the bed. A bullet had severed his spinal cord. He would never walk again. She frowned.

"You say you were lucky?"

Brown nodded. "Yes. Everyone who serves in a tank suffers from the same nightmare, to be caught in a burning tank and to be unable to get out. Any injury to me is better than the fear of burning in a tank."

Scott turned his head to look at Brown. There were some angry burns on his face and a small patch of his hair had been burned away, but his main injuries were to his arms and lower body.

"I'm glad I'm in the next bed to you. At least you know how I feel."

Brown nodded but said nothing, a strange companionship being forged in the silence of shared fears and experiences. Forcing a bright smile, Sarah moved towards the door.

"Right then. While you two get acquainted, I'll go and get your tea."

The next few hours passed swiftly. Sarah brought them their food, propping Brown up so he could eat, then feeding Scott, whose hands were so badly burned that he could not feed himself. Dr. Millard appeared a little later to check over the new patients before Sarah settled them down for the night. She did not go off duty until midnight and so settled herself at the nurse's station where she could hear if any of the patients in the four small wards along this part of the hallway needed her. A small lamp burned on the desk, and she made herself comfortable with a magazine and a hot cup of tea. All was quiet. The patients were asleep and there was nothing to hear save the odd snore or rustle of bedclothes as someone turned over.

She looked at her watch. It was 9-35 p.m.

The screaming began at 10-30. For a moment Sarah was frozen with shock, and then she rose to her feet and ran in the direction of the sound. The screaming was coming from her ward, and as she rushed in she was able to distinguish words amidst the screams.

"Get me out! I'm burning! I'm burning!"

Scott was flailing his bandaged arms wildly as though to beat back encroaching flames. Sweat stood out on his forehead and his face was a mask of terror, although his eyes were tightly closed in sleep. Sarah glanced quickly at the other patients in the room to see if they were all right. Their pale faces were staring at Scott in shock.

"It's all right. I'll look after him. You lie down and try to get back to sleep."

Sarah made her way to Scott's bedside, and laid a cool hand on his brow. She was surprised to feel him shaking violently.

"Shhhh. It's all right. It's all right," she whispered softly. Slowly Scott's body relaxed a little, and his eyes opened.

"Are you an angel?"

Sarah forced a smile, tears threatening to spill from her eyes.

"No, I'm a nurse. Don't you remember?"

"I was in my tank. I was burning up." His voice rose hysterically as he spoke. "I could feel my flesh melting when I touched the walls, they were so hot. The smoke was choking me. I couldn't see, and the smell…" He gagged as though his nostrils were filled with the sickening aroma of burning flesh. "I could smell my friends as they burned. I heard the fat dripping from their bodies, sizzling on the hot floor. I was in hell!"

Sarah stroked his brow soothingly. "It was just a dream. You're safe now. You're in hospital in England. You're safe. It's all right."

The soothing monotony of the words calmed him at last. He gazed at Sarah with clear eyes that held the horror of pain and death.

"I'm sorry," he whispered. He closed his eyes and slowly shook his head. "The dream was so real. I felt as though I was back in the tank. You can't know what it was like." His voice was little more than a whisper. "I felt my hands burning as I clawed at the hatch, I could see them blackening, but I had to go on. If I didn't get out, all of me would have burned up like that." He shuddered. "The screams. I'll never forget the screams of my friends, and I couldn't help them." Tears seeped out from under the closed eyelids. "I couldn't help them. Why did they die while I'm still alive? I should have gone back for them. I should be dead too."

As Sarah spoke softly to the young man, he slowly relaxed and eventually fell into a fitful sleep. Sarah rose and made her way thoughtfully back to her station. The doctors would be able to heal the physical injuries of the soldiers, but she suspected that there were mental scars from this war which would never be healed.

As the war dragged on Sarah's duties increased. From being little more than a cleaner and cook during those first frantic weeks after Dunkirk, she had developed into a competent auxiliary. She was often entrusted with duties which should have been given only to trained nurses, but her skill and natural ability had been recognised and harnessed, so her days were now filled with a variety of tasks. Sarah loved the work Before the war she had not considered taking up a career. She had always thought she would marry and have children and that would be all. But now she knew her life would never be the same without the challenge of nursing. She was saddened by all the wounded men she saw, hating this war which caused so much death and destruction. Yet when it was over she would continue nursing, dedicating her life to serving others.

Scott's burns were healing well, but the damage to his mind would take much longer to put right. As Sarah was massaging Brown's useless legs one morning, he spoke to her about the young man in the next bed.

"Scott was lucky, you know. Once a tank goes up like that, the men have little chance to get out."

"Do others who have escaped react like him?" Sarah continued to knead the numb muscles as Brown nodded.

"Yes, the nightmares are common, but I think they fade as time goes by." He looked across at the empty bed; Scott was down in the burns treatment room. "From what he tells me, he's getting more sleep now he's back in England. His memories of here are from before the war and before the fire. That should help."

Sarah nodded. "What about you? How are you feeling?"

Brown shrugged. "All right I suppose. At least I don't suffer any pain."

"What did you do before the war?"

"I was a bank clerk," Brown smiled, "and I never had a beautiful woman massaging my legs then!"

Sarah smiled too as she began to knead the muscles of his calf. "I must say you're taking all this remarkably well."

"What else can I do? That bullet did permanent damage. Not even the most skilled surgeon will be able to repair my spine, so I just have to get used to the idea that I'll never walk again." His eyes clouded a little. "That's not to say that I won't miss playing rugby, or walking with a pretty girl on my arm. But at least I should be able to do my old job from a wheelchair. It will give me a link with my past, back to the days before this damned war spoiled everything." He met Sarah's eyes. "Sorry, that's not quite the way to talk to a lady, is it?"

Sarah laughed. "Don't worry, I've heard much worse than that on the wards!" She straightened her back for a moment and stretched her tired arms. Brown grinned.

"I suppose I shall have to have my legs massaged for the rest of my life?"

Sarah nodded. "That's what the doctor says."

"Then how about coming home with me, and being my private nurse? You make such a good job of it!"

Sarah looked at him wide-eyed for a moment, then noticed his smile. She laughed gaily. "You shouldn't tease the nurses like that, you know. One day one of them just might accept!"

"Who said I was teasing?"

Sarah frowned, and it was Brown's turn to laugh."

"Don't worry, I have a gorgeous fiancée who'll be more than willing to do that for me!"

Sarah smiled sadly. "Perhaps you're lucky after all. You have a future ahead of you with the woman you love. At least Hitler didn't spoil that for you. Now," Sarah was more matter of fact as she covered his legs, "I must be about my duties."

Brown watched her go with a puzzled frown.

73

Britain was not only suffering defeats in North Africa. In the Far East the situation gradually deteriorated during the first quarter of 1942. The empire hungry Japanese, keen to take advantage of European powers weakened by their war with Hitler, landed in Indonesia on 6th January. The Dutch fought bravely but could do little to halt the Japanese advance without the aid of the British, but this aid never came. On 8th February, the Japanese launched a massive attack against the British in Singapore. The fighting was fierce but the situation was hopeless, and the garrison fell on the 15th with eighty thousand British taken as prisoners of war. The Dutch continued to fight, but without reinforcements defeat was just a matter of time. Two months after the Japanese invaded, on 8th March, the Dutch surrendered Indonesia, and ninety-eight thousand prisoners of war were taken.

74

Tony returned to Heronfield on leave in early March. It was the first time he had seen Sarah for almost two months and he could not hide the smile of delight that lit his face when she met him in the orchard. The bare branches of the trees were swelling with buds, a promise of new life soon to break forth, and Sarah reached up to run a finger over the hidden leaves.

"I've always liked spring." She smiled at Tony. "It's a sign of hope for the future, and we need all the encouragement we can get at the moment."

"What's wrong?" Tony frowned at Sarah. She seemed cheerful enough, but under her calm exterior he detected a deep sadness. "You seem a little depressed."

Sarah shrugged. "No more than anyone else." She sighed. "We were so full of hope at the end of last year. America came into the war and it only seemed a matter of time, maybe only a few months, before the war would be won. We could have peace at last. But things haven't got better, they've got worse. It was the loss of Singapore that brought it home to me. It's still going to be a long time before we can defeat Germany and Japan." She gazed sadly at Tony. "I can hardly remember the times before this all started, and it now seems as though it will never end. How much longer can we go on like this?"

"As long as it takes." He took Sarah gently in his arms, glorying in the feel of her body pressed close to his. "Don't worry, Sarah. We'll win in the end."

Sarah pressed her cheek against his comforting shoulder. Since the Christmas dance, she had come to realise just how much a part of her life Tony had become. Her feelings for him had grown steadily over the months, and years, that she had known him. Life would be duller without Tony around. Sarah sighed deeply.

"I know we'll win in the end; it's just that it seems to be taking so long."

"What you need is something to take your mind off the war for a while. Something to cheer you up."

Sarah extricated herself from his arms and looked up into his smiling face. "What do you suggest?"

"When's your next day off?"

"Friday."

"Good. I'll still be on leave then. Why don't we go out somewhere for the day and enjoy ourselves?"

Sarah smiled. "That sounds lovely. Where shall we go?"

Tony was thoughtful for a moment, watching the grey clouds scudding across the sky. Then he grinned. "How about Bath? Have you ever been there?"

Sarah shook her head.

"Good. Then we'll go there for the day. It's a beautiful place. I can guarantee that you won't be feeling depressed when we come home."

For Sarah the days until Friday seemed to drag by. She told herself it was because she would be seeing another city, somewhere other than Coventry or the small town of Marlborough which were the only places she had seen in her twenty three years. But deep down, she knew the excitement came from knowing she would be spending a whole day with Tony. Would he kiss her again? He had not done so since the dance on Christmas Eve, perhaps sensitive to her loss of Joe, but now she hoped he would. The very thought of his kiss sent shivers of excitement down her spine.

Friday morning dawned bright and clear, though chilly, and Sarah decided to wear

211

trousers. They were becoming more fashionable now. Certain women, such as the Land Army girls, wore them during working hours, and other people were following suit. Sarah had not long had her trousers, and they had taken all of her coupons. She hoped Tony would approve. She finished getting ready as quickly as possible, and made her way down to the huge gateway at the entrance of the estate where she had arranged to meet Tony.

The little red sports car was already there with Tony waiting beside it. As he watched Sarah walking down the drive in brown trousers that showed off her figure to perfection, he smiled. She wore a brown jacket to match and underneath, visible at the neckline, a cream sweater which set off the outfit perfectly.

"You look lovely." He opened the door for her. He had never seen anyone looking quite so lovely, and he could hardly believe that he was lucky enough to be spending a whole day in her company. Sarah, divining nothing of his thoughts, slid into the car and pulled her collar up in an attempt to hide the blush which coloured her cheeks.

"Thank you."

She settled herself comfortably while Tony walked round to the other side of the car where he climbed in without going to the trouble of opening the door. Sarah gave him a sidelong glance, trying not to look too obvious as she took in the smart trousers and cashmere sweater beneath the sheepskin jacket. A lock of brown hair fell over his forehead. He absently brushed it aside, revealing the scar above his left eyebrow from the injury he had received in the cliff fall. Sarah found it strangely attractive, and thought how handsome he looked. She could not believe that this was really her, sitting in a sports car with the heir to this vast estate beside her. Tony turned and smiled.

"I'm glad you wrapped up warmly. This car looks nice but it can be rather cold. Would you like me to put the roof up?"

Sarah shook her head.

"No. I'm looking forward to travelling at speed with the wind in my hair."

Tony smiled. "Good. Well, there's no point in wasting time here." He started the car and put it into gear. "Right then, let's go."

The car slid smoothly down the drive and out of the imposing entrance. As they roared through the narrow lanes Sarah found the journey exhilarating. Never before had she felt such complete freedom; until she met Tony, she had only experienced transport in the shape of buses, trams and trains, and none of them came anywhere near the open topped sports car for sheer excitement. She was almost sorry when Tony slowed down as they entered Bath. He drove confidently to the centre of the city, parked the car and climbed out.

"Come on." He opened the door and helped Sarah out. "Let's go exploring."

He led the way first to the huge stone building which had been erected over the site of the Roman baths and was now the Pump Room.

Sarah took a sip of the water and grimaced.

"It tastes funny!"

Tony laughed. "Funny taste or not, this water was very special for thousands of years. The Celts probably worshipped here. The Romans believed the springs down below us have special healing properties. People have been coming here ever since in the hope that the waters would heal their aches and pains." He sipped his water and pulled a face, making Sarah giggle. "Come on, drink up. There's lots to do and see!"

Sarah drained her glass. "So much for magical properties! I don't feel any different at all!"

Tony laughed. "Neither do I! Come on!" He took her by the hand and pulled her to her feet. Sarah clung tightly to him as they made their way down to the remains of the old Roman baths, where she was delighted by the ancient stonework and statues. She ran her fingers lightly over the stonework, tracing the outline of the head of a Roman god.

"It's hard to believe this has all been here for seventeen hundred years!" She found the concept awe inspiring, and a little frightening. "I wonder if our generation will ever build anything that will last that long?"

Tony almost said that it was unlikely, as the present generation seemed more bent on destruction than construction. But as he gazed at her face, wide-eyed in wonder, he remembered this was a day to forget wars. He smiled.

"I'm sure we shall. In the years to come there'll be a great deal of building, but what we build will be nothing like this. It will contain the spirit of our age. A spirit of hope that will reach out in knowledge and peace, to fill the whole world with beauty."

Sarah turned her serious gaze to his, knowing he wanted to use the words to wipe away her depression about the war. She smiled, a warm intimate smile and her eyes expressed her gratitude in a way that words could not. She reached out and placed a hand on Tony's arm, engulfed by a feeling of closeness which she could not find the words to express.

"Thank you, Tony."

Her voice was little more than a whisper, yet it seemed to echo in Tony's mind as he lost himself in the beauty of her eyes and her smile. His mouth felt dry, and he felt dizzy with the desire to kiss the woman beside him. Sarah saw the look of longing in his eyes. She reached up to kiss him on the lips. It was a soft kiss, little more than the brush of the wings of a butterfly, but it made Tony's lips burn. He knew that he would feel that kiss for the rest of his life. Leaning down he kissed Sarah tenderly, her warm lips responding to his, and for a moment time stood still for the young couple who had found their future in the ruins of the past.

The rest of the day passed in a dream for Sarah. They lunched at an expensive hotel. Although Tony said the food was not up to the pre-war standard, she found it delicious, revelling in the good food and wonderful atmosphere of the old hotel. In the afternoon they walked along the crescents of Regency houses, through the parks and beside the river. They stood on the old stone bridge which had served the citizens of Bath for centuries, and looked at the spring flowers that covered the banks of the river with their gay colours. Sarah felt a contentment deep inside, a feeling which she had not known since Joe's death, and she knew she was falling in love. Looking at the strong profile of the man beside her, a young man any girl would be glad to be seen with, she pondered on what the future might hold for her. While she knew Tony was very fond of her, she doubted that he loved her, and if he did he would never entertain the idea of marriage to her. His father was Sir Michael Kemshall, and he would expect his son to marry someone of similar standing. Her brows puckered in a slight frown. Maybe she should not be feeling so happy after all. If she had thought that Tony was setting out to court her, she would have hardened her heart to him knowing that there could be no future for them. But he had crept in beneath her guard. He had been a friend while Joe was still alive and, as any good friend would, had comforted her during her loss. It was during that time that the seed of her love for him had started to grow and she had not realised it until too late. Now she found herself in love with a man who liked her but would find her most unsuitable as a wife. She vowed never to let Tony know the depth of her feelings for him. Over the last year she had learned how to cope with sorrow and loss. She knew the pain that awaited her when their relationship finally came to an end, but she also knew that she was strong enough to cope with the loss and come safely through the other side; Joe's death had taught her that. She sighed. She would continue her relationship with Tony for as long as possible, and she would allow him to dictate its pace. Never for one moment would she allow him to see that she loved him. When he finally decided to end this little wartime romance in favour of finding a wife, she would be ready for it; even though it broke her heart she would part from him with a smile and in friendship.

Tony heard Sarah sigh and turned to her, puzzled by her frown.

"Is something bothering you?"

Sarah shook her head and smiled, banishing the melancholy thoughts from her mind.

"No, of course not. I'm having a wonderful day."

"Good." Tony took her hand and led her across the bridge. "Come on, let's find the car. I know a lovely little pub on the way back where we can stop for dinner."

Sarah smiled but said nothing. Her enjoyment of the day and the happiness caused by finally recognising that she loved Tony was now tempered with sadness as she contemplated her inevitable future alone.

75

Tony returned to Beaulieu the following Monday, his heart filled with joy. Friday in Bath had been the beginning of something wonderful for him; when he had kissed Sarah her response had been tentative to begin with but then, when her lips moved more firmly against his, he had felt a deep happiness. He knew Sarah would not have kissed him like that if she did not really care for him. On the way home they had stopped for dinner at a delightful little pub, and kissed beneath the bright stars of a cloudless spring sky. Knowing that his leave would be over on Sunday evening, Tony had arranged to meet Sarah and walk with her over the estates of Heronfield on both Saturday and Sunday mornings. They spent all too brief a time together, but Tony knew he would never forget the happiness he had enjoyed during those few hours. He was gentle with Sarah, sensing she would not want to rush too quickly into a relationship after her loss of the previous year, but they had held hands when they walked, and kissed gently in the quiet secluded places where Tony had played as a boy. He had felt they were drawn even closer together. There was some sort of inevitability about their relationship, a rightness which meant that once the war was over, they could spend the remainder of their lives together.

Now Tony stood outside Captain Dawson's office, nervously shuffling his feet as he awaited the interview which he had requested. He had wanted to go back to France ever since he was found fit again, but now he felt an added incentive. He knew he could not ask Sarah to marry him while he was working for the SOE. The chances of him not coming back were too great, and he did not want Sarah to suffer again the loss of a fiancé, or husband, if she accepted his proposal. As far as he could see, the only thing he could do about it was to get back to France as soon as possible, do his bit to shorten the war, and then come back and ask Sarah to marry him.

The door to Captain Dawson's office opened. An orderly left the room shuffling a bundle of papers.

"Captain Dawson will see you now, Lieutenant."

Tony nodded. "Thank you."

Straightening his shoulders, he entered the room and closed the door behind him before standing to attention in front of the Captain's desk with its neat piles of files. There was silence for a moment while Dawson finished reading the file in front of him. Then he closed it and looked up.

"Well, Kemshall, what can I do for you?"

Tony licked his lips. "I want to go back to France, sir."

Captain Dawson nodded slowly. "I thought as much. Do you think you're up to it?"

"I'm perfectly fit, sir, if that's what you mean."

"I know you're physically fit, Kemshall, but what about mentally? That last incident out there hasn't made you lose your nerve, has it?"

"On the contrary, sir!" Tony was indignant. "It was a good piece of work, faultless except for the accident. That's part of the reason I want to go back. I managed to set up a small team and we worked well together. I know that those people are waiting to do something else towards driving the Germans out, and I want to go back there to help them. Without the right kind of guidance, they'll either end up doing nothing or, which is more likely, take too many risks and end up losing their lives. I can channel their enthusiasm in a way that will help to shorten the duration of this war."

Captain Dawson leant back in his seat. "You've thought about this a lot, haven't you?"

Tony grinned. "I've thought about little else since I got back, sir."

"Well, then you'll be glad to hear that we shall be sending you back."

Tony's grin widened.

"When do I leave, sir?"

"In a month. This time we want you to set up a proper group. Your aims are not specific, merely to harass the enemy at every opportunity, and to pass on any intelligence you may come across."

"Yes, sir." Tony frowned. "Can't I go back sooner than that? A month is a long time."

"That's how long it will be before we get our new lot of radio operators ready to go. You're taking a radioman with you this time, and he'll be in charge of the transmitter. His only contact will be with you, so if he gets taken we won't lose the whole group."

"Yes, sir. I'll see if I can come up with some letter-boxes during the next month."

"Good man." Dawson smiled. "You know as well as anyone that a good contact point is essential. You can spend the next two weeks here, giving pep talks to the new recruits, before taking a couple of weeks leave. By that time you should have a cover story sorted out for your family."

"Yes, sir. Thank you, sir."

"That will be all."

Tony saluted, turned and left the room.

.

Two days later, Tony was called back to his commander's office. As he entered his eyes fell on a plump woman, aged about thirty, who sat opposite the desk. Her short dark hair framed a homely bespectacled face. She reminded Tony of the matron at the boarding school he attended as a child - plump, warm, familiar - a person to feel at ease with. Tony saluted the officer behind the desk.

"Ah, Kemshall. I would like you to meet Lieutenant Anna Weston."

The woman rose and held out her hand. "Pleased to meet you Lieutenant Kemshall."

"You too." Tony took the proffered hand, noting the lack of uniform. "Lieutenant Watson?"

The woman smiled and nodded.

"Allow me to explain." Dawson waved Tony to a chair, and the two younger officers sat down. "Lieutenant Watson will be your radio operator in France. She has completed basic training and parachuting quite well, but passed out of our wireless school as top of her class. She's a natural."

Anna smiled at the compliment but said nothing. Captain Dawson continued.

"She has another couple of weeks to go to finish sabotage training then you'll both get ten days' leave before flying out." He perused the two agents. "Any questions?"

"No, sir."

"None at all, sir."

"Good. Right, Kemshall. From now on you'll only refer to Lieutenant Watson by her code name - Angeline. She'll only be here for a couple of hours, so I want you to go over some maps of Saint Nazaire with her and sort out your post-boxes."

"Yes, sir." Tony rose to his feet and saluted, closely followed by Angeline. As they left the room he turned right down the corridor and made his way to the map room.

"What made you join SOE?" he asked.

"The same things as you, I would imagine." Angeline smiled. "My father's a business man. Between the wars, we lived on the Atlantic coast of France, a bit further south than Saint Nazaire but I know the area quite well. I loved living there. I hate to think of the Germans trampling all over my favourite places; so I'm going out there to get rid of them."

Tony laughed. "You're right. I suppose we're all doing it for the same reasons." He stopped and opened the door to the map room. "Please, come in."

They stepped inside. Tony went to a unit filled with map drawers, opened one and withdrew a map of the Saint Nazaire area. Spreading it out on the large table in the centre of the room, he weighed down the corners.

"Right." He took a deep breath. "Obviously neither of us should visit the other's safe house in case we're followed, so I've thought of two post-boxes where I can leave messages for you. The first is here." He jabbed a finger at a church on the northern edge of the city. "You'll be living somewhere in the outskirts of Saint Nazaire, so this is ideal. I shall leave any message inside the fourth prayer book from the aisle, in the third row from the back on the left hand side. The message will be placed there some time in the morning, so you should never be in the area then. Try to cycle past everyday sometime after 2p.m. - you could be on your way to the shops, a café, anything really, just make sure that you have a destination in mind, in case you're stopped."

"Do I have to go into the church every day? Won't that be a little suspicious?"

"You're right, it would be. If there's a message for you I will leave fresh flowers on the second grave from the gate on the left. But don't only go in if there is a message. Go in sometimes when there are no flowers there. That way no-one will be able to see a pattern in your visits."

Angeline nodded. "What if someone else puts flowers on the grave?"

"It's highly unlikely. I know that church, and all the graves in that area are over a hundred years old."

"Is that the only letter box?"

Tony shook his head. "No. The other is here." He pointed to a small fishing village some two miles north of the city. "I'll leave messages there some time before 10 a.m. and you can use the excuse of going out there to see if you can buy fresh fish for dinner. People will cycle miles for good food in France at the moment. Make your pick-up after 11 a.m. There's a rotting boat at the end of the dock - the Jeanne d'Arc - and you'll find the message slipped down behind the nameplate. It'll be easy enough to lean against the boat while watching the fishermen, and pick it up then. If there's a message there you'll see an empty wine bottle fifty yards further along the wall."

Angeline nodded. "I think I've got all that." She had made brief notes as Tony spoke. "I'll memorise and destroy these instructions."

"Good."

"Will you be the only one leaving messages?"

"Yes, it's safer. I have four other people working with me out there, but I don't want to take the chance of you seeing them. The less contact between us, the less danger there is. Though, of course, I'll give details of the drops to one other member of the group, in case something happens to me."

Angeline nodded. "Good idea. How do I get in touch with you if I have a message for you?"

"If I give you a message that will need a reply from London, put the reply in the church - same book, same routine - and I'll pick it up between eleven and twelve the following morning. Any message that comes from London unexpectedly and needs to reach me urgently should be left here." He pointed to a small farm track on the map. "Two hundred and fifty yards down that track is a rotting log. Leave the message in the north end of the log and a handkerchief caught in the bush at the end of the lane. I'll check the bush every afternoon."

"Right." Angeline smiled. "That's it, then. All I have to do is finish learning how to blow things up, then we can be on our way."

Tony smiled. She was not what he had expected in a radio operator at all. She looked more like a schoolteacher than a spy, which wasn't a bad thing. Yet she was full of enthusiasm and obviously knew what to do. He felt instinctively that he could rely on her. Angeline smiled at him, a little nervously.

"I hope you don't mind me asking, but haven't you already been out there as an operative?"

Tony nodded. "That's how I've managed to get a group together already."

"What was it like?"

"You have to be on your guard all the time, and it's strange to see the Germans walking about as though they own the place. Knowing what they would do to me if I was caught kept me on my toes, but at least I had friends who knew what I was doing there, who I could talk to if I felt it all getting on top of me." He frowned. "You know, it's you I really feel sorry for."

"Me? Why?"

"Because, as a radio operator you'll be on your own. You'll live alone in digs with no contact with other groups or agents. And each time you leave to send and receive you'll have to sneak the transmitter out, find a safe place to work and then sneak back. The tension will be intense when you're working, and the boredom unbearable when you're not."

Angeline smiled. "Don't worry about me. I like to be alone. I'll take this opportunity to read a lot of French novels I've always wanted to read but have never had the time to before!"

As Tony replaced the map of Saint Nazaire in its drawer, he thought what a remarkable woman Lieutenant Anna Watson was. He was glad she was part of his team.

76

During 1941 and early 1942, the British losses to German U-boats in the Atlantic were high, causing shortages of all manner of goods in the beleaguered island kingdom. In retaliation for these losses Churchill ordered the bombing of German cities. Hitler responded with the Baedeker Raids, named after the holiday guides that Hitler used to choose his targets. Each city hit was of outstanding historical value and beauty, raids designed to hit at the very core of British morale. The raids began on 24th April at Exeter, then Bath, York, Norwich, Exeter and Norwich again. There were a number of raids on Canterbury, and finally again on Norwich towards the end of June. The raids were serious and the effects long-lasting, but they did not break Britain's spirit as Hitler hoped. Instead they strengthened the resolve of the people to stand against the aggressor, and to turn the tide of the war.

Tony was held up at Beaulieu, giving lectures to a new group of recruits, and did not return to Heronfield until 24th April, with just one week to go before he was due to drop into France. The excitement he felt at the prospect of returning to enemy held territory was overpowered by the thrill of knowing he would soon be seeing Sarah again. Since their visit to Bath, he now knew where his life was taking him. He could see a bright future for him with Sarah by his side, once Germany was defeated. He often found himself wondering how Sarah felt, and would have been surprised at the similarity of their emotions. While Tony was away, Sarah thought deeply about their relationship. She too dreamt of a future together in that distant time 'after the war', but she believed that she was realistic enough to see this was nothing more than a dream. She decided that she would continue to see Tony. Why deprive herself of his company while she could still enjoy it? But she would not reveal the depths of her feelings to him. She would let him dictate the pace of their relationship, whether he chose friendship or romance, she would abide by his choice, enjoy what time she could with him, and be ready to say goodbye when the freedom which wartime lent to relationship was over, and he returned to his own social class to seek a bride.

Tony was well aware of Sarah's habit of walking in the grounds of Heronfield House every evening, as long as her duties allowed. He made sure he was near the orchard that evening, and was rewarded with the sight of her slim figure slipping out of the back door.

"Sarah!"

At the sound of his voice Sarah turned and waved, a bright smile spreading across her face as she walked over to join him.

"Tony! It's good to see you! I didn't expect you to get leave again so soon."

Tony smiled.

"I have to go to America to liaise for the Ministry next week, so they've given me a few days leave."

"America?"

Tony nodded. "Yes, to get the stocks of weapons moving across the Atlantic as quickly as possible. I'll probably be away for a few months at least, so this was my last chance to visit my family...and you." He took Sarah's hand in his. "I'll miss you while I'm away."

Sarah felt a knot of sorrow constricting her throat. "I...I'll miss you too Tony." She looked into his clear eyes. "You will write to me, won't you?"

Tony's eyes clouded and a slight frown puckered his brow. Write? He had not thought she would ask that. How would he be able to write to her from France? Sarah noticed his hesitation. She was angry with herself for trying to push him too far; he obviously did not want to write to her, she was not that important to him. Tony wished he could explain why it was so impossible for him to write. Finally, he smiled.

"I'll be very busy and have little time for writing, but I promise to get in touch with you whenever I can." Maybe, somehow, the SOE would be able to pass on messages for him. He squeezed her hand. "I'd much rather be with you than have to write letters. I never was much good at that."

Sarah smiled though, deep in her heart, she felt saddened. She had obviously misread Tony's feelings for her, and had now made an utter fool of herself. She turned from him slightly.

"Come on, let's go for a walk."

Tony fell in step beside her as they walked down towards the river. The estate was now coming to life beneath the magic touch of spring. Trees were clothed in mantles of fresh green, whilst the grass under foot was studded with spring flowers. Tony took Sarah's hand in his and, slowly, the closeness they had felt in Bath enveloped them once more.

The river was high, rushing between its banks, swollen with the previous day's rain. The weak afternoon sun reflected from the water in glittering rays, and the willow trees were covered in bud.

"It's so beautiful here." Sarah sighed. "People who live in cities don't know how much they're missing."

Tony watched her radiant face, and he felt his heart filling with love. He reached out a hand and gently touched her cheek.

"The city breeds beauty of its own."

Sarah saw the tenderness in his eyes. Surely that could not be false? She smiled and leant her head to one side so his hand was caught between her shoulder and her cheek. The warmth of his fingers brought life to her cold cheek, and to her aching heart. Slowly she reached up and traced the fading scar on his forehead with a gentle fingertip. Tony smiled as he leant forward and kissed her, warm lips gentle, exploring. Sarah found herself responding to his kiss, and slipped a hand behind his head to hold him close. Tony's lips became more insistent with the encouragement. His arms slid close about her, holding her slender body tightly to his chest. At last the moment was over and he drew away, smiling.

He could hardly believe the look of love which flooded her eyes. Could she really care so much for him at last?

"I'm so glad I met you, Sarah."

"And I'm glad we met too."

Sarah buried her head against his shoulder. The strong arms around her made her feel safe and secure. She felt wanted and loved for the first time since Joe. She found that she could think of him now without tears and, somehow, she felt he would wish her well and tell her to take any chance of happiness. He would want her to be happy with Tony. As she snuggled up closer, a heron rose from the reeds with a whirring of wings, rising like a phoenix from the flames. It seemed to symbolise a new love rising from the pain of the old. Feeling Tony's arm tighten around her and seeing the smile on his face as he watched the heron in flight, she realised he could feel the new beginning too. Sarah smiled as she felt the ghost of her previous love for Joe buried at last, and a whole bright new future spreading out before her.

The final few days of Tony's leave passed in a dream for Sarah. The hours she was on duty seemed to drag, while her off duty hours spent with Tony flew by. They spent hours walking together, indulging their shared love for the countryside; and pleasant evenings in the local pubs Tony had known all his life and now delighted in showing Sarah. Sarah's happiness was not confined inside but shone from her eyes, and was there in the constant smile on her lips. It was inevitable this change in her would be noticed. It was Jane who brought it out into the open.

"You're looking happy, Sarah."

Sarah smiled as her roommate sat down beside her upon the bed. "Yes, I suppose I am."

"And you seem to be spending a lot of time with Tony."

Sarah blushed slightly. "What of it?"

"I thought you said you weren't interested in him?"

"That was when Joe was still alive, and Tony and I were just good friends. But after Joe's death Tony was very supportive. I suppose he knew how I was feeling, because he'd lost his brother. I'm not sure how our friendship changed, it just grew over the months until we went to Bath a few weeks ago."

"And?"

Sarah glanced across at Jane and smiled at the inquisitive look in her friend's eyes.

"And what if I don't tell you anymore?"

Jane looked crestfallen and Sarah laughed.

"All right, I'll tell you. After all, I think you've probably guessed already." Her eyes took on a dreamy, faraway look. "While we were in Bath I realised that, over the months, Tony had worked his way into my heart. I love him."

"And what about him? How does he feel?"

Sarah shrugged. "I'm not sure. When we're together we seem so right for each other, and he seems so happy and in love with me. But he hasn't said so yet."

Jane frowned. "I don't want to be a wet blanket, Sarah, but can you be sure of his feelings? I know I've joked about you two having a relationship before, but that was while Joe was still alive and I knew it wouldn't really happen. I'm sure Tony is very fond of you, it's obvious from the way he looks at you, but there is a wide gulf between your life and his. I don't want to be cruel, but do you think he would want to marry someone of your social background?"

Sarah nodded, her face suddenly solemn. "You're not being cruel Jane. I've thought of all these things myself. I don't think he will marry me, but I don't see why that should stop me spending time with him now. As long as he's honest with me about his feelings, I shall continue to see him and just take it one day at a time."

Jane sighed. "I suppose you're right, but it's going to be difficult."

A grim smile played on Sarah lips. "I know. You don't have to tell me that."

77

Sarah was subdued as she pulled the thick woollen pullover over her head before making her way down to the river. It all seemed so quiet and peaceful; it would be so easy to forget the war here at Heronfield, where life continued as it had for countless centuries. Yet people could not cut themselves off from what was happening in the outside world. The radio was on constantly so that no news bulletins would be missed, and it was this that had so depressed Sarah. It had become a habit with her to go into the staff common room to listen to the news when she came off duty, and today she had been shocked to hear of the raid on Bath. At first she did not want to believe it, but as the truth sank in she felt numbed by what the Germans had done. She hardly saw her surroundings as she made her way down the path. Instead her mind saw again the beautiful old houses of the city which she had so recently visited with Tony, and the ancient Roman baths which had given the city its name and which she remembered with such fondness. Wondering how much damage had been done, she found herself hating the Germans more than ever for this senseless destruction. However much she detested it, she could understand the bombing of industrial centres that were contributing to the war effort. But places like Bath had no military value, and bombing them would not bring Germany's war aims closer to fruition. It was a case of destruction for the sake of it, an assault not only on Britain's heritage but upon the heart and will of the British people as well. She found her hatred of the German action strengthening her resolve, and hoped that all the British people felt the same as they contemplated the news of the Baedeker raids. Yet she could not fail to take the bombings personally. The city of Bath held a special place in her heart after her visit with Tony, and, although the wanton destruction could not destroy her memories, this attack touched her soul in a way that no other news of the war had done since the bombing of Coventry.

Sarah found herself standing beneath the spreading branches of the old willow tree which leant over the bank of the river as though attempting to reach out and touch the gently flowing water. She sighed wearily and sat down, back against the textured surface of the tree trunk, leaning her head back to glance up through the gently swaying branches. It all seemed so peaceful here. Why could men not live in peace and harmony as demonstrated by nature? Sarah closed her eyes, picturing the city of Bath as it had been when she walked the streets with Tony. In the peace and tranquility of the countryside she drifted slowly into sleep.

A tender smile lit Tony's face when he found her there half an hour later. She looked so peaceful, so beautiful, and he felt his heart swell with love for her. Tony leant down and kissed her gently on the lips, then watched as the touch brought her slowly awake. Sarah stretched languorously then slowly opened her eyes.

"Tony!"

The young man smiled as he sat down beside her.

"Sorry I'm a little late, Sarah." He leant over and kissed her again, still finding it hard to believe that she would want to kiss him. "You look beautiful when you're asleep."

Sarah blushed, feeling vulnerable after being found like that, as though Tony had been able to see all of her hidden fears and emotions. Tony seemed to sense her unease and smiled.

"I'm sorry I was late, but I had to take a telephone call just before leaving the lodge." He was quiet for a moment, recalling the voice which had told him that conditions over the next couple of days would be perfect for a drop into France so he must return immediately to prepare for his mission. His feelings at the news were mixed. He wanted desperately to get back to France and to continue the fight against the Germans, but at the same time he wanted to remain with Sarah. Now that their relationship was developing, he wished he could have just a little more time with her to be sure of her feelings. He frowned slightly. "I have to return to base tonight, and leave for America in the next day or so." He turned to face Sarah, his emotions plainly visible on his face. "I'm going to miss you, Sarah."

Sarah reached out and took his hand in hers. "How long do you think you'll be away?"

Tony shrugged. "I don't know. At least three or four months, I suppose, maybe even longer. It all depends on how things go."

Sarah felt saddened at the prospect of not seeing him again for months, but at least it would give him time to think about their relationship. She felt that by the time he came back she would know, one way or the other, if their relationship had any chance of lasting.

"Will you write?"

Tony felt uneasy about the question. He had thought about that a lot over the last week but still had not come up with a way to keep in touch with Sarah while he was in

France. His voice was halting as he spoke.

"I'll try to keep in touch, but I can't promise anything. I'm going to be very busy for the next few months."

Sarah frowned. It did not sound too encouraging.

"Will I be able to write to you?"

"I'm not sure where I'll be. I'll be moving around a lot, you know."

Sarah felt crestfallen. It sounded as if he didn't want to write to her, and neither did he want to receive letters from her while he was away. Tony saw the sadness in her eyes and felt helpless as to how to explain the situation to her without giving too much away.

"I tell you what," he said at last, with a forced cheerfulness. "I'll give you the address I told you about in London. You can write to me there, and they'll forward the letters."

Sarah smiled. "All right." She supposed it was better than nothing, and she determined not to let it spoil her last few hours with Tony. As she leant her head against his shoulder, Tony slipped an arm around her, holding her close. It felt so good to have her in his arms. He knew that through the long lonely moments he would endure during the next few months it would be a treasured memory that he could take out and enjoy once more. His arm tightened around Sarah's shoulders, as he thought about the possibility that he might not come back at all. This could be the last time that he would ever hold her.

At the pressure from his arms, Sarah looked up. She felt her breath taken away by the look of longing in his eyes. There was no need for words as Tony leant down and kissed her, softly at first but then more insistently. As Sarah responded to the warming pleasure of his lips, he reached a hand behind her head, softly stroking her hair. His lips became more insistent, pressing harder against hers as his fingers tangled roughly in her hair. Slowly, his hand slid down her back to her waist then, of its own volition, under the thick woollen sweater. Sarah caught her breath and pulled away slightly, breaking the contact of their lips as his fingers stroked the bare skin of her back.

"I'm sorry, Sarah." Tony's voice was husky with desire. "I care for you so much. I just wanted to touch you, to hold you, before I leave. I shouldn't have pushed you. We'll have all the time in the world for that in the future."

Sarah was in emotional turmoil. Her skin burned where his fingers had stroked, crying out to be touched again. Yet she also felt uneasy, not quite sure if she was ready for this change in their relationship. But at Tony's words, her muddled thoughts cleared. Once before a man had touched her and she had stopped him, saying that they had all the time in the world. But time had run out and she had never been able to indulge her love for him. Now Tony's touch excited her in such a way that she did not want him to stop. She longed to feel his hands exploring her body, to feel his naked flesh beneath her fingers. Yet she had pulled away, just has she had done with Joe. She would not make the same mistake again.

Taking Tony's hand in hers, she looked at his long, beautifully shaped fingers, wondering at their softness, wondering how they would feel against the hidden depths of her flesh. Looking up into his eyes, she raised his hand and placed it gently on her breast.

A loan moan escaped Tony's lips. "Are you sure about this, Sarah?"

She nodded, and his hand began to knead her breast through the sweater. Tony's mind was on fire. She felt so soft, so yielding beneath his touch, yet he wanted more. As he kissed her, his hand slipped lower until it was inside the sweater, then it was upon the soft skin of her breast. Sarah gasped at his touch. Tongues of fire coursed through her veins and she pressed herself closer to him. She could not let him go without allowing him to share more of himself with her, without touching more of him herself. Her hand slipped inside his shirt and stroked the strong, hard muscles of his back. Slowly, gasping for breath, Tony pulled away.

"You're so beautiful, Sarah, and I want you so much. Are you sure you want this too?"

Sarah nodded, no words were necessary for her eyes spoke for her.

"Come with me." Tony stood and offered her his hand. "Let's go into the boathouse."

Sarah smiled as he led her into the old boathouse. It was dark and quiet, safe from prying eyes. Leading her to a pile of blankets in the corner, Tony gently lowered her to the floor. He smiled a smile so full of love that Sarah's heart melted, and she knew she was doing the right thing. Tony leant down to kiss her again. For a long time nothing could be heard save the sounds of their sighs, and their whispered words of love.

When it was over, Tony lay for a time, gently stroking her smooth, naked skin. Never in his wildest imaginings had he thought that Sarah would be his so completely and utterly. They had shared something so special that he knew that, whatever happened, there would always be an unbreakable bond between them. He sighed, and Sarah reached out to touch his face.

"Happy?"

He opened his eyes and looked into hers, eyes so full of love that he felt he would drown in them.

"Yes." He ran his fingers through her rich red hair. "That was your first time, wasn't it?"

Sarah nodded but said nothing.

"I had thought...I don't mean to pry...but... you and Joe...?"

"I wanted to wait, but I left it too long. War doesn't allow us to wait for anything."

"Do you regret it?"

"Not making love to Joe? Yes, I do. But I don't regret making love with you." She stroked his thigh, her touch gently as a butterfly's wings, and Tony felt the stirrings of desire once more. "Who knows what will happen over the next few months? At least we both know how we feel now, and will have the memory of this to hold when we get lonely."

"I'm going to miss you so much while I'm away. I wish now that I could stay here with you forever. That this boathouse were the whole world, and we could spend the rest of our lives here alone."

Sarah smiled at his words. "I wish that too, but you have to leave soon, and there's nothing we can do to change that. We need the weapons you are going to America for. The boathouse will still be here when you get back. And so will I."

As he gazed into her eyes, Tony wished that the war was over so that he would never again need to keep secrets from the woman he loved. He knew that no matter what physical dangers lay ahead, the biggest burden of this war for him was the secrets he had to keep about his job, secrets he was afraid might drive them apart. Sarah snuggled closer and he smiled as he gazed down at the head resting on his shoulder. He leant over and gently kissed her hair. It smelt so fresh and clean, and he closed his eyes as he savoured the moment.

Sarah pressed her lips against his chest, and gently stroked the hard muscles of his thigh. She had never imagined that making love could feel so wonderful, leaving her fulfilled, warm, aglow with love yet longing for more. As she stroked his thigh, Tony felt his desire rising once more and drew her close within his arms as his lips hungrily sought out hers.

As they explored each other's bodies, shared each touch, each kiss, each look of love, all thoughts of the conflict which raged around the globe were banished from their minds until they were lost in themselves alone.

78

Within thirty-six hours of leaving Heronfield, Tony found himself seated in the fuselage of a Whitley, the roar of the engines filling his ears as the plane taxied along the runway before rising up into the dark night sky. They banked steeply to the right, then levelled out as the plane headed south towards France. Tony smiled across at Angeline, who was leaning back against the metal wall.

"Are you all right?" He had to shout above the noise of the plane and was pleased to see his companion nod in reply.

"Yes. I'm fine."

"Nervous?"

Again Angeline nodded. "Yes."

"So am I." Tony smiled. "I've already parachuted into France once, and I thought it would be easier the second time round, but it isn't. The danger is still as great and my stomach is still churning!"

Angeline smiled. "Thanks."

"What for?"

"For trying to make me feel better." She eyed her packs ranged on the floor around her. Clothing, radio, gun. "I have everything and I'm well trained. I'll be all right."

Tony nodded, and the two people closed their eyes and buried themselves in their thoughts for the remainder of the journey.

Tony had drifted into sleep and was awakened by a hand shaking him gently by the shoulder.

"We're nearly there, sir."

Tony opened his eyes and looked up at the member of the aircrew.

"Right."

Within moments the two SOE agents were ready. Parachute ripcords attached to static lines, packages tied to their belts, standing beside the hole in the floor which would be their access to France.

"I'll go first."

Angeline looked across at Tony. "Right."

The two nervously watched the red light shining on the wall, waiting for it to go out and the green to come on in its place. The wait seemed to be endless as the plane banked slowly to the left until they were over the dropping zone. Then the light changed.

"Good luck." The airman slapped Tony on the shoulder. "Go!"

Tony, hands tightly by his side, stepped forward and found himself falling between the metal edges of the hole. He fell fast through the cold night air, then was brought up short by the pulling of the ripcord. He looked up and watched the silk of his chute billowing open above him as he found himself falling once more through the cold empty skies above war torn France.

MAY 1942

79

It was hard to see where he was falling, for the land was dark beneath its blackout mantle. As Tony stared down beneath his feet, he detected a darker shadow to his left and carefully steered away from it. As he fell further the ground rose up to meet him, and the dark shadow resolved itself into a clump of trees. With cold hands he steered towards the trees so that he would land closer to them, yet not close enough to become entangled in their branches. Suddenly he could make out the land rushing up to meet him. He clamped his knees and feet tightly together. Seconds later he had hit the ground and was rolling to lessen the impact. With practiced movements he leapt to his feet and began to gather the canopy towards himself, fighting the gentle breeze which sought to keep it inflated. Over to his right, he could just make out the shadow of Angeline's parachute as it fell, then he saw her hit the ground and roll with the fall. Within seconds she too was on her feet, gathering in the yards of billowing silk.

"Bring it over here."

Tony's voice was little more than a whisper, but she heard him and nodded, dragging her chute into the dark shelter of the trees. Tony had already rolled away a fallen log and was digging beneath it; soon there was a hole large enough to take the two parachutes. They covered them with earth, the fallen log and, finally, a deep pile of leaf litter. When they stepped back to scrutinise the scene, it was impossible to tell that the log had been moved. Overhead, the sound of the Whitley's engines had faded into the distance and the night sounds of the woods surrounded them. Tony could hear the wind in the branches. Somewhere over to his left, a small animal rooted amongst the dead leaves and overhead an owl hooted its hunting cry, but no other sounds disturbed the stillness. Tony smiled.

"It looks like we've made it without being seen."

Angeline nodded. "Do we split up here?" She looked around, trying to get her bearings. "I think I have to head south for the city."

Tony nodded. "That's right, but we don't have to split up yet. I have to come with you as far as the coast road. I'll leave you there." He began to skirt the trees as he spoke. "Come on, I'll lead the way."

Falling in behind his dark shadow, a bag with some clothing in one hand and the wireless set in the other, Angeline followed her companion quickly and silently through the deceptively peaceful countryside of Occupied France. It took them little more than half an hour to reach the road, where Tony stopped and crouched behind a sheltering hedge. Angeline knelt beside him.

"Right. This is where we split up." He looked up at the sky as he spoke. Clouds blocked out many of the stars and there was no moon to light the way. "It's dark enough for you to use the road without being seen, but don't forget to listen out for any German vehicles. They use only minimal lighting at night and could be on you before you know it."

Angeline smiled. "Don't worry. I'll be all right." She held out her hand and he took it, his eyes on the determined features which showed not the slightest trace of fear. "Good luck, Albert."

He squeezed her hand. "Good luck to you too, Angeline. And take care. You'll be in a far more vulnerable position than me."

She shrugged. "Each job has its own dangers. Now, I'll be off."

Without another word, the plump bespectacled woman wormed her way through the hedge and started off southwards down the road. After watching her retreating form for a moment, Tony slipped quietly across the road and into the shelter of the trees on the other side. For him it was like coming home. He had spent most of his summers with his Grandmother de Thierry when he was a boy and he knew these woods almost as well as he knew those back at Heronfield. His feet led him unerringly across the northern edge of his grandmother's estate, and then down towards the small cottage inhabited by the Boues family. It was 3.30 in the morning when he slipped past the vegetable patch, noticing the prepared soil and one or two crops already beginning to show. Then he was beside the pig pen. He found the small hiding place still waiting, and stashed his revolver and Sten gun before hurrying over to the dark, silent cottage. He tried the door, but it was bolted from the inside. Slowly he circumnavigated the building until he found a window that had been left ajar in the kitchen. Slipping silently inside he sat in Jean-Paul's chair and settled down to wait.

Tony must have dropped off to sleep. He was woken by a hand on his shoulder, and opened his eyes to see the cold light of dawn flooding the room. He looked up into Jean-Paul's eyes which registered surprise, incredulity, delight.

"Albert! What are you doing here?"

Tony stood up and embraced his host. "Jean-Paul. It's good to see you again. I'm sorry I broke in like this, but I didn't want to make a habit of waking you up in the middle of the night!"

Jean-Paul laughed. "You shouldn't worry about that, my friend! Sit down and I'll make you a coffee, or at least what passes for coffee in these troubled times."

Tony smiled. "We have the same trouble back at home."

He watched as Jean-Paul put on the kettle and took down two bowls from the shelf before turning back to look at the young Englishman.

"We were worried about you, Albert. You don't know how difficult it was, not knowing if your injuries were healing well, or even if you had arrived back in England safely."

"Thank you for your concern, Jean-Paul. There's not much to tell really. The submarine got me back without any trouble, then I was sent to hospital to convalesce. Would you believe they actually sent me home for that!"

"Then your family now know what you're doing?"

"No. They were told I'd been injured in an air raid. They think I'm over in America at the moment."

"But what are you doing here?"

"I've come to re-establish our group, so that we can fight the Germans more effectively. I brought a radio operator with me who will be living in Saint Nazaire, and will have no contact with us. I shall send any messages to London through that channel." He was thoughtful for a moment. "Would you take the risk of knowing how to contact the radio operator, just in case anything happens to me?"

"Of course I will. It's sensible for more than one to know how to contact him."

Tony was about to correct him and say 'her', but then he thought better of it. The less Jean-Paul knew, the safer he, and Angeline, would be. He smiled at the Frenchman.

"What have you and the others been up to?"

Jean-Paul shrugged. "Very little I'm afraid. Claude has been able to cause some disruption by tampering with a few German vehicles, but it has not really caused any damage."

Tony frowned. "Tell him to stop that. I don't want him to be taken and shot for

226

stealing starter motors. He has much more useful work to do.

Jean-Paul nodded. "Yes, of course. It's just that he felt so useless after the excitement of the attack on the U-boat base. We all did. We all wanted to continue the fight."

"What about the others?"

"Charles has been 're-directing' the odd lorry load of German food supplies."

Tony shook his head, exasperated. "Childish tricks. If he's not careful he'll be taken and shot as a black-marketeer. Doesn't he understand that I want us to do big things? One hit causing a lot of damage, not stupid dangerous pranks which will not really help."

"We all know that, Albert, but you weren't here." Jean-Paul smiled gently. "You had fired us up to fight, and it was hard to settle back into dull routine again after you left. Claude and Charles will be only too happy to stop what they're doing to work with you again."

Tony smiled sheepishly. "Sorry Jean-Paul. You're right, of course. What about you and Madeleine? What have you been doing?"

"We have been behaving ourselves."

Tony laughed. "Point taken Jean-Paul. I'm really looking forward to working with you again."

The door to the kitchen opened, and Theresa came in.

"Papa, I..." She stopped when she saw Tony, her face breaking into a wide grin of pure delight. "Albert!" She flung herself into his arms. "I'm so happy to see you fit and well again!"

"And I'm happy to see you too, Theresa." Tony smiled warmly at the twelve year old. "I wanted to say thank you, for all your help on my last visit."

Theresa blushed. "I was glad to help, Albert. And I hope you'll let me help again this time."

Tony smiled. "We'll see, Theresa. We'll see."

The young girl turned and raced from the room, calling excitedly as she went.

"Mamma! Jeanne! Albert is back!"

Jean-Paul laughed. "Welcome home Albert!"

80

Dawn was not far away by the time the dark mass of Saint Nazaire rose up in front of Angeline. The blackout was in force and not a light showed; it seemed the war was the same for civilians everywhere, although Britain did not have to contend with a curfew such as the one which was imposed upon the French. Angeline left the grey ribbon of the road, and hid in the trees that bordered it, waiting for daylight to come and the curfew to be over.

The wait was not long. As she sat with her back to the moss covered trunk of an old oak tree the sky began to grow lighter. She watched for a time, and the suburbs of the city gradually came to life. People were moving about now that the curfew was over, on their way to work, or to the shops, children going to school. A number of people left the city, some on foot and the remainder on bicycles, but none by car for fuel was severely rationed. With the increasing life of the city to cover her approach Angeline made her way out from the shelter of the trees and onto the road. Attaching herself to the tail of a group of farm workers hoping to sell their produce, the English spy slipped into the city.

It was a sombre place, the hand of war heavy upon it. The shops held few goods, and what there were were necessities. Luxuries seemed to have totally disappeared. The people who walked the streets looked serious, as though there was little enjoyment in their lives. Everywhere she looked, Angeline was aware of the occupation - the red, black and white of the Nazi swastika, notices written in both French and German and, above all, the presence of German military personnel. That was the strangest and most disturbing factor for Angeline, to be in amongst the enemy who strutted around as though they owned the city, which indeed they did. With a deep breath and an attempt to appear nonchalant so that she would blend in with the colourless population of the city, Angeline made her way deeper into the suburbs. Stopping outside a small tobacconist's, she perused the advertisements in the hope of finding a room to let, but there was nothing. Pushing open the door she stepped inside.

The owner, rather glum-faced and seemingly suspicious of strangers, glanced over from his position behind the counter.

"What do you want?"

"I'm looking for lodgings. Do you know of any?"

The old man frowned. "You are new in Saint Nazaire?" Angeline nodded. "What brings you here?"

"I'm looking for work." Angeline was not happy with the questioning. Her wireless set seemed heavy in her hand, and she was afraid that someone would recognise it for what it was. She spoke again, feigning confidence. "Can you help me with either a job or a room?"

The man shook his head. "No. I don't trust strangers. But you could try the bakery down the road."

With a swift word of thanks, Angeline left the shop. Turning right, she followed the smell of freshly baked bread until she stood outside the small baker's shop. Although it was still early in the morning, there was already a queue of people waiting to buy bread, ration books in hand. Many gave her angry looks, as she ignored the line of people and made her way inside. The baker was behind the counter, flour up to his elbows, cutting the long loaves in two. He spoke without looking up from his work.

"Can I help you?"

"I hope so. I'm new in Saint Nazaire, and I'm looking for a job and somewhere to live."

The baker looked up and frowned. He was in his late fifties and his face was creased with lines which showed that once, in happier times, he had been more accustomed to smiling than of late. He looked his visitor up and down, noticing the drab clothes of the bespectacled figure. She looked like any other woman after three years of occupation.

"Not many people are moving home now. Why do you want to live and work here?"

Angeline took a deep breath and launched into her cover story. "My name is Angeline Legrand. My husband was killed during the first week of the war. Since then I have been living with my mother in Paris, but she died two weeks ago, and I decided to try to find work elsewhere. Paris is too depressing, seeing the Germans in all the places I used to love to visit."

The baker nodded as though he understood. "Do you have papers?"

"Of course." Angeline nervously handed him her forged papers, but they seemed to pass his scrutiny successfully and he looked up.

"Saint Nazaire is no different from Paris, you know. The Germans are everywhere here too."

Angeline nodded. "I know. But Saint Nazaire is not as familiar to me as Paris. I might find it easier to accept them here."

The baker smiled, a warm friendly smile, and Angeline relaxed.

"I have a spare room you can have. Three Francs a week."

Angeline nodded. "Thank you very much, Monsieur." She smiled. "I'm sorry, but I don't know your name."

"I'm Vincent Artois, but you must just call me Vincent, Madame Legrand."

"Then you must call me Angeline." She looked around the small shop. "Can you show me where to put my things, please? I must go out and find a job, or I won't be able to pay the rent."

"Well," Vincent smiled, "I've been struggling here. I can manage the selling alone, but the bakery is not so easy without a helper, and I'm not willing to ask people to break curfew to help me bake during the night. If you lived here, you wouldn't have to break the curfew if you worked for me."

Angeline smiled. "That would be wonderful!"

"Not all that wonderful. You would have to be up at three o'clock and work until about ten. Could you do that?"

Angeline nodded, hardly able to contain her excitement. Not only had she found lodgings, but also a cover job which would allow her to have time free during the day, she would be able to check the post-boxes for messages from Tony without too much difficulty.

"Thank you very much, Vincent."

"You are most welcome, Angeline. Now, if you could put your things in the corner and help me to sell my bread, then I'll show you to your room."

81

It took two days for Jean-Paul to make contact with the other three members of their group for Claude had been out of the city collecting car parts. They finally met, in the same secluded clearing in the woods which was the scene of Tony's first introduction to the three French nationals who were risking their lives by associating with him. He perused the small group, and smiled. Claude Corver had lost even more of his hair in the few months since Tony had last seen him, but he appeared as fit as ever. Charles Durand, much the same age as Tony, still had the light of fanaticism in his eyes, but Tony knew that he could temper this by giving the young man constructive work to do. And finally Madeleine Thibault, as slim and as beautiful as ever, seemingly more relaxed now that she had played a part in striking back at the hated Germans. The attack on the submarine pens must have gone a long way towards avenging the death of her husband and helping her to come to terms with that sad loss. As Jean-Paul and Tony stepped from the trees, the three occupants of the clearing turned towards them and smiled.

"Albert!" It was Madeleine who spoke for them all. "We're so glad to see you fit and well again. You can't believe how worried we've been about you."

Charles stepped forward and shook Tony's hand."

"I'm glad to see you again, Albert. Now you can lead us against the Germans once more."

Tony grinned, the boyish smile making him appear younger than he was. "It sounds as though you really do need me, Charles. I've heard about the escapades which you and Claude have been indulging in; too dangerous for the very little advantage they give us, if you ask me."

Charles' welcoming smile wavered, and Tony laughed.

"Don't worry, I'm not really angry; in your place I would probably have done the same. But we are now in a position where we're able to inflict much greater losses and damage on the enemy. We must all work together. Understood?"

"Yes, Albert." Claude sat down on an old tree trunk. "What are your plans for us?"

Tony found a comfortable perch, and indicated that the others should do the same.

"Well, Saint Nazaire is an important port for the Germans, so we could do worse than disrupt the facilities."

"How?"

Tony smiled at Charles.

"That's where I need your help. I don't want to go into the city more often than I have to I'll need you, Claude and Madeleine to get a good look at the docks. I want to know where they store their fuel, food supplies, spare parts for ships, ammunition, and anything else you can come up with."

Madeleine frowned. "That will not be easy Albert. We were all familiar with the port before the war, but all the facilities which you are talking about are in an area where only Germans are allowed to go."

Tony nodded. "I understand, but we must know the layout before we go in there or we could be in trouble. It will be necessary to spy from the roofs of nearby buildings. It would be nice if we could get inside, but I think the danger is too great. Don't take too many risks." He looked pointedly at Charles as he spoke. "We don't want to alert the Germans to our interest." He sat deep in thought for a moment then spoke again. "Claude and Charles, you can give me a rough plan of the interior of the port and try to find a way in. I would like Madeleine to concentrate on the guards."

Madeleine raised a quizzical eyebrow. "Concentrate on the guards? In what way?"

Tony grinned again. "Don't worry, I'm not asking you to give up your honour for France. Just spend a lot of time in the area, and see if you can work out the guard routine - how long are they on duty? When do they change guard? Are any of the guards less alert than the others? That sort of thing."

Madeleine nodded. "Consider it done."

"What about weapons?"

Tony turned to Jean-Paul. "I know the things we need, and I'll get a message to London to arrange a drop."

"Do we use the same place as before?"

Tony nodded. "It's remote enough, and we know it now, as do London. We can use it at least one more time before we have to think of another site."

"When will the drop come?"

"It will probably take about a week, Claude. I'll let Jean-Paul know, and he'll get a message to you all to meet us at the site at 10p.m on the night."

"Will you want our information then?"

Tony shook his head. "No, Charles. When the drop comes I want us to hide the stuff and get away as quickly as possible, in case the plane is spotted. Let's arrange to meet here again on Saturday at the same time. All right?"

The others nodded. "We should have some information by then."

"Good. Then let's get going. The less time we spend together, the less danger we are in. Goodnight, and good luck."

With a chorus of good wishes, the five people disappeared into the trees, leaving the clearing deserted once more.

Tony spent part of the next morning encoding his message for Angeline. It would be a long one, longer than he liked, but it was necessary. With his request for a drop, he included the co-ordinates where he would be waiting and a list of the items he needed, including gammon grenades, limpet mines, plastic explosives, pocket incendiaries, Sten guns and thermite bombs. He was glad that the signal which would be given over the radio on the night before the drop had been arranged before he left England so he would not have to take time sending that too. Late in the morning, he borrowed Jean-Paul's bicycle and set off through the misty rain for the outskirts of the city.

There were few people about, the damp air driving them from the streets, and Tony felt conspicuous. He pedalled on, not so fast as to draw attention to himself, but fast enough to appear as though the rain bothered him and he wanted to get to his destination quickly. Shoulders hunched and head down, he turned into the road where the church was situated, only to find a German checkpoint. Swallowing nervously he stopped his bicycle and dismounted.

"Papers."

The young German soldier looked wet and fed-up. He took Tony's papers and perused them. He frowned, and Tony's heart caught in his throat. Was there something wrong with them?

"Name?"

"Albert Fouquet."

"Address?"

"22 Rue Blanc."

"Occupation?"

"Labourer on the de Thierry estate."

"What are you doing here then? Should you not be working?"

Tony shrugged in typical French fashion. "The rain was interfering with my work so I took a couple of hours off."

"What for?"

Tony indicated the bunch of flowers in the basket attached to the front of the bicycle. "I'm going to pay my respects at the family grave."

The young soldier nodded, his face softening. "You may not think we Germans have a heart, but we do. We too have families. We would love to spend time with them, or caring for their graves as you are able to, instead of standing here in the rain, fighting for a man like Hitler." He handed the papers back to Tony. "On your way."

Tony put the papers back in his pocket, mounted the bicycle and rode away. He was frowning as he rode. Since Dunkirk, he had thought of the Germans as little more than vermin which needed exterminating, but now he saw just how naive that attitude was. The young man who had checked his papers was obviously unhappy in Hitler's army, probably a conscript, and his longing for home was obvious. Tony began to realise that the war was not quite as black and white as he had thought. There were probably many Germans who opposed Hitler but could do nothing about it. Young men like that soldier probably had no choice but to join the army if they wished their families to remain safe. Tony found himself sympathising with the young conscript, who was obviously in uniform against his will, and felt his hatred of the German becoming tempered with compassion. It would make no difference to his job, however. The war must be won, and if innocent Germans died as well as innocent British and French, then that was the price to be paid.

Tony cycled along to the church, then dismounted and propped the bicycle against the railings. Taking the flowers from the basket he went through the gate, turned left and stopped at the second grave he came to. Stooping, he placed the flowers on the grave then stood for a moment as though deep in thought, in case anyone was watching. Then he turned and made his way up the path and through the door of the church. It was dim inside, lit only by the candles in front of the altar and the muted light which came through the stained glass windows. Tony made his way slowly up the aisle and into the third row on the left. Moving along the row, he sat down in front of the fourth prayer book along. He knelt down as though in prayer. Taking the prayer book in his hands, he carefully slipped his message to Angeline inside its front cover. After a few moments' contemplative silence Tony found that he was really praying; praying for Angeline, that she would not be caught when she set the message, praying for his group, that they would not be hurt in the planned attack, praying for his parents and Sarah back in England. Tony had rarely been in a church since childhood, but now he found it calming and peaceful. He wondered why he had not tried praying before.

Rising from his knees, Tony made his way out of the dimly lit church. It had stopped raining and a weak sun was peeping out from behind a cloud. With a smile, Tony retrieved the bicycle and set off in the direction of his grandmother's estate. With the weather brightening up, Jean-Paul would need his help on the farm.

82

Angeline settled quickly into life at Vincent Artois' bakery. To begin with, she found it difficult to rise at three in the morning to help Vincent light the ovens and mix the dough, but she soon got used to it. Indeed she found that she enjoyed the tasks he set her, particularly the kneading of the dough. She used it as a release for her pent-up emotions. Kneading and pulling at the dough calmed the nerves she sometimes felt, being in enemy held territory and without personal contact with her own people. The isolation forced her closer to Vincent, who appreciated Angeline's help in the house as well as in the bakery and shop. A close friendship was developing between the two, like uncle and niece, and Vincent was surprised to find that life was more enjoyable for him than it had been at any time since the spring of 1940. He had not realised just how isolated he, and other people, had become under German rule, how lonely it was for someone alone at a time when families were moving closer together, and he thanked God for bringing Angeline to him.

Angeline found it easier to settle into life in Saint Nazaire than she had expected. She had a good safe house, a cover story and a cover job which seemed to hold up well under scrutiny, while giving her time to continue with the activities which were the real reason for her being in France. She finished working in the bakery and shop each morning sometime after ten o'clock, then always went out for a cycle ride to 'clear her head'. Vincent thought nothing of it, unaware that she cycled to a small fishing village to check for messages from a British agent. After lunch, she would shop for their meagre rations, making sure that her route passed the small church in the suburbs.

Life had quickly settled into the routine that was a wireless operator's life. Called on only infrequently to pass on messages, it became necessary to focus the concentration on living a totally French life, so that no action would give her away. Angeline had settled into this way of life so quickly and so well that it was almost a shock for her to see the small bunch of flowers on the grave, bright colours caught by a ray of weak afternoon sun, as she cycled past the church. She stopped, leant her bicycle against the railings and carried her basket of groceries up the path and into the church. The building was empty. She made her way slowly up the aisle and slipped into the pew which Tony had occupied an hour earlier. She placed the basket on the seat beside her. No-one in occupied France would be silly enough to let their food out of their sight even in the hallowed precinct of a church. She knelt down as though to pray, lifting the prayer book down and opening its front cover. There, as she had expected, was the small piece of paper with Tony's message. Her heart was beating rapidly as she slipped the piece of paper deep into her pocket, not daring to read it where she knelt in the church. The palms of her hands were wet with sweat, and she wiped them on her skirt before smiling ruefully. Whoever would have thought that an ordinary looking woman like her would find herself in such a situation.? At least she did not look like a spy, or her idea of what a spy should look like, which was of some comfort to her as she nervously replaced the prayer book.

Angeline heard a door close somewhere over on her right, and had to fight to stop herself jumping at the sound. Taking a deep breath, she slowly lifted her head to see the local priest, who must have been working in a room adjoining the main body of the church, make his way to the altar, his black robes swishing against the stone floor. At the altar rail, he genuflected and knelt to pray. Angeline let her breath out in a slow sigh, she had been unaware that she had been holding it, then rose to her feet, picked up her basket and slipped out of the church. By the time she had secured the basket to the bicycle, her hands had ceased their trembling. She was feeling much more in control of herself. The sight of the priest had been a shock; she had thought herself alone in the church. But the experience reinforced for her the fact that she should be on her guard at all times. With a deep breath, and a mask of confidence, Angeline mounted the bicycle and made her way back to the bakery.

Angeline spent the afternoon and early evening in her room, reading and restlessly pacing back and forth. Her contact time with London was not until five minutes past midnight, still hours away. It would only take her thirty minutes to reach the bombed out warehouse she had chosen to send her first message from. Allowing time for hold ups en route, she would not need to leave the bakery until eleven fifteen. She glanced at her watch. Only seven p.m. What was she going to do for the next four hours? Her stomach was a knot of excitement and fear, closely entwined like the roots of a tree. Aware that her restless pacing might alert Vincent to the fact that she was up to something, Angeline forced herself to sit down on the edge of her bed. But she could not relax. Finally she rose and went downstairs to talk to Vincent, trying to keep her mind away from the fact that she was planning to break curfew and send a radio message to England. Either of those on its own was enough to mean death at the hands of the Germans. Vincent noticed her nervousness, but said nothing. In war-time one did not pry too closely into someone else's affairs.

At nine o'clock, the Frenchman and his lodger retired to bed as was their custom. It was only six hours before they needed to rise to light the ovens and bake the meagre ration of bread for their neighbourhood. Vincent went to bed and immediately fell asleep while Angeline, alone in her room, gazed out over the dark city of Saint Nazaire, the blackout giving it the appearance of a brooding monster. From time to time she saw a German patrol in the streets, or the dark shadow of a cat slinking from rooftop to rooftop, but there was no other movement. Once night fell and curfew took effect, Saint Nazaire was like a city of the dead. The slow minutes and hours ticked by until, at last, it was time for Angeline to leave. Dressed in dark sweater and trousers, she picked up the case containing her radio set, and slipped quietly from her room.

As Angeline crept down, it seemed to her over sensitive ears that every tread of the stairs creaked, that every movement she made would give her away. But she had been well trained, and soon found herself out in the delivery yard behind the bakery, without alerting Vincent to her movements. Now came the difficult, and most dangerous, part. Stealthily she crept from shadow to shadow, sticking to narrow alleyways and the deep cover provided by the piles of rubble in the bombed-out warehouse district. Her progress was slow. Twice she had to crouch deeper into the shadows as German patrols approached, her mouth dry with the fear that she might be discovered, but each time they passed by without being aware of her. Finally, at ten minutes to midnight, she slipped into the bombed-out warehouse, one of six sites she had selected to send from, and moved deeper into the piles of rubble, until she was so far from the road that there would be no chance of anyone overhearing her signals.

Angeline was surprised to find that her hands were not shaking as she opened up the case, attached the battery leads, plugged the crystal into the set with the tongs provided and put on her headphones. Sitting back on her heels, she looked anxiously at her watch, waiting for the hands to reach five minutes past midnight.

At last the moment arrived and Angeline's finger began to tap the key.

"Angeline. EODFNZLGRZ."

Her home station was ready and waiting. Hardly had she ceased sending her name and code than the reply came.

"Receiving."

Angeline's finger tapped rapidly on the key. It sounded loud to her, but she knew that it would not carry too far. Swiftly the message asking for supplies and specifying the drop zone was sent. The reply was immediate.

"Received. Out."

There was no time to waste on pleasantries. A message must be sent quickly, then contact broken before the enemy could trace the sender. Angeline packed away swiftly so that by ten past midnight the warehouse was deserted once more. She had covered only half of the distance back to the bakery when the air-raid sirens sounded. Despite the curfew, people began leaving their homes to head for the nearest shelter and Angeline found that she could now move with less fear of discovery. She still had not reached the bakery when the first of the British planes flew overhead. The sound of their bombs falling on the docks could be heard like the distant rumble of thunder drawing ever closer. Angeline broke into a run. She had managed to evade the German patrols, how ironic it would be if she were now injured or killed by a British bomb. Turning into the delivery yard behind the bakery, Angeline cannoned into a dishevelled Vincent.

"Angeline! Where have you been? I looked for you in your room but you weren't there!"

Angeline took a deep breath. "I'm sorry Vincent. When I heard the sirens I was afraid and ran. Then I realised that I'd left without you, so I came back."

Vincent nodded, and she was glad to see that he accepted her story in the heat of the moment, not even wondering why she was fully dressed.

"All right, but you can't take all your belongings to the shelter. Give that to me." He took the case containing her radio and thrust it into the bakery. "It will be as safe there as anywhere else. Now, come on. Let's get to the shelter!"

The two ran down the street and into the cellar beneath the café on the corner. Angeline was terrified, but not of the bombs. Her radio was sitting in the doorway of Vincent's bakery, where anyone could find it. She leant back against the wall of the cellar and closed her eyes, trying to suppress the fear. What if someone entered the shop? A burglar? A German soldier? What if the shop were hit and the radio found in the ruins? What if Vincent discovered what was in the case? Her heart was thumping wildly. Her mouth was dry with fear, yet her hands were cold and clammy. She breathed deeply, mentally struggling to control her nervous tension, her fear of discovery.

Mistaking the cause of her fear, Vincent laid a hand on her arm.

"Don't worry, Angeline. We are quite safe here."

She opened her eyes and smiled weakly. "Thank you, Vincent."

The raid was thankfully short, aimed at the ships in the docks. In less than thirty minutes the sound of exploding bombs fell silent; moments later the All Clear sounded. Vincent led the way up from the cellar and back through the darkened streets to the bakery, where he handed Angeline's case back to her. Her relief was enormous. She had come so close to discovery, yet here she was, safe at last. Angeline smiled wanly at Vincent, who indicated the case with a wave of his hand.

"Remember next time. Just leave everything and run. Now, get to bed, we have to be up in a couple of hours."

Angeline returned his smile.

"Goodnight, Vincent. And thank you."

As she made her way back up the stairs to bed, she wondered what on earth had induced her to volunteer for this job.

83

Madeleine sat at a pavement table in front of the Café de Maritime, a cup of what passed for coffee in occupied France on the table in front of her. Clothes, along with everything else, were rationed, but she still managed to look smart, despite the age of her charcoal grey suit. One or two heads turned her way as she sat reading the paper and taking occasional sips of her coffee. But she did not notice the effect that her obvious good looks had on men. Seemingly engrossed in her newspaper, Madeleine sat on long after her cup was empty. But if anyone had been watching her closely, they would have noticed how her eyes strayed from the paper to take in the fencing, and the guards who protected the docks.

This was her fourth visit to the Café de Maritime. Every evening she came to drink coffee and read her newspaper, where she could watch the routine of the guards at the time of day when it was most likely that the group would try to enter the docks. As curfew drew closer each evening, she made as if to go home, but then returned and hid in a dark alleyway, watching the guards throughout the night. On all three previous visits the routine had not varied at all. She knew the placing of the guards and the times they were changed, she knew when they left their posts to walk around the fence, and she knew when they slipped away for a warm coffee during the long cold night.

Madeleine smiled. Her time spent watching the docks had been very productive. As she folded her paper and rose to her feet, turning away from the sea front and heading back to her apartment in the centre of Saint Nazaire, she hoped the others had been equally successful in their tasks.

Claude also spent a great deal of time studying the docks. With the blackout, he would have found it difficult to see anything of value at night, so he spent his afternoons in the attic of a deserted house no more than ten yards from the fence surrounding the docks. From this vantage point he had been able to see a great deal of what went on inside the docks, although certain areas were outside his line of sight and he was unable to see what happened there. He now carried in his head a fairly accurate plan of the docks. As far as he could see, there had been little damage caused by the recent air raid. Many of the bombs had missed their target, either falling into the sea or on the buildings surrounding the docks. From his secret eyrie, he could see that the majority of the stocks of fuel and supplies in this part of the docks had hardly been touched. He wondered if it was really worth sending planes all this way for so little gain. It was obvious why Albert wanted them to get inside the docks; any sabotage that they perpetrated would do far more damage than half a dozen air raids.

After seeing all he could, and memorising it carefully, Claude abandoned the derelict house and returned to work at his garage, eager for the days to pass and their meeting on Saturday to arrive.

Charles also began his study of the docks from an attic, but he was younger than Claude and impatient. The things he saw from there were not detailed enough to satisfy him, and he decided to have a closer look. Waiting until after dark, the young Frenchman crept to the fence that surrounded the docks and climbed over it. He was surprised how easy it was. He could see no guards, and was able to hide in the deep shadows created by the blackout. With slow, careful deliberation he crept silently from one warehouse to another. Inside he found everything the Germans would need to re-fit and re-equip any of their warships which put into Saint Nazaire. One warehouse was crammed with ammunition; - shells for the huge guns of the battleships of the German navy, depth charges, ammunition for machine guns and small arms. In another warehouse he found spare engine parts and drums of engine oil; another contained food supplies; another was filled to capacity with drums of diesel.

Charles spent a whole night surveying the docks. Sometimes he was forced to hide from guards or workers who had a task to complete that could not wait until morning. But at other times he moved freely amongst the shadows, surprised how complacent the guards seemed to be. As dawn's pale light began to paint the sky, Charles slipped quietly out of the dock area and made his way home to bed.

It was Saturday evening. As usual after dinner, Tony and Jean-Paul listened to the BBC broadcasting the war news and messages to British agents in occupied territories. It was a peaceful time. The sound of Marie and the children washing up after dinner giving a sense of normality to a situation that could cost them their freedom if they were to be found with the radio. But they did not fear that. Jean-Paul's cottage was too isolated for the Germans to come to, unless they were looking for something specific.

The two men leant forwards to listen to the news, Tony translating any items which Jean-Paul did not understand. Then came the messages. It was a short list, just four items.

"Bring the dog a bone...Peter Pan has grown...The man in the moon...Lady Godiva."

Tony looked at Jean-Paul and the two men smiled. 'The man in the moon'. The drop would take place the following night.

"It's a good job we're meeting tonight, I won't have to try to contact everyone tomorrow."

Tony nodded and looked at his watch. "Yes. Perfect timing from London. Now, if we're not going to be late for our meeting, we had better get going."

Jean-Paul nodded and rose to his feet. Switching off the radio, he lifted it up and crossed to the other side of the room where the corner of a rug had been thrown back and two floorboards lifted out. He put the radio in the cavity underneath, then replaced the floorboards and the rug before turning back to Tony.

"Right, Albert. We have an hour until we meet the others."

Tony nodded.

"Yes, they should have got some useful information about the layout of the docks by now." He grinned boyishly. "As long as everything goes to plan, we should have made our mark on the docks by the end of the week."

Jean-Paul laughed. "I certainly hope so. It feels so good to be doing something to help my country."

In an ebullient mood, the two men left the cottage and set out for their rendezvous in the woods.

The clearing in the woods was now familiar to Tony, a place where he could meet and plan in safety with the French members of his group. When Jean-Paul and Tony arrived, their three companions were already waiting for them.

"Bonsoir."

"Bonsoir, Albert"

"Right. Let's get down to business." Tony crouched on the ground as he spoke and spread a piece of paper out in front of him, holding it in place with a rock at each corner. "This is a plan of the perimeter of the docks. What I want to do tonight is to get your information onto it." He turned to Madeleine. "What did you found out?"

"The guards are situated here, here and here." She pointed to the map. "They're changed every six hours. Those who go on at seven p.m. are always the same, so I have got to know their routines. They tend to stay at their posts, and only walk the perimeter once an hour on the hour. The guard here," again she pointed at the map, "sneaks off to have a quiet cigarette after he has done his patrol at eleven, while the guard at the main gate always seems to disappear at ten thirty for ten minutes or so."

Tony nodded. "Good. That information could prove useful when we are planning how to get in and out of the docks." He turned to Claude. "What did you find out?"

Claude quickly catalogued the stores and guards he had seen from his hiding place, while Tony marked them on the map, filling most of the eastern part of the docks. The western end still remained a blank.

"Thank you, Claude. That's very useful. Now," he turned to Charles who was eagerly awaiting his turn to speak, "what have you found out?"

Charles grinned impishly as he began to point out the sites and guards he had seen at the docks. After a few moments Tony stopped writing and looked up, a frown furrowing his brow.

"This is all very detailed, Charles. How did you come by this information?"

Charles' face broke into a broad grin. "I found a stretch of fence that seemed to be unguarded, so I climbed in and spent a whole night surveying the docks from the inside."

His four companions looked at him incredulously, mouths agape.

"You bloody fool!"

The grin left Charles' face at Tony's exclamation. He looked like a schoolboy who had got a beating instead of the praise he had been expecting.

"What do you mean?" His voice was puzzled. "I got the information, didn't I?"

"Yes. But I told you not to take any risks!" Tony fought hard to control his rising anger. "You did some foolish things while I was back in England, Charles, but I thought you were going to be more careful now that I'm back. Don't you understand?" His voice became less angry and more persuasive as he spoke. "Not only could your action have jeopardised the whole operation, it could have cost you your life too."

Charles nodded. "I'm sorry, Albert."

"Sorry is not good enough." Tony's voice was hard. "If you get taken by the Germans, it could lead them to the rest of us. Do you want to have our deaths on your conscience?"

"I didn't think about that, Albert. I just wanted to help."

"Well, if you want to continue working with this group, you must think carefully about it. You are to obey my orders and take no stupid risks that could endanger our work, or our lives. Do you understand?"

Charles lowered his gaze and nodded. "I understand Albert. I give you my word that if you will allow me to continue to work with you, I won't do anything like this again."

Tony looked at the dejected Charles, then at the other three members of the group who had said nothing during his tirade. Their safety lay in their ability to work closely together and to trust each other, and the last thing he wanted was for this incident to drive a wedge between them all. He smiled and laid a hand on Charles' shoulder.

"All right, Charles. I know you only did it to help us. And let's face it, the information you've brought us is extremely valuable. Let's get it all on the map, shall we?"

Charles looked up, the relief that he was to be allowed to remain with the group evident in his eyes. Noticing the relaxing of the atmosphere as the other three leant over the map, Tony breathed an inward sigh of relief that the situation had turned out as well as it had. He had no training in how to deal with difficulties created by members of his group and had worried that he might do or say the wrong thing. But everyone seemed happy with the outcome, and eager for the plans to go ahead. For a time they worked over the map, until they were sure that all of the information that they had on the docks was there. Then Tony sat back on his heels and grinned.

"Right. I'll study this and plan the attack." He glanced over at Jean-Paul as he spoke. "Now we have some good news for you all. Don't we?"

Jean-Paul nodded.

"Yes. The weapons will be dropped tomorrow night. We meet at ten in the same place as before."

There were smiles all round at the news, and Tony was pleased with their eagerness.

"Tomorrow night we'll hide the weapons and get out of the drop zone as quickly as possible in case the plane has been spotted. We'll meet back there on Tuesday at ten, so I can show you how to use the weapons." He folded the map of the docks. "I should have the plan of attack ready by then, so be prepared to go into action at the end of the week." He was thoughtful for a moment then spoke again . "On Tuesday, you'll have to take some of our equipment back into the city with you. Make sure you have something to carry it in, and a good hiding place ready. It must be somewhere where the equipment can be kept dry and be reached fairly easily. I'm sure I don't have to tell you to be careful. If those weapons are found, it will cost us our lives."

The other four nodded seriously as Tony rose to his feet.

"Right. Now let's get out of here. Take care on your way back to the city. Bonne nuit."

"Bonne nuit."

The sabotage group faded into the trees. Moments later the clearing was empty once more.

Sunday night was clear, with only a sliver of moon to light the sky. As Tony made his way up to the drop zone, he thought what perfect conditions these were for the plane bringing their supplies from England. He and Jean-Paul arrived at the high pasture shortly before ten, and were cutting turfs for a fire when the others arrived. With everyone helping, the bonfire was soon ready, only waiting for the sound of the approaching plane for Tony to put a match to the tinder.

As Tony perused his companions, he noticed that they did not appear as nervous as they had done at the time of the first drop. He smiled. They were moulding together as a unit, and he felt confident that they would be able to work well together.

Jean-Paul first heard the plane as it flew in from the north. The fire was lit and, moments later, the first parachute was seen. Tony counted them as they came down. One...two...three...four...five...six. It would take some time to get them all hidden away in Jean-Paul's cave. As the plane turned away and headed back towards England, Tony shouted out his instructions.

"Madeleine, get that fire out and replace the turfs. The rest of you, get these containers into the edge of the woods over there." He pointed as he ran. "Detach the chutes and leave them for Madeleine to bury, but don't open the canisters. We don't have time. We'll have to carry them up to the cave as they are."

Within minutes, the six containers were concealed beneath the sheltering branches of the trees. Each was almost six feet long and one foot in diameter, weighing about one hundred kilograms.

"It will take all four of us to carry each of these. Let's get going."

They lifted the first cylinder and made their way off in the direction of the cave while Madeleine removed all traces of the signal fire. It took them a little over twenty minutes to reach the cave, where the four men concealed the container at the rear before going back for the next one. It was almost three hours before the back-breaking task of carrying all six cylinders up to the hiding place had been completed. By the time they had finished they were tired and their bodies ached, but everything was safely concealed, and Madeleine had ensured that the drop site carried no traces of their activities. Tony glanced at the pile of rocks hiding their new supply of arms.

"We will have to wait until Tuesday to see what they've sent us. Right now, I think we had all better get home to bed. We can't afford to break our routines in the morning."

With tired smiles, the group split up. Charles, Claude and Madeleine made their way towards the darkened port of Saint Nazaire, while Jean-Paul and Tony went back to the de Thierry estate. As Tony lay in his bed some time later, his mind wandered back to the days he had spent on the estate when he was a child, days of happiness and contentment which he had thought would never end. Now he felt as though the war had been going on for most of his life, and still the end was not in sight. As he drifted into sleep, he had an image of himself as a bearded old man throwing a grenade at a German tank. He smiled at the absurdity of it as he slept.

Tuesday night was cloudy and cold, with the smell of rain in the air. Tony wished he could remain seated in front of the fire in Jean-Paul's kitchen, but the arrangements for meeting the remainder of the group were already made. He could not let them down. Wrapping himself against the cold, damp air he trudged his way up to the high meadow and the cave where the weapons were hidden, with Jean-Paul striding along beside him. They were the last to reach the cave, and Tony smiled at the others' obvious eagerness to get their hands on the weapons. He edged into the confined space, looking at the expectant faces in front of him.

"Right then. Let's get to work."

The six containers were hauled from their places of concealment, and opened along the long axes, looking like coffins filled with jumble. Tony ran a critical eye over the contents and nodded approvingly.

"Good. Now, sit down and I'll explain what we've got here."

His four companions seated themselves and watched eagerly as Tony delved into the first canister. He lifted a cumbersome object the size of a steel helmet, which he held up for them to see.

"I'm sure you all recognise this limpet from our last escapade, and you all saw plastic explosive before the attack on the submarine base, but I was the only one to use it. This time I want you all to feel confident about handling it and setting charges." He took a package wrapped in oilskin from a second cylinder and opened it up. It held a shapeless mass which looked, and felt, much like butter. Breaking pieces from the large block he passed one to each of his companions. "As you can see it's easily moulded which can be very useful when you are laying charges."

He put down the explosives and reached into the cylinder again.

"Remember these pencil fuses?" He held up a bundle of thin, pencil shaped objects. "The timers on them vary from ten minutes to one month. Push one of these hard into the plastic" he demonstrated as he spoke, "then all you need to do is depress the ridge here and the detonator is set. I'll preset the timers for you so you don't need to worry about that.

"This strange contraption," he held up a small bakelite box with a cloth bag suspended beneath it, "is a gammon grenade. The fusing mechanism is in the top, and you fill the bag with plastic. It takes just over a kilo. Throwing it arms the extra sensitive fuse. It will explode as soon as it hits anything. Dropped from an upper window or an embankment it can create a great deal of damage.

"These are pocket incendiaries." He held up a small device barely the size of a pocket diary. "It will burn fiercely for one minute, which is long enough to set a petrol tank or vehicle on fire. We won't be using these or gammon grenades at the docks, so I'll show you how they work another time. The same goes for these clams." He held up another small item as he spoke. "It's a pre-shaped charge, enough to bend a railway line, or crack a cylinder block, or break an axle.

"These are thermite bombs, and we will be using them in the docks." He held up a one kilogram package. "These will, when used with incendiaries, ignite the stacks of petrol drums and machine parts." He grinned. "There was a lot of information there. Any questions?"

His companions shook their heads.

"It all seems fairly straightforward." Jean-Paul spoke for them all. "But what about guns?"

"I can see a number of the new Sten guns in there. I'll show you how to use them before we leave, but have you noticed what was packed into the spaces to stop all the equipment moving around?"

His companions shook their heads as Tony retrieved cigarettes, socks, and even tins of coffee, to the delight of those watching.

Charles grinned excitedly. "We must be the best equipped group in the whole of France!"

Tony nodded. "Yes. But this is not all for the docks. I'll sort out what each of you is to take, then bury the rest until we need it."

The group set to work. Jean-Paul and Claude each took a Sten gun, then joined the others packing their bags with thermite bombs, incendiaries, detonators, fuses, plastic explosives and limpet mines. Then Tony took his map of the docks from his pocket and spread it out on a large rock.

"Right. Here's the plan. We attack on Friday at eleven forty-five. I want you to work in pairs. Charles, you and Jean-Paul will take the western docks area, while Claude and Madeleine make up the second pair in the east. I'll work alone down the centre. We'll go over the fence at the same point that Charles did. The fuses will all be pre-set to go off at two o'clock, so we shall have plenty of time. Work through your area slowly and carefully. Put two thermite bombs in each stack of oil drums, and two or three in each stack of engine parts. In the oil stack, add just one kilo of plastic to each bomb, but you'll need twice that amount for the engine parts as they'll take some time to ignite. For stores of food, use two kilos of plastic placed in four different areas of each warehouse." He looked at them all, face serious. "Take your time. If you haven't set all of the charges in your area by one o'clock, forget about the rest and get out. We'll meet back at Claude's garage at one fifteen. Don't stay in the docks later than one. We have to be well away before the first explosions, and I don't want you getting caught. Leave the areas that are well patrolled. Once the charges start going off we can hope that the fires will spread there."

"Can you show me our area on the map?"

Tony nodded. "Yes, Madeleine. You and Claude will work the eastern side." He pointed to the map as he spoke. "Start with these warehouses here, they contain fuel supplies and have priority, then work your way back to the fence." He looked at the other two. "You have a lot of machine parts on your side. I want them taken out first."

"All right, Albert. And I promise to be careful."

Tony smiled. "I'm sure you will be, Charles. Just remember, if in doubt follow Jean-Paul's lead."

"What will you be doing, Albert? You seem to have split the whole of the docks between the rest of us."

Tony nodded. "That's right. You are to concentrate on the warehouses and stores, while I take care of the transport. If there are any ships in the docks, I'll try to get limpet mines on them. A few clams will also be useful for damaging the railway line into the docks, as well as any rolling stock. With a few pocket incendiaries I should be able to damage, or at least disable, most vehicles within the dock area, from trucks to tankers. Any questions?"

"Yes. Where do we meet?" Charles grinned and Tony laughed.

"In all the excitement I forgot that one crucial point! We'll meet at Claude's garage at half past eleven. Got that?" They all nodded. "Good. Now let's get outside, and I'll show you how these Sten guns work. There's one for me, and one each for Jean-Paul and Claude, but you all need to know how to use them in case of emergencies."

The five members of the group left the cave, and soon the empty hillside echoed to the sound of Sten gun fire.

84

To Tony's immense relief, Friday evening was cloudy with no moon to cast its light on their activities. He and Jean-Paul wore dark clothing, and smeared their faces and hands with mud so that there was less chance of them being seen. It was ten o'clock when they removed their stash of weapons from its hiding place in the manure pile. They put the necessary items in packs, which they shouldered before turning their backs to Jean-Paul's cottage and heading off into the woods at a steady jog.

Madeleine carefully dressed herself in some of her dead husband's clothing, her mind full of conflicting thoughts and emotions. She was scared, more scared than she had ever been in her life before. But the touch of her husband's clothing fired her resolve to take part in the attack on the docks and avenge his death. Careful not to leave marks which might betray her if her room was ever searched, she lifted the boards of the false bottom she had fitted inside her wardrobe, and removed the explosives Tony had placed in her care. She looked at them carefully for a moment, mentally reviewing the use of each item and how to detonate them. Once confident that she knew what to do, she placed them in a pack and glanced over at the clock beside her bed. Ten forty. Time she was on her way. Shouldering the pack Madeleine took a deep breath to calm her nerves, and slipped out of the house.

Charles was dressed and ready to leave home long before the necessary time. His heart beat wildly with excitement every time he thought of the task which lay ahead of them. This was what he had been waiting for throughout the long months since the attack on the submarine base, and he was eager to be off. Aware of Tony's exhortation to take no unnecessary risks, he stayed quietly in his room until ten forty-five, then he carefully lifted the floorboards, taking care not to make any noise which might attract the attention of the people in the neighbouring house. After lifting out his pack, which was already filled with thermite bombs, plastic explosives, incendiaries, fuses and his spare clips for Jean-Paul's Sten gun, Charles replaced the floorboards and rose to his feet. His excitement was now under tight control. Tonight he would prove to Tony just how efficient and reliable he could be. With a grim smiled, he hoisted the pack to his shoulder and slipped from the room.

Claude locked the doors to his garage, made sure that all the blackouts were closed, then switched on the lights. Now that the actual time of the attack was fast approaching, he felt more nervous than he had anticipated. His mouth was dry, and his hands shook as he rolled up his sleeves before delving deeply into a tank of used engine oil he had drained from cars during the past two weeks. His hand groped wildly for a moment before making contact with a slick package. With extreme care he lifted it from the drum and held it aloft to allow much of the excess oil to drain off before placing it in a tray on the workbench which he had placed there for that purpose. He carefully opened the oilskin wrappings to reveal his haversack, still packed with everything he needed for the raid. He was glad to see that no oil had seeped into the package to damage the equipment. Leaving the haversack where it was so as not to get oil on it from his hands, he went over to the sink and began to wash away the oil that coated his skin from his fingers to his elbows. He was drying his hands when there was a gentle knock at the door. Putting down the towel and picking up a tyre iron in its place, he walked cautiously towards the door.

"Who is it?" His voice was little more than a whisper, but his visitors heard it for their reply was prompt.

"Albert and Jean-Paul."

Without another word Claude switched off the light, unlocked the door and opened it just wide enough to admit the two men before closing and locking it once more. When the light was switched on again, he grinned at his two co-conspirators.

"You're the first to arrive," he said as he made his way back to the workbench. "I was just getting my pack ready."

He lifted the haversack from its small nest of oil skins and carefully placed it on one side as he spoke.

"Has that been hidden in the oil drum?" Claude nodded. "A good idea. Well done."

242

Within the next five minutes the remaining two members of the group had arrived. They listened as Tony went over the final details.

"Right," he said. "This is just a reminder, which I'm sure you don't really need but it will probably help us all to calm our nerves. Two thermite bombs in each stack of oil drums." He held up a bomb as he spoke. "Two or three in every stack of engine parts. You only need plastic for the food and clothing supplies, they should start burning on their own. Now, the fuses." He held up one of the pencil fuses as he spoke. "Remember to push it well into the plastic. I'll pre-set a number of them for us. See the colour codes on the side? We'll be using the white, which is pre-set for two hours. I'll give you twelve pre-set fuses each. It should be enough. If you don't use them all leave them in the docks as they will explode at the same time as the others. I'll give you some that haven't been set just in case you don't have enough. Set them just as I've explained to you here using the white code. They will obviously detonate some time after the others but don't worry about that, it will just add to the chaos and confusion. I hope." He grinned at his companions. "Any questions?" There were none so Tony led his small sabotage group out of the garage and off in the direction of the docks.

They moved swiftly and silently, staying hidden in the shadows as much as possible, and found themselves in a bombed out warehouse opposite the docks at ten minutes past midnight. Tony expertly set the pencil fuses before handing them out, giving them the maximum time possible to work in the docks before they exploded. He looked round at the tense, determined faces and felt a surge of pride. He was responsible for bringing them together, and any destruction of the dock would be a direct result of his work. Yet with the feeling of pride came an overwhelming sense of responsibility. He was responsible for their lives, too, and he felt that this was something which he would never get used to. Noting the nervousness of his companions, he smiled reassuringly.

"This is where we strike a blow for Free France. I'll see you back at Claude's garage at one fifteen. Let's get to it."

With that he crept across the open space to the fence that surrounded the docks. Charles showed them where he had previously gained entrance and they slipped inside before splitting up into three groups and moving off to their designated areas.

Claude had his Sten gun in his hand and his pack slung over one shoulder, so he would be able to reach it quickly if necessary. He led the way into the eastern part of the docks, closely followed by Madeleine, a look of grim determination on her face. Claude planned to start at the far end of their assigned area and then work back towards the fence, so he led the way down to the edge of the dock, ignoring the warehouses on either side. The first warehouse which they did enter was dark and cavernous. It took a few moments for their eyes to become accustomed to the pitch black interior, then Claude's face split into a wide grin, his white teeth shining in the gloom.

"A fuel warehouse! Let's get to work!"

The two saboteurs separated, and began to work methodically down either side of the warehouse. Two thermite bombs each with its attendant charge of plastic explosive were placed as far inside the stack of drums as was possible, with the pencil fuse pushed firmly into place. Madeleine was surprised at how steady her hands were. She had expected to feel much more nervous, but the necessity of working quickly and carefully with the explosives calmed her and she was feeling an intense excitement at the thought of the destruction she was helping to perpetrate. Within five minutes, the two were out of the warehouse and moving silently through the shadows towards their next target. It all seemed to be going well, too well perhaps, and it was not until they had planted bombs in one more fuel store and three warehouses containing food supplies that they came across their first German patrol.

Claude was about to leave the warehouse where they had finished planting explosives moments before, when he heard two voices talking softly in German. He peered round the door, his heart in his mouth, and saw two soldiers standing no more than five yards away, talking quietly together. They were standing in the open and would see him long before he had time to creep up on them. He did not want to use the gun gripped tightly in his hand unless their lives depended on it. He motioned for Madeleine to move back into the warehouse and slipped in quietly behind her. He put his mouth close to her ear and whispered.

"Germans. We'll have to wait until they've gone."

Madeleine nodded, and sat down as Claude looked at his watch. Twelve twenty-five. They needed to leave the docks by twelve fifty if they were to make their way back to the garage in time to meet the others. He peered round the door at the Germans, who were deep in conversation. Low laughter reached his ears, and he slipped back inside, exasperated. It looked as though they were going to stand there all night, and as there was no other way out of the warehouse he and Madeleine would have to wait until they had gone. With a knot of fear growing in his stomach, he sat down beside Madeleine to wait, Sten gun held loosely in his hands but ready for use at a moment's notice.

Jean-Paul and Charles worked their way methodically down the western side of the docks. They had covered half their assigned area, planting bombs in warehouses full of engine parts and fuel, when disaster struck. Moving through the shadows between two warehouses they heard the steady crunch of approaching footsteps and pressed themselves against the wall in the forlorn hope that whoever was approaching would fail to see them. Despite their dark clothing and dirt-smeared faces, the German saw them as soon as he turned the corner less than two yards away. For a moment he stood in stunned surprise at the sight of the two intruders, and the two Frenchmen took full advantage of the few seconds of time his shock gave them.

"Now!"

At Jean-Paul's whispered instruction the two men moved rapidly, running forward with a speed which took the guard by surprise. He was only opening his mouth to call out when he was struck. Charles, being the younger of the two saboteurs, had reached the German first and frantically clasped one hand across his mouth to prevent him calling for help. The other arm was clamped firmly around his neck. As the German guard struggled to throw off his attacker and detach his rifle strap from his shoulder, Jean-Paul reached him. The guard's eyes widened in fear as he saw the gleam of Jean-Paul's knife. For a moment the French farmer found himself held by the pleading eyes. He had never taken a man's life before, and he felt unsure. His hand began to shake and he licked his lips. The guard began to struggle in Charles' grip.

"Hurry, Jean-Paul! I am not sure I can hold him!"

Jean-Paul hesitated no longer. With a grunt of exertion he thrust the knife into the German's abdomen and forced it upwards. The German stared at him, eyes wide, as his attempts to scream in agony were lost beneath Charles' forceful hand. Trying not to think, Jean-Paul pushed again, forcing the point of the knife up into the chest cavity where it sliced through the lung and ruptured the heart. The German's eyes slowly lost their spark of life, and his body hung limp in his attacker's arms.

Jean-Paul pulled the knife free, feeling sick as he felt the resistance of the body which seemed reluctant to part with the shining metal which had caused its death. The knife grated against bone as Jean-Paul tugged harder. At last it was free. Unable to stop himself, he looked at the lifeless face of the German. The image of the dead staring eyes, and the blood which frothed from its mouth and seeped through Charles' fingers, would haunt him for the rest of his life. Taking a deep breath to calm his shaking, he wiped the knife on the German's uniform and slipped it back into the sheath at his belt.

"We must hide him. Quickly."

Charles nodded, as stunned by the death as Jean-Paul, and unable to speak as he helped to drag the body behind a pile of oil drums. Wiping his bloody hands on the dead man's uniform, he looked across at Jean-Paul. There was blood on the front of his clothes, and his hands shook slightly.

"Where did the knife come from?"

Jean-Paul's face was grim.

"It's the knife I take with me when I go rabbit hunting. I use it for skinning." He shuddered. "I never dreamt I would ever use it on a man."

The younger man laid a hand on Jean-Paul's shoulder.

"It was necessary."

Jean-Paul nodded. "I know, but I've never killed a man before. Still," he forced the picture of the Germans agonised face from his mind as he spoke, "there will be time for me to come to terms with that later. Right now we have work to do." With that he led Charles away from the hidden body, on towards the next warehouse they had to sabotage.

They continued to work methodically back towards the fence and their exit from the docks. Jean-Paul forced his mind to stay on the job in hand and away from the German guard. Charles also found it difficult to concentrate. He was still as determined as ever to drive the Germans from his country, and he knew that that would involve the deaths of some of the enemy, but he always imagined those deaths to be at a distance. He had never dreamt he would actually hold a man still while another knifed him to death. The night's events had brought home to him just how dangerous it was to be working with Albert, and he realised now that the young Englishman had been right to ask him to curtail his individual activities. The dead German could just as easily been himself, if he had been caught reconnoitring the docks. So the two Frenchmen worked steadily along the row of warehouses, and were soon climbing over the fence out of the docks, making their swift, silent way back to Claude's garage.

Tony made his way down the dockside, a humourless smile on his face. It was so much like his training at Arisaig, but this time it was for real. Any guards he saw would not be other members of his course in German uniforms, but the real thing. As he ran, crouched low to stay in the deeper shadows cast by the buildings, he felt the adrenalin flowing through his system, an intense excitement and expectation which pushed his fears to the back of his mind and left his head clear to deal with whatever lay ahead of him.

When he approached the quay, the dark bulk of moored ships rose up before him. As he ran closer, they became more distinct in the grey of the night, the black silhouettes of three ships. Tony smiled. Crouching down in the shadow afforded by a deserted truck, he rummaged in his rucksack and extracted two limpet mines. They were heavy and bulky, and he had room for only six, so he could afford to use only two on each ship. Carefully setting the timers, he ran the few remaining yards to the dock and peered over the side. A gap of four feet separated the ship from the quay. Floats were hung in these gaps to prevent the ships rubbing against the wall. With a gleeful smile he slipped over the side, holding tightly to the rope of one of the floats. As he lowered himself carefully, his feet touched the oily surface of the water and he leant over, pushing his head and shoulders beneath the surface and pressing the first mine against the hull. There was a dull thud as the six magnets surrounding the pre-shaped charge took hold, and Tony raised himself carefully from the water so as not to create any unnecessary noise. Moving carefully from float to float, he worked his way to the bow of the ship, and planted the second limpet mine in the same manner. Tony raised his head above the edge of the quay, and surveyed the area of the docks immediately surrounding him. About one hundred yards to his left, a guard stepped from the shadows and gazed searchingly along the docks. Seeing nothing, he turned and made his way back the way he had come. Tony smiled. He had not expected security to be so lax at such an important installation. The Germans obviously felt safe from attack by land. Their only fears were of British air raids, and these had proven ineffectual. Tony's smile widened, imagining the consternation and recriminations which the actions of his group would cause. Someone, somewhere, would suffer for the lax security at the docks. With a smile still on his lips he moved on to the next ship.

Working along the quayside, he had the four remaining limpet mines in place fifteen minutes later and, after careful reconnaissance, climbed back onto the dock. Over to his right he could see a transport pool. He moved off in that direction, leaving a trail of wet footprints behind him and praying that the guards would not notice them for another hour. By that time it would be too late.

The transport pool was beyond his wildest expectations. A dozen lorries stood in orderly rows. Behind them was parked a fuel tanker and, on the eastern side, a fire engine. Marvelling at how his hands automatically knew what to do, Tony planted a clam on each truck. The explosive charges, the size of a small box of chocolates, fitted neatly onto the cylinder block. When they were detonated they would render the vehicles inoperative and Tony hoped they would be destroyed by the fire he planned to start in the petrol tanker. He set a clam under the fuel tank of the vehicle, this would explode causing the petrol to leak out and form a pool beneath it. In the area where the fuel was likely to pool, Tony placed an incendiary device, which would ignite the petrol and blow the tanker apart. Keeping low, he moved to his next target, the fire engine.

The large engine stood ready for use, its water tank full. As Tony planted the explosives, he reflected that just one fire engine would be able to do very little to quench the fires he hoped would be raging within the next few hours, assuming that the fire engine was fit for use. As he placed a clam on the cylinder block and axles of the machine he, determined that in no way would it be ready for use that night.

Tony got his first close contact with a guard just as he was about to leave the fenced-off area housing the transport pool. A lone guard was making his slow way down the fence, intent it seemed on everything but the job in hand. Tony climbed into the back of the nearest truck. He watched as the guard passed the gates and moved on for a few yards, before stopping and kneeling to look intently at the ground in front of him. He then stood and glanced towards the docks before turning and following something inside the fence.

Tony cursed silently under his breath. The guard had obviously spotted his wet footprints and was aware that someone was moving around within the fence. The Englishman realised that he must silence him quickly, or the whole operation could be in jeopardy. He watched, poised ready for action, as the guard made a slow study of the row of trucks. As he moved closer, Tony took a deep breath and held it for a few seconds to calm the rapid beating of his heart. Soon the guard was within feet of his hiding place, and moving closer. As he drew level with the truck, Tony reached out in a lightning quick movement, clamping one hand over the guard's mouth and pulling him closer to the truck with the other. The hours of intense training in Scotland paid off. Almost without thinking, Tony twisted the head violently to the left and heard the sharp crack as the guard's neck was broken. With some effort, Tony dragged the body into the truck. Taking a moment to calm his ragged breathing and still his shaking hands, he climbed out once more and moved off silently in the direction of the railway siding which serviced the docks.

Claude looked at his watch. Twelve thirty-four. He was tight lipped as he peered carefully out of the warehouse. The two German soldiers were still there. He could not hear what they were talking about but by the low laughter which occasionally reached his ears, he knew that it was not work. The sky was still cloudy, keeping the night shadows dark on the land. He was just wondering what his chances of survival would be if he tried to sneak up on the two men through the black shadows, when he heard a voice calling out in German. The two guards looked over their shoulders, then stood to attention as an officer approached. Raising his voice angrily, he berated the two sentries who looked sheepish and saluted smartly, before hurrying off to continue with their patrols. After watching them move away, the officer shook his head in exasperation, then he walked briskly back the way he had come.

"What's happening?" Madeleine whispered. Claude turned to her, a broad grin on his face.

"That was an officer; the two guards got a good telling off for standing around talking instead of doing their job." He chuckled softly. "They will certainly be in a lot of trouble when this lot goes up!"

Madeleine rose swiftly to her feet. "Come on then, Claude. We've got time to plant a few more charges before we leave."

The saboteurs moved rapidly about their work once more. After planting charges in one more warehouse, they came across three fuel pumps used to fuel the trucks that worked the docks. Smiling at their good fortune, Madeleine placed charges of plastic explosives on each of the pumps, while Claude dropped thermite bombs into the underground tanks storing the fuel. After replacing the covers over the storage tanks, Claude looked at his watch.

"It's time we were getting out of here, Madeleine."

With a brief nod his companion followed him back to the fence. They ignored any targets they had been unable to sabotage because of the delay caused by the German guards. In moments they were out of the docks and making their way back to Claude's garage.

Tony positioned himself in the cover provided by the darkened walls of the locked customs office, and surveyed the railway siding. As far as he could see, there was little rolling stock in the yard, one engine and half a dozen trucks was all that he could make out, but it was better than nothing. He slid down the embankment, and moved along the lines to the mammoth bulk of the waiting train. He worked swiftly, placing a charge of plastic explosive on the engine boiler, and a clam on the axle of each pair of wheels supporting the empty trucks. Tony marvelled at his own calmness, he could almost imagine himself back in England practising on obsolete rolling stock. But this was no practice. The stock he was sabotaging served a deadly purpose, supplying the ships and submarines which quartered the Atlantic, seeking out Allied prey to destroy. 'Well,' thought Tony as he moved along the tracks, setting small clams at intervals along the lines 'now the prey has entered the wolf's den, and will be doing some destroying of its own.'

Soon he had done all he could in the time available. He exited the docks as the hands of his watch pointed to twelve fifty. The streets were dark and empty as he made his way back to Claude's garage His almost empty haversack flapped against his shoulders as he ran, and his footsteps sounded loud in his ears. Once he saw a German patrol moving down the street towards him, but he easily slipped into a side street and detoured around them before they had a chance to see him. It was one fourteen when he slipped inside Claude's garage, to find the remainder of the team waiting for him. Breathlessly he sat down on an oil drum, and gave them all a quizzical look.

"Well? How did it go?"

Madeleine shrugged. "It went well enough. I didn't realise how tense I was in there until I got back here. Now I'm shaking all over. But we managed to plant almost all of our explosives."

Claude nodded. "Yes, we were held up for a time so we had to leave without putting charges in every building on our patch."

Tony nodded. "Good. I'm glad you didn't try to stay to finish them all. It would have been too dangerous. If what we have planted goes according to plan, the whole dock should be ablaze in a couple of hours, and the fires will spread to any warehouses we've missed. Particularly," he smiled as he spoke, "as I've managed to disable the only fire engine I could find." He turned to look at Jean-Paul and Charles. "What about you two? Is that blood on your clothes, Jean-Paul?"

Jean-Paul nodded. "We had to kill a guard who saw us." He closed his eyes as he spoke, as though he could still see the eyes pleading for mercy. "I used a knife so no one would hear."

"Are you all right, old friend?" Tony had risen to his feet and placed a hand on Jean-Paul's shoulder. Jean-Paul opened his eyes and nodded.

"Yes, Albert. I'm all right now. We knew that people would die in this attack. But we didn't think we would have to do it at close quarters. Charles and I were shaken up by it, but we are all right now."

Tony turned to Charles, his eyebrows raised quizzically, and the young Frenchman nodded.

"Yes, we're fine. I suppose it just brought it home to me that this is not a game, and next time it could be me with a knife in me."

"Do you want to get out of all of this?"

Jean-Paul and Charles shook their heads in unison.

"No way." Charles spoke for them both. "This is what I joined you to do."

"Good." Tony looked at his watch. He had been in the garage for six minutes. "Right, we had better be going. We have forty minutes until the bombs go off, which should give you all time to get home, Jean-Paul and I will be out of the city by then. Make sure you hide any explosives you have left, and keep your heads down. We will meet again in the usual place next Friday at nine p.m. Understood?"

Charles and Madeleine nodded before slipping away.

"Good luck, Albert." Claude held out his hand to Tony. "I'll lock the doors when you have gone, and put my pack back in the oil drum."

Tony nodded. "Take care. The search will be fiercest here, near the docks." With that he and Jean-Paul turned and left the garage. They moved through the blackout and were out of the city and on the road to the de Thierry estate when Tony laid a hand on Jean-

Paul's arm and pointed at his watch.

"It's almost two o'clock."

They turned back towards the city and were just in time to hear the first explosions from the docks. Seconds later more explosions began to ring out, and the sky above the western part of the city began to take on an orange glow. The two men laughed out loud before turning and running towards the safety of Jean-Paul's cottage.

The docks were in turmoil. On all sides warehouses were in flames, broken vehicles were strewn everywhere, men ran around aimlessly as they sought to make sense out of all of the confusion. A staff car with the red, black and white flag of the SS on its bonnet screeched to a halt outside the gates, and a man in the uniform of an SS Major stepped out. He was tall, blonde and blue eyed, Hitler's ideal of an Aryan man, and the imposing uniform fitted his aristocratic frame like a glove. His features were angular, and his brows knitted together in anger as he surveyed the destruction all around him. A sergeant got out of the car and stood beside him.

"Dante must have imagined something like this when he wrote his description of hell's inferno Karl."

The sergeant nodded but said nothing. They had thought themselves so safe from enemy attack, yet here was one of their most important Atlantic ports, blazing furiously like a funeral pyre.

"Come, Karl."

The tall major led his subordinate through the gates, into the chaos reining inside the fence. The air was thick with roiling clouds of black, choking smoke; the smell of burning fuel filled his nostrils; over to his right the wall of a warehouse slowly collapsed outwards and the figures of men, silhouetted against the brilliant glare of the roaring fire, ran from its falling. The officer stalked with long angry strides down to the dock, where the sight of three ships listing badly at their moorings aroused a cold fury in him.

"Who is in charge here, Karl? I want to see him. Now!"

A soldier was running past, and Sergeant Dresner grabbed him by the arm.

"Fetch your commanding officer! Now!"

"Yes, sir!"

The soldier ran off into the fiery hell of the docks, while Dresner turned back to look at the major. He was standing with his back to the crippled ships, feet apart and hands clasped behind his back, watching the running, shouting figures. Slowly, some sort of order was coming out of the chaos. Teams were salvaging what they could from warehouses which were already alight, and carrying their burdens to the quay where no fires burned yet. Pitifully small piles of food and clothing were being assembled, while the infinitely more valuable machine parts and fuel were consumed by the flames. Some warehouses had not yet caught fire, and there were groups of sailors trying valiantly to stop the flames spreading to them, while others fought the fires which raged all around. Pumps had been set up on the quayside to pump sea water onto the voracious flames, and chains of men passed buckets of water to the more inaccessible parts of the docks. To the major's trained eye, it was obvious that the fires made the destruction look worse than it really was, but he knew that, in the cold light of day, the damage would be considerable, and someone would have to pay.

A Werhmacht captain approached through the clouds of smoke and saluted the SS officer.

"Major Steinhauser."

"Are you in charge here?"

"Yes, sir."

"How did this happen?"

"It must have been a sabotage team, sir."

"I know that, you damned fool!" Steinhauser's voice was raised in anger, and the officer before him cringed. "Did they come from the sea, or is this the work of a resistance group?"

"I don't know, sir."

"Then find out, and find out fast!" He looked around. "I see no fire engine. Surely there should be one here?"

"It's been destroyed, sir. I've sent for more from the city, and hundreds of men are coming from the barracks to help fight the fires. We'll soon have it all under control."

Steinhauser nodded, his eyes icy. "I expect to see you in my office at midday, with a full explanation and a damage report."

The young captain saluted and turned back to the fires with an inaudible sigh. Facing the roaring inferno was infinitely preferable to facing the SS Major.

As Steinhauser watched the billowing clouds of smoke and leaping flames, he spoke in a voice full of anger to Dresner.

"Someone will pay for this, Karl. Someone will pay."

Angeline and Vincent sat with steaming bowls of coffee in front of them, the smell of baking bread wafting in from the open door to the bakery. Vincent took a sip of the scalding liquid, then smiled at his companion.

"It sounds as though someone was striking a massive blow for freedom last night."

Angeline raised a quizzical eyebrow, her heart in her mouth. Was he just talking out of sheer delight at the sounds of destruction coming from the docks during the early hours of the morning, or was he trying to link her with it? She forced a smile. There was no way he could know about her connection with the Resistance, it was all in her imagination.

"Yes" she spoke eagerly, "it sounded as though someone had planted some bombs at the docks. I wonder how much damage they've done?

"We'll know soon enough."

Angeline frowned. "How?"

"Because the reaction of the Germans will be in direct proportion to the damage sustained. The more damage, the more difficult life will be for us for the next few days."

"I hadn't thought of that." Angeline's eyes widened. Would someone else be punished for the part she had played in the attack? It was a sobering thought.

Vincent drained his bowl of coffee and rose to his feet.

"Come on now. That bread should be ready, and our customers will be arriving soon."

Angeline followed the baker back to work.

85

Major Steinhauser sat at his desk with Sergeant Dresner standing behind his right shoulder. The hands of the clock on the wall opposite were pointing to twelve o'clock when there was a knock at the door.

"Enter."

The door opened to admit a young German secretary in military uniform.

"Hauptman Schmidtt, sir."

"Show him in."

The young captain entered nervously. Since speaking with Steinhauser at the quayside, he had been busy trying to salvage what he could from the mess at the docks. His uniform was dirty, even though he had attempted to smarten himself up before the interview.

"Well, Schmidtt, what have you to say?"

Schmidtt swallowed hard and licked his lips.

"As far as we can tell, sir, it was a group of saboteurs who must have got into the docks over the fence. Three ships moored at the quay have been damaged, but we can have them all sea worthy again within the week. All the transport at the docks has been damaged, mainly by small charges placed on the cylinder blocks. They will need new engines. There was damage to the rolling stock. That will take a long time to repair, so I've commissioned a civilian train to do any necessary work. Some of the tracks were damaged, but they are being replaced now. The siding should be back in use tomorrow."

"What of the stores?"

Schmidtt glanced at Dresner, but he showed no signs of being aware of the conversation, and Schmidtt looked back at Steinhauser. It was obvious he was going to take the blame for this, so he might as well get it over and done with.

"Forty per cent of food stores were destroyed. Ten per cent of clothing destroyed, and a further fifty per cent damaged. Seventy per cent of engine parts have been damaged in one way or another, and thirty per cent of the fuel supplies are gone."

Steinhauser's face looked like thunder as he rose to his feet, his voice booming.

"Where was your security when all this happened?"

"Security was at its usual levels, sir. I don't know how they got in."

"We can't afford this amount of damage!" Steinhauser thumped his fist hard on the desk. "I shall be recommending a transfer for you, preferably to the Eastern Front. Now get out of my sight!"

Schmidtt saluted, turned on his heel and marched from the room. As the door closed behind him Steinhauser sat down again.

"Well, Karl, that is how we deal with our own. But what about the French swine who are responsible for this?"

"Our informants have nothing for us." Dresner moved round to the front of the desk as he spoke. "We can offer a reward, but I have little hope of it being taken up."

"Do that. At the same time, I want you to take two hundred men to be shipped back to the labour camps in Germany. When these stinking French pigs see their families being taken away, they might be more inclined to help us find the bastards who did this."

Karl Dresner smiled.

"A brilliant idea Herr Major. I'll get to work at once."

The notices were pasted up before curfew that day and were soon surrounded by silent crowds.

ATTENTION!

A reward has been posted for information about the enemies
of the state responsible for the hostile act perpetrated against
the Reich last night. Furthermore, the following men will report
to the railway station for transportation to labour camps at 10 a.m.

tomorrow. If any of these men fail to turn up at the appointed time 10 other members of their family will be taken in their place.

Signed

Major Steinhauser. SS

Below the notice was a list of two hundred names picked at random from the German files; the youngest a boy of fifteen, the oldest a man of seventy. As Angeline studied the notice, her eyes filled with tears. So many to suffer for the work of just a few. She felt a hand on her shoulder, and turned to face Vincent who stood by her side.

"They must have done a great deal of damage to make the Germans do this."

"Is it worth it?"

Vincent frowned as he looked at her. "Of course it is. For the sake of all our countrymen who have died and for those of us who now suffer the occupation. Of course it will be hard for those who have to go, and for their families, but I'm sure that the majority of people are glad that the docks were attacked last night."

Angeline looked at the list again. It seemed so long. "Do you think they will all turn up?"

Vincent shrugged. "I don't know. They've very little choice really do they? They can't hide all the members of their families from the Germans."

Angeline shook her head, unable to speak. When she had joined the SOE she had been prepared to put her life in danger, but had not anticipated that others would suffer the punishment which should rightly be hers. Steeling herself, Angeline turned and walked steadily back towards the bakery. Being an agent was going to be difficult, in more ways than she could ever have imagined.

Angeline tossed and turned through the night, trying to come to terms with the German reprisals. She wished there was someone she could talk to about it, but knew that it would be too dangerous to try to contact Tony. She would just have to try to come to terms with the situation herself. As ten o'clock approached, she found herself cycling slowly in the direction of the railway station. She had not intended to go there, but something compelled her to go and witness the scene.

She arrived to find that she was not the only one who had come to see the deportation. A large crowd had gathered, silently lining the square in front of the station entrance. A table had been set up, and an officious looking SS officer was seated behind it, checking off the names of the deportees as they arrived. They came slowly in large family groups, and all round the square small scenes of farewell were acted out. Angeline got down from her bicycle and stood at the back of the silent crowd, watching. In one corner a teenager hugged his mother and father, fighting manfully to overcome the tears that threatened to spill from his eyes. Not far away a man in his late twenties stood beside a woman, obviously his wife, whose eyes were red from crying; a small boy of five or six clung fiercely to his leg while he desperately clasped a little girl to his chest. With a sob, the man handed the child to her mother before kneeling to embrace the boy. As Angeline watched he stood and took his wife in his arms, his eyes closed as though to hold the memory tight within him for the rest of his days.

Angeline's eyes roved over the square and its pathetic occupants. An old man clasped his wife to his chest; he was grey haired and weak, and it was obvious from their expressions that they did not expect to meet again in this world. Angeline looked at the faces of the people in the crowd. They were expressionless save for the eyes, which held all the anger, hatred and hostility which they were afraid to show openly in front of their

German masters.

Soldiers began to separate the family groups, ushering the men with their one small pathetic bag up the steps and into the station. There were tears and final embraces, but no sound. The whole scene was enacted in silence, save for the tramping of soldiers' boots and the murmured voices of German officers. As the final group of men made their way dejectedly into the station, a pathetic voce rang out.

"Papa! Papa! Come back! Papa!"

Angeline looked at the small boy who had so recently kissed his father goodbye. His mother was still holding his little sister in one arm, while gripping the boy's hand tightly. He struggled to pull away and follow the man who had disappeared from sight.

Angeline mounted her bicycle and began to ride away, tears streaming down her face as the hysterical voice echoed around the otherwise silent square.

"Papa!"

Tony decided to stay on his grandmother's estate over the weekend. Word of the German reprisals had reached them on Saturday evening. With the deportation due to take place on the Sunday morning, Tony wanted to stay out of sight. It was Monday before he managed to leave a message for Angeline at the fishing village.

The sun was bright, beating down on the water and making the reflections sparkle and dance as Angeline cycled down the road to the harbour. The smell of fish hung heavy in the still air and the day promised to be hot. Angeline's white cotton dress was already beginning to stick to her in the humid atmosphere. As she reached the rotting boat at the end of the beach, she saw the bottle by the wall and knew there would be a message waiting for her. Leaning her bike against the wall, she made her way nonchalantly along beside it until she was right next to the boat; swinging her legs over the wall she sat for a while watching the fishermen unloading their catch, and surreptitiously made sure that no-one was watching her. When she was certain she was unobserved, Angeline casually reached a hand behind the nameplate of the boat. She retrieved the piece of paper, slipping it into her pocket without reading it. After sitting for a while longer, she slid down from the wall and made her way to the nearest fishing boat where she bought a small piece of fish for herself and Vincent before mounting her bicycle and riding back towards the bakery in Saint Nazaire.

In her room Angeline took the paper from her pocket and carefully de-ciphered it.

"Attack on docks success. German reprisals against civilians. Will plan another raid in two weeks."

She smiled. Brief and to the point. She would encode it there and then and send it home that night.

As Angeline made her way through the darkened streets she marvelled at how calm she felt. She was still very much aware of the dangerous situation she was walking into, but her senses were keen-edged. She would be aware of any danger soon enough to avoid it. Finding herself in the secluded spot where she planned to send her transmission, she considered herself lucky not to have come into close contact with any Germans. Patrols had been increased since the attack, but they tended to concentrate their attention on the dock and other military targets so that Angeline felt relatively safe in the bombed warehouse where she set up her radio and began to transmit to England. Within moments the message was sent, and Angeline was on her way back home.

86

Captain Dawson sat at his desk late at night, trying to get his paperwork finished before retiring for a well-earned rest. The desk lamp cast a pool of yellow light on the files in front of him, and he rubbed his tired eyes. Perhaps it would be better if he left it for the night and made an early start in the morning. There was a knock at the door and Dawson looked up.

"Enter."

The door opened to admit a WREN carrying a piece of paper.

"We've just received a message from Angeline in Saint Nazaire."

She held out the paper which Dawson took eagerly. "Thank you."

As the WREN turned and left the room he read the message, a slow smile spreading across his face. The attack had been a success. Of course it was not such good news for the Frenchmen affected by the German reprisals, but that was only to be expected. It looked as though Tony Kemshall had got himself a good team already, and Anna Weston, or Angeline as she was known, was proving to be a good radio operator. As long as things continued to go well for them, they should be able to make a great contribution to the SOE's work in occupied France.

Pushing the files away from him, Dawson rose to his feet and switched off the desk light. He was tired. The paperwork would have to wait until the morning. Picking up the files he locked them in the safe before leaving the office, a contented smile creasing his tired features.

87

It was a week since the attack on the docks. Apart from his experiences during the retreat from Dunkirk, it seemed the longest week of Tony's life. His feelings alternated between elation and despair: elation at the apparent success of the mission and the obvious possibilities open to his group, despair at the knowledge of the Germans' arbitrary reprisals. He had not been able to go into Saint Nazaire to judge the mood of the people. He worked hard with Jean-Paul on the estate, burying himself in the work. Yet always at the back of his mind was the thought of how the people were taking the German reprisals. Would the people of Saint Nazaire be opposed to further Resistance attacks against the Germans out of fear of what might happen to them and their families? Would any of the members of the group feel so guilty about what had happened that they would no longer want to work with him? As he made his way through the woods, silently following the dim figure of Jean-Paul who was leading the way to the appointed rendezvous, he wondered what the mood of the group would be.

The other three French members of the group were already waiting in the clearing when Tony and Jean-Paul arrived. Tony surveyed their faces for a moment before sitting down.

"Good evening, everyone."

The three people opposite returned his greeting then settled down to listen.

"First of all, I want to congratulate you on your excellent work last week. I'm proud of you all. Secondly, I want to know what the people of Saint Nazaire, and you, think of the German actions."

Charles shrugged. "People are angry of course, but I don't think they blame us for it."

"Are you sure?" Madeleine frowned. "Did you see the scene at the railway on

Sunday? I did, and many people there were as angry with us as they were with the Germans."

"Don't they want us to help drive the Germans out?" Charles sounded exasperated. "They seem to forget that we are at war. The Germans are our enemy. We must be prepared to make sacrifices if we are to win!"

"Yes, but you didn't make the sacrifice. You didn't lose a father or brother, husband or son to the labour camps."

"Are you saying we should stop our activities?"

Madeleine turned at Tony's question. "No, that's not the way. Charles is right when he says that we must continue to fight until we have won, but we should be aware of the effect our actions will have on other people."

"We should be aware, but we should not feel guilty." Claude spoke for the first time. "Unlike the rest of you, the reprisals affected me directly. My nephew, my sister's son, was taken. He is nineteen. Of course the family were angry and upset to see his name on the list, but despite his fear he said he was prepared to go, because it showed his support for the Resistance. His parents and sister are angry and afraid, but they have said that the Resistance must continue to fight. We will regain our freedom, and the enemy won't be able to do this to us again."

There was silence for a moment as the group came to terms with what Claude had had to say, then Jean-Paul reached out a hand.

"You know that we feel for you and your family, Claude. Do you wish to leave the group?"

Claude shook his head. "That would make my nephew's transportation and sacrifice worthless, wouldn't it? He said that he was proud to go because that would leave the Resistance free to fight on. No, I don't like what has happened, but I'm proud of him, and even more determined to fight the Germans now."

Tony nodded. "Good. I take it you all feel the same way?" The others nodded and Tony continued. "Right, then let's get down to business." He smiled at their expectant faces. "The next target on my list is the rail yard. Are you all with me?"

The smiles and murmurs of agreement were what he had been hoping for and, with a lighter heart, Tony began to outline his plan.

JUNE - JULY 1942

88

May began with a bombing raid by a thousand aircraft over Cologne, in retaliation for the Baedeker Raids which had taken place at the end of April. In the Far East British forces were in full retreat from Burma on a road that led them one thousand miles into Assam. At sea, the Americans surrendered the Philippines at Corregidor with the loss of one hundred and forty thousand men while, on a more successful note, they won the battle against the Japanese navy which was fought in the Coral Sea.

During June, the campaign in North Africa went from bad to worse. The British forces continued to withdraw towards El Alamein. Thirty-five thousand of them were taken when Tobruk fell. In the Far East the news was better. Japanese aircraft attacked the Americans at Midway, but lost the initiative and the Americans won, losing only one carrier, while the Japanese lost four carriers and three hundred and thirty planes in five minutes. The decisive American victory helped to raise spirits a little in an England bowed down but not crushed by three years of war.

89

"Sarah! Sarah!"

The door was flung wide and Jane rushed in breathless and smiling. Sarah laughed.

"What are you so excited about?" She put down her pen. Knowing Jane, she would have to finish the letter to her mother later.

Jane threw herself down onto her bed. "It's the Americans. They've arrived in the area at last. There's a new camp down the road."

"Is that all?"

"Is that all!" Jane sat up, her face a picture of incredulity, and Sarah laughed again.

"Oh come on, Jane. We're not all man mad like you."

"It's not just the men, though I bet they're gorgeous. Haven't you heard of all the goodies they've brought with them?"

Sarah nodded. Like everyone else she was aware of the smart, loud G.I.s who had invaded Britain since the disaster at Pearl Harbour. They came from a land of plenty. They had only just come into the war and their homeland had not been threatened by bombs so that their standard of living had hardly changed from pre-war days. They came to England with their stockings, their excellent tinned foods and their chocolate, and the people who had already suffered through almost three years of war were justifiably envious. The impact of the Americans was great, not least upon the young women on whom they showered their gifts, and the young men of Britain were getting jealous. Sarah wondered if England would ever be the same again.

"So, what are you going to do to get yourself introduced?"

"That's easy. There's to be a welcome dance on Saturday night, and we're going."

"Now hold on. I never said I wanted to come to a dance."

"Well you can't stay here locked up like Rapunzel in her tower waiting for her prince. I'm sure Tony wouldn't mind you going to a dance while he's away."

Sarah frowned. "I suppose not. It's just that I don't really feel like going."

Jane looked knowingly at her friend. "Has Tony written to you yet?"

Sarah shook her head. "No. He's probably very busy, and I suppose it would take a long time for a letter to reach me from America. I expect I'll get one soon."

"And what if you don't?"

Sarah shrugged. "I suppose I'll just have to wait until he gets back to find out what he's been up to."

Jane said nothing. She knew Sarah well enough to realise that she was upset because Tony had not written and, privately, she thought that it was because of the difference in their social class. Jane had never believed that Tony was interested in more than a fleeting relationship with Sarah, and she thought the lack of correspondence proved her right. She lay down on her bed again.

"Don't bother arguing, Sarah. You know you'll be coming with me on Saturday."

Sarah smiled as she picked up her pen and continued with her letter to her mother. Jane was right. It would be fun to see the American G.I.s and find out what the fuss was all about.

Saturday evening was warm and sticky, and the two off duty nurses wore thin cotton dresses to the dance at the new American base. The hall was festooned with bunting, and music blared from the gramophone in the corner. Jane turned to Sarah and smiled.

"Even their music is different."

Sarah nodded as she listened to the big band music. It had an interesting sound and a rhythm which made her want to dance. Perhaps the evening wouldn't be so bad after all.

Seeing the two young women standing by the door, a young G.I. detached himself from the small crowd around the bar and made his way over to greet them.

"Hi, gals."

Jane giggled and Sarah nudged her in the ribs, although she was inclined to smile too. It was the first American they had ever spoken to and his accent sounded strange to them. They had only ever heard an American voice at the cinema before and, somehow, it did not sound quite the same. The G.I. was not put off by their reaction. He grinned broadly.

"My name's Ed. Do you want to come over and meet some of the others?"

Sarah nodded while Jane took care of the introductions. The two young women soon found themselves in the centre of a crowd of G.I.s and fresh-faced English girls who were taking advantage of the chance to break the dreadful monotony of life in a country at war.

"Were you talking about the music when I came over?"

Sarah nodded. "Yes, it's very good. I haven't heard anything quite like it before."

"Really? That's what we call the Big Band sound. It's the Glen Miller Band, the best in America."

Sarah smiled. "I think it's going to be really popular over here."

"Great." Ed got a drink for his two English companions and led them to a table where they all sat down.

"How are you all coping after so long at war?"

Jane shrugged. "All right, I suppose. Everything is rationed and luxuries are non-existent, but we manage."

"What about the bombing?"

"That's mainly in the large cities and industrial areas. It has been pretty bad at times." She turned towards her friend. "Sarah has seen more of that than me."

"Really?"

"Yes. She was in Coventry when it was bombed early on in the war."

Ed raised an eyebrow. "Really? So you've seen action already!"

"You could say that." Sarah was reluctant to talk of her experiences during and after the bombing, the memories were still too deep and cutting. "I was in a shelter during the actual raid. Then I spent the next few days helping the injured."

"Were the hospitals damaged?"

Sarah smiled grimly. "Hospitals? They were totally destroyed. I spent three days in a bombed-out school treating the wounded. It's not like in the movies, you know."

"Sorry. I guess you don't want to talk about it." Ed grinned. "At least we're getting better news of the war now. Did you hear of the Battle of the Coral Sea? Our Fleet and the Japs were over a hundred miles apart, and they fought with planes from carriers. We lost a heavy carrier but we halted the Jap advance towards Australia. They would be there now if we hadn't won that one. Then there was the Battle of Midway. We caught the Japanese Fleet with all its planes on deck. We sank the four large Jap carriers with something between three and four hundred planes in five minutes. Those Japs are sure taking a licking from us out there."

"How do you know all that?" Jane looked surprised. "The details weren't on the radio."

"It was in all the papers back home, and we get it from the letters from our folks."

"Letters?" Sarah was surprised. "You've had letters from home already?"

"Sure. It only takes a week or two. We don't have to lose touch with our families, just because we're at war."

Sarah's heart was pounding and she felt dizzy. Suddenly all she wanted was fresh air and some peace and quiet to think.

"Excuse me. I think I'll just go outside for a moment. It's too hot in here." Sarah rose as she spoke and made her way to the door, unaware of the couples on the dance floor as she passed between them. Jane frowned as she watched her go, sensing something was wrong but not sure what. Ed laid a hand on her arm.

"Do you wanna dance?"

Jane nodded and led the way onto the dance floor, putting all thoughts of Sarah out of her mind.

The night was cooler now. The feel of the air on her brow helped Sarah to collect her jumbled thoughts. She made her way across the car park to a solitary tree and leant with her back against it, gazing out over the countryside which she had come to know and love during her years at Heronfield.

Ed said that letters from America did not take long to reach England. There had been plenty of time for any letter that Tony had written to reach her. She closed her eyes as though to block out an unwelcome thought. The truth was, if she had not received a letter then he had not written one. All the things he had said to her, all their time together had meant no more to him than a passing interlude. He did not really care for her and she realised now that there was no future in their relationship. It was like a physical pain deep inside her. She loved Tony despite his apparent fear of going into action, and the fact that he had used her merely to fill time. The tears flowed from beneath her closed eyelids as she thought of the last time she had been with him. He had given her an address in London and she had written a number of times, hoping that they would forward the letters to him. But he had not received them, or if he did, he had not bothered to reply.

Sarah's features creased in pain as she remembered how he had held her, so tenderly, and kissed her in a way that convinced her that he really did love her. She remembered the touch of his hands upon her naked flesh as they made love, first passionately then slowly and tenderly. Now she realised with a deep abiding pain that she had been fooling herself. Tony had just been playing with her, using her. How many other women had he used like that? Was he with someone else now? Some beautiful American who could offer him so much more than she could? She had shared something very special with Tony. Something she had withheld from Joe had been given to someone who did not value the gift, who had never really cared for her. Sarah felt dirty, used; she didn't really want to believe that Tony could be capable of such deceit, but what other reason could there be for him not writing?

With a deep sigh, Sarah straightened up and wiped her eyes. She knew it would be difficult when next she saw him but, no matter what the cost, she would not let him hold her and kiss her again. The feel of his arms around her and the promise for the future which his kisses gave would be too painful, knowing that he did not really care for her at all. As she looked out across the fields through eyes blurred by tears she vowed she would never fall in love again. It made her too vulnerable. First the pain and sorrow of Joe's death, then the slow coming to terms with life without him; then the dawning awareness that Tony had insinuated himself into her heart and would always hold a place there, no matter what happened. Now she felt his apparent rejection of her all the more keenly. She vowed to live alone, as her mother had done, with only the memory of love to lighten the darkest night.

90

The group met in Claude's garage once again as it was within striking distance of the railway yard which was their target for the night, and only half a mile from the docks where their previous attack had been such a great success. Tony proudly studied his companions. They looked business-like, ready for anything which the night might hold in store for them, and Tony felt a rush of affection for them all.

"Tonight's attack will be in three distinct areas," he began. "Madeleine and Claude, you are each to take a bag of clams and do as much damage to the lines as possible. Place the clam where two rails join. The explosion will buckle them both, so the Germans will have to replace two instead of one. There are four lines coming into the yard. I want damage on all four, and then on all the sidings you can manage. The idea is to leave no track available for use in the morning. Understood?"

Claude nodded as he slipped his haversack onto his shoulders. He picked up his Sten gun while Madeleine placed her bag at her feet, waiting until it was time to leave before hefting it onto her back. Tony indicated two more identical bags.

"These are for you, Jean-Paul and Charles, and you are to carry out the second thrust of this attack. I want as much rolling stock as possible put out of action. You may think these clams are too small to do much damage, but you would be wrong." He smiled. "Placed in the right position, they can disable a train and cause the enemy a great deal of trouble. I want a clam on each axle of each wagon or truck or carriage that you can reach. There won't be anything like enough to replace them in stores. With any luck the Germans will have to send to their factories in the Rhur for more. The stock could be out of action for weeks, if not months."

As the two Frenchmen picked up their packs, Tony lifted his own. "I'm going to do as much damage to the engines as I can." He settled the pack on his shoulders and picked up the Sten gun which fitted so comfortably in his hand. "Right, the last thing. There are plenty of fuses in your bags, they aren't set because I want you to use the red tonight. That means that they will explode thirty minutes after you've set them."

Madeleine frowned. "That's not long. It won't give us much time to get clear."

Tony nodded. "I know. But after our attack on the docks, I expect the rail yard to be more heavily guarded. There is every chance that we might be seen. If we are lucky and manage to set the charges without bumping into a guard, there's still the possibility of a sentry coming across one of the charges, particularly along the rails. We must be in and out of the yard in twenty minutes. It doesn't give us long, but we should be able to plant enough charges in that time if we work quickly and methodically. Once we get back out of the yard I want you all to head straight for home. Don't come back here. Get your stuff hidden fast and get into bed. The Germans will be after us, and if they start house-to-house searches, your beds must appear slept in and warm. It's no good just pulling the covers back, because they will probably check. Understand?"

The others nodded.

"Good. We'll leave it a week again before we meet. This time I think we'll meet up at the cave at ten." He perused the group once more, each member confident and ready, each pair in possession of a Sten gun to protect themselves should the necessity arise. A group to be proud of. "Good luck to you all. Now, let's go."

The light was switched off and the five saboteurs slipped out into the warm June night. It was eleven o'clock, dark enough for them to slip through the streets unseen, avoiding the few patrols they saw. Eventually they arrived at the deserted Station Master's house, on top of the embankment which overlooked the yard. As Tony scrutinised the target, he noticed a number of sentries moving about.

"They look more alert than they did at the docks."

Tony nodded at Jean-Paul's comment.

"Take a good look, everyone. Madeleine and Claude, you move down the bank on the left and get to work on those lines. Jean-Paul and Charles will come with me on the right. Keep an eye on those sentries, and keep out of sight." He looked at his watch. "Check your watches. I want you out of the yard twenty minutes from now. If you haven't completed your task, just leave it and get clear. Split up and head for home. Don't under any circumstances gather here first. Got that?" Four heads nodded in unison. "Good." Tony licked his dry lips. "Right, let's get going. Good luck to you all."

The saboteurs split into two groups before making their way swiftly and silently down the embankment. Madeleine and Claude began setting their clams on the main tracks, then moved back towards the sidings. Each clam was placed where two rails met, the fuse inserted and set within seconds, and Madeleine was pleased with their progress. Further along the sidings, Jean-Paul and Charles were making their way along two lines of stationary trucks, fitting clams to the axles of each. Tony was setting charges of plastic on the boilers of the huge steam engines, when a furious barking broke out. Looking around and finding himself unobserved, Tony jumped down. He was met by Jean-Paul and Charles, who slipped between the stationary trucks to stand beside him.

"It's Madeleine and Claude, Jean-Paul whispered "They've been spotted by a guard with a dog."

"Damn!" Tony's mind was working furiously as he slipped his pack onto his back. "Let's get back to the embankment now, before this place is swarming with Germans. Follow me."

The three men made their way along the lines in the direction of the barking. In the pale light cast by the moon, Tony could see the dim shapes of Claude and Madeleine running towards the embankment closely followed by a guard with a huge German Shepherd dog on a leash. The dog was barking, straining at its leash in an attempt to reach the two fleeing saboteurs, jaws dripping saliva. Another guard ran forward, raising his rifle as he ran. A shot rang out, and Claude threw his arms up into the air as a bullet slammed into him and threw him to the ground. To Tony it all seemed to be happening in slow motion. He ran as fast as he could towards the action. Madeleine stopped running and knelt beside Claude, picking up his Sten gun with one hand and helping him to his feet with the other.

Tony was relieved to see that Claude was still able to run, but his pace was slow despite the urging of his companion. The sentry sighted along his gun again as the second German knelt to release the leash on the dog. With a cry of anger, Tony raised his Sten gun and began to fire. He took the sentry with the gun completely unawares. As the man crumpled to the ground his companion turned and raised his gun, but was taken by the second burst of fire from Tony before he could bring his own weapon to bear. Tony turned his attention to the dog but as he raised the gun again, the chatter of gunfire came from his left. The dog fell in mid-leap. He turned and grinned mirthlessly at Jean-Paul, who lowered his Sten gun and followed Tony towards the embankment.

Madeleine had Claude halfway up the slope when there was the sound of shots behind them. Tony turned to see a crowd of Germans running towards them, too many to count. Raising his gun, Tony shouted his instructions.

"Charles! Help Madeleine to get Claude up the embankment. We'll cover you!"

Jean-Paul and Tony opened fire on the advancing Germans, felling a number of them before replacing the magazines in their guns. Behind them, Charles helped Claude to stumble up the embankment, blood pouring from the wound in his shoulder, while Madeleine ran on ahead. She breasted the slope at a run and turned, flinging herself to the ground and bringing her Sten gun to bear on the Germans advancing towards Jean-Paul and Tony. They were retreating slowly up the embankment, firing as they made their way backwards up the slope. Claude and Charles slid over the lip of ground which sheltered Madeleine as she began to fire on the men below her. At the sound of her gun, Tony and Jean-Paul turned their backs on the Germans. They ran up to join the remainder of the group. Tony reached them first and thrust his gun into Charles' eager hands.

"Use this." He slipped his pack from his shoulders and began rummaging in it as Jean-Paul joined them. The three Sten guns fired down on the advancing Germans, a number of whom fell. But there were still about a dozen approaching.

Tony carefully lifted a gammon grenade from his pack. The black skirt below the bakelite top was distended by a kilogram of plastic explosive. Tony pushed in the extra-sensitive fuse. The grenade was armed when he threw it down towards the advancing Germans and exploded on impact. The effect was devastating. Four of the enemy fell unmoving to the ground while five others screamed and writhed in agony. The rest of the sentries looked up at the top of the embankment where the Sten guns were firing again, then retreated towards the cover of the stationary trains.

"Quick, before they regroup. Charles and Madeleine, get home quickly. We'll meet as planned next week. Leave Claude to me and Jean-Paul."

"Right, Albert."

The two young French patriots made their way towards their homes as Tony knelt beside Claude.

"How are you?"

"I've been hit in the shoulder but I can still run."

"Good." Tony helped the older man to his feet. "Help me, Jean-Paul. We'll get him back to his garage, then decide what to do."

. The two men supported their wounded comrade though the streets towards his garage. It was not far, but the journey seemed to take forever. Claude stumbled along, pain racking his body and his vision blurring, supported on either side by his comrades who were all too conscious of the trail of blood they were leaving behind them, but aware that the time it would take to stop and dress Claude's wounds would probably cost them all their lives. At last they reached the garage and slipped inside the double doors. Claude sank gratefully to the floor, only semi-conscious, while Tony fumbled for the light switch. The bulb sprang to life at his touch, to reveal a blood stained Claude smiling weakly at him.

"Sorry, Albert. This makes things difficult, doesn't it?"

Tony smiled, exuding a calmness and confidence which he did not really feel. "Don't worry Claude, everything is going to be all right." He carefully removed the bloodstained jacket and opened the shirt as he spoke while Jean-Paul fetched a first aid box from the work bench. Tony frowned as he set to work bandaging the wound. "I don't think it's too serious, Claude, the bullet entered from the back and exited at the front. But anyone can see this is a bullet wound so we can't leave you here for the Germans to find, especially with a trail of blood leading straight to your door."

There was the sound of explosions in the distance. The charges they had laid were beginning to go off, and the Germans would be more eager than ever to find them now. Claude grimaced as Tony tied the last knot in the bandages.

"Albert, you and Jean-Paul must get away. I'll be all right."

His two companions shook their heads in unison. "No Claude, we're in this together." Jean-Paul helped his compatriot to his feet. "Get into this car. I'll drive you to a safe place where we can get a doctor to you."

Tony knew he was thinking of the hut down near the beach, where he had hidden out after the accident on the cliffs. He nodded approval.

"Yes, Claude. You'll be safe there." He switched off the light and opened the double doors. The sound of running feet on the street greeted him, and he signalled for Jean-Paul to hurry. As the engine of the car roared into life the first of the Germans came into view. Tony opened fire on them, hitting no one but causing them to duck back round the corner in surprise. The black car drove slowly past Tony, who leapt inside, letting off another burst of machine-gun fire for good measure. Jean-Paul gunned the engine and the car roared off down the road and round the first corner, trying to escape the fire from the guns of the soldiers who were re-emerging into the street.

More explosions could be heard behind them and Jean-Paul increased speed. Claude gritted his teeth at every jolt. They had travelled for almost a mile when they sighted their first patrol. Tony opened fire on them without warning and saw one of the soldiers fall to the ground as they flashed past. The second soldier opened fire on the rear of the car and they could hear sound of bullets thudding into the body work.

The tyres of the car screeched as Jean-Paul threw the vehicle round the next corner and onto the main road. With a muttered curse he saw that the road had been blocked on the edge of the city, at the very point where he believed himself safe from pursuers. With a grim look, he pushed the accelerator all the way to the floor. The engine roared as the car approached the wooden barrier. German soldiers began to fire at them and the windscreen shattered as Tony leant out of the side window to return fire. Bullets flew thick and fast, but Jean-Paul ignored them, his mind focussed on the barrier ahead. They hit it at top speed. Claude was thrown from the back seat, a cry of agony escaping his tight-pressed lips. The sound of tearing metal and splintering wood rent the air, but then they were through. The Germans behind them fired wildly but did not have vehicles to pursue the fleeing saboteurs.

Tony smiled grimly as he laid aside his gun and helped Claude back up onto the seat.

"Well. It looks like we've made it. But I think I owe you a new car!"

Claude forced a smile, more of a grimace really, at Jean-Paul's voice.

"Don't worry, my friend. I won't hold you to that!"

Tony looked back out of the shattered rear window.

"No pursuit yet, Jean-Paul, but they'll be after us soon. Get us to the path leading to the hut as quickly as you can. I'll help Claude to walk down there while you drive on until you're at least five miles past the doctor's village. Then dump the car somewhere. Make your way back to the doctor's, pick him up and bring him to the hut when you feel it's safe. Claude should be all right until then."

"All right, Albert." Jean-Paul nodded as he spoke. "You stay with Claude. Anyone moving around will be questioned. Don't worry if I can't get back to you until later tomorrow. I don't want to risk being followed."

"I trust your judgment."

They continued their journey in silence, until the pathway leading down into the woods came into view. Jean-Paul stopped on the road, not pulling onto the small track which led down to the fishing hut for fear that the Germans might notice the tyre tracks and decide to search the apparently deserted area. Tony helped Claude out of the car, checking that no blood was seeping through the bandages to leave a trail which might be followed, then he began to help his friend down the overgrown pathway. Claude stumbled, suffering from loss of blood and shock. Tony heard the sound of the car fading into the distance, and he wondered if he would be able to get the Frenchman down to the hut alone. Patiently he coaxed the injured man along. Tony hardly noticed his incoherent mumbling as he struggled onwards.

They were about half-way to the hut when the roar of a motorbike engine intruded into the silence, closely followed by the sound of a number of trucks. Tony listened anxiously as the vehicles approached the entrance to the path, then sighed with relief as they roared past. It was now up to Jean-Paul to shake them off and get to Leclerc for help.

The two men stumbled on, the elder supported by the younger. Tony heaved a sigh of relief as the solid bulk of the fishing hut finally hove into view. He opened the door and helped the semi-conscious man onto the bed, then closed the door and lit the lamp. As he looked round the single room, he experienced a strange mixture of emotions. The last time he had seen this hut with its simple wooden bed, table and single chair, he had been the injured one, receiving attention from Doctor Leclerc and waiting for a submarine home. It seemed strange now to have the roles reversed. He gazed down at Claude. The man's face was pale and drawn and he had fallen asleep At least Tony hoped he was asleep and not unconscious. The hastily bandaged shoulder had begun to bleed again, the dark red stain spreading on the blue shirt. Tony rummaged around and found some of the bandages which had been left behind after his sojourn in the hut and used them to rebind the shoulder as best he could. Placing a blanket over the Frenchman, he picked up the bucket from behind the door and went outside to fill it from the stream. On his return he laid a fire in the hearth and lit it. Once the flames were established, he put some of the water in a pot and set it to heat. He checked on Claude again, then settled himself in the chair by the table and fell asleep.

It was almost dawn when Jean-Paul returned with Leclerc. The doctor smiled at Tony.

"Well, Albert. I hadn't expected to see you here again. I'm glad to see you looking so well."

Tony shook the doctor's hand. "It's all thanks to you. I would have died if it hadn't been for you."

Leclerc shrugged. "All part of the job. Now, I had better attend to my new patient." He made his way over to the bed and examined Claude's shoulder. "The bullet passed straight through. I'm afraid it took a piece out of the bone on the way. I'll bandage it. It should heal well enough, but he will always find that shoulder stiff."

"He's going to be all right, then?"

Leclerc nodded at Jean-Paul, who was busy stowing the packs and Sten guns he had carried with him since abandoning the car. "Yes, but it's obviously a bullet wound. He can't go back to his home."

Tony nodded. "We know. But where can he go? Where can we hide him for the rest of the war?"

Leclerc shrugged in reply, but Jean-Paul smiled broadly.

"I can help you there. Claude has a sister living in a small village some thirty miles south of here. We can hide Claude in this hut until the hue and cry about our attack on the railway yard has died down, then we can move him down to his sisters."

"What will he do there?"

Jean-Paul had a ready answer for Tony's question "I think his brother-in-law owns a farm, so he can help there. His days of working with the Resistance are over."

Tony nodded. "He's done well. Even if he does no more in this war, his contribution will be remembered." He turned to his two companions. "I'll stay with Claude while you two get back home. You come back and take over from me later, Jean-Paul, and don't forget to bring some food!"

Jean-Paul arrived in the early evening with a young companion. Tony smiled.

"Theresa! Don't tell me you are going to play nurse again?"

The young girl grinned. "Yes, Albert. When we heard about the attack on the rail yard and Papa came home without you, I knew it must have been your work. For a moment I was afraid that you might have been hurt, but Papa said it was Monsieur Claude. I want to help if you will let me. See." She held up a bag. "I've brought plenty of food. I'll try to look after Monsieur Claude as though I were a proper nurse."

"Well, if you nurse him as well as you did me, we have nothing to worry about."

Theresa beamed at the compliment, and Tony smiled.

"I'm proud of you, Theresa." The girl turned to her father as he spoke. "But please be careful. If you hear anyone moving about in the woods, get out of here and hide."

"What about Monsieur Claude?"

"If he can't walk, you will have to leave him here."

"But Papa!"

"But nothing, little one. We don't want to lose Claude. But if the Germans come, it's better to lose one than two. How do you think your mother and I would feel if you were captured?"

Theresa nodded. "I understand, Papa. I won't take any risks."

"Good. Now, Albert," he turned to Tony as he spoke, "we'd better get back. I'll come daily to check on Theresa and Claude. It would be better for you if you stay out of sight."

Tony nodded. "Right." He leant over and kissed Theresa on the forehead. "Take care, little lady. France will never be defeated while she has children like you."

With that the two men turned and left the hut, leaving Claude to the tender ministrations of his nurse.

91

Major Steinhauser glared at his sergeant on the other side of the desk.

"Well, Karl. What have you got to say about all this?"

Dresner stood to attention, recognising his superior's mood. He was well aware that their usual informal relationship was suspended for the time being.

"Well, sir, after the attack on the docks, the number of sentries at important sites was increased."

"I know, but that didn't stop the saboteurs, did it!"

"It did slow them down, sir. We think they were spotted before they had planted all of their explosives, so the damage could have been worse."

"There should have been no damage at all!" Steinhauser slammed his fist down on the desk in anger, then sat back in his chair in exasperation. "Sorry, Karl. I shouldn't be taking it out on you. It wasn't your fault."

Karl Dresner relaxed noticeably. "I've spoken to the sergeant who was in charge last night. He says they wounded at least one of the saboteurs, then trailed him back to his home." Steinhauser raised his eyebrows in surprise, glad for some good news, but his feeling of elation was soon deflated. "We assume he is the garage owner Claude Corver, for that's where they followed him and at least one other man. They broke away by car and escaped."

"Damn! Can't these regular soldiers do anything right?" Steinhauser showed the usual contempt of an SS officer for the Wermacht soldiers who made up the majority of the German army. "Did they lose anyone?"

Dresner nodded. "Yes. Six dead, ten hospitalised and four more with minor wounds."

"What!" Steinhauser leapt to his feet. "We lost that many, while they only had one wounded?" He walked over to the window and stood for a moment in silent contemplation, hands clasped behind his back. His mind was working furiously as he gazed down at the drab people pursuing their ordinary lives on the streets below. At last he turned back to his subordinate.

"Karl, I'm assuming that the same group of people made both the attack on the docks and the one on the rail yard. What do you think?"

"I would have to agree, sir. Both attacks were extremely well organised."

"Yes, too well organised and too well armed for it to be a group of locals working alone. I think we had better start thinking along the lines of a British agent working somewhere in the Saint Nazaire area, supplying arms and training to the local Resistance. I want you to increase radio monitoring. He must have some contact with England. Also make more spot checks on the civilians. We might be lucky and catch someone with forged papers."

"What about reprisals for last night?"

"I want the family of Corver questioned to find out if they know anything. And it wouldn't hurt if a few people were roughed up a bit on the streets. That might bring an informer out into the open." He frowned across at Dresner. "I want this group found, Karl. Particularly the leader."

"Yes, sir. I'll get on with it right away."

The sergeant saluted and left the room.

The next few days in Saint Nazaire were difficult for everyone. The Germans were angry and frustrated about the attack on the rail yard, and vented their feelings on the civilians. Beatings were common for minor infringements of German laws, sometimes for no infringements at all. No-one dared intervene for fear of disappearing into the prison cells, which already housed a number of people taken for questioning about the attacks. Members of the Corver family were prominent among them.

Dresner took charge of the interrogations, starting with Claude's mother and working through his brothers, nephews and nieces. No-one said anything. Despite the beatings, the lack of sleep, the cold, the hunger, the rapes, everyone denied knowledge of Claude's activities, which was true for none of them had known that he was working for the Resistance. Now that they did know however, and were aware he was wounded, a number guessed where he might go to hide out, but his sister's name was never mentioned. Dresner had to report to Steinhauser that the trail to the Resistance had gone cold.

During the time of reprisals, work to repair the rail yard continued. The damaged tracks were removed and replacements laid within two days, but the repairs to the rolling stock were going to take much longer. Tony had not managed to plant charges on all the engines, so there were still two running, but the others would be off the rails until new boilers could be brought in. The carriages for the passenger transport had not been damaged, but the supply trucks for the army had all had their axles broken. Steinhauser had a number of others brought in from nearby towns, but there were not enough, and the transportation of supplies to Saint Nazaire was severely disrupted.

Tony was pleased with the success of the raid, but the beatings and imprisonments weighed heavily on his conscience. During the excitement of the planning and execution of a raid, its repercussions were pushed from his mind, but afterwards there was always the guilt and wondering if, in the end, it was all worth the suffering. This time Tony was also worried about Claude. His wound was healing well, but Tony wanted him out of the area as soon as possible and did not know how that could be accomplished. In the end it was young Theresa who came up with the only viable plan to get Claude to his sister's without drawing too much attention to the fact that he was wounded.

Tony stood on the pavement opposite the station.

"Are you sure you know what to do?"

Theresa nodded. "Don't worry, we'll be all right."

Tony smiled reassuringly. "I know you will." He turned his attention to Claude. "Ready?"

The older man nodded. "Yes. It seems strange to think we attacked the railways six days ago, yet now we're going to use them for my escape route out of here. Maybe the damage wasn't as great as we'd thought."

Tony smiled. "Don't worry, we did enough. Passenger transport is almost back to normal, but the goods rolling stock is still trapped in its siding with bent axles and broken couplings. The Germans won't be happy about that. We did enough to leave our mark!"

"And you are sure it is safe for me to leave this way?"

"I don't see why not. They're still searching for you, but the heat has gone out of it. They've neither seen nor heard anything of you since the attack, so they must assume you are either dead or have already left." Tony smiled grimly. Little did the enemy know that the man they were searching for was boldly walking into their hands. Only his courage, and that of the twelve-year-old girl who accompanied him, stood between them and the firing squad.

"Right. I see no reason to wait any longer." Tony looked at his watch. "If you don't go now you'll miss your train, and that would be a disaster!"

"I'll see you when I get back, Albert."

Tony smiled. "Take care, Theresa. I don't know what we'd do without you!" He turned to the older man. "And good luck to you, Claude. Just keep your head down and you'll be all right." He took the proffered hand. "You've worked well, and I look forward to seeing you in more peaceful Times."

Claude smiled. "Thank you for all you've done for me, Albert. You've made me feel like a man again. What is more, a Frenchman!" He gripped the young Englishman's hand. "Goodbye, Albert, and good luck. I'll be thinking of you and the others constantly."

With that he turned away and crossed the square, the diminutive figure of Theresa at his side.

Tony's heart was beating wildly and his palms were sweaty as he watched them go, but outwardly he gave the appearance of not having a care in the world, other than the cares heaped upon all of the citizens of an occupied country. Looking at him, no one would have imagined that his ears were pricked for the first sound of raised voices or shots coming from the station. Claude had been well aware of the risks he was running when he joined the group, but Theresa was only a young girl. Much as he admired her great courage, presence of mind and determination to drive the Germans from her homeland, Tony knew that if she were taken she would soon break under the brutal interrogation of the SS He had come prepared. I anything went wrong he would be able to buy some time for the young girl to escape. His hand closed around the grenade in one pocket and the butt of the pistol in the other, and he prayed as he waited, prayed that nothing would go wrong and prayed that he would not be searched on his way out of the city. If he was, his life would be forfeit.

Theresa led Claude over to the ticket desk, his arm resting in a sling with no attempt to conceal the fact that he was injured. As they waited, Theresa smiled at the man.

"Come on Grandpa, give me your papers. They'll need to see them at the desk."

Claude fumbled in his pocket with his good hand and finally handed the papers to Theresa. A German soldier watched with interest as, with each person in front of them buying their tickets, they approached closer to the desk. Then it was their turn.

"Can I have two tickets to Pontchateau, please? One for my Grandfather who will be staying there, and one for me. I shall be coming back on my own." Her voice was loud enough for the soldier to hear, and carried just the right note of pride for a girl of her age who had been entrusted with an important job. The man in the ticket office smiled and gave her the tickets.

"Your train will be leaving soon. You'd better hurry. Platform Four."

"Thank you, Monsieur."

As Theresa turned to leave, she felt a hand on her shoulder. She looked up into the stern face of the German soldier.

"Papers."

She handed them over. Two sets which had been prepared in England and dropped in the containers. All Tony had had to do was to affix their photographs, fill in their false details and add the correct rubber stamp, also painstakingly prepared in advance in England. The guard studied the papers.

"Robert St. Julien?"

"Yes."

"You live in Pontchateau?"

"Yes."

"What are you doing here?"

"Grandpa came to visit for the summer because Grandma just died," interrupted Theresa. "Grandpa has to go back now to see Uncle Paul, but he fell down the stairs to our cellar so Papa said I can go back with him to make sure he's all right."

"You are Bridgit St. Julien?" The soldier looked at the papers as he spoke. You live in Saint Nazaire?"

"Yes. I live with Mamma and Papa. I have got two sisters, and Mamma is going to have a baby." Theresa chatted on gaily. "Papa wants the baby to be a boy. So do I. Do you, Grandpa?" She turned to Claude. "I think a baby boy would be nice. I would call him..."

"That's enough." The soldier roughly pushed the papers into her hand, irritated by the incessant childish chatter. "Hurry, or you will miss your train."

Claude and Theresa made their way out onto the platform and boarded the train at Platform Four. Five minutes later the train pulled out. Claude let out a sigh of relief. With a broad grin on his face, he turned towards the young girl at his side.

"You were magnificent, granddaughter."

Theresa giggled. "Yes, I know how annoying I can be if I won't stop talking. I thought it might work."

Out in the street, Tony heard the sound of the train pulling away and felt some of the tension in his body draining away. The first part of the escape plan had been carried out, apparently without a hitch. He only hoped that the rest of the plan would work as well. Unfortunately that was out of his hands now. As he turned his back on the station and began to make his way out of Saint Nazaire he sent up a silent prayer that there would be no problems.

The remainder of that day and night was spent in a state of nervous tension. No one in the Boues' household mentioned Theresa and her absence, yet it dominated all their thoughts. Ten-year-old Jeanne was not really sure where her sister had gone. She just knew that she was expected home the following day, and so asked no more questions. Tony marvelled at the quiet fortitude of Jean-Paul and Marie. They acted as though nothing was wrong so as not to worry their youngest daughter, yet Tony knew that their hearts and minds must be filled with conflicting emotions about Theresa; pride, fear for her safety, love. He wondered if he would have been able to stand up to it so well, if it had been his child who had gone off to play a deadly game of hide and seek with an enemy - an enemy who thought nothing of beating, raping, torturing and finally murdering young girls who dared so much for the country they loved.

Jean-Paul left just before midday the following morning, to go to the station to meet Theresa's train. Tony tried to bury himself in work on the estate, but no matter how hard he pushed himself he could not get Theresa out of his mind. What would he do if she did not come back? How would he be able to live with Jean-Paul and Marie, face them each day knowing he was responsible for the loss of their child? Finally he threw down the spade he had been using and made his way over the fields to his Grandmother's house. As he sat concealed in a clump of trees and watched the swastika hanging limp in the still summer air above the old house, his mind wandered back to the days he had spent there as a child. Those days seemed so long ago now, as though they were a part of another life lived by a very different Tony Kemshall from the one who sat there now. He closed his eyes, remembering. Those memories could never come to life again, but they would stay forever in his heart, a precious memory of a time when boyhood seemed to stretch ahead to infinity, and adulthood seemed so far away. Now he sometimes wished himself back in those days, days without fear or death, days spent with David as a constant companion by his side. He still missed his brother deeply; it was a wound in his heart which would never completely heal. But the pain of David's death had mellowed a little in the growing love he felt for Sarah. He saw in her a kindred spirit, someone who knew what he was thinking and feeling, and could help to bear his pain. He wondered what she was doing now. He envied the soldiers whose wounds had taken them to Heronfield and her gentle ministrations. He hoped that none of them were becoming too close to Sarah, or she to them. He felt a moment's anger at the S.O.E. for sending him out here to France, where he was unable to contact her. Just a letter was all he wanted, to know that she cared for him and to tell her that he loved her deeply, passionately, more than life itself. Missing her was like a physical pain in the centre of his being, as though a part of him was missing which could only be replaced when he held her in his arms once again. Slowly the anger at his superiors faded. It was not their fault that he was in France, unable to keep in touch with his loved ones. He had volunteered for the job and knew that, given the choice, he would do the same thing again. Opening his eyes, he gazed down at the house where he had spent so much of his childhood. One day he would bring Sarah here, tell her all about his work and how he had helped to push the Germans from a land he loved almost as much as he loved Heronfield, almost as much as he loved her.

There was the sound of movement in the trees behind him. Tony leapt up and spun round to see who was there.

"Jean-Paul! Theresa!" He took the young girl in his arms and hugged her tightly before kissing her on both cheeks. "I'm so glad to see you safely home!"

"Papa said you would probably be here so we came up to let you know that everything is all right." She grinned impishly. "You grownups make such a fuss about everything. It all went so easily."

Tony laughed in relief. "Tell me all about it."

"Well," Theresa's eyes sparkled as she spoke, "we were stopped by a soldier in the station, I think he was suspicious of Monsieur Claude's arm, but I chattered so much that he got fed up and let us through! The train to Pontchateau was slow, but we got there without any trouble. Then changed trains and took the one south to Pornic. When we got there we got a lift in a hay cart to Monsieur Claude's sister's farm." Theresa giggled. "You should have seen her face when she saw us! She was so surprised I thought her eyes would pop out of her head!"

Tony laughed. "I can imagine! Did she let you stay the night?"

"Yes. I left early this morning. I caught the train to Nantes, then changed to the one for Saint Nazaire. It was easy"

Tony shook his head, a broad grin on his face. "You are amazing. Your father must be very proud of you."

"I certainly am." Jean-Paul hugged his daughter. "Now let's get home to your mother."

Theresa wriggled free from her father's arms. "Before we go, you had better have these, Albert." She handed him her false papers. "Monsieur Claude kept his papers, he's going to be Robert St. Julien for the rest of the war. I thought that if you hide these I might be able to use them again, if you need my help."

"Thank you." Tony took the papers back, marvelling at the girl's resilience. With French people like her around, the Germans did not stand the slightest chance of winning this war.

92

One week after the attack on the railyard, Tony found himself at the cave where the arms for the group were stashed. Around him were seated the remaining members of the group. They had arrived early, and were waiting impatiently for him to speak. Charles settled down when he saw Jean-Paul's relaxed demeanor, but Madeleine's face was pale and she looked anxious.

"How is Claude? Is he alive?"

She had been waiting a week to ask that question. Tony's awareness of the pressure that the members of the group were under increased. He nodded at her.

"Yes, he's alive. He lost quite a lot of blood, but the shoulder will heal eventually, although he will have some permanent damage."

"Is he still in Saint Nazaire?"

Tony grinned across at Charles. "No, we've got him to a safe place. We won't tell you where, in case either of you is ever captured and questioned, but it was a wonderful piece of bluff. I'll let Jean-Paul tell you all about it."

So Jean-Paul explained to his two companions how his daughter had managed to get Claude out of the area right under the noses of the Germans. Charles frowned.

"It's a great story. You must be proud of your daughter, Jean-Paul, but getting him out by train just proves our attack was a failure."

"No it wasn't!" Madeleine was vehement. "We didn't set out to disrupt the civilian transport, just the transport of war supplies and I think we succeeded in that. I've not seen a freight train come in all week."

"Madeleine's right." Tony explained. "Civilian trains are moving, which means that troops can be moved too of course. But there are no spare freight wagons in the area, so the Germans can't supply their ships, submarines and soldiers. If I could be a fly on Major Steinhauser's wall, I bet I would hear him saying the raid was a success."

"You can be a fly on his wall. Or, at least, plant one there."

Tony frowned. "Sorry, Charles. I don't know what you mean."

Charles grinned. He had a surprise for the group. He hoped it would make them all very happy, and increase their chances of more successful raids in the future.

"Whenever people have been out of sight or sound of the Germans this week, they've been talking about the two attacks our group have made." The others nodded, already aware of this. "Well, I was talking with two friends who are really impressed by what we have achieved so far. They both want to join the Resistance and fight the Germans."

Tony frowned. "Do you mean you've told them about us?"

"Oh, no!" Charles shook his head vigorously. "We just talked about the attacks and how they were upsetting the Germans. Georges said it must be wonderful to be able to be a part of it, and Alain and I agreed. As far as they are concerned I am just like them, a young man who would like to join the Resistance if only I knew how!"

"What are these two men like?"

"They're much like me, Albert. We are all twenty-two years old. We were friends as children and went to school together. Alain lost his father in the first few days of the war, and is determined to avenge his death." Tony nodded. It was a familiar story. "Georges works as a cleaner at the German H.Q. in Saint Nazaire."

Tony's eyes widened and he leant forward eagerly. "Can he help us there?"

Charles nodded. "Yes. When we were talking, he said he's sometimes able to see papers which should have been locked away but which are left unsupervised on the desk for a moment."

Tony bit his lower lip, deep in thought, then he came to a decision.

"Right. I'll meet these friends, and see if they can be of help to us. We'll meet again when I have details of our next attack. Jean-Paul will get a message to you all to meet here." He turned to Charles. "How soon can you arrange a meeting?"

93

Tony sauntered down the street, his seemingly aimless gaze paying careful attention to the small group of tables on the pavement outside the cafe opposite. Two tables were occupied, one by a young lady and someone who looked as though she might be her grandmother, the other by Charles and his two friends. Tony continued down the road. There were two German soldiers talking further along the street, and a Gendarme standing outside the bakers. None of them seemed to be paying attention to the people in the cafe. When he reached the corner, Tony crossed the road to the opposite side, spent a moment looking into the almost empty windows of the butchers shop, then made his way back towards the cafe. As far as he could see, no one seemed to be acting suspiciously. He glanced at his watch. Three thirty-seven. Exactly on time. He approached the table occupied by the three young Frenchmen and sat down.

"Ah, Albert!" Charles reached across and shook his hand. "Please let me introduce my old school friends, Georges Monet and Alain Blanc. Georges, Alain, this is Albert Fouquet." The three men shook hands and the introductions were complete.

Charles' two companions perused Tony for a moment, obviously surprised that he appeared to be no older than them. The waiter brought another glass and left.

"Charles said we should speak to you if we want to join the Resistance." said Alain. "Do you know how to get in touch with them?"

Tony leant back in his chair and smiled. "It's wise to speak quietly, Alain, but don't lean over the table like that. Such a position looks very suspicious and can be seen from a great distance. Sit as though we are discussing nothing more important than the weather."

"Sorry." Alain sat back and looked around to see if anyone had noticed.

"First of all," Tony took a sip of the red wine which Charles poured for him before he continued, "are you really serious about helping?" The two men nodded. "Do you have any skills which the people in question might be able to use?"

Alain shrugged. "I'm a carpenter. I don't know if that would be of any use."

Tony smiled. "It might. What about you Georges?"

"I'm a cleaner for the Germans. I should be able to get my hands on some useful information."

"Good."

Georges seemed about to say more, but then frowned and shook his head slightly as though thinking better of it. Tony felt uneasy. There was obviously more to Georges than he seemed willing to admit, and that could be a threat to them all. His voice was stern when he spoke.

"Please don't hide anything from me Georges. I'll not be able to pass on your name to the Resistance if I feel that you are hiding something."

The young man cast a worried glance at his two friends who nodded encouragingly, obviously aware of what was troubling him. The young man took a deep breath then began to speak.

"First of all, please believe me when I say that I am a patriotic Frenchman and hate to see my country overrun by the enemy." Tony nodded but said nothing. Georges reluctantly continued. "I'm partly German."

Tony raised his eyebrows in surprise as he turned to Charles.

"You knew this?"

"Yes Albert, I've always known."

Tony thought for a moment. He knew that Charles would do nothing to endanger the group so he must feel that Georges was not a threat. Finally he met the young mans worried gaze.

"Tell me about it."

"My grandfather was a sailor and met my grandmother in Hamburg. She is German. They married in 1890 and moved to Saint Nazaire to live. My mother was born here. My grandmother's sister continued to live in Hamburg where she married. Her husband died in the Great War and she lived the rest of her life as a widow. My grandmother insisted that mother should learn to read and write German as well as speak it so, after the war, she was able to open a guest-house for German sailors which she ran whilst father was at sea." He smiled. "My grandmother was a bit of a tyrant and also insisted that I should not forget my birthright. She considered it her duty to make sure that I was as fluent in German, written and spoken, as I was in French. She made me write letters to her sister in Hamburg, but when the aunt died I had no further contact with Germany and don't know of any relatives there."

"Is your grandmother still living?"

Georges shook his head at Tony's question. "No, she died a few years ago. It would have broken her heart to see the two countries she loved at war with each other again."

Tony was quiet for a moment, considering what Georges had said.

"I'm not a German spy if that's what you are thinking. I'm…"

Tony raised a hand, halting the words in mid-flow.

"I respect your honesty Georges, and I can see that you love your country as much as the next Frenchman. There are plenty of people in France, and England, and America with German grandparents. That doesn't mean that they are all spies and traitors. I trust the judgment of your friend who brought you here. I don't think that you are a spy. If I did, I would have gone by now. I was merely thinking that your knowledge of the German language could be useful to the Resistance. You speak it well?

"Yes. Not only did I converse with mother and grandmother, but also with the sailors who stayed with us. I can also read German almost as well as I can French."

"Do the Germans that you work for know that you speak their language?"

"No."

"Then keep it that way; it could prove useful to us."

Georges was smiling broadly.

"Thank you for your trust. I won't let you down."

Tony smiled at his eagerness. "I'm sure that my trust will be repaid. Now, I think it would be best if this meeting were to close, we've been here long enough."

Georges frowned. "You've asked Alain and myself what we can do; why don't you ask Charles what he can offer to the Resistance?"

Tony and Charles both grinned.

"Because I know what he can do." The two men looked surprised by the reply and strained to hear Tony's whispered words. "He is already part of my group. He was part of the group that attacked the docks and the rail yard, and last year he helped to attack a submarine base and saved my life."

"Mon Dieu! Why didn't you tell us, Charles?"

Charles smiled. "Because Albert asked me to keep it secret. You two must promise not to say anything either."

272

His friends nodded.

"Of course."

"On my honour."

"Good." Tony watched two German soldiers who were moving towards the cafe. "When we hold our next meeting, Charles will lead you to the place. Georges, if you have any information for me I want you to leave it here." He pushed a small map across the table to the young man as he spoke. "It's a small farm track. If you go down the track for two hundred and fifty metres, you'll find a rotting log. Put your message in the north end and leave a handkerchief in the bush at the end of the lane. I'll check the bush daily. Now, memorise that then pass it back." Georges stared at the paper for a moment, nodded, then pushed it back towards Tony who slipped it into his pocket.

"You're very careful, Albert."

"Of course. It's all part of his training."

Alain frowned at Charles. "Training?"

"Yes. I'm an English spy." Tony rose to his feet and, with a broad grin on his face at their incredulous expressions, he walked away.

94

Three days after Charles had introduced him to Georges and Alain, Tony took his usual afternoon walk in the direction of the farm track to see if there were any messages from Madeleine or Georges. For the first time, he noticed a handkerchief caught in the hedge. His heart quickened with excitement. Was it a message from London, or from Georges at the German H.Q.? With a quick look around to make sure that he was unobserved, Tony retrieved the handkerchief and pushed it into the pocket of his trousers. He made his way nonchalantly down the farm track, being careful to look as though he were just going for an afternoon stroll. When he reached the log, he stopped and put one foot on it. Making a pretence of tying his shoelace, he glanced up and down the farm track. There was no one about. The place was deserted, in fact he had only ever seen one other person in the vicinity during the weeks he had been checking the post-box daily. Certain now that he was alone and unobserved, Tony reached down into the end of the log and retrieved the piece of paper which had been left for him. He slipped it into his pocket, and continued his walk along the farm track.

Despite his curiosity, Tony did not stop to read the note but continued to the Boues' cottage and up to his room. He closed the windows which had been opened to allow some fresh air into the hot stuffy room, and took the piece of paper from his pocket. A broad smile spread across his face as he read.

'Because of the disruption to the trains the Germans are bringing in a convoy of fuel and arms on the 28th. It will use the road from Nantes.

There will be 20-30 trucks + escort of troops - one lorry at each end of the convoy, and motorbike outriders.

Convoy due to reach Saint Nazaire around 3.15 p.m.'

The 28th. It was already the 26th, so they would have to move quickly. Tony rushed outside and across the fields to where Jean-Paul was making hay. The older man was swiftly dispatched to the city with a message for Madeleine and Charles to meet, with the new members of the group, at the cave at 10 the following evening. While Jean-Paul was gone, Tony continued with the hay making but his mind was not on his work, instead it buzzed with plans and ideas for attacking the convoy.

"Madeleine, Jean-Paul. Meet Alain and Georges. They will be working with us from now on."

The introductions were swift and Tony soon continued.

"Georges has provided us with information about a convoy of fuel and arms coming into the city tomorrow. The plan is that we attack it, and destroy as many of the supplies as possible."

"Attack a convoy!"

Tony grinned. "Yes, Madeleine."

"But that's very different from anything we've ever done before. Do you think we can do it? Are there enough of us?"

Tony nodded. "Yes, we can do it. And with good planning and surprise on our side, a small group like ours can do plenty of damage."

"I, for one, am ready for it." Charles spoke with barely concealed excitement.

"Me too." Alain grinned. "That is what I joined you for!"

"Good." Tony could see that the whole group were ready for this next step, although they all looked forward to it with a mixture of excitement and trepidation. "If we're all agreed, then let's get down to work and get away as soon as we can. Tomorrow is going to be a long and busy day for us all."

The group met at the appointed place at one fifteen. Georges, as promised, arrived in a car which he had 'liberated' from a German officer who was billeted a quarter of a mile from his home. The group piled in, each carrying his or her own haversack containing all they needed for the attack. As they continued along the road towards Nantes, Tony went over the plan.

"Georges will drop us off, then go and hide the car. You will all take up your positions behind the hedges bordering the road, while I set the explosives and detonators in the road itself. I'll detonate mine first when the leading troop carrier reaches it. Charles will set his off when the troop carrier behind reaches him, then I'll set off the others. The rest of you know what you have to do. Just be careful not to hit each other in the crossfire. Don't stay too long either. Inflict as much damage as you can, then get out fast."

The others nodded as the car rounded a bend. Georges indicated a narrow lane on their right.

"The car will be waiting there."

Half a mile further on they rounded another bend and stopped at Tony's chosen ambush site. He perused it critically, then smiled. Perfect. A long straight stretch of road, bordered by wheat fields and thick hedges, which ran all the way along the road to the lane. Georges would hide the car there, offering them extensive cover for their retreat. He climbed out of the vehicle with the others close behind. As Georges turned the car round and headed off to conceal it, Tony looked at his watch.

"Assuming the convoy is on time, we have an hour. Get to your positions and check your weapons." He pointed down the road as he spoke. "Charles, down at the end on the far side of the road; pace it out as you go, leaving enough space from this point for about thirty trucks. Alain, you will be halfway between Charles and this point; Jean-Paul will be just here." He looked at the other two. "We take this side of the road. Madeleine down near Charles, Georges about opposite Alain and me here. Make sure you know where everyone else is; we don't want any of us to be shot by our own group. Now get going. And good luck."

The group dispersed as Tony knelt in the road and opened one of the haversacks at his feet. With a shovel he dug a shallow hole in the road, filled it with explosives, fixed a detonator and wire then covered it before paying out the wire behind him as he made his way backwards up the shallow bank, and into the hedge which would be his hiding place. His well-trained hands swiftly attached the wire to the plunger. He left it unarmed as he ran down the road to set a similar charge in front of Charles, hoping that it would be in the correct position to knock out the troop carrier bringing up the rear. He played out the wire once more, and attached it to the plunger Charles had brought with him.

"Right, it's all ready to go. You just raise the plunger, twist it one half turn to the right and then it's armed. All you need to do to detonate it after that is to push down the plunger."

"Yes, Albert."

Tony looked at the other preparations which Charles had made, and nodded approvingly. Six hand grenades were laid out in a row, and beside them four full magazines for the Sten gun which lay by Charles' side. Everything was within easy reach. Charles was fully prepared for the ambush. Tony hoped the others were equally well prepared. He had issued everyone with a Sten gun for the attack as well as a number of grenades. If everything went well, their attack would be devastating.

"Good luck."

Tony slipped back through the hedge and made his way back to his assigned position, stopping at regular intervals to lay another charge in the road. The charges were linked together on one detonating wire so that when the second plunger was pressed, they should all go off at the same time. Tony fed the wire through the hedge and laid it ready beside the plunger before checking his Sten gun and laying it down beside him. Now everything was ready.

As Tony lay in the leaf litter, his mind wandered back to his days in Scotland. He remembered being back at Arisaig, preparing to blow up one of the targets set by his trainers. Yet he had never felt so tense in the Scottish Highlands. This was the real thing, and he had two inexperienced new members in his group with him. He had done his best for them, putting each of them between two more experienced members of the group, who could protect their flanks and chivvy them along during their escape; he hoped that would be enough. Glancing down the road at the hedges bordering both sides, he was relieved to see no sign of his companions. They were well concealed, as were the charges in the road. It would take careful scrutiny to see them. They certainly would not be spotted by people in vehicles.

Tony heard a sound like low rumbling thunder in the distance, but the sky was blue and the sun was shining. Unlike thunder, the noise was continuous. The convoy was approaching. Tony peered carefully through the hedge. In the distance he saw the leading motorbike approaching, closely followed by the troop carrier and the first of a long line of supply trucks. With a twist, Tony armed the detonator and waited, watching with grim determination as the targets approached. The motorbike passed in front of him, with the troop carrier following close behind. Tony depressed the plunger as the truck passed over the explosive charge and the earth erupted beneath it. Time seemed to slow. He watched as the truck disintegrated, flinging men and bits of machine in all directions while his fingers removed the first wire from the plunger, attached the second and armed it. As he was preparing to depress the plunger, there was an explosion at the rear of the column. Charles must have set off his charge. As he depressed the plunger a second time, Tony watched six geysers of dusty earth erupt beneath some of the trucks, throwing them and their contents high into the air. Then the whole area burst into life with the sound of grenades and machine-gun fire. The motorbike at the front screeched to a halt. The rider looked back over his shoulder to see what was happening, before revving the engine and riding, head down, in the direction of Saint Nazaire. Tony let off a burst of Sten gun fire after him, but from that distance was not surprised to miss. The rider would go into the city for help. But by the time help arrived, Tony and his comrades would be long gone.

At the far end of the ambush, Charles had depressed the plunger to detonate his explosives a second too early in his eagerness and watched the cab of the truck blow apart, flinging the men into the road dazed but unhurt. With a muffled oath, he reached for the first of his hand grenades, pulled the pin and threw it into their midst. As the men were struggling to their feet the grenade exploded, flinging men, and parts of men, in all directions. Charles picked up his Sten gun and raked the remnants with bullets. Within seconds the threat from the soldiers was eliminated. Charles began to throw his grenades with casual ease at the trucks nearest to him, which were so far undamaged. Along the whole line of trucks, the members of the Resistance group were throwing grenades. The sound of explosions mingled with screams. The smell of burning rubber and flesh hung heavy in the summer air. Huge palls of smoke rose into the sky above the burning wreckage strewn across the road. A number of Germans began to return fire, leaping down from the cabs of their blazing vehicles, only to find themselves trapped between the banks of the road and their attackers. It did not matter which side of their vehicles they tried to hide, for each side was raked with fire from the Sten guns concealed in the hedges. A small handful of soldiers from the first troop carrier had taken refuge beneath the first supply truck, which was unscathed. They began to fire indiscriminately into the hedges on either side of them.

Tony studied the length of the convoy and grinned. Of the twenty or thirty trucks which had driven into their ambush only three remained undamaged, the remainder were burning fiercely or had crashed into the banks. The soldiers who had survived the initial onslaught were trying to regroup. They were now returning fire more accurately, while the motorcyclist must by now be well on his way to the city. Tony realised that it was time to withdraw. As if by telepathy, Charles also decided that it was time to go. Rising to his feet he ran along behind the hedge, stopping at intervals to fire at the few soldiers who were wandering dazedly in the road. On the other side another Sten gun kept pace with him. Madeleine, too, was withdrawing towards Tony's position. As she ran the smell of burning flesh reached her nostrils causing her to retch and she fired into the cabs of the burning trucks from which screams were issuing. She hated the Germans but found that she did not have the heart to leave them burning to death and hoped that her bullets would put a few of them out of their terrible agony. Georges saw her coming and rose to his feet. His supply of grenades exhausted but still with plenty of rounds left for his Sten gun, he joined Madeleine in raking the sides of the trucks. He grinned at her, a triumphant light in his eyes.

"This is great! At last I feel as though I'm doing something to free my homeland!"

"Shut up and run!"

Georges looked at the woman beside him. Her face was twisted with revulsion at the smell, yet she was calm and in control. He admired her courage and grinned at her before continuing to run towards Tony. On the far side of the road, Charles reached the position where Alain had remained concealed. Grabbing his friend by the shoulder, he pulled him to his feet.

"Come on, Alain! We need to get out of here! We've done a damn good job, and to stay would only endanger our lives!"

Alain nodded, released a final burst of fire into the blazing truck opposite and set off at a run.

Madeleine and Georges came up to Tony as he swung the haversack containing his detonator onto his back.

"Are you two all right?" They nodded. "Good, then let's go!"

The three young people ran swiftly along the shelter of the hedge and soon arrived breathlessly at the hidden car. They climbed aboard and Tony wiped sweat from his eyes.

"Start the car, Georges."

"What about the others?" Georges' breath was coming in gasps.

"Don't worry, we're not leaving them. I just want the car running so we can leave as soon as they get here."

Georges nodded and started the car. Madeleine was kneeling in the back seat, gun trained along the hedge in the direction from which their friends would come.

"Any sign of them?"

"No, Albert."

Tony lifted his gun. "I'm going back for them."

His face was grim as he alighted from the car. The people back there had grown to mean a great deal to him in the short time he had known them. He would not turn his back on them now.

"Wait as long as you can, Georges, but if we're not here soon, get away without us. We'll just have to make it back on foot."

Tony turned and began to run back towards the carnage on the road.

Jean-Paul was waiting for Charles and Alain as they approached.

"Come on, you two! There's no firing from the other side of the road, so I think the others have already left! There are some Germans sheltering behind that truck," he indicated an undamaged truck which stood incongruously in the road, "so keep your heads down and run like hell!"

The three set off at a fast pace and the sound of firing fell silent. All that could be heard was the roar of flames and the cries of the wounded. The small group of Germans who had managed to survive the attack slowly crossed the road. When they were not fired upon, they climbed the bank to push their way through the hedge in time to see the three Frenchmen retreating round the bend. The Germans set off in pursuit and opened fire as the Frenchmen came into sight once more. Charles cried out and fell to his knees. Jean-Paul turned and began to fire on their pursuers.

"Help him up, Alain! I'll cover you!"

Alain pulled Charles to his feet. His face was pale but he managed to force a grin.

"Come on," he spoke through clenched teeth, "we mustn't keep the others waiting."

With one arm around his old school friend's shoulders and Alain's arm around his waist, Charles made his way at a stumbling run in the direction of the lane and the hidden car. Behind them Jean-Paul was firing at the Germans, who had now taken refuge in a cornfield. He retreated slowly, step by steady step, face to the enemy, praying he would be able to hold the Germans back long enough for Charles and Alain to reach the car. The Germans were attempting to return his fire, but it was half-hearted, as though they were in a state of shock after the ambush. When another machine-gun opened up on his right they ceased firing altogether. Jean-Paul turned to see who it was and was greeted by Tony's boyish grin.

"Come on, let's get going. The others should be back at the car by now."

The two men ran side by side to the waiting car, and jumped aboard. Jean-Paul and Tony squeezed into the front. The rear seat was taken up by a pale but still conscious Charles, Alain and Madeleine, who was still kneeling with her gun trained behind them.

"Let's go, Georges. I can hear a motorbike coming."

"That must be the one from the rear of the column." Charles' voice was strained. "I killed the rider, but someone else must be using it now."

Someone else was. A soldier had mounted the motorcycle, weaved his way unsteadily between the burning vehicles and was now roaring down the road towards them. Georges accelerated as fast as he could, but the car was overloaded and their pursuer steadily gained on them. Madeleine watched and waited until the bike was close enough to ensure that she would hit him first time. Then she fired. The front tyre of the motorbike exploded. Its rider threw his arms into the air as a crimson stain spread across his tunic. As the German fell from the motorbike which continued on its side until it was brought to a halt by a tree, Madeleine turned round and sat down.

"Well, what are we waiting for? Let's go home."

The huge doors of the barn had been left open in readiness, and Georges drove straight in. Even before the car had ceased to move, Jean-Paul and Tony leapt out and ran to close the doors behind them.

"Right." Tony's mind was racing as he explained what was to happen next. "The car will remain hidden here, as will all weapons and munitions. If we're caught with them we're dead. Pile everything here," he indicated a corner of the barn as he spoke, "then help me to cover it all with these bales of hay."

As the others leapt to do his bidding, Tony climbed back into the car.

"How are you, Charles?"

The young man smiled wanly. "It hurts like hell, but I think I'll live."

Tony helped him to remove the bloodstained shirt, and examined the wound.

"The bullet went in the back and came out the front. It seems to have passed between your ribs. Jean-Paul!" He called across to his friend as he continued to examine the wound. "Bring across the first aid kit we hid here earlier."

Jean-Paul was at his side moments later. "Is he going to be all right?"

"Yes, as long as he doesn't lose too much blood." Tony began to pad and bandage the wound. "We'll have to take him back to your place, while the others make their way across country to the city. He'll never manage to walk that far."

Jean-Paul nodded. The other members of the group had finished concealing their weapons and come back to join the three in the car. Tony smiled reassuringly at them.

"You'll be glad to know that Charles is going to be all right." Smiles replaced their worried frowns as they gathered round. "You've all done extremely well. I'm proud of you. Now, get back home as quickly as you can by your pre-arranged routes. Try not to do anything to draw attention to yourselves. There will be Germans everywhere, but there is nothing to link you to what has happened. If you are stopped, bluff it out. Jean-Paul will be in touch when I want to arrange another meeting. Now get going, and good luck."

As Alain, Georges and Madeleine left the barn Tony and Jean-Paul helped Charles to his feet.

"Can you make it?"

Charles nodded and Tony led the way out. In the distance he could see the swastika flying above the roof of his grandmother's home, and he grinned. The Germans would never dream of looking for a stolen car and illegal arms so close by. With a deep breath, he took one of Charles' arms and Jean-Paul took the other as they set off on the two mile walk back to the Boues' cottage.

It was a long and difficult walk, each step seemed to set Charles' chest on fire. His brow was beaded with sweat and an involuntary groan frequently escaped his tightly clenched, bloodless lips. They arrived at last, weary but in one piece and settled Charles in the cool barn. He lay back in relief, as waves of pain and nausea washed over him. Jean-Paul hurried off to make the necessary arrangements to get Charles home, while Tony talked quietly to his companion.

"Don't worry about anything, Charles." His voice was reassuring. "We won't be able to get you to the hut where we hid Claude because all the roads in that area will be crawling with Germans after our attack, but we'll get you home all right. Dr. Leclerc will come in to see you as soon as possible, probably tomorrow. You should be all right until then." He examined the bandages he had put on earlier. Fresh blood was beginning to seep through, but rather than disturb the wound by redressing it, Tony merely wrapped another bandage tightly around the Frenchman's torso.

"Sorry...to be so...much...trouble."

Tony grinned at the pale face.

"You're no trouble, Charles. You're a valued member of this group and I don't know what I would do without you. We're all in this together: and I'm only doing for you what you did for me."

Charles smiled weakly. "You don't know how...happy I am to...hear you...say that. At times I have thought you...didn't want me in...the group."

"We all have our ups and downs and make mistakes, but that's all in the past now, Charles." Tony smiled. "I can't imagine the group without you as a member."

The Frenchman nodded. "I'm glad because I enjoy working with you." He closed his eyes and leant back weakly as a wave of dizziness washed over him. "How do you plan to get me home? I don't think I can walk far."

"You won't have to." Jean-Paul entered the barn as he spoke. "You'll be going in my pony and trap." He held out a hand and a diminutive figure joined him. "This is Theresa. She'll drive you into Saint Nazaire. If you're stopped, she'll say that she picked you up on the road because you wanted a lift. She's never seen you before."

"Is that safe?"

Jean-Paul shrugged at the question. "I think so. The Germans will hardly suspect a girl of her age of being involved in the ambush. Nor will they expect a member of the Resistance to come so openly back into the city. If you are stopped though, please try not to incriminate my daughter."

Charles' eyes sparkled with unshed tears. "I can't believe that you're willing to take such a risk for me. Believe me, Jean-Paul, I won't let you down."

"It's nothing." Jean-Paul spoke gruffly to hide his emotions. "Now, get this clean shirt on and get moving. Theresa has to be back before curfew."

Theresa left the barn ahead of the three men, and was already seated in the trap when they came out. The pony, which Jean-Paul had only been allowed to keep because of its contribution to the farm work on the estate, tossed its head and pranced lightly on its feet, sending up a little cloud of dust.

"Come on, Monsieur Charles. The pony is in a hurry."

Charles grinned at the young girl as his two companions helped him up into the cart.

"Now make sure that you keep as still as possible," Tony warned. "If you move too much you may start the bleeding again."

"Do not worry. I don't intend to move!" Charles settled himself gingerly into the seat as he spoke. "If I do start bleeding, I'll leave Theresa and hide up somewhere until dark.

Once the Germans see a man in a blood-stained shirt, his companion wouldn't stand a chance."

"But Monsieur Charles!"

"No buts." Jean-Paul's face was severe as he spoke to his daughter. "You are to do whatever Charles tells you. What you are doing is very courageous but also very dangerous. I don't want you to take any unnecessary risks. Understand?"

"Yes, Papa."

Jean-Paul smiled. "Good. Now be careful, Theresa, and hurry home."

"Thank you both for everything." Charles' pain-filled eyes perused his companions. "I owe you my life."

"Don't mention it, that's what friends are for. Now, get going." Jean-Paul slapped the pony lightly on the rump and it leapt forward at a brisk trot.

Theresa guided the pony along the country lanes towards Saint Nazaire, avoiding the main roads wherever possible. It was bright and sunny, even though the afternoon was drawing to close. Charles grimly held on to consciousness as the pain shot like a knife through his body. He was fearful and uncertain as to whether they would be able to enter Saint Nazaire unnoticed. He marvelled at the calm assurance of the girl by his side, and realised that the deep hatred of the enemy from one so young would shape the rest of her life.

At last, the trap reached the end of a narrow lane which joined the main road into Saint Nazaire, and Theresa drew the pony to a halt.

"Right, Monsieur Charles, we can no longer avoid the main road. It's only half a mile into the city now. Are you ready?"

Charles gave a weary nod, the pain and loss of blood taking a toll on his strength.

"Yes. Let's get it over with."

Theresa shook the reins and urged the pony out onto the hard surface of the road at a steady trot. They had covered barely half the distance to the outskirts of the city when the sound of roaring engines reached them, followed swiftly by the looming shapes of trucks racing along the road. Theresa reined in the pony and jumped down to hold his head as the huge trucks hurtled past, and he reared and neighed in alarm. There were five trucks, each filled with soldiers who spared not a glance for the trap and its passengers as they sped past. At last the final truck had gone by. Theresa patted and soothed the frightened pony. When he was calm, she climbed back up beside Charles.

"Where do you think they were going, Monsieur Charles?"

"Out to the site of our ambush I would think. They'll flood the whole area with troops to try to find us." He smiled at the young girl beside him. "If it weren't for you and your father and Albert, they would find me out in those fields."

Theresa grinned. "As it is they won't find anyone, will they?"

She shook the reins and the pony broke into a trot, taking them in a matter of minutes to the outskirts of the city. Charles frowned as they approached.

"A road block. I'd better get down here."

Theresa shook her head. "No. They would notice and want to know why. Sit still please, Monsieur Charles."

As Theresa continued towards the road block, Charles had little choice but to sit still. His palms were sweaty and he wiped them surreptitiously down the sides of his trousers. The trap drew to a halt beside the sentry and the young German perused them.

"Where have you come from?"

"The estate where my father is working."

"Let me see your papers."

Charles and Theresa handed down their papers to the sentry who perused them carefully.

"Where are you going?"

"I have to get some flour and sugar for the family. Mama sent me shopping. I'm a big girl now so she trusts me. I want to see my friends as well while I'm here. Have I got time before curfew?"

The soldier shrugged. "I suppose so, if you hurry." He handed back the papers as he spoke. "Have you come all the way down the main road?"

"No, down the lanes. It's really pretty with all the flowers and trees. I saw a rabbit and some sheep. Do you like rabbits? I had a pet one before the war."

As Theresa continued to chatter a car drew up behind the trap. The soldier, fed up with the noisy child and not at all suspicious of someone who was willing to sit and talk for so long, waved them on.

"Get moving. I have work to do."

Theresa urged the pony on. As it pulled away, Charles glanced over his shoulder to see the guard approaching the car and taking the papers of its occupants. He shook his head in disbelief.

"I don't believe it, Theresa. You seem more calm and relaxed than me. How do you do it?"

Theresa shrugged. "I suppose I enjoy playing games where I pretend with my sister."

Charles nodded thoughtfully. Maybe it was so. Children lived in a world of make-believe, to them it was all a game, not a lie to the enemy. He did not doubt that Theresa realised the seriousness of their position, yet she was able to detach herself in a way that he found impossible.

Theresa glanced across at her companion and frowned. "You're looking pale, Monsieur Charles. Are you all right?"

Charles shook his head slightly. He could feel a warm wetness spreading on his back. His wound was burning and he felt faint.

"I think the bleeding has started again," he whispered.

Theresa glanced at the steadily spreading bloodstain on his back then reached behind her into the trap. She found an old jacket of her father's, which she placed over Charles' shoulders.

"Hang on, Monsieur Charles. We're nearly there."

She drove steadily on, a worried frown creasing her brow as Charles slumped in the seat beside her. But her father's directions had been accurate. Within ten minutes she was drawing to a halt outside Charles' house. She climbed down and tied the pony's lead rein to a lamppost. Charles held out a hand to her.

"Here's the key. Open the door."

Theresa took the key and opened the door, before helping the wounded man down from the trap. He leant his hand heavily on her shoulder as they made their way across the pavement, trying to look as inconspicuous as possible. Once inside, Theresa closed the door and helped Charles to a seat. Removing the jacket from his shoulders, she blanched at the sight of the red patch spreading over his back.

"Sit still, Monsieur Charles. I'll re-bandage this for you."

Theresa hurried upstairs and rummaged around, but could find no first aid kit. Eventually she settled on an old clean sheet which she brought downstairs. With a pair of scissors from the kitchen she cut it into three long bandages, and folded the remainder into two thick pads. After boiling some water and setting it ready in a bowl, she carefully helped Charles out of his shirt. He winced in pain but said nothing. With gentle care, the young girl unwound the bandages and removed the bloodstained dressings. With a cloth dipped in the warm water, she carefully washed both wounds, front and back, and watched as they began to bleed once more. Pressing one of the pads to each wound she managed to smile weakly, though her stomach churned at what she had seen and done.

"It's not bleeding too fast, Monsieur Charles. If I bandage it tightly it should stop. But you mustn't move around." She began to wind the bandages around his torso as she spoke. "I'll help you upstairs to bed before I leave."

At last the bandage was tied and Theresa helped the wounded man up the stairs and into his bed. As she smoothed the blankets, Charles smiled weakly.

"You would make an excellent nurse, Theresa."

The young girl smiled shyly at the handsome man in the bed, one of her heroes from the Resistance, and she felt a blush darken her cheeks.

"You never know, Monsieur Charles. I may become one when the war is over."

Theresa turned and left the room, her mind and body stirred by emotions which she had never felt before. Down in the kitchen, she placed the bloodied bandages and cloth in the fire and watched them burn, while all the time her thoughts were on the man upstairs. She smiled and her heart beat faster; she wondered if she was falling in love. She was too young to understand the feelings which engulfed her. She did not realise that it was a combination of excitement in the face of danger, hero worship of a man wounded in the defence of his country, the feeling of having someone totally dependent on her, all mixed with a genuine attraction towards the older man, which had set her in such a spin. All she knew was that she wished she were ten years older, and that Charles would see her as a young woman instead of a little girl.

With a sigh, Theresa busied herself about the kitchen. She could do nothing about her age, but perhaps she could make Charles see how indispensable she was so that he was willing to wait for her to grow up. In no time at all she had a tray made up for him, with a bowl of hot soup and a piece of bread, a cup of hot coffee, a glass and jug of water and two apples. With a skip in her step she made her way up the stairs once more. Her heart missed a beat as she entered the bedroom and saw the pale face on the pillows. With a forced smile, she put down the tray and helped Charles to sit up.

"I've brought you a hot drink and some soup. You should have them now, and save the apples and water for when you're alone. Can you manage to feed yourself?"

Charles nodded. "Yes. Thank you, Theresa. You should go now or you'll be breaking curfew. I'll be all right until the doctor comes tomorrow, thanks to you." He smiled and noticed the blush which coloured the young girls cheeks.

"I'll try to come back tomorrow and cook you a proper meal. Be careful, Monsieur Charles."

Charles smiled at the young girl. "Thank you, Theresa."

As the child turned and skipped down the stairs he marvelled at her qualities of self-control under stress, and the way she seemed to know just what to do in an awkward situation. He was saddened that war should come along to force youngsters like Theresa out of their childhood and thrust them forward into an adulthood and maturity for which they were not prepared. He hoped she would not be hurt by this war.

95

Georges slowly pushed his broom along the corridor, listening to the sound of voices coming through the open office door.

"We have to do something, Karl!" Major Steinhauser's voice was raised in anger.

"This sort of thing can't go on!"

"Yes, sir. We have hundreds of troops combing the area."

"That's no good, Karl. If we didn't find them in the first hour we're not likely to find them now, twenty-four hours later."

"The guards said they shot at least one."

"Yes, but he still got away and he was not seen trying to get back into the city, which probably means that they have a hideout somewhere out in the country."

"We will find it, sir."

"How?"

Georges moved closer to the door. From his position he could see Steinhauser pacing back and forth across the room.

"They seem to be able to hit us whenever they want and then just disappear into thin air. Even the wounded seem to just vanish. I don't care what it takes, Karl, we have got to get them. If we can't flush them out with our soldiers, we will have to rely on informers." He rubbed his chin thoughtfully. "I want posters all over the city, a reward of fifteen thousand francs for information received. I also want another train load of workers sent to the factories. That might encourage someone to come forward with information"

Sergeant Dresner nodded. "Yes, sir. Men or women?"

"Women this time, Karl. We must keep a fair balance after all!" Steinhauser laughed, a sound without mirth which sent a shiver along Georges' spine. "And Karl, I want you to work on some ideas to trap this group of bastards. They cannot be allowed to get away with it. They have wiped out a whole supply convoy, killing or wounding upwards of forty Germans, with only one of their group wounded and the rest getting away scot-free. We've got to get them, and when we do, Karl, they'll wish they'd never been born!" He laughed again, a laugh which brought no light to the cold ice blue of his eyes. "I am looking forward to having them in my power. It will give me great pleasure to extract every possible piece of information from them."

A German orderly turned the corner of the corridor ahead of Georges, a sheaf of papers in his hand, and the young Frenchman began to push his broom faster, working his way down the passageway until the sound of voices from Steinhauser's office receded into the distance. His face was grim. It looked as though the people of Saint Nazaire were going to suffer once again for the group's activities. But rather than making Georges feel guilty it made him angry. He determined that he would work harder than ever to drive the hated Germans from his homeland.

"Are you sure Leclerc said he would come here?"

"Of course, Albert. Now sit down and relax."

Tony stopped his pacing of the kitchen and turned to face Jean-Paul.

"I'm sorry. I'm just so worried. What if something has gone wrong?"

"We'll know soon enough. I know Theresa isn't experienced, but she seemed to think that the bleeding was stopping when she left Charles last night. And Leclerc said that he would get there this morning. All we can do now is wait."

Tony sighed and flung himself into a chair. "It was the right decision. Too many people coming and going to Charles' house would be unusual and draw attention to him, and that's the last thing we need at the moment. But," he stood up and began pacing again as he spoke, "I hate the waiting most of all."

Jean-Paul nodded. "I know what you mean."

"What's that?" Jean-Paul made his way over to the door as the sound of a car reached his ears. He looked out and a broad grin spread across his face.

"It's the doctor! At last!"

The two men went out to greet their visitor, who kept the engine of the car running and did not get out.

"Bonjour, my friends."

"How is he?"

Leclerc smiled at Tony's question. "Don't worry, it's good news. I've seen Charles and, although very weak from loss of blood, he's doing fine. He was lucky, the bullet seems to have caused very little internal damage. It entered from the back and exited at the front. Both clean wounds. It shouldn't be long before he's up and about again, although he'll be stiff for a few weeks to come."

"Thank God for that! And thank you, doctor, you've saved us yet again."

"Don't think about that, Albert, you won't have to do without me as long as this war lasts."

Tony reached across and shook the older man's hand. "Thank you."

Leclerc gave an embarrassed smile as he continued. "Charles should be all right on his own, but he won't be able to go out to the shops for a while. Do you have any plans to help him?"

Tony nodded. "Yes, we will take care of that, don't worry."

"Good." The doctor put his car into gear. "I'll try to get in and see him again in a couple of days." He smiled at his comrades. "Don't hesitate to call on me again if you need me. It makes me feel good to be able to do something to avenge my son's death."

"What are the Germans saying about the attack?"

"They seem to be at a loss to know who and where you are."

"Good."

"Not so good." Leclerc frowned. "They're offering a reward for your capture, and they're shipping a train full of women to the labour camps."

"The bastards!"

Jean-Paul laid a comforting hand on Tony's shoulder.

"We knew it might happen. We just have to accept it."

Tony's face was grim. "I know, but that doesn't mean I have to like it."

Leclerc nodded. "I know what you mean. Now, I have to go. If I miss my surgery the Germans might become suspicious. Good bye and good luck."

"Goodbye, my friend, and thank you."

"Take care, doctor." Tony smiled. "We really appreciate all your help!"

With a smile and a wave Leclerc drove away. The two younger men watched him go. When the car had disappeared from sight, Jean-Paul turned to his companion.

"What now?"

"We follow the plan. Tomorrow you will take a load of vegetables into the city to sell. I want you to try to gauge the feelings of the civilian population."

"And Theresa?"

"That's up to you, Jean-Paul. Charles would no doubt benefit from having someone to look after him. But if you feel that it will be too dangerous then she stays here."

Jean-Paul set off for the city soon after dawn had painted the sky with its rosy palette. Theresa was seated beside him on the horse-drawn wagon, once again eagerly offering her services as nurse to the group. This time the young girl was looking forward to her duties with an eagerness which she hid from her father. He would never understand how a girl her age could be so fond of a man who was ten years older. How she wished she could grow up overnight!

The journey into the city was uneventful. Jean-Paul drove through the streets of the suburbs at a steady walk, finally halting two streets away from Charles' home.

"Right, Theresa. You get down here. I don't want to stop outside the house." He helped his daughter down, then handed her the basket of food which her mother had prepared earlier that morning. "I'll meet you back here in two hours."

"Yes, Papa."

Jean-Paul smiled fondly at his daughter. "Just be careful."

Theresa nodded and began walking down the street, the summer sun warm on her bare arms as she happily swung the basket to and fro. Jean-Paul watched her for a moment and then drove away, wishing that the war had not come to disrupt her childhood yet proud of the way she was helping the Resistance movement.

When Theresa reached Charles' house, she entered without knocking and ran up the stairs. The bedroom door was open. As she approached she saw Charles struggling to rise to his feet. When he saw her, he relaxed back onto the pillows.

"Oh, it's you, Theresa."

Theresa raised a hand to her mouth in alarm.

"Oh! Monsieur Charles! I'm so sorry! I should have called up from downstairs!"

Charles grinned weakly. "Don't worry, Theresa. Just remember to call out next time. I thought you were the SS coming to get me!"

Theresa placed her basket on the floor and approached the bed. She smiled shyly at her patient as she plumped up the pillows and helped him to settle comfortably.

"How are you feeling today, Monsieur Charles?"

"Sore. But it won't take long for the wound to heal. Then I can get back to fighting with the rest of the group."

Theresa sat on the edge of the bed, a faraway look in her eyes.

"I wish I could fight too. I want to help get rid of the Germans."

Charles smiled. "You're doing a vital job as it is, Theresa. Don't wish the years ahead of you away. I hope the fighting will be over long before you're old enough to carry a gun."

Theresa sighed. She knew what she was doing was worthwhile, but it was a job for a girl not a young woman. She looked at the handsome man in the bed, certain that he would show her more attention if she were able to fight by his side.

"Age has nothing to do with it." She grinned impishly. "I can use a gun. I've helped Papa to keep the rabbits away from the crops in the past. Surely shooting the Germans would be no different."

Charles laughed at the refreshing naiveté of the girl, then winced at the pain.

"When you're older, you'll understand how different it is when you have a man in your gun sights."

Theresa frowned. There he was, talking about her age, or lack of it, again. She climbed down from the bed and made her way over to the door where she picked up her basket.

"You just relax Monsieur Charles, I'll go downstairs and get some food ready for you."

As he watched her go, Charles grinned. Jean-Paul was lucky to have such a daughter.

96

Angeline, with flour up to her elbows, was kneading dough vigorously, while Vincent was removing another tray of bread from the oven. It was hot. She brushed a damp wisp of hair out of her eyes with her arm, leaving a streak of flour on her brow. When Vincent saw it he grinned.

"Don't worry, this is the worst time of the year. It's hot enough without the ovens."

Angeline continued to knead the dough. "Don't worry, Vincent. I shan't give up the job, if that's what you're afraid of." She stopped her work for a moment and turned to face her older companion. "At least I'm being paid for this work. Not like those poor women Steinhauser had transported to the work camps last week. Just think of the poor children who are now without mothers! I sometimes wonder if it's all worth it."

Vincent nodded. "I know what you mean. They don't seem to give in, do they." He wiped the sweat from his brow. "But it is all worthwhile. We will win in the end. We just have to persevere."

Angeline smiled. "I know. I suppose I'm just hot and tired." She frowned. "Do you think anyone will betray the Resistance for fifteen thousand francs?

Vincent shrugged. "I suppose there are always people who will do anything for money. But most people won't betray them, always assuming that they know where they are."

Angeline smothered a smile. She knew. As she continued to knead the dough, Vincent was working thoughtfully. When he finally spoke, Angeline was surprised at his words.

"I wish I knew where to find them."

"Why?"

"Maybe I could do something to help." He grinned. "I was feeling old and useless until you came along. But having someone to talk to and help me with my work has helped me to realise that I have more to offer my country than I thought." He shrugged. "Still, I don't suppose they would be able to use someone like me."

Angeline smiled. "You never know." She was glad that he wanted to help, but knew she would not take the risk of approaching Tony on his behalf. Having an English agent operating an illegal transmitter from his home was dangerous enough, even though he did not know that it was happening. To have an active member of the Resistance group there as well would make the risks unacceptable. As Angeline continued with her work she mused on the irony of the situation. Here was someone with whom she could talk about her clandestine activities and relieve some of the burden which rested on her shoulders, yet she was unable to say anything to him. Strangely, she found that more difficult that the job itself.

97

The next two weeks passed quickly. All places of military importance were under increased guard by the Germans, who still sought the Resistance group which was causing them so much trouble. They knew that their chances of stumbling on the saboteurs by accident were slim, so they concentrated their efforts on the civilians of the city. Checks on papers were increased and beatings common. The families of the three hundred women who had been deported were slowly coming to terms with their changed circumstances. Anger at the Germans seethed hidden in every heart.

The members of Tony's group continued to lie low, doing nothing to vary from the routine of the lives which they had been pursuing ever since the German Occupation began. Charles was the only one whose life changed to any extent, though no one knew, for he never ventured from his house. As Leclerc had said, the wound was healing quickly. With the help of Theresa, who visited every other day, he was soon up and about. Theresa was in her element, providing food and caring for the man she idolised. Charles grew increasingly fond of her, treating her very much like the little sister he had never had. Soon, too soon for Theresa, Charles was well enough to care for himself, and was able to return to the routine of his life. The wound had healed, leaving angry red scars and a stiffness which Leclerc said would fade in time. Charles began to exercise, gently at first but building steadily until he felt that he was well enough, despite his wound, to participate once again in the activities of the group. He found himself looking forward to the next call to action. He did not have long to wait.

98

Georges worked his way steadily along the corridor, sweeping as he went. Most of the office doors were closed, while those that were open showed rooms which were occupied, and so he continued on his way without a second glance. As a cleaner he was ignored by the Germans who worked at the SS Headquarters. It was as though he was not there as far as they were concerned. That gave him ample opportunity to look around and try to glean information which might be of some use to the group. As he shuffled on, blue overalls blending with the dull background of the painted corridor, he finally found what he was looking for, an empty office with its door left invitingly open.

Georges glanced along the empty corridor, then slipped inside the office. It was tidy, with rows of filing cabinets along the walls. He knew from experience that they would all be locked. The office was used by the transport officer, who arranged for all supplies of food and munitions to be brought into Saint Nazaire. Since the débacle of the supply convoy, all information had been carefully filed and locked away. Georges doubted that there would be anything of any use to him. He searched the desk quickly, and his face broke into a broad grin as he spied a piece of paper lying on top of the green blotter. As he studied it, easily deciphering the German words, he heard voices through the door which connected this office to the next. The door was ajar. Georges realised that the transport officer was just next door. He read the paper quickly, then moved back towards the door as the voice drew closer.

"Thank you, Franz. Why do I always run out of ink in the middle of the day? I shall have to get onto supply about it!"

There was a muffled reply which Georges did not quite hear. Then the connecting door opened wider to admit a German officer. He glanced at the paper on his desk, then glared at Georges who was sweeping the floor close to the door.

"What are you doing?" The officer spoke in German and Georges shook his head as though he did not understand. The officer frowned and struggled to speak French. "What here you do?"

"Cleaning, sir." Georges held out his broom. "May I do your office?"

The officer shook his head and waved his hand towards the door.

"No. Go. Come later."

Georges nodded and retreated from the room as the officer made his way over to the desk and perused it carefully. It did not look as though anything had been touched. He placed the new pot of ink on the desk, and frowned thoughtfully in the direction of the door. Then he shrugged. He had only been out of the office for a few moments, hardly time for the Frenchman to get into his office, and even if he had seen the papers, he obviously could not speak German. He began to re-fill his pen. He had better get the paper signed and on its way, before someone who could speak German saw it.

As the transport officer signed the paper on his desk, Georges made his way down the corridor. He grinned. Albert would be pleased with the information he had gleaned today.

Tony studied the message Georges had left for him in the hollow log, and felt the excitement building inside him. This would be a wonderful opportunity to impede the build-up of defences on the north coast of France. Everyone knew that the invasion of Europe would come that way sometime in the future, and the Germans were obviously doing their utmost to strengthen their defences. According to the message, a train carrying tanks would be moving north to be deployed along the Brittany coast. Tony intended to destroy it. According to the communiqué which Georges had read, there would be two carriages of soldiers travelling as guards to the thirty tanks. But forewarned is forearmed as they say, and Tony was sure that they would be able to neutralise them. His mind working overtime, he called Jean-Paul and asked him to arrange a meeting of the group. This was an opportunity not to be missed.

Tony lay concealed behind some bushes and glanced to his right where Madeleine and Georges were also trying to hide in their appointed places. The cover was sparse but sufficient; he turned to his left, where Jean-Paul, Charles and Alain were lying. Each of the group was well prepared, grenades laid out in front of them and Sten guns at the ready. Tony had already laid the explosives on the tracks and he glanced at the detonator box beside his right hand. The wires were attached and ready. In the distance, Tony heard the first sound of the approaching train and peered along the tracks to his left. A smudge of smoke appeared above the horizon, closely followed by the black bulk of the engine. Tony gave the plunger of the detonator a half turn, arming it in readiness. The train approached slowly, the weight of thirty tanks on their open flatcars holding the engine back.

All along the line the group of saboteurs checked their weapons. They watched eagerly as their target approached. Alain, on the far left, glanced across at Charles on his right. He was surprised that his friend was fit enough to take part in the attack. But knowing Charles as he did, he realised that he would have allowed nothing to stand in the way of him attacking the hated Germans. Charles glanced at Alain and waved a hand, before ducking back down as the huge bulk of the train approached. To his right, Jean-Paul frowned. He knew that Charles' wound had healed well, but he still doubted the wisdom of allowing him to fight again so soon. What if the wounds opened again with the activity? He shrugged. It was too late to worry about that now. On Tony's right, Madeleine was aware of Georges' eyes on her but did not turn to look at him. Instead she continued to watch the approaching train. Georges was also aware of the train drawing closer, but found it difficult to keep his eyes from the beautiful young woman lying prone on the ground ten feet away from him. It still amazed him that she could be dressed in trousers and shirt for ease of mobility, with a gun in her hand and grenades at her side, yet still look so feminine. He was proud to be able to fight at her side. The sound of the engine grew louder, and Georges turned his attention back to the track as Tony's hand gripped the plunger tightly.

288

The train reached the point where Tony had concealed the explosives, and he forced the plunger down. The ground beneath the engine rose up, lifting the behemoth with it and throwing it to one side. As it slid along the ground on its side, wheels still turning, the engine dragged the carriage behind it from the tracks, throwing the soldiers inside into a jumble of broken arms and legs. The leading flatcar came after it; the tank broke free from its moorings and rolled forward onto the carriage, crushing the soldiers beneath its heavy tracks. While they were still moving, Tony leapt to his feet and began to throw his grenades with studied accuracy at the tanks which slid past him, carried forward by their own momentum. On either side of him, the other members of his group were also standing, beginning to throw grenades. They created havoc among the tanks, whose broken and buckled shells littered the sides of the track. For a moment the Sten guns which the group possessed remained unused. The mangled soldiers in the first carriage offered no threat. The few who were not already dead were in no position to retaliate. Trapped, bleeding and broken, they felt the life oozing from their bodies as the grinding, crashing, screeching of the derailed train continued all around them.

As the grenades continued to fall amongst the shattered tanks the huge mass of the moving train finally came to rest. The flatcars carrying the last two tanks and the carriage behind them were derailed but still upright, while all in front of them were crushed and broken. Tony smiled. It had gone better than he had expected.

"Come on! Let's get out of here!"

The shrill chatter of a machine gun rent the air. Turning in surprise, he saw a flood of soldiers leaping down from the rear carriage, their rifles raised. They began to fire at Alain and Charles, the two who were closest to them. Alain fired again, the sound of his Sten gun a counter-point to the single shots of the German rifles. Charles turned towards Tony and cupped his hand to his mouth.

"Get back to the trees, Albert! We'll cover you!"

Before Tony could reply Charles had turned to face the Germans and was firing once more. Tony stood undecided for a moment. There must have been fifty soldiers climbing down from the carriage, too many for them to defeat. They must retreat to the trees where they would have better cover, then cover Alain and Charles as they retreated. Tony waved the others on.

"Come on! Run!"

His three companions followed him at a run towards the trees. As their feet thudded on the dry summer grass and their hearts pounded with exertion the sound of gunfire continued behind them. Tony reached the trees first and turned to survey the scene of the attack. The destruction of the train was total. Tony would have been well satisfied with the afternoon's work, if it were not for the skirmish taking place at the rear of the train. At least ten of the Germans lay still upon the ground, their blood soaking into the dry earth. Others sat holding their wounds, but the remainder were advancing relentlessly. Alain and Charles stood side by side, retreating one step at a time, and Tony felt frustrated and angry. There was little he could do to help from where he stood, and he contemplated going back to help them.

Georges and Madeleine reached the trees beside him just as Tony saw Alain throw up his arms in pain and fall back, the Sten gun falling from his hands. Tony's face was grim. He clutched his gun tightly as he stepped forward once again. He had to do something to help them. A hand gripped his arm.

"Hold it, Albert. There's nothing we can do for them now."

Tony recognised the truth of Jean-Paul's words, but it did not help. He and his companions watched the Germans slowly surround Charles. From where they stood it appeared that Charles had been hit; he was standing awkwardly as he fired into the ranks of the approaching soldiers. As his ammunition ran out, he knelt down to pick up Alain's gun. But before he could raise it to fire at his attackers, two bullets caught him almost simultaneously and he slid to the earth. The Germans approached at a run. They began firing into the two bodies on the ground.

"Animals!"

Georges turned towards Madeleine as she spoke. His heart went out to her as he watched the tears fall. Laying his hand gently on her arm, he turned her away from the scene.

"Come on." His voice was gentle, comforting, and Madeleine saw her pain mirrored in his eyes. Georges had grown up with Alain and Charles yet even in his grief he could spare sympathy for her. It helped her to get a firm hold on her feelings, and she nodded weakly.

"Yes. There's nothing we can do here now." Tony turned his back on the brutal scene. "We must get back to the car and out of here, before the Germans get on our trail."

"They're coming now." Jean-Paul had continued to watch the scene. He saw twenty of the Germans head towards their cover at a run. "We must go, Albert."

Tony ran, leading the diminished group towards the hidden car. But he left part of his soul back on the battlefield.

99

Major Steinhauser sat across the dinner table from Sergeant Dresner and poured a glass of cognac for each of them.

"You know, Karl, one of the few good things about the French is their cognac." He put the bottle down and picked up his glass, holding it to his nose to breath in the bouquet. He took a sip from the glass then set it down on the table. His face was serious. "That attack on the train caused a great deal of damage but, for once, we have managed to make them pay for their audacity." He sighed. "If only the soldiers had not been so quick to finish off the two they shot, we might already know where this group is hiding out. As it is, I have a feeling that things are beginning to go our way at last."

Karl nodded. "Yes. Their group can't be very big. Two deaths will be a serious blow to them." He frowned. "The weapons we found on them were British. I wonder if one of them was the spy who led this group?"

Steinhauser shrugged. "I don't suppose we will ever know. But just to be on the safe side, I want you to assume that the group leader was not amongst them. We'll keep looking." He smiled. "You know, Karl, I have a good feeling about this now. I think we'll have our hands on this group before long."

Dresner nodded, but said nothing. He hoped they would wipe out the Resistance group soon; Steinhauser's temper had been on an unusually short rein since the attacks had begun, and he could not wait to get back to normality.

100

The deaths had a salutary effect on the group. It hit Georges hard. To stand and watch as his two oldest friends had been killed in front of him had not been easy. It had taken all of his strength of will not to go rushing back, gun blazing, to help them. But he knew it would have been useless. He would have been left in a pool of blood with them. With fierce determination he had held back, swearing that he would live to avenge the deaths of Charles and Alain.

As Madeleine watched the Germans shooting down her comrades, her mind slipped back into the past. She imagined herself back at the beginning of the war and, instead of Charles, she saw her husband gunned down during the invasion. She had never known how he died, but guessed that it must have been like this. As the group retreated from the railway leaving their dead behind them, the old familiar pain and loss hit her again, as though a dam holding back her feelings had been breached. She was truly able to mourn her husband, without her anger and hatred of the Germans getting in the way. The hatred was by no means diminished, but she had it under control now. It was swamped in the wave of grief at the loss of her husband and her friends. Awash with her feelings she was glad of Georges' guiding hand at her elbow.

Tony decided that the group should lie low for a while, until the German search died down again and they had their feelings under control, so they did nothing rash to avenge the deaths. He had hardly known Alain, but as leader of the group he felt responsible for his death. They were all well aware of the risks they ran as members of a Resistance group, but to see the Germans finishing off their helpless comrades in cold blood as they lay wounded on the ground nauseated him. His hatred of the Germans reached a depth he had experienced only twice before, on the road to Dunkirk, and on hearing of the David's death. He felt the loss of Alain as any commander would feel the loss of one of his men, but the loss of Charles was the loss of a dear friend. Charles had been so like himself in his eagerness to fight and, after one or two early shows of over-zealousness, had proved a reliable comrade. Tony did not doubt that he would have died at the submarine pens if Charles had not risked his life to save him. It cut him deeply to stand and watch the young Frenchman killed, unable to do anything to help, and having to put the needs of the whole group ahead of the needs of one comrade and friend.

Although no one was aware of it, Theresa was the one who suffered most on hearing of the deaths. Jean-Paul told her that Charles had been shot, unaware of the conflicting emotions which his simple statement was to cause his daughter. She knew that she was only a child, even though she helped the Resistance group with the calmness and courage of an adult, the adult which she had wanted Charles to see in her. If she had spoken to her mother about her feelings, Marie would have offered her comfort by telling her that she did not really love Charles, it was just the childish infatuation for an older man that all girls experienced as they approached adolescence. Even so, Theresa would not have listened. To her, Charles was all that was wonderful and brave and worthy in her countrymen. She was sure that if Charles had waited for her to grow up, he would have come to love her as she loved him. But now that would never happen. Instead he would remain forever youthful, while she grew older, reaching his age and passing it. When she died and saw him once again, he would still be the same handsome young man whom she had loved, while she would be an old woman, though still with the heart and spirit of the young girl who now mourned his death. Theresa felt a depth of loss such as she had never felt before, had never even imagined. She knew that the only way to overcome it was to fight, and maybe to die, to avenge Charles. Children grew up quickly in occupied France.

101

Four days after the attack on the train transporting the tanks, Angeline received her first message from London. Each night at 9.45, she set up her radio in her room and listened. Any message for her would be transmitted between 9.49 and 9.54 pm, but so far she had listened in vain. Angeline sat on her bed, headset on, and listened. Suddenly, the beep beep sound of a message in Morse code jolted her. She grasped her pencil, writing swiftly as the message came through. It was coded, as she had expected, but it would not take her long to decode it after she had hidden her transmitter. The message came to an end. She tapped out one word, 'received', on her key, then signed off. Lifting the earphones from her head, she turned towards the door and froze.

Vincent stood in the doorway, his mouth agape and eyes wide in amazement. With a sinking heart she realised that her cover had been broken, and she was well aware of what that could mean to her. Laying the earphones down with a pretence of calmness she did not feel, Angeline rose to her feet.

"So now you know."

With an effort, Vincent pulled himself together. "Who were you speaking to?"

"England." Vincent, still overcome by surprise, said nothing. Angeline realised that she was going to have to take the initiative. "I'm a British agent. Are you going to turn me in?"

Vincent shook his head in disbelief. Then, as her words finally registered, he held up a hand in protest.

"No! Of course not! You know my feelings about the Germans!" He shook his head again. "I had no idea."

Angeline forced a grim smile. "That was how it should be." She frowned. "Do you want me to leave? It will be dangerous for you to knowingly harbour an enemy agent in your home."

""Of course not! You must stay here as long as you wish." Vincent was beginning to recover his senses. "Can I help in your work? Surely you can use me? After all, I'm no more unlikely a candidate to be a spy than you!"

Angeline smiled. Her non-descript appearance had obviously fooled Vincent, as intended. Turning her back on him, she thought swiftly. She believed he was safe, but her cover was still blown. She would have to tell Tony, and let him decide what had to be done. Composing herself she turned back to Vincent.

"I'll see what can be done. Now, if you'll excuse me, I have work to do." Vincent raised a quizzical eyebrow, and she smiled. "I have a transmitter to hide and a message to decode."

Vincent turned and left the room while Angeline quickly packed away the transmitter and sat with her pad, expertly juggling letters to decode the message. The completed transcript was soon lying on the bed beside her.

'High ranking General to visit S.S. 31st July. Attempt assassination.'

It was brief and to the point. Angeline frowned for a moment then added a message of her own.

'Cover blown. Vincent Artois, baker and landlord, caught me using set.
Offered help. Believe him to be safe. Please advise.'

She looked at it for a moment, aware that Tony might choose to eliminate Vincent to protect the safety of the group. She had grown fond of Vincent during her months with him, and regretted that she should be the one to endanger his life. But this was war. Decisively, she re-encoded, then folded the paper and hid it, ready to drop the following morning.

Tony and Jean-Paul watched the bakery from the cover of the shop opposite. Tony had retrieved Angeline's message from the drop site, and his frayed nerves had taken another battering. Far from being able to lie low as he had planned, he was now ordered to try to assassinate a German General. He had no misconceptions as to how dangerous this would be. To make matters worse, Angeline had informed him that her cover had been blown. Marshalling his scattered thoughts, Tony swiftly formulated a plan. That was why he and Jean-Paul were watching the bakery. It was almost two o'clock, and Tony expected Angeline to leave at any moment to check the post-box at the church. Right on cue she wheeled her bicycle out of the yard, clambered aboard and set off down the road. Tony nodded at Jean-Paul.

"Right. Let's go."

The two men left the shop, sauntered nonchalantly across the street and into the bakers. Vincent was wiping down a counter empty of goods, and looked up as the two men entered his shop.

"Can I help you? I'm afraid we don't have any bread left."

Tony perused the man. He looked harmless enough. The skin on his face was loose as though he had lost weight, but that was normal at a time when rationing gave people only the bare essentials to survive. His eyes were wary but not hard, and Tony detected a hint of sadness in them. He turned to look at Jean-Paul who nodded, then faced Vincent as they began the planned questioning.

"Monsieur Artois. We are French patriots. Can you say the same?"

Vincent nodded. "Of course, Monsieur. My country is vitally important to me."

"Then you must realise that the future of our country can only lie with the Germans."

Vincent said nothing, but Tony noticed the slight frown and was encouraged.

"We work for the SS" he continued, "and have had a certain member of your household under surveillance for some time."

Vincent felt cold. He struggled not to show the fear which settled in the pit of his stomach like a lead weight. Finally he found his voice.

"I don't understand."

"We mean the young lady who has been living and working here for the past few months. What do you know of her?"

Vincent turned to answer Jean-Paul's question. "Very little. She was looking for lodgings and work, and I was able to provide both. That's all."

"Where is she now?"

"Shopping."

Tony approached the counter and placed his hands on it, putting all his weight on them as he leant forward and glared directly into Vincent's eyes.

"Some of her movements have been suspicious. We believe she may be working against the interests of France. Are you willing to help us to trap her?"

Vincent's mind was in a turmoil. Of course he was not willing. But if he were to say so then his life would be forfeit. The best he could hope for was to try to gain some time and warn Angeline. After a moment's hesitation he nodded.

"Of course. What do you want me to do?"

"Keep a note of her movements and the people she meets. One of us will call back each day to see if you have any information for us." Tony's face was inscrutable as he stepped back from the counter. "France will not forget what you do."

'Neither will she forget you' thought Vincent, but he said nothing as his two visitors turned and left the bakery. He wiped his clammy hands on his apron and moved round the counter to close the door and put up the closed sign. The two men were standing talking on the pavement. He turned away, not wanting them to see him watching. A deep frown furrowing his brow, Vincent made his way upstairs to change. Somehow he had to warn Angeline.

"So far so good." Tony smiled grimly at Jean-Paul. "Either he's a good liar, or he is willing to sacrifice Angeline. Let's see what he does next."

The two men slipped into the baker's yard, and hid while they waited for the return of Angeline.

When Angeline entered the baker's yard she was not aware of Jean-Paul and Tony. They had concealed themselves well. With a worried frown, the radio operator leant her bicycle against the wall and made her way towards the kitchen door. She had expected a message from Tony to tell her what to do about Vincent, but there was nothing at the drop, and she did not know what to do. Pushing open the door, she made her way inside. She found Vincent sitting at the table. He was staring at a cup of coffee which had long since gone cold on the table in front of him. At the sound of the closing door he started, a frightened look in his eyes. Then he relaxed slightly as though he had been expecting someone else, and was relieved to see that it was only Angeline. He stood up and began to pace agitatedly across the floor. Outside in the yard Tony and Jean-Paul made their way over to the window. They crouched below its sill to hear what, if anything, Vincent told Angeline about his two visitors. They did not have long to wait.

"Angeline! I'm glad it's you!" He stopped pacing and faced her across the kitchen table. "I've had a visit from two men working for the SS. They say they've had you under surveillance, and they want me to help them spy on you!"

Angeline was stunned. She thought she had been so careful. How had they managed to get on to her?

"I shall have to leave."

Vincent nodded. "It's the only solution. You should pack and go now, before they come back. Don't tell me where you're going. If you don't tell me, I can't give you away."

"Aren't you coming too? Surely they'll suspect you if I disappear now?"

Vincent shrugged. "Maybe. But I've lived here all my life, and I don't want to leave. I'll say that you must have become aware of them watching, and you left without speaking to me."

"What happens if they don't believe you?"

"I won't be able to tell them where you've gone. You'll be safe. Do not worry about me, I can take care of myself." Vincent walked around the table and put a comforting arm around Angeline's shoulders. "Now pack your things and go."

"That won't be necessary." The voice came from the doorway and the kitchen door opened to reveal Jean-Paul and Tony. Angeline opened her mouth to say something, but Vincent did not give her a chance. Pushing her behind him, he grabbed a bread knife from the kitchen table.

"These are the men I told you about, Angeline. Get away from here while I hold them off."

"But I don't understand!" Angeline looked blankly at Tony, then Vincent, and finally back to Tony. "I don't know the older of these two men, Vincent, but the younger one is a British agent too." She laid a calming hand on the Frenchman's arm. "Put down the knife, Vincent."

The baker frowned but did not give up his weapon. Neither did he take his eyes from Tony, who was now smiling at him.

"That's right, Vincent. Angeline sent me a message when you caught her with her radio. We paid you that little visit this afternoon to test you."

"To see if I would betray Angeline?"

Tony nodded. "I'm glad to say you passed the test with flying colours."

"What would have happened if I hadn't? No...don't tell me. I think I can guess." Vincent hesitated for a moment, then put the knife back onto the table.

Angeline glared angrily at Tony. "That was a pretty mean trick, Albert."

Tony and Jean-Paul came fully into the room, closing the door behind them.

"I know, but I needed to be certain that you were safe. I could have taken the easy option, you know."

Angeline nodded, and Vincent frowned.

"You mean kill me without putting me to the test?" When Tony nodded in reply, Vincent sat down. "This has all happened so quickly. But now perhaps you'll believe me when I say that I can be trusted and that I want to work with the Resistance."

Tony laughed. "We have no doubt about that at all. I'll let you know when and how we can use you." He held out a hand to the Frenchman, who stood and shook it warmly. "Welcome to our little group, Vincent."

102

Karl Dresner stood to attention, tight lipped and silent, wishing he could be anywhere else but here. The communiqué he had brought for Major Steinhauser, the cause of the man's displeasure, lay innocently on the desk, studiously ignored by Dresner and the object of Steinhauser's furious outburst.

"Did you read it, Karl?" He did not wait for an answer. He paced the width of his office, his usually handsome Aryan features contorted by his feelings. "They're sending General Wolffe here to visit us. They make it sound like a normal visit, but what they're really saying is that we've had too much trouble from the Resistance in the last few months. General Wolffe is coming to find out why we haven't crushed this group by now. It makes me so angry!" He stopped his pacing and faced his subordinate. "They'll say that we haven't tried hard enough, that we're bringing the SS into disrepute."

"I'm sure that the General will say no such thing."

Steinhauser laughed mercilessly at Dresner's comment.

"Of course he won't say it outright. He'll just say how unfortunate it is that this rabble is still freely roaming the countryside, maybe a fresh outlook would help? Damn it! Next he'll be suggesting that I might like to apply for a transfer to the Russian front! We have got to do something, Karl, and do it before General Wolffe arrives."

He frowned. "Wolffe is merciless, Karl. He has been stationed in northern France. A good number of British planes have been shot down there. They couldn't find most of the pilots. Wolffe eventually narrowed down his suspects to a small village. No-one would give up the people who were helping the pilots, so he had the whole village shot. Over three hundred men, women and children, Karl. Then he burned the place to the ground."

"You think he is coming here to do something similar?"

"Who knows? But the chances are that someone thinks we are not doing a good enough job."

Suddenly the Major stopped his tirade. His eyes narrowed as his thoughts came together. After a moment he smiled, a smile of malicious humour.

"Maybe we can use the Herr General's visit to help to show us in a good light."

"Sir?"

"If you were in the Resistance, or an enemy agent, what would you do if you knew that a high ranking general responsible for such actions was about to pay a visit?"

"I suppose I might try to assassinate him, sir"

"Good. That's what I thought."

"But the Resistance doesn't know that General Wolffe is coming."

"No, not yet. But they will, Karl." Steinhauser made his way over to his desk and sat down. He leant back into the leather chair and put his feet up on its highly polished surface. "I want you to spruce up all of our troops, ready for inspection. I want them to know that the general is coming. The information is bound to leak out. I also want you to plan a route of entry for him, make sure it has two or three positions along it ideal to conceal an assassin, then leave copies of that lying around H.Q. There's bound to be some scum here who would sell such information to the Resistance."

"Won't we be putting the general's life in danger?"

Steinhauser laughed. "Of course! But this is war! We will do everything in our power to ensure that he is not hurt. But," he grinned, "the death of Herr General Wolffe would be no great loss in my eyes. It may even help to speed up the promotion I've been seeking, especially if I manage to catch the assassin."

He took his feet from the desk and sat up, leaning forward to hold Dresner's eyes with his own icy blue ones.

"I want our best men watching all possible sites an assassin might use. If anyone tries anything, they are to move in. Make sure that they know that I want this man alive, Karl. They can shoot to wound and slow him down, but if anyone kills him I'll have him transferred to the Russian Front. And I'll make sure that he doesn't come back. Understand?"

"Yes, sir."

"Good. The leader of this group is mine, and I want him alive." He grinned. "Alive when I get him, that is. By the time I've finished with him he'll wish he was dead!"

103

"Are you sure you want to do this, Albert?"

"No. I'm not sure. But London wants him out of the way, so I have to do it. They must have their reasons. They will know the dangers. I'd rather be lying low with the rest of you. This is too much of a risk, but it has to be done."

"Are you sure your plan will work?"

Tony shrugged as he walked along the lane beside his friend. "I don't know, Jean-Paul. The details of the general's movements which Georges got are pretty good, as long as they are accurate; but it's still very risky and I don't want to put anyone else in danger. I have to make this hit alone."

"Maybe so, my friend. But we must have someone else there to know what happens, to report to Angeline if things go wrong, or to cover your back on your escape."

"You will not cover me, Jean-Paul, I forbid it. I can see that I won't be able to persuade you to stay away, but you mustn't get involved, no matter what happens. Is that clear?"

The Frenchman nodded sadly. "Yes, Albert. But I won't pretend that I like it."

"No one expects you to. But it's the safest way. You have too much to lose, a wife, children. This is far too dangerous for you."

"Surely no more than any other attack we've made?"

Tony frowned. "I don't know. The information that Georges got for me is too detailed. It seemed too easy for him to acquire. I have a funny feeling about all this."

"Then don't do it."

"But I have to, Jean-Paul. I don't know what this general has done. But if my bosses want him out of the way, then I must do all I can to accomplish that. No one else need risk their life. It's probably not a bad idea for you to be in the area, in case something goes wrong. But you will be unarmed, and there will be nothing to link you with me. That is how it has to be."

"All right, Albert. You're the boss."

"If it is a set-up and something goes wrong, you'll be able to take over the running of the group for the time being and get a message to Angeline."

The two men entered the outskirts of the city and moved through the suburbs towards Tony's chosen spot. They were half a mile away when Tony stopped.

"Right, Jean-Paul. This is where we split up. You go to the café where you can watch what happens, but don't get involved. Understand?"

"Yes, Albert."

The two men looked at each other for a few moments; there was so much to say yet no words to say it.

Jean-Paul held out his hand. "Good luck, my friend."

Tony took the hand and gripped it tightly. "Good luck to you too. It's been a pleasure working with you."

He turned and walked away.

Tony stood by the intersection of two roads, and reviewed his plan. The general's car would come along one street, then slow to turn left. That was when Tony would shoot him, before making his getaway down the alley behind him, dumping the gun and mingling with the customers at one of the pavement cafés. He did not really like the plan. Too many things could go wrong, and his chances of getting away were slim. But he had no choice. Slipping his hand into his pocket, he felt the smooth outline of the pistol, his only weapon for the attack. He wondered again if he was doing the right thing. He glanced around him, his casual movements masking the careful scrutiny as he noted all details of the people around him. Were any acting suspiciously? Was he under surveillance? He saw Jean-Paul sitting at a pavement cafe across the road but showed no sign of recognition.

Tony heard the sound of an approaching vehicle, and turned towards it. An open-topped staff car flying the red, black and white flag of the Third Reich, was moving towards him. He slipped his right hand into his pocket to grip the butt of his gun and pull it to make sure it was not caught on the material. It moved freely. He breathed deeply, once, twice, and concentrated on the approaching car. The general was seated in the rear. The only other occupant was his driver, while the car was flanked by four motorcycle outriders. The car slowed as it approached the corner. Tony pulled the gun from his pocket and levelled it, arm stretched out straight in front of him. As the car

297

drew level, he pulled the trigger once, twice, three times. In the rear of the vehicle the general threw up his arms in pain and horror, a deep red stain spreading on the front of his tunic. At the sound of the shots, the driver of the car put his foot down hard. The vehicle leapt forwards, too late for the general, whose blood pooled on the floor of the car as he slumped over the back seat.

As Tony turned to run, he saw the four motorcycles screech to a halt. The riders reached for their weapons as they leapt free and began to pursue him. It was as Tony had expected, and he was ready. As long as he was able to get to the end of the alleyway before they began shooting, he should be able to make it. He threw his head back, opening his airways to take gulp after gulp of air to feed his muscles. His legs and arms pumped, forcing him down the alleyway faster than he had ever run before in his life. Behind him he heard the footsteps of the outriders, and waited for the sound of their guns. He felt so vulnerable, his back a huge target for them to aim at, but to stop turn and fire on them would be suicidal. He would just have to keep running and hope that they missed. As he neared the end of the alleyway, his mind was racing. Why had they failed to open fire? His breathing was ragged and there was a sharp pain in his chest when he saw a group of shadows moving at the end of the alleyway, yards ahead. Tony slowed to a walk then stopped. Six soldiers barred his way, rifles levelled at his chest.

Slowly Tony turned around. The four soldiers who had been chasing him also stopped, guns levelled. Tony's heart sank. He was cornered. It was obviously a trap, why else would they have held their fire? Slowly he dropped his arms to his sides, his fingers releasing the gun. It fell to the ground at his feet with a clatter. Over the shoulders of the soldiers who were now walking towards him, Tony could see a crowd gathered in the entrance to the alley, the figure of Jean-Paul prominent in their midst. For a moment their eyes met and held, then Tony broke the contact. Turning to meet the gaze of the closest soldier, he raised his hands above his head and waited.

AUGUST 1942

104

The summer of 1942 produced many a dark day for the people of England. In June, the North African army eventually gave up the unequal struggle to retain control of Tobruk. They withdrew, falling back to El Alamein and leaving some thirty-five thousand of their number en route, to be taken by the advancing Germans and incarcerated for the remainder of the war. The shattered British people saw it as a bad omen, almost as bad as the fall of Singapore. Britain was retreating in all theatres of war, the only Allied successes seemed to come from the Americans in the Far East. In July, Convoy PQ17, taking badly needed supplies to beleaguered Russia, supplies which the British could hardly spare from their scant resources, was hit by submarines which sank twenty-four out of the thirty-five merchantmen, and further depressed the spirit of the British people. Rations were cut even further, Those who had felt that they could not survive on the food they were allowed now found themselves managing on even less. Coal was running short. Priority went to fuelling the power stations to provide electricity for vital war industries leaving little for domestic consumption, a fact that did not matter in the summer heat; but thoughts were already turning to the cold winter months ahead. Those who could began to build up pitifully small stocks of coal to see them through the days to come. Things looked bad. The euphoria of America's entry into the war faded quickly in the face of the harsh realities of life in war torn Britain. Little did the people realise that more disasters awaited them just around the corner.

105

It was such a hot summer's day that Sarah and Jane decided to walk down to the river. The weeping willows leant low over the bank, the tip of their branches trailing in the slow-moving water; there was a rustling in the reeds to their right and a heron took to the air, long legs stretched out behind it, neck tucked in. As Sarah drank in the beauty of the scene, she sighed. Why had she been sent to Heronfield? It was true that if she had been sent to a different hospital she would never have grown to love the countryside as she had, to feel at one with the peace and beauty of the Heronfield Estate; but also she would never have met and grown to love Tony. Where one of the loves brought peace and tranquility to her soul, the other brought nothing but pain. She was resigned to the fact that although she loved Tony and always would, he, despite his assurances to the contrary, cared little for her. It puzzled her. From what she had come to know of the young man who was now heir to the Kemshall fortune, he was kind and considerate; he was aware of other people's feelings and tried hard not to upset them. So why had he not written to her from America? Even if her letters had not reached him, he had no excuse not to write to her; after all, the address was his own home. If he had not written, it was because he did not want to. Either his relationship with her had been nothing but a sham, a pretence of love to fill the empty hours of his leave, or he had cared for her but had now found someone else to take her place. However much it might hurt to know that he had found someone he loved more than her, it would be nothing to the pain of knowing that he had used her, that he had never cared at all, never meant any of the things he said. With a sigh she tried to put it all to the back of her mind. The reasons for his not writing were irrelevant. She knew that their relationship was over. She would have to come to terms with that, though it would not be easy living and working in his home, surrounded by memories of their time together.

The two friends walked on in companionable silence. Jane realised the direction of Sarah's thoughts and did not want to intrude, content to be there as moral support. She felt sorry for Sarah. To have loved two men, only to have one killed and the other leave her, was a pain she hoped she would never have to contend with. She knew little of love. She was still waiting for her 'mister right' to come into her life. But she knew she would be careful in her relationships, after seeing the heartache her friend had endured.

The quiet of their walk was disturbed by a shout, and the two girls turned to see another nurse running down the grassy slope from Heronfield House, waving as she ran. The friends waited for the nurse to approach. When she arrived she stood breathlessly for a moment before beginning to speak.

"Sister wants you back at the hospital."

"But we're off duty. What does she want?"

The nurse shrugged at Jane's question. "I don't know exactly. All I can tell you is that there's some sort of emergency. Everyone who's off duty is to get back into uniform, then report to the entrance hall where we'll be briefed."

Sarah frowned. "Has there been some bombing in the area? I haven't heard any planes."

"I don't know. All I know is that you're to report immediately. Sister will be giving her briefing in half an hour."

A little over twenty-five minutes later, the two young women made their way down the curving staircase into the crowded hall. They had just had time to change into their uniforms, though they could see from the odd splash of colour that some people had not. As they joined their colleagues, there was intense speculation about what was happening. A few minutes later Sister Freeman appeared, and an expectant hush fell on the assembled nurses. After perusing them for a moment she began to speak.

"I'm sorry to call you all here, but it's an emergency. There's been an Allied landing somewhere on the northern coast of France." Murmurs of astonishment swept through the assembled nurses. They were soon silenced by a wave of the sister's hand. "I'm sorry to have to report that it was a failure. Thousands of wounded are expected back here in the next few hours. I'm afraid it will be a little like Dunkirk all over again. Most of the wounded will have received little or no treatment before they reach us." There was silence as the sister's sad eyes scanned the upturned faces. "We're moving all of our convalescing patients to hospitals further north. It will only be hospitals like ours in the south of England who will be taking the wounded. You're to help transfer the convalescing patients, prepare beds and operating theatres, then get what rest you can. We expect the first wounded in three or four hours. Any questions?"

There were none, and Sister Freeman dismissed them. Those who had seen the wounded from Dunkirk moved silently, aware of what was coming, while those who had not been at Heronfield during the evacuation were chattering excitedly. Sarah frowned grimly. Little did they know how harrowing the next few hours would be.

To those who had no experience of treating the wounded who had come directly from the battlefield, the following twenty-four hours were like a nightmare. Bloodstained bandages were wrapped around bullet and shrapnel wounds in arms, legs, torsos, heads. Uniforms had to be carefully cut away and the wounds of the suffering casualties washed, before they were sent down to the operating theatre where the doctors worked to repair flesh torn by the stupidity of man. Yet for those who had treated the evacuees from Dunkirk, the situation was not as dreadful as they had anticipated. This time there were no filthy uniforms of men who had spent days on the beaches and in sea water; no bandages stuck to wounds with an encrusting film of sand, dirt and blood; no weakness from lack of food and water; no smell of rotting flesh and putrescence from wounds left too long without medical attention. This time the nurses were able to deal with fresh wounds, and patients whose strength had not been sapped by days and nights of fear.

It was the late afternoon of the following day when Sarah finally had time to sit back for a moment and take stock of the situation. All of the beds in her ward were occupied by soldiers now cleaned of the grime of battle, wounds dressed, bodies finally sedated and at rest. She still did not know exactly what had happened at Dieppe, no one did. But from what many of the wounded had said, or screamed, in their pain wracked beds, it had been a shambles. No cover from sea or air! How could they have been expected to make progress?

Sarah was seated at the desk in the small ward. She leant back in her chair, closing her eyes and massaging her temples as though to drive away the tiredness and pain. It had been so like the days she had spent in Coventry after the bombing, only this time there were enough medical supplies, beds and food. Yet the pain and suffering of recent injuries were still the same. As she sat, her mind on the edge of sleep, she again saw Tony lying in a hospital bed while his injuries from the bombing raid were treated, accidental wounds rather than wounds caused in the heat of battle. Opening her tired eyes, she looked from one patient to the next. Each individual was suffering because he had laid his life on the line for his country. Unexpectedly, she felt a deep up welling of anger. Not only had Tony failed to keep in touch with her while he was in America, but it seemed to her that he had spent the entire war trying to avoid action. Maybe his father was right. Maybe Tony was a coward. Perhaps his experiences at Dunkirk and the loss of his brother had driven him to seek out a safe job for the duration. How could a healthy young man like him not take his place beside the brave young men who had stormed the beaches of Dieppe?

For the first time, Sarah believed that at last she saw Tony for what he really was, a shallow young man who did not take his relationships seriously, who was not willing to make sacrifices for his country but was prepared to let others fight, and die, for him. A coward of the worst kind. Deep inside her a voice whispered, 'No, you're wrong. That's not the Tony you know. You're just tired.' But she determined to ignore the voice, ruthlessly burying her true feelings for Tony and in her mind, though not in her heart, finally making her break from him. Tears flowed down her cheeks and she brushed them away, blaming it on tiredness after twenty-four hours on her feet, determined not to relate it to the crushing pain she felt deep in her heart.

106

Whilst the disastrous assault on the beaches of Dieppe were still in the planning stages, Tony Kemshall was taken from the alleyway where he had been taken prisoner. The German soldiers pushed him roughly into the back of an armoured car, and climbed in beside him before closing the doors. The engine was already running. It was revved up and the vehicle shot forward taking back streets to avoid the crowds gathered at the scene of the shooting. Within twenty minutes it pulled up outside the Headquarters of the SS. As the car drew to a halt, the rear doors were flung open and the soldiers jumped down, dragging Tony behind them by the collar of his jacket. He fell to the road. His hands were grazed by the rough surface, and he grimaced. The pain was slight, but he saw it as a forerunner of what was in store for him in the huge building in front of him. As he knelt in the road a rifle butt descended. It caught him a crushing blow in the side which caused him to fall prostrate, biting his lip to keep from crying out. Tony struggled for breath as a hand grabbed him by the arm and began to drag him towards the steps.

"Schnell! Schnell!"

At the harsh cry, Tony hauled himself painfully to his feet. He stumbled across the pavement and up the steps which led into the dark interior of the building. As the door closed behind him, Tony felt as though the world he had known had been closed to him forever. All he had to look forward to was here in this dark, depressing building. He had no misconceptions about what lay ahead. The SS would do all that they could to force him to divulge information on his group, and he knew that if they ever found out that he was British he would be severely tortured before they executed him. Offering a silent prayer that he would be able to stand up to the interrogation, he allowed himself to be marched away, an armed soldier on either side, along corridors and up stairs until they halted outside the office of Major Steinhauser. The door was open, and Tony could see the major sitting at his desk. At the sound of their footsteps the officer looked up from the papers he had been signing, a broad grin on his face.

"Ah, Karl, see what we have here."

Sergeant Dresner, who stood behind the Majors chair, grinned too.

"It seems that you plan worked, Herr Major."

"Dismiss the guards, Karl, and bring the prisoner in."

Dresner withdrew his gun from its holster and held it pointing directly at Tony, before ordering the guards to wait outside. He waved his hand with the gun in it, indicating that Tony should enter. The young Englishman took a deep breath and stepped forward into the room. Dresner closed the door behind him.

"Name?"

Tony boldly held the gaze of the SS major.

"Albert Fouqet."

Address?"

"22 Rue Blanc Saint Nazaire."

The major leant back in his chair, a thin-lipped smile on his face which did not reach the icy cold depths of his blue eyes.

"I don't suppose for one minute that that is true. Do you wish to elaborate?"

Tony said nothing, standing straight, tall, defiant.

"From your demeanour," continued Steinhauser "I would guess that you are a soldier." He waited for a moment, but Tony said nothing. "Are you a soldier of the French army or from another country?"

"I am not a soldier. My name is Albert Fouqet. I live at 22 Rue Blanc, Saint Nazaire."

"Do you believe him, Karl?"

Dresner shook his head.

"Neither do I. Take him down to the cells. He's to have no food, water or sleep until I see him again at this time tomorrow." His eyes bored into Tony's. "While you're down there, young man, I suggest that you think carefully about your situation. You have attacked an officer of the Third Reich, and you must pay the consequences. You could make it easier for yourself if you tell me all there is to know about your Resistance group." He looked across at his sergeant. "Get him out of here, Karl. Once he's locked up safely, we must find out what has happened to General Wolffe."

Tony sat on the cold stone floor of what had once been a cellar, but which now served as a prison for the SS who had commandeered the building above. He was cold, hungry and thirsty, but most of all he was tired, so very, very tired. He had been in the room for twenty-four hours, it had been thirty six hours since he last slept, and the guards would not allow him to sleep. He was not even allowed to sit down. As soon as the key was turned in the lock, he would have to leap to his feet and look as though he had not sat down at all. He knew that the door would be opened any moment now. The guards rarely left him alone for more than two or three minutes. There had been someone with him almost continuously since he had been taken, and although the guards were able to get their rest and food at regular intervals, there were no such luxuries for him. The cold of the cellar had crept into his bones, and he found it painful to move. His feet had gone through a period of icy painfulness, but now were mercifully numb. His hands, tied behind his back, had lost all feeling, as had his lower arms, and he wondered if he would ever be able to move them again. His eyes were dry and itched terribly, the eyelids heavy and continuously falling as his body sought to find relief in sleep. He licked his dry lips and tried to swallow. The welcoming arms of sleep were reaching out to him, and his head began to fall forwards onto his chest. The sudden harsh grating of the key in the lock caused him to jerk fully awake once more. He climbed painfully to his feet as the door opened, to admit two guards who pointed their guns menacingly at his chest.

"Come. Schnell."

Tony stumbled towards the door at the order. He was afraid, more afraid than he had ever been before. His experiences on the road to Dunkirk and on the beaches had been frightening, but then the destruction and hate had not been directed towards him as an individual, merely as one of a heaving mass of humanity. Those thousands of men suffering the same fears as him had helped him to remain strong, had supported him in his hour of need. Now he was alone. There were no soldiers to help him. Indeed he had to try to conceal the very fact that he was a soldier, to pretend to be someone and something he was not. This time the hatred and the violence were aimed directly at him. Upstairs a major in the infamous SS was awaiting him, ready to use any means within his power to make him talk, and Tony was not unaware that his means and his malice were great. Tony's face remained impassive, betraying nothing of the fear which filled his heart and his mind. Head held high, he marched between the two soldiers and up the cold stone stairs to the third floor where he had met Major Steinhauser for the first time twenty-four hours before. That had been a brief encounter, but he knew that today's would be longer and far more painful. As the two soldiers marched him through the open door, he focussed his mind on his cover story, determined he would give nothing away under interrogation. 'I am Albert Fouqet. I am Albert Fouqet. I am Albert Fouqet.' The mantra whirled round and round in his mind, and, as he faced the figure across the desk, he felt he was ready.

The door closed behind him with an ominous thud. Tony was conscious of the two soldiers standing behind him as Steinhauser rose from his seat and walked round to the front of the desk. He leant back, sitting on the edge of the polished wood and stretching his long legs, encased in shiny leather boots, out in front of him. Folding his arms across his chest, he surveyed the prisoner in his French peasant clothing. Finally he spoke.

"What is your name?"

"Albert Fouqet."

"You still insist on using that name? Never mind." His lips twisted into an evil smile. "Well, Monsieur Fouqet, General Wolffe is dead." He waited to see if there was a response, but Tony said nothing. The expression on his face did not change, but his mind was racing. He would be executed for the assassination, but at least it had been successful. Steinhauser watched him closely

"You fired the fatal shot, did you not?"

"It would be pointless to deny it. Your men followed me from the ambush and took the gun from me."

"Just so. Didn't you wonder how they got to you so quickly?"

Tony said nothing.

"We knew that you would try it. So we set up our own little ambush at all the places where you might make the attempt."

Tony still did not respond, and Steinhauser's temper began to rise. He wanted the prisoner to admit that he had been outwitted, but he refused to talk. The major stood up and took a step forward, so that he was separated from Tony by only a few inches.

"You see that we know who you are." His voice was icy, full of malice, and Tony had to fight hard to remain calm before the direct gaze. "We guessed that whoever was leading the local Resistance must be a foreign spy, and we knew that you would have to try for the General. Now tell me about your Resistance group. I promise that your death will be swift and relatively painless."

"My name is Albert Fouqet. I shot the General, but I know nothing of the Resistance or foreign spies."

Steinhauser stepped back and signalled one of the soldiers, who stepped forward and turned to face the prisoner. Tony blanched at the sight of the rubber truncheon.

"I warn you, this is going to be very painful. You will tell me what I want to know in the end, they all do. Make it easier on yourself, Monsieur Fouqet. Answer my questions now."

"I have nothing to say."

The soldier turned an enquiring look at Steinhauser, who nodded. With a malicious grin the soldier raised the truncheon and brought it down across the Englishman's ribs. Tony's body jerked, and he stumbled, his tied hands making it difficult for his tired body to retain its balance. The soldier raised the truncheon again and brought it down methodically, each blow landing with a sickening thud. The implement was well designed. It was hard but had enough flexibility to prevent it from breaking bones. The poor soul who was on the receiving end would be severely bruised, but bruises heal quicker than breaks, and he would soon be well enough to undergo a similar treatment once more. The soldier carried out the beating slowly, steadily, as though he were striking a piece of wood, caring nothing for the pain he was inflicting. Tony stood straight, staring directly at Steinhauser as the beating began, his lips tight and a frown furrowing his brow as he fought desperately against the need to cry out at the agony flooding his body. Every inch of his upper body was subjected to a blow; the sensations of pain filled his mind, and his body, weakened from lack of food, water and sleep began to succumb to the terrifying treatment. Slowly his head fell forward onto his chest, jerking up again at each blow. His eyes were closed and his legs weak and shaking, but he still refused to cry out. Finally he could take no more and slumped to his knees. As his breath came in ragged gasps, his head bowed low upon his chest, he gradually became aware that the blows had ceased. He raised his head and opened his eyes, to see Major Steinhauser standing above him.

"Who are you? What are the names of the rest of your group?" barked the SS officer.

Tony forced his answer through teeth clenched tight against the pain which suffused his body, but his eyes were direct.

"I am Albert Fouqet. I belong to no group."

Steinhauser was angry and kicked out, the toes of his well-polished boot contacting with Tony's stomach and knocking the air from his lungs. Tony doubled over in agony as Steinhauser's boot caught him again and again in the ribs. His vision was blurred and there was a terrible racing noise in his ears. He fell onto his side, hitting the floor hard as he was unable to use his hands to save himself. Steinhauser continued to kick the prostrate form three, four, five times, but now there was no response. Tony was barely conscious, his eyes closed and the sounds of the room coming and going like waves upon a distant shore. He vaguely heard the major's voice as though it came from miles away.

"Get him out of here. I'll see him again in the morning." The two soldiers stepped towards the battered and bloodied figure. As they reached down to haul him to his feet, fresh waves of agony coursed through Tony's tortured body. As he slipped towards blessed oblivion, the last thing he was conscious of was Steinhauser's voice.

"And send someone up here to clean my boots. This filthy pig has bled all over them!"

107

Jean-Paul walked determinedly down the street towards the bakery. Ever since the moment when his eyes had locked with Tony's his mind had been in turmoil. He stood for a time in the midst of the silent crowd, subliminally aware of their feelings of happiness, however well-disguised, at the death of a German officer. All the time his mind was a whirling confusion of thoughts. What would the group do without Tony? Who would lead them? More importantly, would he betray them? Jean-Paul knew that he would not do it in order to save his own life, but what if others were threatened? What if they tortured him until he could no longer resist? As he turned and began to make his way home, sick at heart at having to leave Tony in the hands of the SS, the thoughts whirled around Jean-Paul's mind until he finally came to the inevitable conclusion. However much he disliked the idea, there were only two choices. Either they must help Tony to escape or make sure that he was unable to talk.

Jean-Paul spent the remainder of that day and the long hours of the night deep in thought at his home. But no matter how hard he tried, he could find no other solution. They should try to get Tony out, there was no other way. After a long sleepless night, Jean-Paul set out for the city at dawn. He approached the bakery later in the morning after Vincent's regular customers had been. It would give him time to be alone with Angeline and Vincent, to discuss what should be done. The bakery was empty when he entered. He closed the door, put up the closed sign and made his way behind the counter and through to the living area beyond. He found Vincent and Angeline sitting at the kitchen table. They looked up in surprise as he entered.

"Jean-Paul! What are you doing here?"

"I'm sorry to intrude, Vincent, but I must speak to Angeline."

Angeline looked up from her coffee.

"We heard about the shooting, and that the assassin was arrested. It was Albert, wasn't it?"

Jean-Paul nodded, glad that he would not have to be the one to break the news.

"What do you plan to do?"

Jean-Paul turned to Vincent and shrugged. "I'm not sure. All I know is that we have to get him out of there. Do you have any suggestions?"

Angeline gave a sad smile which did not quite reach her eyes. "We've thought of little else all night. We think we have a plan. Do you think someone in the group could get hold of some German uniforms?"

Jean-Paul shrugged. "I don't know. I suppose it's possible."

"Good. The plan is that your friends dress up as German soldiers and pretend that they've taken me prisoner. We go into SS H.Q. and down to the cells, where we release Albert."

"Then what? The whole German army will be looking for him. Where can we hide him?"

"Leave that to me." Angeline poured a coffee for Jean-Paul as she spoke. "I'll get in touch with London, and try to arrange for a plane to pick him up. I'll leave you to get the group organised. As soon as London let me know when the pick-up will be, I'll be in touch."

"You will tell them to be quick, won't you? I doubt if Albert is having an easy time of it."

Angeline frowned. "I know, but he's trained to cope with this sort of thing. We'll just have to hope that he can hold out until we get to him."

"You've been trained too, Angeline. If the SS find out you're a spy, you will be dead, and we would have no more contact with England. Maybe you shouldn't come with us on the rescue."

"But I must help! Albert would do the same for me!"

"Perhaps you haven't thought it out fully." Jean-Paul sat at the table and leant earnestly towards her. "Madeleine or one of the others could just as easily pretend to be a prisoner, but would any of them be able to set up a runway to allow the plane to land?"

Angeline bowed her head and sat silently for a moment before finally nodding.

"You're right, Jean-Paul. If the runway isn't set up properly it will jeopardise the whole operation. I'll get in touch with London and make all the arrangements. You get the group organised and I'll be in touch. Do you know the log where I leave messages for Albert?" Jean-Paul nodded. "Good. I'll leave a message for you there. I'll only have twenty-four hours notice of the plane coming, and that could change with adverse weather conditions. So we must be flexible. Understand?"

Jean-Paul nodded. "Yes. There's just one problem. If Georges and I pretend to be Germans and take Madeleine as our prisoner, we'll have to leave the car unattended. How can we be sure it won't be moved while we're in the SS H.Q.?"

"Easy. I'll drive."

Angeline and Jean-Paul both turned towards Vincent.

"Are you sure?"

Vincent nodded. "Of course. I told you I wanted to help, didn't I? I may not be young or fit anymore, but I can still drive a car."

Jean-Paul smiled. "Thank you. Now," he rose to his feet as he spoke, "I'd better be going. I have a lot to do." He walked towards the door then turned to the couple seated at the table. "I'll wait to hear from you, Angeline."

With that he turned and was gone.

108

Tony lay on the cold stone floor of the cell, his body wracked with pain. Thinking that he might be forced to stand for hours at a time once the guards realised that he was conscious, Tony kept his eyes closed and began to make a mental check of his condition.

Someone had untied his hands and he wriggled his fingers experimentally. They all moved and did not appear to be damaged. His whole torso ached where he had been beaten by the soldier, but there was a far more searing pain in his chest. Slowly he took in a deep breath, expanding his lungs to the maximum, and the agony increased. Apart from using his hands to check the damage, a movement which would obviously attract the guard's attention, there was no way of finding out how badly hurt he was. He guessed that his ribs had been badly bruised, some of them probably fractured, by the boot of the SS major.

Tony was stiff and cold. His body cried out for warmth, for food and for water, but he made no move. He realised that the beating was just the beginning of the interrogation. Things would get much worse before the Germans executed him. His mind and his body needed to rest as much as possible. He needed to hang on to whatever reserves of strength he had, in order to resist the coming questioning.

As he lay on the floor, Tony's mind sought refuge in happier times. He imagined himself at Heronfield, basking in the warm summer sun. The strength of his longing and the weakness of his body helped to banish the chilling cold from his thoughts, and gave him respite for a time. His closed eyes saw everything brighter, clearer than it really was. But he did not care. The image he had created to comfort him in his suffering allowed him to walk hand in hand with Sarah, beside the crystal waters of the river, and watch as a heron took flight from the lush reed beds. In his mind Sarah squeezed his hand gently, and he turned to look at her as a brilliant smile danced across her lips. The sun behind her head caught the auburn hair, shining through to create a golden halo about her head. Her eyes fixed on his, full of love and longing, and he leant down to kiss the soft, warm, welcoming lips.

The guard by the door frowned. He had watched over many prisoners who had been beaten, but this was the first to have smiled in his agony.

Tony was not able to keep the fact that he had regained consciousness from the guard for more than an hour. As he lay still upon the floor the pain increased, and forced the images of home and of the woman he loved from his mind. Finally he had had to move to relieve his discomfort. The guard was swift to pounce.

"On your feet, swine."

He dragged the battered man to his feet, forcing an involuntary cry of pain from his lips in the process, then looked him over. Eventually he smiled grimly.

"You'll live. For a time."

Tony said nothing, but began to slowly flex his arms and legs to relieve the tension in his muscles, then he paced back and forth across the cell to bring warmth back to his chilled body. Finally he stood beneath the naked light bulb and waited. The hours passed slowly, hours when in his mind he relived the horrors of the war as he had seen it, the road to Dunkirk, the beaches, David's death, the brutality of the occupying forces in Saint Nazaire, the swastika flying above his grandmother's home, the injuries and deaths of his comrades who had fought beside him. He reviewed the facts again and again, focussing on the horror and the pain, determined to build up his hatred for the Germans so high that he would never give in. But he tired quickly in his weakened condition. As the hours passed, his thoughts became less coherent. His head began to fall onto his chest as he slipped towards the welcoming arms of sleep only to be brought brutally back to the present by a punch from the guard, causing fresh agony to sweep through his bruised and battered body.

Tony did not know how many of those endless hours passed before the routine was finally broken, and the door opened to admit a second soldier. For a moment, Tony thought that it was just the regular changing of his guard, but then he noticed that the other man was carrying a small card table, which he placed on the floor to the right of the door. He went out, only to reappear moments later with a jug of water and a glass which he placed on the table, and a bucket which he put on the floor. Tony licked his cracked and dry lips, his eyes focussed longingly on the water. He did not see the two men who entered next. He became aware of them as the first placed a chair beside the table. It was the soldier who had administered the beating to Tony, a face he would never forget and which would haunt his nightmares for months to come, if he lived that long. The last to enter the cell was Steinhauser who walked casually over to the chair and sat down, legs stretched out in front of him in his habitual manner. He perused the prisoner.

"Do you wish to answer my questions now?"

"I have nothing to say." Tony's voice was cracked and hoarse.

Steinhauser slowly poured a glass of water. The sound was torture to Tony as he watched the crystal clear liquid flow from one receptacle to another. He would have licked his dry lips, but his tongue felt too swollen to be of any use and besides, he did not want to give his adversary the satisfaction of seeing the extent of his thirst. Steinhauser stood up slowly and walked towards Tony, glass in hand.

"You'd like some of this, wouldn't you?" He took a sip of the water, noting the longing which Tony was unable to conceal from his eyes. Then the SS officer held the glass in front of Tony's eyes. Slowly, so very slowly, he poured the contents onto the floor, where they formed a small puddle and splashed Tony's lower legs. A malicious smile lit the German's face, as the longing in the prisoner's eyes turned to anguish and hatred.

"Let's talk first, shall we?" He made his way back to the table, put down the glass and resumed his seat.

"Now, who were you working with?"

Tony said nothing.

"Where did you get your weapons from?"

Silence.

"Are you in contact with London?"

Tony still refused to speak.

"If that is the way you want it, I have only one course of action left open to me." Steinhauser's voice was pleasant, almost conversational as he waved a hand to indicate the soldier, whose rubber truncheon was now held prominently before him. "Are you going to answer my questions, or must I ask this man to persuade you?"

"I have nothing to say."

Steinhauser nodded imperceptibly. Tony tensed as the soldier stepped forward. There was a gleam in his eyes and a smile on his face. Tony realised that he liked his work. The truncheon was raised. Tony watched as it fell towards his shoulder anticipating the impact. When it came with a sickening crunch, it sent waves of agony coursing through his battered body. The blows continued to fall. Tony stood with eyes closed, brows knotted as he fought against the pain. When the truncheon connected with his broken ribs he cried out in agony. Steinhauser's face broke into a broad grin, though Tony did not see it through the red agony which clouded his brain. After that first cry, Tony took his lower lip between his teeth, determined not to cry out again. The blood flowed where his teeth broke the skin. Suddenly, from no-where, a blow caught Tony on the temple and he slipped into unconsciousness.

"You imbecile!" Steinhauser's voice was hoarse with rage. "You know that I don't want him hit about the head! How can he tell me what I want to know, if you damage his brain!"

The soldier cringed before the major's tirade.

"I'm sorry, Herr Major, but he moved as the blow fell, and I didn't have time to stop."

"Don't give me excuses! You should be better at the job than that. Wake him up; I want to continue with his interrogation."

"Yes, sir."

A second soldier stepped forward. He picked up the bucket, throwing its contents of icy cold water onto the figure on the floor. The shock of the water dragged Tony back to consciousness, and a groan escaped his lips. He dragged himself up onto his hands and knees and then to his feet. His knees buckled and he almost fell, but with an incredible effort of will he forced his legs to stand firm. He straightened his shoulders before carefully opening his eyes. The light from the single bulb hung suspended from the ceiling seemed blinding, sending arrows of pain knifing through his brain. The sound of a voice seemed to come closer and then recede, but he was unaware of what it was saying.

"Will you answer my questions?" Steinhauser frowned at the man who was almost unconscious on his feet. "Do you want some water?" It was obvious that his words were not registering, and he turned angrily towards the soldier with the truncheon. "Do that again, and you will be on the Russian Front before you know it! You!" he indicated the guard who had so far taken no part in the interrogation, "he's of no use to me in that condition. Give him some water and let him rest. But don't give him any food. I want his mind clear but his body weak, the next time I see him."

Steinhauser turned and stormed from the cell, followed by his two companions. The guard poured some water and held it to Tony's cracked and bleeding lips. Some of the cool, refreshing liquid slipped down the parched throat before Tony realised what it was, then he reached out trembling hands, took the glass and drank greedily. Half of it spilled down his front, but he was unaware of that as the life-giving liquid flowed through his body. He held out the glass for more. The soldier took it, but before he could fill it Tony slumped to the floor. He was unconscious before he hit the ground.

109

Jean-Paul sat at the back of the darkened church and watched as the priest genuflected and rose to his feet, before going out of the side door and leaving the Frenchman alone. He had received a message from Angeline asking him to meet her here to discuss the plans for Tony's rescue. He found the environment calming. Church had always been able to soothe him in times of stress and he was grateful to her for the choice of location. He had been waiting for only a few moments when he heard someone slip into the pew behind him. A voice whispered into his right ear.

"It's me, Jean-Paul. Don't turn round." Angeline got down onto her knees as she spoke and bowed her head as though in prayer. "Have you managed to make your arrangements?"

Jean-Paul picked up a prayer book and opened it, pretending to read as he answered the Englishwoman.

"Yes. Georges has got two uniforms, the car is ready and the tank is full."

"Do you have swastikas on it?"

Jean-Paul shook his head.

"Fix a couple of small flags to the front. It might help if you need to get through a road block."

Jean-Paul nodded imperceptibly.

"Does everyone know what they have to do?"

"Yes."

"Can you reach them quickly?"

"Yes. All of the arrangements are made. We can be ready to move as soon as you give the word."

"Good. London is sending a small plane. It will land just south of Montoir, to the west of a small wood with a lake on the other side of it. Do you know the place?"

Jean-Paul nodded. "Yes. You mean the plane will land between the wood and the lake?"

"Yes. On the night of the rescue you should arrive there at 10.40. The plane will come in at 10.45."

"Will it wait if we're late?"

"It can only wait five minutes at the most, Jean-Paul."

The Frenchman frowned. "It's going to be difficult. We have to time things so that we get Albert out and get to Montoir by 10.40, but we can't be too early. We're sure to be pursued."

"No-one said it would be easy, Jean-Paul. Do you want to call it off?"

Jean-Paul was thunderstruck. "Of course not!" His exclamation was louder than he had intended.

"Shhhh."

"Sorry." His voice was a whisper once more.

"When will the plane come?"

"As soon as possible. Listen to the BBC at 7.30 each day. The code 'the flight of the heron' means that it's all on for that night. Got it?"

"Yes. 'The flight of the heron.'"

"Good. Let's go. You leave first. I'll hang on for five minutes."

Jean-Paul nodded and rose to his feet. As he turned to leave the pew, he glanced down at the bowed head of the young woman and smiled. Who would ever have thought that she was an English spy?

"While you are down there," he muttered, "perhaps you can say a prayer for Albert and the rest of us. We're going to need all the help we can get!"

110

Karl Dresner watched as his superior officer poured himself another cognac and settled himself comfortably in his chair. The major smiled across at the sergeant and raised his glass in salute, though he did not offer the younger man a drink.

"You know, Karl, I was not absolutely certain when we first took the assassin that he was a spy. Or even if he was connected with the Resistance at all for that matter. But the more I see of him, the more I'm convinced that we have an Englishman amongst us."

"How can you be sure, Herr Major?"

"He's too good, Karl. He hasn't said a word yet, not even to curse us. You should see him. He's just one big bruise, yet he still refuses to talk." Steinhauser grinned. He obviously enjoyed the suffering of his prisoner and looked forward to seeing it continue.

"Will you be able to make him talk?"

"Oh yes, Karl. So far we've just been softening him up. When we get round to the really serious questioning, he'll talk. He'll beg to be allowed to tell us all that he knows." Steinhauser took a sip of his cognac and smiled appreciatively. "It may take as long as a week, but by then we'll have wrung him dry. We will know who was working with him, where they store their weapons, where the weapons came from originally. We may even lay our hands on a British radio operator and his equipment. Just think how useful that could be." He leant back and closed his eyes, his feet stretched out in front of him. "Ah, Karl, this could be just the break I've been looking for. With Wolffe gone, they'll need to promote someone else. Just think how much better my chances will be, if I manage to expose a secret British spy ring."

Dresner said nothing. He was well aware of his superior officer's ambitions and hoped his plans would come to fruition; after all, if the Major moved up the hierarchical ladder he would take his sergeant with him. But Dresner was always the pessimist. If this Albert Fouqet was the leader of the Resistance group, and nothing to that effect had yet been proved, then he may not talk at all, no matter what the means of persuasion. As he watched the Major enjoying his cognac, he hoped that nothing would go wrong. Steinhauser in a temper was not a pretty sight.

111

Tony was feeling weak from lack of food. The water which he had been given over the last twenty-four hours had relieved some of his suffering, but his stomach was now cramping for lack of solid sustenance. But the gnawing emptiness in his stomach, however, did not compare with the pain in his bruised and battered body. His torso and arms were a patchwork of red, black and blue. He ached all over, although some of the stiffness was easing. During the times of most intense pain, he retreated into an idyllic dream, where he and Sarah walked through a world which knew nothing of war. He would not have been able to stand up to the brutal use he had been subjected to if it had not been for his love for her. He had not known that the love of a woman could impart such inner strength, but he resisted for her, to prove to her that his country and his love for her were far more important to him than his own life. He was determined to survive if he could, but he had no misconceptions about Major Steinhauser and what he planned to do with him. He was coming to terms with the fact that he probably would not leave the SS. H.Q. alive. He regretted that he would not see England again, his home, his family and his friends; but most of all he regretted that he would never see Sarah again. He longed to hold her in his arms once more, to know that her feelings for him were equally strong. He would close his eyes and see the glowing auburn hair, sparkling green eyes and infectious smile of the woman he loved. His heart wept with the pain of missing her, and he would whisper 'Wait for me, Sarah. I'm coming home to you, my love.'

The guard often heard him muttering under his breath, but could not make out the words. If he had, he would have wondered at the force of love which kept his prisoner's mind from the pain and humiliation he had already suffered, and the brutality that was yet to come.

When the door opened to admit Steinhauser and his two companions once more, Tony had a sinking feeling in the pit of his stomach. His mouth was dry with fear of the anticipated pain, but he let none of his feelings show. He stood silently and watched, as a heavy chair was carried in and placed in the centre of the floor beneath the naked light bulb.

"Sit down."

Tony complied silently. He sat still and tense as first his hands were tied to the arms of the chair, and then his ankles to the legs. The ropes were tight and bit deeply into his flesh so that the blood flow to his extremities was restricted. But Tony paid it little attention, his mind focussing instead on what was coming next. Why was he tied? What did Steinhauser plan to do to him? One of the guards stepped forward and ripped open the prisoner's shirt to expose his bruised and battered torso. Tony shivered, whether as a reaction to the cold air of the cell or to his fear even he did not know. Steinhauser lit a cigar and smoked for a moment. His evil eyes took in the battered appearance of his victim.

"Shall we continue with our interrogation?" His voice and his gaze were as icy as the air in the cell.

"I still have nothing to say to you."

Steinhauser stepped closer until he stood before the chair with its bound occupant, drawing on the cigar until its tip glowed red. Taking it from his mouth he exhaled a stream of smoke into the air so that it swirled around the naked light bulb in a blue haze. Holding the glowing tip of the cigar close to Tony's eyes, he smiled his evil smile.

"Are you sure about that?"

He lowered the cigar and pressed it against Tony's shoulder. The flesh blistered and steamed. Tony bit his lips to stop himself from crying out.

"What is your name?"

"Albert Fouqet."

The cigar was lowered once again. Tony watched, unable to take his eyes from the glowing tip which approached his flesh. As the burning cigar touched his skin, his eyes screwed tightly closed in agony.

"Your name?"

Tony's voice was filled with pain. He forced the words through gritted teeth. "Albert Fouqet."

Steinhauser's brow creased in anger as he pressed the tip of the cigar against Tony's chest again. Once. Twice. Three times. Tony was rigid with pain, his back arched and his limbs straining against the restraining bonds. But he still did not cry out. When Steinhauser stepped back, Tony's head lowered onto his chest and his breathing came in painful gasps.

"Name?"

"Albert Fouqet."

"Who were you working with?"

"I work alone."

"Are you in touch with England?"

"No."

Steinhauser stepped forward again, puffing on the cigar until the end glowed redly once more. Tony closed his eyes in anticipation of the pain. When it came, he clenched his teeth tightly together so that the muscles in his jaw and neck stood out like corded ropes. He lost count of the number of times he felt the touch of the burning cigar before the questioning began again.

"Did you sabotage the docks?"

"No."

"Where did you get your weapon?"

"I found it." Tony looked defiantly into the eyes of the SS major, who spluttered in anger.

"You bastard! You think you're strong, but you can't stand against me! Sooner or later you will answer my questions!"

He stepped forward again, the cigar held out in front of him, but this time he pressed it against the extra sensitive skin of the Englishman's nipple. He laughed when his action was rewarded with a scream of agony.

"See, 'Monsieur Fouqet'," his voice was full of derision, "I still have many ways to inflict pain on you. Indeed I have barely scraped the surface of ways to make you suffer. Now will you answer my questions?"

Sweat stood out on Tony's brow despite the chill of the room. His body shook as he fought to control the pain, but as he looked at his tormentor, his eyes were still defiant. The SS major embodied all that he hated about this war. The blue-eyed, fair haired man had been indoctrinated with the myth that he, and other Aryans like him, were the superior race, destined to rule the world. Tony knew that if the Germans did win, they would treat all of the people they subjugated in the same manner as they treated the French, and all resistance would be met with treatment similar to that which was being meted out to him. He knew that no matter what the consequences to himself, he would do nothing to help the hated Germans in their conquest. He would give his life to protect Jean-Paul and his family, and the rest of their group. As the waves of pain washed over him, he saw the whole conflict in black and white, good versus evil. Knowing what would happen to him would not influence what he said next.

"No. I will not answer your question. Not now. Not ever."

With a cry of frustrated rage, Steinhauser stepped forward and forced the red cigar tip into Tony's navel. He ground it round and round until the burning tobacco was extinguished. The screams of his victim rang in his ears. Stepping back, he threw away the cigar butt, and signalled one of the soldiers who accompanied him to step forward.

"The nails."

With an evil grin the soldier knelt on the floor and removed Tony's shoes and socks, not an easy task with his ankles still bound tightly to the legs of the chair. The other soldier stepped behind Tony, holding onto the back of the chair as though to brace it against some violent movement. Tony's heart beat wildly with fear. Standing directly in front of him, Steinhauser removed a match from the box in his hand. He gave it to the soldier, who knelt at Tony's feet.

"Begin."

The soldier gripped Tony tightly by the right ankle, and forced the match down beneath the nail of the big toe. Tony fought and screamed, unaware of Steinhauser's malevolent gaze, but he could do nothing to prevent the excruciating pain as the thin piece of wood was forced down to the root of his nail. He took in huge gulps of air as the soldier released his ankle, and the pain gradually began to subside. Blood poured from the shattered nail and torn flesh. As the curtain of red pain began to recede, he thought that no more painful form of torture could be devised. But he was wrong. He opened his eyes to see Steinhauser gloating above him; slowly he withdrew another match and struck it against the box so that it burst into brilliant flame. As he began to crouch down in front of him, Tony suddenly, with a flash of terrible insight, knew what he was going to do. He struggled and fought, his body bucking and straining at its tethers. But it was useless. His torturer held the flame to the end of the match which had been thrust under Tony's nail. The sulphurous end burst into life. As the flame consumed the wood, Tony screamed and writhed in agony. Never in his wildest nightmares had he imagined such pain.

"No! My God! No!" he cried, his back arching in agony, but unable to move further because of the restraining bonds. "In God's name, stop!"

But the fiery pain did not stop, not until the flame was so far under his nail that it lacked the oxygen to burn, and the wood was too soaked with Tony's blood for the fire to take hold. So the flame died, but the smouldering stub of the match was still embedded in the lower portion of the nail continuing the agony.

When the pain had receded enough for him to control it, Tony opened his eyes and frowned at the triumphant smile on Steinhauser's face.

"So, Monsieur Fouqet cries out in English when he is in pain!" He laughed.

Tony blanched. Had he? Had he really cried out in English? The agony had been so all-encompassing that he knew that it was possible. He bowed his head in shame and defeat, but then straightened once more. So, he had cried out in English, but he had told Steinhauser nothing else, he could still resist.

"So...you know that...I'm English but that...won't help...you." His voice was little more than a whisper, his words disjointed by pain.

"Tell me about the group you worked with."

"No."

Steinhauser slowly took another match from the box, conscious that Tony could not take his eyes from it, his eyes filled with pain and fear. He handed the match to the soldier. He took hold of Tony's left ankle, and began to force the thin piece of wood down beneath the nail of the big toe. Tony took his lower lip between his teeth, drawing blood as he tried to suppress his cries, but the pain was too great and he screamed once more. Once the match was in place, Steinhauser waited for the pain to recede a little. He watched as the blood from the broken toe pooled on the floor. Then he lit another match and held the yellow flame close in front of Tony's eyes.

"Now will you talk?"

Fighting his fear Tony shook his head. He closed his eyes as Steinhauser bent down and lit the match. The burning agony began again, and Tony began to scream.

"No! No! Sarah! Oh my God! Sarah!"

As the name of his beloved echoed in his ears, he slipped into merciful unconsciousness.

Tony gradually became aware of the hard stone floor beneath his right shoulder. He tried to move, and groaned as his body was engulfed in pain. Opening his eyes, he saw that the guard had left the room. Apparently he was no longer under constant supervision. They no longer needed to keep him awake for twenty-four hours a day now that Steinhauser had decided to use pain rather than deprivation as a means of making him talk. Tony had no idea how long he had been lying on the cold stone floor. It could have been hours or even days. He struggled to sit up, each movement caused his burned torso to bend and sent waves of excruciating pain coursing through him. But it was nothing compared with the agony which emanated from his feet. His head spun. He closed his eyes in an attempt to retain a hold on consciousness and to fight the pain. When he opened his eyes, he looked fearfully down at his abused body. His shirt still hung open, and though he was cold he was glad that the guards had not buttoned it. The thought of the material touching his tortured flesh sent shivers down his spine. He surveyed the damage which had been inflicted upon him. His body was swollen and bruised, showing every colour that could conceivably be imagined. The patchwork was only relieved by the whitened bubbles of burnt and blistered flesh where Steinhauser had pressed his cigar. Tony was finding it painful to breathe, and though he could detect no damage to his ribs with his eyes, the pain told him that some of the bones must be cracked or broken. He hoped there were no more serious internal injuries.

Tony kept his gaze on his upper body for a moment wanting, yet fearing, to look at his feet. Finally summoning the courage, he took a deep breath and let his eyes travel down his legs to his bare feet. When the full horror of what he saw finally registered on his brain, he felt sick and turned away. Violent shivers shook his body, and a look of revulsion passed over his face. His two big toes were swollen to more than twice their normal size, the nails broken, the flesh torn and bleeding, the skin blackened and blistered where it had been burned. He could still see the charred remnants of the matches embedded deep in his flesh.

Tony looked across at the bucket in the corner of the room which he had been using as a toilet, and he wondered how he was ever going to manage to make his way over to it. He tried to struggle to his feet, but waves of nausea washed over him. There was no way he would be able to stand. He contemplated crawling, but the thought of his damaged toes catching on the stone floor filled him with fear. Eventually he shuffled over to the bucket on his backside. He used his hands to propel himself along, trying to drag his feet by the heels and hoping to jar the damaged toes as little as possible. Movement was slow and painful, but he finally managed to reach the bucket and relieve his discomfort, though he could not find the energy to drag himself more than a few feet away from the stinking receptacle before he collapsed on the floor. When he awoke again it was to find a guard standing over him. He helped Tony to sit up and held a tin mug of water to his lips. Tony drank thankfully, aware of a look of pity in the soldier's eyes. When he had finished drinking, the German shook his head sadly.

"Why don't tell him what he wants to know?"

"I can't."

The soldier inclined his head towards Tony's feet. "Don't think that this is the end of it. You have eight more toes, and then ten fingers. If you still have not talked by then, which I doubt, he will begin to torture other parts of your body even more sensitive than your nails."

"I can tell him nothing."

The German shrugged. "Then you'll be responsible for your own suffering."

As his captor rose and left the room, Tony buried his head in his hands. He did not know how much more pain and humiliation he could stand, and he was afraid that he would soon betray his friends. Tears filled his eyes as he contemplated the hopelessness of his situation, but he determined to be strong and to hold out for as long as he possibly could. He called forth an image of Sarah, and knew that it was their love which helped him to stay strong. Without the memories of her or the hope of returning to her some day, he knew that he would not survive.

112

The rescue team sat in the car just half a mile from the SS Headquarters. Jean-Paul perused his companions. Georges had been able to get hold of another German uniform for Vincent, who now sat in the front, hands tightly gripping the steering wheel.

"Do you know where to take us when we get Albert out?"

Vincent nodded at Jean-Paul's question. "Yes. We cycled out there this afternoon. You don't need to worry about that, just make sure you get Albert out safely."

Jean-Paul, looking strange in the uniform of a Werhmacht Sergeant, grinned nervously. He glanced across at Georges, who had managed to get the uniforms out of the laundry. He would be their guide once they were inside the building, the success of their mission would depend a great deal on him.

"You know where they're holding him, Georges?"

The young Frenchman nodded. "Yes. There has been a lot of gossip amongst the Germans. It appears that they know that Albert is English, but he's told them nothing about us. At least that was the rumour in the offices today."

"How do you know this?"

Georges smiled at Madeleine. "As far as the Germans are concerned we French don't exist. As long as I look as though I'm working, it's not too difficult to listen in to conversations."

"Will they recognise you when we go in? It could give the whole game away."

"I've thought about that," Georges countered, "I don't think it's a problem. They might think my face is familiar, but they will probably assume that I've recently been posted here. I doubt if they will link a vaguely familiar face in German uniform to an obscure French cleaner. Anyway, it's a risk we have to take. I'm the only one who can speak German."

"Georges is right," concurred Jean-Paul, "it's a risk we must take. Are we all ready?" His three companions nodded. "Good, then let's get going. We're working on a tight schedule."

As Jean-Paul finished speaking, Vincent turned the ignition key, and the engine roared into life. With swastikas flying in the gentle breeze, the car with its three German soldiers and their companion slipped into the main road, and made its way towards the headquarters of the dreaded SS.

The atmosphere in the car was electric. Its occupants were all aware of the danger into which they travelled, and the consequences to themselves and their families if their plan failed. Yet they were all determined to carry on. The driving force behind them was not only the fear of what would happen if Tony was forced to talk, but also their concern for his safety. Most of them had only known Tony for a short time. Only Jean-Paul had known him before the war and knew his true identity, but they all admired him and the way he had led them to so many successes. He had given them back their self-respect in a country occupied by a brutish force, and given them hope that the occupation would not continue overlong. He had brought out the courage and strength hidden deep in each one of them, and focussed it so that they had been able to help their country, albeit in a small way. With their leader taken, they could do no less than to utilise the qualities which he had brought out in them, to free him or die in the attempt. As the car made its way towards its destination, its occupants were silent, each coping with their fear and trepidation in their own way. As they rounded the final corner the faces of each of them were calm, grim, determined.

Vincent drew the car to a halt in front of the steps which led up to the entrance, the black, white and red of the huge swastika billowing above it. Jean-Paul leaned forward and spoke softly to the driver.

"Wait here and keep the engine running. We won't be long."

Jean-Paul climbed down from the car, closely followed by Madeleine and finally Georges. The two men posing as German soldiers held their rifles in their hands as they flanked the young woman and escorted her up the steps, into the huge imposing building. As they passed the sentries at the door, their hearts were in their mouths, but no one said anything as they walked confidently past, as though on their way to an important meeting. Once in the entrance hall, Georges whispered to his colleagues.

"We turn right here, then go on until we reach the stairs that go down to the cellars. That's where they're keeping him."

Jean-Paul nodded and followed as Georges led the way. There were not many people about. Although some of the soldiers looked curiously at them, they were not challenged until they reached the stairs. The young soldier on duty blocked their way, and looked them up and down questioningly.

"Where do you think you're going?"

"To the cells."

The soldier glared at Georges. "You know that's forbidden."

"We're under orders from Major Steinhauser. He thinks this woman can identify the prisoner."

"Then why isn't he with you?" The soldier glared at Madeleine, then looked back at Georges. "I'll have to check with the Herr Major before I let you down."

"Of course." Georges forced a smile as he spoke. "I'll come with you."

The guard nodded and turned towards the entrance hall. Jean-Paul clamped a hand over his mouth and put his other arm around his neck. Madeleine grabbed the German's gun as he struggled with his attacker, while Gorges slipped his knife from its sheath and thrust it hard into the soldier's chest. The blade slid in between two ribs and found the heart. Georges gave it a twist to free it and pulled back. He heard the metal grate against bone. A gush of blood flooded the front of the sentry's uniform. A groan, muffled by Jean-Paul's hand, escaped the young man. He slumped into his attacker's arms, lifeless eyes staring.

"Get him down the stairs. Quick." Jean-Paul began to drag the body down the stairs, and was closely followed by his companions.

"We must hurry." Madeleine's voice was little more than a whisper. "Once they notice that the guard is missing, we won't stand a chance of getting out of here."

Georges nodded. He fumbled with a bunch of keys attached to the dead German's belt.

"Albert is the only prisoner down here at present so he'll be in the only room that's locked."

Jean-Paul began trying all the doors flanking the underground corridor. The third one on the right resisted his efforts to open it. He motioned his companion forward.

"Get this one open, Georges."

Georges struggled with the keys for a moment until he found the right one. As the key grated in the lock, he turned the handle and pushed the door open.

"Mon Dieu!" His face lost all its colour and his hand on the door began to shake. Madeleine wondered what had caused such a reaction and pushed past him to see. The sight which greeted her caused her to stop in her tracks and she felt nauseous. In the far corner of the room was a huddled form. The torso was black and blue from bruising. Huge blisters covered the skin where something had burned him. The feet of the figure lay in a pool of blood, the toes blackened, the nails shattered.

"Albert?" Madeleine's voice was little more than a whisper. She could not believe what her eyes were seeing, did not want to believe it. How could anyone stand up to such punishment and live? She took a hesitant step into the room, then rushed across to the still form. Her two companions in the doorway stood silently for a moment before joining her. They had not known what to expect, but none of them had anticipated anything like this.

"We should have got him out sooner." Jean-Paul crossed the room quickly, his vision blurred by tears. Kneeling down, he forced a smile to his anguished face as he gazed down into the pain -filled eyes.

"Jean-Paul?"

"Yes, Tony. I'm here." In the heat of the moment he used Tony's real name, and the others looked at him.

"You know who he really is?"

Jean-Paul's eyes opened in surprise at Madeleine's question, then he cursed himself.

"You keep it a secret from the Germans, even after they've done this to you, then I have to let it slip."

Tony forced a smile. "Don't worry Jean-Paul, it won't make any difference now. I'm just so glad to see you all."

Jean-Paul helped the Englishman to sit up, and looked down at his tortured feet.

"How are we going to get you out of here? I'd thought you'd be able to walk with us, and we'd just have to bluff our way out."

"I won't be walking for quite a while, Jean-Paul. You can't carry me. We'd never get out like that." He closed his eyes for a moment, and took a deep breath. He looked deep into his old friend's eyes, and reached out to grasp his hand. "Thank you for coming, all of you, it was a very courageous thing to do. But as you can see, it's hopeless. If you try to get me out of here, you'll all be taken. Kill me, Jean-Paul, and then get out of here."

"No. Tony, I can't do that."

"You must, Jean-Paul. If you leave me here they'll make me talk eventually. You must kill me. It's the only way."

"We'll find another way, Tony. I'm not leaving you here, and I'm not going to kill you. How would I explain that to your family?"

"There might be another way." Georges found it difficult to speak around the lump in his throat. "There's a first aid post not far from where the sentry stood at the top of the stairs. I could get a stretcher from there and we could carry Albert...Tony out."

Tony's face creased into a pain-wracked semblance of a grin.

"Continue to call me Albert, Georges, Tony is a name best forgotten. Do you think your plan could work?"

"It must." Madeleine spoke for the first time since she had rushed to Tony's side. She took his free hand in hers and squeezed it gently. "We're not going to leave you here to these animals. We knew the risks when we came to get you and we'll not back out now. There's a plane coming for you tonight, and we're going to make sure you're on it."

"A plane?"

Jean-Paul nodded as Georges slipped from the cell to find the stretcher.

"Angeline. We have to get moving if we're to meet her on time."

"How do we get past the guards?"

"Bluff. We'll just say that Steinhauser has ordered you to be taken to hospital. If the Germans don't believe us, we'll just have to kill them."

Tony smiled weakly. "I certainly came to the right man when I came to you, Jean-Paul. Thanks."

There were footsteps in the corridor. Madeleine leapt to her feet, gun in hand. She relaxed visibly as Georges entered with the stretcher and a folded blanket.

"No one has noticed that the guard is missing yet, but I don't suppose it will be long before they do. We had better hurry."

"The guard?"

"No time to explain now." Jean-Paul gently lifted Tony onto the stretcher, noticing the grimace of pain which clouded his friend's features.

"I'm sorry, Albert, but I must cover you." Madeleine gently laid the blanket over his tortured body as she spoke. "I know it must hurt, but if we cover you the Germans might not know who is on the stretcher."

Tony felt dizzy with pain. Nausea threatened to overcome him as the blanket brushed his shattered feet. He closed his eyes and fought to control his breathing as the two Frenchmen lifted the stretcher, each movement bringing renewed pain to his abused body.

"Wait." Madeleine slipped the slain guard's gun beneath the blanket so that Tony's hand rested on the butt. "You might need this."

Tony nodded his thanks as Jean-Paul and Georges carried him out of the cell and along the stone passageway. His eyes fell on the bloodied body of the sentry but he said nothing as the small party began to make its way up the stairs, each step a jarring agony for the man on the stretcher. As they reached the top of the stairs, Jean-Paul let out a breath he did not know he had been holding.

"No one around. They've not noticed the missing guard yet."

The group made their way along the passageway and into the entrance hall, where a sentry stopped them.

"Who is on the stretcher?"

"A clerk. This woman is a nurse. She thinks he has appendicitis. We're taking him to hospital."

The sentry nodded and waved them on. "Good luck to him."

Moments later Jean-Paul and Georges lifted Tony from the stretcher into the back of the car, where he sat flanked by Madeleine and Georges. Jean-Paul climbed into the front next to Vincent.

"Go."

The car roared away and as it turned the first corner its occupants heaved a collective sigh of relief.

"I don't believe it!"

"We did it!"

"It's a miracle!"

Vincent didn't join in the self-congratulation. "How is he?"

"In a bad way." Jean-Paul glanced over his shoulder as he replied. There was no sign of pursuit. "If he'd been there much longer, he would have either told them everything or died." He looked at the young Englishman. The jolting of the car had increased his pain, and he had slipped into merciful unconsciousness. "Get to the rendezvous as fast as you can, Vincent. They're bound to discover the dead guard and missing prisoner soon. Then the whole German army will be on our tails."

Vincent took the road north to the outskirts of the city, then slowed the car.

"Roadblock."

Jean-Paul frowned. "They know we've been there. They must have radioed ahead to have all roads out of the city sealed off." He laid his gun unobtrusively on his lap. "Slow down and stop, Vincent. The rest of you get your weapons ready. We must kill everyone at the barrier, or pursuit will be so close that we won't be able to meet the plane."

The others nodded, releasing the safety catches on their guns. Vincent slowed the car, and stopped at the barrier as six soldiers approached. They were relaxed, as though expecting no trouble from a car flying the swastika and carrying three German soldiers.

"The SS have lost a prisoner," called the closest of the approaching soldiers. "Have you seen anything?"

"Yes!" Jean-Paul leapt to his feet and opened fire. A fusillade of shots came from either side of the rear of the car. The Germans fell before they even had time to bring their weapons to bear on their attackers. Vincent pressed his foot to the floor and the car leapt forward, throwing Jean-Paul back into his seat.

"On to Montoir!"

The car sped into the night and towards its rendezvous with the English plane five miles away.

Angeline was busy by the small lake outside Montoir. Between the water and the woods was a narrow patch of meadowland. It was ideal as a runway for the Lysander which was due to arrive within the next half hour. It was Angeline's job to make sure that the ground drill was carried out correctly, so that the plane could land and take off safely in as short a time as possible. The plane was unarmed. The only weapon was the pistol which the pilot carried. The pickup would be dangerous ,and the pilot would want to spend no more than two or three minutes on the ground.

Angeline checked the direction of the wind and began to set up the landing lights. With the wind in her face, she placed a bicycle lamp on the ground and began to pace out the grass in front of her. After four hundred yards she put down another lamp, turned to her right and paced out a further fifty yards. Then she placed the third and final lamp on the short turf. All she had to do now was wait until she heard the sound of the approaching plane and then switch on the lamps. Although they were small they would be easily seen by the pilot, as all of the surrounding land was obsidian in the blackout. The plane would come down into the wind, landing as close as possible to the first light. Then it would taxi to the second light. It would turn in the space designated by the second and third lights, before taxiing back to its landing point. The passenger would be picked up there, and the plane would take off into the wind, in the direction of the second light. Angeline would then only need to retrieve the lights and make her way back to Saint Nazaire.

Once the lights were all in position, Angeline waited anxiously, surveying first the sky and then the road. Time was running out and the plane would not be able to wait. Where was the car? Had they managed to get Tony out of the hands of the SS? Had they been caught en route to the rendezvous point? Angeline paced nervously back and forth across the springy turf. If they did not come soon, it would be too late.

It was 10.41 when Angeline heard the sound of the approaching car. She let out a sigh of relief. Right on time. The plane was due in four minutes. The car pulled onto the meadow and drew to a halt, as she ran across to it.

"Keep the engine running, Vincent, we'll want to get away as quickly as possible." Jean-Paul climbed out of the car. "It's good to see you, Angeline. Is everything ready?"

The young Englishwoman nodded. "Yes. Where's Albert?"

Jean-Paul's face creased with worry.

"In the back of the car. He's in a bad way, Angeline, and we don't know what he might have told them."

Angeline moved to the rear of the car where her compatriot was propped up between Madeleine and Georges, who eyed her curiously. Tony had not regained consciousness. The lack of food and water, compounded with the pain and injuries kept him in a blissful state where he could feel no more hurt. Angeline frowned. Tony was wrapped in a blanket with only his face showing. That appeared to be uninjured, so what had the Germans done? As though reading her thoughts, Madeleine gently removed the blanket and Angeline gasped. The injuries to his body and feet looked appalling, even in the dark. She wondered if he could possibly have sustained so much damage without betraying her and the remainder of the group. But there was no time to think about that now. The plane was due any moment.

"What are you going to do, Angeline?"

The young woman gazed questioningly at Vincent.

"What do you mean?"

"He may have given them your name. Do you want to end up like him?"

Angeline shivered with fear but said nothing.

"You should go back with him."

"I can't. I have no orders to return."

"You have no orders because this situation was not foreseen," said Jean-Paul. "It would be safer for you, and for us all, if you were to return to England. If they wish to send you back, you can always parachute in again. Besides, Albert will probably need you during the flight."

Angeline thought silently for a moment, then nodded.

"I suppose you're right, though I don't want to leave." She looked at Madeleine and Georges for the first time. "I'm going to need your help. There are two bicycle lamps further along the field, I'll show you where. I want you to switch them on when we hear the plane. Then when it has taken off again, switch them off and get back to the car as quickly as possible. Jean-Paul," the Frenchman looked at her as she spoke, "I want you to take care of the one at this end."

Jean-Paul nodded and moved across to the lamp which she pointed out to him.

"Were you followed, Vincent?"

He shook his head. "No, but we had to kill some soldiers at a roadblock so they must know by now which direction we took. They could be here any minute."

She nodded. "Keep the engine running. And when you get home, hide my radio."

He smiled sadly. "I'll miss you, Angeline."

"Don't worry Vincent. I'll be back. After all, I'll have to retrieve my property won't I?" She leant over and kissed him on the cheek. "Right, you two," she looked at Madeleine and Georges as she spoke, "the plane will be here any moment. Follow me."

The two members of the French Resistance followed her into the darkness at a run, and were soon stationed beside their bicycle lamps. As they watched the Englishwoman turn and run towards the car once more, they marvelled at her. She looked so plain and ordinary, yet she had taken command of the situation swiftly and expertly. She had come to their country at great risk to herself in order to help them, and they regretted that they had not had a chance to get to know her. Yet they knew that, as long as they lived, they would never forget the plain bespectacled woman who had so briefly intruded into their lives.

As Angeline ran, she heard the engine of the monoplane approaching from the north. In front of her Jean-Paul switched on his light and the beam leapt towards the star-studded sky. Looking back over her shoulder, Angeline saw the other two lamps burst into life. She heard the plane banking to the west. It had seen the lights and was beginning its approach run. The young woman quickened her pace and arrived at Jean-Paul's side just as the small monoplane touched down yards away from them. There was a roar from the engine as the pilot applied the brakes and the plane bumped its way towards Madeleine and Georges. Moments later, they saw its black silhouette turn in a tight circle and begin to taxi back towards them.

"Get Albert."

Jean-Paul made his way over to the car. He lifted his young English friend gently into his arms like a child, and made his way back to Angeline. The Lysander was turning, once more facing Georges and Madeleine. Jean-Paul approached it and helped Angeline to lift the inert bundle which was Tony into the rear cockpit. The British agent tapped on the window of the front cockpit. The pilot opened it.

"I'm coming back with you!" She called loudly to be heard over the sound of the engine.

The pilot gave the thumbs up sign and Angeline climbed aboard.

"Good luck, Jean-Paul."

He nodded. "And you too. Take care of him!" He leapt down as the engine roared and the plane began to move. As he watched it moving across the bumpy ground, he was glad that Tony was unconscious and unable to feel it. Then the wheels lost contact with the springy turf, and the plane was airborne. Jean-Paul picked up his lamp, switched it off and leapt into the car.

"We have company."

On hearing Vincent's words Jean-Paul looked over his shoulder and saw an armoured car approaching at breakneck speed. With a curse, he put down his lamp and picked up his gun.

"Drive on to pick up the others! Fast!"

As the car leapt forward. Jean-Paul opened fire on their rapidly approaching pursuers. Ahead of them, Madeleine and Georges were racing towards the car. Vincent screeched to a halt, and they leapt into the back. They turned to rake the armoured car with bullets as its occupants began to return fire. The car raced off once more. The plane banked above the trees and headed north. Angeline looked out of the window of the cockpit and watched in horror as the vehicles raced away. The flash of guns could still be seen as the cars disappeared behind the trees and headed east. She wished there was something she could do to help, but there was nothing. She would not even know the outcome of the chase. Turning back to her unconscious colleague, she checked that his belt was securely fastened and wrapped the blanket around him once more. There was nothing she could do to help their French colleagues, but at least she could do her best to make sure that Tony was still alive when they arrived back in England.

SEPTEMBER - DECEMBER 1942

113

Tony's body sought protection from pain, fatigue and hunger in unconsciousness. He felt nothing of the discomfort of the flight, nor the following ambulance journey to a small military hospital in the south west of England. The ambulance arrived just as dawn was painting the sky with the delicate shades of an artist's palette and its sole occupant was carried on a stretcher into a small private room, where his injuries were examined and tended. He was finally left to sleep in a comfortable bed. With no jolting to cause additional pain and new strength imparted to his body by the injected drugs, Tony slowly regained consciousness at around midday. He opened his eyes and his features creased into a puzzled frown as he slowly focussed on the young nurse seated beside his bed. His vision was blurred but he thought the figure was familiar, particularly the uniform.

"Sarah?" His voice was hoarse and grating. The nurse leaned over him solicitously with a glass of cool water.

"No. My name isn't Sarah." She held the glass to his cracked and dry lips. "Try to drink a little of this."

He lifted his head from the pillow. A groan escaped him as pain coursed through his body. The nurse slipped a hand beneath his head to support him as he took a few sips of water, and then lay back, exhausted.

"I'll fetch the doctor. He wanted to be informed as soon as you woke up."

Tony watched the nurse as she put down the glass and left the room. Now that his vision was clearing, he could see that she did not resemble Sarah at all. His mind had been clinging on to thoughts of her throughout his ordeal in France. Regaining consciousness in comfortable surroundings had allowed his imagination to run away with him. His features softened and he smiled. It would not be long now before he could see her again, hold her, kiss her. His whole body ached for her with a longing that had kept him sane and strong under the brutal torture of the SS. and could no longer be denied. He wondered if he would be transferred to Heronfield to convalesce. He certainly hoped so.

The door opened, shattering the idyllic image his mind was creating. He smiled weakly at the grey haired figure who approached him.

"Good morning, Lieutenant. I'm glad to see you awake. You're at a hospital which is often used by the S.O.E. if a patient has arrived somewhat unexpectedly."

"Then I'm right in thinking I'm back in England?"

The doctor smiled.

"You certainly are, young man and if I may say so you're damned lucky to be alive." He shook his head. "If I hadn't seen your injuries for myself I wouldn't have believed that people could be so brutal."

"How bad is it?"

"Well, your minor cuts and bruises will heal well enough by themselves, and the burns to your torso should cause little problem, although I must warn you that you will probably be scarred for life."

Tony nodded weakly. "I'm not surprised."

"You also have three broken ribs," the doctor continued, "and are extremely lucky that your lungs weren't punctured by the sharp ends of the bones. If that had happened, you wouldn't be here now."

"Will they heal?"

The doctor nodded. "Given time, and plenty of rest, and food to build up your strength."

"Food has been sadly lacking for me since the Germans took me."

"I'd guessed as much. A word of warning though. Say nothing of the Germans to anyone, not even the staff. I know where you've come from, and I'm sure that given your injuries some of those who nurse you will guess what has happened. But you are not to speak of it until Captain Dawson has debriefed you."

"Captain Dawson? Is he here?"

"No, but I've spoken to him on the telephone. I expect him to arrive sometime tomorrow."

"I can't make a phone call?"

"Not until you've seen Captain Dawson."

Tony sighed. Seeing Sarah, even talking to her, would have to wait a little longer. He moved slightly in the bed. He felt an arrow of pain shoot along his foot and leg, and drew a swift breath in through gritted teeth.

"You haven't said anything about my feet," he managed to say through the waves of pain. The doctor shook his head as though in disbelief.

"I've never seen anything like them before. What did they do to you?"

Tony closed his eyes. The pain intensified as he forced himself to live through the agony once more.

"They pushed matchsticks down under the nails, then set them alight."

"That explains your injuries. The nails are torn and splintered, and there are pieces of charred wood embedded in the flesh which is obviously cut and burned." He suppressed an unethical shudder. "I'm afraid we'll have to take them off."

Tony's eyes opened wide and he stared in horror. "Take them off? But I won't be able to remain on active service without my toes!"

The doctor laid a restraining hand on his shoulder. "Calm yourself. I mean to remove the nails not the toes. You'll be in pain for a while and it will be some time before you can walk normally again, but we've got you in time. The toes should heal eventually."

Tony relaxed into the pillows, the vision of permanent disability fading.

"When will you do it?"

"Now. You've had no food for some time, which means we can administer the general anaesthetic without any danger. Once the operation is over, we can start to feed you again and build up your strength."

"Good. Let's just get it over with. I could do with a good meal."

The doctor nodded and walked towards the door. "Right, I'll send in a nurse to prepare you."

At the door he stopped, hand on the knob, and turned towards his patient. "You know, Lieutenant Kemshall, I really admire you, and the others who do your line of work. Not many could do it. But it's vital to the war effort. I feel privileged to know you."

As the doctor turned and left the room, Tony managed a weak smile. Now that his work in France seemed to be over, he should be able to tell his father all about it. Imagining the pride he would see on his father's face as he learnt of his youngest son's work, Tony found himself content.

Dawson entered the room the following morning. He gazed down at the pale young man in the bed. He looked tired and thin, but there was a sparkle of life in his eyes.

"Well, Kemshall, I'm glad to see you, though I wish it were under different circumstances." He pulled up a chair and sat down beside the bed. "I've spoken with the doctor. He said that your operation went well." He shook his head sadly. "He told me the full extent of your injuries. We won't speak of them now, I would think the memory is too painful. All I will say is that I feel responsible in a way. I sent you out there, and I sent the order for the assassination, although I wasn't happy with it. You may be glad to know that the powers that be have decided to put a hold on all assassinations for now." He sighed. "I just wish they'd made that decision sooner."

"There's no reason for you to feel responsible, sir. I knew what I was getting into when I joined SOE, and I knew when I dropped into France that something like this might happen."

His commanding officer nodded but said nothing.

"I've spoken to Angeline. She's given me details of what has been going on in your area."

"You've spoken to her?"

Dawson nodded. "Yes, of course. She flew back with you. Didn't you know?"

Tony shook his head. "I was unconscious from the moment we left the SS HQ until I woke up here. I have no idea what's been going on."

"Well, Angeline is to be given some leave. She'll come and visit you in the next day or two, and she can tell you all the details of the escape. For now though, tell me what you've been up to. What is the make-up of your group, details of your attacks, plans for the future? You know the routine."

Tony smiled. "Yes, sir, I certainly do."

Tony related all that his group had accomplished in France, holding nothing back. He told of the successes, the deaths, the hopes, the fears and finally of his days at the mercy of SS Major Steinhauser. When he had finished, Dawson was quiet for a moment, as though digesting all that had been said. Finally he spoke.

"Of course I shall want a full written report, but that can wait until you're feeling better. I'm proud of you, Kemshall. You're a credit to the S.O.E. I shall be recommending that you be decorated for your service."

"Decorated?" Tony was surprised. "That isn't necessary, sir. I was only doing my duty."

"What you've been doing is above and beyond the call of duty for an ordinary soldier, Tony. You deserve everything you get."

"Thank you, sir." Tony looked questioningly at his superior officer. "Will I be able to go back to France, sir? Now that I've been a guest of the SS, it would be unwise for me to go back to Saint Nazaire, and I don't know any other area half so well."

Dawson nodded. "It's hard to say, Tony. At the moment I see your future career as a training officer at Beaulieu. You've learnt a great deal during your two trips to France. All that will prove extremely useful to new recruits."

"Does that mean I can tell my family about what I've been doing?"

Dawson shook his head. "No. You're still a member of the S.O.E. You must keep your work secret. Is that a problem?"

"Not exactly, sir. It's just that my father would like to see me on active service. He hates the thought of me in an office job, when I should be out there avenging the death of my brother."

"Keeping your work a secret is a problem?"

Tony nodded. "Yes, sir."

"I'm sorry, but there's nothing I can do. S.O.E. activities must not be made public until after this damned war is over."

"Well, sir, if I can't tell him what I've been doing, can I at least request a transfer to an active unit?"

"You can make your request, but it will be turned down. You're far too useful to us as a training officer."

"I understand, sir."

"Good."

"When will I be allowed to get in touch with my family?"

"Not until you're well again, I'm afraid. If they were to see you in this state then they'd begin to ask questions. We can't have that." Dawson smiled at the frown which furrowed Tony's brow. "It's not just your family you're thinking about, is it? Am I right in thinking there's a girl?"

Tony nodded. "According to my cover I've been over in America. I had to promise her that I'd write, but of course that's been impossible."

"Don't worry, she hasn't forgotten you."

Tony raised a quizzical eyebrow.

"You obviously gave her our London address. I have some letters for you." He handed Tony a small bundle of letters as he spoke. "I'll leave you to read these in peace, but please don't reply to them, or she'll want to know why you can't get to see her if you're back in England."

Tony nodded. "Yes, sir. Thank you, sir."

Captain Dawson rose and left the room, leaving the young man to his correspondence. Tony looked at the postmarks and frowned. The first six letters had been posted in May, the following four in June and the last two in July. There had been none since. With rapidly beating heart, he tore open the first envelope and began to read.

Half an hour later Tony was staring silently at the sheets of paper spread out on the bed in front of him. His eyes picked out random passages. They seemed to piece together a story which he did not want to believe, but which his heart told him was true.

> 'My darling Tony,
> I'm missing you so much. When the missing becomes too much to bear I close my eyes and think of Bath, and it always seems to bring me closer to you.'

> 'Life here goes on in its normal vein. So many wounded! I hope your work will help to bring this war to an end soon....When I feel lonely I think of those last few hours we spent together and I feel you close to me....Please write soon, I'm missing you so much.
> With all my love,
> Sarah.'

> 'You've been gone for over a month now and I'm getting used to your absence but it still hurts. I miss you. The Americans based near here are always getting letters from home. Why don't you write?'

> 'I am beginning to feel foolish. I write to you so often but you don't write to me. Is there someone else? It's hard for me to take the old familiar walks alone. So often I have felt that you were walking by my side but now even that feeling is fading. Are you no longer with me even in spirit, Tony? Maybe you didn't really want me to write to

you. I don't know what to do.'

Finally his eyes rested on the last letter once more, his vision blurred by tears

'Dear Tony,
I'm sorry that I've bothered you with so many letters. It's obvious to me now that you didn't really want me to write. I can no longer deceive myself by saying that you are too busy, or that your letters have got lost. You've been gone for three months now and I miss you as much as ever but, if anything, this war has taught me to be a realist. I was happy with you, Tony. My memories of those days we spent together will stay with me for the rest of my life, but I will not try to force love where there is only friendship. Why do I say is? Perhaps the word should be 'was'. Surely you would have written by now even if we were just friends? At least I now know where I stand.
Thank you for the memories Tony.
I wish you all the luck in the world.
Goodbye.
Sarah.'

Tony closed his eyes, his face creased in an agony of hurt and rejection. Yet as the tears began to fall, he knew that Sarah had been feeling this same pain for months. He rested his head on the pillows and let his tears flow freely, weeping with an agony of spirit for the love which had kept him alive in the cold, damp prison in France, and which now seemed lost to him for ever.

114

The fields were a golden sea of waving corn. Sarah watched from the bus as two shire horses plodded steadily along in front of a farmer making his way home after a long day's harvesting. It was a beautiful, idyllic scene, something that had happened time and time again over the centuries. The horses and the abundance of the land imparted a sense of peace and plenty, but both commodities were actually in short supply in a country bowed down by more than three years of all-out war. Sarah felt at one with the countryside. It always made her feel safe and at home. Yet she knew that once the war was over she would probably return to Coventry, all dreams of marrying and settling in this beautiful corner of the country lost forever.

"Cheer up. We're supposed to be going to a dance to enjoy ourselves."

Sarah turned and smiled at the young woman beside her.

"Sorry, Jane. I was miles away."

"Thinking of Tony, no doubt." When Sarah made no reply, she continued in a gentler vein. "Come on, Sarah, you have to get him out of your system. Isn't it obvious that he was just using you?"

Sarah nodded. "I suppose I should have expected it from the beginning, but he was so convincing. And he filled a hole in my life that I thought would never be filled after Joe died."

Jane took her hand and squeezed it gently. "Just remember, if a man like Tony Kemshall can do that, there must be many others much more worthy of that place."

Sarah managed a wry grin. "I suppose that next you'll be telling me I'll meet 'Mr. Right' at the dance tonight!"

Jane shrugged her shoulders and laughed. "You never know!"

The bus finally pulled into the small town of Marlborough where the two young women alighted, and made their way to the Town Hall for the weekly dance. As was usual now, the American GIs in their smart uniforms far outnumbered the few remaining young Englishmen who stayed at home. There was a great deal of resentment towards them from several quarters of the community. They had too much money, too many luxuries, too many of the young English girls and, worst of all, too much spare time. The most frequently-voiced question was why there were so many of them in England who had never seen active service? Were they going to stay there until the Second Front came, when that could be a year or more away? Of course few of the young women asked such questions. They were just glad to have so many escorts to choose from, now that the local boys were all away from home.

Sarah and Jane had barely bought a drink and found a seat before they were approached by two GIs.

"Hi, gals. Would you like to dance?"

Jane smiled up at the shorter, slimmer of the two Americans, black hair slicked back above angular Latino features. "Yes. Thanks."

As Jane rose to her feet and was escorted towards the dance floor. Sarah shook her head at the other GI, dashing his expectations.

"Sorry. I don't feel like dancing at the moment."

The American shrugged. "OK, lady."

He turned and walked away. Sarah watched her friend out on the dance floor. She wished she could be out there too, but did not want to dance with anyone but Tony. So she watched, a solitary figure whom none of the Americans approached, perhaps sensing her need for space in the way she sat. But she was not unhappy. The music was lively, causing her to tap her feet along with the beat. She enjoyed watching the couples dancing, imagining all sorts of stories of their lives and their involvement with each other. After a while, a breathless Jane rejoined her at the table. She dropped into her seat and relaxed visibly.

"Gosh, it's hot on the dance floor tonight."

"Do you want me to get you another drink?"

"No thanks. Al is getting one."

"Al?"

"Yes, Al Ginelli. That gorgeous GI I've been dancing with." Her eyes sparkled, and her voice was breathless, whether from the dancing or from excitement Sarah could not tell. "He comes from Boston. His father owns an Italian delicatessen. His family went over to America at the turn of the century, and he was born there. When the war is over, he says he's going into the family business and open another branch."

"How long have you known him?" Sarah laughed as she spoke. "I could have sworn that you only met him half an hour ago. But you already seem to know his whole life story!"

To Sarah's immense surprise, Jane began to blush.

"Yes, it does seem as though I've known him longer." She looked nervously across at her friend. "Please don't laugh, Sarah, but I feel that I could grow to like Al rather a lot."

"Of course I won't laugh! It's about time one of your dates lasted more than one night!"

"Shh, he's coming!"

Sarah looked up to see the beaming GI approaching with two drinks. As he set them

328

on the table, he turned to her with an apologetic smile.

"Sorry, did you want a drink too?"

Sarah shook her head. "No, thanks."

To her surprise the American held out his hand.

"My name's Al. You must be Jane's friend Sarah. I'm pleased to meet you."

Sarah smiled warmly as she shook his hand. "I'm pleased to meet you too, Al."

As the young man sat down. Sarah could not help noticing the way he looked at Jane. She responded to him with a warm smile which seemed to light her eyes with a special kind of radiance. Rarely had Sarah seen her friend so ebullient. She felt she was watching the beginning of a very special relationship. With a warm smile, she hoped that things would go well for her fellow nurse.

115

Tony sat in his wheelchair, gazing listlessly out of the window at the orchard. It was so similar to the orchard at Heronfield that it gave him a vague sense of coming home. But that did not lighten his heart. Depression had settled upon him when he had read Sarah's letters and it had not lifted over the intervening days. It was now a week since the operation on his feet, and he was beginning to feel better. The bruises on his body had begun to fade and the cuts were healing nicely. The broken ribs were knitting together well, so he was now able to move a little easier and the pain was diminishing, but the pain in his heart remained as deep as ever. There was a gentle knock at the door. Tony hesitated for a moment. He was not expecting anyone. No-one knew that he was back in England yet, and he felt like being left alone. The knock came again and he relented.

"Come in."

The door opened, and Tony's tired features broke into a smile of welcome.

"Jim! I thought you were out in France!"

"I was, but I got back about two weeks ago. Captain Dawson gave me leave to come and visit you, as your family don't know you're back."

"I'm glad you came. I could do with some company." He truly meant that. Seeing no one but the doctors and nurses had been limiting. He needed to talk with someone about his experiences in France. And about Sarah. Someone who would understand what he had been through, and would listen with consideration to his worries and problems. "Sit down Jim, we've got a lot to talk about."

Jim sat down, his welcoming smile fading to a frown.

"How are you feeling? Dawson told me about what they did to you. The bastards!"

Tony shrugged, feeling the tightening in his ribs as he did so. "I'm not too bad, all things considered. I'll admit I look a bit of a mess underneath these pyjamas, though. The burns are healing, but they're not a pretty sight. Neither are my feet if it comes to that."

Jim looked down at the offending members swathed in snow-white bandages.

"Will they heal?"

"Oh yes. I should be able to get around on crutches soon. The only thing holding me up in that department is the broken ribs. When they've healed I'll be up on my feet; the sooner I can walk normally without sticks, the sooner I'll be allowed home."

"Dawson said you wouldn't be allowed home until all visible signs of your injuries are gone. That's rough."

Tony shrugged. "I suppose so; but there's nothing much to go home for."

"Really!" Jim grinned. "What about that nurse you were so enamoured with? Don't you want to see her again?"

"Of course. But she doesn't want to see me."

Tony's answer lacked life. His eyes clouded with sadness.

Jim frowned. "Do you want to talk about it?"

"Why not? There's not much to tell." Tony told his friend all about his experiences in France, how he had to break his promise to Sarah and not write. Then he told of the letters Dawson had brought, and how through them he had witnessed Sarah's fall from happiness into despair. "So you see," he finished, "it's all over between us, before it really had a chance to begin."

Jim was touched by his friend's sadness. He wanted to reach out and help him in some way.

"Come on, Tony, surely it's not as bad as all that. You're not feeling yourself at the moment. When you're better you'll be able to see her again and explain everything. I'm sure she'll understand."

"Will she? How can I explain it all to her, Jim? You know I'm not allowed to talk about what I've been doing. She'll think I couldn't be bothered to write, and now I'm making excuses. To be honest, I can't really blame her for feeling like that, can I?"

"I suppose not. But at least you won't be going back to France again. Staying in England will give you an opportunity to win her back."

"Will it?" Tony was doubtful, but allowed a small seed of hope to lodge in his heart. Maybe, just maybe, he would be able to make her understand.

"Perhaps being based at Beaulieu will have its advantages. Though I'd rather be going back to Saint Nazaire, if I could." Tony smiled and changed the subject. "So what have you been up to? Why are you back here?"

"I was flown out with one of the leading members of the Resistance in my area. The top men wanted to talk to him to see what is needed, though why they couldn't just ask me is a mystery!"

The two men laughed. The rapport which had existed between them since the retreat from Dunkirk was as strong as ever.

"Who knows what the boys upstairs think!?" Tony clutched his ribs, a stabbing pain coursing through his chest.

"Are you all right?"

Tony looked at his friend's concerned features and grinned. "It only hurts when I laugh!"

He was glad Jim had been able to visit. Having someone to talk to was just what he needed to put all his problems into the proper perspective. With a contented sigh, he leant back into his wheelchair, new hope for the future lightening his heart.

As the weeks went by, Tony's healing continued. His first attempts at walking were short and painful, even with the aid of crutches. But time is a great healer and as the days passed he was able to walk further and, eventually, unaided. To begin with his steps were uneven as the pain coursed through his feet, but soon that too was gone. The broken ribs healed, the bruises disappeared and the blisters where he had been burned turned to angry red scars. Eventually the doctor was satisfied that, save for the scars beneath his shirt, there were no outward signs of Tony's injuries. This good news was followed by a telephone call from Captain Dawson. Tony could go home on leave at last.

Tony gathered together the few personal items he had accumulated during his seven long weeks in hospital and convalescing - toothbrush, flannel, shaving equipment, brush and comb. Into his pocket he slipped the slim package of envelopes which contained the letters from Sarah. He gazed thoughtfully at himself in the mirror. Much as he wanted to go home and see Sarah, he was afraid to face her. What if she would not listen? What if she wanted their relationship to end permanently? He felt a cold shiver down his spine as he contemplated life without her by his side. That would be harder than anything, for it was thoughts of Sarah that had kept him strong in France. What would keep him strong if she no longer wanted him? With a deep breath Tony picked up his cap and placed it on his head. There was no point worrying about it. The only way to find out how Sarah felt was to confront her. Picking up his pitifully small bag, he turned and left the hospital room.

116

Sarah grimaced at Jane across the table.

"I'll be glad when this war is over. I'm getting fed up with the limited menu."

Jane nodded. "I know what you mean. I've almost forgotten what oranges taste like, and as for bananas! I can hardly even remember what they look like!"

Sarah laughed. She finished her dinner and pushed her plate away.

"What are you doing this evening?"

"I'm going dancing with Al."

Sarah grinned. "You've seen a lot of him over the last few weeks."

Jane blushed. "Yes, I guess I have. You know, Sarah, he's really special, so kind and considerate, not as pushy as most of the Americans you meet. I feel as though I've known him all my life."

"It sounds as though you're in love with him."

"I don't know, Sarah. It's all happening so quickly. I think I love him, but how can I be sure? He's over here in a strange country, and obviously missing his family. What if he's just using me as a substitute?"

Sarah smiled encouragingly. "Do you really think that?"

"Well...no, I don't think so."

"Then stop worrying. Just go out and enjoy yourself."

Jane laughed. "You know me, that's my main aim in life!" She rose to her feet. "I'll just go and take a quick bath, or I'll be late."

Sarah smiled sadly as her friend left the dinning room. Things seemed to be looking up for Jane. Maybe, finally, she had found her 'Mister Right'. Sarah only hoped that her friend would be luckier in love than she had been herself. When Joe was killed, she felt that her capacity to love died with him, until Tony slowly taught her to love again. Her love for him had been like the slow unfurling of the petals of a flower, growing from a small insignificant bud into a thing of great beauty. His subsequent rejection of her had been like a sudden unexpected frost which had caused the petals to curl and die. But at least he had shown her that it was possible to love again. With a sigh she rose from the table, and followed her friend from the room. Maybe she would fall in love again. But first she had to bury her love for Tony deep in her heart and lock it away there, where it could not rear its head to trouble her ever again.

117

The taxi pulled in through the empty space where the huge iron gates once hung, then drew to a halt outside the lodge. Tony climbed out, paid the driver and watched as the black cab turned in the wide drive and went back out of the gateway. Turning to look along the drive to the distant house where he had grown up, Tony was tempted to go straight there, to confront Sarah as soon as possible. But common sense took over. He had not seen her for almost six months, so another hour or two would make no difference. And he knew how hurt his mother would be if he did not call in to see her first. With one last longing look at the home of his youth, he turned and made his way up the shallow steps. He opened the door and stepped inside, closing it quietly behind him as he listened to the sound of voices coming from the drawing room. With a smile he put his small bag of belongings down, and made his way over to the door.

"Hello, Mamma. Bonjour, Grandmamma."

The room was filled with an electric silence as the two women turned towards the door.

"Tony!" The exclamation came from his mother's lips as she stood and hurried towards him, tears starting in her eyes. "Oh, Tony! I'm so glad to see you!" She hugged her son tightly, then stepped back to study him. "When did you get back?"

"Yesterday. I came down as soon as I could." His glance strayed to his grandmother, who remained seated. She looked older than he remembered, as though the enforced exile from her home had taken all the strength from her. Tony made his way over to the chair and bent down to kiss her cheek. It seemed fragile, papery thin beneath his lips. Kneeling down beside her, he took her hand in his.

"How are you, Grandmamma?"

"Not too bad, mon cher." Her voice was thin. Where was the robust woman whom he had put on the boat in Saint Nazaire just two years before? He could see that this war would have more casualties than those who had been injured by bullets or bombs. Tony flashed a questioning glance at his mother.

"She misses her home."

Tony nodded. What else was there to say? Turning back to his grandmother, he smiled encouragingly.

"Don't worry, the war will soon be over. When it is, I'll take you back home to Saint Nazaire."

"But will it still be there, Tony? How much of it will have been destroyed by the bombing? What about my home? I do not even know if it is still standing, and if it is, who is living in it." Her eyes took on a faraway look as though she could see her home as she spoke. "And what of the people, Tony? How are the Germans treating them? Will any of those I remember still be alive if I ever return? What of the Boues?" She looked down at him, and he felt the tears start in his eyes. "Do you remember Jean-Paul and his family?"

Tony nodded. "Yes, Grandmamma. I remember them."

"They worked for me. Their family had worked for my family for generations and it was my responsibility to protect them. But I let them down." She gazed into the distance again. "I ran away, Tony, when I should have stayed with them, should have helped them."

The tears stood out on her cheeks and Tony noticed that his tears were falling too.

"But you are old now, Grandmamma. What could you have done to help them?"

"My duty. I am Madame de Thierry and I should be there. There should be a de Thierry there to help them in their troubled times. I have failed in my duty."

Tony could say nothing. He wanted to take her in his arms and tell her that it was all right. There was a de Thierry looking after her people. He, Tony, had been there and helped them in a way that she never could. He wanted to tell her that Jean-Paul, Marie, Theresa and Jeanne were all alive and well. He wanted her to know that her people were fighting back. When the end came and they were finally victorious, a fact of which he had no doubt, they would proudly hold their heads high as they welcomed their Countess home. No-one would say that she, or the de Thierry family, had failed in their duty. But he was sworn to secrecy. All he could do was to watch her anguish and his heart ached because he was unable to help her.

Rising to his feet, he brushed the tears from his cheeks and looked helplessly at his mother.

"She has been like this for some time now, Tony. Nothing we do or say seems to help."

Tony saw the pain in his mother's eyes, and put his arms around her to comfort her. How difficult it must be for her to stand by and watch her mother deteriorate. They embraced in silence for a time. Then his mother stepped back and dabbed at her eyes with a delicate lace handkerchief. She smiled through her tears.

"I am sorry, Tony. This is not the homecoming I would have planned for you."

Tony returned her smile. "I'm so glad to see you again, Mamma. I've missed you." His mother looked tired. The worry of his grandmother, and probably the lack of news from him, had worn her down. He decided to lie to her so that she would not think that he had forgotten her. "Did you get my letters from America?"

His mother frowned and shook her head. "No. We had no letters from you."

"Damn the Post Office!" Tony turned towards the window as he spoke so that she would not see the lie in his eyes. "I wrote to you three or four times. I wondered why you didn't reply."

Louise Kemshall sighed. "That explains it. Your father was very angry that you did not write. He said you were too busy enjoying yourself in the land of plenty to think of us."

Tony turned to her, tight lipped. Enjoying himself? If only she knew!

"Is he in his study? I suppose I ought to speak to him."

Louise shook her head. "No. He went up to town yesterday. He is coming back on the afternoon train. He should be here in about an hour. That will give me time to get some dinner ready."

Tony raised his eyebrows. "Retreating into the kitchen? I thought you might want to talk with me. After all, we haven't seen each other for almost half a year."

Louise smiled conspiratorially. "Yes, and it is half a year since you saw that nurse up at the big house who you seemed so fond of. Why not take a walk up there and see if she is free?"

"You don't mind?"

Louise laughed, the first laugh since his return. He was glad to hear it.

"No, of course not! I was young myself once, believe it or not!"

Tony hugged his mother. "Thank you Mamma! I'll be back in time to meet Father."

He turned and hurried from the room, rushing out into the chill October afternoon and walking briskly towards the welcoming facade of Heronfield House. But as he approached the only home he had ever known, his steps slowed. Sarah's letters were like a lead weight in his breast pocket, close to his heart, and he began to worry about the reception he would receive. His feet were almost dragging as he finally entered the hall, his heart beating wildly and his palms sweaty. He was afraid, far more so than when about to set out on a sabotage raid. If he had not been so nervous, he would have laughed at himself. Turning towards the reception desk, cap in hand, he spoke to the young nurse who looked up at his approach.

"Is it possible for me to see Nurse Sarah Porter, please?"

The nurse looked down at her papers. "I'm afraid she's on duty at the moment. But if you'd care to wait in the library, I'll see if she can be spared."

"Thank you." Tony turned away.

"The library is over..."

"Thank you" interrupted Tony, "I can find my own way."

He crossed the hall and went through the door into the library. As he closed it gently behind him he was thankful to be alone. He would not like to have this talk with Sarah with someone else present. Perhaps he should take her for a walk in the grounds? It might help to talk in places that held happy memories for them both. He went over to the window and looked out. It was beginning to rain, so the idea of a walk was out. As he waited he wondered what to say to her, his mind full of thoughts and ideas which would not come together. How could he explain, when he was not able to tell her the truth?

"Oh, it's you."

Tony spun round. He had been so engrossed in his thoughts that he had not heard the door open. Sarah stood in the doorway, a frown furrowing her brow. Tony felt his heart stand still. She looked puzzled, maybe a little annoyed. But it did not matter to him, all he saw was her beauty. He just stared for a long moment, drinking in the sight of her, wanting to hold her and thank her for the love they shared, a love which had kept him alive during the darkest hours of his life. Then he noticed the frown was still there, and his warm welcoming smile faded.

"I've just got back home, so I came straight round to see you."

"Why?" Sarah's voice was hard. Tony was the last person she had expected to see. She was not prepared for the conflicting emotions she felt. Her most overwhelming feeling was relief to see him safe, a love so strong that she wanted him to put his arms around her and hold her close, to kiss her and tell her that he felt the same way. Yet, beneath those feelings was the hard core she had forced herself to build in her heart, knowing that he did not care for her. To get involved with him once more would only cause her more heartache.

"I just wanted to see you and talk to you." Tony realised that this was going to be far more difficult than he had anticipated. "Please come in and close the door,"

"What have we got to talk about?"

To Tony's relief, Sarah stepped into the room and closed the door behind her as she spoke. He smiled and stepped towards her.

"It's so good to see you, Sarah. I've missed you so much."

The words touched Sarah deeply. He sounded so sincere. His eyes seemed to speak to her of the depth of his feelings. Yet she would not allow herself to believe him.

"If you missed me so much, why didn't you reply to my letters?" Her words were harsh, filled with pain and rejection. Tony's heart went out to her as he reached into his breast pocket and took out the small bundle of envelopes.

"I've only just got them, Sarah. They weren't forwarded to me as I'd requested. They were waiting for me when I arrived back in England."

Sarah looked deep into his eyes and could see there that there was no dishonesty in his words. It was true then; he had not received her letters. She took a hesitant step towards him, then stopped.

"That's no excuse, Tony. You knew where I was. If you'd missed me as much as you say, you could have written to me here."

"I'm sorry, Sarah. I was just so busy, and when I didn't get a letter from you, I didn't know if you wanted me to write." Tony knew it was a feeble excuse and hated himself for lying, but he did not know what else to say. Sarah seemed so far away from him now. She had been much closer to him in the cell in Saint Nazaire, and he did not know how to breach the barrier between them.

"Did you meet someone else? Is that it, Tony?"

Tony was stunned. "No! Of course not! You know how much I love you, Sarah!" His eyes were soft, warm, inviting. Sarah wanted to rush into his arms, forget about the past and look forward only to a future with him. But she held back. There was no getting past the fact that if he really loved her he would have written at least one letter in the six months they had been apart.

"How can I be sure that you love me, Tony? How can I know that you're not just using me?"

Tony felt as though the walls were rushing in on him. What could he do? What could he say? An idea exploded in his mind. His eyes lit up in excitement and he opened his mouth to speak. Then he closed it again, as the fire in his eyes was quenched by reason. He had been about to ask her to marry him. Surely that would prove his love for her? But what would happen to their relationship when he had to lie to her again? What would he tell her if he were sent back to France? He wanted to marry her, more than anything in the world he wanted that, but he knew that they could never build a lasting marriage on a foundation of lies. Finally his shoulders slumped in defeat. He shrugged.

"All I can do is say that I love you, and hope that you will believe me."

She wanted to. She saw the fear of rejection in his eyes and wanted to believe him. But that would leave too many uncertainties, too many unanswered questions. Sadly Sarah shook her head.

"I'm sorry, Tony. I don't know what to think or believe any more." She frowned. "You've been gone so long, and I don't know what you've been doing or anything. How can I be expected to believe you if you won't tell me the truth?" She waited, heart in her mouth. She had done what she could. It was up to Tony now.

"Please understand that this is war, Sarah. I can't tell you." Tony's eyes were pleading.

Sarah felt her anger rising. Why was he deliberately making it so difficult for her?

"Surely you can tell me something? The soldiers upstairs tell me what they've been doing. I've seen so many while you've been away. Have you heard what happened at Dieppe? So many dead and wounded while you were off enjoying yourself in America!" She was almost shouting now.

"Enjoying myself? It was hardly that!"

"Have you asked for a transfer to active service yet?"

"Yes, but it was refused. What has that got to do with it anyway?"

"Everything. I'm sure that if you had been insistent they would have given you a transfer, but you don't seem to care about anything important. You're prepared to let other people do the fighting, while you take the easy way out. It's the same with our relationship. You pretend you care when you're here, but once you're away it's out of sight out of mind. And you haven't got the courage to tell me!"

"Are you saying I'm a coward?"

Sarah said nothing. That was not what she had intended to say at all. She just wanted to push him into doing or saying something to prove that he really did care. But it was obvious to her now that that was not going to happen. There was silence for a time as they each struggled with their emotions. Finally Tony spoke.

"Don't you love me anymore, Sarah?"

His voice was soft, gentle, full of pain. In his eyes she saw the Tony who had befriended her, whom she had grown to love through the caring way he had helped her to get over Joe's death. But she was no longer sure that the man she saw now was the only Tony. There were so many facets to his character that she did not understand. She knew she could never be happy with him, knowing that so much of his life was a secret to her. She closed her eyes and her shoulders slumped. She looked so dejected that Tony wanted to reach out and take her in his arms, to hold her close and never let her go again. If he had, maybe things would have turned out differently. But life is not built on maybes.

"Yes, I still love you." Sarah opened her eyes and looked directly at him, tears blurring her vision. "I think I shall always love you, but it's not enough. If you can't trust me enough to tell me your secrets, then you can't love me."

"But I do!" Tony cried out, sensing that she was drawing away, and trying desperately to prevent that. His worst nightmares seemed to be coming true, and he did not know what to do.

Sarah shook her head. "No, Tony. Perhaps you think you do, but your actions don't show it. Maybe one day you'll be able to put others before yourself. When you find yourself able to fight for your country, to do what your family want you to do, to love me as much as I love you without holding back, then perhaps I'll believe you."

"Just give me a chance, Sarah. I'll prove it!" Tony was frantic. He could feel her slipping away from him. The only way to stop her was to tell her why he hadn't written, why he had not applied for active service. For a moment he was tempted. Tell her everything, and damn S.O.E.! He had a life too, didn't he? Surely he was entitled to some happiness after what he had been through? He held out his hands, imploring her to see his love for in his eyes and not to turn away. But it was hopeless.

"I'm sorry, Tony. You're just not ready for the kind of love and commitment I need. I don't feel I can settle for anything less."

Tony felt as though the world had stopped revolving, as though life itself was ending. The tears welled up in his eyes.

"Please don't end it like this, Sarah."

Hearing his imploring words, seeing his unhappiness, sensing a pain which she could not understand, Sarah almost relented. Then she remembered the long weeks and months waiting for a letter that never came, while sacks of mail from America were arriving every day for the GIs down the road. He had not cared enough to write. His excuse had just been an act. Maybe his professed love for her was just an act too. She shook her head sadly.

"I'm sorry, Tony. Goodbye."

Without another word Sarah turned and left the room. As Tony watched her walk away he felt as though he were dying inside. All he had held in his heart, all that had shone as a beacon, keeping him alive and drawing him home, lay shattered on the rocks of hurt and misunderstanding. In that moment, he wished that he had died in France believing that she was waiting for him. It would have been far less painful than this rejection. He watched Sarah mount the stairs, stiff-backed and erect. But he did not see her crumple as she turned the corner out of his sight. Nor was he aware of her anguished sobs. All he knew was that Sarah was no longer his and that life had no meaning now.

Tony found himself on the steps leading up to the lodge and wondered how he had got there. His clothes were soaking wet and his hair was plastered against his skull so he knew he must have been walking in the light rain for some time. But he did not know where he had been, or for how long. His mind was a blank. With a sigh he made his way inside, only to be confronted by his father with a face like thunder.

"There you are at last! Where have you been, boy? Your mother had dinner ready hours ago! You've been away for six months, then come back late for your first meal at home! I think we'd better have a talk in my study."

Tony felt tired, too tired for another confrontation, but he knew it could not be avoided. He forced a smile.

"It's good to see you too, Dad."

Sir Michael glared, then turned to lead the way into the study.

Tony followed his father into the room where Sir Michael positioned himself with his back to the window, hands clenched behind him. Tony decided to take the initiative. The last thing he wanted now was an argument with his father. He smiled weakly.

"It really is good to see you, Dad. I've missed you while I've been away."

Sir Michael's features softened a little.

"We've missed you too, son. We need someone young to bring a little life back into this house." Sir Michael was struggling to keep his voice even, confused by his emotions. He really had missed Tony and was glad to see him safe. But at the same time he felt angry and resentful. Why? Surely he did not resent his younger son because his first-born had died in battle? What was he doing, always picking an argument whenever his son paid one of his rare visits home? He wanted Tony to stay at home, to be safe and to come through this war alive, yet at the same time he felt that no one was trying to avenge David's death. It was as if he were the only one who cared, the only one who had been hurt by the family's loss in the Battle of Britain. As he struggled with his conflicting emotions a frown creased his brow. Tony mistook it for returning anger.

"I'm sorry I missed dinner, Dad. It was Mamma's idea that I go up to the house and let my friend know I'm here."

"But she expected you back for dinner! As soon as you left the house she searched the larder for all the special things she had saved. She made the best meal she could as a welcome for you, but you couldn't even be bothered to turn up!" Sir Michael found his anger and confusion rising again, but did not seem able to control them. "Do you care so little for your mother? You didn't even write to her while you were away. David would never have behaved like that!"

"But I'm not David, Dad. I'm Tony. Anyway, I did write but my letters don't seem to have arrived."

"Do you expect me to believe that? Surely one of your letters would have got through?"

Tony had nothing to say. His father was right, it was a feeble excuse.

"I don't think you realise just how difficult things have been here in the last few months. Your mother needed to hear from you."

Tony was deeply hurt by Sarah's rejection, tired by the constant jibing from his father. It seemed as though no one appreciated what he had done, that the whole world had turned against him.

"I've had a difficult time too, you know!"

"Difficult?" Sir Michael snorted in disgust. "We all know what it's like in America, the GI's are always so pleased to tell us. Few shortages, no bombing, life going on as normal. You call that difficult? Try living here with a poor old woman who feels guilty about leaving her home and responsibilities and wants to return to an occupied country! Try living with a woman who mourns the death of her first-born son! Try being a father who would give anything to put on a uniform and avenge the death of that son!"

Tony's heart went out to his father, and he tried to bridge the gulf between them.

"I miss David too, Dad, we all do. And I promise, his death will be avenged."

"When, Tony? And by whom? It should be the duty of his family to go out there and finish what he started. To defeat the Germans and make sure his death was not in vain!" He looked quizzically at his younger son. "When are you going to apply for a transfer to active service?"

Tony had known it was coming, had sensed that the argument would take the usual turn. Why should he be banned from telling the people he loved that he had already seen active service, that he had already avenged David's death many times over? He wished he had never joined S.O.E. but had gone straight into a conventional active unit; then he thought of the comradeship and the successes, and knew he could do nothing else. He decided to tell a part of the truth. But, deep inside, he knew it would not be enough.

"I've already applied for a transfer, Father."

Sir Michael's face was transformed. It was as though the sun had come out from behind a black rain cloud, flooding his features with light and hope.

"When will it come through, son?" His voice was eager, more alive than Tony had heard it since David's death. He hated to do what he must do next.

"Captain Dawson turned me down."

"Turned you down? Why? What about the Second Front?" Sir Michael was confused. Why had Tony built him up, only to knock him down again?

"They don't think the Second Front will come for some time yet, Dad. But when it does, they say I can do more good in my present job than by joining the invading forces."

"Can't you speak to this Captain Dawson again? Surely if he knew how much you wanted the transfer, he would agree. Shall I speak to him? They can't refuse if you are persistent."

"There's no use talking about it. I'm not being transferred, now or when the Second Front comes."

"You mean you don't really want to be." Sir Michael crossed to the desk and picked up a framed photograph of David in his RAF uniform. He looked at it in silence for a moment, then held it out for Tony to see. His voice was cold and hard when he spoke again. "Look closely, Tony. Your brother was a man to be proud of. I could not have wished for a better son. If he and others like him had not fought so long and valiantly throughout the summer of 1940, we would have been invaded. The Germans would now be in our towns and villages, living in our homes, and there would be nothing we could do against them. Can you imagine that, Tony?" Tony said nothing, instead he saw again the city of Saint Nazaire. Yes, he could imagine it. "You and I, the whole of England, owe David so much," his father continued. "When are you going to repay that debt?"

Tony closed his eyes. 'I am repaying it! I have already!' he wanted to scream, but the words did not come. He wanted to open his shirt and show his father the scars of his repayment, to show him the feet which had been torn and bloodied in the fight against his brother's killers. He wanted to tell him all that he had suffered for the people and land he loved. Instead he said all he would be allowed to say.

"I am repaying the debt in my present job. I won't ask for a transfer again."

"Coward!" Sir Michael's voice was angry as he spat out the word. "You're not fit to call David 'brother'. You're not fit to be my son. I have fathered a coward. It makes me ashamed of myself too!"

Tony closed his eyes and fought to hold back the tears which threatened to overwhelm him. 'It's not fair!' His mind screamed his anger and frustration. 'It's not fair!' He took a deep breath and opened his eyes to look directly into those of his father, eyes filled with contempt.

"I'm not a coward, Father. I would hope that you could take my word for it. But as you can't, we will just have to wait for events to prove me right. I'm sorry, Father, but as long as you feel this way, I can no longer live in this house."

"Then go, Tony, and don't come back. From this day on I have only one son, and he is dead."

Sir Michael turned to look out of the window but he saw nothing through his tears. Tony stood in silence, watching the ramrod back, hoping his father would turn, but nothing happened. Finally he turned away, rejection and despair showing in his every movement. Out in the hall he picked up his kitbag. He had not even had time to take it to his room, let alone unpack. He let himself out silently through the front door, and made his way down the drive. When he reached the road he turned and looked back at the lodge and at Heronfield House, both shrouded in misty rain. He no longer had the home he loved, or the people he loved. His life stretched out before him, an empty wilderness which he must wander alone. As he turned away and began the long walk along the empty road, the tears began to fall at last.

Sir Michael turned from the window at the sound of the closing front door. He wished he had handled things better, had not called Tony a coward; but he honestly believed that what he said was true. Yet he loved the young man. That was something he could deny to Tony, but never to himself. He still had two sons, one dead and one alive, but so alienated from him that he might as well be dead. He crossed to the desk once more and picked up another photograph, not of David alone this time but of the two brothers together. Two young boys in short trousers sitting side by side, holding up the trout they had caught. Both boys were smiling. Their eyes held an innocence which had been lost long years ago. Sir Michael remembered taking the photograph. He remembered how close they had all been that day, and he mourned for that lost heaven. One son dead but the memory of him bright and true, one son alive but the relationship broken beyond repair. Sir Michael lowered himself slowly into a chair and watched his tears splash on the glass covering the photograph. His whole world was shattered and he did not know how to repair it.

118

While all hope in Tony's personal life seemed to be lost, hope was rekindled in the hearts of the British people by the news from North Africa. On October 23rd, the British launched an attack against Rommel's forces, setting in motion the Second Battle of El Alamein. The battle raged back and forth across the burning sands for almost two weeks, before the British tanks finally broke through the lines of the Afrika Korps. That made it possible for Britain and America to land forces in French North Africa. More good news filtered through from the Eastern Front. The German advance towards the Caucasus was stopped because of snow. On November 19th, six Russian armies broke through the German lines at Stalingrad, leaving the invading forces trapped. As 1942 began to draw to a close, British forces in the Far East began a land offensive towards Burma. Although the Germans finally moved into unoccupied France and the French fleet was scuttled at Toulon, it looked as though the war might have reached a turning point at last. As 1943 moved ever closer, the hopes and expectations of the embattled Allies were raised.

Sarah had been out walking, a practice she still enjoyed although she avoided the walks she had taken with Tony, still finding constant reminders of his presence too painful. Now she raced up the stairs and burst into the room she shared with Jane, a safe haven in times of need. It was 15th November, 1942.

"Jane! Jane!" she called as the door banged shut behind her. "Guess what! They're ringing the church bell in the village!"

Jane, who had been busy writing a letter, paled visibly. She put down her pen unsteadily.

"Invasion?"

Like everyone else, she knew that the church bells had not been rung since the outbreak of war and would only do so if England was invaded. Yet Sarah was radiant, she was even laughing.

"No! It's good news! Monty has defeated Rommel at some place called El Alamein! Mr. Churchill said the bells should be rung to celebrate this great victory!"

Jane leapt to her feet excitedly. "Oh Sarah, isn't it wonderful! Perhaps the war will soon be over."

Sarah shrugged. "I don't know about that, we still have a long way to go. But it is good news. The Germans will be defeated in the end, no matter how long it takes."

"You're right of course, but I think Monty's timing is lousy."

Sarah frowned in puzzlement. "What do you mean?"

Her friend grinned broadly. "I have some good news to tell you, but it hardly compares with Monty defeating Rommel. Perhaps I'll save it for another day."

"Don't be silly, Jane. Tell me now."

Jane blushed slightly but her smile was radiant. "Al and I are getting married."

"What! Married!" Sarah's face broke into a brilliant smile. "Oh Jane, I'm so pleased. He's just the right man for you."

"I think so too." Jane flung herself onto the bed and stretched out, hands behind her head as she looked up at the ceiling. "I never thought I'd be so happy. Isn't it wonderful to be in love?"

Sarah grinned. "It certainly is. When will you get married?"

"Soon. There's no reason to wait. We want to spend as much time as possible together, before the Second Front comes and he's sent to France."

Sarah nodded. "Will you go home for the wedding?"

"Yes. We've both applied for leave. With any luck we'll be able to get married before Christmas."

"That's wonderful. Can I come to the wedding?"

"Of course. I want you to be my bridesmaid."

"Me? Are you sure?" Sarah was thrilled to be asked.

"Of course! Who else?"

"Thanks! Oh!" Sarah's face suddenly fell and Jane looked worried.

"What's wrong?"

"What on earth am I going to wear?"

Jane laughed. "I've got the same problem too!"

Sarah joined in the laughter. It was good to have friends, and she was glad Jane had finally found the right man for her. But Sarah's happiness was tinged with sadness. Would she ever be as happy in love?

November passed quickly for Sarah and Jane, as they planned the wedding. Hoarded coupons were spent on food and clothes so that, although most things were rationed, they were able to provide all that was needed. November became December. Only four weeks after she announced her engagement, Jane became Mrs. Ginelli. It was a small family wedding full of joy and excitement, there had not been many things to celebrate since the outbreak of the war and everyone was glad to be able to join in the festivities. The day passed quickly. In the early evening Jane and Al left for their brief weekend honeymoon in London. Sarah travelled back to Heronfield alone, feeling empty, as though her life was being wasted, and she vowed she would do something about it.

Wartime places all sorts of restraints on people. Once the weekend in London was over, Jane returned to the room she shared with Sarah, and Al rejoined his fellow Americans at the base just outside Marlborough. Although time together was limited, it was not wasted. While awaiting the Second Front, Al had a fair amount of spare time and spent as much of it as possible with Jane at the local hotel. It was there that Jane first heard of the Christmas party that the GI's were planning for the local children and evacuees. It took no time at all for Jane to become involved in the planning. Sarah, finding in the enterprise something to occupy her loneliness, agreed to help.

The party was held on the Saturday before Christmas. The dance hall in Marlborough had been commandeered for the occasion. It had been transformed into what every child's idea of Christmas should be. In the corner stood a huge fir tree, hung with streamers and tinsel and tiny lights that flickered brightly. Around the walls were flags, bunting and balloons, creating a gay atmosphere for the children. Down the length of the hall, trestle tables had been erected and were laden with food, food from the American base which had not been seen in England since the outbreak of war. There were tinned fruits of every possible variety, some of the children had never heard of them, let alone tasted them. There were cakes made with real eggs, full of currants and cherries and covered with sweet sticky icing to look like snow. Over in the corner, a freezer held ice-cream. As Sarah perused the hall waiting only for the children to bring it to life, she smiled. She was not sure who was anticipating the party more, the children or her! The clock in the square chimed three. The doors opened and the children came rushing in, their eyes bright with excitement, their cheeks flushed. They gazed wide-eyed and open-mouthed at the beautiful decorations, and stopped for a moment just inside the door, not sure what to do next. Then the GIs took over.

"Hi kids! Come in! It's time for games!"

The children rushed excitedly over to the group of American soldiers. There were running games, singing games and team games, and the noise was incredible. Jane and Sarah were laughing, having almost as much fun as the children as they helped to put the finishing touches to the spread on the tables. The children, although enjoying the games, could not stop their eyes from straying to the food. The Americans were lavishing all of the affection which they would normally have shared with their families at Christmas on this group of children, who had been deprived of so much during the years of their childhood. They could see the excitement and anticipation in the eyes of their small guests, and it filled their hearts with festive cheer. Grinning broadly, the GIs indicated the tables.

"Right, kids. Let's eat!"

With excited cries, the children made their way across to the tables and sat down. At each place was a party hat, which they put on before tucking into the food. Christmas carols were played on the gramophone, while the GIs passed round plates of sandwiches, cake, fruit, jelly and ice-cream. Sarah watched as Jane and Al worked together, laughing as they shared their first Christmas party. It was a wonderful atmosphere, full of joy, excitement, giving; just as Christmas should be. Sarah did not doubt that the Germans had such parties, and she wondered why men who could be so kind and giving one minute could then go out and kill people. She watched the soldiers laughing and joking with the children while the food disappeared from the tables, and hoped that this would be the last Christmas of the war, the last Christmas when people would be separated from their families, fearing for the safety of their loved ones.

When the food had all been eaten, the base commander climbed onto a chair and blew a whistle to attract attention. Silence fell upon the hall. He smiled down at the eager faces turned towards him.

"Are you all having a good time?"

"Yes!" The answer was deafening.

"Do you like Christmas?"

"Yes! Yes!"

"Well, I know someone else who likes Christmas. He's usually very busy just about now, but he's managed to come to see us this afternoon. Shall I ask him to come in?"

"Yes!"

The children could hardly contain their excitement. No one had said who the mystery visitor was, but most of them thought they could guess. As the base commander made his way over to the door and opened it, they knew they were right. It was a tall man dressed in red trousers and a coat trimmed with white fur. There were shiny black boots on his feet and a red fur trimmed hat on his head of white hair. A full white beard flowed down onto his chest, and he carried an enormous sack flung over his shoulder. The cheers which greeted his appearance left the ears of the adults ringing and their faces wreathed in smiles as he began to delve into the sack, and hand out presents wrapped in brightly coloured paper.

Sarah smiled happily. Here was the future of the world. This generation was growing up during a war. Hopefully they would remember the deprivations as well as these happy times, and make sure that nothing like this would ever be inflicted upon their own children.

121

Tony perused the group of men and women who sat in the main body of the hall gazing expectantly at him. Here he was, giving advice when he longed to be back in the field. It was a strange and disconcerting situation. Captain Dawson stepped forward and spoke to the group first. Tony, resplendent in uniform, waited nervously for his turn.

"This is Lieutenant Kemshall," Dawson began. "Not so long ago he was sitting where you are now. At the time we had not yet sent agents into France, so what we told him about the conditions was pure speculation. Lieutenant Kemshall has recently returned from his second stay in France, and now has firsthand knowledge to pass on to you. Listen carefully to what he has to say. What you learn from him now might save your life."

Dawson's audience looked at each other. A real agent who had been to France and, they assumed, fought the enemy on occupied ground. This seemed worth listening to.

"That's all I have to say. I'll leave you now in the capable hands of Lieutenant Kemshall."

Tony smiled wanly. Capable? He had never felt less capable in his life. He watched as Captain Dawson left the room, then cleared his throat.

"Bonjour."

He smiled at the chorus of French greetings that came back to him.

"I find it almost easier to think and talk in French after months in France," he began, "and you have to train yourself in the same way. The slightest slip of the tongue could cost you your life. In France it's a question of fading into the background. You have to look as tired and dispirited as the rest of the people around you or you will attract attention to yourself. Always be ready with an answer, because you never know when you will be stopped and questioned. You must be able to say who you are, where you're going, what you're doing." He paused for a moment, thinking back to his time in France, trying to pick out the things which would be most helpful to the new agents.

"Of course you won't be working alone," he continued. "Ideally you'll be sent to an area you already know well. There make contact with one person you knew before the war and believe you can trust. That person will help you to build your own group through his acquaintances. Of course, some of the areas you will be sent to already have their own Resistance groups, and where possible prior contact will be made with them. You'll find that the members of your group will be like your family to you. You can relax with them, talk with them, share with them in ways which are necessary to relieve the pressures of being a secret agent in Occupied France. You can never totally relax. Never tell anyone your real name, don't give any more information than is absolutely necessary. You will be responsible not only for your own life but the lives of your group as well, so always be on your guard."

Tony frowned, thinking of the disasters which had befallen members of his group. He hoped that the people now seated in front of him would not have to experience such terrible feelings of self-doubt, anger, fear, self-condemnation and despair.

"I can't emphasise to you too much how important it is to act naturally. I will be setting up little role-plays for you over the next week or two to give you a feeling of what it will be like, and experience in how to handle particular situations. Before that, are there any questions?"

A tentative hand was raised and Tony nodded in recognition.

"Yes?"

"You've spoken rather broadly about groups, but can you give more detail? What about the group you worked with?"

Tony took a deep breath. This was going to be difficult.

"I first made contact with a man I've known all my life. He worked for my French grandmother." He paused as he remembered that first meeting with Jean-Paul, and how excited he had felt at being in France at last. "That friend," he continued, "introduced me to three other people and we worked together during my first spell in France. When I returned, one of them brought two others to the group. My radio-operator finally introduced a third new member. So the group grew slowly. New members were only admitted when I was convinced that they were safe."

"Did any of them let you down?"

Tony frowned at the young man who had asked the question. "No, on the contrary. They saved my life twice, by getting me out of France when things became too difficult."

"Are they still working together, now that you're back in England?"

Tony was silent for a moment, seeing once again the bullets ripping into his friends after the railway ambush. He swallowed hard at the lump in his throat.

"What's left of them, yes," he finally managed to say. "One was wounded and his cover blown, so he was moved to a safe place. Two others died during an operation."

There was silence for a moment, the new agents mourning the loss of people they had never met. As Tony watched their reaction he realised that his openness, however painful to him, would prove invaluable to the recruits. Rather than lofty ideals, they were learning what it was really like to live, fight and possibly die on enemy soil. After a few moments another question was put forward.

"What was it like to lay an ambush?"

"Frightening," Tony answered honestly, "but exhilarating too. To be honest, I preferred the sabotage work - we could sneak in, plant our explosives and get out again without being seen. But ambushes are necessary too. Just make sure that you don't take on something bigger than you are equipped to handle."

"What was it like to see the Germans on the streets?"

Tony smiled grimly. "Believe it or not, that was one of the most difficult things to cope with." As he spoke he almost felt as though he was back in Saint Nazaire amongst the despair of a people suffering a brutal occupation. "To see the enemy on the streets, acting as though they own the place and there is no danger of them ever being usurped; to have to walk past them without lifting a finger and without looking resentful. Controlling your emotions in the face of the enemy is going to be hard."

"Is it easy to cope with the Germans? My one fear is that I'll be taken and will be forced to talk."

"Thank you for your honesty." Tony's gaze held that of the young man who had spoken. "When I sat where you are sitting now, I felt the same. I didn't think I would be able to stand up to interrogation. But let me tell you that when the worst possible thing happens to you, you will find hidden depths to your character and the strength to bring you through."

"How can you be sure of that?"

"Because I was a prisoner of the SS." Tony took a deep breath, fighting to control the trembling which threatened to overrun his body at the thought of the cellar beneath the S.S. H.Q. in Saint Nazaire. "I was afraid that I would talk. But I thought of my friends whose lives would be forfeit if I spoke, friends who had already saved my life once, and that gave me the strength to remain silent."

His audience were silent, wide-eyed and agog as Tony continued to speak, almost as though he did not see them but saw again the brutal faces of his torturers.

"I won't lie to you. The SS know some diabolical ways of inflicting pain, and I don't suppose I could have held out for ever. Just remember this if you are taken. You have friends on the outside. If they are anything like my group, they will move heaven and earth to get you out of that hell hole." There were tears in his eyes as he finished speaking. You could have cut the atmosphere in the room with a knife. He could see how moved the assembled agents were, and hoped that he had not put them off. But then, if he had, they were obviously not the right material for the S.O.E.

"Any more questions? No? Right then, let me explain your first training exercise."

122

Tony soon settled into the routine at Beaulieu. He found that he enjoyed running the training exercises, although he missed the excitement and camaraderie of active service. Tony worked himself until he was so tired that all he wanted to do in the evening was to eat and go to sleep. This had the advantage of keeping his mind busy and giving him little time to dwell on his personal problems. He knew that it would be a waste of time for him to go home again. That would only lead to more arguments with his father. Yet he felt that he understood Sir Michael better now, his anger and frustration at being unable to fight the men who had killed his son and the disappointment of the belief that his only remaining son was a coward. Tony knew that once he was allowed to speak openly to his father about his activities, Sir Michael would be proud of him. That would go a long way to healing the wound of his own inability to avenge his son's death.

Coming to terms with his relationship with his father was one thing. But Tony's relationship, or lack of it, with Sarah was something else completely. He knew how hurt she had been about his not writing. He knew that she still loved him, that was obvious from their last painful confrontation. What he did not know, however, was how to heal the hurt, and make her understand that he loved her too. Two people who felt so spiritually close as they did could not have secrets from each other without damaging the trust that was the basis of all lasting relationships. He realised that any affair between them was doomed to failure while his wartime activities remained a secret. He cursed Adolf Hitler. If it had not been for him, his life would not be in such a mess. But then again, if it had not been for the war, he would never have met Sarah. He had come to the conclusion that his personal relationships would have to be put on hold for the duration of the war, however long that might be. The only way to ensure that he and Sarah did not drift apart was to try to put their relationship on a purely platonic footing. With Christmas fast approaching, he had the ideal opportunity.

Tony chose his Christmas card for Sarah with great care, finally deciding on one which portrayed an old country house not unlike Heronfield. The landscape was covered in a blanket of snow, while a group of carol singers holding yellow lanterns sang in front of a door which had been opened to reveal an interior full of warmth and light. He hoped that it would make Sarah feel a part of Heronfield, as though she really belonged there. Tony wrote his Christmas greeting inside, then sat for a time chewing thoughtfully at the end of his pen, before writing a short note.

> 'Dear Sarah,
>   Merry Christmas! I want to say sorry once again for hurting you, and ask that you will forgive me and remember me kindly for the sake of the happy times we shared. Can we be friends, Sarah? I know you don't want a steady relationship and I respect that, but I have come to value the talks we shared and the way you so often seemed to understand me and help me. I know that you are aware that I would like more from our relationship than just friendship, but I would rather be just your friend than to never see you or speak to you again.
>   Please say you forgive me and will allow me to be your friend.
>   May God bless you and keep you this Christmas.
>   Tony.'

After he re-read the letter, Tony put it with the card inside an envelope and took it down to the desk. Once it was given to the officer on duty it was out of his hands. He could only wait and see if the bond which had been forged between him and Sarah was strong enough to hold fast during difficult times as well as good, and allow them to continue in friendship.

123

Tony's emotions were a mixture of puzzlement and excitement as he waited outside Captain Dawson's office. They met each Saturday afternoon to discuss the exercises which had taken place during the preceding week and the agents who had taken part in them. They also took the opportunity to plan exercises for the weeks to come. If Dawson wanted to speak to Tony at any other time of the week, he usually did so in the dining room or out on exercises. Never before had he sent a message ordering Tony to report to his office on a Wednesday morning. Tony wondered what it was all about. Perhaps they had decided that he could go back to France after all.

He knocked on the door and waited.

"Enter."

Tony went inside, closing the door quietly behind him before taking up a position in front of the desk. He saluted and stood to attention.

"Stand easy, Lieutenant Kemshall."

Dawson was seated behind his desk, the corners of his eyes crinkled with the smile that lit his face.

"I have some good news for you, Tony."

"I can go back to France?" Tony's voice was full of eager expectation. Dawson pursed his lips.

"No, I'm afraid not. Now that the SS know who you are, you can't go back to Saint Nazaire, and you're not well enough acquainted with another area of France to fit in. Besides, we need you here."

"If I could get in touch with the Resistance in a new area, they could help me settle in."

Dawson shook his head. "That's what you're training these recruits for."

"What about my group? Who will handle them?"

"You're persistent, Tony, I'll give you that. Angeline has returned to France and is managing quite well. She liaises with Jean-Paul Boues, who will lead any attack which she plans. She has been ordered not to go into action, because she's needed to operate the radio. They will not be doing much, just disrupting things for the Germans a little. We want the group to remain intact for when the Second Front finally comes."

"Will I be allowed to go back then, sir?" Tony was disappointed that he would not be allowed straight back into France but he wanted an assurance that he could go back later.

"We'll see." Dawson was non-committal. "I can't plan any operation until I know where the Second Front will be, and I don't think even the Prime Minister knows that yet."

"I see, sir."

Tony looked disappointed and Dawson grinned. "I still haven't told you the good news yet."

Tony returned his smile.

"No, sir. Sorry I interrupted."

Dawson waved a dismissive hand. "That's all right, Tony." He shuffled the papers on his desk until he found the one he was looking for. "I received this letter from the War Office this morning. It confirms your Distinguished Service Order."

"My what?" Tony's expression was incredulous.

"Your Distinguished Service Order." Captain Dawson stood up and held out his hand as he spoke. "Let me be the first to congratulate you."

Tony took the proffered hand and shook it, lost for words at the unexpected honour.

All he could think of was 'won't Father be proud!' As he released Dawson's hand, he realised that his father would probably never know.

"Thank you, sir. I suppose I must keep this secret from my family, or they'll want to know what I've been doing to deserve it."

Dawson nodded. "I'm afraid so Tony. But don't worry, once the war is over you can tell them anything you like."

"It can't be over soon enough for me!" said Tony with obvious feeling.

124

Sarah's reply to Tony's letter arrived two days before Christmas. She had been surprised to receive the card and letter, thinking that he did not really care for her at all. She had agonised for almost a week before she decided what to do about it. Although they were no longer going out together, she still missed Tony dreadfully. She agreed with him that it was too good a friendship to waste. She knew that it would be difficult to be in his company, remembering the way it had felt to be in his arms, the way his lips felt when they pressed against hers, the way it had felt when they made love, yet to remain just friends. Being honest with herself, she was not sure she could cope with the emotional turmoil it was likely to create. But she was willing to give it a try, remembering the closeness of their friendship in the early days.

Tony sat in the privacy of his room to read the letter.

> Dear Tony,
> Thank you for your letter. While I'm sure you didn't deliberately set out to hurt my feelings, it happened. I'm not going to let it happen again.'

Tony's heart began to beat faster and the letter in his hands began to shake. Surely she would not say no! He continued to read, his eyes rapidly scanning the paper.

> 'I'm willing to give our friendship another try as I, too, value it. But please don't let me down again, Tony. I've been hurt too much by this war already.'

Tony thought of Joe, the young man he had only seen once from a distance, but who had meant so much to Sarah before the war cut short his life. Yes, she had been hurt and he did not want her to be hurt ever again. All he wanted to do was to take her in his arms and promise that he would always be there to protect her and to love her. But he knew that such a promise was impossible. He continued to read, and a flicker of hope began to burn in his heart.

> 'This war had put many pressures on us all. It makes us do and say things that we would not otherwise dream of, and it changes us. Maybe it will change us further before it's over. Who knows where we will be or what we will be like before it is finished. Until then I would like to be your friend. We must promise that until the war is over we will not talk about your work, or anything else that might drive a wedge between us.

Merry Christmas.
Your friend,
Sarah.'

Tony re-read the letter and smiled. She could only commit herself to friendship now, but for him that was enough. He was in no position to offer anything more.

125

It was New Year's Eve. 1942, a year of constant warfare, was drawing to a close and 1943 dawning with no prospect of peace in sight. Yet in a country at war, people could always find time to put their cares aside and enjoy themselves. All over the country, people were out celebrating on New Year's Eve, forgetting the war for just one night. As he drove towards Marlborough in the car which had once belonged to his brother, Tony was glad that he was working at Beaulieu. It meant he could spend the evening at the dance which had been arranged for the nurses and local soldiers, and still be able to return to base before dawn. He was feeling nervous. He hoped that Sarah would be at the dance, and would be happy to see him. He had not written to tell her he would be coming, indeed it had been a spur of the moment decision. As he approached the hall, he wondered if he had done the right thing. What if she were there with someone else? As the thought took hold, he felt a knot of fear in his stomach and a frown creased his brow. What would he do if she were not alone?

Tony parked the car and made his way across the road and into the hall. The music was loud and the floor a swirling mass of dancers. Tony frowned. There were only one or two other British uniforms like his own, the rest were smart American uniforms, and the girls obviously found the GIs attractive. It was ten o'clock and the party was in full swing. Tony looked anxiously around the room searching for a familiar head of auburn hair. At last he saw her. A relieved smiled spread across his features, only to be wiped away when he saw that she was sitting with an American GI. Her eyes were bright and she was laughing gaily. Tony felt a stab of jealousy. He was tempted to turn and go back to Beaulieu without even saying hello. But if he left now, he would never know who the American was, or what he meant to Sarah. Taking a deep breath, Tony worked his way around the edge of the crowded dance floor until he was standing behind Sarah's chair.

"Hello, Sarah." He laid a hand on her shoulder, and she jumped in alarm as she turned towards him.

"Tony! You startled me! What are you doing here?"

"Sorry to make you jump like that." Tony was sheepish. "I just came across for the evening to wish you a Happy New Year." He looked questioningly at the GI. "I hope I'm not interrupting anything."

Sarah smiled, knowing what he was thinking and enjoying his discomfort.

"Let me introduce you to Al Ginelli."

The American stood up and held out a hand which Tony felt obliged to take. "Hi. Glad to meet you."

"Hello. I'm Tony Kemshall."

Sarah smiled as Al resumed his seat. "You remember my friend Jane?"

Tony nodded. "Of course."

"Al is her husband. They were married just a few weeks ago."

Tony felt relief wash over him like a flood, and for the first time a broad grin split his face.

"Congratulations Al. Jane is a nice girl."

"You're right there." Al grinned. "I expected nothing but trouble from this war, but instead I found myself a wonderful wife. And here she comes now."

Jane was approaching from the direction of the powder room. She frowned slightly when she saw Tony standing beside Sarah's chair, wondering what unhappiness he was bringing her way now. But she wiped the frown away and forced a smile of welcome as she reached the table.

"Hello, Tony. Happy New Year."

"Thanks Jane, and congratulations on your wedding."

Jane glanced at Al. "Shall we dance?"

"I thought you were tired?"

"I'm feeling better now. Let's go." She took her husband's hand and pulled him to his feet, before leading him determinedly out onto the dance floor.

Sarah looked at Tony, so handsome in his uniform. She was glad that she had a few moments in the company of others to get her muddled feelings under control. When she first heard his voice and felt his hand on her shoulder, her heart missed a beat and her hands began to shake but now she was more in control of herself. She smiled.

"Aren't you going to sit down?"

"If you don't mind?"

"Of course I don't mind."

Tony grinned, pulled out a chair and sat down. "I got your letter, Sarah. I'm glad we can be friends."

Sarah smiled nervously, not wishing to discuss their relationship. She retreated onto what she thought was safer ground.

"Have you been to see your parents yet?"

Tony frowned and shook his head. "No. Dad and I had a bit of an argument. I won't be going back there."

"What! Never?"

Tony shrugged. "At least not until after the war."

Sarah was shocked. "But that's awful!" What about your mother?"

"I write, and phone when I can. Believe me, it's better for her than to have to put up with our constant bickering."

Sarah looked at him carefully and saw the unhappiness in his eyes. She knew him well enough to realise that this split with his family hurt him deeply, and that he did not want to talk about it. Her heart ached for him. She wanted to take him in her arms, smooth the frown from his brow and tell him that everything was going to be all right. Instead she smiled comfortingly.

"Do you want to dance?"

Tony grinned his boyish grin, and Sarah felt her heart fill with love for him.

"Yes. That's what I came for!"

Smiling happily, they made their way onto the dance floor where Tony took her in his arms. It felt good, as though they had never been apart, as though they belonged together, and the hours flew by. They talked and danced as though there had never been anything wrong between them. Sarah wished it could always be like this. So the time passed and midnight approached. Suddenly the band stopped playing and a GI leapt up onto the stage.

"OK. everybody. Ten seconds to go. Ten...Nine..."

All over the dance floor people began to join in the countdown.

"Eight...Seven...Six..."

Tony turned and smiled at Sarah, who smiled back as the counting continued.

"Five...Four...Three..."

Without quite knowing how, Sarah found her hand in Tony's. It felt so right that she didn't want to pull away.

"Two...One...Happy New Year!"

Streamers were thrown. The air was soon thick with them, and balloons floated down from the ceiling.

"Happy New Year, Tony."

Sarah looked radiant. Her eyes sparkled and her smile was warm and inviting. Without thinking, Tony leant down and pressed a gentle kiss on her lips. After a moment's hesitation, Sarah's lips began to move beneath his. She closed her eyes as his arms slipped around her, and gave herself up to the sensations washing over her. It felt so good, so right to be in his arms once more. Tony could hardly believe it was happening. He could hardly believe that after all that he had been through he was holding her, and feeling from the depth of her response that she really did love him. Then it was over. Sarah opened her eyes, placed her hands on his chest and pulled gently away.

"Sarah?"

She shook her head, her eyes a confusion of longing, hurt and regret.

"No, Tony. That kiss changes nothing. I can be no more than your friend."

It hurt Tony to hear the words, but the pain did not cut as deeply as before. He had held her and kissed her, and he knew from the way she had responded that she felt drawn to him in the same way that he was drawn to her. That was all he needed, the confirmation that she still loved him. Now he had that, he was content to wait until the war was over. Then he would be free to ask her to share the rest of her life with him.

JANUARY - DECEMBER 1943

126

The war seemed to be going well at last. In January Churchill and Roosevelt met in Casablanca to continue planning for the Second Front, while the Germans were facing defeat in Russia. The assault on Stalingrad which had begun in the middle of August 1942 had failed, and the Germans finally surrendered at the end of January. In the Far East, the sea battle for Guadalcanal which began at almost the same time as the assault on Stalingrad, finally ended on 7th February 1943 with the Japanese withdrawing from the Solomon Islands. For a time North Africa looked as though things might go wrong when Rommel struck back at the Americans in Tunisia and the British at Medenine, but Montgomery led a counter-attack, and the Afrika Korps was defeated on 20th March. While the global picture was becoming more hopeful, life for Tony Kemshall continued in its less successful vein.

127

Tony found the work at Beaulieu tame compared with life in the field. He longed to return to France. Yet being in England did have its advantages. During the first two months of 1943 he was able to get over to Marlborough four times to join Sarah at the local dances. They were close again, in the way they had been close when Joe was alive. Being in England also gave him the opportunity to write to Sarah, which he did frequently, always in a chatty vein, talking of the war news and his social life in camp but steering safely away from personal relationships. Little did he know that far from smoothing the way for his relationship with Sarah, the letters and visits were only adding to her confusion. Each time Sarah went to a dance she hoped yet dreaded seeing Tony. She wanted to be with him, yet feared the turmoil of emotions which he awoke in her. The letters, too, were disquieting. Surely he was no less busy now than he had been in America. So how did he manage to write so often? And why in such an impersonal way? Sarah did not know how to respond. How was she to keep his friendship without letting him break her heart again? The solution presented itself one evening in early March.

"We don't get anything like this back home." Al surveyed the pub decorations of horse brasses and foxes heads with bared teeth.

Sarah smiled. "That could be a good thing! I still find them slightly unnerving. It seems strange that people should come out to enjoy themselves amongst these grim trophies."

"Don't be silly, Sarah. I thought you loved the country life?"

"You know I do, Jane. But I love the beauty. I love the animals running around, not stuck on a wall!"

"I shouldn't say that too loudly, or we'll get thrown out!" Jane laughed.

Sarah let her gaze wander around the pub. It was a cold evening. A log fire burned brightly in the hearth, going some way towards dispelling the gloom of the pub. A few locals leant against the bar quietly drinking their pints. In a shadowed corner a courting couple sat close together, oblivious to the world around them. Sarah smiled a little uncomfortably at Jane.

"Surely you and Al would prefer to be alone. Why don't I go back to the hospital?"

"No, stay with us. I hate to think of you brooding alone."

Sarah laughed. "I don't 'brood' and I certainly won't be alone. Why don't you and I come here again, some time when Al can't get away?"

Sarah could tell by the way the young couple looked at each other that they would prefer to be alone. Rising to her feet, she smiled at the newlyweds. "I'll see you later Jane; and you Al, please try to persuade her that I don't need looking after, so she should spend as much time as she can with you. Alone."

Al laughed. "Thanks, Sarah. I sure will."

"Well, goodnight then."

Sarah turned and made her way towards the door of the pub which opened to admit a GI who bumped into her, knocking her sideways.

"Gee, I'm sorry. Are you all right?"

Sarah nodded, unable to speak. There was something about this man which seemed so familiar, and made her heart beat faster. Then she realised what it was. The way his hair fell softly over his brow, the hidden depths of his eyes, his overall build and the way he moved, all reminded her of Joe.

"Hey, are you OK?"

Sarah nodded. The American voice brought her back to the present, and to the realisation that this was not Joe. She would never see Joe again. Seeing someone who reminded her so much of him made the pain of his loss so real that she paled as she made her way to push past him and leave the pub.

"Yes. I'm fine, thanks."

"I don't think you are, miss. It seems I gave you a bit of a fright. Can I buy you a drink to make amends?"

Sarah wanted to say no, but deep inside she wondered just how like Joe he really was. Would he think the same way? Have the same sense of humour? If she walked away now and did not give herself a chance to lay this ghost of Joe to rest, it would haunt her for the rest of her life. She nodded.

"Yes. Thank you."

The American led her to a table. Sarah was so flustered that she did not see the smiles directed at her by Jane and Al.

"Sherry?"

"Yes. Sherry would be nice."

The young GI was at the bar for a few moments which gave Sarah a chance to compose herself as she watched him. Yes, he was very much like Joe, yet with an air of confidence and jauntiness which she had only ever seen displayed by the American GIs based nearby. Perhaps it was the difference between being born in the old and new world. Sarah recovered by the time he returned to the table, and she smiled haltingly.

"Sorry to put you to all this trouble. My mind was miles away, and I didn't expect to bump into anyone."

The American handed her the sherry and placed his whisky on the table.

"Are you sure you're OK?"

Sarah nodded. "Yes."

The American's frown was smoothed away, and his face lit by a brilliant smile.

"Good. It's not the best way to meet someone, but I'm glad it happened." His eyes were appreciative as he spoke, and Sarah blushed slightly. "My name's Bobby Wilson, by the way."

"I'm Sarah Porter."

There was silence for a moment as each tried to think of something to say. Then...

"How long...?" Sarah began while

"Do you...?" said Bobby.

They both laughed.

"Sorry. You first."

Sarah smiled. "I was going to ask how long you've been in England."

"One week, so I haven't had much time to explore the country yet. What I've seen seems small compared to America, yet very beautiful and full of history. I'd like to get to know the place much better" 'And you' said his eyes although he did not say the words yet. "Do you live around here?"

"Yes and no." Sarah smiled at his puzzled expression, and went on to explain. "I was born and brought up in Coventry, but I came down here at the outbreak of the war to be a nurse. I've been living here for three years now."

Bobby sipped his drink. "You know, I still find it hard to believe that England has been fighting for so long, and we've only just joined in."

"So do we."

Bobby frowned slightly. "Is that a criticism?"

Sarah was tempted to say no, but somehow she could not lie to him.

"I suppose it is really. We've felt for a long time that you Americans could do more to help us."

"Still, we're here now. The war can't go on much longer."

"That sounds rather arrogant."

Bobby laughed. "Sorry, it wasn't meant to. I just meant that Germany has only limited resources, and can't hold out for ever. Still, enough of this. Tell me about yourself."

Sarah began to talk about her life and how the war had affected her. But she kept the most personal part of her life secret. She was not ready to share that with a stranger, no matter how much he reminded her of Joe, or maybe because he did remind her of her dead fiancé. How would she tell him that he resembled a man she had planned to marry, but who was now dead? And as for Tony, she was still so mixed up about her feelings for him that it felt better not to mention him at all. So she talked of her mother and her childhood, and of what it was like to receive the wounded from Dunkirk and be caught up in the bombing of Coventry.

Bobby shook his head in amazement. "You know, you make the war seem so much more alive and personal," he said when she had finished. "It makes me feel a little ashamed that America has sat on the fence for so long. My life over the last few years has been nothing in comparison with yours."

"What have you been doing?"

"Pa owns a small farm in North Carolina, and I've been helping him to work it."

"A farm?"

"Yes. Nothing big. Just a few acres of corn, some cows and a few horses, but it's a beautiful place. I'd never really been away from it until I joined up. I miss it."

Bobby went on to describe life for a child on the farm, a life which Sarah found hard to imagine. As they talked, they felt a closeness which belied their short acquaintance. Neither of them saw the pub filling up, or Jane and Al leave. It was only when the publican called last orders that they realised how many hours had gone by.

"I really must be getting back! I'm on duty at six in the morning." Sarah rose to her feet.

"Can I walk you home?" Bobby stood up and helped her into her coat. Sarah smiled her thanks.

"Yes, I'd like that."

They left the pub, and as they made their way down the road to Heronfield, Sarah felt Bobby's arm slip around her waist. She did nothing to deter him. She liked the man, and during the evening she had come to know him as an individual, rather than a copy of Joe. It was only in physical attributes that they were so similar, and Sarah was glad that his character was so different. She liked him for who he was, not who she would have liked him to be.

The huge stone pillars guarding the drive to Heronfield House rose up before them sooner than either would have hoped. They lingered for a moment in the chill March air.

"I hear they have a dance in Marlborough every couple of weeks. Would you like to go with me?"

Sarah smiled warmly.

"Yes, Bobby, I would. As long as I'm not on duty."

"Can I call you here?"

"Yes, anytime. If I'm not available just leave me a message."

She stood for a moment looking into his eyes, which reminded her so much of Joe's. Bobby was puzzled by her expression, a mixture of longing and pain. He reached out a tentative hand to touch her cheek. His touch seemed to break the spell which held her. Sarah smiled warmly again, and he leant down to brush his lips against hers. For a moment she did not respond, Then she closed her eyes and returned the kiss.

Bobby found her warm, soft lips incomparable. It was good that he could not read Sarah's thoughts, for as they kissed she found herself thinking. 'This is not like his kiss'. To her surprise, she realised that she was not comparing his kiss to Joe's, but to Tony's.

In the weeks that followed, Sarah and Bobby met often, sometimes at dances or in the pub, sometimes just walking together to enjoy the spring weather and explore the English countryside. Sarah felt warm and comfortable in his presence. She enjoyed his company, his sense of humour and the way he treated her, without impinging too deeply on her already wounded heart. She no longer saw Bobby as a substitute for Joe, but as an individual who could be more to her than a friend yet less than a lover, someone who did not make her want to commit herself more than she was capable of. She felt safe in a way she had not for a long time. She thought briefly that she might be using Bobby to cushion her feelings for Tony, as a buffer between him and her heart. But she had not seen Tony since the end of February, and had not been able to put her theory to the test. He had written to say that he had been moved to another part of the country for a while. He continued to write, although his letters were more infrequent. She was glad. She knew how he would react to Bobby, and she needed to sort out her own feelings before confronting his. As it was, fate lent a hand, and Tony did not return to Beaulieu until the end of May, seven weeks after Sarah and Bobby first met, and their relationship was well established before he appeared on the scene to torment Sarah's heart once more.

128

Tony had been in Arisaig for two months. The Scottish spring was wet and cold, and the exercises he led were extremely uncomfortable. He was glad to be back in the south once more, the soft rolling landscape of home. Taking the first opportunity which presented itself, he arrived at the dance hall in Marlborough on a warm evening at the end of May. As he walked through the door he was greeted by the swirling rhythm of the American dance band. He found his heart beating faster and his face beginning to break into a smile. It was so long since he had seen Sarah, and he was looking forward to spending the evening in her company. His eyes eagerly scanned the crowded hall, hoping that she would be there. His relief was incalculable as he finally saw her, seated alone at a table. He made his way across the crowded hall towards her, shouldering his way through the numerous American uniforms. He pulled out a chair and sat down beside her.

"Hello, Sarah."

Sarah smiled in welcome, ignoring the increased beating of her heart as her happiness at seeing him washed over her.

"Hello, Tony. How are you?"

Tony smiled. She was as beautiful as ever. He never tired of looking at her. She seemed so alive, as though the whole world was her playground, and he was glad to see her looking so happy again.

"I'm fine. How are you?"

"OK."

Tony raised his eyebrows. OK? Where had Sarah picked up such an Americanism?

"OK?"

Sarah laughed. "Sorry. I suppose I've picked that up from Bobby."

"Bobby?" Tony's smile faded. His earlier happiness evaporated as he waited for her answer.

"Yes. Here he comes now."

Tony turned to see the GI approaching with two drinks. There was something familiar about him which Tony could not put his finger on, but he felt vaguely threatened. When he saw the way the American looked at Sarah, he knew that his fears were justified. Sarah was smiling at the soldier, and Tony saw an easiness and confidence in their relationship which left a cold pit of fear in his stomach. He rose to his feet as the American placed the two glasses on the table.

"Bobby, this is Tony Kemshall. His father owns Heronfield House. Tony, this is Bobby Wilson."

The American held out his hand. "Pleased to meet you. It must be hard for you to give up your home for the war."

"I suppose so, but I'm not home often enough for it to matter to me." Tony was trying his best to appear friendly, only Sarah could see that his smile was forced. She felt sorry for him. She wished she had told him about Bobby in a letter, but it was too late for that now. Anyway, she did not have to explain her life to him. The two men sat down, each instinctively seeing the other as a rival. Sarah felt uncomfortable and broke the uneasy silence.

"Would you like to dance, Tony?"

Tony smiled in relief. "Yes. I'd love to."

As Bobby watched the English couple make their way onto the dance floor, he frowned. Sarah had never mentioned Tony to him. But he could see from Tony's reaction and Sarah's nervousness that there had once been something special between them. As he watched them in each other's arms they looked right together, and he worried that he might be about to lose the English girl who had stolen his heart.

Tony took Sarah in his arms and began to move to the rhythm.

"That American seems a nice enough chap."

"Yes, he is."

"How long have you known him?" Tony tried to make the question sound casual but Sarah noted the tension in his voice.

"About two months."

Two months! His heart sank. No wonder they seemed so at ease together. How could he have been so foolish as to think that she would wait for him until he was able to tell her the truth about himself? As he looked down at the girl in his arms, he realised that the very things that attracted him to her were what the American found so attractive too. He tried to smile.

"You seem to get on well with him."

"Yes, he's fun to be with."

"You know," Tony frowned. "I'm sure he reminds me of someone."

"Yes. Joe."

As Sarah said the name, his heart sank. Yes, of course. He had only seen Joe once from a distance, but he could see the similarity. If he was so much like her fiancé, it was no wonder that she wanted to be with him. He had never thought that the dead man would come back to haunt him, but it seemed that he had. Tony knew he could not compete. It looked as though he had lost her forever. He smiled, a sad smile that did not hide the pain in his eyes, and Sarah felt her heart go out to him.

"I suppose I'd better get back to base."

"Surely you don't have to leave yet."

"I don't want to intrude on your evening with Bobby."

Sarah looked over at the American where he sat at the table anxiously watching the dancers, and then turned her attention back to Tony. Bobby never made her feel the way she felt with Tony. But at least with him she was safe, and that was how she wanted to feel right now.

"Bobby won't mind if you join us."

"I think he will." Tony stopped dancing and stepped back, breaking the contact with Sarah. "Can I still write to you?"

"Of course. And please keep visiting me."

He shrugged his shoulders. "If I can." He was not sure that he wanted to. Sarah seemed to have made her choice and it was not up to him to try to change her mind. He felt as though his heart would break, and he knew he would have to leave before he made a fool of himself. He looked back at the American. He seemed a decent enough fellow. Maybe he was just the man to make Sarah happy, something he had never been able to do himself.

"Goodbye, Sarah. Be happy."

He turned and walked away. Sarah stood and watched him, an island of stillness in the midst of the dancers, not noticing the worried glance that Bobby threw at her. She knew that Tony was not the man for her, but it hurt to finally admit that their relationship was over. As she watched him walk away, she felt as though her future was leaving with him, and she wondered if she was doing the right thing. Still, it was done now, and her future was about to take a new direction. She watched the door close behind Tony, then turned back towards the table where Bobby waited for her. It was as though she had turned her back on a storm tossed sea and turned her face towards a safe harbour. She smiled as she made her way back towards the American. Sometimes the most difficult decisions were made for the best, and she had just made hers. No longer would she allow Tony to dominate her thoughts and her heart, now she would link her life to someone who could make her happy. As she reached the table, she leant down and kissed Bobby on the cheek.

"Will you dance with me?"

He stood without speaking and took her in his arms, a smile of happiness wiping away the anxiety. She had sent the Englishman away, and now her future belonged to him.

129

The war continued to ebb and flow back and forth across the world. The Allies made advances only to meet setbacks at a later date. The biggest setback in 1943 was the final withdrawal of British forces from Burma, leaving the Far Eastern theatre mainly to the campaigning of the Americans who still held a savage hate in their hearts for the Japanese who had bombed Pearl Harbour. On the Eastern Front, things were beginning to go well for Russia at last. Although the siege of Leningrad which had begun in September 1941 still continued, the Russian victory at Stalingrad in March gave new hope to the Russian people. In July a seven day tank battle between the Germans and the Russians took place at Kursk, leaving the Germans defeated and in retreat. In their rear, the Russians began an offensive towards Germany itself. The North African war reached its climax at the end of May, when the Allies entered Tunis on the 8th. The remaining Axis troops surrendered on the 13th. War in North Africa was over at last, ending in triumph for the Allies who used it as a stepping-off point for an attack on the southern extremities of Europe. In July the Allies invaded Sicily, taking Palermo in only ten days and causing King Victor Emmanuel III to dismiss the dictator Mussolini. At the beginning of September Montgomery landed in southern Italy and the heart went out of the Italian people, who surrendered on the 8th. But the German troops in Italy fought on. The battles raged for the remainder of the year, the Germans fighting every step of the way along the road of their retreat while the indigenous population watched, no longer involved in a war which still ravaged their homeland. By the end of the year, the Allies were still eighty miles short of Rome. But their eventual victory seemed certain, particularly now that the Allied bombing of the Ruhr, which had begun in March and continued throughout the rest of the year, was continuing to disrupt Germany's capacity to wage war.

130

The sound of machine guns to his right caused Bobby to duck his head, until his face was almost touching the grass. He inched forward on his elbows and knees, dragging his rifle clumsily beside him. The pack on his back was barely an inch below the barbed wire criss-crossing the air above him. To his right and left, other soldiers in American uniform were crawling forward. Dirt and stones showered down on them as mortar fire landed close by, causing the earth to erupt into geysers of dust, dirt and clumps of grass. Somewhere ahead of them, a sergeant's voice could be heard calling out orders. Then, at last, they were free of the barbed wire. Bobby rose to a crouching position and ran forward, rifle held closely against his chest.

"Get your head down!"

Bobby heard the call. He crouched lower as a burst of gunfire came from his left. Ahead of him was a steep slope. He struggled up, his breath coming in painful gasps. He reached the summit to find a number of straw-filled dummies dressed in German uniforms, hung from a wooden frame. Over to Bobby's right, a voice called out.

"Don't just stand there! You won't have time to catch your breath in battle! Get moving!"

Bobby held the rifle in front of him, bayonet pointing menacingly at the dummy ahead of him. As he ran forward, he gave a yell and plunged the bayonet into the chest of the effigy. It swung crazily at the violation. Withdrawing the sharp weapon, he ran on wondering if it would be as easy to run a bayonet into a living, breathing human being. The training exercises were getting him and his fellow soldiers used to the sound of enemy fire, and the difficulties of moving when loaded down with equipment. But they would not help when he came face to face with his first German, and had to kill before he himself was killed. As he made his way down the far side of the hill, he wondered how he would stand up to a real battle situation.

131

The months rolled on, through spring and summer towards the autumn of 1943. Bobby and Sarah spent as much time as possible together. The area around Heronfield was new to both of them. Although Sarah had been there since the outbreak of the war, and had taken a few trips out with Tony, she had spent the majority of her time at the house and in the extensive grounds of the Heronfield Estate. Now the couple took trips out together, finding secluded country pubs and small restaurants where the rationed fare was more palatable than the norm. They visited Salisbury, Andover, Melksham, Devises and Newbury, as well as Stonehenge, the stones of Avebury and many other attractions. At times they could almost forget the war as they strolled contentedly together. Bobby found himself falling in love with the rolling green hills of England, the neatness of it all compared with the sprawling vastness of America. He was falling in love with Sarah too. The auburn-haired young nurse reached a spot in his heart that no one else had ever touched before, and as the months passed, he knew she was the one whom he wanted to spend the rest of his life with. He still wondered about Tony Kemshall, but she had never mentioned him, and he did not know how to bring up the subject, taking comfort from the fact that she had not seen him again.

Sarah had not thought she could be so relaxed in the company of a man so soon after ending her relationship with Tony, yet she felt she had known Bobby all her life. True, he did not bring quite the sparkle to her existence that being with Tony did. His kisses did not excite her in quite the same way. But he felt comfortable and safe to be with. She had not seen Tony since the dance, but he still wrote to her fairly frequently, friendly letters which Sarah enjoyed reading. She felt that they never quite said enough, though that helped her to put her relationship with him in the right perspective. The past was behind her now. Her future seemed to lie in the hands of the American who looked so much like her first love. As the weeks and months passed, the pain of losing Tony diminished, and in its place grew a quiet contentment. She had experienced the best and worst of love. Her relationship with Bobby, while lacking in excitement, seemed to hold all that was best of love, yet with none of sadness of her life with Tony. Maybe what she needed from life was trust, stability and safety. Bobby gave her all of these. Life seemed to be improving and she was glad to let it take its course.

132

"This is much better than being in Italy."

Sarah smiled at the captain, who leant back against his pillows, face relaxed and smiling.

"Don't get too used to it. Once you're better you'll have to move out, and let someone else have your bed."

He grinned in return. "I can't say I won't be happy for that to happen, but it's great to be able to just lie back and relax after what we've been doing out there."

Sarah sat on the edge of the bed. "I thought things were going well for us in Italy?"

The soldier nodded. "They are. Since the Italians surrendered at the beginning of September we've only had to fight the Germans. But they're determined not to give up Italy without a struggle. They retreat slowly into easily defended positions in the mountains where we have to shell them heavily to get them to move. Once they do move back, we can't rush them because our bombardment has made such a mess of the roads. By the time we can get moving, they've got themselves into another defensive position and the whole thing starts all over again."

"It sounds very frustrating."

The young officer smiled. "It is, especially as we can all see that the outcome is inevitable." He shifted his position slightly to make himself more comfortable. "I know that we've been at war with Italy, but they are out of it now, and it seems a shame that we have to continue destroying their country. So many beautiful things are ending up in ruins."

Sarah shrugged. "That's no different to what's been happening to us over the last few years." In her mind's eye she could see again the beautiful cathedral which once stood in the centre of Coventry, now no more than a heap of rubble.

The captain nodded. "I agree, but it just seems so futile for the Germans to keep fighting us in Italy, when they know they can't win." He smiled. "As far as I'm concerned, this is the beginning of the end for Hitler. I just wish that he'd see it and give up now, instead of dragging things out to the inevitable conclusion."

"I can't see him doing that." Sarah rose from the edge of the soldier's bed and moved over to the window. She gazed down at the trees, vibrant in the reds and golds of autumn, and at old Madame de Thierry, Tony's grandmother, who walked slowly between the trees, cloaked in a veil of sadness. "Hitler won't surrender until we've re-taken France and pushed his armies back to where they came from. That won't be easy."

The Captain nodded. "I know, but we will do it. Next year, or perhaps the year after. With the Americans on our side, we can't lose. They have so many resources. Germany's resources are limited, and growing less all the time."

Sarah smiled at the mention of the Americans. She would be seeing Bobby again that evening, and he would be glad to hear the news from Italy. Sarah turned her back on the autumnal scene beyond the window, and briskly straightened the covers of the bed.

"At least you'll be home for Christmas, not suffering in the cold and snow of the Italian mountains."

"It will be my first Christmas at home since 1940."

Sarah could see the mixture of longing and delight in his eyes. She smiled. It looked like this Christmas was going to be a happy one, despite the war.

Autumn gradually changed to winter. As the festive season approached, Sarah found herself looking forward to the time she would spend with her mother and with Bobby. She rarely thought of that other Christmas when Joe had proposed to her. Her life was now so changed that she felt like a different person. Three years had passed since then, and now her future stretched before her to horizons she had never dreamed of.

Sarah alighted from the train into the bustle of Coventry station and stood for a moment to take in the sights and sounds. The platform was full of people, mainly uniformed men returning home on leave for Christmas, their relatives waiting eagerly to welcome them. Kit bags were balanced against arms filled with brightly wrapped parcels and there was an air of life and gaiety. It was subtly different from the other Christmases since 1939, maybe because people now really believed that Germany could not win and there would not be many more Christmases celebrated under the constraints of war. With a smile, Sarah made her way through the crowds and out onto the streets, where she was lucky enough to get straight onto a bus heading towards her home. As the bus bumped along its way, she gazed sadly at the bomb damage, like raw wounds of the face of the city of her birth. In some places there were piles of rubble where homes and shops had once stood. In others, buildings which were far too unsafe to use stood derelict. The boarded windows seemed to stare sightlessly down on the mass of humanity which inhabited the city. Sarah determined not to let the destruction and the drabness of a city where rationing precluded bright materials bring her spirits down. It was 21st December, and she had to return to Heronfield again on the 23rd. There was no time to waste on looking at the negative things that war brought. Her mother was waiting and this Christmas was going to be as enjoyable as those before the war, if she had anything to do with it. The bus finally stopped at the end of the road where Sarah had lived her whole life until the outbreak of war. She climbed eagerly down, walking briskly through the cold winter air towards the small terraced house that was home. She bounded up the steps and pushed open the door without knocking.

"Mum! It's me!"

She placed her bag on the floor and made her way into the kitchen. She expected to find her mother there but the room was empty, though the kettle was on the stove, which meant she could not be far away. Sarah went over to the window and looked out. A washing line was strung from the Anderson shelter to a pole on the other side of the garden. Alice was hanging out washing, which flapped wildly above the leeks and Brussels sprouts in what had once been the rose bed. Sarah smiled and turned away. She took off her coat and hung it in the hall, before returning to the kitchen where she took down two cups and saucers and began to make the tea. When the back door finally opened, the pot was on the table covered with its cosy, and the milk and sugar stood beside it with a small plate of biscuits. Alice's face broke into a wide grin.

"Sarah!"

She put the laundry basket down onto the floor and held out her arms to her daughter, who rushed into them, happy to be enfolded once more into the warmth and security of home.

. "It's good to see you, Mum." She kissed her mother warmly on the cheek. "Gosh, you're cold! Sit down and I'll pour you a cup of tea."

Alice sat down gratefully. "Thanks, love." She smiled happily. "You're looking well. Nursing seems to suit you."

Sarah nodded happily as she poured the tea. "Yes. I love it. It's a really rewarding job, Mum. You don't know how good it feels to care for someone who is sick and injured, to watch them slowly improving until they're able to leave your care."

Alice smiled. "Of course I understand. Who looked after you when you had chicken pox? Who nursed you through all your childhood ills?"

Sarah laughed. "I suppose all mothers are nurses then, aren't they!"

"Yes, being a mother is a very fulfilling job." Alice looked quizzically at Sarah. "Have you any plans in that area? You can't mourn Joe forever."

Sarah nodded. "Yes Mum, I know. But I'm not sure where I stand at the moment."

Alice smiled. "Are you still seeing that American?"

Sarah nodded. "Yes. He's really kind and considerate and fun to be with but..."

"But you don't love him the same way as you loved Joe?"

Another nod. "I knew you'd understand, Mum. Especially as you lost Dad in the last war."

"That was different, Sarah. We were married, and I had you. We were a small family, and I was not alone as you might be when I've gone."

"Mum! What an awful thing to say! You'll be around for a long time yet!"

Alice smiled. "Of course, I plan to be. But you can't wait forever. Bobby's not the one for you, then?"

Sarah shrugged and took a sip of tea as she thought. "I don't know. I don't suppose I'll ever love again the way I did with Joe."

"You seemed to be close to it last year with that Tony Kemshall you were always writing to me about. What happened to him?"

"Our lives were too different, Mum. His father is Sir Michael Kemshall, and Tony will inherit all his businesses and estates one day. You can hardly expect someone like that to marry a poor working- class girl from Coventry."

Alice sighed. "I suppose not. That doesn't mean you're not good enough for the likes of him, just that rich people are too blind to see it."

Sarah laughed.

"Oh, Mum! Can you really imagine me as the lady of the manor, riding horses and ordering servants around?" She smiled, a little wistfully. "I don't see much of Tony now, but we keep in touch. We're still friends, which is more than a girl of my background can expect."

Sarah put her empty teacup back into its saucer where it settled with a gentle clatter.

"How come relationships never seem so easy in wartime? I'm very fond of Bobby, but I can't help remembering Joe and how he died. Bobby will be fighting when they open the Second Front, and I have to face the fact that he could be killed. Maybe that's why I'm not allowing myself to fall in love with him. I don't want to lose the one I love again."

Alice frowned. "That's one way of looking at it, Sarah. But if I'd thought that, I'd never have married your Dad and you wouldn't be here now. Of course it hurt to lose him but at least I had happy memories of our time together, and I had you. I wouldn't have given that up for any amount of peace of mind. You mustn't deprive yourself of love, just because you fear you might lose it. Do you wish you'd never loved Joe?"

Sarah shook her head sadly. "Of course not." She sighed. "I suppose you're right. If you really love someone, you have to take a chance."

"And you do love Bobby, don't you?" It was more a statement than a question.

Sarah shrugged. "I don't know. I enjoy being with him, and I'm sure we could be happy together. Maybe that's enough to start with, and love will grow from there."

"Well, it gives you something to think about. Now come with me to the living room, I've got something to show you."

Alice rose from the table and led her daughter into the living room, smiling happily at the surprised gasp which escaped her daughter's lips.

"Mum, it's beautiful! Just like when I was a little girl!"

The room was hung with paper garlands. Some of them were patched, but that only added to their beauty for Sarah, for she could remember each chain made, each tear lovingly repaired. In the corner stood a small Christmas tree, bedecked with tinsel and tiny wooden figures which Sarah remembered from her childhood. At the top was a fairy, her white dress now yellow with age and her wand slightly bent. Sarah remembered carrying the paper bag with its precious cargo home from the shops, and putting it in its rightful place at the top of the Christmas tree for the very first time, when she was four or five years old.

"As you won't be here for Christmas Day, I thought we might as well celebrate a few days early."

Sarah hugged Alice warmly. "Oh Mum, it's wonderful! It makes me feel like a little girl again!"

Alice gave her a motherly pat on the shoulder and smiled. "You'll always be my little girl, Sarah, no matter how old you are."

The two women stood with their arms around each other, wrapped in the memories of the past. A quiet peace settled on the small house, in a bomb ravaged city, in a war torn country. An oasis of stillness where the coming of a little baby to bring peace and joy to the world could be contemplated far from the madness and hate which engulfed the globe. Maybe one day in the not too distant future, there would come a time when there really was 'Peace on earth goodwill towards men'.

Sarah strolled amongst the shops, gazing at the somewhat meagre window displays, wondering what to buy for her mother for Christmas. She was enjoying the relaxed feeling she had, now that she was away from Heronfield and not on call at all hours. She had lain in her bed until late, revelling in the freedom to do so in her old familiar room, and now she was shopping for the few items she needed for Christmas. She had already made some of her purchases - a small silver photograph frame for Jane and Al, a book about English history for Bobby, who seemed so interested in the country of her birth - and these items bulged comfortably in her shopping bag. Sarah's eye was caught by a splash of colour in the corner of one window, and she went over to have a look. It was a bolt of dress fabric, creamy white with pink roses set against pale green leaves. Sarah knew that she had found the ideal present for her mother. It took no time at all for her to go into the shop to make the purchase.

As she came out of the shop, Sarah wondered what to do with the rest of her morning, and decided to take another look at the cathedral before going home. The sight of its spire standing above the rubble always inspired her to look beyond the end of the war to a brighter future. As she walked in the direction of the bomb site which had once been a beautiful place of worship, she continued to gaze into the shop windows, until her eyes were drawn to a small gold tie pin in the front of a jeweller's window. It was shaped like a heron in flight, and transported her back to a day when she stood on the banks of the river at Heronfield with Tony, and watched as a heron took flight from a bed of tall reeds. She could almost feel Tony's lips against hers, and the warmth of his embrace. For a moment it was as though all the misunderstanding had never happened, that she and Tony were together again. She gazed at the tie pin until the cold December air penetrated her dream and brought her back to reality. Tony was no longer a part of her life, but the small golden heron was still there, striving to reach the heights above. As Sarah stared at the beautiful simplicity of its lines, she knew she must have it. She carefully checked her purse and, finding that she had just enough money, she entered the shop, feeling that the heron was made for her. It had been sitting in the shop waiting for her to pass by.

After leaving the jeweller's, Sarah walked in the direction of the Cathedral. But her mind was no longer on the church which had been destroyed on the night she had been caught up in the bombing three years ago. She was thinking of Tony, wondering what he was doing for Christmas and if he would be going back to Heronfield. She was so deep in her memories that the familiar face did not register at first. She thought it was part of her daydream, then reality hit her and she frowned in puzzlement. Surely it was not him. What would he be doing here in Coventry looking at the burnt out Cathedral? She slowly approached the uniformed man and spoke hesitantly.

"Tony?"

The young man whirled round in startled surprise and she knew that she had been right.

"Tony! What on earth are you doing here?"

Tony's features worked with a mixture of emotions. Surprise, delight, a touch of sheepishness, almost as though he felt guilty at being caught out in something.

"Sarah!" His face broke into a smile and his voice filled with warmth. "I didn't expect to see you here!"

"Come on, Tony, this is my home town. Where else would I go on leave at Christmas?"

Tony grinned. "I suppose so. I just didn't know you were going to be home on leave."

"So, what are you doing here?" Tony looked at the destroyed Cathedral, unable to meet Sarah's direct gaze.

"To tell you the truth, I came here because it is your home town. You've told me so much about Coventry that I wanted to see it for myself. I thought it might make me feel closer to you."

Sarah was surprised and remained silent. She gazed at Tony's profile. He looked so vulnerable. Laying a tentative hand on his arm she drew his attention away from the cathedral and back to her.

"Would you like to talk?"

Tony nodded. "Yes, why not. But not here, it's too cold. Is there somewhere we can get a cup of tea?"

Sarah grinned. "Yes. Come on."

Sarah led him along a bomb damaged street and round the corner to a small tea shop. The bell above the door tinkled as they entered the cosy environment. There were not many people there and they took a seat by the window, ordering tea and cakes from the waitress and indulging in small talk until their order came. Then Sarah took a deep breath.

"How much leave do you have for Christmas?"

Tony smiled across the table at her. He was glad that he had suggested tea. It had given him a chance to get his feelings under control. He was surprised to hear Sarah call out his name, he had thought she would be at Heronfield for Christmas. He was not going home, so his only chance to feel close to her was to come to places that she knew, and imagine she was there with him. But now he did not have to imagine it. She was there, warm and vibrant, the woman he loved.

"I'm not due back until Boxing Day."

"When are you going down to Heronfield?"

He frowned. "I'm not. Things are no better, Sarah. I can't go back until my father is willing to accept me for who I am, not who he wants me to be."

"What about your mother? And your grandmother? Don't you think they would like to see you?"

"Of course. And I feel the same way about them. But it's not worth the trouble it will cause."

"So what are you going to do for Christmas?"

"I'm staying at a hotel here in Coventry."

Sarah was puzzled. "Why not London? You don't know Coventry at all. You'll be lonely here."

"Any big city is lonely when you're alone. I wanted to be somewhere I could feel close to you." Tony watched Sarah's face anxiously as he spoke. Would she be angry with him for trying to read more into their relationship than she was willing to give?

Sarah felt a strange mixture of warmth and frustration. She was glad Tony felt so strongly about her, but nothing had changed in their relationship. She did not want to feel pressured again. Tony sipped his tea as he watched her, then put his cup down decisively before speaking again.

"How long do you have for Christmas?"

"I go back to Heronfield tomorrow. I was just doing my last bit of shopping."

Tony's happiness at seeing Sarah again after so long lost some of its edge. He frowned.

"Will you be seeing Bobby over Christmas?"

Sarah nodded. "Yes. When I'm not on duty."

Tony felt a hot flame of jealousy. So she was still seeing him after all these months. He had to know how much of a threat the American was.

"You obviously get on well with him. Do you love him?"

Sarah shrugged. It was the second time she had faced that question in only two days, and she was still no nearer an answer.

"I don't know. We get on well together. That's a start."

Tony reached across the table and tentatively took hold of Sarah's hand.

"Will you do something for me? Please?"

Sarah was flushed. Tony's hand around hers felt comforting, and she was so happy to be with him again. Why was life so complicated?

"What do you want?"

"Will you promise not to make any commitment with Bobby until the war is over? You must know how I feel about you. I want the chance to make you happy, without all the problems which the war has placed between us."

"But I have no such problems with Bobby. I know what he does, and he's always honest with me."

"Don't you think I'd like our relationship to be like that too?" Tony's voice was pleading. Sarah shook her head.

"To be honest, Tony, I don't know what to think. I sometimes think that you are two different people. There's the Tony who was my friend at the beginning of the war, the man I got on so well with, the man who came back from Dunkirk so fired up with wanting to fight the Germans, and so angry and hurt at the death of his brother. Then there's the other Tony, the man with secrets, the man who says he'll write but then doesn't, the man who seems afraid to take up a gun and fight. I'm never really sure which of the two Tony's I'm going to see. The confusion's unsettling."

Tony's eyes were sad as he gazed into hers.

"The first one is the real Tony, Sarah, I promise you that. It's the war that has created the second, and I can't explain how or why until it is all over. Please, just say you'll wait until I can explain. Then, if you don't like what you hear, make your life with Bobby and I'll wish you all the happiness in the world. What do you say, Sarah? Will you give me the chance, for the sake of what we've meant to each other?" His hand tightened around Sarah's as he spoke, as though he felt that by the force of his will he could make her do what he wanted.

Sarah was quiet for a moment. She wanted to believe him. She wanted the old Tony to take control again, the man whom she had fallen in love with and, if she was honest with herself, the man she still loved. But what about Bobby? She knew she could never love the American in the same way that she loved Tony. But at least she knew he would not hurt her. She shook her head in confusion.

"I don't know, Tony. I don't know if I can promise to wait for you when I can't be sure of what you want from me."

"Just promise that you'll think about what I said."

Sarah nodded slowly. "All right, I'll think about it."

Tony gave a relieved sigh. If she was willing to think about it then there was hope for him yet. They sat in silence for a moment, their hands still clasped across the table, then Sarah carefully extracted her fingers from his and stood up.

"I have to go now. Mum's expecting me for dinner." Her face broke into a sudden smile. "I know. Why don't you come back with me? We're going to celebrate Christmas early, so you can join with us. That way you won't spend Christmas entirely alone."

Tony was flustered. "I don't know, Sarah. I don't think your mother would like me to intrude in your celebrations."

"Don't be silly! Christmas is a time for sharing. She'll be glad to have you. We both will."

Tony grinned happily, the boyish features taking on the familiar pattern which Sarah loved.

"Then yes, I'd love to come. Thank you."

The smiling couple left the tea shop and made their way to the Porter home, chatting along the way as though the difficult times between them had never existed.

Sarah led the way up the steps to the front door. Tony followed behind, eager to see the place where Sarah had been born and grew up. Sarah pushed the door open and called out.

"Mum! I'm home! And I've brought someone back for dinner!"

Alice Porter appeared in the kitchen doorway wiping her hands on a towel, her face flushed from the heat of the kitchen. She smiled warmly at Tony as he stepped forward to greet her.

"Hello, Mrs. Porter. I hope you don't mind me intruding on your Christmas dinner?"

"Of course not." Alice grinned at her daughter. "Well, aren't you going to introduce us?"

"This is Tony Kemshall, his father owns Heronfield House. Tony, this is my mother."

"Pleased to meet you."

"And you too. I've heard a lot about you."

Tony turned a quizzical look towards Sarah, who blushed at her mother's words. Thankfully she did not have to explain herself, for Alice spoke again.

"Take our guest into the other room, love. Dinner will be about half an hour."

Sarah hung up her coat and took Tony's greatcoat from him, then led him into the room decorated for Christmas. Tony looked around at the paper decorations and the small tree and smiled. Mistaking his feelings Sarah was somewhat defensive.

"I know it's not as lavish as the Christmas decorations you're used to, but this is how Christmas has always been for me."

Tony turned and smiled warmly at the young woman by his side, and Sarah could see the depth of his feelings for her in his eyes. She was unable to turn away as he spoke.

"That's what I like about it. It's so homely, and has obviously been put together with a great deal of love."

Sarah's feelings, which had been under control for so many months, were now threatening to overwhelm her. Tony gazed at her, seeing the firelight reflected in golden highlights from her hair. He noticed the confusion in her eyes and reached a tentative hand, but Sarah turned away.

"Please sit down and make yourself comfortable, Tony. I must set the table for dinner."

Tony sat on the sofa and watched as Sarah busied herself setting a clean linen cloth on the table and taking the best china from the cupboard. It did not take long. When she had finished she had her feelings under control once more.

"Will you excuse me a minute, Tony? I just want to freshen up for dinner."

"You look beautiful as you are."

"Nevertheless I must change." Sarah was blushing as she left the room and carried her shopping upstairs. Ten minutes later she returned, clean and fresh in a pale blue dress, and carrying a parcel wrapped in Christmas paper in her hands. She placed it under the tree and turned smiling towards Tony.

"It's for Mum."

At that moment Alice came into the room. She too had changed. She placed a covered dish on the table, and Sarah excused herself to help. In the kitchen, Alice smiled warmly at her.

"He seems very nice, love. Are you sure you prefer the American to him?"

"Mum!" Sarah's face was red. "We're just good friends. Honest!"

"When did you last invite a friend for Christmas dinner?"

Sarah grinned. "Never before, but he's on his own. You don't mind?"

Alice shook her head. "Of course not. I was just teasing. Now carry this dish for me."

Sarah carried the dish into the other room. Within minutes the table was full, and the three people sat down. Tony smiled appreciatively at Alice.

"What a wonderful spread. How do you manage it?"

"Most of the vegetables come from the garden, so it wasn't too difficult." She carved the small chicken as she spoke, passing the plate to Tony. He helped himself to potatoes, carrots and sprouts and covered the whole with thick rich gravy.

"Mm, this is lovely." He smiled as he ate, and the conversation continued as they enjoyed their meal.

"We're having Christmas dinner today, because Sarah goes back to Heronfield tomorrow."

Tony nodded. "Yes, I know. She's lucky, she'll be getting another Christmas dinner there in a few days."

"Won't you?"

Tony shook his head sadly. "I'm afraid not. I won't be going home for Christmas."

Alice wore a puzzled frown. "If you're on duty at Christmas, what are you doing here instead of visiting your family now? You're not working in Coventry, are you?"

Tony looked a little uncomfortable and Sarah intervened.

"Mum, I'm sure Tony doesn't want to talk about this."

"That's all right, Sarah." Tony smiled gratefully. "To tell the truth, Mrs. Porter, I don't get on very well with my father at the moment. I think I'll probably go back to camp for Christmas. At least that way I can share it with some of my friends."

"Don't you think you ought to make an effort with your family? After all, who knows what might happen during the next year. Nothing is safe or sure while we're at war."

"Mum!"

Alice smiled apologetically at Sarah. "I'm sorry love, I didn't mean to embarrass Tony. It's just that I know what it's like to lose someone in a war. I don't know what I would have done if your father and I had parted on bad terms, and never had a chance to make it up."

Tony nodded. "That's all right. I'm sure your mother meant well, Sarah." He turned towards his hostess. "The truth is Mrs. Porter, I would love to go home and put things right with my family, but I can't see that happening with Dad so mad at me. I shall really miss Mamma this Christmas. That's why I appreciate your generosity so much."

Alice smiled. "Well then, let's enjoy this Christmas together." She gathered together the empty plates. "I'll just take these plates into the kitchen and fetch the pudding."

Sarah turned an embarrassed face towards Tony.

"I'm sorry about that. Mum can sometimes be a bit outspoken."

Tony grinned. "Don't worry. In fact, I like her openness. You obviously get on well together."

Sarah nodded. "I had no father, so we've always been extra close."

Alice returned with the Christmas pudding as Sarah spoke. It was a beautiful round pudding with a sprig of holly stuck jauntily in the top, just like the traditional pre-war puddings.

"Mm, that looks, and smells, delicious."

"I only hope it tastes as good. It's a recipe I got from the paper. There's a few things in it you wouldn't expect to find in a traditional Christmas pudding, but it's the best I can do with the rationing."

"It looks wonderful, Mrs. Porter."

And so it was. In no time at all the pudding was eaten, and the three people rose from the table.

Tony smiled his appreciation at Alice. "I'll help you with the washing up."

"You'll do no such thing! You're our guest! Sarah and I will do it later. Now, sit down and relax."

Alice sat in her favourite chair by the fire as Tony seated himself on the sofa. Sarah fetched the present from beneath the tree.

"Happy Christmas, Mum." She kissed Alice on the cheek as she handed the present over. "I hope you like it."

"I'm sure I will, love." Alice opened the parcel carefully and gazed at the beautiful cloth. "Oh Sarah, it's lovely." She placed it on one side and stood up to hug her daughter, before taking a much smaller present from beneath the tree. "This is for you, love."

Sarah took the present and unwrapped it, to find a pair of gold earrings in the shape of small bluebirds. Her eyes shone with delight as she carefully put them on and admired herself in the mirror.

"They're lovely."

"They really suit you."

Sarah turned to Tony who smiled as he watched the two women exchanging gifts, although his happiness was tempered with sadness as he thought of the coming Christmas Day when he would be unable to share such moments with his own family. Sarah seemed to guess his thoughts and, suddenly, an image came into her mind.

"Will you excuse me for a moment?"

Alice and Tony exchanged a puzzled glance as Sarah hurried from the room and rushed upstairs. Once in her room she took out the small gold tie pin she had bought that morning. As she held the tiny heron in the palm of her hand she felt once again the warmth of the summer sun and Tony's lips on hers. She felt a deep certainty that the tie pin was not meant for her. Destiny had led her to it that morning, so she could buy it for Tony. It would not compensate him for spending Christmas away from his family, but it might help. She put the golden heron back into its box and carried it downstairs. As she entered the room, Alice gave her a quizzical look then rose to her feet.

"I'll just go and make some of that counterfeit coffee they sell now."

She closed the door quietly behind her, leaving the two young people alone together. Sarah smiled shyly at Tony and held out the small leather box.

"I bought this this morning, and I'd like you to have it. Happy Christmas, Tony."

Tony took the box and opened it carefully. He sat silently for a few moments lost in his thoughts.

Sarah frowned.

"Don't you like it?"

Tony fought to control his emotions as he looked up. "Like it? It's beautiful Sarah. It reminds me of home, and the times we shared together there."

Sarah felt an overwhelming desire to hold him,. Tony's thoughts were so like her own. She felt so close to him, and she wished this could last forever. Tony saw her emotions reflected in her eyes, and slowly stood up. He placed the small leather box on the arm of the sofa and reached out to touch her cheek. This time Sarah did not pull away. She stood, frozen, not knowing what to do. At this moment she wanted to be with Tony, the Tony she loved. But who knew what he would be like next time they met? Should she give way to her feelings and leave herself open to hurt once more? Or should she play safe and stay with Bobby? Tony leant forward and gently brushed her lips with his. For a moment Sarah responded, but then caution won over the feelings of her heart and she pulled away.

"No, Tony." Her voice was little more than a whisper as she compared his lips with Bobby's. She knew which she preferred.

Tony frowned. "Are you thinking of Bobby?"

Sarah nodded, unable to speak. If she did, she would tell Tony that Bobby could not compete with him in her thoughts or her heart. Tony stood silently for a moment, remembering the feel of her lips beneath his and the way she began to respond. Then he smiled. She had responded, and earlier that day she had promised not to commit herself to Bobby until the end of the war. Why spoil a pleasant day by trying to rush things? Sarah relaxed as she saw Tony's smile, though she was puzzled as to why he should smile at her rejection. Tony turned and picked up the small golden heron and looked at it once more.

"It's so beautiful, Sarah, almost as beautiful as you are." He looked up at her. His eyes held hers so that she could not turn away. "I'll keep this with me, and whenever I look at it I'll think of home. But more importantly, I shall think of you. As long as I have this with me, I'll feel I have a part of you with me too."

Sarah smiled and sat down on the sofa, and Tony sat beside her. They gazed at the small decorated tree and watched the tinsel throw back the reflected light of the fire. As Alice opened the door and entered with the coffee, they were both thinking this was a Christmas they would never forget.

133

"Hi, Sarah. Are you coming to the dance tomorrow night?"

"I'm sorry Bobby, but I'm on duty tomorrow evening, and on Christmas afternoon."

"But it's Christmas Eve tomorrow. I want to see you."

Sarah laughed at the sound of his voice on the end of the telephone. "You sound like a little boy who can't get his way!"

The sound of Bobby's laughter reached her.

"Sorry. But I was so looking forward to spending Christmas with you, and now I shall have to ditch all my plans."

"Perhaps we could meet for lunch tomorrow?" suggested Sarah.

"Sure! Anything! As long as I get to see you!"

"OK, lunch it is then." Sarah smiled. "Our first Christmas together."

"I like the sound of that. Does it mean we can look forward to lots more?"

"Who knows. No one can make plans until this war is over."

"Sure we can, if we want to."

Sarah smiled. "Well, maybe."

"No maybe, Sarah. I'm making plans already "Bobby's laughter echoed down the telephone again.

"OK then, see you tomorrow."

"You're on."

Sarah walked into the pub. Bobby's present was wrapped in gay paper, tucked safely under her arm. The pub which seemed so dim at their first meeting was bright and full of life. Christmas decorations hung across the low ceiling. Bobby was already waiting for her, and rose eagerly to his feet, smiling broadly.

"Over here, Sarah!"

Sarah smiled and waved as she made her way through the crowd to join him at the table. She sat down gratefully.

"I got you a sherry. Is that OK?"

Sarah nodded. "Yes, lovely."

She sipped the drink, then settled back in her seat. "Sorry I can't make it to the dance tonight."

"That's OK. I'm sorry I made a fuss yesterday. The boys at the hospital need to enjoy their Christmas too. I'm sure I'd appreciate you being at my bedside, if I had to be in hospital for Christmas."

"I hope that never happens."

"What ? You hope you're never in a position to help me if I'm hurt?"

Sarah laughed. "Don't be silly. What I meant is that I hope you are never in hospital, needing my help."

Bobby looked thoughtful. "Who knows who will be in need of help next year. I'm sure the Second Front must come soon. I like to think that if I'm hurt, there'll be people like you to help me."

Sarah felt a shiver run down her spine.

"Don't talk like that, Bobby, I don't want you to tempt fate." She picked up the present. "We're here to celebrate Christmas, not to be morbid. Here, this is for you."

Bobby smiled warmly as he reached out and took it. He felt the gift carefully, like a little boy, and Sarah could not help laughing.

"Aren't you going to open it?"

"I guess I shall have to, if I'm to find out what it is."

He eagerly opened the present, and smiled as the book was revealed.

"Gee, Sarah, this is great. I need this to help me learn more about your beautiful country. I'll be sorry to leave when this war is over. But I can't wait to get home." He looked quizzically across the table. "What are you going to do after the war?"

Sarah smiled. "That's easy. I'm going to train to be a proper nurse. I love my work."

Bobby nodded. "That doesn't surprise me. Have you decided where you're going to study?"

Sarah shook her head. "No. There'll be plenty of time to think about that when we're at peace again."

"We have a lot of good hospitals in America. You could always do your training over there." Bobby's voice was hesitant, as though he was not sure he should have made the suggestion. Sarah felt uncomfortably nervous and shook her head.

"Why should I want to do that?"

"Perhaps you might like to be near me?"

Sarah did not know what to say. She sat silently as Bobby took a small leather box from his pocket. He held it out nervously.

"What I'm trying to say is that I love you, Sarah. I'd like you to be my wife."

He opened the box, and Sarah gazed at the beautiful sapphire ring in its nest of white satin. She dared not raise her eyes to Bobby's in case he saw her confusion. If he had asked her to marry him a few days previously, she would probably have said yes, choosing the safety and security he offered. But now that answer was impossible. She had seen Tony again and promised not to make a commitment to Bobby or anyone else until hostilities had ceased, when he felt that he would, in some mysterious way, be in a position to put their relationship back to where it had been before he had been changed so much by the war. If she was honest with herself however, she knew that, even without the promise, her answer would have been the same. After spending time alone with Tony, relaxing, sharing their thoughts, a brief tentative kiss, she knew she loved Tony with all her heart. She could not agree to marry anyone else. Now she was going to have to hurt Bobby, a man who had never done anything to hurt her. She sighed sadly.

"What is it, Sarah? Why don't you answer?" Bobby's eyes were pleading, full of love and fear. "You'll still be able to nurse if you marry me. I promise I'll never stand in the way of anything you want to do. I love you too much to do that. I only want to make you happy."

At last Sarah raised her eyes to his, and Bobby's heart sank. She did not have to say anything. He knew what her answer would be. But he was determined not to let her go without a fight.

"Do you love someone else?" Bobby was thinking of Tony Kemshall. He remembered how he had looked when he found out that Sarah was seeing the American. The sick feeling he felt then returned once more as he awaited Sarah's answer.

"Yes...No... Oh it's difficult to explain." Sarah said in answer to his question. Bobby closed the box and put the ring carefully back into his pocket.

"Take as much time as you like, Sarah. But I must know why."

Sarah closed her eyes and took a deep breath. It seemed the time had arrived for her to tell Bobby everything she had kept from him. She opened her eyes. It was going to be hard, but it had to be done.

"It all started long before the war," Sarah began, her eyes looking into the distance and seeing not Bobby, but the man whose features so closely resembled his. "I fell in love with Joe. He lived in Coventry like me. We were so close, we knew each other so well." Her eyes filled with tears, but she did not notice them. "When war broke out I came down to Heronfield. Joe joined the Home Guard because he was found unfit for active service." She smiled a soft sad smile which tore at Bobby's heart, but he did not interrupt her as she continued. "Joe and I were engaged, but before the wedding Joe was killed in an air raid." Now the tears began to flow but Sarah still did not seem to notice. "I loved him so much. It broke my heart to lose him, and I thought I would never love again. Joe left a hole in my life which took a long time to fill."

Bobby reached out and took Sarah's hand in his. The warmth of his touch brought Sarah back to the present. She looked down at his hand enfolding hers.

"I can try to make you forget him, Sarah, if you give me a chance."

Sarah carefully removed her hand from his and searched her handbag for a handkerchief. After wiping her eyes, she took a deep breath and looked at Bobby. He looked so full of sorrow at her loss that she did not want to continue with her story. But she knew she must. She shook her head sadly.

"No, Bobby, I can't say yes. Do you remember Tony Kemshall?"

Bobby nodded. How could he forget him?

"Well, he helped me to get over Joe. For a time we went out together. We were happy; I thought we were in love, but somehow Tony doesn't seem able to cope with the war. One minute he's a kind, generous, heroic man whom I can love. The next he's thoughtless and seems to be a coward. I couldn't take the contradictions in his character. I didn't want to be hurt anymore, so I said I wouldn't see him again."

"Then you met me?"

Sarah nodded. "Yes. I don't think I would have stayed for that first drink if you hadn't looked so much like Joe.'

"I look like Joe?" Bobby was feeling confused. Sarah had obviously been badly hurt emotionally, first by the loss of her fiancé and then by Tony Kemshall. He had hoped to be the one to help her get over that. But now it seemed that she only went out with him because he reminded her of Joe. What about all the good times they had shared together? Had she spent all her time with him wishing that he were someone else? It seemed that Sarah had read his thoughts, for she smiled sadly.

"You look like Joe, but apart from that you're nothing like him. You're kind and warm and fun to be with in your own way. You make me happy, and you make me feel safe."

"Then why not marry me?"

"Because it's not enough. I need to love the man I marry."

"Surely love could grow? I'm willing to give it a chance." Bobby frowned. "Do you still feel more for Tony Kemshall than you do for me?"

Sarah nodded sadly. "I saw him while I was on leave in Coventry. He was his old self again, the one who helped me to get over Joe. He asked me to wait until after the war before making plans. He said he hoped we might have another chance together then."

"And are you going to wait for him?"

Sarah shrugged. "I promised to wait until after the war before making any commitments. I didn't promise that any commitment I made would be to him."

"But you would like it to be?"

Sarah nodded sadly. She kept her eyes on the table, unable to meet Bobby's gaze and the pain that she would see.

"Sarah, look at me."

Reluctantly she lifted her eyes. To her surprise she saw that he was smiling. It was a sad smile which tugged at her heart, and made her wonder if she was doing the right thing.

"I'm glad you told me all of this. It helps me to understand you better. If Kemshall is willing to leave you here with me until after the war, and then let you make your choice, then I'm willing to accept that too. But let me warn you, Sarah, I won't let you go without a fight. I'll do my best between now and the end of the war to make you fall in love with me. Do you understand?"

Sarah nodded. "Yes, but..."

"No buts. I don't want to hear them. I know Kemshall has a head start on me, but while you're single I can live in hope. All I ask is that you'll continue to see me until I'm shipped out."

"You still want to see me, after all I've said?"

"Of course I do. I love you. I'm prepared to do whatever's necessary to make you fall in love with me too." Bobby smiled sadly. "Now, let's put all of this behind us and get on with what we came here for." He lifted his glass in salute. "Happy Christmas, Sarah."

Sarah smiled too as she raised her glass. "Happy Christmas, Bobby. And thank you."

Although he smiled, the happiness had gone from Bobby's Christmas, but he would not let her see that. He vowed that, no matter what it took, Tony Kemshall would not be the one to marry the beautiful girl opposite him. The Englishman had his chance, and he had blown it. Now Bobby knew what he was up against he could fight back. He was determined he was the one who would spend the rest of his life with Sarah.

134

1944 began with good news for the Russian Allies, when Leningrad was finally relieved after a siege of more than two years. The city, now known as the Hero City, was in a shocking state. Over a million inhabitants had died of starvation, while the rest were in very poor condition; but they had survived. Their defiance and tenacity against the Reich was a shining example for all those who struggled for freedom. No matter how bad the situation, how hopeless the future looked, as long as people held on they would eventually overcome the aggressor. On January 5th the Russian army crossed the pre-war frontier with Poland, and went on to clear the Ukraine of the hated Germans. The push continued, and by May, the Crimea had been liberated.

In the south of the European continent, the Allies staged a landing at Anzio on 22nd January. It went ahead almost totally unopposed, but instead of advancing while they had the advantage, they chose to consolidate their position. By the time they moved on over a week later, the Germans had built up a great strength in opposition. To relieve the pressure on the beachhead at Anzio, the Gustav line in the south began a bombardment of the monastery at Monte Casino, attempting to drive out the Germans whom they were convinced were garrisoned there. However, the intelligence was inaccurate. One of the greatest historical monuments in Europe was systematically destroyed for no reason. At last, after such a disastrous start on the part of the Allies, the Germans began to fall back. Each time they moved back to well-prepared defensive lines so that the Allied progress was slow and painful. The advantage they hoped to gain from the landings at Anzio was lost in a welter of confusion and lack of drive.

In England, the preparations for the invasion went ahead. Much had been learned from Dieppe, Anzio and numerous other attacks which began before they were fully prepared. This time, meticulous attention was paid to each detail of the landing. A great deal of dis-information was relayed to the Germans by their agents who had been turned and were now working for the Allies. Their masters in Berlin were uncertain where to focus their attention - the Pas de Calais or the beaches of Normandy. In April, the Allies began bombing the bridges over the Seine and the Loire, as well as the French railway system, in an attempt to disrupt German supplies. Back in England the soldiers who would be the first to go ashore on the D-Day beaches continued with their training. In the land around Marlborough, Bobby and Al underwent intensive training. They had less time than they would have wished to visit the women they loved, but there was a positive feeling in the air, wanting to get on and do the job in hand, and they were content with their lot.

Sarah saw Bobby whenever she could and still enjoyed being with him. Tony managed to get down to see Sarah twice during the first few months of 1944. He was glad their relationship was back to its old friendly footing, though he wished Sarah would trust him more. He knew that if he ever held her and kissed her again, he would force her to recognise her love for him, but she would not allow him into a position where he could pursue the matter. He also found it difficult to visit his home neighbourhood, without calling in at Heronfield to see his family. He longed to see his mother again, not just to write to her and receive her letters. He also wanted to see his grandmother, and try to encourage her hope that France would soon be free once more. But most of all, he wanted to see his father. They had always been so close before the war came, and Tony's work had driven them apart. But, instead of confronting his family, Tony had to be content with training S.O.E.'s new recruits for the work they would be doing prior to the invasion of France. He hoped that he would be allowed to go out there with them.

135

Jane almost bounced into the room, her eyes shining, and Sarah smiled. There was something subtly different about her friend. She was always full of life, but over the last few weeks she had felt there was something more. She sat down on the bed, drawing her feet up beneath her, and smiled across at Sarah who was writing a letter at the desk.

"Are you writing to your Mum?"

Sarah shook her head. "No. Tony."

For a moment Jane's eyes clouded, and she frowned at her friend.

"I thought you'd got over him last year."

Sarah's smile was rueful. "So did I, Jane; and it's easy to pretend that he means nothing to me when we are apart. But when we are together I feel so alive."

"And confused."

Sarah nodded.

"Right as usual, Jane, but I can't help it. Tony seems to think that things will be different after the war and I have to give him a chance."

Jane frowned. She was very fond of Sarah, and hated to see her life in such a muddle. Yet what could she do to help?

"I think he's just using you like before. When he gets bored or finds someone else he'll stop writing and visiting again. Besides, I think you're being unfair to Bobby. He's so good to you. Yet you keep writing to Tony, and sometimes seeing him, behind his back. I could never do that to Al, and I don't think you should to Bobby."

Sarah carefully put down her pen and turned to face her friend. Jane was so defensive of Bobby, so hurt for the hurt that he might feel. Sarah knew it was time for honesty.

"I know what you mean about Bobby. We are very close and I think that if it weren't for Tony, I could fall in love with him, or at least we could be happy together. But you're wrong about me doing it behind his back. Bobby knows all about me now. I told him about Joe and about Tony. He's willing to let me have time to make up my own mind, even if it takes until the end of the war."

"What? He must be mad! He should be forcing you to make your choice now." She turned her questioning gaze on Sarah. "When did you two discuss all this?"

"At Christmas. When he proposed."

"He proposed? And you turned him down? I take it all back, Sarah. You're the one who's mad!" Jane stood up, shaking her head in disbelief. "Bobby must be really hurting."

Sarah nodded sadly. She knew how much she had hurt the American, but could see no other course of action that would not eventually end in more heartache.

"I know. I offered not to see him again until I'd sorted things out with Tony, but he wouldn't hear of it. I suppose if I'm still seeing him he thinks he has still got a chance."

"And has he?"

Sarah threw up her arms in exasperation, her muddled emotions no nearer to resolution than they had been months before. "I don't know, Jane. If I could be sure of Tony I'd say no. But you know what Tony's like. One minute he can be kind, caring, heroic, loving and the next he seems to cast me aside and be afraid to fight. I want the Tony I love to emerge from this war, not the other one or a mixture of both. I don't think I could live with that. But it wouldn't be fair to Bobby for me to agree to marry him now, only to find out I've made a mistake."

Jane sighed. "I'm glad my life's not as complicated as yours. I think I'd just give up and become a nun!"

Sarah laughed. "Oh Jane, I do like your sense of humour! I don't know what I'd do without you here."

"Well, you'll have to manage without me soon."

Sarah nodded sadly. "Yes. I suppose you and Al will live in America after the war?"

Jane nodded, a mischievous glint in her eye as she smiled happily at her friend.

"Yes, I'm sure Al will want to build up the family business for the three of us."

"The three of you?" Sarah frowned in puzzlement, then suddenly her eyes widened and her mouth opened in a circle of surprise. Now she knew what had been different about Jane in the last few weeks. She had been hiding a secret.

"You're pregnant!"

Jane's grin reached almost from ear to ear

"Yes, I'm going to have a baby in October."

Sarah rushed across the room and hugged her friend tightly. "That's wonderful news, Jane. Does Al know?"

Jane nodded excitedly. "I've just told him. That's where I've been. He's so excited and we're both so happy. I can't wait until the war is over and we can go over to America and live together as a proper family should. I hate being apart from him."

Sarah nodded, but said nothing. The mention of the war had sent her mind racing ahead to the coming Second Front. She wondered if Al might not come back at all. She could almost see Jane in the same position as her own mother had been in, a war widow with a small child to bring up alone. She felt a shiver of apprehension run down her spine. Smiling brightly, she kept her fear out of her eyes. She would not spoil Jane's happiness now. There would be time enough over the coming months to think of the danger Al would be facing and to cope with the fear that he might not come back. Right now, all Sarah could do was share her happiness.

"It's wonderful news!" she exclaimed happily. "Come on, let's celebrate!"

The two friends left the room laughing together. No one could tell the future, so they put thoughts of it from their heads and determined to enjoy the present.

136

Tony knocked on the oak panelled door and waited. Captain Dawson wanted to see him, probably about the new batch of recruits who were ready to go out. He was glad he would be able to give a good report of them all.

"Come in."

Tony pushed open the door and entered the office, where Dawson watched him thoughtfully from behind his desk. Tony saluted and closed the door, and Dawson waved a dismissive hand at him.

"This is just an informal meeting, Tony. Sit down." He indicated a chair on the opposite side of the desk and Tony sat down, puzzling over what it could be all about.

"When do you think the Second Front will come?"

Tony was surprised at the question. "I don't know, sir, but I suspect it will be this summer. Surely it won't be put off until next year?"

Dawson shook his head. "No, indeed not. We're sending out as many agents as possible to disrupt lines of communication and hamper the Germans in their attempts to reach the beachheads, wherever they might be." He smiled at Tony. "Of course I don't know, and if I did I certainly wouldn't tell you."

Tony laughed but said nothing as the officer continued.

"We are particularly concerned with making life difficult for the Germans in certain ports, to confuse them and to try to stop them sending ships and U-boats into the Channel, where they'd be in a position to disrupt our lines of communication. Now we get to the point." He leant forward across the desk as he spoke. "Which of the agents we've just finished training do you think would fit in best with your old group in Saint Nazaire?"

Tony thought back to what he had been through with those brave French people, and felt his heartbeat quicken. He frowned, wanting to be as objective as possible in his choice of agent, while wishing that it could be him. After a few moments thought he began hesitantly.

"I suppose Cooper would do well, or maybe Wallis. But neither of them really knows the area. And of course they don't know the people involved."

Dawson sighed as he leant back in his chair. "That's the answer I thought I'd get. They would take too long to get acquainted with the area. Isn't there anyone else?"

Tony thought hard for a moment then shook his head. "No, sir. Only me."

Dawson's eyes narrowed thoughtfully. "You were the first person I thought of, Tony, but I couldn't order you back there. Not after what happened last time."

"I understand, sir. You couldn't order me. But I could volunteer."

"You do realise how dangerous it would be for you? The SS know you're a British spy. With the invasion in full swing, they wouldn't waste much time on interrogating you again. I'm afraid that if you went back and were caught, you would be executed on the spot."

Tony swallowed hard and nodded. "I know, sir. I've given this a great deal of thought over the last few weeks, in the hope that I might get a chance to go back out. I know the dangers, but I also believe that I'm the best man for the job. I know the area well. I know the members of the group, and we've already proved we can work together as a team. As long as I'm careful and stay out of sight, I should be safe."

Dawson's expression was grim. "You're not the only one who has given this a lot of thought. I wanted to ask you to go back. But I didn't want to put you in a position where you felt you had no choice."

"You mean I can go?" Tony was smiling, his eyes full of eagerness. "I know my work here has been useful, sir, but it doesn't compare with life in the field. You can't imagine how much I've wanted to be back there."

"Even knowing the dangers?"

"Yes, sir. I built up that group. It would mean a lot to me to fight with them for the final liberation of their homeland and, I might add, the final liberation of my own family estates."

Dawson nodded. "Right then. You're the one who will go. Now come with me. I'll show you what we want you to do."

Tony eagerly followed his commanding officer from the room, and down the hallway to a small office. Dawson unlocked the door, then led him across to a filing cabinet. Unlocking the bottom drawer, he took out a brown manila folder. He placed it on the desk where they could both see its contents. Dawson spread a detailed map of the Saint Nazaire area and indicated certain points.

"These bridges will need to be destroyed before the landings. And as many stretches of railway as possible need to be put out of action." Tony nodded as the captain continued. "If there are any transport trains in the area, I want them destroyed. All this before the landings. Then, to keep the Germans busy, attack the docks and cause as much chaos as possible."

"How will I know when the landings are coming?"

"BBC radio." Dawson's answer was simple. "There will be so many groups waiting to go ahead with their final attacks that we're going to use one blanket message. When you arrive, I want you to begin disrupting the transport lines. When you hear the first message, which will come on the first day of the planned month of invasion, you'll know to get ready for your attack on the docks."

"What's the message?"

"The first line of Paul Verlaines' Chanson d'automne. 'Les saglots long des violins d'automne'."

"How will I know what day the landings will be?"

"You won't, not exactly. A second message will be transmitted to indicate that the landings will begin within the next forty-eight hours. That will be your signal to launch your attack on the docks."

"What...?"

Dawson grinned as he interrupted.

"The message will be the second line of the same song. 'Blessent mon coeur d'une langueur monotone'."

"Good." Tony perused the map in front of him for a time, trying to form some idea of what would be needed to accomplish his task. Finally he spoke.

"I assume the group still have the Sten guns, but I'm sure we could do with some more ammunition." He began to mentally tick off the things he would need. "I'll need gammon grenades, clams, probably more plastic and some time switches, some abrasive grease would come in useful and probably some PIATs if you have them."

Dawson nodded. "You'll get them. We're going to drop you by parachute, so we can drop the containers at the same time. We'll be in touch with Angeline, and make arrangements for the group to meet you."

"Suggest a zone somewhere near the cave we used to use, if it's still safe."

"All right. Anything else?"

Tony's brow furrowed in concentration. "I don't think so. When do I go?"

"As soon as possible. Within two weeks at most. You'll be in France before the end of April, in plenty of time for the invasion when it comes."

Tony had a faraway look in his eyes. "It seems rather fitting. I was there at the beginning, during the German invasion and Dunkirk. It seems only right that I should help drive them out again, and help to avenge those who are no longer alive to have that opportunity."

Dawson nodded his understanding. "Then you're determined to go on with this, despite the added risk of being known to the SS?"

Tony nodded.

"Then make sure that you have everything in order here before you go. I don't want to be a pessimist, but we must be realistic."

Tony nodded. "Don't worry, sir. I'll be ready."

137

Tony held the delicate golden heron in his hands, and gazed at it longingly. It meant so much to him. Each time he looked at it or held it, he felt close to Sarah. He remembered the times they had shared together, particularly the Christmas meal they had enjoyed and how they had felt the old closeness once more. He remembered the look in her eyes as she had given the tie pin to him, the look of love tempered with caution. He was going to hurt her again with his unexplained absence, but this would be for the last time. Once the invasion was over, he would have to keep no secrets from Sarah and he knew that she would finally understand him. He looked again at the heron, contemplating whether or not to take it with him. He turned it over. One look at the English assay mark told him that would be impossible. He sadly placed the heron in its box, and carefully closed the lid before slipping it into a large envelope with a folded sheet of paper. He stuck it down and looked at the address

Miss Sarah Porter. Heronfield House Hospital.

He placed it next to another bulky package on his desk, this one addressed to his parents. He was aware of the dangers which lay ahead, and the two envelopes contained his final goodbyes to the people he loved. He fervently hoped they would never need to be delivered. Picking up both packages, he placed them together in a larger envelope, and sealed it down. He gazed thoughtfully at his own clear handwriting.

Captain Dawson.
In the event of my death please deliver the enclosed letters to the people concerned.
Lieutenant A. Kemshall

With a sigh he rose from the desk, and picked up the small bag he had prepared to take with him. With one last look at the room which had been home to him for so many months, he turned and left Beaulieu training centre for the last time.

138

Tony sat in the body of the Halifax, thinking back to the time when he had prepared for his first parachute jump. He grinned ruefully. He had been so frightened then, not of the jump but of actually going up in the aircraft. It was like second nature to him now to be flying above the Channel towards enemy-held territory. He looked around him at the three cylinders which were to accompany him on this jump. They contained all he needed, or so he hoped, to wage his war of disruption on the German lines of communication. He shifted his position to try to get more comfortable, the parachute making it difficult for him to lean back with any ease. He grinned at the crew member sitting opposite.

"It won't be long now, sir." The youngster threw a questioning glance at Tony. "Are you nervous?"

Tony nodded. "Yes, I'm nervous. You can never be sure that the Germans won't see the plane, and get to the jump zone before you get clear. Then there's the constant fear of being in enemy held territory. Above all that there's the anticipation of seeing old friends again, and the excitement of feeling that you're doing something wonderful. It's always the same."

"You've done this before?" The young man looked surprised as Tony nodded. "If you feel like that, why go back again?"

Tony shrugged. "Because it's my job and I'm good at it, I suppose. It's frightening, but so worthwhile. Believe it or not, it's enjoyable in a strange way. Still, I'll be glad when the war is over and I can visit France without having to sneak in at the dead of night."

"I've never been to France."

Tony smiled. "You must go after the war. It won't be the same as before '39, but I'm sure you'll enjoy it."

The young man grinned. "I'm sure I'll enjoy it more than you do on this visit!"

Tony nodded. "If it turns out anything like the last trip, you'll soon be hearing me calling you to get me back out!"

"Was it that bad?" Tony nodded. "If it turns out anything like the last trip, you'll soon be hearing me calling you to get me back out!"

"Was it that bad?"

Tony thought of the cell where he had been held; the cold, the hunger, the endless light, but most of all the pain. He felt the fear once again as he thought of the information he now carried about the D-Day codes. He could not allow himself to give that information away. He felt with his tongue for his L pill, the cyanide capsule which had been hidden inside a tooth hollowed out for that specific purpose. It was comforting to know it was there, though he prayed he would never need to take it.

"Sir?"

Tony dragged his mind back to the present.

"It could have been worse." He smiled as he spoke. "They could have run out of cognac!"

The young man shook his head in disbelief. "You know, they talk about our soldiers who fight on the ground, in tanks, in the air, at sea, but they never mention blokes like you. I think you're the real heroes. I could never do what you do."

Tony shrugged. "If someone had told me four years ago what I would be doing now, I wouldn't have believed them. But in war you do what you have to do. That isn't heroic, just a matter of necessity."

A red light came on above the crew members' head, casting an eerie glow over the interior of the plane and bringing their conversation to an end. There was no need for words. The two men rose to their feet, removed the hatch, fixed static lines to the parachutes attached to the containers and pushed them close to the edge. As Tony attached his own static line, the light changed from red to green, and the two men pushed the containers one by one through the hole. As Tony sat on the edge, the airman smiled encouragingly at him.

"Good luck, sir!"

Tony grinned. "See you in France after the war!"

The dispatcher's arm swept down as he cried "Go!" Tony leapt into the night air above a France eagerly awaiting its liberation.

He floated down through the cold night air, no lights below to show how far he had fallen or how far he had yet to go. A little to his right he saw the mushrooming canopy of the nearest container. He altered his direction slightly, so that he was falling closer to it and would land not too far away. He did not worry about the other containers. Angeline had received the message saying an agent was coming, and Jean-Paul was sure to have arranged a reception committee for him and the canisters. Although he could not yet make out any landmarks, those on the ground would have seen the parachutes, and would already be splitting up and moving off to intercept them. Then Tony saw the dark shadow of the land approaching fast, and took his landing position. As he touched the ground he rolled, then was back on his feet in seconds, fighting to deflate the balloon of his canopy and gather in the yards of silk. As he pulled the material towards him he heard the sound of running feet behind him. Turning anxiously, he recognised the approaching figure and grinned broadly. The Frenchman halted in surprise, his face a mask of incredulity.

"Mon Dieu! Albert!" Suddenly his face broke into a broad grin, and he quickly covered the remaining few yards to embrace the British agent. He stepped back and shook his head in disbelief.

"We were told to expect an agent, but I never dreamt it would be you! What made you come back?"

"I'll explain everything later, Jean-Paul. For now, just help me to get this parachute out of sight and find the cylinders."

Jean-Paul helped Tony to bundle the silk under his arm.

"We're not far from the cave. We'll hide your parachute there." He looked around. "We saw four chutes. Was that all?"

Tony nodded. "Yes. Mine and three containers."

"Good." Jean-Paul pointed to their left. "Georges took the one over there, Madeleine the next and Vincent the one that fell closest to you."

Tony was surprised. "Vincent is here?"

"Yes." Jean-Paul grinned. "You wouldn't believe how helpful he's been. Now let's get you to the cave."

The next half hour was spent moving the containers into the cave. There was little time for exchanging news, but once all signs of the drop were out of sight, they settled themselves on the rough stone floor and took stock of their situation. All the members of the group were as surprised as Jean-Paul to see Tony back in their midst, and he could not help grinning at them.

"Yes, it really is me."

"It's good to see you again, Albert, but do you think it was really wise of you to come back? The Germans were furious at your escape. We had to stop all activities for months because of the increased checkpoints, spot checks and downright nastiness. Your picture was plastered on every wall in the city, and there's a large reward out for your capture." Jean-Paul looked worried. "It's not just the Germans we have to worry about, even some French people would hand you over if they saw you, either for the money or for favours for their families."

Tony nodded. "I know. I considered all that, but I was the only agent who knew the area well enough to help you to cause the maximum amount of disruption, in preparation for the invasion." He grinned at the expressions on their faces, varying from hope to relief and joy. Madeleine spoke for them all.

"The invasion at last! When will it come, Albert?"

Tony shrugged. "I don't know. All I can say is that we'll be given a warning at the beginning of the month. Before that we must cut the German lines of communication - bridges, railways and telephones. Then we attack the docks to coincide with the landings, to prevent troops being moved up to the front.

"But it will be soon?"

Tony nodded. "Yes, Vincent. By the end of the year, there will be no more Germans in France." He looked across at Georges and Madeleine, who were smiling delightedly at each other with the news, then looked back at Vincent. "I'm glad you're all here together tonight. It gives me a chance to thank you for what you did for me, last time I was here.

You shouldn't have taken such risks for me, but I'm glad you did! It was a wonderful piece of teamwork. If you hadn't done it, I would be dead."

"As might the rest of us. We did it as much to protect ourselves as to help you."

Tony smiled at Jean-Paul. "I know, but it would have been easier if you'd just silenced me, instead of trying to smuggle me out. I thank you for taking that decision, and you, Vincent, for helping."

The older man smiled happily. "I've enjoyed working with these people. It's good to be doing something for my country other than complaining about the Germans."

"What have you been up to?" He aimed his question at Jean-Paul who, as always, was spokesman for the group.

"We've hit a few small convoys and blown a few tracks. Enough to keep our hand in, and keep the Germans on their toes, but no big attacks. Hopefully that will change, now the invasion is coming."

Tony nodded. "It will." He looked quizzically at Georges and Madeleine who were holding hands, not too discreetly. They smiled at him.

"I'm afraid you missed our wedding, Albert."

Tony smiled in delight. "You're married? That's wonderful!" He crossed the cave and embraced the couple. "I'm really happy for you both!" He thought of Madeleine as she had been when he first met her, angry, bitter, full of pain and hate, and was glad that love had found a place in her life once more. It was good to see that although the Germans had conquered the land, they had not conquered the spirit of the people. There was still life and hope and love, and while these three existed the people could never really be defeated. Dragging his thoughts back to the present, he addressed his small, tightly knit group.

"You had all better get back home. We'll continue to use the same contact points as before. Jean-Paul will be in touch to give you details of the planned attacks." He smiled at them all. "Thank you all for coming tonight. You don't know how good it feels to be back amongst my friends again."

Tony and Jean-Paul wished the others goodnight, and watched as they slipped out into the darkness. Then the Englishman turned to face his companion.

"Well, Georges and Madeleine always seemed friendly, but I didn't expect to find them married when I got back."

Jean-Paul smiled. "That's the only good thing I have seen come from the occupation." Tony raised his eyebrows questioningly and Jean-Paul continued. "They both took the deaths of Charles and Alain very hard. Georges had known them for most of his life and was bitter and angry, but what struck him and Madeleine the hardest was the sheer brutality of their deaths. For a while I thought their hate was so great that they might do something stupid and become a liability to the group, but then they began to spend time together, and managed to talk out the extremes of their feelings. They still hate the Germans for what they did and want revenge. But they managed to get those feelings under control. Love seemed to help to heal their wounds."

Tony nodded. "I understand. We all need someone to share our hopes and fears with, or we're lost." He was thinking of Sarah, and wishing he could share his life and heart with her as Georges and Madeleine did. He made an effort to put Sarah to the back of his mind. Thinking of her and wishing he were with her would only distract him from the important things he had to think about. He could not let his love for her become a liability, putting his and other people's lives at risk. He knew it would be hard, but it had to be done. He brought his thoughts to bear on the present situation.

"You'd better be on your way, Jean-Paul."

"You'll stay with us again, Albert." It was a statement not a question.

Tony shrugged. "I don't know. I don't want to put you and your family in any greater danger. I had thought of staying here in the cave."

"That won't be necessary. The Germans very rarely come out as far as us, as long as they get their produce. If they do come, there are many places where you can hide until they've gone. You know you're more than welcome in my home."

Tony grinned. "Thank you, Jean-Paul. I must admit, I find the idea of sleeping here rather unappealing. And it will be good to see Marie and the children again."

Jean-Paul put his arm around the younger man's shoulders.

"Come on. Let's go home."

139

It was close to midnight when the two men arrived back at Jean-Paul's home, but Marie was still waiting for her husband. She never went to bed until he returned home safely from his work with the Resistance. When she saw Tony, tears sprang to her eyes and a welcoming smile lit her face.

"Albert! It's so good to see you! Let me get you a drink!" She bustled around as she fought to control her emotions. She had not expected to see Tony again until after the war, if at all, and her surprise at his sudden re-appearance was overwhelming. Soon there were three glasses of red wine on the table, and she had regained her composure. "Jean-Paul told me what the Germans had done to you. When they put you on that plane, they didn't expect you to live. But then we received a message to say you had arrived safely, and were expected to survive." She closed her eyes, as though to shut out the memory of those dark days. "We didn't know what sort of recovery you would make and I felt so sad for your grandmother and parents. With David dead and you so badly injured, they must have suffered greatly."

Tony shook his head sadly. "They didn't even know." His two companions looked questioningly at him, and he tried to explain. "The work I do is secret. It has to be kept as much a secret in England as here in France. My family don't know what I do. They thought I was in America trying to obtain arms. When I got back to England I was kept in hospital until all signs of what I had been through were gone. Only then was I allowed to go home, and say I had just got back from America."

Jean-Paul looked disbelieving. "I'm sorry, Albert. I didn't realise it was like that for you. It must be very difficult to keep all this from the people you love." Tony nodded but said nothing, and Jean-Paul continued. "You had no visitors in hospital?"

"I had some. People who know what work I do. They helped me a great deal."

"But no family?" Jean-Paul shook his head in disbelief.

"They will be very proud of you when they find out," Marie smiled comfortingly at Tony. "While you're here, you're not without a family who understands. You're a part of us now, and you have constantly been in our prayers since we last saw you."

Tony was touched by the concern and understanding shown by the Boues.

"Thank you, Marie." He raised his glass. "Let's drink to family and friends. Those with us now, those far away and those who only live in our memories."

The three people raised their glasses, uniting a family divided by distance and misunderstanding. They prayed for a speedy end to the war, so that peace would come and heal all wounds.

When Tony came down to breakfast, he found the whole family at the table and was touched by the welcome he received from Theresa and Jeanne. The two girls were growing quickly, despite the meagre rations which life in Occupied France allowed. They seemed full of life as they clambered down from the table to rush across the room to embrace him.

"Albert! I've missed you!"

Tony ruffled the hair of the twelve year old. "I've missed you too, Jeanne."

He turned and smiled at Theresa. "You've grown too. You're a proper young lady now." He took her hand and kissed it gallantly. Theresa smiled warmly. At fourteen she was developing a woman's body. Her childish features were softening and maturing. Despite the war, Tony felt there were probably many young men seeking to court this teenager.

"I'm glad you are well enough to come back to us, Albert. We've missed you."

Jean-Paul smiled warmly at his daughters.

"If you two have finished your breakfast, will you please leave Albert in peace to enjoy his. Don't you have any chores to do?"

Jeanne, as impulsive and affectionate as ever, ran across to her father and kissed him on the cheek.

"Of course, Papa. I'll gather the eggs." With that she turned and rushed through the open door.

Tony laughed. "What a ray of sunshine she is!" He turned to the older girl. "Do you have work to do too?"

"I want to help with your work."

"My work?"

The teenager nodded. "Yes. I'm sure you wouldn't have come back if you didn't have plans to fight the Germans once more. I want to help."

Tony nodded solemnly. "Yes Theresa, I'm sure you do. I'll try to find work for you."

"I want to fight this time, Albert. I'm fourteen, almost grown-up. I have more to offer than nursing skills."

Tony looked across at Jean-Paul, who shook his head imperceptibly, a movement which was not lost on Theresa.

"Please don't try to stop me, Papa. It's something I have to do." She turned back to Tony. "You will give me a chance to prove myself?"

Tony was silent for a moment, then nodded. "All right. I won't promise anything, Theresa, but if a suitable job presents itself, you can have it."

"Thank you." Theresa turned and followed her sister from the kitchen. Tony sat down at the table with a shake of his head.

"She's changed, Jean-Paul. Much more adult. She seems to hate the Germans in a more adult way too."

Jean-Paul nodded sadly. "She's been like this since the death of Charles."

Tony frowned. "What has Charles got to do with this?"

Marie put a large cup of coffee on the table in front of him and sat down.

"Charles has everything to do with it," she said softly. "Theresa idolised him. He was her hero. And she fell in love with him."

"In love? Surely she's too young for that?"

Marie smiled. "She was just the right age. All girls as they reach their teens fall in love for the first time, and usually with an older man. It's all quite natural. In time they grow up a little, and realise it's just an infatuation. That man will always have a special place in their memories, but they will go on to fall in love with boys of their own age. That's how it should be. Only with Theresa, that didn't happen." She sighed sadly. "Charles was killed before Theresa could grow up. She was still in love with him, and hates the Germans for what they did. I do too, for they took away her childhood before she was ready to give it up."

"It must have been hard for you."

"She hasn't talked about it, but Marie and I know what she feels and try to be understanding. It is hard though. She has constantly asked to come out on ambush with me, but I think she is too young. Besides, I love her too much." Jean-Paul sighed. "If only I could find a job to satisfy her thirst for revenge, while keeping her relatively safe."

Tony nodded. "A difficult task. I'll see what I can do, but I promise that I won't ask her to do anything that will put her in too much danger, and of course, I'll discuss it with you before asking her to do anything at all. But you must both come to terms with facts. She is growing up fast, too fast perhaps because of this war, and she must be allowed more freedom to choose her own way. Just guide her with love and you won't go far wrong."

Marie smiled and covered his hand with hers.

"Wise words, Albert, surprisingly wise for one your age. You've obviously given a great deal of thought to the subject of parents and children."

Tony thought of the endless hours he had spent pondering the problems in his relationship with his father but said nothing. He turned to his hosts.

"You've both been so kind to me. I want you to know that I'll do my best to make sure that neither of your daughters is endangered because of what I ask them to do."

Jean-Paul nodded. "We can't ask for more. Now drink your coffee before it gets cold!"

140

Tony spent his first week back in France reconnoitring the land. During the day, he and Jean-Paul spent hours poring over maps, trying to identify targets. At night they moved silently around the countryside, getting a closer look at the places they intended to sabotage. By the end of the week, Tony had a list of places he felt must be disrupted. He intended to start with the ones which would take the longest to repair. He did not know exactly when the invasion would come, but there was no point blowing things up now which might be repaired before the landings. At the top of his list were the two bridges, which carried the railway from the south into the Saint Nazaire area. If they could be destroyed, it would make it difficult for the Germans to move troops up to the area of the landings. Road bridges, too, were high on his list of priorities, as were the rail tunnel, and the bridges on some of the minor roads. That would cause disruption to the vehicles detoured from the main routes which should have been blocked by earlier attacks. Finally, as the day of the invasion approached, the group would attack as many of the railway points as they could, and the telephone exchange. If they took their time and did not try to do too much damage on each sortie, they should get away with it. He was already working on his plans for the attack on the docks, the culmination of his work in preparation for D-Day. He knew that was where the real danger to himself and his friends lay.

Careful plans were laid. Jean-Paul conveyed instructions and arms to the other members of the group and, on the last day of April, the attacks were launched on the two railway bridges. Jean-Paul, together with Georges and Madeleine, took the bridge just south of Dognes, while Vincent joined Tony in his attack on the bridge to the west.

Everything went like clockwork. The bridges were not heavily guarded. It took only a little time and patience for the saboteurs to place their charges of plastic at the points indicated by Tony, set the pencil fuses and retreat to their homes. They were all back in their warm beds when the bridges were blown at 6.30 a.m. on the morning of May 1st. Tony's bridge was totally destroyed, and although Jean-Paul's had part of its frame intact, it was completely unsafe. There was no way that the Germans would be able to move trains over it for months to come. Although Tony was unable to go back and check the bridges carefully for himself, he was satisfied as to the success of the mission by observing, from a distance, the reaction of the Germans. Patrols were increased and searches made, but the occupying forces had nothing to work on. Tony knew that his group was safe, although the increased security would make subsequent attacks more difficult.

That evening Jean-Paul and Tony sat in the barn with the radio playing softly, awaiting the BBC messages. Jean-Paul smiled at his companion.

"The attack went well."

Tony nodded and lay back in the hay. "Yes, but the others won't be quite so easy. There'll be additional guards at vital points. I'm sure the Germans are as aware of the coming invasion as we are. They will rightly assume that our attacks, and the other ones all over France, are all part of the general build up." He picked up a wisp of hay and began to chew it thoughtfully. "We'll have to space the attacks about a week apart, and make sure we get in and out fast."

"Shhh. Here come the messages."

Tony sat up and leant eagerly towards the radio. He was not expecting the invasion to come yet, but it paid to be alert. He listened carefully, and his concentration was rewarded with the second message.

"Les sanglots longs des violins d'automne."

In a daze Tony leant across and switched off the radio.

"Albert? Was that it?"

Tony nodded slowly, unable to believe that he had just heard the message heralding the invasion. Then his face broke into a broad grin.

"Yes! The invasion will come this month!" He was thoughtful for a moment, then continued. "We have to listen each evening for the next message. That will give us forty-eight hours warning. If we have to be ready sometime this month, we'd better move the next attack forward. We'll hit the bridge on the Nantes - Vannes road in three days time. By then I should have finished finalising my plans for the attack on the docks and will be able to let everyone know what their job will be."

Jean-Paul hid the radio in a small secret compartment in the barn wall. He was grinning broadly.

"I can't believe it's really happening! The invasion! Soon we'll be free at last!"

The two men left the building happily together, unaware of the confusion which raged in S.O.E. Headquarters after hearing the first line of the Chanson d'automne broadcast by the BBC.

141

On 2nd May, Angeline listened in to her radio at 10 p.m. as usual. She had received very few messages from Britain. Her main task was to send information back, but this evening was one of the exceptions. Right on time the steady tap, tap tapping of Morse code filled her headphones. She wrote down the list of letters quickly, sent the received signal and hid her radio, before settling down to decode the message. It did not take long. When she finished she frowned in puzzlement at the words. They meant nothing to her.

'Urgent. Albert. Disregard Chanson d'automne. Not May.'

With a shrug she hid the message safely away. It was bound to mean something to Tony, and that was all that mattered.

Angeline slept well that night. Immediately curfew was over, she set off to deliver the message. She left it in the same post-box as before, knowing that Tony would check the log before the day was over.

That afternoon, Tony walked along the track as usual and was surprised to see a handkerchief caught in the hedge. He had not expected a message from London. His features creased in a worried frown as he made his way down the track to the hollow log. A brief check told him that he was unobserved, and he quickly retrieved the message from the north end of the log. Slipping it into his pocket, he made his way back to the farm. He was eager to read what London had to say, yet to read it in the open would be to court disaster.

Back at the cottage he went into the empty kitchen and took the message from his pocket. He scanned it quickly, and was not sure that he understood it, so he read it again. The meaning was abundantly clear. Someone, somewhere had made a mistake and now, all over France Resistance groups were preparing for an imminent invasion which would not arrive.

Tony screwed up the paper and threw it into the fire. He was angry that his expectations had been built up, his plans changed, risks taken, all for nothing. He watched the paper shrivel and blacken as the fire took hold and consumed it.

"Damned BBC."

"Is anything wrong?" Tony whirled round in surprise, his heart beating wildly, then he smiled sheepishly at Jean-Paul.

"You gave me a fright."

"Sorry, Albert. Is anything wrong?"

Tony sighed. "Yes Jean-Paul, I'm afraid so. It's nothing bad," he hurried on as he saw the Frenchman's worried frown, "it's just that someone in London made a stupid mistake. The message put out by the BBC two days ago should not have come."

"So there will be no invasion?" Jean-Paul looked crestfallen, and Tony smiled comfortingly.

"Oh yes, it will come. It's just not going to happen this month, that's all."

Jean-Paul nodded. "At least it gives us a little more time to disrupt the Germans. That reminds me, do we still go ahead with tomorrow's attack?"

Tony nodded. "Yes, it is well planned and the others are ready to go. It might be dangerous to call it off now." He smiled. "Don't let the false message get you down. The invasion will come."

"I know." Jean-Paul was pensive. "But if they can mess up sending a simple message by radio, what other mistakes will be made, with even more lives at risk? Another stupid mistake like that could be costly. We might never know about it until too late."

Tony's smile did not waver. "You could be right, but I doubt it. A lot of time and effort has gone into organising this. It will go without a hitch. Just wait and see."

The group met at some distance from the Nantes - Vannes road. There were some crestfallen faces when Tony explained that the Allied landings would not be coming for at least another month.

"Don't worry," he concluded, "the landings will come this year. Having at least one more month gives us more time to disrupt the Germans. Tonight's little outing will be to destroy the bridge on the main Nantes - Vannes road, or at least damage it so much that no heavy trucks or tanks will be able to use it. There is also a stretch of road about two miles further north, where it runs close against a steep hillside. If we plant charges there too, we can cause a landslide to block the road as well." He turned to Jean-Paul. "I want you, Georges and Madeleine to take that one, and meet back here in three hours' time. Vincent and I will take the bridge. Set your pencil fuses for a six hour delay. The further we are from here when they go off, the better."

The others shouldered their packs.

"Good luck, Albert. Keep your head down."

Tony smiled. "You too, Jean-Paul. Now get moving."

Vincent and Tony watched the small group of people disappear into the night. Then Tony led the way towards the road bridge.

"How's Angeline?"

Vincent smiled. "She's fine. She works hard and no-one suspects her true identity. She has also improved my life considerably."

Tony raised his eyebrow questioningly and Vincent chuckled.

"Not like that. Having Angeline around is like having a daughter in the house. I feel my life has a purpose again, now that I have a surrogate family. I would do anything to help her in her work."

Tony inclined his head towards a black shadow which loomed ahead of them. "Right. There's the bridge. Let's see how far you're prepared to go."

The two men approached the bridge slowly and silently. The huge brick pillars reared above them, supporting the road where it spanned the wide ravine. The sound of footsteps came from above. Tony listened as they crossed and re-crossed the bridge. A guard. He frowned. That made things more difficult. Motioning Vincent to hide and wait, Tony silently shrugged off his backpack and began to make his careful way up the steep sides of the ravine. It was slow, painful progress as he tried not to attract the guard's attention to himself. At one point his foot slipped. He waited in silence, heart beating rapidly, as a small shower of stones slithered down the ravine. The guard halted his pacing and peered over the parapet for a few moments, but could see nothing moving. With a shrug he turned away from the ravine and recommenced his measured pacing. With a silent sigh of relief Tony continued his ascent. For a moment he had imagined himself back in the SS cells. . He felt as though a black cloud had engulfed his very soul. A fear which he had not felt for months washed over him. He would do anything to make sure that he was never in such a situation again. He continued to climb silently until he was crouched behind the parapet of the bridge where he slipped his knife with its razor sharp blade from its sheath and waited.

The guard's measured tread was approaching, and Tony crouched, ready to pounce. He heard the footsteps draw level with his position and then move past. That was his cue. He straightened and leapt over the wall with one practised movement. His arm was around the guard's throat and he guided the blade of the knife between the ribs and into the heart before the German knew what was happening. Tony felt the body go limp, and the soldier's rifle clattered to the ground. He dragged the dead weight to the end of the bridge and into some nearby bushes. The body rolled over, and he saw the German's face for the first time. He froze in shock. The fresh face hardly showed any stubble; the eyes wide in fear were frozen in death, a boy's features, a boy who should still be at school, not dying for his country. Tony felt tears spring to his eyes. The boy could not have been more than sixteen years old. He had not stood a chance against Tony, with all his sophisticated training. Then Tony's features hardened. He had a job to do. No matter what his age, the German soldier was his enemy. He turned and went back out onto the bridge to retrieve the rifle. Then he slid back down into the ravine to re-join Vincent.

"Is everything all right?"

Tony nodded. "The guard is dead. We go ahead as planned, but use shorter fuses. If they plan to change the guard before the bridge goes up and can't find him, they'll get suspicious. They might find the charges."

Vincent took the first charge from his pack and handed it to Tony.

"Let's get moving, then."

Tony began to place the charges around the base of the supporting piers, setting the timers as he went. It helped him keep his mind from the image of the boy lying dead at the head of the ravine. Soon all the charges were set. The two men made their way back to the rendezvous point, where Jean-Paul and the others were already waiting.

"Did everything go all right?"

Jean-Paul nodded. "No problems at all. When that hillside comes down, it will totally block the road. It will take them weeks to clear and repair it."

"Good."

"What about you, Albert?"

"Just a slight problem. The bridge was guarded, but I took care of him. I shortened the fuses though. We have just under two hours before they go off. We'd better get out of here."

Tony led the way back to the empty barn where they had hidden the car, and they were soon on their way back to Saint Nazaire.

Long before dawn the ground shook with the force of the explosion at the bridge. But by then, the Resistance group were all safely back home and unable to see the evidence of another mission successfully accomplished.

142

May was half over when Tony and Jean-Paul set out to destroy the railway tunnel to the west of the city. It was a cool night for the time of year. They were well wrapped in warm, dark clothing, their faces blackened, packs of explosives on their backs and Sten guns in their hands. As they moved silently along, parallel to the tracks, Tony smiled. With the rail and road bridges down, the destruction of the tunnel would cause havoc in the German transport system and he was proud of the part he was playing in the preparations for D-Day. They were approaching the tunnel when Tony saw a siding branching off to the left. He stopped to stare at the deeper shadow of the trucks which occupied it. His indrawn breath hissed through his teeth. Jean-Paul laid a questioning hand on his shoulder.

"What is it?"

Tony inclined his head towards the train. "Tanks."

Jean-Paul looked more closely. He too could see the huge bulk of the war machines with the long muzzles of their guns held low for ease of transportation. He could not see the full length of the train, but he estimated there must be twenty trucks, each with their heavy load of a single Panzer. The thought of all the destruction they could unleash on any invading force filled him with fear. He turned to the Englishman at his side.

"What do we do about them?"

"Nothing tonight. But I have an idea how to put them out of action. I'll tell you all about it later. Meanwhile let's concentrate on the tunnel."

The two men moved silently on the grass which edged the stone chippings close to the rails. Soon the black maw of the tunnel revealed itself as a deeper patch of darkness in the night, and Tony led them in until total blackness engulfed them. The two men felt their way carefully along the wall, until the curve of the tunnel hid them from the entrance. Tony took out his pencil torch, and shone it into the blackness ahead of them.

"We'll lay charges in four places. There's no way they'll be able to clear up all that mess." He led the way deeper inside. When they were almost a hundred yards from the tunnel entrance he stopped, removed his pack and knelt down beside it on the sharp stones of the tunnel floor. Quickly removing the first package of plastic explosive he began to fix it to the tunnel wall.

"You take the other side."

Jean-Paul crossed the tracks to place a similar charge on the opposite wall. Soon all was ready, timers inserted, and they began to make their way back towards the entrance. After twenty yards, Tony stopped.

"Let's put the next ones here."

The two men worked as an efficient team. Both knew what to do, and could get on with it swiftly and silently. Within three minutes the charges were laid and the saboteurs were about to move on when they felt a strange vibration in the tunnel. A train.

"Find an alcove! Quick!" Tony yelled as he ran along the tunnel, searching its surface for one of the recesses put there to offer safety to rail workers who found themselves in the tunnel with a train approaching. The sound of the approaching train grew louder, and Tony was relieved to see the black opening of a recess in the narrow beam of light from his torch.

"This way, Jean-Paul! Hurry!"

The two men threw themselves into the narrow opening as the sound of the train reached a mighty roar. A blast of hot wind pressed them back against the wall. They closed their eyes and mouths against the stinging smoke and soot which engulfed them. The huge bulk of the train rushed by like a denizen of hell, sparks flying, steam burning. It seemed endless, rolling past the two men, who struggled to keep as much distance as possible between themselves and the terrible monster. At last it passed. Tony cautiously removed his hands from his ears, still ringing after being assaulted by such noise. He wiped some of the soot and smoke from his eyes, and opened them to see Jean-Paul grinning at him, his teeth dazzling white and eyes sparkling in the blackness of his face.

"We didn't need camouflage tonight, the train has done it for us!"

Tony grinned too. "Yes, but it could have done much more." He noticed Jean-Paul's puzzled expression and continued. "If we hadn't been using plastic explosives, the vibrations could have set the charges off."

"You mean...?"

"I mean we would now be buried under half the tunnel."

Jean-Paul felt a shiver run down his spine. "I don't know about you, but I want to be out of here as soon as possible."

"Let's go, then."

The two men retraced their steps along the tunnel. They planted the third pair of charges just inside the bend, and the final set a mere twenty yards from the tunnel entrance. Greatly relieved that no other train had passed through, they made their way out into the fresh night air where they drew in deep breaths which washed the smoke and dust from their lungs.

"Let's go."

Jean-Paul led the way and, ten minutes later, they passed the siding with its trainload of tanks.

"Can we destroy them, Albert?"

"Possibly, but I have a better idea."

As the two made their way home, Tony described the plan to his French companion. Jean-Paul was reluctant at first, but finally he agreed that it would be the best solution to two of their problems. All he was worried about now was how he was going to explain it all to Marie.

143

Jeanne was already in bed when Theresa came into the kitchen. Jean-Paul and Marie were seated at the table talking quietly. Tony stood staring pensively into the fire. Being with a couple like the Boues, who were still obviously very close after many years of marriage, made him lonely for Sarah. He wanted to hold her and kiss her, to share his thoughts and feelings with her. He missed her terribly, and was unhappy that he was not even able to bring the small gold heron she gave him. Just holding that would have helped him to feel closer to her.

"I hear the railway tunnel was blown up last night."

Theresa's words brought him back to the present.

"Was it?"

Theresa threw him an exasperated look. "Yes. And there have also been attacks on bridges in the last few weeks. It wouldn't all have something to do with you, would it, Albert?"

Tony smiled. "What if it did?"

"You said you would find me something to do to help." Theresa's eyes were pleading. "I've tried to be patient and not keep asking, but you still haven't said anything. I wondered if you'd forgotten."

Tony looked at Jean-Paul, who had reached out to take Marie's hand in his. Marie looked as though she did not want to hear what would be said next, yet found it impossible to leave the room. Tony turned back to Theresa and smiled.

"No, I haven't forgotten, and you have been very patient. It was just that nothing suitable seemed to come up. Would you have been able to plant explosives to blow up the bridges or the tunnel?"

"No, but you could teach me like you taught Papa," she answered stubbornly.

Tony nodded. "Yes I could, but I don't think your mother would have liked that."

"But Mamma agreed that I could help."

"If the right job came up." Jean-Paul smiled tenderly at his daughter. "It's only because we love you that we don't want you getting into danger."

"But I want to help!" Theresa was exasperated. "The Allies are bound to come soon and I want to do my part."

"What damage do you think twenty Panzers could do to the Allied landing forces?"

Theresa frowned, puzzled by the apparent change of subject.

"A great deal, I should think. It would be better if they were kept out of any battle."

"I agree." Tony smiled. "We saw about that many tanks entrained in a siding last night. If they had been on the other side of the tunnel, they would have been of little use to the Germans because they would have been trapped. But as it is there's open track ahead of them all the way to the Channel coast. We could blow them up, but that would give the Germans time to bring up replacements. What we really need to do is disable them, so that the enemy would be unaware of it until they tried to move them, and by then it would be too late." He smiled at the teenager. "Would you like to be responsible for disabling them?"

Theresa's eyes opened wide in surprise.

"What? Me?"

Tony nodded, and with a cry of delight she threw herself into his arms.

"Thank you, Albert! You don't know how much this means to me!"

"I think I do!" laughed Tony, giving her a quick hug.

Suddenly Theresa frowned, and turned towards her parents.

"What do you think, Papa? Mamma?"

Jean-Paul looked at Marie then back at his daughter. He spoke for them both.

"We realise that you want to help, and that you're old enough to make your own decisions. There's obviously danger involved and we are worried about you, but Albert thinks you'll be relatively safe. So, if you want to do it, we won't try to stop you."

Theresa nodded solemnly. Tony wondered again at her surprising maturity.

"Thank you, Papa, and you Mamma." She crossed to the table and put her arms around her mother's neck. "I know how difficult it is for you. I promise not to let you down."

Marie had tears in her eyes as she hugged her daughter.

"Just keep yourself safe, dear, that's all I ask."

Theresa turned back to Tony with a look of eager anticipation.

"Right then, Albert. What do you want me to do?"

"Sit down and I'll explain."

Tony and Theresa joined Jean-Paul and Marie around the table. The young girl leant forward to listen to the Englishman as he began his careful explanation.

"When I parachuted in last month, some supplies were dropped as well. Among them were a number of cans of abrasive grease."

"What is that?"

"It looks like heavy motor oil, but in fact it has finely ground carborundum in it. If we replace lubricating oil with this, it will cause the moving parts to seize up. What I want you to do is drain the oil from the axle boxes of the trucks, and replace it with the abrasive grease. The Germans won't know it's been done until they try to move the train. When they do, the axles will seize up and the train will be stuck. Although the tanks won't be damaged, they will be unable to reach any battlefield. As an added bonus, they will block the railway so nothing else can get through."

"That's a devious plan. I like it."

Tony laughed at Theresa's eagerness. "Right. I'll get everything you need from our stores. You can begin your work tomorrow night."

Theresa cycled along the road with the two cans hidden in the basket on her bicycle. Tony had given her one empty can to drain the oil into, so she would leave no trace of her work behind her, and another full of the abrasive grease to replace it. The Englishman told her there was only enough for two or three carriages in the can. She would have to make anything up to ten trips to complete the job. Ideally she should disable all of the carriages, but if that was not possible, she was to make sure that those at either end were sabotaged. If they were unable to move, those in the middle would be stuck too.

As Theresa approached the railway she saw a German guard outside the signal box, and she slowed as he stepped out into the road in front of her. With a wave of his hand, he indicated that she should stop and show him her papers. He took them and perused them carefully.

"Theresa Boues?"

She nodded.

"It is only one hour to curfew, little girl. Where are you going?"

Theresa was annoyed at being called a little girl, but she did not show it. The soldier was probably as old as her father, so it was only natural of him to think of teenagers as 'little girls'. He was smiling at her and looked friendly, but Theresa was not taken in by his demeanour.

"I've lost my puppy and I'm looking for him."

The soldier frowned.

"You think he is over here?"

"Yes." Theresa nodded. "I got him from a lady near here. He might be trying to find his way back to his mother."

The German soldier nodded. "It is possible. You had better hurry if you are to get home before curfew. Do not go down to the railway lines though. We have patrols down there, and you will get into a lot of trouble if you go where you are not allowed." A fleeting smile lit his face. "I would help you look if I could, but I cannot leave my post. Good luck."

He waved at Theresa as she cycled on, trying to control her shaking hands. When the guard had stopped her, she had been afraid he might search her bicycle and find the cans. She had no illusions as to what would have happened if he found out what her real mission was. She felt a deeper appreciation of her mother's fears as she continued on her way. But not once did she think of turning back, even with the knowledge of German patrols on the lines. She had a job to do, and she intended to do it well. As she approached her destination, she thought of Charles and how hard he had worked for the Resistance. He was her hero, her ideal. What she did was as much for him as for France.

As Theresa approached the siding, she looked carefully around. No one was in sight. She quickly hid her bicycle in the bushes, took the cans from the basket and made her way down the steep slope to the railway tracks. She stared in awe as she approached the train in the siding. The tanks looked huge and threatening. It chilled her to the core to think of the death and destruction they could wreak on France's liberators. The huge metal monstrosities gave her a fuller appreciation of the trust Tony had placed in her, and she was determined not to let him down.

Moving swiftly forward, she slipped between the wheels of the first carriage and crouched down beside the axle box. It took her a few moments to free the drainage hole, but the oil was soon flowing freely into her can. The thick black substance poured like treacle in a seemingly endless stream. Finally it began to slow, then stopped as Theresa closed the drainage hole. Unscrewing the cap, she began to pour the abrasive grease. It took half the can to fill the box, then she screwed the cap back on. Her hands were shaking as she quickly made her way to the second truck and set to work. What if a patrol should pass? What if she spilt some of the oil on her clothes, would the German sentry notice? Within fifteen minutes, which seemed like fifteen hours to the young French girl, the job was complete. A nervous Theresa made her way back up the bank, to the bushes where her bicycle was hidden. The road was still deserted. With a relieved sigh, she wheeled out the machine and began cycling back towards her home.

She approached the guard at the signal box with trepidation, her palms sweaty with a fear she dare not show in her face. To her immense relief, he was smiling.

"Did you find your puppy?"

"No, Monsieur."

His smile faded a little. "Oh, I am sorry to hear it. I will bring it over to your home if I find it. You live on the de Thierry estate, do you not?"

Theresa swallowed hard then nodded.

"Yes , monsieur."

"Well, good luck then. Now be on your way, or you will not be back before curfew."

Theresa nodded in relief as she began to pedal away. "Thank you. Goodbye, Monsieur."

"Goodbye, little girl."

As Theresa cycled home, she was glad it had been such an old and friendly guard on duty. She surely would not have got away with her deception so easily if it had been a younger, more enthusiastic soldier. As she cycled, she decided to use a different route to the siding in future. She could not afford the danger of coming into contact with any more guards while sabotaging the train.

144

The days passed swiftly. In the early evenings, Theresa set out with her cans to work on the train. She took the long route now. It avoided all contact with the Germans, so was well worth it. Only once was she surprised by a patrol making its way along the siding where she was working. Heart in her mouth, she slipped into a small cavity between the tracks of the megalithic tank on the truck above her. The space was filled with the deepest of shadows. The two guards passed, talking quietly between themselves. They were unaware of the oil cans hidden in the long grass, and the young girl holding her breath not five yards from them. Theresa was not disturbed again, and it was not long before she had completed her assignment.

She was immensely proud of her accomplishment. So were her parents and Tony, who could see a subtle change in her attitude now she was doing something to help. While Theresa disabled the train, Tony and Jean-Paul, together with the rest of the group, continued their nightly sabotage work. Now the main targets had been destroyed, they were concentrating on the bridges on the minor roads. Any transports forced to make detours would have additional problems when they tried to arrange alternative routes. Although the group were striking frequently, there was no pattern to their movements. The Germans did not know what to do, apart from increase patrols and hope to stumble on the Resistance group by chance. But they could not patrol all the minor roads, nor the railway junctions, where the group frequently blew up the points to disrupt train transports even further. The Germans eventually settled to the usual solution, harassment of the population, but this was not as severe as it was earlier in the war. They were preparing for the Second Front, which they expected to open up soon, and this thankfully gave them less time to practice their brutality on the population of occupied France. Steinhauser also needed his limited supply of trains for military transportation up to the Channel coast, so the numbers of those deported to labour camps dropped rapidly. Things were not easy for the French, but the re-percussions were certainly not as severe as Tony had feared.

Things appeared to be going well for Tony, until the day the German came to the cottage.

It was Jeanne who first saw the man approaching the cottage, wobbling along on a
bicycle. She rushed into the kitchen where, luckily, the whole family were gathering for
dinner.

"A German is coming!"

Tony leapt to his feet, fearful that someone had given him away, putting the whole
Boues family in danger. His mind was crystal clear as he barked out instructions in an
effort to protect the people who were like family to him.

"Marie! Clear my place from the table! The rest of you, act naturally. I'll slip out of a
window at the back, and hide in the woods until it's safe!" He rushed from the kitchen
to a room shielded from the approaching soldier by the bulk of the barn. Clambering
through the opening, he ran close to the wall, crouched low so that he would not be
seen, until he reached the corner. Peering carefully round it he saw the German. He
frowned in confusion. It was a lone man in his early forties, riding a bicycle. His rifle was
slung across his back and he pedalled slowly, balancing a cardboard box on the
handlebars. It did not look as though he were coming to arrest an English spy. But if he
did not know about Tony, what was he doing here? The soldier stopped the bicycle and
got off. Lifting his precarious burden he placed it gently on the ground. He propped his
transport against the pigsty wall and took a good look around the small yard. Then he
picked up the box and walked hesitantly towards the cottage door. Tony felt that he was
relatively safe where he was, and decided not to move. That might draw attention to
himself. Besides, he wanted to hear what the German had to say.

Inside the cottage Marie had cleared away all traces of Tony's presence. She was
smoothing her apron when a hesitant knock came at the door. The two adults looked at
each other in some confusion. It did not sound much like the heavy-handed Germans
they were expecting. Jean-Paul licked his lips nervously, and crossed the kitchen to open
the door. He frowned at the sight of the German who stood nervously outside.

"Yes?"

"You have a teenage daughter called Theresa?" His French was remarkably good.
Jean-Paul had no excuse to pretend that he did not understand. He squared his
shoulders defensively.

"Yes, I do."

"I checked her papers two weeks ago, by the railway."

Jean-Paul paled visibly. At the corner of the house, Tony felt nauseous. Had they
discovered the abrasive grease in the axle-boxes of the train trucks, and linked that with
Theresa's presence in the area? He carefully lifted his trouser leg and removed his knife
from the sheath strapped to his lower leg. Leaning back against the wall he listened
carefully, ready to leap out if necessary, determined to keep his promise to Marie and
Jean-Paul. He would allow no harm to come to their family because of his activities.

"May I see your daughter?"

The German's request was polite, but Jean-Paul knew that he had no option. He
turned back to the interior of the cottage.

"Theresa. Will you come here, please.?"

Theresa appeared at the door with Marie's arm protectively around her shoulder.
Jeanne stood a little back from them, wide-eyed in fear. When Theresa saw the German
with the box in his arms, she recognised him instantly. Her palms were sweaty with fear.

"Bonjour Madame, Mademoiselle." The soldier smiled, and the family did not know
what to think. "I have the right house at last. This is the third place I have visited in

search of your daughter, Madame Boues."

"What do you want with her?" Jean-Paul's tone was abrupt, but the soldier appeared not to notice. He was used to getting such a response from the French.

"She was searching for a puppy when I met her." He turned to Theresa. "Did you find it?"

Theresa shook her head. "No, Monsieur. I did not."

"Then I did right to bring you this." He placed the cardboard box on the ground, and stepped back a pace. "Please open it. It is for you."

Theresa frowned and took a hesitant step forward. Tony, unable to contain his curiosity, peeped cautiously around the corner. The soldier was watching with a smile as Theresa knelt and carefully opened the box. Her face lit up instantly in a smile of wonderment. She reached in and lifted out a small bundle of brown fur. As Jean-Paul watched his eldest child cuddle the little puppy, he was filled with mixed emotions. Who was this soldier? Why should he give a gift to Theresa? There was only one way to find out.

"Why have you done this?

The German turned towards Jean-Paul, and his expression was serious.

"Because, Monsieur Boues, not every German is evil. Some of us agree with you French that the world would be a better place without Herr Hitler. But while we do not like him we are patriotic, just as you are, and when we are called on to fight for our country we do it." He sighed. "I sometimes wish I could run away, or be captured. I would rather spend the rest of the war in a prison camp than fight and kill. But I know that is impossible, and I must do my duty. Doing my duty does not make me a monster, though." He looked sadly at Theresa. "I once had a daughter. She and her mother died in an air raid on Cologne, two years ago. If she had lived she would have been much the same age as your girl." There were tears in his eyes. "I promised to buy her a puppy for her next birthday, but she did not live long enough for me to give it to her. When I saw this puppy yesterday I bought it to give to your daughter, if she had not yet found her own." He turned questioningly towards Jean-Paul. "You will allow her to keep it?"

Jean-Paul had a lump in his throat. He nodded silently, and Theresa rose to her feet beside him, the puppy cradled in her arms.

"Thank you, Monsieur. It was most kind of you to think of me." As she thought about what the German said, she came to a deeper, more mature understanding of the futility of war. That did not mean she would not continue to fight for her country. But it showed her that her hate should be directed more to the tyrannical regime which had started the war, than to the German people themselves. Like the French, there were good and bad in their nation. She would find it hard to hate this particular German soldier, or others like him. She smiled hesitantly. "I will call the puppy Pax. Maybe one day when there is peace between us, you can visit him as a friend, not as an enemy soldier."

The Germans eyes were sad. "I would like to be a friend now, but you are right, I am supposed to be your enemy."

Impulsively Jean-Paul held out his hand. "We may be on different sides in this war, but we will always think kindly of you."

Hesitantly the German took the proffered hand, the first that had been held out to him in peace since his arrival in France.

"Thank you, Monsieur Boues. Now I must get back to Saint Nazaire." He smiled down at Theresa as she held the squirming puppy. "Take good care of him."

Theresa smiled. "I will."

Tony slipped the knife back into its sheath. He watched the German retrieve his bicycle, mount it and set off down the road, much steadier now he did not have to balance the box on his handlebars. Jeanne came out of the cottage to stand with her parents and sister. They silently watched the man cycle away then, unable to contain their excitement, the two children took the puppy into the kitchen. Jean-Paul shook his head wonderingly as he put an arm around his wife's shoulders.

"We all have something to learn from that man."

Marie nodded, her eyes sad as she thought of the Germans lost family.

"Yes. And we don't even know his name."

145

"You know you're mad don't you."

Sarah and Jane were sitting in the pub waiting for Bobby and Al to arrive. Jane sipped her drink and looked at her friend thoughtfully.

Sarah grinned. "Whatever makes you say that?"

"The faraway look in your eyes, that's what. I wouldn't win any prizes for betting that you are thinking of Tony Kemshall."

Sarah nodded. "I was just wondering what he's doing."

"He hasn't written, has he?"

Sarah shook her head sadly. "No, it's been some time since his last letter."

"How long?"

"About six weeks."

Jane shook her head in exasperation. "I told you he'd let you down again. But you wouldn't listen."

"Perhaps he's too busy to write. After all, the Second Front is bound to happen sometime this summer."

"Oh, I've no doubt he's busy, Sarah. But I'm sure he could find the time to drop you a line or even telephone you, if he really wanted to. I don't know why you persist with him, when you have someone like Bobby around. He's kind and reliable, and I'm sure that deep down you really like him."

"Yes, I really do like him, but he isn't Tony." Sarah smiled sadly. "You're just going to have to leave me to sort this out for myself."

"Just be careful that you don't drive Bobby away in the process."

The door opened to admit Bobby and Al, looking handsome and smart in their G.I. uniforms. Bobby waved at Sarah as he crossed to the bar to get the drinks, while Al moved over to his wife. He kissed her on the forehead and smiled fondly.

"Hi. How are you feeling, sweetheart?"

"I'm fine, darling."

"And what about Junior?"

Jane smiled. She smoothed a hand over her abdomen, which was now showing its burden.

"He's fine too."

Al grinned broadly as he sat down.

"I still can't believe I'm going to be a father!"

Sarah smiled, happy for the love this young couple so obviously shared.

"It will be a lucky child, to have parents like you."

"Gee thanks, Sarah."

Bobby joined them at the table with a tray of drinks. He sat down as Al continued. "I hope this war will be over, and we'll be back in America before he's born."

Sarah frowned. "Do you know something we don't?"

Bobby shrugged in response to her question. "Well, yes and no. We're to be confined to barracks after tonight. We're getting ready to move out. The Second Front can't be far away now."

Sarah felt a well of emptiness opening inside her, as she thought of these two men facing the landing beaches. Her job had shown her what that could do to a man, particularly after the disaster at Dieppe. She did not want to think of either of them lying wounded or dead upon the sand. Impulsively she covered Bobby's hand with her own.

"You will be careful, won't you?"

"Of course I will."

Sarah looked across at Jane. Her face had paled. Her eyes were filled with fear as she contemplated pregnancy and the birth of her child without Al beside her. Maybe she would even be left to bring up the child alone. The fears and anxieties she had buried deep over the last few months rose to the surface, and she turned to Al with tears in her eyes.

"I wish you didn't have to go."

"But that's my whole reason for being here, sweetheart. If it hadn't been for this war, I would never have met you."

Sarah's heart filled with compassion for her friend, but there would be plenty of time to comfort her later. Turning to Bobby, she inclined her head towards the door. He nodded.

"I think we'll just take a walk." Bobby rose to his feet. "See you back at camp, Al."

Bobby leant down and hugged Jane gently.

"Take care of yourself and the baby. Make sure you invite me to the christening."

Jane smiled at him through her tears. "Thanks, Bobby. Take care of yourself too."

He nodded. "I will. And don't worry about Al, I'll make sure he comes back home." He turned back to Sarah. "Come on then, we've got a lot to talk about."

Sarah walked with the G.I. out into the cool night air. She shivered, then felt his arm slide comfortingly around her shoulders as he led her through the gateway into the hay field they must cross on their way back to Heronfield.

"Cold?"

She shook her head. "No, just scared." She turned her worried gaze to his. "You know how much I care for you. I hate to think of the danger you'll be facing."

"I'll be fine, Sarah. Don't worry."

"That's what my dad said to my mum, and he never came back."

Bobby reached out and touched her cheek tenderly. "I'm glad you care enough to worry about me." His eyes were serious. "Why don't we get married, or at least engaged, before I go?"

Sarah shook her head sadly. "I'm sorry, Bobby. I can't."

The young American smiled wistfully, unable to hide the hurt in his eyes.

"Somehow I knew you'd that. Still, I had to try." He brushed a stray wisp of hair from her forehead. "Say you'll wait for me, Sarah. Don't marry anyone else until I get back."

Though he did not say the name, Sarah knew that he was thinking about Tony. She wished there was some way she could make them both happy, or at least, she wished she could choose between them. How much easier life would have been, if Joe had not died. She would be happily married now, maybe with a child or two of her own, not facing a future where one of the men she cared for walked boldly into a battle from which he might never return, while the other seemed intent on ignoring her and shutting her out of his life. She smiled sadly.

"Just make sure you come back, Bobby. There'll be time enough after the war to think about the future."

Bobby's eyes were filled with longing. He enfolded Sarah in his arms. "I love you so much, Sarah, I just don't want to lose you."

He pressed his lips hungrily against hers and Sarah responded, sliding her arms up and around his neck as he kissed her, knowing that it might be the last kiss they ever shared. Bobby gently lowered her to the ground. He kissed her with a passion he had fought to control for months, but which now threatened to overwhelm him.

Bobby's hands began to roam hungrily over her body. Sarah tensed and made to pull away.

"What's wrong?"

"I can't do it, Bobby."

"But Sarah, I might never come back. Surely you could love me just this once. Please I need the memory of you to take with me."

Sarah shook her head sadly. "I can't. I have to wait." She thought of Joe, how she had waited for him until it was too late. Would the same happen with Bobby?

"I suppose you're thinking of Tony." Bobby voice held a bitterness which Sarah had never heard before. She reached out to touch his face.

"No. I was thinking of Joe. I never made love with him. We were going to wait until we were married. It didn't feel right then, no matter how much I wanted it, and it doesn't feel right now." She kissed Bobby tenderly. "Making love won't change our feelings one way or another. We have to wait."

Bobby began to stroke her breast through the thin cotton blouse. "Are you sure, Sarah?" His voice was mesmerising. "Just this once to say goodbye?"

'To say goodbye'. She had made love to Tony to say goodbye, the only time she had ever given herself to a man, and she knew that what she felt for Bobby now could never come close to that. Even thinking of making love with Bobby felt as though she were betraying Tony. She pulled away.

"No, Bobby."

Bobby stood up. He looked down at her, anger and longing clouding his eyes.

"It's not because of Joe, is it? It's Tony. He treats you so badly, yet you still care more for him than you do for me. In that case, Sarah, I'll go now. You have to make a decision soon, and stop playing with my feelings as if they don't count!"

Sarah struggled to her feet as he began to walk away.

"I'm so sorry Bobby, I never intended to do that. I would never want to hurt you! You must believe me!"

Bobby stopped walking, then turned slowly, his sorrowing gaze meeting her eyes, a world of longing in his features. "I know, Sarah. I'm sorry. I should never have lost my temper. Please forgive me."

"There's nothing to forgive." Sarah stepped closer, then reached up and kissed him tenderly. "You are the kindest, gentlest man I have ever met. I will pray for you every day while you're away. Make sure you come back, Bobby. Please."

He reached out and enfolded her in his arms.

"I will. You'll always draw me back here, Sarah." As he stroked her hair gently and kissed her with a tenderness born of love, Sarah lost herself in the moment. She pushed all thoughts of Tony, of tomorrow, from her mind. Nothing mattered but the here and now.

146

Bobby and Al were part of what was to become known as Force O, destined for Omaha beach. They were held in readiness for embarkation with the rest of the soldiers at Poole, Portland and Weymouth. The whole of the south coast of England was a heaving mass of men and machines, as the Allies made their final preparations for the assault on France. The troops were confined to their camps, and for security reasons were told little of what lay ahead of them; it would not be until they were well on their way that Bobby and Al would know their destination, and the full scale of the invasion force of which they were such a small part.

147

It was early evening on June 1st 1944. A cool breeze was beginning to blow after an unseasonably hot day, but it did not reach the interior of the barn which was still stifling hot. Tony and Jean-Paul sat comfortably on the hay, with the radio beside them broadcasting the news from England. Tony listened to the quiet voice of the BBC. He looked over the edge of the loft, and out through the open barn doors to where Theresa was playing with Pax in a pool of sunshine. As the puppy gambolled, it uttered an excited high-pitched bark. The sound of Theresa's laughter could be heard; it made Tony smile. The war had made her grow up far too quickly. She had experienced many things that a child should not have to go through, but inside there was still a little girl who surfaced from time to time, and Tony was glad to see it.

The war news on the radio was coming to an end. Tony turned his full attention to the voice as the S.O.E. messages relayed by the BBC began. He was tense with nervous excitement. Would the message come? Were the Allied forces ready to cross the Channel at last, and push back the Germans? He glanced across at Jean-Paul, whose expression mirrored his own. He nodded understanding as the messages came over the airwaves.

"The blue sky brings rain. The blue sky brings rain...Snow in September. Snow in September... Les sanglots longs des violins d'automne. Les sanglots longs des violins d'automne."

Tony reached over and switched off the radio. His hands were trembling. He gazed stony- faced at Jean-Paul, then his face broke into an infectious grin.

"That's it, Jean-Paul! The invasion will be this month!" His voice was filled with excitement. He stood up, needing to move to express his joy.

"As long as it's not another mistake."

Tony laughed out loud. "Don't worry, Jean-Paul, even the British couldn't make that mistake twice! The Allies are coming!"

Suddenly Jean-Paul was laughing too. The two men embraced, sharing their joy at the knowledge that freedom for the French could not now be far away. Jean-Paul began to pack the radio away, his face wreathed in smiles as Tony spoke thoughtfully.

"We have a lot to do to make sure we are ready. The landings may not take place for four weeks, but they could be tomorrow. We should be ready for the earliest possible date. I want the telephones out of action as soon as possible. You and I will hit the exchange tonight." The Frenchman nodded. "We must meet at the cave tomorrow evening. I'll explain the plans for the attack on the docks once the next code is received. That means we must monitor the radio each evening." His face lost its serious look, and he grinned again. "At last, Jean-Paul. It seems so long since Dunkirk. At times I thought this moment would never come, but the Allies will be here soon. Let's go and make sure that everything is ready for them!"

The radio was hidden away, and the two men descended the ladder from the loft and began their preparations.

Tony went to one of the small caches of arms, hidden in the woods close to the cottage and removed the explosives and detonators he needed for the attack. He was glad he did not need to go to the cave every time he needed arms. The less activity in the area, the less chance of anyone noticing that something unusual was happening there; besides, it was a much shorter walk. He now lay concealed in the ruins of a bomb-damaged building opposite the telephone exchange, which had been under German control since the débacle at Dunkirk. At his side, Jean-Paul checked that his Sten gun was fully loaded and in working order, before turning his serious gaze towards Tony.

"I'm ready."

"Good. You know what to do?" Jean-Paul nodded. "Then let's go." Tony carefully studied the road before making a move. Though it was dark, he could tell that nothing and nobody was moving. The guard on his rounds was now checking the rear of the building, which gave them time to gain entrance before he returned. Rising to his feet, the British agent ran lightly across the road, with Jean-Paul close on his heels. Within seconds they were in the darkened doorway where Tony carefully pushed the door open. There was nobody in sight, and they slipped silently inside. It was late at night. The reception area was unattended, although Tony could hear the murmur of voices coming from a room at the end of the hall. Motioning silently for Jean-Paul to follow him, he cautiously approached the closed door. There was a lull in the talking. He pushed the door open, entering the room with his Sten gun held unwaveringly in the direction of the voices. Two men in uniform were sitting at an exchange criss-crossed with wires, which carried messages to all parts of France and beyond. The two men looked up in surprise at the intrusion and began to rise to their feet.

"Don't move!"

They looked at the muzzles of the two machine guns aimed directly at them, and froze. "Take off your headsets!"

The Germans immediately complied, never taking their eyes from the guns as they placed the headphones on the table.

"Now move over to the wall. Hands on your head." The two soldiers did as they were told. Tony's eyes flicked momentarily towards Jean-Paul. "Make sure you keep them covered."

The Frenchman trained his gun on the two Germans. From the corner of his eye, he saw Tony put down his gun and begin to take the plastic explosives from his pack. Each console soon had its own lump of plastic moulded to it. Tony took out the pencil fuses, setting them to red, thirty minutes. Wishing there were shorter fuses available, he pushed them carefully into the putty-like mass of the explosive. Within minutes, all was ready. He turned back to Jean-Paul and the Germans.

"We'll have to tie them up, and keep them quiet for half an hour."

Jean-Paul nodded and was just about to move over to them when the door behind him opened. As Tony swung round, there was a sharp intake of breath from the young man who had entered with a tray bearing steaming mugs of coffee. He dropped the tray, turned and ran back into the hall.

"Resistance! Resistance!"

Tony followed closely behind him, instinctively pulling the trigger of the Sten gun. It burst into life, spitting out a lethal hail of bullets which tore into the back of the fleeing soldier, flinging him against the reception desk in a shower of blood and gore. As Tony turned back towards the room, he saw the two Germans lowering their hands from their heads and leaping forward. Jean-Paul's gun roared into life, and the two soldiers were thrown back against the wall. As they slid down it, leaving a red trail of blood behind them, the two Resistance fighters quickly reloaded their Sten guns.

"Damn!" Tony pushed the ammunition clip into place as he spoke. "This place will soon be crawling with soldiers. They'll have time to remove the charges before they go off." He was thinking swiftly. "Get down the hall and take cover behind the reception desk. Shoot anyone who tries to get in. I'll join you in a minute."

Jean-Paul ran to do Tony's bidding. The young Englishman delved into his pack and removed four hand grenades. Placing two beneath each console, he put his pack on his back, then pulled the pins. Grabbing his gun, he ran from the room, closing the door behind him, and joined Jean-Paul behind the desk. The door to the street burst open. The guard who had been checking the rear of the building entered with his rifle held threateningly in front of him. He saw the young soldier lying dead in a pool of blood beside the reception desk. He had just become aware of the two men crouched behind it, when the grenades exploded. The door at the end of the hall was blown open by the force of the blast, emitting clouds of dust and smoke. Instinctively the soldier looked in that direction. By the time he had turned back to the threat behind the desk, it was too late. Tony was on his feet, firing the Sten gun as he raced towards the door.

"Come on, Jean-Paul! Run!"

The two men were out on the street before the soldier hit the ground. Shots were fired from their right. Tony turned to fire on the three approaching soldiers, and Jean-Paul sprinted for the bombed out building which had concealed them earlier. Tony saw one of the soldiers fall before Jean-Paul began his covering fire from behind a pile of bricks. He turned and ran, leaping what was left of a wall to fall beside his French companion. Swiftly reloading his weapon, he raised his head cautiously to look over the wall. Two of the soldiers lay unmoving, while the third was trying to crawl to the shelter of a nearby shop doorway. Jean-Paul lay with his back against the wall, fitting a new ammunition clip into his gun. Tony crouched down beside him.

"Let's get the hell out of here!"

The two men raced through the debris of the house and out into the street beyond. Behind them, they heard the roar of approaching vehicles and the occasional shout in German. But they had a head start, and Tony knew they could make it. Grinning broadly, the two men disappeared into the darkness.

Theresa made her way down the street with a shopping bag over her arm and Pax bounding along beside her on his lead. Jean-Paul had dropped her on the outskirts of the city, promising he would pick her up again later in the day. He and Tony had not been followed the night before. They felt relatively safe, but he did not want to go back into the city and run the chance of being recognised by the soldier they had left wounded in the road. Theresa approached Vincent's bakery and joined the queue waiting for their daily bread rations. The line of people moved slowly. Theresa occupied herself with playing with her puppy. One or two people watched with smiles on their faces, but the majority seemed not to notice, as though the trials of the years of occupation had robbed them of their humour as well as their freedom. Gradually the queue moved on and Theresa found herself inside the shop at last. Moments later it was her turn to be served. Vincent smiled at the young girl and her dog.

"Yes? What can I get you?"

Theresa smiled.

"A loaf please." She looked behind her as she spoke. There were four other people waiting. Turning back to Vincent she took the proffered bread. "Thank you, Monsieur. Do you have a gateau?"

Vincent shook his head.

"Oh. I was hoping for one for a celebration tonight. It is Mamma's birthday. Do you not have anything at all, Monsieur Vincent?"

Vincent frowned at the use of his name. He did not recognise the child, so how did she know who he was? She smiled innocently at him, but he detected a strange intensity in her eyes.

"Wait a moment. I'll see what I can do. Angeline!" Vincent turned to call through the open doorway, and moments later a homely form appeared.

"Yes, Vincent?"

"Can you finish serving here? I have to see what I can do to help this child."

"Yes, of course."

Angeline watched Vincent lead the girl into the back room, then turned to serve the next customer. Vincent turned to Theresa and frowned.

"Who are you, and how do you know my name?"

"I'm Theresa Boues. Be at the cave at 9 p.m. tonight. It's urgent."

Vincent's eyes widened. "Jean-Paul's daughter? Aren't you a little young to run messages like this?"

"Papa trusts me. Don't you?"

Vincent grinned. "Of course I do. I'll be there." He turned to the table and picked up a small cake which he had baked for himself and Angeline. "Take this with you, just in case someone out there is curious." He put the cake into her basket, then led the way out into the shop. He smiled broadly.

"I hope your Mamma enjoys her birthday cake."

Theresa smiled and waved happily. "Thank you, Monsieur Vincent. I'm sure she will."

She turned and left the bakery, Pax pulling on his lead at her side, and made her way towards the far side of Saint Nazaire, where she was to deliver a similar message to Georges and Madeleine.

Tony smiled at the assembled members of his group, who were waiting expectantly to find out why he had called them together. He began without preamble.

"There was a message on the radio last night. The Allies will begin a Second Front, somewhere on the northern coast of France, sometime this month."

His words were met with looks of incredulity, then smiles of joy. Georges leaned over and kissed Madeleine happily, while Vincent leaned over and shook Tony by the hand.

"At last! We thought it would never come!"

"What can we do to help?"

Tony turned to Georges. "We'll get a warning to say that the invasion will take place within the next forty-eight hours; that's when we attack the docks. The idea is to worry the Germans into leaving as many men as possible to defend the port, so they won't send reinforcements north until the beachheads are well established."

"Do we do it like the last time?"

"Well, Madeleine, yes and no. We will try to get in and plant some explosives. But instead of getting straight out of there, we'll wait for the Germans to come and try to sort out the mess. Then we hit them. The idea is to make them think we're a larger group than we actually are, or maybe even give them the impression that we are an Allied commando force. It's risky, but we have to keep them busy."

"How do we know when the invasion is coming?"

"Well Georges, the B.B.C. will broadcast a message in the evening to say that the landings will come in the next forty-eight hours. The message is 'Blessant mon coeur d'une languer monotone'." He looked at Georges thoughtfully. "Do you have access to a radio?"

George and Madeleine shook their heads.

"I know Vincent does. Vincent," he turned to the oldest member of the group, "you must listen to the evening broadcasts. When you hear the code, you must let Georges and Madeleine know immediately. The attack will happen that night."

Vincent nodded. "No problem, Albert. I won't let you down."

"Right." Tony took a sheet of paper from his pocket and spread it on the stony floor of the cave. "Here are the details of the attack. Pay close attention. Our lives depend on us getting this right."

The group leant forward and listened intently as Tony began to draw on the piece of paper and describe the contribution they would make to the liberation of France.

148

It was early evening, 5th June 1944. Tony and Jean-Paul listened to the radio, trying to keep their excitement under control. Each evening it was the same as they anticipated the message they were awaiting so eagerly and then were disappointed when it did not come. As usual, the BBC news from all corners of the world came first. Then the messages began.

"Blessant mon coeur d'une langueur monotone. Blessant mon coeur d'une langueur monotone."

Jean-Paul reached over in silence, and switched the radio off. His heart was thumping wildly, but his face showed no emotion as he looked across at Tony.

"This is it, then."

Tony nodded. He was feeling nervous and excited at the same time. His mind raced as he reviewed the plans for the attack on the docks. He hoped he had thought of everything and nothing would go wrong, but it was too late to worry about that now. He watched Jean-Paul put the radio away.

"Right. Let's get our equipment ready. We have four hours to reach the rendezvous point."

As Tony and Jean-Paul made their way out of the barn, Angeline was running excitedly down the stairs and into the kitchen. Vincent looked up as she burst into the room.

"Did you get the message?"

She nodded. "Yes. The invasion will come in the next forty-eight hours."

Vincent was beaming broadly as he rose to his feet. "Right. I'll get across to Georges to let him and Madeleine know. Then I'll come back here and get my things ready." He looked across at her. "Four hours. That gives me plenty of time."

He quickly left the room, picking up his coat to keep out the gentle rain which had begun to fall. It was overcast, which promised to be helpful to the saboteurs, and he was glad of that. He hurried through the streets to deliver his message, and was back home within the hour. He retrieved the plastic explosive and pencil fuses, incendiaries, Sten gun and ammunition from the false-bottomed flour barrel where they had been hidden. At the same time, Georges and Madeleine were removing their cache from beneath the kitchen floorboards. Everything was going to plan.

It was dark. A fine rain was still falling, but Tony did not mind. German sentries tended to be less observant in such conditions, seeking to keep warm and dry rather than patrol their routes. He looked at the group, gathered round him in the bombed out building.

"You all know what to do?"

The others nodded, their faces stony as each contemplated the danger they would be facing in the next few hours, but none of them considered not going ahead with the attack. The Allies were coming to fight for the liberation of France and, as patriotic French citizens, they wanted to strike their own blow for freedom. Tony looked at them, and felt a deep sense of pride. This was his group, these were his people, each willing to fight and to die for what they believed in. He wondered if all of them would survive the night, or if some of them would pay the ultimate price. He wanted to embrace them all, but instead he smiled encouragingly.

"I know that you will all do well tonight. Get in, set your charges for midnight, then get out again to set up your ambushes." He took one last long look at each one of them. "Be careful. I intend to share my victory dinner with all of you."

The others nodded in understanding. No one wanted to move. It was a moment of shared comradeship they would all remember for the rest of their lives. At last, Tony made the first move.

"Come on then, let's go."

The five people disappeared into the gentle rain.

Jean-Paul and Vincent slipped through the fence around to the docks, and began to work methodically. From time to time they saw Germans hurrying through the rain, but they had plenty of time to conceal themselves in the shadows of the darkened dockside, continuing to work when the danger had passed. They placed plastic explosives in a number of warehouses, and small incendiary devices amongst the pyramidal piles of fuel tanks. It took them little over an hour to complete the task. Then they slipped out of the docks and made their way to an empty building overlooking the approach road. This was their assigned position for the ambush on the relief forces, which would come once the explosions began. Making their way up to the second floor, Jean-Paul and Vincent positioned themselves by an open window. They carefully laid out the four gammon grenades Tony had given them, then checked their guns and settled down to wait.

Georges and Madeleine entered the docks at the opposite end to their two compatriots, and began their work in the transport pool. It took very little time to fix the small clam mines to cylinder blocks and axles, ensuring that the majority of vehicles would be put out of action. Then the young couple turned their attention to the nearby warehouses. Stocks of food and ammunition were piled in boxes in the huge darkened warehouses and they had soon set as many charges as they needed. It was while they were working their way back towards the fence that disaster struck.

George was crossing an open space when a cry came from the shadow to his left.

"Halt!"

The Frenchman stopped and turned slowly to see a German, rifle levelled at him, stepping out of the shadows.

"Put down your gun!"

Georges complied, conscious of a deeper shadow behind the soldier, and praying that Madeleine would stay out of sight. They had both seen what the SS had done to Tony, and he was determined to let nothing like that happen to his wife. If Madeleine was in danger, he would risk everything to save her. He stayed tense, ready to dive for his gun if necessary but hoping he would not have to use it and bring even more Germans running, alert to the fact that there were intruders in the docks. That would put the lives of the rest of the team in danger.

Suddenly the soldier half-turned, as though he heard a noise behind him. Georges reached down to pick up his gun. He ran towards the soldier, who had dropped his rifle and was clutching at his neck with both hands. As Georges drew to a halt, he saw the man slide to the ground, eyes wide with terror and blood pouring through fingers clutching at his severed jugular vein. His mouth was open as though screaming, but the only sound was an eerie bubbling noise. Slowly the light in his eyes dimmed. He fell forwards to lie still at Madeleine's feet. Georges looked at his wife. The hand holding the knife was shaking violently.

"Are you all right?"

Madeleine nodded but said nothing. Georges took her by the arm and led her to a pile of boxes.

"Sit behind these while I hide the body." Madeleine watched as Georges first dragged the soldier against the wall, then fetched his gun and placed it beside him. Finally he moved some boxes into a position where they would hide the body from a casual observer. Satisfied that it was well concealed, he went back to Madeleine and knelt beside her.

"You should have stayed hidden and got away."

Madeleine shook her head and smiled weakly. "I couldn't let him take you."

Georges smiled and embraced her. "I'm so lucky to have you. Now, let's get out of here."

The young couple made their swift but careful way out of the dockyard and, into the house which was their assigned post for the ambush. They settled down to wait.

Tony lay once again in the bombed out building which overlooked the approach road to the docks. His mission of sabotage had gone without a hitch, his charges placed in fuel dumps and on the dock's petrol pump before he retreated out of the area, silent and unseen. Now he carefully checked the PIAT by his side: it was a long tube weighing a little over thirty-four pounds, which fired rockets weighing two-and-a-half pounds, with a hollow charge in the head. He checked the small pile of rockets first then the tube, slightly over three feet long, which he would use to launch them. The Projector, Infantry, Anti-Tank, or PIAT, was effective up to about fifty yards. The hollow charge, though small, had great penetrating power. A light tank hit by a PIAT was not likely to move again.

Tony checked his watch. Five minutes to midnight. He had barely settled himself prone on the ground, with the launch tube loaded and ready, when the first charges went off. From the position of the writhing column of black smoke, Tony judged them to have been planted by Jean-Paul or Vincent. They were a few minutes early, but not enough to affect his plans. Suddenly more and more explosions were heard. They sent clouds of smoke mushrooming into the air, causing fires which the light rain had no chance of dampening. Tony was looking in the direction of the petrol pump when his charges went off in a burning flash of light which spewed burning fuel in all directions. He closed his eyes, but continued to see the red after-image of the fire.

There was shouting and the sound of people running. Tony opened his eyes to see the dark silhouettes of German soldiers attempting to bring order to the chaos in the docks. The fire engine, which Tony had been unable to sabotage, was working on the fiercest fire. In the distance he could hear the sound of others approaching. The first relief fire engine roared round the corner, closely followed by an armoured personnel carrier. Tony levelled the PIAT. He fired the first rocket, which struck the fire engine, bringing it to a shuddering standstill. The driver of the following vehicle swerved wildly to avoid it, while Tony swiftly re-loaded the weapon and brought it to bear once more. As he fired and watched the armoured personnel carrier blown apart, his pulse was racing and the adrenalin flowed. He re-loaded, aware of the chatter of a machine gun over to his left, where Georges and Madeleine were shooting the few soldiers who emerged from the stricken vehicles. A lorry roared in from the opposite direction. Tony turned in time to see the dark shape of a gammon grenade arcing through a night lit by fires, to fall in amongst the soldiers in the transport. It erupted in a geyser of flames, human flesh and bones.

Jean-Paul and Vincent tossed three more gammon grenades at the vehicles approaching the docks, causing chaos in the streets below. Over to their left, they heard the last two of Tony's rockets being fired. They saw two light tanks halted in their tracks. Jean-Paul grinned at Vincent. He picked up his Sten gun and turned back to the window.

"This is a night we will never forget!" He depressed the trigger and flame burst from the muzzle of the gun. The bullets caused mayhem amidst the wounded and dying below them. Vincent too began to fire. Between them they laid down a devastating fusillade of bullets, until their ammunition was almost gone. Each slipped a full clip into their pocket, and fitted the last ones to their guns.

"Right. Let's get out of here."

Vincent led the way out of the room and down the stairs, Jean-Paul close to his heels. Within moments they were outside, heading off into the darkness. A single shot came from their rear and Jean-Paul cried out in pain. Vincent turned to see his companion fall, wounded by a German soldier who approached rapidly. As the soldier raised his gun to shoot the wounded Frenchman, Vincent raised his and pulled the trigger. Nothing happened. Cursing the weapon, he ran back in the direction of Jean-Paul, surprised to see that the German had lowered his gun and was kneeling beside the saboteur.

"Boues?"

Jean-Paul looked up through pain filled eyes. He recognised the German soldier who had given Pax to Theresa. He nodded as he saw the indecision in the man's eyes.

"Yes, I'm Boues. Do what you must."

The soldier shook his head and reached a decision. "You are only doing what I what do if I were in your place. We both know this war is over in all but name. Each new death is a senseless waste of life. Though I have lost a daughter, it would be wrong of me to deprive your children of a father in the name of Hitler. Good luck, Boues." The soldier stood up. With a final look at the injured Frenchman, he disappeared into the night.

Vincent drew up beside Jean-Paul, a frown furrowing his brow.

"Who was that? Why didn't he kill you?" His voice was breathless.

"I'll explain later." Jean-Paul looked down at his injured leg. Blood poured from the wound and he knew that the leg would not support his weight. "Just help me get out of here."

Vincent bent down to help his companion to his feet.

On the far side of Tony, Georges and Madeleine fired into the German soldiers who were arriving at the scene. They were easy targets silhouetted against the fires raging in the docks. A few Germans fired back. Bullets thudded into the brickwork. Soon some organisation came out of the chaos and a number of soldiers ran in the direction of the

French couple. Madeleine turned to her husband.

"I think we'd better get out of here."

Georges nodded and led the way from the scene of conflagration. The rain was falling harder now, and the night was dark. Within minutes the pursuing Germans had lost sight of them and reluctantly turned back towards the area of the city which lit the night like a beacon.

Tony had fired off the last of his rockets. He was now throwing grenades down onto the soldiers, who were shouting orders above the cries of the wounded and dying. He felt hot, despite the cold rain which drenched him; exhilarated by the success of the mission, he could have stayed there forever. But he was almost out of grenades, and the Germans were beginning to close in. Leaving the rocket launcher, he turned and ran, crouched low to the ground. He had not gone far when he saw Vincent helping Jean-Paul. He rushed over to their aid.

"Are you all right?"

"I have felt better." Jean-Paul forced a grin.

Tony turned to Vincent. "Get him clear of here, and try not to leave too obvious a trail of blood. I'll cover you."

Jean-Paul had seen the Germans closing in. "What about you?"

"Don't worry about me. Just get out of here!" Tony pulled the pin from a grenade and threw it at the approaching Germans, then took cover behind a heap of rubble. Behind him, Vincent supported Jean-Paul and helped him to hobble away. They heard, and felt, the grenade explode, but they did not stop. As they moved further away from where Tony held the Germans at bay, they heard one, two more grenades, closely followed by the distinctive chatter of a Sten gun. Jean-Paul took a final look over his shoulder. Tony was almost totally surrounded. As he limped away, supported by Vincent, he had a sinking feeling that he would never see Tony again. Tears coursed down his cheeks, and they were not tears of pain.

Tony threw his last grenade at the approaching soldiers. He felt the dust and débris of its explosion rain down on him. Ears still ringing, he lifted his Sten gun. He began to sweep it back and forth, watching the hail of bullets tearing into the Germans. Many of them fell beneath the attack, but more kept coming. A cold knot of fear filled his stomach, as he loaded the last magazine into his gun. There was no way out now. He thought fleetingly of Sarah, of her gently smile, her warm loving eyes, her tender embrace. Then he concentrated on the situation in hand. The Germans were closer now, and he fired again. Seeing the fires raging in the distance, he knew that his night's work was successful. When the invasion came, the Germans would not dare to strip the garrison of Saint Nazaire. He fired again and again, vowing that he would not die until he had taken more of the enemy with him.

149

Bobby and Al waited in their holding area as the terrible storm raged, wondering if it would affect the date of the invasion. The rain lashed down in sheets from the black sky, and the wind blew to almost hurricane force. It seemed to be never ending as the emotionally charged soldiers waited in their confined space. The storm raged for three days, and only began to abate late on 5th June. The assembled masses would have been relieved, if they had known that those in charge of the invasion forces had decided that now everything and everyone was in position and ready to go, the D-Day landings could not be halted. If they waited four more weeks for the next favourable moon and tides, it would cause almost insurmountable problems with the masses of men and equipment concentrated on the south coast of England. It was logistics which finally convinced them to go, whatever the weather. The D-Day force consisted of one thousand two hundred ships against fifteen German destroyers, ten thousand aircraft against Germany's five hundred, four thousand one hundred and twenty-six landing craft and eight hundred and sixty-four transport ships. There were tanks with flails for clearing mine fields, amphibious tanks, tanks to destroy concrete bunkers, tanks that laid their own carpets and tanks for bridging dikes. To back up all of these machines, there were almost two hundred thousand men. It was a magnificent exercise in logistics, but to hold everything in the same place for almost another month would be impossible. Eisenhower, showing rare wit for him, said that 'Only the great number of barrage balloons floating constantly in British skies kept the islands from sinking under the waves'. As the force of the storm finally began to abate on 5th June, the go-ahead for D-Day was given and the troops began to embark in the still-falling rain.

Bobby and Al boarded their transport with two days of rations in their packs as there would be little chance of re-supplying the forward troops in the first forty-eight hours after landing. The 1st Infantry Division and two Ranger Battalions made up Force O, under the command of Major-General Clarence R. Huebner. He sent his officers to explain the plans of the imminent invasion to their troops. The American soldiers who had been stationed near Heronfield listened intently to their instructions.

"There will be five beaches," the captain explained. "The British will take Sword, Juno and Gold in the east. The US will come ashore on Omaha and Utah beaches in the west. We are destined for Omaha. The beach has been further divided into four - Fox, Easy, Dog and Charlie. 2nd Ranger Battalion, with the 5th as reserve, will come ashore in the centre of Dog. 116th RCT will come ashore on Dog and Easy, while 16th RCT with 18th as reserve will come ashore on Easy and Fox. Charlie will be hit by the forces from Utah."

He perused the thousands of men who listened to his words in silence. Most of them would be seeing action for the first time when they hit the beaches of Normandy. He wondered how they would fare. Their faces showed determination but little fear, and he was encouraged.

"You each have two days' rations. Barges with four thousand tons of ammunition will be beached with the invasion forces, as an immediately available reserve. Once all the troops are landed, a huge flotilla of ships will re-supply you. Everything is ready. Nothing can go wrong, so hit the beaches fast and hard. We will be in Berlin for Christmas."

A rousing cheer greeted his words, and the officer smiled. "Right. For now relax and get some rest if you can. We hit the beaches at dawn."

Bobby made his way to the side of the ship, and looked off into the dark night. The huge bulk of the ships rose up ahead of and behind him and he hoped the air cover was sufficient. If the Luftwaffe got in amongst this lot, it would be a disaster. Bobby need not have worried. The skies were totally under Allied control. RAF Coastal Command had one thousand and seventy aircraft in forty-nine squadrons, patrolling around Iceland and into the Eastern Atlantic as far as the Western English Channel, where they concentrated their efforts. Air Defence of Great Britain was covering all shipping and convoy routes to a range of forty miles from the British coast. The Allied Expeditionary Air Force, with 69 and 171 fighter squadrons, was to give protection to the invasion forces; five squadrons of American planes were permanently over the swept channels, five further American squadrons would be used as high cover for the beaches while five

British squadrons would provide low cover for the ground troops.

As the transport ship moved further on its way, Bobby was unaware of the number of ships in the waters surrounding him, and the perfect timing and control it would take to get them all safely into the right place at the right time. The assembled invasion fleet moved down four swept lanes, from the south coast to Main Assembly Area 2, about eight miles south-east of St. Catherine's Point. All the ships en route to France were to pass through this area, known euphemistically as Piccadilly Circus, and pick up its route to France. From Piccadilly Circus they would follow two hundred and forty-five minesweepers down five marked channels which were assumed to be free of mines, one channel leading to each of the beaches. South of latitude 50 North the minesweepers began to clear and mark two lanes for each assault force, one for fast traffic and one for slow ships, leading to transport areas where the assault craft were to be lowered, and the various amphibious vessels arranged into attack formation. The British transport areas were seven miles off-shore while the Americans had to be eleven miles out, because of the danger of converging fire from the two adjacent coasts of their beaches. It would take the Americans three hours to make touchdown from the transport area. They needed to begin assembling in the area four hours before touchdown. Between the time of assembly and assault, the minesweepers were to clear lanes for the bombarding force, and assault vessels. Bobby stood at the rail of the ship unaware of any of these complicated arrangements. He could see four other ships, and occasionally heard the muted engines of aircraft overhead. It seemed so calm and peaceful. The rolling of the huge transport vessel left him with a feeling of safety and security. He wondered how he would react when the quiet of the night was rent asunder by the sounds of war, by bombs and mortars, gunfire and screams. He breathed in the salty sea air, wondering how far from the French coast they were, and hoping that when he finally did reach land, he would not let the side down.

It was still dark when Bobby made his way down the ladder and into the landing craft. As it hit the water, he was conscious of the change in motion from the gentle rocking he had felt on the transport ship. The landing craft was much smaller. It rose and bucked in the waves, the final vestige of the storm which had raged for so long. He looked around at his grim faced companions waiting for whatever lay ahead of them. Each had a pack on his back, rifle in his hand and helmet on his head. Some had already done up the chin straps in anticipation of the beaches, but most left them hanging loose. All was still. The only movement was the rocking craft, and the ceaseless movement of American jaws as they chewed gum.

At last the landing craft carrying V Corps were on their way to Omaha beach, a seemingly endless line of craft, like a column of army ants on the move. The approach to the beaches seemed to go on forever. Three hours can seem an eternity when you know that each moment your life could be in danger from enemy patrols. But miraculously the flotilla approached the beaches unobserved and unopposed. The sky was beginning to brighten with the grey light of dawn as the order came to prepare for the assault. Seconds later, the scream of shells high above their heads could be heard, followed by the dull roar as they hit the coastal defences. Bobby was on his feet now, one of a line of soldiers who waited with shoulders hunched and heads bowed low for the ramp to be lowered. So far, it was just like a training exercise, with the roar of friendly fire to their backs and, as yet, no enemy in sight. But Bobby knew that was all about to change. He tightened his grip on his weapon, and said a swift prayer that when the day was over he would still be alive to tell the tale.

410

High above, unseen and unheard, Allied planes approached and dropped their lethal cargo onto the enemy defensive positions. The ramp was quickly lowered, covering those closest to it with fountains of sea water. A cry came from the officers in the rear.

"Let them have it, boys!"

Bobby shuffled forwards, then found his feet on the unstable surface of the ramp. He moved on, jumping into the waves which reached above his knees. Rifle held high above his head, he waded ashore as the enemy opened up with a withering defensive fire. On all sides of him Bobby saw men fall, arms flailing wildly as the bullets ripped into them and they struggled to keep their footing. The water was shallower now. Bobby made his way onto the hard-packed sand, and looked wildly around him. Up ahead, the German 352nd Infantry Division was sited in commanding defensive positions which the air and naval bombardment had failed to destroy. From there, they were creating havoc amongst the force struggling to come ashore.

Bobby spied some sand dunes which would offer limited protection. He sprinted in their direction, but before he was halfway there the sand around his feet was thrown up in a stinging spray as bullets tore into it. He threw himself down beside another soldier, and pushed his helmet tighter onto his head.

"Gee! This is hotter than I expected!"

The soldier made no reply. Bobby turned to look at him in the early dawn light. Half of his chest was missing, and the sand around him drank the red blood as swiftly as it flowed from the gaping wounds. Bobby paled. He felt his stomach churn. He released his hold on his gun to wipe nervously at his mouth, and realised that he had not yet fired a single shot. Lying prone and using the body of his dead compatriot as cover, he sighted on the defensive positions which were becoming more visible as the sun rose higher. Carefully, methodically, he began to fire.

Bobby was reloading for the third time when a hand tapped him on the shoulder. He turned his head towards the lieutenant who had crawled up beside him.

"They're backing up behind you, soldier, and have no cover. They're sitting ducks at the water's edge. Move on up the beach."

Bobby perused the wide expanse of sand, littered with broken and bleeding humanity.

"Where do you suggest I go, sir?"

The lieutenant pointed to the sand dunes Bobby had tried to reach earlier.

"Try to get up there. You need cover just as much as the lads behind you. If you don't get moving soon, they'll be using you just as you're using this G.I."

Bobby looked at the soldier whose body had sheltered him, then back at the lieutenant.

"I'm on my way, sir!"

It took him almost thirty minutes to travel the one hundred and fifty yards to the sand dunes. He crawled on his belly, stopping to fire off a few rounds at the enemy, cowering low as the enemy mortars rained down on the beach. When he finally reached his destination, the relative safety of the dunes was already packed with soldiers who could see no way ahead. Those who were hit, or died of their wounds after reaching the dunes, were mercilessly pushed clear to make room for the living who crowded the blocked beach with nowhere to go.

"Where the hell is the armour?"

Bobby looked at the soldier beside him and shook his head. "I don't know, pal."

Looking down the beach he could see a few tanks. Most of them had been damaged by German mortar fire, and the only contribution they now made to the battle was to provide cover for those soldiers unfortunate enough to be stuck out in the open expanse of the beach. Those who were in the relative safety of the dunes were still under pressure from the masses of soldiery behind them, and eventually moved forward once again. So it went on throughout the day, small movements forward followed by long periods of lying low and trying to pick off the enemy. It was like a slow game of leapfrog amidst a field of dead and dying. By the evening of D-Day, the forces attacking Omaha beach had penetrated at their furthest point little more than a mile inland. In places opposite the main landing sites they were still within a thousand yards of the beaches. As darkness fell, Bobby found himself on the edge of a road. American forces stretched on either side of him into the distance, and the German 352nd Division still opposed them heavily ahead. He wondered, in his tiredness tinged with fear and frustration, if the whole invasion had been as disastrous as the small part in which he was involved.

To either side of Omaha the soldiers who landed on Utah and Gold beaches were luckier. They managed to get ashore without the strong opposition which had greeted the U.S. 1st Infantry Division. Further east, the British on Juno and Sword had been opposed by the 21st Panzer Division, which lost almost half its armour to the fighter-bomber and artillery attack. By the end of the day, one hundred and fifty-six thousand men had been put ashore on the beaches of Normandy. Although Major General Huebner said that his 1st Division were only digging in on Omaha beach with their fingernails, the Allies once more had a foothold on North Western Europe, the first since the disaster at Dunkirk. They were determined that nothing would drive them back into the sea again.

150

There was a knock at the back door. Angeline nervously looked up at the clock. It was just after midday. Vincent laid his spoon down beside the bowl of onion soup, and reached out to squeeze her hand.

"I'll go."

He was nervous as he slowly approached the door. It had been a difficult night. He had eventually managed to get Jean-Paul back to his home at 3.30 that morning, then slipped back into Saint Nazaire with the early morning workers, soon after dawn. The Germans had spent the morning rushing around in a frenzied attempt to get the fires raging in the docks under control, and seeking clues as to who had carried out the attack. Surely they hadn't made the link between him and what had happened? Vincent would not expect the Germans to come knocking quietly on his back door, but you never knew. Breathing deeply to try to control the rapid beating of his heart, he reached out and opened the door. His breath escaped in a sigh of relief as he saw who was standing there.

"Oh, it's, you. Come in quickly."

He stepped back to admit a nervous and serious faced Theresa. She quickly looked around the room. Seeing Angeline and only two places at the table, she frowned.

"Is Albert here?"

"No. Didn't he return to the farm?"

Theresa shook her head, and tears sprang to her eyes. Angeline immediately rose and put a comforting arm around her shoulders.

"Come and sit down, dear, and tell us all about it."

Theresa allowed herself to be led to the table and sat down wearily.

"How is your father?"

Theresa looked at the baker.

"He'll be all right, Monsieur Vincent. Mamma took out the bullet in his leg and bandaged it. We waited and waited for Albert to come back but when he didn't, Papa asked me to come to see if he's hiding here."

"No Theresa, I'm sorry. I've been out today. As far as I can make out, the Germans have not said that they took any prisoners last night. Albert could be injured, hiding somewhere between here and your home."

"Or dead."

Theresa was the only one who put their fears into words. They all knew what a risk the attack had been, the more so for Tony because he was a known British agent. Angeline did not say anything, but she realised that if Tony had been taken he would be facing a firing squad in the very near future. She knew that if he did not turn up soon, it must be assumed that they would never see him again.

It was Theresa who eventually broke the gloomy silence. "Papa asked me to come past the railway on my way here, to see if they had tried to move the train."

Angeline frowned. "Which train?"

"The tank transport. Albert had said that it must be out of action for the invasion, so I sabotaged the axle boxes."

"You did that?"

Theresa nodded at Vincent. "Yes. It wasn't too difficult. Papa said that if the train had moved I was to tell you, and you would let the radio operator know."

Angeline frowned. "And had it been moved?"

"Yes. They hooked it up to an engine and moved it from the siding onto the main line heading northwards. Then the axles froze. It's now stuck there, blocking the line." For the first time since her arrival, Theresa smiled. "Albert would have been happy to know that."

Angeline turned to Vincent excitedly. "If they've tried to move the train, it must mean that the tanks are needed in the north. And that would mean..."

"The invasion!" Theresa leapt to her feet in excitement. Angeline laid a restraining hand on her arm.

"Shhh." She looked at Vincent. "Fetch the radio."

He disappeared into the storeroom and retrieved the radio from its hiding place in the false bottom of the flour bin. Within minutes it was tuned in to the BBC. The three people listened eagerly to the news.

"...this morning. Allied troops are even now on French soil, and the freedom of Europe cannot now be far away..."

Theresa squealed in delight, and threw her arms around Angeline's neck. The Englishwoman smiled and inclined her head towards the radio. Vincent nodded, switched it off and concealed it once more. Angeline hugged the French girl, then gently disentangled her arms. She looked her nervously in the eye.

"Remember, Theresa, we are not supposed to know that. Tell no one but your parents, or the Germans will be suspicious."

Theresa nodded, still unable to stop smiling. Angeline continued. "Tell your father that last night's attack was a great success. Vincent and I will make sure that the radio operator tells London about that, and the train. You have all done well."

Theresa nodded, and her smiled faded. "We wouldn't have been able to do any of it without Albert."

Angeline nodded comfortingly. "I know. Either Vincent or I will bring you news of him, as soon as we hear anything. The most important thing for you to do is to ac normally."

Theresa nodded. "I understand. I'll be going now, I don't want my parents to worry And I can't wait to tell them the news!"

She hugged Angeline impulsively once more then smiled. "Goodbye."

Vincent re-entered the room as she was leaving. "Goodbye. And take care."

Theresa nodded and waved, then was gone. As the door closed behind her, Vincen turned to Angeline with a broad grin on his face.

"The invasion at last! Our freedom can't be far behind!"

Angeline nodded. "Yes, but at what cost? You said that Albert was surrounded wher last you saw him?"

Vincent nodded. "Just about. It would have been difficult for him to get out of tha position and, if I'm honest, I don't believe the Germans were in any mood to take prisoners."

"Then we should fear the worst?"

Vincent nodded sadly. "I'm afraid so."

Angeline's face was determined. "I am going to spend the afternoon down by the docks and outside the S.S. H.Q. to see what I can find out."

"Is that wise?"

"It's my job." Vincent nodded but said nothing as Angeline continued. "I'll get in touch with England tonight."

151

Captain Dawson paced the length of the radio hut and back again, time after time. The operators were working hard. There seemed to be a message from every agent in France. Each operator wrote swiftly on the pad in front of them, then de-coded the message before handing the transcript to a runner, who took it across to Dawson. Each time a piece of paper was handed to him, the officer stood still and read it, before giving it back to be filed or placed on his desk for further action. It was a busy night. The messages all brought good news. The sabotage work had gone well, and the invasion seemed to be going more or less to plan, so he was unprepared for the message which came a few minutes after midnight.

> 'Attack on docks success. Tank transport train out of action
> and blocking line. Albert missing. Presume worst.
> Angeline'

For a moment the full meaning of the message did not sink in. Then he read it again. 'Presume worst'. His face was stony as he looked at the message without really seeing it. It was bound to happen. You could not send hundreds of agents behind enemy lines without expecting to lose some, but each time it happened it came as a shock. To many it would seem like just one more casualty in a war where millions had lost their lives. But this casualty was personally known to him, as was his great contribution to the war effort. Dawson continued to cling to the thin shred of hope that Tony might still be alive, but deep down he knew that Angeline would not have sent such a message if she did not think he was dead. He turned and left the hut, still clutching the flimsy piece of paper, so small a thing to represent the loss of a human life.

152

On Omaha beach and beyond, the battle raged throughout the night of June 6th and into the following morning. The tanks finally seemed to be coming ashore in usable numbers. They were moving forward to where the U.S. 1st Division had stubbornly clung on to their tiny beachhead during the night. As the huge behemoths thundered past Bobby, he smiled wearily. At last they appeared to be gaining the upper hand. Falling in behind a tank, he shuffled forward with the other GIs. In over twenty-four hours since hitting the beaches they had managed to snatch only a few moments of sleep. They were exhausted, but it felt good to be moving forwards at last.

The 5th Rangers came ashore and relieved the 2nd on Pointe du Hoc, then surged forwards to secure Grandchamp. The 175th Infantry drove along Route 13 towards Isigny during the night. By dawn on the 9th, the town was in their hands, while the German infantry was beginning to withdraw from its positions on the Arnes.

Behind the troops, the beaches which had seen such fierce fighting on D-Day now became transport depots. The Allies knew it would be some time before they had access to port facilities on the French coast, so they had planned to provide all five beaches with breakwaters called Gooseberries, behind which the merchantmen could shelter and unload. Work on these portable harbours began on 8th June, with the sinking of block ships on the fifteen foot line. It was hoped that the harbours would be in full working order by the 11th, to supply the thousands of men with the equipment they would need to rid France of its occupying forces. By the end of the 9th, the beachheads had linked up although all of the objectives had not been achieved. Caen was supposed to have fallen on the first day but was not in fact taken for four weeks, but the Allied forces were well established, filled with the confidence that the end of a war which had cost so much in suffering and death was now immeasurably closer.

153

Bobby moved cautiously along the narrow lane. The thick hedges on either side reached high above the sunken roadway. They offered ideal protection for the slowly retreating Germans to mount ambushes on the Americans, who sought desperately to reach the port of Cherbourg, where the enemy were equally vigorous in their defence. Ahead of Bobby and his platoon the road turned sharply left, hiding what lay ahead from the approaching soldiers. Suddenly there was the sound of gunfire. The GIs threw themselves against the sides of the bocage, frantically surveying the hedges, hoping desperately that there were no Germans waiting above to fire down on them in such an enclosed place. All was still, and Lieutenant Cooper waved an arm to indicate that his men should climb up the steep banks and through the hedges, so they could attack the ambushing Germans from the flank.

Bobby slung his rifle over his shoulder, and began to scramble up the impossibly steep bank. He clung tightly to exposed roots and the slim trunks of saplings, as he hauled himself upwards and pushed his way through the dense undergrowth. At last he found himself in a small field; crouching low he unslung his rifle and held it ready in front of him. As silently as possible the Americans made their way forwards in the cover of the hedge, moving steadily closer to the sound of gunfire. At last they saw the Germans. A machine gun had been set up in the shelter of an enormous oak tree and from there the enemy were firing down into the bocage on the entrapped soldiers, who could do nothing to relieve their predicament. If they tried to move from what little cover they had found, they were sitting ducks to the enemy in their superior position.

Bobby glanced across at the lieutenant, who held up a hand in readiness. The two Germans operating the machine gun, and the soldiers who surrounded them and were using their rifles to fire on the Americans, had not sensed the danger to their flanks. When Cooper dropped his hand and the GIs rushed forwards, guns blazing, they took the enemy completely by surprise. With fierce determination the Americans moved forwards, bullets slamming into the enemy as they turned with startled eyes to see the harbingers of their doom. The element of surprise was so great that they wiped out the enemy position, while only one of their number was injured.

The relieving Americans climbed down into the bocage, where they began to help their wounded comrades, binding wounds and comforting the injured. They were still there when a soldier appeared at a run, with further orders for the advancing forces. He saluted Cooper and began to speak breathlessly.

"The 101st Airborne have now linked up with the 29th Infantry, sir, and are moving on Carentan. You're to swing your men around to the southwest, to outflank and encircle the town. With any luck, we'll be able to cut off the entire garrison."

Cooper unfolded his map and perused it carefully, then nodded.

"OK. Tell the captain we're moving in. Will we link up with other groups from our division down there?"

The runner nodded. "Yes, sir."

"Good. Then you get back to HQ." He folded his map and put it carefully away. "Come on guys, we have a job to do."

It was late afternoon of June 11th when Lieutenant Cooper's group came within sight of Carentan. The officer studied the situation, then pointed to a small copse of trees.

"Bivouac down there, lads. Wesson and Garland on guard. I'm going to try to find HQ, and see what they want us to do now."

As Cooper and two accompanying soldiers moved off, the remainder of his platoon moved into the copse, only to find that it was already occupied by other GIs. Wesson and Garland joined those already on guard, while the remainder settled down to rest. Bobby removed his helmet, and was lying down to sleep when the sound of boots rustling in the leaf litter alerted him to someone approaching, but he was too tired to socialise. He lay there with his eyes closed, waiting for them to pass by.

"Are you deliberately ignoring me?"

Bobby's eyes opened wide in surprise and he sat up.

"Al!"

Al grinned broadly and threw himself onto the ground. "So you've managed to get this far, Bobby. I can't tell you how glad I am to see you."

"I'm glad to see you too, pal. After our group split up, I didn't know what had happened to you." He frowned. "I've seen so many men go down over the last few days. I was afraid you might not have made it."

Al nodded. "I know what you mean. There were times when I thought I'd never get off that beach alive." He shuddered as he thought of all the death and destruction he had witnessed. "We might be moving now," he continued, "but it's still slower than I thought it would be."

"Yeah." Bobby grinned. "It seems strange for us to be moving west and then north when Germany lies to our east. But I suppose the brass know what they're doing."

"You're damn right they do, Wilson." Bobby looked round to see Lieutenant Cooper miling down at him. "We have to take Cherbourg before we can join the British going ast. We attack Carentan in the morning, then head on up the Cotentin Peninsular. Once ve have the port in our hands, supply will be easier. And we won't have to worry about n enemy at our backs." He looked around at the soldiers relaxing in the copse. "For onight we stay right where we are. Get some rest. It will be quite a fight in the norning."

For once Lieutenant Cooper was proved wrong. During the night the German garrison quietly evacuated Carentan and moved up to join with the garrison defending Cherbourg. The American soldiers were in hot pursuit, but could not bring the fleeing roops to battle.

154

The Allied attempts to confuse the Germans into thinking that the invasion would come in the Pas de Calais rather than Normandy had worked well. Even a week after the landings, Hitler still thought that Normandy was just a diversion. He was waiting for the forces to come over the narrowest part of the Channel. That was the area where part of his new 'secret weapon' was situated and, on 13th June, the first V-I set out on its deadly mission. The small pilotless planes carried a heavy load of high explosive. They flew on until their fuel ran out, then they would dive straight to the ground. The ensuing blast was enormous, causing high casualties because most of them came over during the day when it was impossible for the majority of people to take shelter. Once again the children of London were evacuated to safer areas. Once the new menace was fully understood, anti-aircraft defences were moved out towards the coast. They helped to contain the threat by firing shells with proximity fuses, while fighter aircraft brought the flying bombs down in the air. It seemed strange to the British to be under such constant attack again, particularly now that the war seemed to be going so well for them, but they soon became used to the threat. They continued their daily lives in the same stoic fashion which had characterised their reactions since the outbreak of war so long before.

155

The nurses and auxiliaries at Heronfield and other hospitals throughout Britain were under a great deal of pressure as the wounded flooded back from the beaches of Normandy. But the days passed, and the flood slowed as the Allies gained a firmer foothold. No longer was Sarah dealing with wounded who had only been treated at a Forward Dressing Station before being sent to Heronfield. After twelve days they were converting back to their usual role as a convalescent hospital, and the staff had more time to themselves. Sarah and Jane took advantage of this as they walked through the orchard. The apples on the trees were growing fast in the dappled sunlight, and Sarah wondered if the war would be over before it was time to pick them. She watched a butterfly flitting through the trees searching for flowers, and smiled.

"I like it here, Jane. It's so peaceful."

"Yes. I suppose northern France was like this once." Jane's voice was wistful, and Sarah turned sympathetically towards her friend. "I know what you're thinking, Jane, but you must try not to dwell on what might be happening."

"That's easy for you to say." Jane's voice held a sharpness which Sarah had rarely heard before. "You're not carrying the child of a man fighting out there. Each time new patients arrive, I find myself looking for Al. I have to stop myself asking every one of them if they've seen him, or know what's happened to him. I'm so worried, Sarah."

"I know." Sarah's voice was soft, comforting. "I worry about Bobby too. But that won't help him. It just distracts me from doing my job properly. We owe it to them to carry on as normal."

"It's different for me. I love Al, and I want him to be with me when our child grows up. You don't love Bobby like that. How can you know how I feel?

Sarah turned away from Jane. She gazed with unseeing eyes through the trees to where the river reflected the sunlight in the distance. She supposed Jane was right. What she felt for Bobby was different from how Jane felt about Al. She loved him in a quieter, less passionate way. She was concerned for his safety, and it would leave a great hole in her life if he were to die. But it was not the same as if Joe had ever gone into battle, or how she would feel if Tony was in Normandy, instead of safe behind a desk somewhere in England. Sarah felt a gentle touch on her arm and looked round. Jane had tears in her eyes.

"I'm sorry, Sarah. That was unfair of me. I know how much Bobby means to you."

Sarah smiled gently.

"It's all right, Jane. Of course you're more worried than I am. You're worrying for two. But believe me, I do know how you feel. I would have felt the same if Joe and I had married and he'd gone out there."

"Do you think of him often?"

Sarah shrugged. "Now and then. Sometimes I don't think of him for weeks at a time. Then something reminds me of him and the memories come flooding back."

"It must be hard."

Sarah nodded. "Yes, but as the months and years pass the pain does ease. I can smile at my memories." She looked thoughtfully at Jane. "I suppose finding someone else to love has helped too."

"Are you trying to tell me that if Al dies I'll fall in love again, and have nothing but happy memories?" She grinned, the impish grin Sarah knew so well. "Let me tell you this, Sarah Porter, I won't need to fall in love again. Al is going to come home to me and the baby." She touched her stomach where it swelled with its precious cargo, and her eyes softened with the misty look of love. "He cares too much not to come back."

"That's the attitude." Sarah smiled. "Be positive. Al and Bobby will both come back, and all of our worries will be over."

Jane laughed. "Mine will, but yours will just be beginning!"

Sarah frowned for a moment then joined in the laughter. "I suppose you're right. One day I shall have to choose between the two men in my life. But I don't know how to do it!"

"It shouldn't be that difficult. Which of the two has supported you best during this war? Who has been the most honest? Which one tries to keep in touch? Which one has caused you the least unhappiness? Which one..."

"All right! Enough!" Sarah held up a hand, laughing. "Are you trying to tell me that Bobby is the better of the two?"

"What do you think?"

Sarah frowned. "I suppose he is. But do we always fall in love with the best?" She was quiet for a moment, deep in thought. When she spoke again it was as though a weight had been lifted from her shoulders. "I know Bobby would make me happy and would always be there for me, not like Tony. It's weeks since I heard from him or saw him. When I do see him it often ends in tension. But when things go well with him, it's so much better than being with Bobby."

"How often do the good times come?"

Sarah sighed. Jane was so perceptive.

"Not really often enough." She frowned. "I can't break my promise to Tony to wait until after the war. But if things haven't improved between us by then, I shall go to America and start a new life with Bobby. I know from experience that I can get over him in time. I don't see why I should commit myself to an uncertain future, when I have security and love waiting for me with someone else."

"I think that's the right decision. I'm sure you won't regret it."

The two women stepped out from the shelter of the trees and walked towards the river in silence. Sarah felt that the difficult decision had now been made. It saddened her to think that her future would not be with Tony, but she convinced herself that she must be strong, or she would regret losing Bobby for the rest of her life. As they walked a strange sound could be heard in the distance, a harsh, grating sound. The two women stopped as the sound grew louder, and looked around to see if they could pinpoint its source. For a moment they could see nothing. Then Jane pointed to a small black dot in the sky to the southeast.

"What's that?"

"A plane, I think. It sounds as though there's something wrong with its engines."

The flying object approached swiftly until they could see its outline, and Sarah's heart sank.

"It looks like one of those new flying bombs we saw on the newsreel. What did they call them?"

"Doodlebugs." Jane did not take her eyes off the object. It was passing south, heading away now. The noise, which had risen in pitch to an unbearable sound, was beginning to recede. Then it stopped. The silence was almost painful after the harsh sound of the V-1's engine. The women watched the nose point towards the earth and the bomb began to fall. A whistling sound began, growing in pitch until they had to cover their ears. Sarah grabbed Jane's hand and they ran back into the shelter of the trees. Behind them, Hitler's secret weapon hit the ground and exploded in a geyser of earth. Sarah turned to see that it had fallen beyond the trees, probably in a field on the other side of the river. She was thankful that no one lived in that direction. She turned shakily towards Jane, whose face was ashen.

"How can we defeat something like that?"

Sarah shook her head. "I don't know, but we will. It's only a machine, and no machine will defeat us."

It was as though Jane had not heard her. "Are they sending them against our men? Will they be able to shoot them down?"

Sarah took her gently by the hand. "Come on. Let's get back."

Jane nodded and walked along beside her friend towards the people who were flooding out of Heronfield house to see what had happened. The new V-1s instilled a feeling of uncertainty and fear into people who felt that this weapon could prolong the war. Yet if they had been aware of the weapons vulnerability they would have felt easier in their minds as they made their way inside and back to their normal everyday routine.

156

Bobby tried to wrap his coat closer around himself, but it was a fruitless exercise. After four days of torrential rain, the worst recorded storm for forty years, he was wet through and the coat gave no protection. The water dripped from the rim of his helmet, splashing into the liquid mud where he had sat for four days, since 19th June. The whole Allied advance ground to a halt as the rain lashed down. Thunder roared overhead like artillery fire, and lightning split the sky. Beside him, Al was eating corned beef from a tin with a spoon. The food was cold again because they could not light a fire. He grinned across at his comrade.

"What a way to earn a living!"

Bobby wiped water from his face with a hand that had not felt warm for days. Reaching out, he took the half eaten meat from Al, and began to spoon the cold damp mess into his mouth. He smiled.

"If I'd known it was going to be this much fun, I would have invited the girls to our picnic!"

Al reached down for his tin mug. Huge raindrops were splashing into the cold coffee. He grimaced as he drank. Over the rim of the mug, he spied a tiny patch of blue, and knocked Bobby with his elbow.

"Hey, will you look at that."

Bobby looked up. The sky did seem slightly less grey. The small patch of blue was growing as the rain began to slacken. He sighed.

"Do you think it can really be over?" He smiled as the wind began to clear the rain-clouds from the sky. "Do you realise we could actually be dry tomorrow!"

Al laughed. "You'll be dry but we'll have to move out, so you'll complain about your sore feet instead!"

"And why not? We have to complain about something!"

The sky finally cleared, leaving a land wet and steaming. And two armies ready to meet in conflict once more.

With the storm finally over the Americans began to move forwards once again, heading inexorably towards Cherbourg. In the east, the 15th Scottish Division pushed on until, by 26th June, they were within striking distance of Odon. On the following morning they secured the bridge, and began moving their armour across, only to face the largest ever assembly of Waffen SS armour around the Cheux salient. The sight of hundreds of tanks was daunting. But the British had intercepted the German signals and a map from a motorcycle courier, so they knew the German plans well in advance. As the 9th and 10th Panzer Divisions rolled forward to attack the British forces around Cheux on three sides, in an attempt to push them back and re-take the bridge over the Odon, they were swamped with British artillery fire, against which they were helpless. Shell after shell fell amongst the tanks, throwing metal and bodies into the air while the Allies dug in to await the outcome. It was hopeless for the Germans. Tank after tank was destroyed as they attempted to push on towards the river, but finally they had to halt and try to retreat through the shattered remnants of their own forces. It was a heavy defeat for the enemy, leaving the British in control of the bridge, poised to push on towards the German homeland.

News of the great British victory at Odon was well received by the Americans as they made their way towards Cherbourg and, with increased vigour, fought onwards up the Cotentin Peninsular. The Germans were trapped in and around the port and fought valiantly, but were eventually forced to surrender. Organised resistance at Cherbourg ended on 27th, but the final forces on the breakwater did not surrender for two more days. The Americans took thirty thousand prisoners, and entered the port to find that the Germans had wrecked the dock installations and obstructed the harbour. It was a disappointment to the forces who had wanted to use the harbour to aid their supply operations, but at last it was in Allied hands. Once repairs were made, it would soon be in a position to receive supplies for the advancing armies.

Bobby stood silhouetted against the sky, his helmet pushed towards the back of his head, pack heavy on his back and rifle on his shoulder. He looked tired yet triumphant, standing on the quayside surveying the destruction around him; the twisted metal of cranes, hulks lying low in the water, buildings blown apart by bombs and artillery. It was a dismal scene, so much destruction and death. He looked north across the English Channel, as though trying to see the peaceful countryside he had explored with Sarah. For a moment he smiled as he thought of her, wondering what she was doing, then he turned eastwards, and his gaze was stern. Over there lay Germany, and he could not see Sarah again until that country was defeated. Between him and his objective were thousands of men who would try to stop him. With grim determination, he moved away from the water's edge towards the unnumbered battles which still awaited him.

158

Angeline stood still and silent in the shadows of the alleyway, and watched the German patrol marching briskly past. The three weeks since the landings on the Normandy beaches had not weakened the German hold on Saint Nazaire. The docks were still in a mess, but operating in a limited way. The German soldiers showed no fear of defeat, as reports of the fighting continued to come from the north and east. The Resistance group had laid low since the attack on the docks, hoping for more Allied help and searching for clues to what had happened to Tony. But they were disappointed. No Allied attack on Saint Nazaire materialised, and the occupiers soon settled back into their normal routine. Some civilians had been taken in retaliation for the attack, but the Germans seemed more intent on building up their defences, and had not reacted with their usual brutality. No one knew if they had captured Tony on the night of the attack, or if he had been killed. For days they hoped he would make his way back to the farm, or be found wounded and hiding somewhere. But after a week they reluctantly gave up hope. No announcement was made by the Germans, and nobody was found. That led Angeline to the reluctant conclusion that Tony was dead. Surely, if Steinhauser had taken him prisoner he would have bragged about it? If they had captured an English spy, they would have had a public execution? The only other possibility was that Tony was killed before they had identified him, and his body was buried without any fuss. The Germans had so many more important things to occupy them.

The patrol disappeared round the corner, and Angeline crossed the road as silently as a shadow. Within minutes she was hidden deep in a basement, with the radio set in front of her and earphones on her head. Expertly, she began to tap out her message to England.

Captain Dawson sat at his desk and looked down at the piece of paper in front o
him. He had seen many such messages, but experience did not make it any easier. H
read the message once more.

> 'Still no sign of Albert. No German announcement. No execution.
> Must assume killed in attack.
> Angeline'

The words were cold, heartless, but that was only for speed and accuracy. Dawsoi
knew how difficult it must have been for Angeline to send such a message. Th
procedure for such an eventuality was laid down. The family must now receive :
telegram with the news of the loss of their son. Dawson, however, was a goo
commanding officer. He appreciated the calibre of work his men did, the dangers the
faced, the secrecy of their lives. He knew the shock that hearing of this through a
impersonal telegram could cause the family. Reaching down into the drawer beside him
the captain removed an envelope and a bulky package and laid them on the desk in fron
of him. The smaller was addressed to 'Miss Sarah Porter, Heronfield House Hospital' th
larger to 'Sir Michael and Lady Kemshall, The Lodge, Heronfield'. With a sigh, Dawsoi
picked up the packages and left the room. It was going to be a long and difficult day.

The staff car turned in through the gateway. As the wheels of the vehicle crunched
on the gravel driveway, Captain Dawson slowed, then brought it to a stop in front of th
steps which led up to the lodge. He sat in silence behind the wheel for a moment. H
had given his driver the day off so that he could drive himself, anything to keep his min
occupied by thoughts other than what he had to say to Tony's parents. With a sigh h
opened the door and climbed out of the car. Leaning across the passenger seat, h
picked up the packages which Tony had left in his safe-keeping. Then he straightened
and slammed the door. He looked up at the lodge. Inside life was pursuing its usua
course. It would continue until he spoke, and then things would never be quite the sam
again.

"Can I help you?"

Dawson jumped at the sound of the softly accented French voice. He turned to se
who had spoken, and was greeted by a smiling Louise Kemshall.

"I am sorry to have startled you. I was in the garden at the side of the house and
heard your car."

"Good morning." Dawson tried to smile but found it difficult. Her features were sc
like Tony's, and with the French accent, he knew he was addressing one of the people he
had come to see. His next question was reluctant. If he did not say it, he would not
receive the answer which he dreaded. But say it he must. "Are you by any chance Lady
Kemshall?"

"Yes, indeed I am. But there you have me at a disadvantage."

Dawson gave a crisp salute. "My apologies, Madame. My name is Dawson, Captain
Dawson. I wonder, is Sir Michael at home?"

Louise nodded. "Yes, he is in his study. Please come this way."

Dawson followed the lady up the steps into the cool interior of the house. She led
him past the first door on the right, before knocking gently on the second door and
pushing it open.

"Sorry to disturb you, mon cher, but there is a Captain Dawson here to see you."

There was the murmur of a reply, the words inaudible to Dawson's ears. Louise turned towards him.

"Please come in." She stood back to allow him to enter. "Well, if you will excuse me, I must get back to my garden."

"Thank you, Madame."

Dawson entered the room and heard the door close quietly behind him. Sir Michael was standing beside his desk, with a slight frown.

"Captain Dawson? I'm sure that that name is familiar, but I can't think why. Welcome, anyway." He held out a hand which Dawson shook, feeling like a traitor.

"Your son may have mentioned me, Sir Michael."

"David?"

"No, Tony. I am his commanding officer."

"Yes, now I remember. You're from the Ministry for Economic Warfare. You're the one who refused Tony permission to transfer to an active unit." He indicated a chair. "Please sit down Captain Dawson. Tell me what this is all about. Have you granted his request at last?"

Dawson gratefully took the seat. He watched Sir Michael walk back round to the other side of the desk, and make himself comfortable in the large leather chair.

"Sir Michael, I'm afraid I am bringing you bad news." His voice was tentative. How many times had he gone over this conversation in his mind, without coming up with a better way of beginning? "I'm afraid that Tony is missing in action, presumed dead."

Sir Michael's face paled. For a moment he felt that his heart had stopped beating, his lungs refused to take in breath. Then he shook his head emphatically.

"No. You must be wrong. Tony has never seen action. You must be talking about someone else."

Dawson's eyes were filled with sadness and compassion. Sir Michael fell silent before his steady gaze. Would Dawson have come if it were not true?

"But it can't be true! I haven't received a telegram!" He was clinging to straws, and he knew it.

Dawson nodded. "I know. I had to tell you personally. You knew nothing of Tony's work, so I knew it would be hard for you to accept. That's why I came."

"I know all about his work. Liaison with factories. He isn't in danger there."

"That was just a cover, Sir Michael."

Sir Michael looked down at his hands, which were shaking violently on the desktop. He clutched them tightly together and looked back at Dawson. His eyes begged him to say that it was not true, it was all just a cruel joke.

"I don't understand."

Dawson's heart went out to the man.

"I know. Please let me explain. Of course, I would appreciate it if you don't tell too many people the details until after the war." Sir Michael nodded but said nothing. "It all began just after Dunkirk. With France in German hands, we needed men behind enemy lines to send us information, and to disrupt the enemy wherever possible. Because of Tony's excellent French and his knowledge of the Saint Nazaire area, we recruited him to the Ministry of Economic Warfare, a euphemism for the Special Operations Executive. He was given a high degree of training and parachuted into France in September '41."

"My God!" Sir Michael's eyes were wide in amazement. "Why didn't he tell me?"

"He wasn't allowed to. He was assigned to the Saint Nazaire area and set up a Resistance group, with the help of a man he knew from before the war. You know him too, I believe. Jean-Paul Boues."

"Jean-Paul! Of course I know him! He worked with Tony?"

"Yes. On that first mission he was looking for U-boat bases. He found one, and with the help of his group managed to destroy it. In the process he was injured. We managed to get him back by submarine a week later."

Sir Michael was frowning. "Was that around the time he was caught in the air raid?"

Dawson nodded. "Yes, but the injuries were not caused by an air raid, but a cliff fall in France."

"The poor boy." There were tears in Sir Michael's eyes. "All that time I said he was a coward and would not avenge David's death. How I must have hurt him." He frowned. "You sent him back again?"

"Yes, when you thought he was in America in early '42. This time his group carried out a number of attacks. On the docks at Saint Nazaire, railways, convoys. They did a great deal of damage, and had the enemy really worried. They were lucky. But their luck didn't hold out. Tony was taken by the SS"

"God! No!" Sir Michael pushed himself violently out of his chair. "Did they know who he was?"

"They only suspected at the beginning. But by the time they finished with him, they knew he was one of our agents."

Sir Michael brushed tears from his cheeks. "What did they do to him?"

Dawson shook his head. "You don't want to know the details, Sir Michael. His group managed to break him out, and we flew him home. For a time it was touch and go, but he made it in the end. When he was nearly recovered, we let him come home to convalesce."

"And I turned him away. While my own son was still suffering the results of torture at the hands of the SS. I threw him out of my house, because I thought he was a coward! No wonder he was angry and hated me. I wish I'd known, then we could have parted as friends."

"I'm sure he understood, Sir Michael. He was just waiting for the end of the war to tell you."

Sir Michael looked at him accusingly. "But he didn't live to see the end of the war, did he? You sent him back."

Dawson nodded. "Yes. I sent him back, but I had little choice. Please let me explain."

Sir Michael was pacing agitatedly back and forth as Dawson continued.

"After his brush with the SS we planned to keep Tony in England. It was too dangerous to send him back to where the SS could identify him. Then with the Second Front coming, we needed a man in Saint Nazaire. Tony was the best man for the job, but I would never have asked him to go back after what he'd been through. He volunteered for the job, Sir Michael, and I couldn't turn him down. We needed him too badly."

Sir Michael sat down heavily once more. "What happened?"

"He went back to France at the end of April. With his group he destroyed bridges, telephone communications, rail links, anything that could have helped the Germans to push us back on the Normandy beaches. He led an attack on the docks at Saint Nazaire in the early hours of the morning of 6th June, D-Day. The last anyone saw of him, he was fighting alone, surrounded by the enemy."

Sir Michael looked up, desperate hope in his eyes. "There was no body? How can you be sure that he's dead?

"We can't be one hundred per cent certain, but the Germans didn't say that he had been taken prisoner. The Resistance can find out nothing. The only real possibility is

424

that he was killed, and buried without the Germans realising who he was."

"Or they could have taken him and be torturing him now." Sir Michael's voice was low, tortured as he knew his son had been.

Dawson shook his head. "No. He would have talked by now, and the rest of the group would have been taken."

"Tony would never talk!"

Dawson's eyes were filled with compassion. "He would have talked. No-one could stand up to SS treatment for this long."

Sir Michael shook his head. "Until I know for certain, I won't give up hope. Don't you see?" His eyes were filled with pain as he spoke. "I sent him away. I called him a coward. He has to live, so that I can ask him to forgive me! I love my son, Captain Dawson. I won't accept that he's dead!"

Dawson stood up. "I'm sorry Sir Michael, but Tony was aware of the dangers. He asked me to give you this if he didn't come back."

He held out the package. Sir Michael reached out hesitantly to take it. He cradled the parcel in his hands, and gazed down at the familiar writing before meeting Dawson's eyes.

"I'm proud to have known and worked with your son, Sir Michael. The peoples of England and France will never fully know the debt they owe him. He was one of a rare breed of men, Sir Michael, a hero. Be proud of your son." He held out a hand, which Sir Michael took, his firm grip masking his shock.

"Thank you for coming in person, Captain Dawson. I would never have been able to understand if I had suddenly been confronted by a telegram."

Dawson nodded. "Tony deserved better than that."

"If you should hear anything..."

Dawson nodded. "I will let you know immediately, if I hear anything. But don't hope for too much."

"I must hope. That's all I have left."

"Goodbye, Sir Michael."

Sir Michael nodded but said nothing, his hands caressing the package from Tony. Dawson turned and left the room, closing the door quietly on the man whose heart bled for his son, and the way he had treated him.

Sir Michael made his slow way back to his desk and sat down. Placing the package carefully in front of him, he sat looking at it for a few moments, as though not opening it would in some symbolic way deny everything Dawson had told him. If he did not read the letter, it would be easier to believe that Tony was still alive. Finally he reached for his paper knife. He carefully unsealed the package and drew out two sheets of folded paper and a small leather-bound box. Laying the letter aside for a moment, he gazed curiously at the box. Then with tentative movements he lifted the lid. As his eyes fell on the contents, his tears began to fall. His vision blurred for a moment and he wiped roughly at his eyes. Then he lifted the Distinguished Service Order from the box. All the time he thought Tony was a coward, he had been laying his life on the line for his country. He must have shown a bravery matched by only a few to have been awarded such an honour, yet he could never speak to his parents about it. Sir Michael laid the medal to one side and picked up the letter with the familiar writing of his son. What would it say? Would Tony condemn him for his lack of understanding and cruel words, even from beyond the grave? He closed his eyes for a moment as though in prayer. Then, steeled to face whatever recriminations the letter might hold, he began to read.

Dear Dad and Mamma,

If you are reading this then I must assume that I am now dead. I want you to know that I regret nothing of what has brought me to this state. I have been proud to serve my country, and as I prepare to go to France once more, I am aware of all the risks. Who knows better than me what lies ahead, for I have been there before. My one regret is that I will not be able to see you again, to explain for myself why I have kept so many things secret from you during this war.

Dad, you once said that you bitterly resented the fact that no one from our family was actively fighting to free France and to regain Grandmamma's home. Tell her I have been doing just that. Tell her that I have seen the Germans in Saint Nazaire, seen their flag flying from her home, fought beside good friends like Jean-Paul Boues and made sure that the occupation of her home does not go uncontested. Tell her too that her home has not been damaged. Her land still produces food, and her people still love her. When this war is over and she goes home, no one will say that she abandoned them. They knew that she had to go, and they look forward to seeing her again in a free France. You called me coward, Dad. That hurt bitterly, to think that you believed I could sit back and do nothing while our country is at war. But I don't blame you for what you said. I know how much you loved David, and how deeply his death hurt you. You see, I felt the same way too. I am as much to blame for our problems as you are, because I kept my work secret. I hope that you understand that I could not tell you. It was not allowed. You know, you might think that it took a great deal of courage to jump from a plane into Occupied France. But I will tell you that it was not as hard for me as keeping silent in front of you.

This war has caused more hurts than those physical ones brought about by bullets and bombs. It was this hurt that made us lash out at each other, but I believe that underneath it all, there was love. You loved me as a child, Dad, and I cannot believe that that love has died. So do not be hard on yourself. I go to France now, knowing that you love me, and that love and the love of my dear Mamma will be what I remember when the end comes.

Dearest Mamma. I know the hurt my death must cause you. You had two sons who loved you dearly. Now you have none. But remember, our love will still reach out to you from beyond the grave. David and I are together again now. We will await the time when you will join us in heaven. But let that time be long, Mamma. Live the rest of your life with joy. Remember us with pride.

My dear parents. I send you my DSO. You will be no less surprised to receive it than I was! Please put it with David's DFC, and always remember that we earned them fighting for England, and for France. Remember always that I love you both now as I always have, and always will. May God bless you and keep you safe.

You were the best parents anyone could have, I am proud to be your son.

Your ever loving
Tony.

Sir Michael sat in unseeing silence for a long time before laying the letter on the desk. Burying his face in his hands, he gave way to his grief and wept bitterly.

Captain Dawson drove back down the drive from Heronfield Hospital. His meeting with Sarah Porter had been difficult, but not as difficult as the one with Sir Michael. The young woman had taken it well, or so it seemed. He only hoped there would be a friend close by when the full realisation of what he had said hit her. He drove slowly past the lodge. Lady Kemshall was no longer in the garden. He was glad he had not been the one to tell her about Tony, and his heart went out to Sir Michael as he broke the news to his wife. Pulling out onto the road, he turned the car back in the direction of Beaulieu, starting his return journey to the base where other young men and women like Tony were undergoing training.

Sarah sat at Doctor Millard's desk. He had called her into his office. A Captain Dawson had wanted to speak to her, a stranger who had brought unbelievable news about Tony and left her with a small parcel. She recognised Tony's handwriting, but still did not believe what the officer told her. It was just too extraordinary to be true. While she wanted to believe that Tony could show such bravery in the defence of his country, she could not accept it. That would mean accepting the other news, the news of his death. She was not sure she could cope with that

Steeling herself for the ordeal ahead, she carefully opened the large envelope and took out the familiar leather box. As she looked at it, her heart plummeted. She opened it slowly to gaze at the graceful lines of the golden heron. She did not have to read the letter to tell her that what Captain Dawson had said was true, she knew Tony would have kept the heron if he could. To have it in her hands now meant the end of everything. She closed her eyes, remembering again the touch of his lips, and the way his hair felt as she ran her fingers through it. Then she took out the letter and began to read.

> My darling Sarah,
>
> This is the hardest letter I have ever had to write for I know that if you are reading these words I must be dead, and I will never be able to see your beloved face again. I am sure that by now Captain Dawson has told you about the work I have been doing. Do you remember, Sarah? You said you sometimes felt that I was two people in one body; now you know that is true. I sometimes had to bury the real me because I was not allowed to tell you everything, and it caused a wall to grow up between us. I'm sorry, Sarah. I hated lying to you. You must know now why there were times when I did not write or visit, but through those times you were never far from my thoughts. And I firmly believe that through it all you never really stopped loving me. I have to believe it, for it is your love which has made my life worth living.
>
> I love you, Sarah. I have loved you from the very first time I saw you, and I will love you for all eternity. Mourn me a little while, my darling, but never forget what I told you after Joe died. You must not waste your life on what might have been. Bobby is a good man, and he will make you happy. Take a chance with him, and put the past behind you. All I ask is that you take out the golden heron once in a while, and think of me as I have so often thought of you. When I was in France, it

was thoughts of you that kept me strong. I know that whatever happens between now and my death, thoughts of you will never be far from my mind, for you are forever in my heart.

God bless you, my darling Sarah. I thank him daily for allowing me to love you, and to share happy times with you - however brief they may have been.

Good luck, my darling. Be happy.

Tony.

Sarah picked up the heron and traced its outline with her fingertip. If only their love had been allowed to soar with the freedom of a bird. She regretted all the wasted time which she could have spent with Tony, and she vowed to make it up to him. No matter what Captain Dawson said, she would not, could not, believe he was dead, that she would never be able to see or hold him again. He would come home, and then they would spend the rest of their lives together. A small voice deep inside whispered 'Don't believe it. He's dead. He won't be back'. She tried to block out the sound, but however hard she tried, it continued to whisper, forcing her to face a reality she did not want to believe. By the time Jane came to find her at the bidding of Doctor Millard, Sarah was staring unseeingly at the wall, tears coursing down her cheeks and a small golden heron clutched tightly to her breast.

160

Tony pulled the pin from a grenade and threw it with all of his might, before diving down behind a pile of rubble. As the grenade exploded he was showered with dust and small stones. He heard the cries of someone in pain as he laid his three remaining grenades on the ground in front of him, and quickly glanced over his shoulder at the retreating forms of Jean-Paul and Vincent. He was relieved that nobody was pursuing them. Throwing two grenades in rapid succession, Tony then began to fire the Sten gun methodically at the approaching Germans. Some fell in the hail of bullets, but there were always more to take their place. They fired unceasingly at the lone Englishman, crouched low behind a pile of rubble. Tony grabbed his last grenade and threw it. Then he pressed himself against the low wall which was his protection from the force of the blast, and from the advancing Germans. As the débris from the explosion ceased to rain down, he raised himself to where he could see the Germans spreading out around him. There seemed no hope in his situation. He felt a cold fear in the pit of his stomach. Not a fear of dying but a horror of surviving the next few minutes, and being taken once again to the cells beneath the SS Headquarters, to endure once more the full horror of Hitler's depraved élite. The trigger clicked against the empty magazine. Tony ripped it from his gun and threw it aside in desperation. Taking a firm grip on his last magazine, he slammed it into place. He began to fire steadily at the approaching Germans, determined to sell his life dearly. He could see the sky glowing orange and red now, lit by the fires raging within the docks, fires ignited by himself and his group. As he thought of his French comrades, he was relieved that they had all made their escape. They would be able to fight beside the liberating armies now, instead of in secret.

Tony's face was grim. But a light of triumph shone in his eyes as the first bullet tore into his shoulder. He turned to his left and fired awkwardly with one hand, bringing down the man who wounded him. Turning back, he pulled the trigger once more.

Nothing happened. With a roar of frustrated anger, he threw the gun at the approaching enemy and turned to run, only to be confronted by a group of Germans who had circled around behind him. Ignoring the fiery pain in his shoulder, he picked up a brick and threw it at the enemy. It was a futile gesture which could not harm them. But it made him feel better. Then he stood and waited, determined not to show any fear. The approaching soldiers halted, unsure what to make of the unarmed man who faced them so defiantly, left arm hanging awkwardly and dripping blood. Then over to the left, two shots rang out. Tony felt a blow to his left leg just below the knee. He crumpled to the ground as a fiery trail was burned across his chest by a second bullet. Waves of pain engulfed him. He felt his life's blood draining steadily from his body. His eyes found the soldiers who approached him slowly, but already his sight was growing dim, and their figures soon became too indistinct to see. It seemed to take a tremendous effort to hold his head up above the ground, an effort his body could no longer sustain. He lay down, surprised to find that the bricks and rubble, far from being hard, were as soft as a feather pillow beneath his cheek. As his eyes slowly closed, Tony was transported back once more to a grassy river bank beneath a warm summer sun. He seemed to turn his head, and there she was smiling at him, her eyes full of love.

"Sarah! I love you!"

Tony was not sure whether the whispered words actually issued from his lips or if they were only spoken in his mind. But he knew they had been said and that, somehow, Sarah would know that his last thought had been of her.

Tony lay for a long time with his eyes closed, wondering if this was heaven. He tried to move. Sharp knives of pain coursed through his body, and he knew he was not dead after all. Slowly he opened his eyes, and turned his head to survey his surroundings. He was in a small room lit by a naked bulb, which threw the bare stone walls into stark relief. The walls were unbroken by any obstruction, save for a heavy wooden door. The only furnishings, if they could be so called, were a bucket in one corner and the bed on which he lay. With tentative fingers he explored the thin mattress on the base of bare wooden boards. His joy at finding himself still alive began to recede, as he recognised the room for what it was, and the grim truth of his predicament burst on is brain. It was so similar to the room where he had been held before that there was no doubt in his mind that he was once more in the hands of the SS. For a moment he lay still, absorbing the facts of his situation. He knew that he would not be able to hold out under interrogation this time. He felt the hollow tooth with its hidden parcel of death with the tip of his tongue, and took a strange comfort from it. This time he was not solely at the mercy of his captors, but had the freedom to choose the time of his own death.

Summoning whatever reserves of strength he had, Tony moved his right hand, carefully exploring the areas of pain on his body. His chest was swathed with bandages. He probed them gently to reveal a long wound which, though painful, was not too hard to bear. He thought one of the bullets in its flight had cut a groove in the flesh of his chest. He was thankful it had not hit him an inch to the right, for then it would have entered his rib cage, and the chances were that it would have caused his death, through damage to either his heart or lungs. The exploring hand moved on to the left shoulder. Waves of excruciating pain flooded his being as he explored the bandaged wound. He could not determine the extent of the wound, and wrongly assumed that it felt worse than it was. In fact the bullet had entered through the shoulder blade, and as it exited had taken muscle and bone with it, leaving a gaping wound. Whoever had dressed it had cleaned it fairly well, but had not removed all the fragments of bone from the torn flesh nor attempted to mend the torn muscle. When the wound healed, always assuming that Tony would live long enough for it to do so, the shoulder would always be stiff and awkward to move. The only other part of Tony's body to pain him was his leg. A bullet had torn through the top part of the calf muscle, carrying much of it away in a gobbet of blood and flesh. The wound had been dressed, but again no attempt had been made to rectify any of the damage. The leg was bound to be weak when healed.

Tony wondered how long he had been lying in the cell, and who had dressed his wounds, but his questions went unanswered as the minutes and hours slowly ticked by. Gradually the pain was pushed to the back of his mind. Hunger and thirst took precedence in his tortured body, but pain and the loss of blood took their toll and he slowly succumbed to sleep once more.

The sound of a key in the lock and the heavy wooden door opening brought Tony back to wakefulness. He turned his head towards the entrance. His heart sank, though his face remained impassive as the two men walked in. Major Steinhauser's face wore a malicious grin as he looked at the helpless man on the bed.

"So we meet again." Tony said nothing as the major turned to the sergeant who accompanied him. "Well, Karl, what do you think of our brave Englishman now?"

"Like a snake with its fangs pulled."

Steinhauser laughed.

"At least the snake managed to cause you plenty of trouble before you were able to draw its fangs."

Steinhauser stopped laughing and glared at Tony. "Brave words, Englishman, but they won't sustain you when the questioning begins." His voice was harsh as he crossed the bare floor with brisk strides, blue eyes flashing. "You won't get away from us this time."

"That's irrelevant." Tony was defiant. The suicide pill gave him extra courage. He knew that he could always find blessed release if the pain of questioning was too great. "You must realise by now that you have lost this war. It is only a matter of time before the Allies are successful."

"You will never live to see that day!"

Tony smiled mockingly. "I know. But just knowing the day will come is enough for me!"

Steinhauser kicked the wooden bed. The vibrations jarred Tony's body. He gritted his teeth as waves of agony suffused his body. Steinhauser grinned as the Englishman gasped for breath.

"You have an inflated idea of your own worth. You are a worthless pawn in this war, and I won't waste my time with you. You have nothing that can be of any use to me now, so I'll have you moved to a place where they can interrogate you at their will, before executing you for the spy you are." Steinhauser turned on his heel and left the room with brisk strides. Tony frowned at Dresner.

"What does he mean by that?"

"You will be on the next transport to a labour camp, like all members of the Resistance who fall into our hands. We no longer waste our time with such rabble here."

The German turned and left the room. As the door closed and the key turned in the lock, Tony smiled. The Germans seemed rattled. A year ago they would not have considered the interrogation of an English spy as a waste of time. His heart lifted as he realised that this could mean only one thing. The Allies had landed at last, and the Germans were worried. He closed his eyes and willed his injured body to rest in preparation for whatever ordeals lay ahead, and said a silent prayer of thanks that he had lived long enough to see the beginning of the end for Germany.

161

The days passed slowly. Each day saw a small improvement in Tony's condition, as his wounds began the slow process of healing. It was still impossible for him to move his left arm without a pain in his shoulder of such nauseating intensity that it made the room swim around him. He could not put any weight on his mangled leg, but the wound to his chest was healing fast and he was able to sit and feed himself with his right hand.

By the time he had been in the hands of the Germans for a week, he was able to move a few paces, as long as he leant against the wall for support and moved slowly. He was trying to see how far he could walk when the door was opened. Two civilians entered, accompanied by a guard who pointed his rifle at Tony.

"Come now."

"Where?"

"Don't question, scum. Just come."

The two civilians moved forward, one either side of him, and supported Tony as they moved out of the cell. Each step was an agony as they led him along the narrow corridor and up the stairs. In the yard at the rear of the building a truck was waiting. As Tony hobbled forward, he could see that it was already full of tired, weary men, whose heads were held low beneath the threatening barrels of the German guns. The two men with Tony helped him into the back of the truck, the excruciating pain in his shoulder causing him to cry out, and the German guards laughed. Tony lay on the floor of the truck, gasping for breath as the two civilians climbed up behind him and sat down.

"Where are we going?"

"Silence!"

The butt of a rifle caught Tony in the ribs. He slipped into merciful oblivion as the truck began to move away.

Tony had no idea how long he had been unconscious. When he opened his eyes once more, he was in a dark, stuffy place, lying on bare wooden boards. Chinks of light shone through the cracks in the wooden walls. A hut perhaps? He struggled to sit up and felt a hand on his arm.

"Here, let me help you."

He turned his head to see who it was and saw a Frenchman in his forties, one of the two who had helped him into the truck.

"Where are we?"

"On a train."

Tony looked around. The confined space was full of men who stood or sat in the gloom. They looked depressed, as though they had no hope for the future. Tony frowned.

"This is a train?"

The man nodded. "Yes. They put us in a cattle truck."

"Who are all these people?"

"We're just ordinary men who've done something to annoy the Germans. We're being transported to a labour camp in Germany."

"Germany?"

The man nodded. "We are to work, to help the German war effort."

Tony felt his heart sinking. They would be moving east, away from the advancing Allied forces and any hope of rescue. There was no chance of him escaping alone in his present condition, and the future looked bleak. He began to realise why the men with him were so quiet and depressed.

"What's your name?"

"Henri Arnaud. I'm here because I drained the petrol from a German truck." He looked quizzically at Tony.

"What happened to you?" Tony thought for a moment. Should he tell this man who he really was, or should he continue with his cover story? Henri mistook his silence and made to turn away.

"You don't need to tell me. I'm sorry I asked."

"No. Wait." Tony smiled. "I'm sorry, I was just debating what to tell you. You see, I'm English and have been working in France under the name of Albert Fouquet. But now the Germans know I'm English, I can revert to my true name, though I shall tell them nothing else. I am Tony Kemshall and I am pleased to make your acquaintance, Henri."

Henri shook the proffered hand. "I'm pleased to meet you too, Tony." He indicated the bandages as he spoke. "Can you tell me what happened?"

"I sabotaged the docks, and was shot while trying to escape."

"A saboteur! You're lucky the Germans didn't shoot you straight away!"

As Henri spoke the train began to move. As it jolted forward Tony cried out in pain. Henri helped him to lie down again, and tried to make him as comfortable as possible. The truck swayed from side to side as it gathered speed. Henri wondered if the pale Englishman was well enough to withstand the rigours of a train journey that could last as long as two days. If he had known just how bad the journey would be, he would never have believed that Tony would reach their destination alive.

The train was made up of many trucks, and it wound its way eastwards like a slow snake. The hot sun beat down on the cattle trucks. They grew stuffy with the lack of air, for the only ventilation came from small slits high in the sides. During the first day, the prisoners ate and drank freely of the bread and water which had been placed inside the truck with them. But as the train was halted in a siding that night, the huge doors remained tightly locked and the men began to realise that their provisions might have to last them until they reached their destination, so they began to ration themselves carefully. As pressing as the need for food and water was, the suffering men found the need to relieve themselves even more demanding. The small bucket in the corner had overflown early in the afternoon. It was now surrounded by a pool of urine and excrement, attracting numerous flies, which were able to come and go through the cracks in the walls whenever they pleased. The smell was discomforting, and the men hoped they would be able to empty the bucket in the morning.

Before dawn the train moved on again, the bucket still unemptied. With the Allied landings a week old, transport priority went to troops and munitions trains so that the prison transport was shunted back and forth to keep the main lines clear. Sometimes they would travel for hours in an easterly direction, only to be sent south or north at the next town. Twice they travelled west for some indeterminable time before regaining their route once more. All the time, the conditions in the truck deteriorated. The bread, green with mould, ran out on the fourth day, some hours after the last drop of water had been drunk. The atmosphere was oppressive, hot and stuffy. A sickening stench of vomit and excreta filled the air, which was unbreathable. Henri had managed to widen a crack in the walls, so he and Tony could take welcome gulps of fresh air whenever possible. There was no doubt that this enabled them to survive, where others did not. A number of older men had already died by the end of the fifth day, unable to breathe, their bodies desperate for water. When the train stopped, the prisoners cried out and banged on the sides, pleading for provisions and a chance to unload the dead. But they were ignored. The bodies had to be piled beside the offensive bucket, whose filth had long since spread all over the floor so that the men sat in their own excreta. The smell of the dead mingled with the other smells, to create a miasma the like of which none of the prisoners could ever have imagined in their wildest nightmares.

Tony was thankful that Henri Arnaud stayed by his side. The rocking and bumping of the truck filled his wounded body with pain. At times he slipped into unconsciousness. He might have died, save for the ministrations of his new friend. The fresh air which came through the enlarged crack was more than welcome, helping Tony to fight off the fever which struck him on the second day, and did not leave him until three days later. Lying weakly beside Henri, he noticed that the Frenchman had done his best to keep the dressings of his wounds out of the filth covering the floor. But the white bandages were now grey, and he feared that if they were not changed for clean ones soon, infection might set in. It would be ironic if he died from gangrene, before the Germans were able to interrogate him.

The nightmare journey continued until, in the early afternoon of the seventh day, the train came to a halt. Tony pressed one eye to the crack. He looked out to see a marshalling yard full of German soldiers, with dogs barking and straining at their leashes. A sign over the small platform told the grim legend of their destination. BUCHENWALD. They had arrived.

The huge doors of the cattle truck were pushed open, allowing fresh air to enter for the first time in a week. Those who had survived dragged themselves through the muck and over the bodies of their dead comrades, gasping as the clean fresh air filled their lungs. Climbing down from the truck, they blinked hard as the bright sunlight burned their eyes. Tony stood supported by Henri, and stared in amazement. The few dozen men who had journeyed from Saint Nazaire were insignificant compared to the hundreds of people fighting their way out of the trucks of the long train. Trucks which had become coffins on wheels.

There was the sound of whips, the barking of dogs, the screaming voices of guards. It was chaotic, but slowly order was being made out of the chaos as the prisoners were pushed into columns of fives. Tony noticed that all those from the other cattle trucks were wearing a yellow star. Those who were slow to take their places were kicked or beaten, whips rained down on their shoulders and the huge German shepherd dogs bit and snarled at their heels. Tony and Henri found their place in the short column of people who had come from France and waited until the cattle trucks were empty of all, save the dead and those too weak to move. At last the prisoners were marched off.

The track was dry and sandy, lifting dust which settled on their filthy clothes and bodies like a crust. Tony was hardly aware of that, all he could think of was dragging his injured body forwards. Henri was at his side, constantly supporting and encouraging. Tony knew he would never have made it without that help. At last, over the heads of the men ahead of him, Tony was able to see his destination. A huge fence stretched away in both directions. At intervals of a few yards there were posts, with shelters high above them and in each shelter a guard. Beyond the fence were groups of buildings, but Tony was too far away to make out what they were.

The column slowed to a crawl. As Tony approached the huge iron gate, he saw that they were being divided. An SS officer watched those approaching impassively, as though assessing their worth. Some he sent through the gates and into the compound, while others were directed to follow the road as it turned left and continued parallel to the fence. As he watched, Tony felt he could discern the criteria for selection. The young and healthy went through the gates, while the old, children, the sick and those dreadfully weakened by the journey went to the left. The majority of those sent that way wore the gaudy yellow star. Henri and Tony approached the officer, who perused the Frenchman and indicated that he should enter the compound. His eyes roved over Tony's wounded body and pointed left. A young man at his shoulder whispered in his ear. He indicated Tony's injuries, and then a note in the file he carried. The officer held up his hand. Tony stopped. When the German beckoned, he limped forward, flanked by two armed guards.

"Name?" barked the SS officer.

"Albert Fouquet."

The young soldier whispered again.

"That's an alias. You are English?" Tony nodded. "Real name."

"Lieutenant Anthony Kemshall."

The young man beside the officer nodded, and pointed to something written in the file. The officer pointed to Tony, and then to the gates. Without a second glance at the young man, he continued to select which of the new arrivals were to go to the right and which to the left.

Tony hobbled through the gates to where Henri was waiting for him. Together they followed the rest of the column into the building, which they would come to know as the Sauna. Men in prison garb with a red cross painted on the back were yelling orders in German. The prisoners were ordered to take off their clothes, which were taken away to be de-loused and were never seen again. Then they marched into the showers where the lukewarm water washed away the filth of their journey. Tony's once white bandages were filthy. He removed them, and allowed the water to wash over his wounds, hoping that it would clear away any infection before it had a chance to take hold. On leaving the showers, the new arrivals at Buchenwald were dipped in disinfectant, a foul smelling greenish blue liquid. Tony gritted his teeth as the fluid burned into his slowly healing wounds. He felt as though a fire was raging through his skin, and he scrambled out at the far side as quickly as possible.

On the other side, he was greeted by a prisoner with a razor who set to work and shaved his head, the whole operation over in a few seconds. Tony reached up to touch the bare flesh of his scalp. It felt strange and cold. He shuffled forward, to where a huge pile of clothes had been left on the floor and watched as others who had just been shaved dived into the pile and began to put on clothing. Realising that this would probably be his only chance to find something to wear, Tony joined them. He took his prizes to a corner and put them on, a pair of striped trousers which barely reached his ankles, a shirt with the same stripes but no buttons, two odd socks and a pair of wooden clogs. It felt strange, as though he were no longer Tony Kemshall but someone else who had only just come into being, who had been born fully grown into a new and confusing existence. He had little time to contemplate this feeling, before being pushed by one of the prison guards in the direction of some young girls seated at desks. It looked as though they were doing some sort of office work, and he quietly waited his turn.

"Name?"

"Lieutenant Anthony Kemshall."

The girl wrote his details in an enormous ledger next to a number.

"Hold out your left arm."

434

He did so and the girl began to tattoo the same number onto his arm. His shoulder ached as he strained to keep his arm still while the needle dug into his skin time and time again, the pain of the needle nothing in comparison to that in his injured shoulder.

When she had finished, Tony looked down at his arm. 507924. Little did he know just how important that number was to be.

Tony followed the other new arrivals out of the building, then stopped and stared in horror at the sight which greeted him. All around him were people, men and women, who were little more than living skeletons. They walked slowly, dragging their feet. Some even crawled, while others lay still as though they had no energy left to move.

"My God! What sort of place is this?"

Henri shook his head. "Hell, I think."

A camp guard yelled at them. "You will soon have seen so many Muselmenn that you won't look twice. Come now to your block, or you will be beaten."

The two men moved with a smaller group into a section of the camp set aside for the quarantining of new arrivals. Both had been assigned to Block 17. They were told to sit on the lawn, the area of bare earth at the rear of the block, for no one was allowed to enter the building except at night. As Tony lowered himself painfully to the ground, Henri produced a spare shirt from where it was hidden inside his own.

"I got this when I saw that they hadn't redressed your wounds. It's not sterile, but at least it will keep the dirt out, and prevent your clothes from rubbing."

Tony smiled gratefully as the Frenchman tore the shirt and began to bind his wounds.

"Thank you, Henri."

The Frenchman grinned. "It's the least I can do for a man who led an attack on the port of Saint Nazaire."

The group sat on the ground for the remainder of the afternoon, enduring the heat and the dust and the smell until a whistle blew to call them back into the life of the camp.

"Zahlappell. Alles anstellen."

Evening roll call. The inmates stood in rows of five for over two hours until an officer came to count them, checking carefully that the number tallied with that in his book. When all was in order, the new arrivals were allowed to enter Block 17 at last. At the door they were handed meagre rations, under four ounces of bread and a small piece of margarine which they were told would have to serve for breakfast as well as supper. Tony looked at it in disbelief. How was anyone supposed to survive on so little? No wonder so many of the people they had seen were on the point of starvation.

Tony looked around at his new home. On either side of the two gangways which stretched the length of the block were continuous lines of three-tiered bunks. Each was to hold four or five people. The best places, those on the top, were already taken by men who had been there longer than the new party. Tony, Henri and the rest managed to squeeze in somehow on the bottom ones, which were hot and stuffy. Lying head to toe, with one thin straw mattress below them and an even thinner blanket above, they settled down for the night. A voice from the blackness called wearily down.

"Don't take off your clothes or shoes if you want to see them again. And put the rest of your bread ration inside your clothes or that will disappear too."

Tony had arrived in hell on earth.

162

It was four o'clock in the morning when Tony was awakened by the deafening sound of whistles. In the dark, confined space which was his shared bunk, he thought for a moment that he was back in the train. Then as people began to climb wearily from the neighbouring bunks, he remembered where he was, and rubbed the sore spot on his left arm where his number had been tattooed. It was time for morning roll-call. The occupants of Block 17 shuffled out into the dark to stand in rows of five, silently waiting for the time to pass until the count was taken at six a.m. On the way out, Tony was handed a dish of some foul smelling liquid, a herb tea, which he drank rapidly in his thirst, gritting his teeth against the nauseating taste. Fumbling inside his shirt, he pulled out the crust of bread he had saved from the night before. He nibbled hungrily on it, but it barely took the edge off the hunger which gnawed at his belly. As he joined the rest of the block in their regimented rows, there was a harsh whisper from someone close by.

"Don't lose that dish. No dish, no food."

Tony looked around, but could not see who had spoken. Grateful for the advice, he tucked the dish inside his shirt and took his place. The time passed slowly. Before long, his wounded leg began to throb painfully. To take his mind off the pain, Tony thought of home, the green fields, the trees, the river sparkling in the sunlight. Yet as the sun slowly raised its head above the horizon, the reality of the scene forced all thoughts of Heronfield from his mind. The ragged scarecrows of humanity surrounding him looked as though they had come straight from Dante's Inferno. Cheeks sunken, eyes deep set in black shadows, straggly hair growing in where it had been shaved, ill-fitting and ill matched clothes hanging from their skeletal frames. Tony glanced along the row of new arrivals to Block 17. He realised just how fit and healthy they must appear, to anyone who had been in Buchenwald for any length of time.

At last the count was taken. The new arrivals were ordered back to the large bare area behind the block, where they were to spend their day before evening roll call and being allowed inside once more. It was a hot day, with no shade. The new inmates sat or lay so that they would expend less energy. Some moved over to the walls of the block, where there was some shade, but this was sparse and the sun soon moved round, catching them with its full glare again. It was almost midday by the time the monotony of the day was broken. Henri pointed at some buildings on the far side of the compound.

"Something's happening over there."

Tony looked up as enormous drums were carried out of the kitchens. He watched in horror as men from the nearby blocks rushed forward. Some soup had been spilled, and the men lay on the ground, trying to lick it up before it soaked into the dry dusty earth. Others rushed over to the dustbins and delved deeply, in the hope of finding a scrap of potato peel. Tony shook his head in disbelief.

"Those poor devils must be starving."

"How long do you think it will be before we're like them?" Henri shuddered as he spoke. "Do you think their plan is to kill us by slow starvation?"

"I don't know, Henri. But I do know that I'll do my utmost not to end up like them. I intend to go home when this war is over." He looked over towards the drums of soup again. "Let's make sure we get our soup. It's the only way to make sure we don't end up like those Muselmanns."

The two men rose to their feet and made their way with the other members of Block 17 to the kitchens, where a single ladle of soup was slopped into their dishes. It was thin and watery to look at, with a few tiny pieces of what looked like potato and swede floating on top. Tony tasted it and grimaced. It was horrible tasteless stuff which made him want to vomit, but he was too hungry to leave it. There were no spoons so he went with Henri to sit in a small patch of shade beside the block, and sipped the lukewarm concoction straight from the dish. It left him still feeling hungry. He realised that this gnawing emptiness was going to be with him for as long as he remained in Buchenwald. He contemplated his situation throughout the long afternoon in the hot sun which sapped his body of liquid and energy. He was thankful when the whistles for evening roll call sounded once again, followed by the issuing of bread rations and bed.

So the pattern of Tony's first weeks in Buchenwald was set.

All newcomers to the camp were held in the quarantine blocks for six weeks. Tony was to be eternally grateful for this time of enforced inactivity, which gave his wounded body time to heal. By the time the quarantine was over, he could move his left arm without pain, although its movement was limited. He was unable to lift his elbow higher than his shoulder, and the muscles were weak. His leg had healed too, leaving a hollow on the calf muscle where some of the tissue had been shot away. He walked with a permanent limp now, but at least he was able to walk and to stand for the interminable hours necessary for the daily roll calls.

The first six weeks also taught him how to survive in camp, lessons learned from careful watching and overheard conversations. It was obvious from the start that no one could hope to survive on the food doled out to them, so this had to be supplemented in any way possible. He soon became aware of camp currency - food, clothing, bribery - and how to come by those commodities. The first time one of their number died, Tony was surprised to see his body stripped and his possessions stolen by those who had been longer in the camp than him. But then he saw those who had acquired the items with extra food, and realised that bread could be bought for boots. It was hard, the first time he took the coat from a dead man and exchanged it for two rations of bread, but the dead man no longer needed it, and he needed to survive. Once he was lucky enough to find a dead man with some food hidden in his clothes. He took it gratefully, though he swore he would never take from the living, only from those who no longer needed the things necessary for survival. So, gradually, he acquired a spoon, a pullover, and more importantly, extra food. By the time his six weeks' quarantine were over at the end of July, his weight had not fallen as low as many others who had come with him on the nightmare journey from Saint Nazaire and he felt able to survive in Buchenwald for as long as necessary. But that was before he learned about the work parties.

163

Sarah smiled at the young American, who grinned back.

"Thanks, nurse. That was just what I needed."

He handed the empty cup back to Sarah. She placed it on the table, then took the brake off his wheelchair and pushed him down the ramp and into the gardens. A thin blanket lay across his lap, covering the place where his legs had been, legs that lay somewhere in the fields of France. Sarah pushed steadily, taking care not to jar the raw stumps. It was a few minutes before they joined the other Americans in the shade beneath the trees. A table had been set up with a radio on it, and the sound of the Glenn Miller Orchestra enlivened the atmosphere. Sarah looked at the Americans. They were all recovering from wounds received as the Allied armies pushed across France. Many of them would never be the same again, but they took their changed situations stoically. They were ready to accept the sacrifice, now that they had the Germans on the run. Sarah put the brake on the wheelchair and laid a gentle hand on the young man's shoulder.

"Will you be all right here?"

"Yes. This spot's fine." He turned to look over his shoulder, and grinned up at the young Englishwoman. "Why not leave me for a while and get yourself a cup of tea. If I need anything, one of the fellas will lend a hand."

Sarah nodded. "O.K. I'll be back in half an hour."

"An hour?"

She smiled. "No, definitely not. This is your first time out. Dr. Millard says half an hour is quite long enough."

"O.K. You're the boss."

"I certainly am. Now enjoy yourself."

Sarah turned and made her way back inside the hospital. She did not really want a drink, but valued the chance to be alone. As she made her way up to the room she shared with Jane, she realised that she had done a lot of thinking lately, perhaps too much. But she could no more control the thoughts in her head than the feelings in her heart. Sitting down at the desk, she opened the small leather box and took out the golden heron. She remembered the previous Christmas when she had seen it for the first time, and it had symbolised for her all that was good and beautiful in her relationship with Tony. How could she have been so blind? If she truly loved him, surely she would have seen the real Tony who was battling to show himself, even though he was forced to keep so much secret? Surely if she truly loved him, she would have accepted him as he was without need of explanation? She had come to realise over the last long difficult weeks that yes, she did love Tony more than anyone else in the world and yes, she did miss him dreadfully. She did not know what she would do if he did not come back. Yet the overriding feeling amongst all her jumbled emotions was guilt. Tony had been working so hard and had been in need of a great deal of support, but she had not given it to him. Instead, she had heaped many more pressures on him and made a difficult life even harder to bear. Realistically she knew there was very little chance of her ever seeing Tony again. She would have been able to cope with that if only she had had a final chance to put things right with him. Why had she not been able to hold him one last time, to tell him that she was sorry, to let him see that she loved him and that he meant the world to her?

The door opened, and Sarah turned to see who had entered. Jane saw her friend, fingers gently caressing the small golden tie pin, tears in her eyes. She swiftly crossed the room to take hold of her hand.

"Are you all right, Sarah?"

Sarah nodded through her tears. "I guess so. I just can't believe that he's gone and I won't ever see him again."

Jane's voice was soft, her words sympathetic. "You've got to let go, Sarah. You can't waste the rest of your life mourning what might have been." She frowned. "You're really taking this bad, far worse than you took Joe's death."

"But don't you see?" Sarah's voice was pleading, begging to be understood. "Joe and I knew that we loved each other. I mourned him, but at least I had the happy memories

438

of our times together. But with Tony it was different. I sent him away without telling him how I really feel. I'll have to live with the knowledge that he went into danger without knowing whether I loved him or not. I let him down, Jane. I can never forgive myself for that."

"But I'm sure he understood, Sarah. He wouldn't have sent you that letter, or the heron, if he'd not believed that you truly love him."

"But I can never be really sure of that!" Sarah looked down at the heron and traced its outline with a gentle finger. "All I can do is pray that he's alive somewhere, and that one day I'll have the chance to put things right."

Jane squeezed her friend's hand gently. "Don't count on that Sarah. Captain Dawson said you should presume the worst."

"But there was no body! He could still be alive!" Sarah shuddered. "But knowing that is almost as bad as believing he's dead. Captain Dawson said that the SS had held him before and treated him cruelly. So if he's still alive, he must be suffering terribly." She lifted her tear- filled eyes to Jane. "I don't know what to do! Should I hope that he's alive? Or dead, beyond pain and suffering?" The tears began to roll down her cheeks, and a sob escaped her lips. "I just want him back, Jane. I want him back, and I want him to know that I love him."

Jane took her friend in her arms and cradled her head on her shoulders.

"Don't do this, Sarah. Forget the guilt and remember the good times. Remember him and be happy." As Jane whispered the words, she wondered if anyone who had been through what Sarah had since the outbreak of the war could ever be truly happy again.

164

With the Cotentin Peninsular finally in the hands of the Allies, the Americans turned south from St. Lo at the end of July. Within a week they reached Avranches. The Allies moved on into Brittany and had soon lifted the yoke of German occupation from the Bretan people, save at the ports of Lorient, La Rochelle and Saint Nazaire, which were to hold out defiantly for another nine months. So, with their rear secure, the Americans turned east in an attempt to free the rest of France and drive the retreating Germans back into their homeland. But The Germans were not about to fall in with the Allied plans. They launched a counter attack towards Avranches, creating a gap between the American armies and their British allies, who had reached as far as Falise, sixty miles to the east. Pressure was put on the Germans from both sides, and it was only a matter of time before the gap was closed.

165

The company approached Sourdeval in brilliant sunshine. The sky was cloudless, and the bright light reflected in the sparkling rays from the river which ran parallel to the road. Bobby and Al were unaware of the beauty of their surroundings as they moved slowly forwards behind the tank. It offered them some protection from the Germans, who fired continuously at their pursuers during their long, slow retreat. The huge gun on the tank roared as it continued to roll forward. Somewhere up ahead, there was the sound of an explosion as the shell found its target. Bobby was unable to see what it had hit. He felt little inclination to peer round the heavily armoured vehicle to find out. Lieutenant Cooper approached the leading members of his platoon in a crouching run, shouting instructions, his words almost lost in the sounds of battle which raged ahead.

"We're almost on the outskirts of the town! The tanks will go in and try to move out any German heavy armour. As soon as we reach the first buildings, you are to come out from behind the tanks and take cover where you can find it. We'll have to clear Sourdeval street by street, house by house if necessary, and it won't be a pleasant job. But it has to be done." He smiled encouragingly. "I know you can do it, boys."

The tank continued to trundle forwards, its great weight breaking up the road surface beneath its huge tracks. Suddenly Bobby realised that the fields on either side of the road had given way to houses. He glanced across at Al, who nodded knowingly, his face grim.

"I guess this is it."

The two men crouched low and sprinted to their left, where they dived behind the protective cover of a garden wall as bullets thudded into the brickwork all around them. They crawled along to the end of the wall, where they cautiously rose to their knees and peered over the top. The tanks had stopped their advance, and were firing at three Panzers which blocked their route into town. As the two men watched, the Panzers began to return fire, forcing them to crouch behind the protecting wall once more. The explosions rocked the earth for a few moments. The air was filled with dust, which clogged the throat and caused Bobby to cough dryly. Then there was the sound of moving tanks again. Bobby looked over the wall to see two of the Panzers retreating. The third was a flaming wreck, and Bobby could hear the screams of its trapped crew as they burned alive. Oblivious to what was happening inside the enemy vehicle, the American tanks began to move forward, taking away the corner of the house as they skirted the burning wreck. Bobby breathed deeply, taking a firm hold on his rifle and forcing his fears to the back of his mind. He turned to Al and spoke grimly.

"It's time we were gone."

Al nodded and the two men stood. Vaulting the wall they ran along the pavement, bullets spattered into the brickwork above their heads. They turned to fire at the German soldier in the doorway opposite as they ran. Bobby saw him fall, a huge red stain spreading across the front of his uniform, then the two Americans were in the shelter of a shop doorway. Bobby carefully reconnoitred the route ahead. They had lost sight of the tanks now. Every doorway and wall seemed to conceal an American soldier, as the attacking forces made their way slowly but steadily towards the town centre. As Bobby watched, one American soldier on the far side of the street collapsed, his head a fountain of blood. Al laid a hand on his arm.

"I'm sure that shot came from in here."

The two Americans moved quietly forwards. Al opened the door and Bobby slipped inside. It was, or had been, a furniture shop. The ravages of war had left it with virtually no stock, and what there was seemed worthless junk to the Americans, who had suffered none of the deprivations of war which had afflicted Europe. There was the sound of movement from the floor above. Bobby inclined his head towards the stairs, and Al nodded. Slowly, silently they approached. Bobby climbed first. A step creaked beneath his foot and he froze, but the sound had not been heard by whoever was concealed above, so he continued his slow ascent to the landing. Peering round, he saw that the second flight of stairs was clear. He waved to Al, who climbed up to join him. Bobby held his rifle at the ready, covering the stairs as Al climbed the second flight. As he reached the top, he saw a partially open door. Someone was moving in the room beyond, but he could not see who. With rifle trained on the door he nodded, and Bobby climbed up to join him. Within seconds the two men were standing side by side. Al looked across at Bobby.

"Now!"

Bobby kicked the door open as he spoke and the men charged into the room. The sniper in a German uniform had his back to them and was turning to face the intruders when their bullets ripped into him. The rifle slipped from his fingers and fell to the floor. A look of disbelief and fear filled his eyes before they glazed and he saw no more. Bobby stepped forward and gazed down at the inanimate bundle which had so recently been a living, breathing human being.

"God! He's little more than a boy!"

The face, relaxed now in death, was clear skinned. A faint downy growth clung to his top lip, as though he had laboured to grow a moustache to prove himself a man. The uniform hung on a body two sizes too small to fit it.

Al joined his companion and gazed at the pathetic remains, his eyes filled with compassion.

"Poor kid. The Germans must really be on their last legs if they're drafting boys as young as this."

The sound of gunfire from outside finally intruded on their thoughts. Bobby moved over to the window, stepping round the body on the way. As he peered cautiously out, he saw that the battle had moved away from them.

"Come on, Al, or we'll get left behind!"

The two Americans raced downstairs and out into the street. Somewhere over to their right they could hear the chatter of a machine gun, and the sound of an explosion, probably a grenade, which silenced it. Crouched low to minimise their targets, the two men ran forwards, guns held out in front of them at the ready. At the next corner they halted and peered cautiously round. In the small square, a group of Americans had taken cover behind an overturned truck. They were firing across the open space at a building which must have held at least one machine gun, for the return fire was fast and furious.

"Let's move round and try to outflank it."

Bobby nodded at Al's suggestion, and the two men moved cautiously off to the right. As they crossed the open corner of the square, the enemy machine gun fired again. Bobby ran to the nearest cover.

"That was close."

There was no reply. Bobby looked round to see that Al was no longer with him. Peering back from behind this cover he saw his fellow American lying still in the road. For a moment he thought he was dead, then an arm moved as Al tried to drag himself along. Slinging his rifle onto his back, Bobby took a deep breath and rushed out into the open once more. Within seconds he had his hands under Al's arms, and he dragged the wounded man back out of the line of fire. Each movement caused Al to scream in agony. Bobby was afraid the sound would draw enemy fire in their direction, but it was just one more noise amidst the din of battle and they made it safely, the enemy only opening fire when it was too late.

Al lay gasping on the ground, his face pale and creased in agony.

"How bad is it?" he gasped.

Bobby looked down. Both of the legs were bathed in blood. He could not see the extent of the damage, but he knew it must be considerable as he watched the blood pump out. He looked back at Al's face, his eyelids flickering as he fought to remain conscious.

"Don't worry pal, you'll be fine." Bobby wasn't sure that he believed his own words. He took out his knife and began cutting away Al's trousers. "I'll just dress these for you, then get a couple of stretcher bearers."

"Bobby?"

"Yes?"

"Will you do something for me?" His voice was weak, and Bobby had to lean close to his face to catch his words. "If I die, will you make sure Jane is OK?"

"You're not going to die."

"Please, Bobby."

Bobby nodded. "Of course, Al. I promise."

Al relaxed, as though now he knew someone would take care of Jane, he could give in to the pain of his wounds. As he lapsed into merciful unconsciousness, Bobby tore the material away from his legs and looked at the wounds. His left leg had been hit twice, flesh wounds which he thought would heal well. But the right leg was a mass of mangled flesh, with splintered bone protruding at a number of places. Bobby did not know how many of the machine gun bullets had hit the leg, but he knew that there was little chance of recovery for it. Working swiftly, he used the trousers to tie a tourniquet and was relieved to see the flow of blood from the wounds slow and finally stop.

"Stretcher bearers! Stretcher bearers!"

He called loudly for assistance as he bandaged the wounds as best he could, praying that help would not be long in coming.

166

The gap between the British and American armies at Falise was finally closed on 20th August. While most of the German army managed to make good their escape, fifty thousand Germans were taken prisoner. The spirit of the French people was high. After four years of occupation, liberation was now at hand, and those people who had been so suppressed by their conquerors were now able to strike a blow towards their own freedom. On 15th August, the Metro workers in Paris went on strike, to be joined later by the police. The Resistance movement began to fight the Germans on the streets of their capital city. Much as the Allies wanted to be seen bringing liberation to the French people, they finally admitted that the Free French, who had fought bravely throughout the war years, deserved the chance to be the first to enter Paris. A French armoured division under Leclerc was sent to the city which they entered on 25th August, followed later that same day by de Gaulle.

While the people of Paris were celebrating their liberation, Al was lying in a convalescent hospital in Wales. The Forward Dressing Station had tended his wounds, then sent him back down the lines and across the Channel to Britain. He now awaited a ship back to America. He had written to Jane telling her of his wounds, and wondered fearfully what her response would be. He knew that she loved him, but that had been in the past when he had been a whole man. Would he now be able to provide for her and the baby? Would she want him to? He lay in his bed and worried, wondering if his happiness had been destroyed forever in the streets of Sourdeval.

167

Sarah was tired after a long night on duty, and made her way gratefully to the room she had shared with Jane for so long. It seemed strange to think of someone else sharing it with her, but she knew that time could not be far away. Jane's body was swelling with its precious burden. She would soon be giving up work, to move back with her mother until after the birth of the baby.

She pushed the door open and slipped in quietly not wanting to wake Jane, who was not due on duty for another few hours. She was surprised to see her friend cramming her belongings into a suitcase, her uncombed hair hanging loosely and the tracks of tears on her face.

"Jane! What's wrong?"

"It's Al! I have to be with him!"

Sarah's heart sank. Not more bad news. Would this war never end? She took Jane gently by the shoulders and turned her around.

"Sit down, Jane. Calm yourself. Getting worked up like this can't be good for the baby."

Jane tensed as though to pull away, but then suddenly relaxed and allowed Sarah to lead her across to the bed and sit her down. Sarah knelt on the floor at her feet.

"Now tell me what this is all about."

Jane sniffed and wiped her tear-filled eyes on the back of her hand.

"It's Al. I got a letter from him in the early post."

Sarah felt relief flooding through her body. If he had written, then things could not be all that bad. She took Jane's hand gently in hers.

"What did he say?"

"He was wounded." Her eyes, full of love and pain, fixed on Sarah's upturned face. "He's lost a leg, Sarah. My poor Al is crippled." The tears flowed again as she thought of the handsome young GI she had first met and fallen in love with, so tall and straight, so perfect.

There were tears in Sarah's eyes too as she sought to comfort her friend.

"We've seen many men like that, Jane. He can be rehabilitated. His life will be different, but he will still have so much to give."

Jane nodded. "I know that, but Al doesn't. He said in his letter that he didn't know if he could provide for me and the baby. He sounded as though he felt that I might not love him anymore." She managed to smile weakly through her tears. "He's such a fool, isn't he? How could he think I'd ever stop loving him?"

Sarah looked at the partially packed suitcase. "Are you going to him?"

Jane nodded.

"I've spoken to Dr. Millard, and he's given me immediate compassionate leave. I would have been leaving soon anyway, so I won't be coming back."

"Where will you go?"

"To Wales. Al's there at the moment. When he's well enough, they'll ship him back to America and I'll go with him." She looked across at the mess on her bed. "I'd better finish packing. A taxi is coming for me in half an hour."

"Come on, then. I'll help you."

So the two friends worked together, packing away more than four years of memories. They were both tearful as they stood on the steps of Heronfield House half an hour later. The taxi driver put Jane's belongings into the boot, and Sarah smiled at her friend through her tears.

"I'm going to miss you, Jane."

"I'll miss you too."

"You won't have time. Not with Al and the baby." Sarah's eyes filled with compassion. "Make sure you take good care of him."

Jane nodded.

"I will. And don't you let Bobby slip through your fingers."

Sarah shook her head sadly. "I don't know Jane. He's a good man, but I'd rather wait for Tony to come home."

"Hope is a good thing Sarah, but you must be realistic. Don't hope for too much, or you're going to be hurt again."

"I'll be careful."

The two young women stood looking at each other for a moment, then suddenly they were in each other's arms. Their tears fell as they said goodbye. They had shared so much in the years since the early days of the war - sadness, pain, hard work and much joy and laughter. It was a period of their lives that would live on in their memories and in their hearts as the years of war turned to years of peace. They might never see each other again, but they had grown as close as sisters. In their hearts they would never be apart.

"Keep in touch."

Jane pulled back and wiped away her tears.

"I'll write and let you know my new address as soon as I have it."

"Goodbye, Jane. And good luck."

Jane nodded, unable to speak, her heart full. She made her way down the steps and into the waiting taxi. As it drove away, she turned and waved at Sarah, who raised her hand in acknowledgment. It was not the way she had envisioned their goodbye, but as she watched the car go out through the gateway, she thought perhaps it was better this way. It had all happened so quickly that there had been little time for sadness. As she made her way back into the hospital she realised just how strange it was going to be without Jane. She wished her friend all the luck and happiness the world could give.

The letter from Bobby arrived four days later. He had written as soon as he could after Al had been wounded, in the hope of giving Sarah and Jane fuller information than the authorities usually did. He told how they had fought side by side from the beaches of Normandy, although much had been blacked out by the censors, and explained how Al received his wounds. From that point, the letter changed direction, becoming more personal and full of emotion.

> 'It was strange to see Al more concerned for Jane and the baby than for his own wounds. I realised that there's no-one waiting for me like she's waiting for him. It made me feel as though my life has been worthless with no one to leave behind, no-one to miss me if I should die, no one to be there to welcome me if I do come home.
>
> I'm sure you know what I'm trying to say, Sarah. I love you and it would make me feel so good to know that you love me too, and that you're waiting for me and there is some purpose to my life. Being out here amidst all this fighting makes you concentrate your thoughts more on the meaning of life and I know that my life would be meaningless without you. Say that you love me, Sarah. Say that you will wait for me. Say you will marry me, and come home to America with me when this war is over. I will never hurt you, no matter what.
>
> All I want to do is to make you happy, and to feel that you want to do the same for me.
>
> Write soon and say yes.

All my love.
Bobby

Sarah's face was filled with sadness as she read the words. She could not do the one thing that would make Bobby happy. She knew it was going to be difficult, but there was only one thing she could do. Taking paper and pen, she sat down and began to write. She told Bobby all about Captain Dawson's visit, and what he had told her about Tony. Putting it all on paper made it all more real to her, as though the act of writing made the deeds. As she wrote as objectively as she could, she realised that the chances of Tony returning were minimal. But she knew she had to wait. It was hard to tell a living man that you could not marry him because you were waiting for someone else who was probably dead. By the time she had finished the letter she felt drained. Drained, but in control of her destiny once more.

168

The occupants of Block 17 were seated as usual in the open area behind the building, when an SS guard approached with a group of prison guards who bawled and shouted at them. Moving quickly to avoid a beating, the prisoners lined up and waited sullenly for the SS guard to speak. He perused the ragged scarecrows with disgust.

"Today your quarantine is over, and you will be moved into the main camp. Tomorrow you will begin to earn your bread."

He turned and began to walk away. The prisoners followed, encouraged by the camp guards who yelled and struck out at them. Over the weeks, Tony had learnt that these guards were prisoners who had worked their way up to the job, which was considered a privileged position. As far as he was aware, the only criterion for holding the job was that you had to be of a vicious and cruel nature, which revelled in beating those too weak or too afraid to fight back. The column of prisoners shuffled their way along the track, and into the main compound with its rows and rows of huts. The workers had already left for the day so that the only people around were those whose duties kept them in the camp, or those too sick to work, or the Muselmenn, and it was never long before the people of the latter two groups disappeared into a separate part of the camp and were never seen or heard of again.

As they marched past the 'hospital hut' Tony wondered what kind of medical attention a prisoner might receive there. They passed the kitchens and what looked like another shower block, before the SS guard halted at a hut, indistinguishable from all the other huts in the camp.

"This is your hut. You may not enter until after evening roll call." He perused the prisoners. "You are excused work today. 507924." There was silence then the guard spoke again, his voice harsh. "Prison 507924 step forward!"

Suddenly Tony realised that that was his number. He took one pace forward. A camp guard brought his stick down heavily across Tony's back, and he cried out as waves of agony swept through his newly healed shoulder. A voice bellowed in his ear.

"Respond quicker, scum! You don't keep the guards waiting!"

A hand pushed him hard in the centre of the back. Tony stumbled forward until he stood barely three paces from the guard, who glared at him.

"You. Come with me." As he spoke the guard turned and marched away. Ton
glanced back over his shoulder towards where Henri was standing with the othe
prisoners. The Frenchman was frowning, but managed a weak smile of encouragemen
as Tony turned and followed the guard in the direction of the main gate. At the gate wa
a green hut, the SS Headquarters. The guard halted outside.

"Wait here."

Tony watched the guard make his way up the steps and through the door. H
wondered what it was all about, afraid that the questioning was about to begin at las
The guard came out and marched away, without a second glance at Tony. He continue
to stand for almost an hour, the sun beating down on his scalp with its thin covering o
hair which had grown back since his arrival at Buchenwald. At last the door opened an
another guard appeared.

"507924?"

"Yes, sir."

"This way."

With his heart in his mouth, Tony ascended the steps and entered the SS HQ. Th
interior was dim after the brilliant sunshine outside, and it took a few moments fo
Tony's eyes to adjust. On his left was a desk, where a young German in SS uniform wa
pounding away at a typewriter. To his right, another young man was rummaging in
filing cabinet. The guard who told Tony to enter indicated a door in the far wall.

"This way."

The name on the door told Tony all he needed to know. He cringed inwardly. Majo
Hase. Was this it, then? With some trepidation he followed the guard across the oute
office to the door, where the guard knocked and waited. The response was almos
immediate.

"Enter."

The guard opened the door, pushed Tony through, then closed the door behind him
Tony eyed the officer behind the desk, concealing his nervousness beneath a calm
exterior. The major was leaning back in his leather chair, every line of his bod
communicating relaxed superiority. His piercing eyes took in the detail of Tony'
appearance, and he smiled maliciously.

"So, you are the English spy from Saint Nazaire. You don't look so confident now
feel." Tony did not answer. "I see your injuries have healed. Good. We only use fit mer
here. The others are... expendable." He chuckled and Tony felt a shiver run down hi
spine. There seemed to be something inherently evil about this man.

"Do you know why I have called you here?"

Tony shook his head. He felt sweat break out on his brow, thinking of the agony he
had already endured at the hands of the SS. Hase must have read something of his
thoughts in his eyes, for he laughed.

"You think I am going to torture you for information. You are not that important,
507924. Whatever you could tell me now is irrelevant. Saint Nazaire has not fallen to
your weak attempt at an invasion, and shall never do so. You see, spy, your work wa
totally wasted. So, what shall I do with you now?"

Tony spoke for the first time.

"I suppose you will shoot me."

The major's malicious grin returned.

"No, spy. That would be too quick and easy. You will work like all the other
prisoners here, until you are unfit to work any more, like those living skeletons, those
Muselmenn, outside. Then you will be disposed of." He eyes roved over the tall straight
figure of the Englishman. "I warn you, it will be far worse torture than any you endured

in your previous questioning."

Hase looked at his watch and frowned.

"I have no more time to waste on an insignificant prisoner. Get out."

Tony turned and left, his mind in a whirl as he crossed the outer office, and left the SS HQ. He made his way back to the hut which was now his home. Of all the things he had feared in his confrontation with the authorities, this outcome had never featured in his nightmares. To be classed as insignificant, not worthy of wasting SS time. Did this mean that the Allied invasion had failed? Had Hase been telling the truth when he said that Saint Nazaire had not fallen? As Tony walked back through the camp, unable to take his eyes from the living dead around him, he fervently hoped not. If he were to remain in Buchenwald for any length of time, he knew he would be unlikely to survive.

The following morning, with roll call over and the sun barely above the horizon, the inmates of Tony's hut, around eight hundred of them, were divided into four groups. Each group had its own Kapo, who was in charge of the work party. Under him were assistant guards, who each kept an eye on ten prisoners. Looking at their grey faces and their dull expressionless eyes, these people had obviously been in the camp for some time. It was a job no newcomer could hope to attain. The morning was still cool as the work group to which Tony and Henri had been assigned moved off, but the cloudless sky held the promise of another scorching day. As they passed the green hut housing the SS HQ, Tony thought again of his conversation of the previous day. He wondered if the invasion really was going badly, or if Hase had said that to dishearten him. Soon however, as the sun rose higher and the morning grew warmer, Tony stopped thinking of France and concentrated on his surroundings. The group marched with the Kapo in front and the rear guarded by a soldier with a German shepherd dog straining at its leash. They passed nothing but camps with their barbed wire and sentry boxes. Tony wondered how many poor unfortunate souls were incarcerated in Buchenwald.

They walked for almost an hour before the fences finally came to an end and the fields began, fields which had not felt the touch of a plough for years, deserted farms which looked forlorn in the empty landscape. Tony realised that the whole area surrounding the camps must have been evacuated of all civilians, leaving nothing but rabbits and foxes to inhabit the once prosperous farms. At times the work party marched beside a railway, which led off in the direction of Buchenwald. Twice they were passed by trains drawing long lines of cattle trucks such as the one Tony had travelled in. He wondered how many more poor wretches were lying beside their dead comrades inside.

Tony's left leg was aching badly when the Kapo finally called a halt. They had been marching for more than two hours before Tony was finally able to sink gratefully to the dry dusty earth, gasping for breath. Henri dropped down beside him.

"How's the leg?"

Tony massaged the aching calf muscle.

"Painful, but I think it will hold out."

A whip cracked, and Henri felt its sting across the back of his neck.

"Get up, scum!"

The two rose wearily to their feet, and the guard pointed out an enormous pile of rocks beside the road.

"Carry those across the field, to where they are working on the new road."

Tony looked in disbelief at the huge stones which had to be moved. Surely the guard was joking! The whip cracked again. This time Tony felt its sting.

"Get moving!"

He bent over the pile of rocks and instinctively grasped the smallest one. Marshalling all of his strength, he heaved it up into his arms. His wounded shoulder complained at the brutal treatment. But it was now eight weeks since he had been wounded, and the six weeks' quarantine had helped the torn flesh and bone to heal. The shoulder reluctantly held out under the strain, as Tony limped with his burden in the direction of the road builders. He stumbled onwards, sweat pouring from his brow and into his eyes, until at last he reached his destination. He dropped the stone beside a prisoner, whose job it was to split the rock with a hammer until it was in pieces small enough to be used to make a road surface. Tony watched for a moment as he regained his breath. The pain of a wooden club crashing into his ribs forced him to double over.

"Back to work!"

Tony limped back to the huge pile of stones, picked up another and began to make his way back towards the new road. So the morning passed, the heat building up in intensity until it sapped their strength and forced the moisture out through the pores of their bodies. By the time a halt was called for lunch, the specific pains in Tony's wounded shoulder and leg were lost in the general agony which pervaded his whole body. His tongue was swollen in his dry mouth, and he lay panting on the ground, as the drums of cold soup were pulled towards them on little wooden carts drawn by prisoners. Tony reached inside his clothing for his precious bowl, without which he would not be fed, and reached over to tap Henri on the shoulder.

"Come on, let's eat."

The older man groaned loudly. "I don't think I can handle this, Tony."

"Of course you can." Tony helped the Frenchman to his feet. "It's an attitude of mind. If you think you can't survive, then you won't. You must tell yourself that you will live. It's the only way."

Henri stumbled forward to join the shuffling line of men waiting for their rations. When their turn finally came, the usual ladle of thin soup was slopped into their bowls. Henri looked in disbelief at the prisoner who served him.

"Is this all? Don't we get more if we are working?"

The man shook his shaved head. "No. Everyone gets the same ration."

"What about water?" Tony's voice was hoarse.

"You get the usual ration after roll call this evening."

The two friends looked at each other in disbelief, then made their way to one side. They sat down and sipped the cold, tasteless liquid which was their main meal of the day. It did not fill the gnawing emptiness in their bellies, but it went some way towards alleviating their thirst, after all the soup contained little else but water. They had barely emptied their bowls, licking the last drops from them with eager tongues, when the Kapo began to scream once again.

"Back to work, scum!"

Tucking the precious bowls inside their clothes once more, the prisoners rose wearily to their feet and began the endless task of moving the stones. Each time a prisoner halted in his work, he was kicked or beaten until he began again. The sky was still cloudless, and the sun a bright ball of fire. The prisoners prayed for rain to wet their parched lips, but no rain came. The work was arduous, and the day long and weary. But it eventually passed, as all time must, and the long tiring march back to camp began.

Tony felt that he did not have the energy for the march back to the hut. His shoulder ached unceasingly, and his limp was far more pronounced than it had been when they had begun work. Yet he managed to shuffle along with the rest of the column. Those still able to walk helped to drag along the others, who were too weary to make it on their own. The march took appreciably longer than it had in the morning. The bruised and battered, almost unconscious, prisoners arrived back in the early evening to face the inevitable wait for roll call, and stood to attention for almost three hours until the count had been made. Finally making their way back into the hut, their faces lightened for a moment as they received their daily ration of bread and water. Tony was thankful that this was one of the two days of the week when an additional piece of cheese or sausage was given. Tonight he took the tiny morsel of sausage gratefully. He shuffled over to join Henri on the edge of the bunk they shared with six other men. Tony broke his bread in half, tucking one piece inside his clothing for breakfast and began to chew on the second. Although he was hungry, or perhaps because of it, he ate slowly, savouring each mouthful. Nothing was said as he and Henri ate their supper, bread first, then the mouthful of sausage followed by the water. When he had tucked his bowl away, Tony lay down beside Henri.

"I'm still hungry and thirsty."

Henri nodded. "I think that's how we'll feel for the rest of our time here."

Tony was exhausted. His eyes were closing as he spoke to Henri. "One thing is certain, we won't survive long at this job. We must find a way of getting easier work."

There was no reply from Henri. He was already asleep, and soon Tony joined him in that blissful state where pain and hunger could not reach him.

169

Two weeks later the weather broke, changing overnight from burning hot sun to solid drenching rain. The prisoners welcomed the change at first. It felt good to be wet, to hold your face up and feel the cool moisture soaking into parched and dry skin, to stick out your tongue and taste the fresh raindrops. At every opportunity bowls were held out to catch the rain, before transferring it to eager lips which drank thirstily. For the first time in weeks, Tony did not feel that he would die of thirst. The rain continued for days, and soon its novelty wore off. Clothes never seemed to dry. Mud clung to heavy wooden clogs which made the march to work seem even longer. The wet stones slipped and were dropped, exhausting the workers further and causing many injuries.

Tony and Henri had lost a lot of weight. They dragged themselves back and forth to their work area with ever decreasing energy. Finally the day came when Henri could not manage the walk back to camp. Tony half supported half carried his friend for the last half mile. He was totally exhausted by the time evening roll call was over and knew they had reached the point of no return. A number of men in their work group had already collapsed, unable to work. They disappeared, never to be seen again. If that was not to happen to Henri and Tony, something drastic had to be done. Fast.

When Tony was awakened by the sound of whistles the next morning, he had a plan. As he and Henri ate their meagre bread ration, Tony explained.

"I've thought of a way out of our work party. It's simple, but hopefully effective. We can't keep doing the work we have been and survive for much longer. So we just smuggle ourselves into another group. It doesn't matter what work they do, it can't be as bad as carrying rocks."

"But surely we'll be missed."

Tony shrugged. "Maybe, maybe not. They're usually only concerned that they bring back the same number they take out. They rarely know who exactly is in the group. It's a risk I'm willing to take. What about you?"

Henri took no time at all to think about it. "I can't survive this work much longer I'm with you."

So, immediately roll call was over, the two friends slid behind the block to conceal themselves. From their hiding place, they watched the Kapo come to collect his group. The column formed up and moved out in the same manner as usual. No-one commented on the two missing men. When they had marched out of sight, Tony and Henri smuggled themselves into another party.

This time they marched in a different direction through the thin rain, the heavy mud clinging to their feet, and stopped after only one hour. Once they had reached their destination, the group began digging with heavy wooden spades. Each man had his own allotted patch which had to be dug during the day, and the newcomers set to. It was hard. The wet soil clung to the spades, the mud was heavy with retained water, but it was not as hard as the work on the roads. By midday Tony was tired, but not as totally exhausted as he had been before, and he knew they had made a change for the better. He sat next to Henri, as he supped his soup diluted even further with rain water.

"Are you glad we made the change?"

Henri shrugged in typically Gallic fashion. "The work is easier but I don't like it."

Tony frowned. "Why not?"

Henri turned to look quizzically at him. "What are we doing?"

"Digging."

"Digging what?"

It was Tony's turn to shrug. "I don't know. It seems as pointless as everything else about this place."

"We're digging graves, Tony."

"Graves?" Tony looked at the holes, and realised that what Henri said was true. But these were no ordinary graves. They were enormous pits, designed to take scores of bodies at a time. He shuddered at the thought of the Muselmenn who crawled through the camp. So this was their final resting place.

"Perhaps we should try to get out of this work group."

Henri shrugged. "Yes. If the opportunity arises. But someone has to do it, or disease will be even more rampant in the camp than it is now. I know one thing, I won't give up this work to go back to the roads. All that will do is to hasten the day when I shall be filling one of these holes myself."

Tony said nothing. He recognised the truth of Henri's words. Buchenwald was no place to try to make a political or moral statement. Only one thing mattered, survival. He would do anything to stay alive. If that meant digging graves for those less fortunate than himself, then that was what he would do.

The afternoon passed slowly, with the graves growing gradually deeper. Each time Tony stopped to ease his aching shoulder or rest his blistered hands, he would feel the blow of a heavy wooden club adding to the numerous bruises covering his body.

As the dull day was drawing to a close there was the sound of cracking wood, followed by a whimper from somewhere to Tony's right. He looked round, to see that the man digging the area next to him held the two pieces of his broken spade in his hands. His eyes darted wildly around, searching for a means of escape from the retribution he knew was about to descend upon him. But there was no escape. The nearest guard saw he had stopped work and approached. Seeing the broken spade he began to hurl insults, screaming and shouting obscenities as his club came down across the man's unprotected shoulders. The worker scrambled from the almost completed grave. He tried to run, but the SS guard further along the row saw him, and released his German shepherd from its leash. The dog leapt forward, and sank its teeth into the man's leg. With a scream he buckled and fell. The Kapo approached, and rained blows down upon his shoulders and arms, which were raised to protect his head. Gradually the screams diminished to whimpers. The blows began to reach his skull, and the man fought to retain consciousness. As he tried desperately to drag himself away from his tormentor, the dog tore away part of his leg. The man screamed in agony. Tony felt sick as he watched the dog wolf down the human flesh, then leap back into the fray. At last the man's cries ceased. Moments later his body was still. The only sounds to be heard were the dull thud of the club descending on his lifeless body, and the sound of the dog's teeth tearing at his flesh. The SS guard approached leisurely and called the dog back. It went reluctantly, its jowls dripping blood, a length of human flesh still hanging from its jaw. The Kapo finally stopped wasting his energy on the dead man and kicked the body into the grave. The man who had so recently toiled to dig it, was now its first occupant.

The guard had obviously enjoyed his outburst of violence. A huge grin stretched across his face. His eyes were wide and shining with excitement, and he began to look around, searching for another victim. Tony hurriedly began to dig again, studiously keeping his eyes from the pitiful remains of the man beside him. He desperately tried to make his shaking limbs work, and stop his heaving stomach from emptying its meagre contents. Somehow he managed to avoid the guard's attention. He worked on, his mind no longer on his surroundings, but seeking refuge once again in thoughts of home and of the woman he loved.

170

Summer moved inexorably towards autumn. Tony lost himself in the dreary round of life in the camp. He concentrated on what he would have to eat next, how he could avoid work, how long he could survive. Sometimes as he lay in the crowded bunk during the long dark nights, he wondered how far the Allied armies had got. Would they reach Germany this year? Would the war be over by Christmas? Would he still be alive when the liberators arrived? Would they come at all? There was no way of knowing the answers to these questions, so he tried to push them to the back of his mind along with his hunger and pain. Instead he thought of home. How he missed England. How he longed to walk once more beneath the trees of Heronfield, or beside its flowing crystal river. His dreams, waking or sleeping, were haunted by faces; David, dead for four years now, but still as much a part of Tony's heart as he had been in childhood; his mother, so beautiful and loving; his father's stern features, which concealed a caring heart. There was once face, however, which was with him more frequently than the rest. Sarah's. Did she think he was dead? Had she taken the advice of his letter and married that American soldier? Or was she still waiting for him to come home? He clung to the last thought like a leach. He imagined Sarah at Heronfield, waiting for him to come home, eager to take him in her arms and to kiss away his hurts. Dwelling on such thoughts gave him the strength to face each new day, determined to survive and to go home to the woman he loved.

It was almost three months since Tony had arrived at Buchenwald. His shower on arrival had been the last time he had washed. If a relatively clean puddle could be found, he could rub himself down with the water, as long as he was not so thirsty that he would fall down on his knees and lap it up like a dog. His skin was a colourful patchwork, grey where the dirt and grime had engrained itself in the pores, blue where he was bruised, red from sores. His hair grew back and was now home to hundreds of lice which he found quite impossible to kill. They formed into crusts on his scalp and burrowed down under the skin where they itched like mad, but could not be scratched. If the skin was broken, it would undoubtedly become infected. His clothing was alive with fleas which he shook out daily. He watched them run away seeking new homes, leaving his body covered in red spots, like measles. From head to toe he was covered with scabs and boils from which pus had to be squeezed out at regular intervals to prevent further infection. But they would not heal. They left behind holes of increasing size in his flesh, which was wasting away as the calories he used up were not replaced. Tony felt as though he were rotting alive. Yet he was determined not to give in, striving all the time to keep as clean as possible and to drive away the parasites. He knew that if he was to become infected with scabies or any similar condition, he would disappear just as the Muselmenn did, and never be seen again.

After some weeks on the grave-digging work party, Tony had again hidden one morning to avoid work. He joined another group in order to try to find a job that would provide him and Henri with more food. Without it, he feared the Frenchman would not survive the coming winter. He was already much weaker than Tony and often found it almost impossible to manage the march back to camp after a day digging graves. Tony was lucky once again. This time he found himself in a work party digging potatoes, a task that was a little easier than grave digging. At the end of the day he managed to smuggle two potatoes into camp, one under each armpit. As he lay in bed that night, he showed his treasure to Henri.

"What do you think?" He was grinning broadly, an expression Henri had not seen on his face for months. Henri himself was wide-eyed with surprise. He swallowed the saliva which flowed at the sight of the two small, muddy potatoes. He reached out tentatively and touched one. It felt so solid, so real that he knew that this was not one of the hundreds of dreams about food that he had. He looked at Tony.

"Just what you need to keep you going through the winter."

"Not just me, Henri. We're a team. You cared for me on the train and I owe you my life."

He held out one of the potatoes, and Henri took it gratefully. The two men carefully brushed off the dried earth and bit into the vegetables. They were hard, but neither man cared as they chewed on the food, their jaw muscles aching through lack of use. The raw potatoes tasted like heaven to the starving men who chewed each mouthful slowly and with relish. At last the potatoes were finished. They licked the last drops of starch from their fingers. Tony sighed with satisfaction.

"That was lovely. But next time I'll try to cook them!"

"Will there be a next time?"

Tony smiled at his friend and nodded. "I don't see why not. But I really need to bring many more back. That way we can exchange them for other things we might need. Food. Water. Extra clothes."

"Be careful, Tony. If you're caught, you'll be in serious trouble.

Tony nodded. "I know. I'll be careful. I'll just have to think of a way."

As Tony fell asleep that night a plan was forming in his mind. He smiled in his sleep.

During the next week Tony smuggled potatoes back into camp every night, but instead of eating them, he hid them in a shallow hole near the latrine pit. At last he had enough for what he needed. He exchanged the small pile of vegetables for a coat. He smiled as he put it on. It would serve two purposes; firstly to keep him warm as winter approached, while secondly, and more importantly, he would be able to fill the hem with potatoes. He could bring many more into camp each evening. His plan worked well. Over the next few weeks he was able to exchange potatoes for a coat for Henri, new shoes for them both, extra water rations, a little cheese and sausage, as well as having some left over to eat. Gradually the two men felt a little more strength in their weakened muscles. They still did not have enough food to prevent them losing weight, but the weight loss was reduced. Raw potatoes as a staple diet is not exciting, so Tony endeavoured to cook them whenever possible. The difficulties and dangers this entailed because of the curfew did not hold him back. It drove him on to seek ever more resourceful ways of finding fuel, and smuggling it back into the hut in the dead of night. Though he and Henri kept their potatoes for themselves, Tony's activities had added benefits for the other occupants of the hut, who often warmed themselves beside the meagre fire.

A strict curfew was enforced throughout the camp for the hours between evening and morning roll calls. No-one was allowed to leave their hut during that time. Enormously powerful searchlights situated around the electrified fence illuminated the whole camp, so the guards could see anyone moving between the huts. Not only was it difficult to move about outside, but it was difficult to get out there in the first place. The Kapo in each block was held responsible for any infringements of the curfew, so kept watch to prevent the inmates from moving about at night. This did not deter Tony. He would sneak out of the block while the guard was dozing, keep to the shadows as he made his way to the woodpile next to the kitchen, and carry an armful of its precious cargo back to the hut. He made a fire in the chimney breast, and baked the potatoes he had smuggled into camp that day. They were usually still part raw, but that did no matter to the hungry men who would have done anything to keep starvation at bay.

One night at the beginning of October, Tony slipped out as usual. He was making his stealthy way across to the kitchen hut when an SS guard spotted him.

"Halt!"

Tony turned to see the guard running towards him. He stood frozen in fear for what seemed like endless seconds before turning and sprinting back towards the hut, with the guard in hot pursuit. It was not far, but Tony's breath was laboured and his lungs bursting as he arrived and dragged himself back into his bunk. A year before, he would have been able to run that distance without even becoming winded. Now he felt totally exhausted, and his wounded leg ached. He drew the thin blanket over his head and tried to smother the sound of his laboured breathing. The door to the hut was thrown open.

"Who just ran in here?"

The inmates of the hut woke slowly, and looked with bleary eyes at the SS guard who stood silhouetted in the doorway.

"Someone broke the curfew. Which of you was it?"

There was silence, save for the sound of someone trying to smother a cough on the far side of the hut. The guard was angry, but he did not bother to search the hut. There were far better methods of finding out what he wanted to know.

"If the person responsible is not found, the whole block will be transferred to the Straffenkommando in the morning."

The SS guard turned and left, while the hut settled down to rest again. No one spoke, but Tony could feel the questions in the air. Though many suspected Tony, no one was sure that he had broken the curfew. If it was not him, who was responsible? The atmosphere was electric. If the guilty man was not handed over to the SS in the morning, they would all be in the straffenkommando, the work party for offenders, which few people survived. As Tony lay in the silent, oppressive darkness he felt the icy touch of fear at the thought of the punishment that would be meted out to a curfew breaker. But he knew that he could not allow the whole block to be punished for his misdeeds. He spoke in a confident voice which masked his fear. His words echoed in the silent hut.

"I'll hand myself in in the morning."

The silence continued but it changed in nature. It was no longer the silence of fear and speculation, but the absence of sound as the exhausted men sought sleep once more. Tony was the only one to remain awake. The prospect of the coming day drove all thoughts of sleep from his mind.

At four o'clock the whistles for roll call were blown. The men from the hut stumbled out into the cold morning air, to stand in their rows of five until the count was taken at six o'clock. Tony usually found that standing in the cold damp air caused his shattered shoulder to stiffen and ache. But he did not feel it this morning as the guard counted the rows. Satisfied that everyone was present, he addressed the men.

"Have you found the curfew breaker?"

Tony took a deep breath, straightened his back and stepped forward. "It was me."

The guard looked Tony up and down. He beckoned him forward to where he stood beside a wooden trestle. Tony took off his coat and shirt, allowing them to fall to the ground along with his dish as the cold autumn wind whipped his body. He had seen enough punishments to know what was expected of him. He stretched out his arms, so that two prisoners from his hut could tie him down. He looked across at the SS guard, who was smiling as he uncurled his whip.

"Twenty-five strokes."

He flexed his arm and the whip cracked. Tony closed his eyes and waited for the first blow. When it came, it sent a river of fire coursing across his back though he did not flinch. With tightly gritted teeth, he counted the blows as they fell, raising huge red wheals upon his back. One. Two. Three. Four. Five. His body began to jerk with pain each time the lash found his bare flesh. Six. Seven. Eight. Nine. Ten. He cried out as his skin burst beneath one particularly viscous blow. Somehow he lost count, not knowing how many times the lash had fallen. He only hoped he could hold out to the end. The SS guard drew back his arm with relish, savouring each moment. The whip cracked and the prisoner writhed in torment, while the other occupants of the hut watched in silence.

At last it was over. The guard coiled his bloodstained whip, surveying his handiwork with a smile. Tony's back was criss-crossed with raised weals, but the skin had only broken in one place. A trickle of blood ran down the thin wasted flesh, which could no longer conceal the contour of the Englishman's bones.

"You are lucky to escape with twenty-five. Next time the punishment will be worse."

As the guard turned and stalked away, Henri rushed forward to untie Tony and help him back into this clothes. The material of his shirt rubbed against his back. He winced as the heavy coat fell over his shoulders. Henri tucked the enamel bowl into his shirtfront.

"I wish I was on your work party. You need someone to look after you today."

Tony tried to smile, but could not hide the pain in his eyes.

"That's all right, Henri. I'll manage." He turned and joined his work group. Henri watched him go, wondering how he would be able to survive a day's work after such a beating. Tony wondered that too. He struggled to keep up on the march to the field. Once they had arrived and he set to work, each movement was an agony. But he forced himself to work on, for to stop would only draw the guard's attention and ensure another beating. The day seemed endless, but Tony gritted his teeth and refused to give in. He knew that survival in Buchenwald was dependent on a mental attitude, as much as on physical strength. It was a matter of willing yourself to take one more step, dig one more plant, live for one more day, one more hour. He concentrated his mind until all he was aware of was himself, his body and the work he had to do. He did not see or hear those around him. He did not have the energy to focus on them. By the time the whistle blew for the end of work, he was close to collapse.

Shuffling, limping along with the others, he completed the long march back to camp where, he entered the gates with shoulders stooped and bowed, his left leg dragging weakly. A curious guard stepped forward.

"What is wrong with him?"

A prisoner to Tony's right spoke. "Punishment lashing this morning."

The guard grinned as he stepped back and allowed the column through. They made their way back to the open area behind the hut, where Henri was waiting anxiously. He stepped forward eagerly when he saw Tony.

"How are you feeling?"

"Like hell."

Henri helped him to sit down. "You must not take any more risks like that. You might not survive the next beating."

"I might not survive the beating, but I know for certain that I won't survive the camp if I don't take risks." He forced his exhausted features into a caricature of a smile. "There was a suspicious guard at the gate, but he didn't find these." He shook his arms and a potato slipped down each sleeve and into his waiting hands. "Baked potatoes again tonight!"

Before Henri could say anything, whistles blew for evening roll call. They made their way to the front of the hut. While they waited in silence to be counted, he acknowledged that Tony was right. The only way to survive Buchenwald was to try to stay one step ahead. Tony's potatoes would help them to do that.

171

Despite his beating, Tony continued to break curfew to get firewood and trade his potatoes. As he watched the faces in the hut change as men came and went he knew it was the additional food that kept Henri and himself from succumbing to the diseases which were rife in the camp. But the two men were growing weaker and thinner by the day. He was afraid it would not be long before their turn came.

Henri lay awake, strange for him, for he was usually so exhausted when he crawled into the bunk that he fell asleep as soon as his head touched the thin straw mattress crawling with fleas. Tonight he tossed and turned, unable to get comfortable, alternately hot and cold, his body wracked by shivers. Tony was awakened by the erratic movements of the Frenchman. He turned towards him to see what was wrong, and reached out to touch a thin shoulder.

"What is it, Henri?"

Henri turned, his face bathed in sweat and his teeth chattering. "I don't feel too good."

Tony's brow creased into a worried frown. His friend was very ill. He feared that it might be typhus, a disease to which most prisoners fell victim at one time or another. Very few survived. There was nothing he could do to help Henri, save hold him close throughout the night and try to keep him warm. He hoping he had just caught a cold and would feel better in the morning, but deep inside he knew he was lying to himself. The truth of the lie was proved when the whistles blew for roll call. Tony crawled from the bunk and pulled Henri along beside him. "Come on, old friend. You can do it."

Henri sat on the edge of the bunk and shook his head, which sent arrows of pain shooting through his skull.

"I can't do it, Tony. My legs won't hold me up."

His voice was hoarse, and Tony was worried.

"Come on! You've got to make it! You know what will happen if you don't."

Henri did know. The dead, those who would never again rise from their bunks without assistance and all those too sick or weak to make it to roll call, were carried out of the hut each morning. No-one knew what happened to the weak, for they were never seen again. They did not reach the Hospital Block, as they were considered useless to the Germans as slave labour. To stay in the hut during roll call was an immediate death sentence. With a supreme effort of will, he tried to stand but his legs buckled under him. Tony caught him by the arm and helped him across the hut. By the time they were outside, Henri was almost unconscious, but he had made it. He would not be on the death carts today.

Tony stood in his allotted place, never taking his eyes from Henri. The Frenchman was swaying from side to side, desperately struggling to stay on his feet, but as time passed it was obvious that he would not make it to the count. Tony watched helplessly as Henri finally slumped slowly to the ground. He did not dare to make a move to help him, knowing only too well the consequences of getting out of place during roll call. The wait seemed interminable. Tony willed the minutes to pass so that he could help Henri, it seemed like the count would never take place. The SS guards finally made their way along the columns, counting the rows of fives. Today there were no problems. Everyone was accounted for, so by the time the sun was up roll call was over. Tony stepped forward and knelt beside Henri.

"What are you doing?" Tony turned towards the SS guard but did not reply. He knew no reply was expected.

"Get back to your work group."

Plucking up his courage, Tony spoke to the guard. "He needs my help."

The guard seemed surprised to hear a prisoner speak, but at least his response was not brutal.

"It is not your job to take him to Barrack 61. Get to your work group."

Tony rose to his feet and moved away, relief flooding through him. Barrack 61, the hospital compound. Henri was not for the death carts, although his life was still in danger. Like any prisoner in Buchenwald, Tony knew what the hospital was like. The chances of Henri coming out alive were slim, but at least there was a chance. As he marched to work he thought over what he knew of Barrack 61.

The hospital was a hut one hundred and fifty feet by thirty feet, just like the rest of the camp, save that here the wooden walls were windowless. There were areas set aside for specific diseases, the dysentery section, the TB section and the typhus section, where Tony feared that Henri was going. Each area had its complement of prisoner nurses and cleaners, none of whom were trained. Their whole stock of medicine consisted of nothing more than water. As there were no bandages available, they used paper for dressings. Rations were no different from those received in the rest of the camp. Tony was fully aware that a diet of dry bread was not the best way to keep a sick man alive and build up his strength. He was thankful that his workgroup was still digging potatoes; somehow he would smuggle some of them into the hospital and make soup for Henri.

That evening he did just that. After roll call, he slipped out of his hut and made his stealthy way over to the hospital compound, where his belief in a loving God was severely shaken at the sights and sounds and smells which greeted him. He thought life in the ordinary huts of Buchenwald was hell, but it was nothing compared with what assailed his senses as he searched through the section containing the typhus cases for Henri. The sick lay in delirium on the filthy straw mattresses, while those responsible for their care raced back and forth in a vain attempt to relieve the suffering. Each bunk had been made for a single occupant, but most contained three or four poor souls who struggled to stay warm beneath the one thin blanket. Down the centre of the hut ran a heating channel about three feet high and two feet wide. It was connected to a brick chimney at the end but this was, of course, cold. It was known as the stove, but Tony saw that it was used as a seat where the nurses tended the sick. The only positive thing they could do was to squeeze pus from suppurating boils, and stick a piece of paper on to try to keep them clean.

Tony searched bunk after bunk unsuccessfully. He was becoming frantic by the time he found Henri. The glazed eyes of the Frenchman did not recognise him. He cried out for water, he tossed and turned. In his delirium he cursed Tony for not giving him the meat and fruit he imagined he carried. His hands clawed at his head which was filled with an excruciating pain. He cried out for the wife he had left back in Saint Nazaire. After a few moments Tony left the bedside, tears in his eyes as he made his way down to the small fire at the end of the hut. He cooked a little potato soup and took it back, spooning it into Henri's mouth and watching as much of it dribbled out from the uncontrollable lips. Somehow he managed to get his delirious friend to swallow a little Finally Henri lapsed into unconsciousness, his shaking body sweating profusely. Tony sadly left the bedside to speak to the 'nurse' in whose care Henri had been placed.

"Do your best for him."

The exhausted prisoner looked reproachfully at Tony. "I do my best for all of them But it is not enough."

Tony nodded, seeing the tiredness, the hopelessness, the hunger in the face of the man who suffered as much as any other inmate of the Buchenwald camps.

"I understand. I'll come each evening and cook some soup for him."

As Tony looked around at the hundreds of sick men, he realised that Henri was in as much danger from selection as from the disease which ravaged his body. The selections came at random times. No-one had time to hide. They could only wait helplessly as the most sick people were cleared from the hut and never seen again.

"Try to hide him if there is a selection. I'll give you food if you do."

The prisoner looked at Tony through starving eyes. "I'll do my best. But I can't promise anything."

"That's good enough for me."

Sadly Tony made his way back to his own hut, avoiding the searchlights and guards, determined to do all he could to save his friend.

Henri remained unconscious for days. He was kept alive only by the drops of water which the nurse managed to force through his parched lips during the day, and the thin potato soup which Tony prepared and fed to him, with endless patience, each night. When he finally regained consciousness, he was totally unaware of his surroundings, unable to recognise the Englishman who gave up so much of his time to keep him alive. Tony watched helplessly as what little flesh was left on Henri's body slowly wasted away, leaving nothing but protruding bones and loose sagging skin. What hair had grown back on Henri's scalp since his head had been shaved now fell out in handfuls, leaving him totally bald again. As Tony looked at the wasted body, the sunken cheeks and eyes which looked at him out of a living skull he marvelled that anyone could survive such deprivation. But slowly Henri's strength began to return, he learned to sit up once more and Tony began to teach him how to walk again. It was slow work. At first he massaged the wasted muscles, then helped Henri to stand for a short while each evening. Finally, after over a month in Barrack 61, Henri took his first slow, painful step. He collapsed breathlessly onto the bunk immediately afterwards, but it was progress. Tony went to the fire to prepare the potato soup on which the Frenchman's life depended, more confident that he could now survive. When he returned Henri was sitting up, with his back supported by the wooden partition. He looked quizzically at the bowl of soup, then up into the younger man's eyes. A flicker of recognition crossed his face, and he spoke hoarsely.

"Tony?"

Tony could not prevent the smile which lit his face. Henri knew who he was! It was a vital step on the road to recovery. He sat down on the edge of the bunk, and spoke gently to the Frenchman.

"Yes. It's me, Henri."

"What happened?" It was as though Henri's mind had sought refuge in forgetfulness. Only now that his body was recovering did it allow him to question. Tony took a deep breath and began to explain.

"Typhus. You collapsed at roll call, and were brought to Barrack 61."

Henri looked at the filthy hut with its delirious occupants, and then down at his own wasted body. He held up a hand, little more than flesh and bone, and stared at it wonderingly.

"How long have I been here?"

"Almost five weeks."

"Five weeks?" Henri was incredulous. How could he possibly have been so ill for so long and survived? He looked again at the bowl of soup, and understanding dawned. "Have you done this for me every day?" Tony nodded. "Then I owe you my life."

Tony waved a hand dismissively. "Don't worry about it. Now eat this before it gets cold."

Henri ate gratefully. He would have been dead weeks before, if not for the care that Tony had lavished upon him and the risks he had taken in smuggling food. It was a debt he vowed to spend the remainder of his life repaying.

Henri continued to make a slow recovery, each day taking more steps than the day before as a little of his strength slowly returned. Inside the windowless hospital hut he was unable to see how the weather was changing. In Buchenwald one did not notice the seasons. There was no grass, no trees, no flowers. The prisoners knew only by the falling temperatures and the shorter hours of daylight that autumn was passing and winter fast approaching. Prisoners like Tony, whose work took them beyond the confines of the electric fence, saw the leaves on the trees bordering the fields where they worked turn red and gold, and finally fall to the ground where they were driven into piles by the wind. Tony could not help comparing it to the beauty of Heronfield in autumn. He wondered what Sarah was doing now, and how his parents were. But thoughts of home were soon buried beneath the necessities of life. Tony was increasingly grateful for his coat, not only because it made it easier for him to smuggle potatoes back into camp, but because of the added warmth it provided in the bitter wind. He was able to exchange the potatoes for woollen socks and gloves, carrots, a little sausage, even an extra blanket for Henri. Slowly, over the weeks, he was able to see his efforts rewarded. Henri, one of the very few survivors of the typhus epidemic, was now fit enough to offer occasional help to his fellow sufferers.

It was mid-November. Henri was trying to help a man to drink his meagre water ration when the door to the dimly lit hut was opened to admit an SS doctor, accompanied by a number of guards. There was general fear in the hut, as everyone realised what was happening. A selection. Who would be allowed to stay in Barrack 61, and who would never be seen again? There was silence save for the moans and cries of the sick and delirious. Then the doctor spoke.

"Line up beside the stove."

All those well enough to move staggered from their bunks, and lined up beside the barely warm heating channel. It was as much as many of them could manage, but they did it, the fear of what would happen to them if they did not spurring them on to almost inhuman efforts. The doctor called in a work party from outside, and indicated those who were so ill that they had not been able to get out of their bunks.

"Put them in the trucks."

As the living skeletons were carried from the hut by their fellow prisoners, the doctor turned back to those who stood by the stove. Some were so weak that they swayed from side to side, their legs threatening to collapse beneath them. Most looked as though they would be lucky to survive another few weeks. But the SS doctor was not going to leave them there long enough to find out.

"Jump over the stove."

The prisoners struggled to obey. Some, like Henri, managed to clamber over the three foot high conduit with some difficulty, though his breath came in short gasps, his head thumped and his chest ached as his heart pounded under the exertion. Others, by far the majority, were left panting and gasping on the other side. The doctor looked at them dismissively. Too sick to jump, too sick to work. He called the work party forwards.

"Put them in the trucks."

Some of the condemned went willingly, many not understanding what was happening, but many fought, though in their weakened condition it did little good. It was a token resistance. Weeping, they were dragged out, bundled into trucks and driven away to meet their fate. Those left behind watched silently, thankful that they had been spared yet another selection, which routinely depleted the camp of its weakest inhabitants. Slowly they made their way back to the almost empty bunks, knowing they would soon be occupied by more men, suffering and dying as the typhus gripped them.

When Tony returned to the hut that night, he learned of the selection at Barrack 61 and spent an anxious two hours waiting for roll call to pass, so he could go and find out if Henri was still safe. . But that night was one of the not infrequent occasions when the numbers at roll call did not tally. The prisoners continued to stand in the icy wind, teeth chattering, while the guards checked inside the huts. Finally they found the missing prisoner standing outside the wrong hut. This frequently happened with those who were reaching the last limits of their endurance, and could concentrate on only one thing, survival. At last roll call was completed and the prisoners were allowed back into the cold huts. No fires were allowed yet, as the S.S deemed that it was not yet cold enough for the prisoners to need them. Tony collected his ration of bread and water. He lay down on the bunk, waiting for the rest of the hut to settle, so that he could go across to the hospital to see if Henri had survived.

At last the inmates of the hut fell asleep. Tony slid out of his bunk to make his silent way across the floor, slipping past the prisoner whose job it was to guard the door. He was dozing at his post, as usual. Tony crouched low, keeping to the heavy shadows at the base of the hut walls until he came to an open space which separated him from the hospital compound. It was brightly lit by the searchlights. Even a mouse would have been seen moving across the muddy ground. Tony settled himself and carefully surveyed the guard posts, to make sure that there was no one looking in his direction He knew from experience it would be some time before they were all looking away. He had to draw on all his reserves of patience and self-control as he sat in the bitterly cold shadows, awaiting his chance. When it came, he did not hesitate. He ran straight across the yard, taking the shortest route possible, and stopped in the shadow of the hospital hut to gather his breath. He never dreamt during his days of training for the S.O.E. that the skills he was learning would come in useful in such a situation. But stealth and silence were vital to survival if one constantly broke the curfew. He would also have been surprised, four years earlier, that running such a short distance would leave him breathless and close to collapse. His whole body ached from the exertion, and he realised that although the deterioration of his condition was slow, it had not halted. There would come a day when he would not be able to cover the distance in time. He fervently hoped that Henri would be out of the hospital and back in the hut before that day came. That was if he had survived the selection. Tony pushed open the door and made his way into the dark hut.

460

It was strangely silent. He was used to hearing the cries and moans of the sick, the rantings of the delirious, coughing, hushed voices. But tonight there was nothing. As his eyes slowly adjusted to the gloomy interior, he hoped that the whole hut had not been cleared. Over to his right, he heard a familiar voice and let out a sigh of relief.

"Tony. I'm over here."

He made his way across to Henri, and sat down beside him on the bunk.

"Henri! I'm so glad to see you! I thought you might have been selected."

Henri shook his head. "No. Believe it or not I'm one of the fittest, or I should say I was one of the fittest. All those in worse condition than me have now gone."

"Maybe they've been taken to another hospital."

Henri looked at the Englishman, his eyes filled with incredulity. "Do you really believe that?"

Tony shrugged. "I don't know. I can't imagine the Germans caring for them, but what else could they do with so many?"

"Kill them."

Henri's eyes held a strange haunted look, and Tony frowned.

"So many? It would be impossible."

"Maybe, maybe not." Henri's voice was unusually dull. "One of the work party who took the sick away managed to give his guards the slip and hide in here. He said he couldn't go back to that work, or he would go on the fence."

Tony frowned. What could be so bad about the work that the man was willing to throw himself onto the electrified fence and commit suicide? Henri interrupted Tony's thoughts.

"His is a grim story. Do you want to hear it?"

Tony nodded, and Henri slipped off to fetch the man. When he returned Tony was surprised to see a young man barely out of his teens. He appeared to be well fed, at least he was not as thin as most people in Buchenwald, but what really caught Tony's attention was his eyes. Never before had he seen eyes filled with such hopeless terror, as though death was waiting round every corner, and could not be avoided.

The young man sat nervously on the edge of the bunk and looked at Tony.

"So you want to hear about the ovens?"

Ovens? Tony looked questioningly at Henri, who nodded. Tony looked back at the young man.

"Yes, please."

The boy began to speak, his eyes fixed and staring as though he were seeing the atrocities again. Tony listened. He felt the bile rise in his throat. His head pounded, but he did not doubt that the young man was telling the truth, and he did not try to stop the flow of words.

"When the dead are taken from the huts, they go to the crematory, where the ground floor ovens are waiting. There are six of them, with huge chimneys behind. We have to throw the bodies inside and watch them burn. The smell is awful. But we can't move away because we have to feed in more bodies and more coke. Those who are taken from here alive, or who are sent to the left at the selection by the gate when they arrive, are sent to the showers. They strip down and go under the shower heads. But instead of water, gas comes out. They die screaming and writhing. We have to carry their twisted bodies to the ovens."

Tony's head was swimming as he absorbed the terrible facts. He looked across at Henri, who had come so close to selection that very day.

"Thank God you weren't taken."

Henri nodded. "Yes. But there is more to hear."

461

Tony's eyes were wide. What more could the haunted young man tell him? Surely there could be nothing worse than what he had heard already? But there was.

"The ovens are on the ground floor. In the basement they execute those who have been convicted of capital crimes in the camp."

"Capital crimes?"

"Yes. Insubordination. Attempting to escape. Smiling in ranks. Stealing or smuggling food."

Tony thought of the potatoes he had brought into camp each evening and shuddered. He knew that the Germans viewed it seriously. But he had not thought he would be executed if he was caught. He swallowed hard.

"Do they shoot them?"

"Shoot them?" The young man laughed, a hollow empty sound devoid of all humour that made Tony's skin crawl. "They would see that as a waste of ammunition. The guards put a short slip noose around their necks. They hang them from hooks about eight feet above the floor. It takes a long time for them to die. Their faces go red, their eyes bulge out of their sockets, their tongues go black and swollen. If the guards are impatient and think they are taking too long to die, they beat their brains out with a club."

Tony felt physically sick. His body shivered uncontrollably. He closed his eyes as the lifeless voice continued.

"They cut the bodies down. We have to put them into a lift which takes them up to the ground floor. They are put on a miniature railway of metal litters, which takes them from the lift platform to the furnace doors. It is all terribly efficient."

Henri and Tony looked at each other, unable to hide their horror. Henri looked down at the potatoes which Tony had brought to cook. They were now clenched tightly in his fists.

"They had better be the last."

Tony looked down at them. How could two such small and muddy items be responsible for the torture and death of a man? Should he stop smuggling them? He looked at Henri.

"We must eat more than our rations to survive. But I won't bring them every day. And I'll only bring enough for us. I won't be able to trade for other things, but I won't stop bringing in food for you and me. If I get caught I'll be killed. But if I don't bring it in, we'll die anyway."

"I don't want to be responsible for your death."

"You won't be. I'll be bringing them in for myself anyway." Tony looked at the young man.

"Are you all right?"

The young man nodded slowly. "Yes. But I won't go back there."

Tony said nothing. He did not know he would have coped with what this young man had seen and experienced. He was lucky not to have gone insane. But how could they help him to avoid going back? It was Henri who spoke. He put a comforting arm around the young man's shoulders.

"You must smuggle yourself into a work party from one of the huts. Make it look as though you've always been there."

"They'll be looking for me."

Tony thought for a moment then held out his hand. "Let me see your tattoo."

The young man frowned questioningly, but rolled up his left sleeve and held out his arm. Tony took hold of it and looked at the number. 503110. He nodded thoughtfully.

"If you could get hold of something valuable enough, you could bribe one of the

462

tattooists to change that 3 to an 8. I'm sorry, but it's the best idea I can come up with."

The young man looked at him through haunted eyes.

"Thank you. I'll risk anything not to go back there. I'll join another hut, and try to get hold of something valuable." He stood up. "I'll leave you now. Thank you for trying to help me." He turned and walked away.

Tony watched him leave. His hatred of the Germans increased, until it was like a red mist before his eyes. A tyrant such as Hitler who could create such a living hell did not deserve to live. He prayed fervently that the war would soon be over, and Buchenwald and its horrors wiped forever from the face of the earth.

The following morning roll call was completed in record time. Tony wondered if there would be a chance of getting over to see Henri again before the work parties set out, but to his surprise, the men were not dismissed after roll call. The SS guards stood with guns pointed at the prisoners, as Major Hase approached with long, angry strides. Tony had rarely seen him inside the camp. He wondered what could possibly be important enough for him to enter now. The major finally halted, and stood where all the prisoners could see him. His face was thunderous.

"A prisoner has chosen to leave another part of the camp, because he does not like his work. I want that man to step forward now."

No one moved. Tony knew it was the young man he had met the previous evening. He cursed himself for not realising that the Germans would not let him go without a fight. He knew too much about their secret operation. They did not intend him, or the others who worked at the crematoria, to be alive when the war ended. Tony did not know where the young man had gone, and hoped he was well hidden. But deep in his heart, he knew that he had little chance of avoiding a thorough German search.

Major Hase began to tap his cane against the leather top of his boot.

"No-one is willing to step forward? Then we will do this the hard way. Show your numbers."

The prisoners rolled up their left sleeves and held out their arms as the guards began to make their way along the seemingly endless rows, checking each number as they went. Time passed slowly. The guards checked and double-checked to make sure that they did not pass over the missing prisoner. An hour after the checking began, a scuffle broke out, in the ranks stationed in front of the hut nearest the fence. A guard dragged a struggling figure out from amongst his fellows, and threw him down onto the ground. Tony recognised the young man, and his heart went out to him. He could expect no beating or withholding of rations. The only punishment the Germans would think fit was execution, and there was no-one more aware of what that punishment entailed than the prisoner himself.

Major Hase crossed the compound, to where the nameless man grovelled in the dirt.

"Did you think you could escape?" he bellowed, his voice so loud that all the prisoners could hear. "No one escapes from Buchenwald!" He brought his cane down across the young man's shoulders. Once, twice, three times. Then he kicked him in the ribs, before stepping back. "On your feet, scum."

The young man struggled to his feet. His eyes were wild with fear as they darted all around, seeking an escape route which did not exist. The major turned to the guard who had found the missing prisoner.

"Take him back to his own hut for punishment."

"No!" With a cry of despair the young man evaded the guard's grasp. He threw himself at the fence less than ten feet away. As he touched it, he screamed. His body convulsed as the surge of electricity flowed through him. Sparks flew all around him, as he gripped tightly to the only object which gave him some choice in this hell on earth. As Tony watched the young man suffer and die on the wire, the full realisation of his own situation finally hit him. There was no hope of escape by prisoners who were too weak to do anything but work and sleep. And if the rumours of the gas chambers reached the rest of the camp, the Germans would make sure that none of them survived the war to tell the Allies what was happening. With tears in his eyes, he watched the inert body being carried away towards the ovens. He wondered how long it would be before his turn came.

172

Two days later, Henri was released from Barrack 61 and sent back to work. His body and mind, barely healed after the ravages of typhus, were subjected to the gruelling work party once again. Now that November was dragging to a close and December fast approaching, the ground was becoming iron hard and difficult to dig. Henri struggled on, barely able to stand for the roll call each evening. He was determined he would not let the Germans class him as unfit and transfer him to the secret, hidden part of camp, where his life would be measured in hours rather than days. At last the ground became rock hard and impossible to dig with the wooden spades provided. Henri's work party was stood down until spring. The Frenchman doubted that any of them would still be alive when spring came. The rations were not increased to help their weakened bodies combat the cold, and each hut was only allowed enough wood to enable them to light the fire for two or three hours a day. But at least he no longer wasted energy digging the mass graves in the woods.

Tony was also glad that there was no more work for the next few months. The fields were now empty of potatoes, so he was unable to supplement their rations. He knew that their best chance of survival was to sit still to conserve energy, to keep as warm as possible and wait for the long cold winter to pass. It was bitterly cold in the hut most of the time. The two friends were glad of the extra blankets Tony had been able to procure while he still had access to potatoes. Every morning as they crawled from their relatively warm cocoon, they saw the bodies of those who had succumbed to the cold during the night being carried from the hut, and left in a heap for the death carts to collect. The sound of hoarse coughing was now continual. Henri and Tony both contracted an ailment which made their lungs burn, and forced them into long hard bouts of coughing, which made their ribs ache and left them gasping for breath.

The cold seeped into Tony's bones and seemed to settle in his injured shoulder. He now found it painful to move the left arm at all, and what little mobility there was was considerably reduced. He took to tucking his arm inside his shirt, holding it close and immobile against his ribs, which now had nothing but skin covering them so that the contours of each individual bone could be seen. His left leg had held up well. Though he still limped, he was grateful that he could walk, for if he had been unable to reach the kitchen hut, he would not have received his daily ration of the thin watery soup. He would already have been amongst those whose bodies had been reduced to ashes in the crematoria.

Both Henri and Tony seemed to be playing host to hundreds of fleas and lice which burrowed into their skin and sucked their weakened blood but these were minor irritations. The sores which covered their bodies were by far the most dangerous of their ailments. If they were not kept relatively clean they would become infected. They had seen that happen in many others, who had cried in agony as the infection spread. It led to fever and eventually death. The hollow in Tony's calf, where the flesh and muscle had been carried away in Saint Nazaire, had been susceptible to sores ever since he had arrived at Buchenwald. But now the lack of vitamins was taking its effect and his strength was diminishing daily as the sores spread rapidly, eating away at the remaining flesh. All he could do was scrape away the putrescence and try to keep the sores clean. Some, very few, of the sores on his body and arms healed over, leaving scabs and scarred flesh. But he felt that the ones on his leg would never heal, and it was only be a matter of time before gangrene set in.

The enforced inactivity of winter, the cold and the pain, caused his mind to retreat as much as possible from the hardships which surrounded him. He frequently sought refuge in thoughts of home. Often he closed his eyes to feel the warmth of the summer sun on his upturned face and hear the sound of birds singing in the trees. Many times he smiled, as he imagined himself walking with Sarah and watching the heron rise from the reed bed. Somehow that picture seemed to epitomise for him all that was beautiful and true in the free world he had left so far behind. He tried often to reach out and touch Sarah's face with his fingertips, only to feel his hand brush the wooden wall, and to open his eyes to the life which threatened to consume him. At times like that he wished he had taken the golden heron with him into France and could hold it now, to see its beauty and feel some tangible link with home, some proof that this living hell was not all there was to life, and that there was something for him to go back to if he survived. As the endless days dragged by he spent more and more time in the imaginary world inside his head. He sought strength and comfort from a time and life long in the past, but which still had the power to uphold him in his hours of greatest need.

173

While Tony languished in Buchenwald, a place seemingly isolated from the civilised world, that world he had left behind him continued to tear itself apart in a war to which everyone but Hitler could see the only possible outcome. While most of the protagonists were eager for peace, the German Fuhrer continued to wage war as though he still had massive armies at his beck and call, and the eventual victory would be his.

By the end of August, Hitler's first secret weapon, the V-1, was suffering great losses in the skies above southern England. British fighter aircraft and guns were bringing down eighty per cent of the pilotless planes before they could do any damage. The Allies felt that the danger from the rockets was now over. They were wrong. On 8th September, the first of Hitler's V-2 rockets hit London. This time there was no warning. The missile approached high above the city, then dropped with its devastating cargo on a population unaware of its approach. As the days passed and more of the V-2's came over, there was limited panic. People did not know what was happening, only that at any time, day or night, an explosion might occur which could wipe out a whole street killing all in its vicinity. There was no warning, and no time to seek shelter. It was not until 10th November that the Government admitted that the country was being attacked by rockets. Although there was some fear, at least people knew what was happening. They faced the new threat with stoicism.

The Allied offensive in Northern Europe slowed during September, as the supply lines became extended. Troops had to wait for the necessities of warfare to catch up with them, as they moved inexorably onwards. By the end of the month, the German had used the breathing space to stabilise their defences. Although the Allies continued to push the enemy front, they made little progress over the next weeks and months. Whilst the Allies were almost static on the Western Front, in the east the Russians continued to make progress. Finland sued for peace on 2nd September and Romania on the 12th. By October, the Russians had entered East Prussia, and were drawing ever closer to the heart of the Third Reich.

While the war in Europe continued on land, the war at sea in the Far East did not slow. On 20th October, the largest naval engagement in history began, with the Americans defending their beachheads at Leyte in the Philippines. Over the next four days, two hundred and eighty two warships pounded each other with their huge guns. The superior power of the American forces was eventually victorious, and the foothold strengthened. German naval sea power was at an all-time low in the west. Their one remaining battleship, the Tirpitz, sought to evade the British during November, but the unequal struggle was eventually lost. The German navy lost its last vestige of glory as the Tirpitz sank beneath the waves.

On 15th December, the Germans began a massive offensive on the Western Front. They pushed forwards into the Ardennes, through a narrow corridor which divided the Allied forces. In an effort to take Bastogne, the Germans reached within six miles of the river Meuse. The Battle of the Bulge had begun.

174

Bobby pulled the greatcoat tighter around his shoulders. He listened to the captain, who explained the situation quickly, eager to be out of the cold wind.

"The Germans are moving on Bastogne, where our forces have been cut off. McAuliffe is holding out. The Germans seem short of oil. All of our dumps that were in their path were fired, so they have got no supplies from us. Montgomery has been put in charge of the battle. Our orders are to push east as fast as we can, to bring relief to Bastogne. Be ready to move at seven a.m."

As the Captain turned and walked swiftly away, the soldier to Bobby's right snorted derisively.

"Monty! Haven't we Americans got enough leaders of our own, without borrowing from the British?"

"It's their war too, you know." Bobby looked at his compatriot thoughtfully. "Don't forget that they have been fighting for years longer than us. They have the right to be in at the kill."

"Yes. They fought for years, but they made no progress till we joined in."

Bobby shook his head in disbelief. People who thought like that had no idea of what the British had endured while they fought alone. What was worse, they did not want to know. As Bobby made his way back to his makeshift shelter, he looked up at the heavy clouds. If they held out, there would be no air cover again in the morning. It seemed as if even the forces of nature were conspiring to aid the enemy.

The sky was still grey and cloudy the next morning as the Americans moved out, and they had not been on the road for long before it started to rain. As Bobby drew closer to the front line, he passed columns of wounded moving back down the lines. He wondered how bad things were up ahead. At noon they crossed the Meuse, swollen with its burden of rain rushing down the hillsides in overflowing streams. They could hear the sound of heavy guns in the distance, competing with the thunder overhead. The day grew dark long before evening, and Bobby was not sure what time it was when they finally halted and settled for the night. Up ahead the sky was lit by the bright flashes of exploding shells. The earth shook as though in pain from the destruction which men, the least of her children, wreaked upon her.

Bobby was awoken by someone shaking his shoulder.

"Come on. It's time to move out."

He sat up and tried unsuccessfully to shake some of the water from his greatcoat. It was still dark. Some instinct told him that was the darkness of the storm. The day must have begun some time earlier. He opened a can of beef and ate hungrily, before taking a drink of cold water from his bottle. Picking up his rifle, he joined the rest of his company as they moved forward through the widely spaced trees. The line of men stretched away to the right and left. In neither direction could he see its end, each soldier moving steadily forward through the cold, wet landscape. Within an hour they had reached the forward positions, and dug in just over the crest of a low hill. From there they could see the immense German forces surrounding Bastogne. A young soldier to Bobby's right frowned.

"Why don't they send in the planes and bomb them out?"

Bobby pointed to the sky. "The cloud cover is too low. They wouldn't be able to see if they were hitting the Germans or our own men, they're too close together."

The young soldier nodded. "I guess so. We sure could use a wind to clear these clouds."

Bobby shrugged. "It doesn't work that way, does it. God seems to leave the fighting to us. He doesn't bother to get involved, even to the extent of sending a breeze."

The young soldier looked at Bobby.

"Maybe that's because he can't bear to see the mess we're making. After all, he created us and this world. All we can do is destroy it."

"But surely he'd help us? We didn't start this war."

"Didn't we? If the world had stood up to Hitler in the beginning, this war may never have started. We are just as responsible as him."

"What's your name, kid?"

"Zach Abramovitch."

"How old are you?"

"Eighteen."

"Well, you sure know a lot for your age."

"I was born in Germany. My Pa didn't like the way things were going over there, so he moved us all to America when I was six. Since then we've paid close attention to what's been happening in Europe. We discuss it a lot at home."

"Well, Zach, your Pa should be proud of the way you've thought all this through. Most of the guys out here just blame Hitler for it all."

"Don't get me wrong. I blame Hitler too. But I think we could've done more to limit this war."

"Well, we're sure doing our bit now." Bobby grinned at the young soldier. "I'm glad to have you fighting by my side, Zach."

Zach was by his side, but there was no fighting that day. The rain continued to fall. The Americans continued to consolidate their positions, so that the Germans would be unable to advance further. During the following night the rain stopped. The sky began to clear at last, so Bobby woke to see patches of blue for the first time in a week. His face was grim as he looked down at the German forces. While the change in the weather was welcome, it meant that the assault on the enemy would soon begin. He had seen many of his comrades fall in the months since D-Day. He knew that by evening many more of his friends would be gone forever. He hoped he would not be amongst those who would not leave the battlefield alive.

"Morning, Bobby."

Bobby turned to the young soldier. "Hi Zach." He indicated the clearing sky. "The clouds are gone. Maybe God is helping after all. I suppose he thinks we can kick the Germans out today, so we can have a peaceful Christmas."

"Christmas?"

"Sure. It's Christmas Eve today. Had you forgotten?"

Zach shrugged. "What's to remember? Did you forget my name? Zach Abramovitch. I don't celebrate Christmas."

Bobby was sheepish. "Gee, I didn't think. Sorry, pal."

Zach grinned. "Don't worry. It's good to be with someone who sees me as an American first and a Jew second. It wasn't like that back in Germany, when I was a kid."

There was a heavy droning sound in the sky, growing louder as it came closer. Bobby pulled Zach down beside him into a muddy foxhole.

"It looks like those planes you ordered are coming at last!"

The two Americans tightened the chinstraps on their helmets. They crouched low as the bombers passed overhead, and dived down towards the massed German tanks surrounding Bastogne. The guns of the tanks began to swing round and fire on the approaching planes. Puffs of smoke surrounded their muzzles as the shells flew skywards. One of the planes was hit and fell spiralling from the sky, smoke trailing behind it. But the other planes flew on dropping their deadly cargo with unerring accuracy on the armoured behemoths which had sought to push back the might of the American army. The air was filled with screaming bombs as they fell to the earth, then the crash and roar as they reached their targets, blowing tanks apart and setting their wrecks alight. The air above the massed armour was black with smoke, lit from beneath by the flames of their destruction. The vibrations of the destruction radiated through the ground, until the Americans crouched low on the hillside could feel them. Somewhere behind them, a damaged plane which had tried to limp back to base failed in its struggle and fell into the trees with a resounding roar and crash. Those close by covered their ears as they raced forwards to help. But when they reached the burning wreck, it was obvious that no-one would be brought from it alive.

The air battle raged for most of the morning. The Americans lost some planes, but it was nothing compared with the massive destruction they inflicted on the German tanks. When the planes finally withdrew, the signal for the infantry attack was given. Bobby found himself advancing down into the midst of the wreckage of the German armour. There were burning tanks all around. From some came no sound save for the roar of flames and the cracking of metal as it overheated. From others came the screams of men trapped inside the flaming hulks, burning to death. Bobby tried to close his ears to the sounds as he advanced, but it was hard. The smell of burning flesh assaulted his nostrils, and made him gag.

The sound of a machine gun to his left caused Bobby to throw himself to the ground and seek shelter as the Germans on the far side of the tanks began to open fire on the advancing Americans. While most of their armour had been destroyed, the enemy were still there in massive numbers. Their withering fire brought the American advance to a halt. Swinging wide of the burning wreckage, they began to dig in. Bobby saw many Americans fall before they could reach cover. One man fell right beside him with half his face blown away, spraying Bobby with blood. Too busy to do more than push the corpse aside, Bobby and Zach dug frantically, until their position was secure and they were able to fire back on the Germans from comparative safety.

The battle raged throughout that day and the night which followed. When Christmas Day dawned, it was upon a scene of carnage. No peace on earth, goodwill to men around Bastogne, instead the guns continued to fire and men continued to die as the Americans pushed relentlessly forwards. Gradually, inch by inch, they made progress and the Germans began to fall back, fighting every step of the way. So Christmas Day passed with few men acknowledging it any more than Zach Abramovitch. Battle left little time for men to pause and reflect on a God who became man to bring peace.

As night fell, the attacking soldiers sought what little rest they could in infrequent periods of sleep while the battle raged around them. The Germans hung on tenaciously, but they were outnumbered and their position was hopeless. Dawn came. At last the Germans began to retreat as the Allies advanced on three sides. So Bastogne was relieved, and the besieged garrison celebrated Christmas a day late, a day which had seen the change from siege to freedom, and heralded the end of the German Reich.

175

While Bobby lay in his foxhole, cold, wet, tired and under fire from the enemy, Sarah sat in her room overlooking the grounds of Heronfield House, the room she had shared for so long with Jane and which she now shared with Ann. Ann was just nineteen. Although she was only six years younger than herself, Sarah felt immeasurably older than the new VAD. It was hard to imagine that she had been much the same age at the outbreak of the war. So much had happened to her during the intervening years that she felt poles apart from the girl. Sarah brushed her hair, and nervously checked her makeup. Sir Michael and Lady Kemshall had invited her down to the lodge for a drink when they returned from church. She desperately wanted to make a good impression. She had spoken to them briefly on two or three occasions since they had heard about Tony. Captain Dawson had told them how much Sarah had meant to their son, but this would be the first time she met them on a formal occasion. She took the golden heron from its box and pinned it to her blouse. Satisfied with her appearance, she made her way down the sweeping staircase and out into the cold crisp air of the morning of Christmas Day, 1944.

Sarah walked down the drive, and soon found herself knocking tentatively at the door, which was opened by Louise. She smiled at the young Englishwoman, instantly putting her at ease.

"Merry Christmas, my dear! Please come in."

Sarah mumbled her thanks and entered the lodge. It was warm and comfortable, though it must have seemed crowded to the Kemshalls who were used to life up at the big house. Sarah thought it all rather grand. She was a little overawed by her surroundings as Louise took her coat and led her into the drawing room. Tony's father and grandmother were waiting to greet her.

Madame de Thierry smiled from her seat beside the fire.

"Happy Christmas, child."

Sarah smiled. "Happy Christmas. I am so glad to meet you at last. Tony has told me so much about you."

"Merry Christmas."

Sarah turned to face Sir Michael. He was standing straight and tall, with a serious expression, yet Sarah felt that this was a mask which hid his true feelings. She found it hard to reconcile him with the image Tony had given of an unforgiving and domineering man. Perhaps he had changed over the last few months.

"Happy Christmas, Sir Michael."

"Please sit down." He indicated a chair, and made his way over to the drinks tray. "Would you like a sherry?"

Sarah sat down. "Thank you. Yes."

There was an uncomfortable silence. Sir Michael poured the drink and handed it to Sarah. Then Louise spoke.

"Dr Millard said you would not be going home for Christmas. We felt sure that if Tony were here he would have invited you. We do so want to do what he would have liked."

"I wonder where he will be spending Christmas."

Sir Michael turned to his guest, not quite able to hide the hope which flashed across his features.

"Then you believe he is alive?"

Sarah nodded. "I have to, Sir Michael. There were so many misunderstandings between us, I have to believe I will get the chance to put things right."

Sir Michael nodded, acknowledging her honesty.

"I know what you mean. I pray daily that he's alive, and will come back to us. I just regret that we wasted so much time during this war. We didn't even spend his last Christmas in England together."

"Tony was thinking of you last Christmas. He told me he wished he could come home and share it with you."

"You saw him last Christmas?"

Sarah looked at Louise. Should she tell her the truth, or should she lie to save hurting them? But too many lies had already been told. She nodded.

"Yes. I bumped into him in Coventry a few days before Christmas, while I was on leave. He shared an early Christmas dinner with Mum and me. He said he wished he could come home to see you and his grandmother. But there were too many ... problems." She cast a tentative glance at Sir Michael. His eyes were filled with pain and sadness.

"You don't need to be so tactful. He said he couldn't come home because of me, didn't he?"

Sarah sat motionless for a moment, then nodded.

"I was such a fool!" Sir Michael crossed the room and poured himself another drink. "I drove my own son from his home at Christmas time."

"Please don't blame yourself." Sarah's voice was pleading. "He missed you. I think he understood what you were feeling. He wasn't bitter and angry, so you mustn't let the past spoil your future." She touched the golden heron on her blouse. "I gave this to Tony last Christmas. He said it reminded him of home, and of the people he loved here. He left it with Captain Dawson when he went to France. I'm looking after it for him. You must always remember that he thought fondly of you, and talked about you often. I'm sure he's looking forward to coming home to you at the end of this war."

Sir Michael smiled at his young guest.

"I can see why Tony is so fond of you. You have a wise head on your young shoulders. I'm sure Tony would want us to be happy today. Let's forget the past and think only of the future. I don't care what Captain Dawson says, I'm sure Tony will be home soon. So let's drink a toast." He raised his glass high. "To Tony, wherever he is.

May God grant him a happy Christmas, and keep him safe until he returns home to us."

Four glasses were raised by four people whose love reached out across the sea to the young man who would forever be in their thoughts and in their hearts.

"To Tony."

176

Tony knew only that it was winter. It was a long time since he had known what month, let alone what day, it was. He lived from day to day, hour to hour, in the hope that winter would soon be past and spring would bring forgotten warmth to the air. The only part of Buchenwald which showed any sign that this was the festive season was the SS compound. For the rest of the camp, life continued in the usual winter routine, collecting food and trying to keep warm while their bodies slowly diminished in strength and energy. The only break in the routine for Tony and Henri came on 26th December.

Morning roll call was over and the prisoners stood in the cold waiting to be dismissed so that they could seek the comparative warmth of the hut. But today was different. The SS guard in charge cast a derisive look over the prisoners.

"You are filthy dirty, and you smell!" The prisoners said nothing. They were fully aware of their condition, but it was not of their own choosing. "It is six months now since most of you arrived, and it is time for you to be cleaned up."

Tony frowned. Six months? Had it really only been that long? He felt as though his whole life had been spent within the electrified fences. The guard was still talking. As Tony focussed on his words, his body became rigid with fear.

"You are to proceed to the shower blocks, where you will be disinfected and shaved. Move out."

As the column of prisoners shuffled across the compound towards the shower block, Tony looked across at Henri, whose pale haunted features echoed his own fears. Was this the end? Did the Germans intend to gas them, and burn their bodies so that they did not have to feed them during the winter months? He wished now that he had never spoken to the young man who had escaped from the death compound. Then he would be able to approach the showers oblivious to the terror-filled death, which might await him there.

The column of prisoners shuffled along. As they halted at the shower block near the quarantine huts, Tony's fear diminished slightly. Surely they would not use gas in the main compound? Most of the prisoners did not know what went on in the areas of the camp dedicated to death. To kill some of their members openly like this would be foolish, unless they intended to eradicate the whole camp. But Tony would not, could not believe that of them. There were too many prisoners. Surely they would not gas them all?

The men made their way into the shower block. The Kapos were lined up, with their sticks ready to beat anyone who did not comply with their orders.

"Strip off, and leave your clothes in the centre of the room."

Most of the prisoners were only too ready to comply, glad to be rid of their vermin infested clothes and with the prospect of a shower ahead. Henri, Tony and some of the others who had heard rumours of the gas chambers were more reluctant. There was nothing they could do to prevent or avoid what lay ahead. Fearfully, they stripped off their clothes. Tony carefully laid aside his shirt and trousers, the woollen gloves and scarf and the extra blanket which he wrapped around his upper body to keep him warm and make sure it was not stolen from his bunk. He put his acquired leather shoes and warm woollen socks on top of the pile, convinced that he would never see them again.

"Take your bowls with you."

Tony looked around at the naked men who surrounded him. Their skin hung loosely over bones protruding sickeningly from bodies which looked as though they belonged to dead men. The skin was grey, the cheeks hollow and eyes sunken in blackened pits. Most of the eyes held no expression, as though their owners had given up all hope. As he studied them, Tony realised that he must look the same. He wondered if his family would recognise him.

"Get moving!"

A stick came down heavily across his shoulders, and Tony fell to his knees beneath the blow. A foot caught him in the ribs.

"Get up! Take your bowl and follow the others!"

Tony picked up his bowl and dragged himself to his feet. As he held the precious object close to his chest, he wondered if it were a good omen. You needed your bowl to collect your food and water rations. If they were to take them with them, surely that meant that there would be life beyond the showers? Tony limped after his fellow prisoners into a room with shower heads set in the walls. The door closed with an ominous thud behind him. He felt a hand on his shoulder and turned to meet Henri's worried gaze.

"Do you think this is the end, Tony?"

The Englishman shrugged. "I don't know, Henri." His serious eyes held the Frenchman's. "I want to thank you for keeping me alive on the train from Saint Nazaire. I would not have survived without you."

Henri shook his head. "No thanks are necessary, my friend. I would have died many times over in this place, if it had not been for you. The debt was more than repaid." He held out his hand. "If this is to be goodbye, then I want you to know that I'm proud to have been your friend."

Tony reached out and clasped the hand in his own. "Goodbye, my friend."

Suddenly the two men were caught by a deluge of barely warm water which flowed across their bodies, leaving them gasping for breath. They stared at each other in disbelief, then suddenly they were laughing and crying at the same time, arms around each other. It was a shower after all. Their relief was overwhelming, leaving them feeling light-headed and full of an up-surging joy. Life would continue, and where there was life there was hope. They lifted their heads to feel the water falling on their faces, and rubbed their filthy bodies to try to dislodge the accumulated dirt of six months. Almost before it had started the flow of water ceased, amidst cries of frustration from the men. Most of them were barely wet, let alone clean. But Tony and Henri did not complain. They were just glad to be alive.

"Move out! This way!"

Shivering with cold, the naked prisoners followed the sound of the voice to where a drum of the same bluish green disinfectant which greeted them on their arrival at the camp was waiting. Each man dipped himself quickly into the foul-smelling liquid, before lining up for a shave. Tony's hair was scraped none too carefully from his head, and he was glad to lose the filthy locks. There was no home now for the parasites which had lived and bred in his hair for the past months. Freedom from lice would more than make up for the cold of the exposed skin.

"Get dressed."

Tony looked in dismay at the pile of clothing on the floor. These were the same uniform, striped trousers and shirts and heavy wooden clogs. But where were the things he had taken off before the shower? His woollen socks, gloves and scarf? Most importantly of all, where was his blanket? As he helped himself to clean shirt and trousers and struggled into the wooden clogs, he plucked up the courage to address one of the Kapos.

"Where are our other things?"

"They were filthy and infected with parasites. They are being burned."

Tony knew better than to complain, but his heart sank. He had worked hard and taken so many risks to acquire those things he had thought were essential to survival. And now they were being burned! Consumed to ashes, just like the people who were no longer wanted in Buchenwald. He wanted to cry in anger and frustration. Surviving the winter was no longer a foregone conclusion. He had been relying on the added warmth from the acquired clothing. Without it he, and especially Henri who was older and much more vulnerable after his bout of typhoid, were liable to take a trip in the death carts, long before the first flowers of spring pushed their heads through the thawing ground to reach towards the sky in a symbol of hope. Tony's hopes were crushed. His necessities for survival were rising in smoke towards the heavens. He wondered why God did not see and do something to help those whose only future lay in the coke ovens of Buchenwald.

JANUARY – MAY 1945

177

1945 dawned with the Allies convinced that this was the year that would see the end of the war. Although the Germans still fought on, they were short of men and supplies. They could not hope to hold out for much longer, neither could they dream now of the final victory being theirs. January saw the might of the Russian army pushing the beleaguered Reich from the east. Warsaw was liberated on the 17th. While Stalin, Roosevelt and Churchill met at Yalta to discuss how they would divide the inevitable spoils of war, the Germans planned and began a counter offensive. It was doomed to failure, as the Russians continued to push towards the German heartland, and Budapest finally fell to the communists. In the west, the Allies were impatient for final victory. To hurry matters towards a satisfying conclusion, a massive bombing raid against Dresden was launched on the 13th and 14th of February. It did little to hasten the winning of the war, but further crushed the spirit of a people who now stared defeat in the face as the Allies reached the Rhine, that all important barrier which the Americans crossed at Remagen on 7th March. Monty led the British across on the 23rd. It looked as though nothing could go wrong for the Allies. It was with deep shock and sadness that they learned of the death of President Roosevelt on 12th April, a man who had worked so hard during the war years, but whose body could not hold out for the few weeks necessary to allow him to see his forces victorious in Europe.

178

As the long winter months dragged on, Tony felt his body weakening day by day. No longer could he find the energy to move around the camp in search of additional food and clothes. All he could do was watch those in his own hut, waiting for them to eventually succumb to the cold or starvation. He would rush to their bunk to see what he could salvage, hoping to get there before anyone else realised that the man was dead. He felt ghoulish, watching and waiting for men to die so that he could take their clothes, but he buried his hatred of his own actions along with his feelings of guilt. This was a matter of survival, and he was determined that he would survive. Often he took small portions of bread from those who had died during the night, and he would share these with Henri, to supplement their meagre rations. Sometimes he was lucky enough to strip the dead of their clothing. The first few times, he and Henri kept what they took. They soon had extra layers to fight off the bitter cold of the German winter, a cold that could kill them in their weakened condition as easily as starvation. Wooden clogs and extra clothing were also traded for food, though there was little on the black market. A quarter of a loaf of tasteless black bread could cost as much as three shirts, but Tony would not give in. Day by day he watched Henri slipping further and further away. His age and his weakened condition were too much of a handicap for him to fight the inevitable. By the beginning of March he numbered among the Muselmenn, who crawled from place to place because their stick-like legs, devoid now of all muscle, could no longer take the insignificant weight of their bodies. Tony knew that if the Allies did not arrive soon, Henri would not live to see freedom.

One morning there was a sound like thunder muted by distance. A storm was nothing new, so Tony thought little of it to begin with. But the sound continued and the sky stayed clear and bright. Slowly an idea formed in his mind. Was he hearing gunfire? Could the Allies be coming at last? He made his slow way on unsteady legs to where Henri lay in the comparative shelter of the hut wall.

"Do you hear that?"

"Thunder?"

"It could be. But I was in northern France at the beginning of the war. When I approached Dunkirk, I heard heavy guns in the distance. It sounded much like this."

"Guns?" Henri's voice was weak, almost a whisper, totally lacking in feeling as though nothing mattered to him now. His head rested on his chest, his neck too weak to hold it up for long. Tony felt a tightening in his chest. Would Henri make it?

"Yes, Henri. I think the Allies are almost here. We will soon be free."

Henri closed his eyes as he slipped into sleep. He slept a lot now as his body sought to preserve its pitifully few resources. Tony sat down beside him, eyes closed as he listened to the sound of gunfire. Hope grew within him, taking flight like a heron rising.

The whistles blew for roll call at four a.m. as usual the next day. Tony helped Henri out into the compound. He was sure he could still hear the muted sound of gunfire, although maybe it was just his imagination. The wind was in the east, blowing any possible sounds from the Western Front away from him.

Roll call was over by seven a.m. but the prisoners were not dismissed. Trucks were driven into the centre of the compound and SS officers began to make their way along the rows of human scarecrows. Any Muselmann was carried away by the work party and placed in the trucks. Tony whispered desperately to Henri.

"A selection! You don't look too thin with all that added clothing. Just stay on your feet and you'll be all right. Do you hear me, Henri?"

Henri said nothing but his back straightened slightly, and he held his head a little higher as the SS officer approached. He looked carefully at Henri, then passed on taking another fifty from their hut to the trucks. Tony breathed a silent sigh of relief. They had survived! His relief was short lived. The selection took four long hours during which many succumbed to cold and fatigue and fell to their knees. These too were taken to the trucks.

By mid-day fully one third of the prisoners had been driven away. Each time a full truck left for the death compound, another arrived to take its place. Tony tried not to imagine what it must be like at the other end, as the endless lines of prisoners were killed and burned. The SS officers were seated around a brazier in which a fire roared, warming their hands at the flames, just sitting watching and waiting. Each time a prisoner fell, they would point to him, and the work party carried the unfortunate victim to the waiting trucks. Tony was aware of Henri struggling to stay upright in front of him. It was a battle he could not win. Eventually the Frenchman could hold out no longer, and slipped to his knees. Tony bent to try to lift him, but a Kapo caught him across the back of the neck with a whip.

"On your feet, or you go with him."

Tony looked at Henri, his mind a whirl of conflicting emotions. Could he let Henri face the terrible ordeal which lay ahead alone? Should he, for the sake of their friendship, go with him? He felt the hollowed tooth with his tongue. After all, he did still have his suicide pill. He could be with Henri to offer moral support, but end his own life before the agony of death by gas. Henri's vision cleared for a moment. He seemed to see deep into Tony's mind and heart. He shook his head, a weak movement which took tremendous effort.

"No, Tony. You're too close to freedom. I'll be all right."

Slowly Tony stood and watched the work party drag Henri over to the waiting truck. It was only half full. The Frenchman sat so that he could see Tony. Their eyes met and held for the twenty minutes it took for the rest of the truck to be filled with its hopeless cargo. Henri drew strength from the comforting look of his friend, while Tony drew on the quiet courage of the man who knew what manner of death awaited him, and faced it boldly. At last the truck was full. As it and pulled away. Tony's tears began to fall. He had held out for so long. Why the General Roll Call now? Why was Henri not to see the freedom that must be round the corner?

The long afternoon dragged on towards evening. The prisoners still stood in their depleted ranks numb with cold, weak from hunger, desperately thirsty. At six p.m., fourteen hours after they had first been called from their huts for the morning roll call, it was over.

Major Hase stood and addressed the remaining prisoners.

"You will run back to your huts. There are trucks waiting for those of you who cannot. Dismissed."

Tony's mind reeled at the barbarity of it all. Still more to go, still one final selection. He forced his stiffened muscles to move as he took one faltering step after another and broke into a shambling run. His weakened left leg dragged behind him. Much to his surprise he made it, and turned in the doorway to watch the other prisoners. They ran in slow motion, drawing desperate breaths as they forced their weakened bodies to obey them. Most made it, but some did not. They were taken, heads held low in despair, to the last of the waiting trucks, which carried them away to the place of no return.

Tony heard the sound of guns frequently over the next few days, but he thought little of freedom. If it came so be it. But since Henri was taken, he had lost all ability to hope for freedom in the future. It was as though some unseen force conspired to separate him forever from the people he loved. For the first time since his capture he allowed his mind to sink into despair.

179

"What's that?"

Bobby looked across to where an enormous fence seemed to stretch from horizon to horizon. From this distance it was hard to see what was going on. But there seemed to be people moving about beyond it.

"I'm not sure, Zach. It could be a prisoner of war camp. If it is, I'll be mighty glad to get in there, and free any of our boys that have been captured."

Zach nodded as they moved forward. "Yes. But it's so quiet. You'd think they'd cheer or something. They must be able to see us coming."

Bobby only then realised the unnatural silence which seemed to pervade the area, as though all living things had gone, no birds in the trees, no small animals. He shivered.

"This is eerie."

It was 13th April 1945. Bobby and Zach, along with the rest of the United States 3rd Army, were advancing in the vicinity of Weimar. They soon came to realise that what they initially thought was a prisoner of war compound had in fact been built to hold prisoners who had committed crimes against the Reich. It held many dissidents and members of the resistance groups from countries the Germans had occupied at the height of their power. As they approached the electrified fence, the normally voluble Americans fell silent at the sickening sight which greeted their eyes. Men in striped trousers and shirts stood silent and listless, their heads shorn, eyes sunken, hollow cheeked, many of them too weak to close their mouths. It was like a scene from hell, yet without the hideous screams that scene evoked. This place was eerily silent. The gates were opened, and the numbed Americans made their way into the living hell. Their commanding officer stared in utter disbelief at the men, some weighing only fifty or sixty pounds. He wondered how they could still be alive. At last he spoke.

"Do what you can for them." His voice was full of compassion. His men began to move past the wooden carts piled high with skeletal bodies and in amongst the suffering men, offering them water, food, blankets, feeling that their best efforts were useless in the face of the unbelievable suffering.

As Bobby and Zach made their way into Buchenwald, the smell hit them as an almost physical blow. There was a stench of excreta, of disease, of rotting flesh and of death. The two men looked around in disbelief at the pitiful remnants of humanity, who stared at them with eyes that echoed the horrors they had witnessed. As Zach looked at the yellow Star of David which many of the prisoners wore, he began to shiver uncontrollably. He turned his tortured gaze to Bobby.

"This is why my parents left Germany. They knew Hitler wanted to get rid of us Jews, but they never imagined anything like this. If they'd stayed, I could be one of these men. If I weren't already dead."

Bobby reached out and touched his arm in sympathy. "Come on. Let's do what we can to help."

They opened their packs and began to hand out their rations, saving nothing for themselves. It was an insignificant drop in the ocean. How could they provide relief for so many? As Zach did the best he could for a small group of prisoners, he noticed that one of them was watching Bobby, a frown furrowing his features. Finally the prisoner spoke, his voice cracked and hoarse.

"Bobby?" He looked at Zach, his haunted eyes questioning. "Is that man called Bobby?"

Zach was surprised to hear the man speaking English. His eyes widened in disbelief.

"Yes. Do you know him?"

The prisoner nodded. "Yes. I knew him in another life. Long before I came here."

Zach laid a hand on the man's shoulder, and felt the contour of his bones beneath the thin shirt. He shuddered.

"Don't move, pal. I'll be right back."

Amongst all the men in Buchenwald, those newly freed and their liberators, Zach was the only man to move quickly. He rushed over to his compatriot, and pulled him round to face the wasted prisoner.

"That man over there says he knows you!"

Bobby looked hard at the man. His head had been shaved and the hair grown back sparsely in thin strands. The face was skull like, the body skeletal, with folds of skin hanging from bones which had lost all covering of flesh. The man stood rocklike, as though any attempt to move was a great effort. Bobby thought he must be quite old, at least fifty or sixty. He turned to Zach.

"How could he know me?"

The young Jew shrugged. "I don't know. But he spoke to me in English, and asked if your name is Bobby."

"In English?" Bobby turned and looked at the man again. Perhaps he was not as old as he first imagined. The sunken eyes were regarding him almost in desperation, as though pleading to be recognised. There was something about those eyes which struck chord in Bobby's memory. He took a hesitant step forward, then another. As h approached the wreck of humanity a wild thought took root in his mind. He whispered name.

"Tony? Tony Kemshall?"

The prisoner looked back, the despair in his eyes turning to hope.

"Tony Kemshall! My God, it is you!" He crossed the intervening space quickly the stopped, unsure of how to proceed. It was Tony who spoke first.

"You can't believe how glad we all are to see you Yanks."

It was the same voice, though flat and unemotional, as though all feeling had bee forced from this young man who looked so old. Bobby took him by the arm and helpe him to sit down, conscious all the time of the bones which protruded from h translucent skin. He knelt in the dirt before the Englishman.

"So this is what happened to you. Sarah wrote to say you had disappeared in France She told me all about your work."

Tony's features brightened at the sound of her name. His eyes came to life again radiating a love so deep that it tore Bobby's heart to see it.

"Sarah!"

The whispered word was like a prayer, and Bobby felt tears spring to his eyes. A whole world of love and longing had gone into that single word.

The Englishman looked at the American, his breath escaping in a sigh.

"I suppose she thinks I'm dead."

"No!" Bobby shook his head emphatically. "The officer who visited her said that sh should assume that, but she didn't give up hope. She said she won't believe it until sh sees your body." As he looked at this ghost of a man who had suffered so much durin the course of this war, Bobby knew he had lost Sarah forever. She had loved Tony for s long. She would never abandon him now. Though his heart was breaking, he forced smile for the one who had endured far more than most people could and still surviv "She's still waiting for you, Tony."

"Waiting? For me?"

The words were little more than a whisper. Tony closed his eyes as the full realisatior of his situation finally hit him. He was free! Somewhere the Americans were holding th Germans who had made Buchenwald such a hell on earth. There was no one to tell hir what to do, and he could return home at last to Sarah. Tears forced their way beneat his closed eyelids. He wept unashamedly, unaware of the tears the American shed, which he wiped away roughly with the sleeve of his greatcoat. He said nothing for a time allowing Tony to come to terms with the situation. Then he touched him on the arm.

"Come with me. I'm going to make sure you're one of the first out of here."

He took his coat and laid it across Tony's shoulders. It threatened to smother him with its great size and weight. He looked like a child dressed up in his father's clothes and Bobby wondered how he had ever survived such deprivation. How much longe would he have been able to hold out if the Americans had not come? Indeed, was h strong enough to survive long enough to return home to Sarah? As the living skeleton made his way slowly beside him, dragging an almost useless left leg behind him, Bobby realised that Sarah might yet be his, and he was surprised to find that he did not want to win her that way.

"Can you manage a few more steps?"

Tony nodded. He accompanied the American soldier towards a jeep, where a major and captain were deep in conversation. Bobby stopped a few yards short of their objective.

"Wait here while I go talk to the major."

He tidied his uniform, drew himself to attention, took a deep breath then marched over to the two men. Stopping in front to the major he saluted smartly.

"Permission to speak with you, sir."

The two officers turned round, and the captain glowered angrily.

"What are you doing, soldier? If you have anything of interest for the major, you go through the proper channels. Speak to your lieutenant about it. If he thinks it is important enough, the major will hear about it."

Bobby took a deep breath and continued.

"I'm sorry, sir but this can't wait. I must speak with the major now."

"You insolent…"

The major held up a hand and cut off his fellow officer in full flow.

"OK, soldier. Out with it."

Relief flooded through Bobby. All he needed was a chance to speak. Once the major heard his story, he could not fail to help.

"It's about the prisoner over there, sir."

The Major looked at Tony and frowned. He looked no different from any of the other inmates of the camp.

"What of him?"

"I know him, sir."

The Major's eyes widened in disbelief. "Know him? How?"

"I met him in England, sir. We were both in love with the same girl. I heard from her some months ago to say that Tony was missing. He's a British agent, sir. He was at Dunkirk and has parachuted into France a number of times. He was wounded and also taken prisoner by the SS. They tortured him, but the Resistance got him out. He was flown back to England where he was decorated. He went back to France to help prepare for the invasion, and he disappeared during an attack on the port of Saint Nazaire on D-Day."

"And he ended up here." The officer looked at Tony. "He must be a very brave man."

"Yes, sir, I believe he is. I would like to request that he is sent back to England as soon as possible, sir. He deserves to get the best hospital treatment."

"I agree, soldier. Get that man to the medics. When they have finished with him, I'll speak to him."

"Thank you, sir."

"By the way, which of you two did the girl choose?"

Bobby looked at Tony, then back at his commanding officer.

"She hasn't said yet, sir. But I know I can't compete with him."

"Yet you're willing to send him back to her?"

"Yes, sir. He deserves all the happiness he can get." Bobby saluted. "Thank you again, sir."

The major returned his salute. "That's all, soldier. Now get him to the medics."

As Tony lay beneath the thick woollen blankets, he still wondered if he was dreaming. Bobby took him to the medics, who did what they could for him – cleaning and dressing his ulcers, removing parasites, injecting him against disease. They fed him a meat stew which still sat heavy in his stomach, although he had eaten no more than a child. Finally they had propped him up in a bed, so he could talk to the Major. He listened to his story in amazement and horror, before making a note of Captain Dawson's name and of Tony's call sign. He promised to get in touch with England as soon as possible, to arrange for Tony's journey home. As he floated on the edge of sleep, Tony savoured that word. Home. It held so much for him. Heronfield. His parents. Sarah. As he slowly drifted into sleep his worn and weary features relaxed into the semblance of a smile.

180

It took longer than Tony thought it would for the British to be informed of his survival, and for arrangements to be made to get him back to England. Yet he did not worry. He knew he would be going home. Every day he waited, he was able to eat a little more food and regain a little more strength. While he was moved steadily back down the lines, the war in Europe continued towards its inexorable end. He was still in Germany, being carried on a stretcher in the back of an ambulance, when the Russians began their assault on Berlin on the 16th. When the German army on the Rhur surrendered on the 18th, he celebrated with the Americans at one of their field hospitals. During the next week he was moved steadily west and north. On the 25th he crossed over the borders of France as the American and Russian forces met at Tongau on the Elbe. So much seemed to be happening so quickly, yet he was still stuck in Europe, and frustration began to set in. He wanted to get home as quickly as possible now, so he could rest his weary and broken body, and see his family in the flesh once more, not only in dreams which faded on waking. At last on the 29th, as the German forces in Italy capitulated, Tony made his slow unsteady way up the gangplank and onto the hospital ship that was to carry him home to England. He was somewhere on the waters of the English Channel when events in Berlin took the final turn, which presaged the end of the war in Europe. Inside his bunker, Hitler could hear the sound of small arms being fired as the Allies swarmed over his beloved city and knew then that end was in sight. He married his long time mistress, Eva Braun. As Tony's ship sailed into harbour on the morning of 30th April, the man who had brought so much death and destruction to the world shot himself, too much of a coward to face the Allies, who would have put him on trial for the crimes which he had carried out in the name of Germany. With Eva dead beside him, poisoned by her own hand, petrol was thrown upon the two bodies, which were ignited and consumed by flames. The tyrant of Europe was dead.

181

It was a gentle spring morning. Louise Kemshall smiled as she made her way around the garden removing the dead flowers from her daffodils. She always loved this time of year, the bright fresh green of new leaves, the golden daffodils, the promise of new life. She allowed the peace of her surroundings to submerge her, to bury her sorrow beneath the hope of new life which spring always brought. The sound of a vehicle turning into the drive broke into her thoughts. She straightened up to watch the staff car which pulled up in front of the lodge. The driver got out and opened the rear door to allow his passenger to alight. Louise immediately recognised Captain Dawson. Her heart raced and her mind was filled with conflicting emotions. Hope warred with fear as she wondered what the captain was doing here. Had he brought the news that she had prayed for daily, or had they found Tony's grave at last? She made her way with hesitant steps to confront the man who turned to greet her. At sight of her worried frown, his features broke into a broad grin. Though she did not need to ask, she had to say the words.

"He is alive?"

Dawson nodded. "Is your husband home?"

This time it was Louise's turn to nod. "Yes. Please come with me."

She led the way up the steps and into the house, a lightness to her step that had been missing for so long. She floated on a cloud of happiness as she led the way into the study. Sir Michael looked up, and his face paled as he saw the officer. He knew this was it. If it was bad news, he would never be able to put things right with his son. He would go to his grave regretting the things he had said and done.

"Captain Dawson?"

"Sir Michael, it's good news. Tony is alive."

The blood pounded in his ears, and Sir Michael felt as though he could not breathe. Alive! After all these months! Slowly he regained control of his turbulent emotions. He waved the captain to a chair.

"Please sit down and tell us all about it." Unable to sit himself, Sir Michael moved around the desk and put his arm around his wife's shoulders. "Has he been in a Prisoner of War camp all this time?"

Dawson shook his head. "No. I received a radio message last night to say he had been in Buchenwald since July."

"Buchenwald? Where's that?"

Dawson's face was serious.

"It's a Concentration Camp in Germany which was liberated by the Americans five days ago. I don't have all the details, but it seems that the conditions were appalling. The prisoners are all ill and weak from hunger."

"What about Tony? He will be all right, won't he?"

Dawson's eyes filled with compassion as he looked at Louise.

"The Americans say he is very weak, and still suffering from some wounds he received when he was captured. He'll be sent across Europe by ambulance, and then across the Channel in a hospital ship. His condition is not what we could hope for. But they say he should survive the journey, as long as it is steady and they don't try to rush it." He looked at Sir Michael, whose renewed fears were reflected in his eyes. "I'm sorry the news could not be better, but at least he is alive and in Allied hands. He should be home in a week or two. Then it will be a matter of nursing him back to health."

"What were his injuries?"

Dawson shook his head. "I'm sorry sir, I don't know. I must assure you that I'm as concerned as you are. Tony's a friend of mine, as well as a colleague."

Sir Michael nodded and smiled. "I understand. It was good of you to come all the way out here to tell us the news. And it's good news. Far better than you led us to hope for. He is alive. That's all we need to know for now." He held out his hand and shook Captain Dawson's. "You'll tell us when he's due back in England?"

"Of course. Now, if you'll excuse me, I'm sure that you must want to be alone. I must take the good news to Miss Porter up at the hospital."

"Goodbye, captain."

"Sir Michael."

"Yes. Goodbye, captain. And thank you for everything."

Dawson smiled. "I'm just glad I could bring you the good news myself."

As the officer turned and left the room, Sir Michael turned to his wife. She wa
smiling, but tears filled her eyes as she rested her head on her husband's shoulder.

"He is alive, Michael. I can hardly believe it! Tony is alive. He is coming home!"

Sir Michael's arms enfolded the slim figure of his wife. He held her close, his eye
closed as he offered up a silent prayer of gratitude to God. He was to be given anothe
chance after all. This time he would make sure that Tony knew just how much he love
him and wanted him home.

182

Sir Michael and Louise Kemshall stood on Southampton dock as the hospital shi
moved slowly towards its berth. It seemed an age before the ship was finally stationary
the huge cables tying it to the dock, and even longer before the gangplank was in plac
and the first of the wounded soldiers brought ashore.

Captain Dawson had been as good as his word. He informed the Kemshalls of th
imminent arrival of the hospital ship, in plenty of time for them to drive down t
Southampton to meet it. They were the only civilians there. The relatives of the othe
wounded servicemen would not know when their men arrived. The first they woul
know of their loved one's return home to England would be a letter from the hospital
Sir Michael was profoundly glad that Tony's superior officer had cared enough to allow
them to be here to greet their son, and to have arranged for him to be sent to Heronfiel
rather than another hospital.

The couple watched as a steady stream of sick and wounded disembarked. Some
were too ill to walk and were carried down the gangplank, bandages shining a brilliant
white against the dull grey of the military blankets. Some walked down with their arms in
slings, or bandaged heads, or stumbled down with crutches to support their body above
shattered limbs. Sir Michael and Louise eagerly scanned the face of each man who came
ashore, longing for a glimpse of their son. Some were young, mere boys it seemed to a
man who had fought in the trenches of Picardy. Some were old, perhaps old enough to
have served with him in that first war to end all wars. Louise's heart went out to the
wounded men, the shattered remnants of a generation which had given its finest and its
best in opposition to a tyrannical ruler.

She watched one old man hobbled down the gangplank, his left leg dragging almost
uselessly behind him, his left arm in a sling. The man's hair was thin and straggly, and he
was dressed in a uniform too large for his slender frame. Then she noticed the face. His
was not a slender frame, but the body of a man who had been close to starvation, and
only just been dragged back from the brink. The cheekbones stood out above hollowed
cheeks covered with parchment-like yellow skin. The eyes were sunken with black rings
beneath them, reflecting a horror that she did not want to know about.

With a shudder, Louise tore her gaze away from the pitiful wreck of humanity which
limped down the gangplank. She continued to search amongst the hundreds of wounded
men for her son. But something about those eyes seemed frighteningly familiar. She
found her gaze drawn back, almost against her will, to the man who had now almost
reached the bottom of the gangplank. He was looking at her with those sad, weary eyes.
Blue eyes. Her eyes widened as she saw the corners of his mouth turn up in a weak smile
of welcome. Through the hurt, the sadness, the loss in those eyes, she saw a little boy
who had run to her when the world had struck out at him, and who was coming back to
her comforting arms. With a stifled cry of alarm, Louise grabbed her husband's arm, her

fingers tight as she communicated her pain. Sir Michael looked down.

"What is it?"

"Tony."

The word was little more than a whisper, but Sir Michael heard and turned to scan the crowd. Twice his gaze passed over the ragged scarecrow of a man who was limping towards him. Then he realised that was where Louise was staring, and he looked again. Slowly recognition dawned on him. His heart wept at the sight of what this war had done to his son. He crossed the space which separated them with rapid strides, then stopped, unsure what to say in the face of so much suffering. Two pairs of eyes, so similar, locked and searched for what they longed to see. There, in them both, was forgiveness, acceptance and love. Sir Michael opened his arms, and Tony closed his eyes as he stepped into the embrace. His mind raced back to the times when he had sought comfort in his father's loving arms as a boy. Now he was back there. He was home at last.

"Oh Tony, I'm so sorry. I should have believed in you instead of hurting you."

The feel of his son's bones protruding through the flesh caused Sir Michaels to weep bitter tears. They fell in warm saltiness on his son's upturned face. Tony stepped back and smiled.

"That all happened a long time ago, Dad. I've seen and done things which make a few angry words seem insignificant now. I knew you loved me, even when we argued. Those few words are long forgotten. Will you forget them too?"

Sir Michael nodded.

"Thank you, son. Now come and say hello to Mamma, then we'll go home. There's someone waiting for you."

183

Sarah sat beneath an elm tree beside the gravel drive which led up to Heronfield House. Ever since Captain Dawson had come to see her with the news that Tony was alive, she had been longing to see him again, to hold him in her arms and tell him she had no doubts now. She would spend the rest of her life with him if he would have her. Her joy at the knowledge that he was still alive had been tempered by the cautionary news of his wounds and poor physical state. She was determined to nurse him back to health. The war would soon be over, and she would be able to dedicate every waking moment to making him well.

The days had passed slowly since she had first spoken to Captain Dawson. Each time she telephoned him, he could do no more than say that Tony was on his way and would be home soon. Then Sir Michael had come up to the house to tell her that the ship was due in, and to ask if she would like to accompany them to Southampton. Sarah had been touched more than she could say. She knew how desperate the Kemshalls were to see their son again, and they were willing to share that time with a relative stranger. It had been hard for her to say no, but she knew that it was the right thing to do. He deserved time with his family, and she could wait the few extra hours until he was back at Heronfield.

Now the hours dragged like days as she waited for them to return. They had been gone for so long that she was beginning to wonder if Tony had not been on the hospital ship after all. What if someone had made a mistake? She would hardly be able to bear it if he did not come home now. They had been apart for so long, yet she still remembered everything about him. The soft fair hair that she loved to run her fingers through, the laughing blue eyes, the lips that were always curving into a boyish grin. She remembered his tall slim body, the way he walked, the strength of his arms as he held her close. Every day of the past year was spent in remembering, and now she was to see him again. She stood up and began to pace back and forth. Would the car never come?"

At last, as afternoon was turning to evening, the sound of a car could be heard. Sarah stood on the grass opposite the steps which led up to the lodge. She waited breathlessly as the car swung through the stone pillars which had once held the gates to the estate. The tyres crunched on the gravel, then slowed and finally stopped. Sir Michael was the first out of the car, his smile of happiness tinged with a strange melancholy and he would not meet her gaze. He helped Louise from the car, and her eyes held a shadow of sadness as they reached out in sympathy towards the young nurse.

Sarah felt strangely ill at ease as Sir Michael opened to door and helped Tony out. What was wrong? Then Sir Michael stepped back and she saw him. She did not know what she had been expecting, but it was nothing like this. Her eyes filled with tears as she imagined the suffering which Tony must have experienced. As he limped slowly towards her, the sure firm step gone now forever, she saw that the laughter which had always filled his eyes would forever now be tinged with sadness and suffering. Her heart filled with love for this man. She stepped forward to greet him, only then aware that his eyes were focussed on her breast not her face. He stopped walking, and his eyes filled with tears as the spring sun reflected in rays of gold from the tiny heron pinned to her blouse.

"Tony?" Her voice was soft, questioning. He reached out a tentative finger to touch the heron, as though afraid that it was not real and would disappear as soon as he got close enough to touch it. But it did not disappear. He stroked the golden bird with a touch as gentle as a butterfly.

"Whenever things got too bad I thought of this." His voice was a whisper. Sarah did not know if he was talking to her or to himself. Tony raised his eyes to Sarah's face, the face he had dreamed of so often that each contour was indelibly etched on his memory. "Thoughts of the heron and you kept me alive, Sarah." He reached up to touch the auburn hair with its golden nimbus of sunlight. Sarah took his skeletal hand in her own, and held it against her cheek. Her eyes closed as she savoured his touch once more. When she opened them she was smiling, the light of love shining from her eyes.

"Not a day has gone by when I have not thought of you, my love."

Tony smiled at her words, a ghost of a smile, but one which Sarah loved none the less.

"Will you stay at Heronfield when the war is over?"

Sarah nodded, unable to speak for the tears which threatened to choke her.

"Then I'm truly home at last."

Sarah slipped her arm around Tony's waist and turned to lead him back into the lodge. As they crossed the drive, they could hear the distant whirring of wings down by the river. A heron rose from the reeds into the evening sky. As they watched it fly off into the west towards the setting sun, the young people smiled.

Author's Note

'Heronfield' grew out of my love of history. I have tried to remain true to the historical facts, while peopling my novel with characters with whom my readers can identify, with all their human strengths and weaknesses. These characters serve to bring together some of the key moments of the Second World War, which I have described as accurately as possible.

From the beaches of Dunkirk through the bombing of Coventry, the work of the VAD's and the Special Operations Executive, I have tried to remain true to historical fact, allowing some flexibility to enhance the flow of my story. The activities of 7 Squadron are accurate, their bases and number of losses a matter of record. The same applies to the 1st Infantry Division and the two Ranger Battalions of Force O which landed on the Normandy beaches, and the liberation of the concentration camps. On one occasion only have I deliberately strayed from recorded fact – the submarine pen of Saint Nazaire.

Soon after the surrender of the French in June 1940, the Germans built a heavily fortified U-boat base in Saint Nazaire, its 9m thick concrete ceiling capable of withstanding almost any bomb in use at the time. In 1942, 611 British Commandos and Naval personnel launched a raid against the docks, destroying the gates and machinery so that the U-boat pens could not be used for the remainder of the war. 89 decorations were awarded to those who took part in the raid, including 5 Victoria Crosses. The exploits of these men deserve a book of their own. In 'Heronfield' I needed the character of Tony Kemshall to be working either alone or in a small group, so had him searching for and finding submarine pens hidden in a cliff face. My deviation from historical fact on this point is in no way meant to be at the cost of the memory of those brave men who took part in Operation Chariot